OF
LOVE
AND
LIFE

Three novels selected and condensed
by Reader's Digest

The Reader's Digest Association Limited, London

The Reader's Digest Association Limited
11 Westferry Circus, Canary Wharf, London E14 4HE

www.readersdigest.co.uk

ISBN 0-276-44108-7

CONTENTS

the CONSTANT PRINCESS

PHILIPPA GREGORY

Katherine of Aragon's greatest claim to fame
is as the first of King Henry VIII's ill-fated
six wives. But her life story, even before her
marriage to Henry, is one of drama and
excitement, steeped in the history of the
Crusades and the long conflict between
Muslims and Christians.
The Spanish Infanta, Catalina—as Katherine
was called as a child—was groomed to become
a ruler of men. But her destiny eventually took
a very surprising turn . . .

PRINCESS OF WALES
Granada, 1491

THERE WAS A SCREAM, and then the loud roar of fire enveloping silken hangings, then a mounting crescendo of shouts of panic that spread and spread from one tent to another as the flames ran too, leaping from one silk standard to another, running up guy ropes and bursting through muslin doors. Then the horses were neighing in terror and men shouting to calm them, and the night swirled with smoke and rang with shouts and screams.

The little girl, starting up out of her bed in her fear, cried out in Spanish for her mother and screamed, 'The Moors? Are the Moors coming for us?'

'Dear God, save us, they are firing the camp!' her nurse gasped. 'Mother of God, they will rape me, and spit you on their sickle blades.'

'Mother!' cried the child, struggling from her bed. 'Where is my mother?'

She dashed outside, her nightgown flapping at her legs, the hangings of her tent now alight and blazing up behind her in an inferno of panic. All the thousand tents in the camp were ablaze, sparks pouring up into the dark night sky like fiery fountains.

'Mother!' She screamed for help.

Out of the flames came two huge, dark horses, like great, mythical beasts moving as one, jet black against the brightness of the fire. The child's mother bent down to speak to her daughter who was trembling. 'Stay with your nurse and be good,' the woman commanded, no trace of fear in her voice. 'Your father and I have to ride out and show ourselves.'

9

'Let me come with you! Mother! I shall be burned. Let me come! The Moors will get me!' The little girl reached her arms up to her mother.

The firelight glinted off the mother's breastplate, off the embossed greaves of her legs, as if she were a woman of silver and gilt.

'If the men don't see me, then they will desert,' she said sternly. 'You don't want that.'

'I don't care!' the child wailed in her panic. 'I don't care about anything but you! Lift me up!'

'The army comes first,' the woman mounted high on the black horse ruled. 'I have to ride out.'

She turned her horse's head from her panic-stricken daughter. 'I will come back for you,' she said over her shoulder.

Helpless, the child watched her mother and father ride away. 'Madre!' she whimpered. 'Madre! Please!' but the woman did not turn.

She watched the two horses go to and fro among the burning tents. Everywhere they went the screams were stilled and some discipline returned to the terrified camp. The men formed lines, passing buckets all the way to the irrigation channel, coming out of terror back into order. Desperately, their general ran among his men, arraying them in defence formation on the plain, in case the Moors had seen the pillar of fire from their dark battlements, and sallied out to attack and catch the camp in chaos. But no Moors came that night; they stayed behind the high walls of their castle, too fearful to come out to the inferno that the Christians had made, suspecting that it must be some infidel trap.

The five-year-old child watched her mother's determination conquer fire itself, her queenly certainty douse panic, her belief in success overcome the reality of disaster and defeat. The little girl perched on one of the treasure chests and waited for the camp to settle.

When the mother rode back to her daughter she found her dry-eyed and steady.

'Catalina, are you all right?' Isabella of Spain dismounted and turned to her youngest, most precious daughter, restraining herself from pitching to her knees and hugging the little girl. Tenderness would not raise this child as a warrior for Christ.

The child was as iron-spined as her mother. 'I am all right now,' she said.

'You weren't afraid?'

'Not at all.'

The woman nodded her approbation. 'That is good,' she said. 'That is what I expect of a princess of Spain.'

'And Princess of Wales,' her daughter added.

This is me, this little five-year-old girl, perching on the treasure chest with a face white as marble and blue eyes wide with fear, refusing to tremble, biting my lips so I don't cry out again. This is me, raised by a strong woman in armour, on campaign for all of my childhood, destined to fight for my name, for my faith and for my throne. I am Catalina, Princess of Spain, daughter of the two greatest monarchs the world has ever known: Isabella of Castile and Ferdinand of Aragon. Their names are feared from Cairo to Baghdad to Constantinople to India and beyond by all the Moors in all their many nations: Turks, Indians, Chinamen. My parents' names are blessed by the Pope as the finest kings to defend the faith against the might of Islam, they are the greatest crusaders of Christendom as well as the first kings of Spain; and I am their youngest daughter, Catalina, Princess of Wales, and I will be Queen of England.

Since I was a child of three I have been betrothed in marriage to Prince Arthur, son of King Henry, and when I am fifteen I shall sail to England in a beautiful ship with my standard flying at the top of the mast, and I shall be his wife and then his queen. I know my duty.

I am a child of absolute convictions. I know that I will be Queen of England because it is God's will, and it is my mother's order. And I believe, as does everyone in my world, that God and my mother are generally of the same mind; and their will is always done.

In the morning the campsite outside Granada was smouldering, everything destroyed by one candle carelessly set. There could be nothing but retreat. The Spanish army had ridden out in its pride to set siege to the last great kingdom of the Moors in Spain, and had been burned to nothing. It would have to ride back again, to regroup.

'No, we don't retreat,' Isabella of Spain ruled.

'Your Majesty, we have lost for this season,' one of the generals said gently to her. 'It is not a matter of pride nor of willingness. We have no tents, we have been destroyed by ill luck. We will have to go back and provision ourselves once more, set the siege again. Your husband'—he nodded to the dark, handsome man who stood slightly to one side of the group, listening—'he knows this. We all know this. A good general knows when he has to retreat.'

Every man nodded. The battle would keep. It had been coming for seven centuries. Each year had seen generations of Christian kings increase their lands at the cost of the Moors. Another year would make no difference. The little girl, her back against a damp tent post, watched her mother's serene expression. It never changed.

'Indeed it *is* a matter of pride,' she corrected him. 'We are fighting an enemy who understands pride better than any other. If we crawl away

in our singed clothes, they will laugh themselves to al-Yanna, to paradise. I cannot permit it. But more than this: it is God's will that we fight
the Moors, it is God's will that we go forwards. So we must go forwards.'

The child's father turned his head with a quizzical smile but he did
not dissent. 'The queen is right,' he said. 'The queen is always right.'

'But we have no tents, we have no camp!'

He directed the question to her. 'What do you think?'

'We shall build one,' she decided.

'Your Majesty, we have laid waste to the countryside for miles all
around. There is no cloth. There is no canvas.'

'So we build in stone. I take it we have stone?'

'We are surrounded by a plain of arid rocks, my love,' the king said.
'One thing we do have is stone.'

She turned to her husband. 'Then we will build, not a camp, but a
city of stone. It is God's will and mine.'

He nodded. 'It will be done.' He gave her a private smile. 'It is my
duty to see that God's will is done; and my pleasure to enforce yours.'

The army, defeated by fire, turned instead to the elements of earth and
water. Everyone, cavalry officers, generals, the great lords of the country,
was expected to toil in the heat of the sun and lie on hard, cold ground
at night. The Moors, watching from the high, impenetrable battlements
of the red fort on the hill above Granada, conceded that the Christians
had courage. And equally, everyone knew that they were doomed. No
force could take the red fort at Granada; it had never fallen in two centuries. It was placed high on a cliff, overlooking a plain that was itself a
wide, bleached bowl. It could not be surprised by a hidden attack. No
scaling ladders could reach the top, no party could climb the sheer face.

But, amazingly, day after day, week after week, the Christians did the
impossible. First there was a chapel built in the round like a mosque,
since the local builders could do that most quickly; then, a small house,
flat-roofed inside an Arabic courtyard, for King Ferdinand, Queen
Isabella and the royal family: their precious son and heir Juan, the three
older girls, Isabel, Maria, Juana, and Catalina the baby. The queen asked
for nothing more than a roof and walls, she had been at war for years,
she did not expect luxury. Then there were a dozen stone hovels around
them where the greatest lords reluctantly took some shelter. Then there
were stables for the horses and secure stores for the precious explosives
for which the queen had pawned her own jewels to buy from Venice;
then, and only then, there were barracks and kitchens. Then there was a
little town, built in stone, where once there had been a little camp. No

one thought it could be done; but, bravo! it was done. They called it Santa Fe and Isabella had triumphed over misfortune once again. The doomed siege of Granada by the determined, foolish Christian kings would continue.

Catalina, Princess of Wales, came upon one of the great lords of the Spanish camp in whispered conference with his friends.

'What are you doing, Don Hernando?' she asked with all the precocious confidence of a five-year-old who had never been far from her mother's side, whose father could deny her very little.

'It's a secret, Infanta,' said Hernando Perez del Pulgar.

'I won't tell.'

'Oh! Princess! You would tell. It is too big a secret for a little girl.'

'I won't! I truly won't! I promise upon Wales.'

'On Wales! On your own country?'

'On England?'

'On England? Your inheritance?'

She nodded. 'On Wales and on England, and on Spain itself.'

'Well, then. If you make such a sacred promise I will tell you. Swear that you won't tell your mother?'

She nodded, her blue eyes wide with excitement.

'We are going to get into the Alhambra. I know a gate that is not well guarded, where we can force an entry. We are going to go in, and we are going to say our prayers in their mosque. And I am going to leave an Ave Maria stabbed to the floor with my dagger. What d'you think of that?'

'When are you going?'

'Tonight! This very night!'

'I shan't sleep till you come back!'

'You must pray for me, and then go to sleep, and I will come myself, Princess, and tell you and your mother all about it in the morning.'

But in the morning, he did not come. For the first time in her life, the little girl had some sense of the mortal danger he had run, and for nothing but glory and to be featured in some song.

It was time for her mother's audience for petitioners and friends, and suddenly Hernando was there, in his best suit, his eyes dancing, and the whole story spilled out: how they had dressed in their Arab clothes so as to pass for townspeople in the darkness, how they had crept in through the gate, and dashed up to the mosque, how they had knelt and gabbled an Ave Maria and stabbed the prayer into the floor of the mosque, and then, surprised by guards, they had fought their way, blades flashing in the moonlight; back into the night. Not a man lost. A triumph for them and a slap in the face for Granada.

It was a great joke to play on the Moors, to take a Christian prayer into the very heart of their holy place, to insult them. The queen was delighted, the king too, the princess and her sisters looked at their champion, Hernando Perez del Pulgar, as if he were a hero from the romances, a knight from the time of Arthur at Camelot.

Next, they waited for the reply from the Moors. They knew that their enemy would see the venture as the challenge that it was. It was not long in coming.

The queen and her children were visiting Zubia, a village near to Granada, so Her Majesty could see the impregnable walls of the red fort herself. They had ridden out with a light guard and the commander was white with horror when he came dashing up to them in the little village square and shouted that the gates of the fort had opened and the Moors were thundering out, the full army, armed for attack. There was no time to get back to camp.

In desperate haste Queen Isabella climbed to the flat roof of the nearest house, pulling the little princess by her hand up the crumbling stairs, her sisters running behind. 'I have to see! I have to see!' she exclaimed.

It was a raiding party, not the full force. They were led by their champion, a giant of a man, dark as mahogany, riding a huge black horse as if he were Night riding to overwhelm them.

'Madre, who is that man?' the Princess of Wales whispered to her mother, staring from their vantage point.

'That is the Moor called Yarfe, and I am afraid he has come for your friend, Hernando.'

'His horse looks so frightening, like it wants to bite.'

'He has cut off its lips to make it snarl at us.'

'You won't let him hurt Hernando, will you? Madre?'

'Hernando laid the challenge. Yarfe is answering it. We will have to fight,' she said levelly. 'Yarfe is a knight, a man of honour. He cannot ignore the challenge.'

'How can he be a man of honour if he is a heretic? A Moor?'

'They are most honourable men, Catalina, though they are unbelievers. And this Yarfe is a hero to them.'

'How shall we save ourselves? This man is as big as a giant.'

'I shall pray,' Isabella said. 'And my champion Garallosco de la Vega will answer Yarfe for Hernando.'

As calmly as if she were in her own chapel at Cordoba, Isabella knelt on the roof of the little house. Sulkily, Catalina's older sister, Juana, dropped to her knees, the princesses Isabel and Maria, her other sisters, followed suit. Catalina saw, peeping through her clasped hands as she knelt in prayer, that Maria was shaking with fear, and that Isabel, in her widow's gown, was white with terror.

'Heavenly Father, we pray for the safety of ourselves, of our cause, and of our army.' Queen Isabella looked up at the blue January sky. 'We pray for the victory of Your champion, Garallosco de la Vega, at this time of his trial.'

'Amen,' the girls said promptly, and then followed the direction of their mother's gaze to where the ranks of the Spanish guard were drawn up, watchful and silent.

Catalina turned to her eldest sister and pulled at her sleeve. 'Isabel, if God is protecting de la Vega, then how can he be in danger?'

Isabel looked down at her little sister. 'God does not make the way smooth for those He loves,' she said in a harsh whisper. 'Those that God loves the best are those who suffer the worst. I know that. I, who lost the only man that I will ever love.'

'Then how shall we win?' the little girl demanded. 'Since God loves Madre, won't He send her the worst hardships?'

'Hush,' their mother said. 'Watch. Watch and pray with faith.'

Their small guard and the Moorish raiding party were drawn up opposite each other, ready for battle. Then Yarfe rode forwards on his great black charger. Something white bobbed at the ground, tied to the horse's glossy black tail. There was a gasp as the soldiers recognised the Ave Maria that Hernando had left speared to the floor of the mosque. The Moor had tied it to the tail of his horse as a calculated insult, and now rode before the Christian ranks, and smiled when he heard their roar of rage.

'Heretic,' Queen Isabella whispered.

The queen's champion, de la Vega, turned his horse and rode towards the little house where the royal guards ringed the courtyard. He pulled up his horse and doffed his helmet, looking up at his queen and the princesses on the roof. His dark eyes sparkled with anger. 'Your Grace, do I have your leave to answer his challenge?'

'Yes,' the queen said. 'Go with God, Garallosco de la Vega.'

'That big man will kill him,' Catalina said, pulling at her mother's long sleeve. 'Tell him he must not go.'

'It will be as God wills it,' Isabella maintained, looking down at her daughter whose face was flushed with distress. 'You have to have faith that you are doing God's will. Sometimes you will not understand, sometimes you will doubt, but if you are doing God's will you cannot go wrong.

Remember it, Catalina. We are soldiers of Christ. You are a soldier of Christ. If we live or die, it makes no difference. We will die in faith, that is all that matters. This battle is God's battle, and whichever man wins today, we do not doubt that God will win, and we will win in the end.'

'But de la Vega . . .' Catalina protested, her lip trembling a little.

'Perhaps God will take him to His own this afternoon,' her mother said steadily. 'We should pray for him.'

Her mother knelt again and Catalina knelt beside her and her sisters. All of them squinted through their closed eyelids to the plain where the bay charger of de la Vega rode out from the line of the Spaniards, and the black horse of the Moor trotted proudly before the Saracens.

The queen kept her eyes closed until she had finished her prayer, she did not even hear the roar as the two men took up their places, lowered their visors, and clasped their lances.

Catalina leapt to her feet, leaning over the parapet so that she could see the Spanish champion. His horse thundered towards the other, racing legs a blur, the black horse came as fast from the opposite direction. The clash when the two lances drove into solid armour could be heard on the roof of the little house, as both men were flung from their saddles by the force of the impact.

'He is down! He is dead!' Catalina cried out.

'He is stunned,' her mother corrected her. 'See, he is getting up.'

The Spanish knight staggered to his feet. The bigger man was up already, helmet and heavy breastplate cast aside, coming for him with a huge sickle sword at the ready, the light flashing off the razor-sharp edge. De la Vega drew his own great weapon. There was a tremendous crash as the swords smacked together and then the two men locked blades, each trying to force the other down. They circled clumsily, staggering under the weight of their armour and from their concussion; but there could be no doubt that the Moor was the stronger man. De la Vega tried to spring back and get free; but the weight of the Moor was bearing down on him and he stumbled and fell. At once the black knight was on top of him, forcing him downwards. De la Vega's hand closed uselessly on his long sword; he could not bring it up. The Moor raised his sword to his victim's throat, ready to give the death blow, his face a black mask of concentration. Suddenly he gave a loud cry and fell back. De la Vega scrabbled to his feet, crawling on his hands and knees like a rising dog.

The Moor was down, plucking at his breast, his great sword dropped to one side. In de la Vega's left hand was a short stabbing dagger covered with blood, a hidden weapon used in a desperate riposte. With a super-human effort the Moor got to his feet, turned his back on the Christian

16

and staggered towards his own ranks. 'I am lost,' he said to the men who ran forwards to catch him. 'We have lost.'

At a hidden signal the great gates of the red fort opened and the soldiers started to pour out. Juana leapt to her feet. 'Madre, we must run!' she screamed. 'They are coming! They are coming in their thousands!'

Isabella did not rise from her knees, even when her daughter dashed across the roof and ran down the stairs. 'Juana, come back,' she ordered in a voice like a whip crack. 'Girls, you will pray.'

She rose and went to the parapet. First she looked to the marshalling of her army, saw that the officers were setting the men into formation ready for a charge as the Moorish army came pouring on. Then she glanced down to see Juana, in a frenzy of fear, unsure whether to run for her horse or back to her mother.

Isabella, who loved her daughter, said not another word. She returned to the other girls and knelt with them. 'Let us pray,' she said, and closed her eyes.

'She didn't even look!' Juana repeated incredulously that night when they were in their room. 'There we are, in the middle of a battle, and she closes her eyes!'

'She knew that she would do more good appealing for the intercession of God than running around crying,' Isabel said pointedly. 'And it gave the army better heart than anything else to see her, on her knees, in full sight of everyone.'

'What if she had been hit by an arrow or a spear?'

'She was not. We were not. And we won the battle. And you, Juana, behaved like a half-mad peasant. I was ashamed of you.'

Day by day the heart went out of the Moors. The Queen's Skirmish turned out to be their last battle. Their champion was dead, their city encircled, they were starving in the land that their fathers had made fertile, and before them were the Princes of Spain, Isabella and Ferdinand, with a holy war declared and a Christian crusade gathering pace with the scent of success. Within a few days of the meeting of the champions, Boabdil, the King of Granada, had agreed terms of peace, and a few days after, he came down to the iron gates of the city with the keys to the Alhambra Palace and the red fort on a silken pillow and handed them over to the King and Queen of Spain in a complete surrender.

The Spanish family with their officers ahead and the royal guard behind, glorious as sultans, entered the fort through the enormous square tower known as the Justice Gate.

The Spanish guard peeled off to right and left inside the town walls, checking that the place was safe, and no despairing soldiers were preparing a last ambush. Finally, Isabella the queen looked up to the sky, shaded her eyes with her hand clinking with Moorish gold bracelets, and laughed aloud to see the sacred banner of St James and the silver cross of the crusade flying where the crescent had been.

Then she turned to see the domestic servants of the palace slowly approaching, their heads bowed. They were led by the Grand Vizier, his height emphasised by his flowing robes, his piercing black eyes meeting hers, scanning King Ferdinand at her side, and the prince and the four princesses behind them. The king and the prince were dressed as richly as sultans, wearing rich, embroidered tunics over their trousers, the queen and the princesses were wearing the traditional kamiz tunics made from the finest silks, over white linen trousers, with veils falling from their heads held back by filets of gold.

'Your Royal Highnesses, it is my honour and duty to welcome you to the Alhambra Palace,' the Grand Vizier said, as if it were the most ordinary thing in the world to hand over the most beautiful palace in Christendom to armed invaders.

The queen and her husband exchanged one brief glance. 'You can take us in,' she said.

The Grand Vizier bowed and led the way. The queen glanced back at her children. 'Come along,' she said and went ahead of them, through the gardens surrounding the palace, down some steps and into the discreet doorway.

The little doorway is like a keyhole to a treasure chest of boxes, the one opening out from another. The man leads us through them like a slave opening doors to a treasury. Their very names are a poem: the Golden Chamber, the Court of the Myrtles, the Ambassadors' Hall, the Court of the Lions, or the Hall of the Two Sisters. It will take us weeks to find our way from one exquisitely tiled room to another. It will take us months to stop marvelling at the pleasure of the sound of water running down the marble gullies in the rooms, flowing to a white marble fountain that always spills over with the cleanest, freshest water of the mountains. And I will never tire of looking through the white stucco tracery to the view of the plain beyond, the mountains, the blue sky and golden hills.

We move into the harem as the easiest and most convenient rooms for my three sisters and me. We have always worn Moorish dress at home and sometimes at great state occasions so still there is the whisper of silks and the slap of slippers on marble floors, as if nothing has changed. Now, we study where the slave girls read, we walk in the gardens that were planted to delight the favourites of the sultan. We bathe in the hammam, standing stock-still while the servants lather us all over with a rich soap that smells of flowers. Then they pour golden ewer after golden ewer of hot water over us, splashing from head to toe, to wash us clean. We are soothed with rose oil, wrapped in fine sheets and lie on the warm marble table that dominates the entire room, under the golden ceiling where the star-shaped openings admit dazzling rays of sunlight into the shadowy peace of the place. One girl manicures our toes while another works on our hands, shaping the nails and painting delicate patterns of henna. We are served as if we are sultanas, with all the riches of Spain and all the luxury of the East, and we surrender utterly to the delight of the palace.

Even Isabel, grieving for the loss of her husband, starts to smile again. Even Juana, who is usually so moody and so sulky, is at peace. And I become the pet of the court, the favourite of the gardeners who let me pick my own peaches, the darling of the harem where I am taught to play and dance and sing, and the favourite of the kitchen where they let me watch them preparing the sweet pastries and dishes of honey and almonds of Arabia.

My father meets with foreign emissaries in the Ambassadors' Hall, he takes them to the bath house for talks, like any leisurely sultan. My mother sits crosslegged on the throne of the Nasrids who have ruled here for generations, her bare feet in soft leather slippers, the drapery of her kamiz falling around her. She listens to the emissaries of the Pope himself, in a chamber that is walled with coloured tiles and dancing with pagan light.

We live a life that is more refined and more luxurious than they could dream of in Paris or London or Rome. We live graciously. We live, as we have always aspired to do, like Moors. We learn from Muslim scholars, we are attended by their doctors, study the stars in the sky which they have named, count with their numbers which start at the magical zero, and delight in the waters which run through their aqueducts. Their architecture pleases us; at every turn of every corner we know that we are living inside beauty. Their power now keeps us safe; the Alcazabar fortress is, indeed, invulnerable to attack once more. We are the victors but they have taught us how to rule. Sometimes I think that we are the barbarians, like those who came after the Romans or the Greeks, playing with beauty but not understanding it.

We do not change our faith, at least. Every palace servant has to give at least lip service to the beliefs of the One True Church. The horns of the mosque are silenced, there is to be no call to prayer in my mother's hearing. And anyone who disagrees can either leave, convert, or face the Inquisition. We made a solemn promise to poor King Boabdil, that his people, the Muslims, should be as safe under our rule as the Christians were safe under his. We promise the convivencia—a way of living together—and they believe that we will make a Spain where anyone, Moor or Christian or Jew, can live quietly since all of us are 'People of the Book'. Their mistake is that they meant that truce, and they trusted that truce, and we—as it turns out—do not.

We betray our word in three months, expelling the Jews and threatening the Muslims. Everyone must convert to the True Faith and then, if there is any shadow of doubt, or any suspicion against them, their faith will be tested by the Holy Inquisition. It is the only way to make one nation: through one faith. My mother builds a chapel in the council chamber and where it had once said 'Enter and ask. Do not be afraid to seek justice for here you will find it', in the beautiful shapes of Arabic, she prays to a sterner, more intolerant God than Allah; and no one comes for justice any more.

But nothing can change the nature of the palace. It was built first and foremost as a garden with rooms of exquisite luxury so that one could live outside. It is a series of courtyards designed for flowers and people alike. The Moors believe that a garden is a paradise on earth, and they have spent fortunes over the centuries to make this 'al-Yanna': the word that means both garden, secret place, and paradise.

I know that I love it. Even as a little child I know that this is an exceptional place. And even as a child I know that I cannot stay here. It is God's will and my mother's will that I must leave al-Yanna. It is to be my destiny that I should find the most beautiful place in all the world when I am just six years old, and then leave it when I was fifteen; as homesick as Boabdil, as if happiness and peace for me will only ever be short-lived.

DOGMERSFIELD PALACE, HAMPSHIRE
Autumn 1501

'I SAY, YOU CANNOT come in! If you were the King of England himself— you could not come in.'

'I am the King of England,' Henry Tudor said, without a flicker of amusement. 'And she can either come out right now, or I damned well will come in and my son will follow me.'

'The Infanta has already sent word to the king that she is in seclusion, as a lady of Spain,' the duenna said witheringly. 'Do you think the King of England would come riding down the road when the Infanta has refused to receive him? What sort of a man do you think he is?'

'Exactly like this one,' he said and thrust his fist with the great gold ring towards her face. The Count de Cabra came into the hall in a rush, and at once recognised the lean man in his forties threatening the Infanta's duenna with a clenched fist, and gasped out, 'The king!'

At the same moment the duenna recognised the new badge of England, the combined roses of York and Lancaster, and recoiled.

'It is the king,' the count hissed, throwing himself into a low bow. The duenna gave a gasp of horror and dropped into a deep curtsy.

'Get up,' the king said shortly. 'And fetch her.'

'But she is a princess of Spain, Your Grace,' the woman said, rising but with her head still bowed low. 'She is to stay in seclusion. She cannot be seen by you before her wedding day. This is the tradition.'

'It's *your* tradition. It's not *my* tradition. And since she is my daughter-in-law in my country, under my laws, she will obey my tradition.'

'She has been brought up most modestly, most properly . . .'

'Then she will be very shocked to find an angry man in her bedroom. Madam, I suggest that you get her up at once.'

'I will not, Your Grace. I take my orders from the Queen of Spain herself and she charged me to make sure that every respect was shown to the Infanta.'

'Madam, you can take your working orders from me, or your marching orders from me. I don't care which. Now send the girl out or I swear on my crown I will come in and if I catch her naked in bed then she had better pray that she is pretty.'

The Spanish duenna went quite white at the insult.

'Choose,' the king said stonily.

'I cannot fetch the Infanta,' she said stubbornly.

'Dear God! That's it! Tell her I am coming in at once.'

She scuttled backwards like an angry crow, her face blanched with shock. Henry gave her a few moments to prepare, and then called her bluff by striding in behind her.

The room was lit only by candles and firelight. The covers of the bed were turned back as if the girl had hastily jumped up. Henry registered the intimacy of being in her bedroom, with the scent of her lingering in the enclosed space, before he looked at her. She was standing by the bed, one small white hand on the carved wooden post. She had a cloak of dark blue thrown over her shoulders and her white nightgown trimmed with priceless lace peeped through the opening at the front. Her rich auburn hair, plaited for sleep, hung down her back, but her face was completely shrouded in a hastily thrown mantilla of dark lace.

Doña Elvira darted between the girl and the king.

'This is the Infanta,' she said. 'Veiled until her wedding day.'

'Not on my money,' Henry Tudor said bitterly. 'I'll see what I've bought, thank you.'

He stepped forwards. The desperate duenna nearly threw herself to her knees. 'Her modesty . . .'

'Has she got some awful mark?' he demanded, driven to voice his deepest fear. 'Is she scarred by the pox and they did not tell me?'

'No! I swear.'

Silently, the girl put out her white hand and took the lace hem of her veil. Her duenna gasped a protest but could do nothing to stop the princess as she raised the veil, and then flung it back. Her clear blue eyes stared into the lined, angry face of Henry Tudor without wavering.

She was an utter beauty: a smooth, rounded face, a straight, long nose, a full, sulky, sexy mouth. Her chin was up, he saw; her gaze challenging. This was no shrinking maiden fearing ravishment. This was a fighting princess standing on her dignity.

He bowed. 'I am Henry Tudor, King of England,' he said.

She curtsied.

He stepped forwards and saw her curb her instinct to flinch away. He took her firmly at the shoulders, and kissed one warm, smooth cheek and then the other. The perfume of her hair and the warm, female smell of her body came to him and he felt desire pulse in his groin and at his temples. Quickly he stepped back and let her go.

'You are welcome to England,' he said. He cleared his throat. 'You will forgive my impatience to see you. My son, too, is on his way to visit you.'

'I beg your pardon,' she said icily, speaking in perfectly phrased French. 'I was not informed until a few moments ago that Your Grace was insisting on the honour of this unexpected visit.'

Henry fell back a little from the whip of her temper. 'I have a right.'

She shrugged, an absolutely Spanish gesture. 'Of course. You have every right over me.'

At the ambiguous, provocative words, he was again aware of his closeness to her: of the intimacy of the small room, the tester bed hung with rich draperies, the sheets invitingly turned back, the pillow still impressed with the shape of her head. It was a scene for ravishment, not for a royal greeting. Again he felt the secret thud-thud of lust.

'I'll see you outside,' he said abruptly.

'I shall be honoured,' she said coldly.

He got himself out of the room briskly enough, and nearly collided with Prince Arthur, hovering anxiously in the doorway.

'Fool,' he remarked.

Prince Arthur, pale with nerves, pushed his blond fringe back from his face, stood still and said nothing.

'I'll send that duenna home at the first moment I can,' the king said. 'And the rest of them. She can't make a little Spain in England, my son. The country won't stand for it, and I damned well won't stand for it.'

'People don't object. The country people seem to love the princess,' Arthur suggested mildly. 'Her escort says.'

'Because she wears a stupid hat. Because she is odd: Spanish, rare. Because she is young and—' he broke off '—pretty.'

'Is she?' Arthur gasped. 'I mean: is she?'

'Haven't I just gone in to make sure? But no Englishman will stand for any Spanish nonsense once they get over the novelty. And neither will I. This is a marriage to cement an alliance; not to flatter her vanity. Whether they like her or not, she's marrying you. Whether you like her or not, she's marrying you. Whether she likes it or not, she's marrying you. And she'd better get out here now or I won't like her and that will be the only thing that can make a difference.'

I have to go out, I have won only the briefest of reprieves and I know he is waiting for me outside the door to my bedchamber and he has demonstrated, powerfully enough, that if I do not go to him, then the mountain will come to Mohammed and I will be shamed again.

I brush Doña Elvira aside as a duenna who cannot protect me now, and I go to the door of my rooms. Henry of England wants me to meet his son, before his travelling party, without ceremony, without dignity as if we were a scramble of peasants. So be it. He will not find a princess of Spain falling back for fear. I grit my teeth, I smile as my mother commanded me.

I nod to my herald, who is as stunned as the rest of my companions. 'Announce me,' I order him.

His face blank with shock, he throws open the door. 'The Infanta Catalina, Princess of Spain and Princess of Wales,' he bellows.

This is me. This is my moment. This is my battle cry.

I step forwards.

The Spanish Infanta—with her face naked to every man's gaze—walked into the room, only a little flame of colour in both cheeks betraying her ordeal.

At his father's side, Prince Arthur swallowed. She was far more beautiful than he had imagined, and a million times more haughty. She was dressed in a gown of dark black velvet, slashed to show an undergown of carnation silk, the neck cut square and low over her plump breasts, hung with ropes of pearls. Her auburn hair, freed from the plait, tumbled down her back in a great wave of red-gold. On her head was a black lace mantilla flung determinedly back. She swept a deep curtsy and came up with her head held high, graceful as a dancer.

'I beg your pardon for not being ready to greet you,' she said in French. 'If I had known you were coming I would have been prepared.'

'I'm surprised you didn't hear the racket,' the king said. 'I was arguing at your door for a good ten minutes.'

'I thought it was a pair of porters brawling,' she said coolly.

Arthur suppressed a gasp at her impertinence; but his father was eyeing her with a smile as if a new filly was showing promising spirit.

'No. It was me; threatening your lady-in-waiting. I wanted to see my daughter-in-law, and my son wanted to see his bride, and I expect an English princess to behave like an English princess, and not like some damned sequestered girl in a harem. I thought your parents had beaten the Moors. I didn't expect to find them set up as your models.'

Catalina ignored the insult. 'I am sure that you will teach me good English manners,' she said. She turned to Prince Arthur and swept him a royal curtsy. 'My lord.'

He faltered in his bow in return, amazed at the serenity that she could muster in this most embarrassing of moments. He reached into his jacket for her present, fumbled with the little purse of jewels, dropped them, picked them up and finally thrust them towards her, feeling like a fool.

She took them and inclined her head in thanks, but did not open them. 'Have you dined, Your Grace?'

'We'll eat here,' the king said bluntly. 'I ordered dinner already.'

'Then can I offer you a drink? Or somewhere to wash and change your clothes before you dine?' She examined the long, lean length of him consideringly, from the mud spattering his lined face to his dusty boots. 'Or perhaps you don't like to wash?'

A harsh chuckle was forced from the king. 'You can order me a cup of ale and have them send fresh clothes and hot water to the best bedroom and I'll change before dinner.' He raised a hand. 'You needn't take it as a compliment to you. I always wash before dinner.'

Arthur saw her nip her lower lip with little white teeth as if to refrain from some sarcastic reply. 'Yes, Your Grace,' she said pleasantly. 'As you wish.' She summoned her lady-in-waiting to her side and gave her low-voiced orders in rapid Spanish. The woman curtsied and led the king from the room.

The princess turned to Prince Arthur.

'*Et tu?*' she asked in Latin. 'And you?'

'I? What?' he stammered.

He felt that she was trying not to sigh with impatience.

'Would you like to wash and change your coat also?'

'I've washed,' he said. As soon as the words were out of his mouth he could have bitten off his own tongue. He sounded like a child being scolded by a nurse. What was he going to do next? Hold out his hands palms-upwards so that she could see he was a good boy?

'Then will you take a glass of wine? Or ale?' Catalina turned to the table, where the servants were hastily laying cups and flagons.

'Wine.'

She raised a glass and a flagon and the two chinked together, and then chinked again. In amazement, he saw that her hands were trembling.

She poured the wine quickly and held it to him. His gaze went from her hand and the slightly rippled surface of the wine to her pale face.

She was not laughing at him, he saw. She was not at all at ease with him. His father's rudeness had brought out the pride in her, but alone with him she was just a girl, some months older than him, but still just a girl. The daughter of the two most formidable monarchs in Europe; but still just a girl with shaking hands.

'You need not be frightened,' he said very quietly.

She looked down. He stared at the flawless pallor of her skin, at the fair eyelashes and pale eyebrows.

Then she looked up at him. 'It's all right,' she said. 'I have been in far worse places than this, and I have known worse men than your father. You need not fear for me. I am afraid of nothing.'

No one will ever know what it cost me to smile, what it cost me to stand before your father and not tremble. I am not yet sixteen, I am far from my mother, I am in a strange country, I cannot speak the language and I know nobody here. I have no friends but the party of companions and servants that I have brought with me, and they look to me to protect them.

I know what I have to do. I have to seem at ease where I am not, and assume confidence when I am afraid. You may be my husband, but I can hardly see you, I have no sense of you yet. I have no time to consider you, I am absorbed in being the princess that your father has bought, the princess that my mother has delivered, the princess that will fulfil the bargain and secure a treaty between England and Spain.

The king, having washed and taken a couple of glasses of wine before he came to his dinner, was affable with the young princess, determined to overlook their introduction.

'You had a bad voyage,' Henry remarked.

'Very bad,' she said. She turned to Prince Arthur. 'We were driven back as we set out from Corunna in August and we had to wait for the storms to pass. When we finally set sail it was still terribly rough, and then we were forced into Plymouth. We couldn't get to Southampton at all. We were all quite sure we would be drowned.'

'Well, you couldn't have come overland,' Henry said flatly, thinking of the parlous state of France and the enmity of the French king. 'You'd be a priceless hostage. Thank God you never fell into enemy hands.'

She looked at him thoughtfully. 'Pray God I never do.'

'Well, your troubles are over now,' Henry concluded. 'The next boat you are on will be the royal barge when you go down the Thames. How shall you like to become Princess of Wales?'

'I have been the Princess of Wales ever since I was three years old,' she corrected him. 'They always called me Catalina, the Infanta, Princess of Wales. I knew it was my destiny.' She looked at Arthur, who sat silently observing the table. 'I have known we would be married all my life. It was kind of you to write to me so often. It made me feel that we were not complete strangers.'

He flushed. 'I was ordered to write to you,' he said awkwardly. 'As part of my studies. But I liked getting your replies.'

'Good God, boy, you don't exactly sparkle, do you?' asked his father critically. 'There was no need to tell her that you were ordered to write.'

Arthur flushed scarlet to his ears.

'I don't mind,' Catalina said quietly. 'I was ordered to reply. And, as it happens, I should like us always to speak the truth to each other.'

The king barked out a laugh. 'Not in a year's time you won't,' he predicted. 'You will be all in favour of the polite lie then. The great saviour of a marriage is mutual ignorance.'

Arthur nodded obediently, but Catalina merely smiled, as if his observations were of interest, but not necessarily true.

'I dare say your father does not tell your mother every thought that crosses his mind,' he said.

She gave him a long, slow, considering gaze from her blue eyes. 'Perhaps he does not,' she conceded. 'I would not know. But whether he tells her or not, my mother knows everything anyway.'

He laughed. 'She is a visionary, your mother? She has the gift of Sight?'

'She is wise,' she said simply. 'She is the wisest monarch in Europe.'

The king thought it would be graceless to point out that her mother was a long way from creating a peaceful and united Spain. The tactical skill of Isabella and Ferdinand had forged a single country from the

Moorish kingdoms, but they had yet to make everyone accept their peace. He changed the subject. 'Why don't you show us a dance?' he demanded, thinking that he would like to see her move. 'Or is that not allowed in Spain either?'

'Since I am an English princess I must learn your customs,' she said. 'Would an English princess get up in the middle of the night and dance for the king after he forced his way into her rooms?'

Henry laughed at her. 'If she had any sense she would.'

She threw him a small, demure smile. 'Then I will dance with my ladies,' she decided, and rose from her seat at the high table and went down to the centre of the floor. She called one by name, Henry noted, Maria de Salinas, a pretty, dark-haired girl who came quickly to stand beside Catalina. Three other young women, pretending shyness but eager to show themselves off, came forwards. The princess raised her hands and clapped, to order the musicians to play.

Henry noticed at once that she moved like a sensual woman, her hips swaying and her eyes heavy-lidded, a little smile on her face. She had been well schooled: any princess would be taught how to dance in the courtly world where dancing, singing, music and poetry mattered more than anything else, but she danced like a woman who let the music move her; and Henry believed that women who could be summoned by music were the ones who responded to the rhythms of lust.

He went from pleasure in watching her to a sense of rising irritation that this exquisite piece would be put in Arthur's cold bed. He could not see his thoughtful, scholarly boy arousing the passion in this girl on the edge of womanhood.

Henry looked away from her dancing and comforted himself with the thought of her dowry which would come directly to him, unlike this bride who seemed bound to unsettle him and must go to his son. As soon as they were married her treasurer would hand over the first payment of her dowry: in solid gold. A year later he would deliver the second part in gold and in her plate and jewels. Having fought his way to the throne on a shoestring and uncertain credit, Henry trusted the power of money more than anything in life; more even than his throne.

'Do I please you?' she demanded, flushed and a little breathless.

'Well enough,' he said, determined that she should never know how much. 'But it's late and you should go back to your bed. We'll ride with you a little way in the morning before we go ahead of you to London.'

She was surprised at the abruptness of his reply. 'As you wish, Your Grace,' she said politely.

The king nodded and rose to his feet. The court billowed into deep curtsies and bows as he stalked past them, out of the room.

Arthur followed behind his father with a quick 'Good night' to the princess as he left. In a moment all the men in their train had gone too, and the princess was alone but for her ladies.

'What an extraordinary man,' she remarked to Maria de Salinas.

'He liked you,' the young woman said.

'And why should he not?' she asked with the instinctive arrogance of a girl born to the greatest kingdom in Europe.

He is not what I expected, this king who fought his way to the throne and picked up his crown from the mud of a battlefield. I expected him to be more like a great soldier, perhaps like my father. Instead he has the look of a merchant, not a man who won his kingdom and his wife at the point of a sword.

I expected his court to be more grand, I expected a great procession and a formal meeting with long introductions and elegant speeches, as we would have done it in the Alhambra. But he is abrupt; in my view he is rude. I shall have to become accustomed to these northern ways. I shall have to overlook a lot until I am queen and can change things.

But, anyway, it hardly matters whether I like the king or he likes me. He has engaged in this treaty with my father and I am betrothed to his son. I shall live and rule Wales and he will live and rule England, and when he dies it will be my husband on his throne and my son will be the next Prince of Wales, and I shall be queen.

As for my husband-to-be—oh!—he has made a very different first impression. He is so handsome! I did not expect him to be so handsome! He has pale, almost silvery skin, he has fine golden hair, and yet he is taller than me and lean and strong like a boy on the edge of manhood.

He has a rare smile, one that comes reluctantly and then shines. And he is kind. That is a great thing in a husband. He was kind when he took the glass of wine from me; he saw that I was trembling and he tried to reassure me.

I wonder what he thinks of me? I do so wonder what he thinks of me?

Just as the king had ruled, he and Arthur went swiftly back to Windsor the next morning and Catalina's train, with her litter carried by mules, with her trousseau in great travelling chests, her ladies-in-waiting, her Spanish household, and the guards for her dowry treasure, laboured up the muddy roads to London at a far slower pace.

She did not see the prince again until their wedding day, but when she arrived in the village of Kingston upon Thames her train halted in order to meet the greatest man in the kingdom, the young Edward Stafford, Duke of Buckingham, and Henry, Duke of York, the king's second son, who were appointed to accompany her to Lambeth Palace.

'I'll come out,' Catalina said hastily, emerging from her litter and walking quickly past the waiting horses, not wanting another quarrel with her strict duenna about young ladies meeting young men before their wedding day.

The older woman shook her head, but Catalina marched out barefaced, feeling both fearful and reckless at her own daring, and saw the duke's men drawn up in array on the road and before them, a young boy on his horse, helmet off, bright head shining in the sunshine.

Her first thought was that he was utterly unlike his brother. While Arthur was fair-haired and slight and serious-looking, with a pale complexion and warm blue eyes, this was a sunny boy who looked as if he had never had a serious thought in his head. His hair was red-gold, his face still baby-plump, his smile when he first saw her was genuinely friendly and bright, and his blue eyes shone as if he was accustomed to seeing a very pleasing world.

'Sister!' he said warmly, jumped down from his horse with a clatter of armour, and swept her a low bow.

'Brother Henry,' she said, curtsying back to him.

'I am so pleased to see you,' he said quickly, his Latin rapid, his English accent strong. 'I was so hoping that His Majesty would let me come to meet you before I had to take you into London on your wedding day. And call me Harry. Everyone calls me Harry.'

'I, too, am pleased to meet you, Brother Harry,' Catalina said politely.

'Pleased! You should be dancing with joy!' he exclaimed. 'Because Father said that I could bring you the horse that was to be one of your wedding-day presents and so we can ride together to Lambeth. Arthur said you should wait for your wedding day, but I said, why should she wait? She won't be able to ride on her wedding day.'

'That was kind of you.'

'Oh, I never take any notice of Arthur,' Harry said cheerfully.

Catalina had to choke down a giggle. 'You don't?'

He made a face and shook his head. 'Serious,' he said. 'And scholarly, of course, but not gifted. Everyone says I am very gifted, languages mostly, but music also. And, of course, I am a sportsman. Do you hunt?'

'No,' Catalina said, a little overwhelmed. 'At least, I only follow the hunt when we go after boar or wolves.'

'Wolves? I should so like to hunt wolves. Do you hunt them on foot like boar?'

'No, on horseback,' she said. 'They're very fast, you have to take very fast dogs to pull them down. It's a horrid hunt.'

'I shouldn't mind that,' he said. 'Everyone says I am terribly brave about things like that.'

'I am sure they do,' she said, smiling.

A handsome man in his mid-twenties came forwards and bowed. 'Oh, this is Edward Stafford, the Duke of Buckingham,' Harry said quickly. 'May I present him?'

Catalina held out her hand and the man bowed again over it. 'You are welcome to your own country,' he said in faultless Castilian. 'I hope everything has been to your liking on your journey? Is there anything I can provide for you?'

'I have been well cared for indeed,' Catalina said, blushing with pleasure at being greeted in her own language. 'And the welcome I have had from people all along the way has been very kind.'

'Look, here's your new horse,' Harry interrupted, as the groom led a beautiful black mare forwards. 'You'll be used to good horses, of course. D'you have Barbary horses?'

'My mother insists on them for the cavalry,' she said.

'Oh,' he breathed. 'Because they are so fast?'

'They can be trained as fighting horses,' she said, holding out her hand, palm upwards, for the mare to sniff and nibble at.

'Fighting horses?' he pursued.

'The Saracens have horses that can fight as their masters do, and the Barbary horses can be trained to do it too,' Catalina said. 'They rear up and strike down a soldier with their front hoofs, and they will kick out behind, too. My mother says that one good horse is worth ten men in battle.'

'I should so like to have a horse like that,' Harry said longingly. 'I wonder how I should ever get one?'

He paused, but she did not rise to the bait. 'If only someone would give me a horse like that, I could learn how to ride it,' he said transparently. 'Perhaps for my birthday, or perhaps next week, since it is not me getting married, and I am quite neglected.'

'Perhaps,' said Catalina.

'I should be trained to ride properly,' he said. 'Father has promised that though I am to go into the church I shall be allowed to ride at the quintain. But My Lady the King's Mother says I may not joust. And it's really unfair. I should be allowed to joust. If I had a proper horse I could joust, I am sure I would beat everyone.'

'I am sure you would,' she said.

'Well, shall we go?' he asked, seeing that she would not give him a horse for asking.

'I cannot ride, I do not have my riding clothes unpacked.'

He hesitated. 'Can't you just go in that?'

Catalina laughed. 'This is velvet and silk. I can't ride in it.'

'Oh,' he said. 'Well, shall you go in your litter then? Won't it make us very slow?'

'I am sorry for that, but I am ordered to travel in a litter,' she said. 'With the curtains drawn. I can't think that even your father would want me to charge around the country with my skirts tucked up.'

'Of course the princess cannot ride today,' the Duke of Buckingham ruled. 'As I told you. She has to go in her litter.'

Harry shrugged. 'Well, I didn't know. Can I go ahead then? My horses will be so much faster than the mules.'

'You can ride ahead but not out of sight,' Catalina decided. 'Since you are supposed to be escorting me you should be with me.'

'As I said,' the Duke of Buckingham observed quietly and exchanged a little smile with the princess.

'I'll wait at every crossroads,' Harry promised. 'I am escorting you, remember. And on your wedding day I shall be escorting you again. I have a white suit with gold slashing.'

'I am sure everyone will remark what a handsome boy you are,' she said, and saw him flush with pleasure.

'Everyone always cheers most loudly for me,' he confided. 'And I like to know that the people love me. Father says that the only way to keep a throne is to be beloved by the people.'

'My mother says that the way to keep the throne is to do God's work.'

'Oh,' he said, unimpressed. 'Well, different countries, I suppose.'

'So we shall travel together,' she said. 'I will tell my people that we are ready to move on.'

'I will tell them,' he insisted. 'I shall give the orders and you shall rest in your litter.' He gave one quick sideways glance at her. 'When we get to Lambeth Palace you shall stay in your litter till I come for you. I shall draw back the curtains and take you in, and you should hold my hand.'

'I should like that very much,' she assured him, and saw his ready rush of colour once again.

He bustled off and the duke bowed to her with a smile. 'You must forgive his enthusiasm. He has been much indulged.'

'His mother's favourite?' she asked, thinking of her own mother's adoration for her only son.

'Worse still,' the duke said with a smile. 'His mother loves him as she should; but he is the absolute apple of his grandmother's eye, and it is she who rules the court.'

31

'She is an indulgent woman?' she asked.

'Only to her son,' he said. 'The rest of us find her—er—more majestic than motherly.'

'May we talk again at Lambeth?' Catalina asked, tempted to know more about this household that she was to join.

'At Lambeth and London, I shall be proud to serve you,' the young man said, his eyes warm with admiration. 'You must command me as you wish. I shall be your friend in England, you can call on me.'

London, 14th November 1501

On the morning of her wedding day Catalina was called early; but she had been awake for hours, stirring as soon as the cold, wintry sun had started to light the pale sky. They had prepared a great bath—her ladies told her that the English were amazed that she was going to wash before her wedding day and that most of them thought that she was risking her life. Catalina, brought up in the Alhambra where the bath houses were the most beautiful suite of rooms in the palace, was equally amazed to hear that the English thought it perfectly adequate to bathe only occasionally, and that the poor people would bathe only once a year.

'I suppose it is always so cold that it does not matter,' she said uncertainly to Doña Elvira.

'It matters to us,' the duenna said.

Doña Elvira had commanded from the flesh kitchen a great tureen that was usually deployed to scald beast carcasses, had it scoured by three scullions, lined it with linen sheets and filled it to the brim with hot water scattered with oil of roses brought from Spain. She lovingly supervised the washing of Catalina's long white limbs, the manicuring of her toes, the filing of her fingernails, the brushing of her teeth and finally the three-rinse washing of her hair.

'If only we had a proper bath house,' Doña Elvira mourned. 'With steam and a tepidarium and a proper clean marble floor! Hot water on tap and somewhere for you to sit and be properly scrubbed.'

'Don't fuss,' Catalina said dreamily as they helped her from the bath and patted her all over with scented towels. One maid took her hair, squeezed out the water and rubbed it gently with red silk soaked in oil to give it shine and colour.

'Your mother would be so proud of you,' Doña Elvira said as they led the Infanta towards her wardrobe and started to dress her in layer after layer of shifts and gowns. 'This is her day, as well as yours, Catalina. She said that you would marry him whatever it cost her.'

Yes, but she did not pay the greatest price. I know they bought me this wedding with a king's ransom for my dowry, and I know that they endured long and hard negotiations, and I survived the worst voyage anyone has ever taken, but there was another price paid that we never speak of—wasn't there?

There was a man of only twenty-four years old, Edward Plantagenet, the Duke of Warwick and a son of the kings of England, with—truth be told—a better claim to the throne of England than that of my father-in-law. He was a prince, nephew to the king, and of blood royal. He committed no crime, but he was arrested for my sake, taken to the Tower for my benefit, and finally beheaded on the block, for my gain, so that my parents could be satisfied that there were no pretenders to the throne that they had bought for me.

When they told me that he was dead, I said nothing, for I am an Infanta of Spain. Before anything else, I am my mother's daughter. I do not weep like a girl and tell all the world my every thought. But when I was alone in the gardens of the Alhambra in the evening with the sun going down I prayed that I might be forgiven for the death of an innocent man.

And sometimes, when I do not remember to be Infanta of Spain nor Princess of Wales, but just the Catalina who walked behind her mother through the great gate into the Alhambra Palace, and knew that her mother was the greatest power the world had ever known, sometimes I wonder childishly, if my mother has not made a great mistake? If she has not driven God's will too far? For this wedding is launched in a sea of innocent blood. How can such a wedding ever be the start of a good marriage? Must it not—as night follows sunset—be tragic and bloody too? How can any happiness ever come to Prince Arthur and to me that has been bought at such a terrible price?

Prince Harry, the ten-year-old Duke of York, was so proud of his white taffeta suit that he scarcely glanced at Catalina until they were at the west doors of St Paul's Cathedral and then he turned and stared, trying to see her face through the exquisite lace of the white mantilla. Ahead of them stretched a raised pathway, lined with red cloth, studded with golden nails, running at head height from the great doorway of the church where the citizens of London crowded to get a better view, up the long aisle to the altar where Prince Arthur stood, pale with nerves, 600 slow ceremonial paces away.

Catalina smiled at the young boy at her side, and he beamed with delight. He paused for a moment more, until everyone in the enormous church realised that the bride and prince were at the doorway, waiting to make their entrance, a hush fell, everyone craned to see the bride, and then, at the precise, most theatrical moment, he led her forwards.

The prince turned as Catalina came towards him, but was blinded for a moment by irritation at the sight of his brother, leading the princess as if he himself were the bridegroom, as if it were him that everyone had come to see. Then they were both at Arthur's side and Harry had to step back, however reluctantly, as the princess and prince faced the archbishop together and knelt together on the specially embroidered white taffeta cushions.

Never has a couple been more married, King Henry thought sourly, standing in the royal pew with his wife and his mother. Nine times they have been betrothed. This will be a marriage that nothing can break. Her father cannot wriggle from it, whatever second thoughts he has. He will protect me against France now. The very thought of our alliance will frighten the French into peace with me, and we must have peace.

He glanced at his wife at his side. Her eyes were filled with tears, watching her son and his bride as the archbishop raised their clasped hands and wrapped them in his holy stole. Her face, beautiful with emotion, did not stir him. Who ever knew what she was thinking behind that lovely mask? Of her own marriage, the union of York and Lancaster which put her as a wife on the throne that she could have claimed in her own right? The king scowled. He was never sure of his wife, Elizabeth. In general, he preferred not to consider her.

Beyond her, his flint-faced mother, Margaret Beaufort, watched the young couple with a glimmer of a smile. This was England's triumph, this was her son's triumph, but far more than that, this was *her* triumph. It was her plan to bring her son back from France at the right moment to claim his throne. They were her alliances who gave him the soldiers for the battle. It was her battle plan that left the usurper Richard to despair on the field at Bosworth, and this was the marriage that was the culmination of that long struggle. This bride would give her a great-grandson, a Spanish–Tudor king for England, and so lay down a dynasty of Tudors that would be never-ending.

Catalina repeated the words of the marriage vow, felt the weight of a cold ring on her finger, turned her face to her new husband and felt his cool kiss, in a daze. When she walked back down that absurd walkway and saw the smiling faces in the cathedral she started to realise that it was done. And when they went from the cool dark of the cathedral to the bright wintry sunlight outside and heard the roar of the crowd for Arthur and his bride, the Prince and Princess of Wales, she realised that she had done her duty finally and completely. She looked up and smiled and the crowd, delighted with the free wine, with the prettiness of the young girl, with the promise of safety from civil war that could only come with a settled royal succession, roared their approval.

They were husband and wife; but they did not speak more than a few words to each other for the rest of the long day. There was a formal banquet, and though they were seated side by side, there were healths to be drunk and speeches to be attended to, and musicians playing. After the long dinner of many courses there was an entertainment with poetry and singers and a tableau. It was a greater celebration than the king's own wedding, greater even than his coronation. Two new dynasties were proclaiming themselves by this union: Ferdinand and Isabella of the new country that they were forging from al Andalus, and the Tudors who were making England their own.

The musicians played a dance from Spain and Queen Elizabeth, at a nod from her mother-in-law, leaned over and said quietly to Catalina, 'It would be a great pleasure for us all if you would dance.'

Catalina, quite composed, rose from her chair and went to the centre of the great hall as her ladies gathered around her, formed a circle and held hands. They danced the pavane, the same dance that Henry had seen at Dogmersfield, and he watched his daughter-in-law through narrowed eyes. Undoubtedly, she was the most beddable young woman in the room. 'She is delightful,' the queen remarked.

'Let's hope so,' he said sourly.

'My lord?'

He smiled at her look of surprised enquiry. 'No, nothing. You are right, delightful indeed. And Arthur, he seems to be growing and strong? I would to God he had the spirits of his brother.'

They both looked at young Harry who was standing, watching the dancers, his face flushed with excitement, his eyes bright.

'Oh, Harry,' his mother said indulgently. 'But there has never been a prince more handsome and more full of fun than Harry.'

The Spanish dance ended and the king clapped his hands. 'Now Harry and his sister,' he commanded. He did not want to force Arthur to dance in front of his new bride. The boy danced like a clerk, all gangling legs and concentration. But Harry was raring to go and was on the floor with his sister Princess Margaret in a moment. The musicians struck up a lively galliard. Harry tossed his jacket to one side and threw himself into the dance, stripped down to his shirtsleeves like a peasant.

When the two had romped their way through the final turns and gallop, everyone applauded, laughing. Everyone but Prince Arthur, who was staring into the middle distance, determined not to watch his brother dance. He came to with a start only when his mother put her hand on his arm.

'Please God he's daydreaming of his wedding night,' the king remarked

35

to Lady Margaret his mother. 'Though I doubt it.'

'I can't say I think much of the bride,' she said critically.

'You don't?' he asked. 'You saw the treaty yourself.'

'I like the price but the goods are not to my taste,' she said with her usual sharp wit. 'She is a slight, pretty thing, isn't she?'

'Would you rather a strapping milkmaid?'

'I'd like a girl with the hips to give us sons,' she said bluntly.

'She looks well enough to me,' he ruled. He knew that he would never be able to say how well she looked to him. Even to himself he should never even think it.

Catalina was put into her wedding bed by her ladies, Maria de Salinas kissed her good night, and Doña Elvira gave her a mother's blessing; but Arthur had to undergo a further round of backslapping ribaldry, before his friends and companions escorted him to her door. They put him into bed beside the princess, who lay still and silent as the strange men laughed and bade them good night, and then the archbishop came to sprinkle the sheets with holy water and pray over the young couple. It could not have been a more public bedding unless they had opened the doors for the citizens of London to see the young people in their marital bed. Finally the doors were closed and the two of them were quite alone, frozen like a pair of shy dolls.

There was silence.

'Would you like a glass of ale?' Arthur suggested in a voice thin with nerves.

'I don't like ale very much,' Catalina said.

'This is different. They call it wedding ale; it's sweetened with mead and spices. It's for courage.'

'Do we need courage?'

He got out of bed to fetch her a cup. 'I should think we do,' he said. 'You are a stranger in a new land, and I have never known any girls but my sisters. We both have much to learn.'

She took the cup of the hot ale from him and sipped the heady drink. 'Oh, that is nice.'

Arthur gulped down a cup and took another. Then he came back to the bed. 'I shall blow out the candle,' he announced. The sudden dark engulfed them; only the embers of the fire glowed red.

'Are you very tired?' he asked, longing for her to say that she was too tired to do her duty.

'Not at all,' she said politely, her disembodied voice coming out of the darkness. 'Are you?'

'No.'

'I know what we have to do,' she said abruptly. 'All my sisters have been married. I know all about it.'

'I know as well,' he said, stung.

'I didn't mean that you don't know, I meant that you need not be afraid to start.'

'I am not afraid, it is just that I . . .'

To his absolute horror he felt her hand pull his nightshirt upwards, and touch the bare skin of his belly.

'I did not want to frighten you,' he said, desire rising up even though he was sick with fear that he would be incompetent.

'I am not afraid,' said Isabella's daughter.

In the silence and the darkness he felt her take hold of him and grasp firmly. At her touch he felt his desire well up so sharply that he was afraid he would come in her hand. With a low groan he rolled over on top of her and found she had stripped herself naked to the waist, her night-gown pulled up. He fumbled clumsily and felt her flinch as he pushed against her. The whole process seemed quite impossible; there was no way of knowing what a man was supposed to do, and then she gave a little cry of pain, stifled with her hand, and he knew he had done it. The relief was so great that he came at once, a half-painful, half-pleasurable rush that told him that, whatever his father thought of him, whatever his brother Harry thought of him, he was a man and a husband; and the princess was his wife and no longer a virgin untouched.

Catalina waited till he was asleep and then she got up and washed herself in her privy chamber. She was bleeding but she knew it would stop soon; the pain was no worse than she had expected, Isabel her sister had said it was not as bad as falling from a horse, and she had been right.

Catalina came back to the bedroom. But she did not go back to the bed. Instead she sat on the floor by the fire, watching the embers.

'Not a bad day,' I say to myself, and I smile; it is my mother's phrase. I want to hear her voice so much that I am saying her words to myself.

'Is there ever a bad day?' I once asked her.

'Not when you are doing God's work,' she replied seriously. 'There are days when it is easy and days when it is hard. But if you are on God's work then there are never bad days.'

I don't for a moment doubt that bedding Arthur is God's work. It is God's work that there should be an unbreakable alliance between Spain and England. Only with England as a reliable ally can Spain challenge the spread

of France. Only with English wealth, and especially English ships, can we Spanish maintain the defence of Christendom against the terrifying might of the Moors. And once they are defeated, then the crusaders must go on, to India, to the East, as far as they have to go to challenge and defeat the wickedness that is the religion of the Moors.

'What if there is no end to them?' I once asked my mother, as we leaned over the sun-warmed walls of the fort and watched the dispatch of a new group of Moors leaving the city of Granada. 'What if now we have defeated these, they just go back to Africa and in another year, they come again?'

'That is why you have to be brave, my Princess of Wales,' my mother had answered. 'That is why you have to be ready to fight them whenever they come, wherever they come. They will come again and again, and you will have to be ready in Wales as we will be ready in Spain. I bore you to be a fighting princess as I am a Queen Militant. Your father and I placed you in England as Maria is placed in Portugal, as Juana is placed with the Hapsburgs in the Netherlands. You are there to defend the lands of your husbands, and to hold them in alliance with us. Make sure that you never fail your country, as your sisters must never fail theirs, as I have never failed mine.'

Catalina was woken in the early hours of the morning by Arthur gently pushing between her legs. Resentfully, she let him do as he wanted, knowing that this was the way to get a son and make the alliance secure. It did not take long, and then he fell asleep. Catalina lay as still as a frozen stone in order not to wake him again.

He did not stir until daybreak, when his grooms of the bedchamber rapped brightly on the door. He rose up with a slightly embarrassed 'Good morning' to her; and went out. They greeted him with cheers and marched him in triumph to his own rooms. Catalina heard him say, vulgarly, boastfully, 'Gentlemen, this night I have been in Spain,' and heard the yell of laughter that applauded his joke. Her ladies came in with her gown and heard the men's laughter.

'I don't know what your mother would say,' Doña Elvira remarked.

'She would say that words count less than God's will, and God's will has been done,' Catalina said firmly.

It was not like this for my mother. She fell in love with my father on sight and she married him with great joy. What looked like a remarkable unity of two calculating players was deceptive—it was their passion that they played out on the political stage. She was a great queen because that was how she could evoke his desire. He was a great general in order to match her. It was their love, their lust, that drove them; almost as much as God.

We are a passionate family. When Isabel, my sister, now with God, came back from Portugal a widow she swore that she had loved her husband so much that she would never take another. Juana, my second sister, is so in love with her husband Philip that she cannot bear to let him out of her sight, she is quite mad with love for him. And my brother . . . my darling brother Juan . . . simply died of love. He and his beautiful wife Margot were so passionate, so besotted with each other, that his health failed, he was dead within six months of their wedding. I come from passionate stock—but what about me? Shall I ever fall in love?

Not with this clumsy boy, for a certainty. My early liking for him has quite melted away. He forced me to command in the bedroom, and I am ashamed that I had to be the one to make the first move. 'In Spain', indeed! Stupid puppy.

When I first saw him I thought he was as beautiful as a knight from the romances. I thought I could be like a lady in a tower and he could sing beneath my window and persuade me to love him. But I can never get more than two words out of him, and I feel that I demean myself in trying to please him.

Of course, I will never forget that it is my duty to endure this youth, this Arthur. My hope is always for a child, and my destiny is to keep England safe against the Moors. I shall do that; whatever else happens, I shall be Queen of England and protect my two countries: the Spain of my birth and the England of my marriage.

London, Winter 1501

Arthur and Catalina, standing stiffly side by side on the royal barge, led a great fleet of gaily painted barges downriver to Baynard's Castle, which would be their London home for the next weeks. The Mayor of London, the councillors, and all the court followed the royal barge; and musicians played as the heirs to the throne took up residence in the City.

Catalina noticed that the Scots envoys were much in attendance, negotiating the marriage of her new twelve-year-old sister-in-law, Princess Margaret. King Henry was using his children as pawns in his game for power, as every king must do. Princess Mary also would be married, when her time came, either to the greatest enemy that the country faced, or the greatest friend that they hoped to keep.

Catalina also noticed that Arthur was very restrained in his greeting when he met the Scots lords at dinner at the Palace of Westminster.

'The Scots are our most dangerous enemies,' Edward Stafford, the Duke of Buckingham, told Catalina in whispered Castilian, as they stood at the back of the hall, waiting for the company to take their seats. 'The king and the prince hope that this marriage will bind the Scots to

39

us. But it is hard for any of us to forget how they have constantly harried us. We have all been brought up to know that we have a most constant enemy to the north.'

'Surely they are only a poor little kingdom,' she queried. 'What harm can they do us?'

'They always ally with France,' he told her. 'Every time we have a war with France they make an alliance and pour over our northern borders. Every summer they harry the border countries and steal what they cannot grow or make themselves. No northern farmer has ever been safe from them. The king is determined to have peace.'

'Will they be kind to the Princess Margaret?'

'In their own rough way.' He smiled. 'Not as you have been welcomed, Infanta.'

Catalina beamed in return. She knew that she was warmly welcomed in England. Londoners had taken the Spanish princess to their hearts, they liked the oddness of her dress, and they liked the way the princess always had a smile for a waiting crowd. Catalina had learned from her mother that the people are a greater power than an army of mercenaries and she never turned her head away from a cheer.

She turned to find Arthur at her side, ready to conduct her into the hall behind his parents.

The royal family took their seats. The king and his two sons sat at the high table under the canopy of state, to their right sat the queen and the princesses. My Lady the King's Mother, Margaret Beaufort, was seated beside the king, between him and his wife.

'Catalina has become the very centre of the court,' she complained to him. 'The palace is crowded out with people coming to watch her dine. Everyone wants to see her.'

'She's a seven-day wonder. And anyway, I want people to see her.'

The groom of the ewer presented a golden bowl filled with scented water and Lady Margaret dipped her fingertips and then wiped them on the napkin.

'I think her very pleasing,' Henry said as he dried his own hands. 'And the people like her.'

His mother made a small, dismissive gesture. 'She has not been brought up as I would bring up a child of mine. Her will has not been broken to obedience. She thinks that she is something special.'

Henry glanced across at the princess. She had bent her head to listen to something being said by the youngest Tudor princess, Princess Mary; and he saw her smile and reply. 'D'you know? I think she is something special,' he said.

The celebrations continued for days and days, and then the court moved on to the new-built, glamorous palace of Richmond, set in a great and beautiful park. To Catalina, in a swirl of strange faces and introductions, it felt as if one wonderful joust and fête merged into another, with herself at the very centre of it all. But after a week the party was concluded with the king coming to the princess and telling her that it was time for her Spanish companions to go home.

Catalina had always known that the little court that had accompanied her through storms and near-shipwreck to present her to her new husband would leave her once the wedding was done and the first half of the dowry paid; but it was a gloomy couple of days while they packed their bags and said goodbye to the princess. She would be left with her small domestic household, her ladies, her chamberlain, her treasurer, and her immediate servants, but the rest of her entourage must leave. She sent them with messages to everyone in Spain and with a letter for her mother.

From her daughter, Catalina, Princess of Wales, to Her Royal Highness of Castile and Aragon, and most dearest Madre,

Oh, Madre!

As these ladies and gentlemen will tell you, the prince and I have a house near the river. It is called Baynard's Castle although it is not a castle but a palace and newly built. There are no bath houses, for either ladies or men. I know what you are thinking. You cannot imagine it.

Doña Elvira has had the blacksmith make a great cauldron which they heat up on the fire in the kitchen and six serving men heave it to my room for my bath. Also, there are no pleasure gardens with flowers, no streams, no fountains, it is quite extraordinary. At best, they have a tiny court which they call a knot garden where you can walk round and round until you are dizzy. The food is not good and the wine very sour. They eat nothing but preserved fruit and I believe they have never heard of vegetables.

You must not think that I am complaining, I wanted you to know that even with these small difficulties I am content to be the princess. Prince Arthur is kind and considerate to me when we meet, which is generally at dinner. He has given me a very beautiful mare of Barbary stock mixed with English, and I ride her every day.

You will want to know if I am with child. There are no signs yet. You will want to know that I read my Bible or holy books for two hours every day, as you ordered, and that I go to Mass three times a day and I take Communion every Sunday also. Father Alessandro Geraldini is well, and I trust to him and to God to keep me strong in the faith to do God's work in England as you do in Spain. Doña Elvira keeps my ladies in good order and I obey her as I would you.

I will be the princess that you want me to be. I shall not fail you or God. I will be queen and I will defend England against the Moors.

Please write to me soon and tell me how you are. You seemed so sad and low when I left, I hope that you are better now. I pray for you and for Father every day. I hear your voice in my head, advising me all the time. Please write soon to your daughter who loves you so much,

Catalina

The young Prince and Princess of Wales finished their visit to Richmond and started to make their own royal household in Baynard's Castle. Catalina had her rooms at the back of the house, overlooking the gardens and the river, with her household, her Spanish ladies, her Spanish chaplain, and duenna, and Arthur's rooms overlooked the City, with his household, his chaplain, and his tutor. They met formally only once a day for dinner, when the two households sat at opposite sides of the hall and stared at each other with mutual suspicion.

The castle was run according to the commands of Lady Margaret, the king's mother. The feast days and fast days, the entertainments and the daily timetable were all commanded by her. Even the nights when Arthur was to visit his wife in her bedchamber had been appointed by her. Once a week the prince's household and friends solemnly escorted him to the princess's rooms and left him there overnight. For both young people the experience was an ordeal of embarrassment. Arthur became no more skilled, Catalina endured his silent determination as politely as she could. But then, one day in early December, Catalina's monthly course started and she told Doña Elvira. The duenna at once told the prince's groom of the bedchamber that the prince could not come to the Infanta's bed for a week. Within half an hour, everyone from the king at Whitehall to the spit boy at Baynard's Castle knew that the Princess of Wales was having her course and so no child had yet been conceived; and everyone from the king to the spit boy wondered, since the girl was lusty and strong and since she was bleeding—therefore obviously fertile—if Arthur was capable of doing his side of their duty.

In the middle of December, when the court was preparing for the great twelve-day feast of Christmas, Arthur was summoned by his father and ordered to prepare to leave for his castle at Ludlow.

'I suppose you'll want to take your wife with you,' the king said, smiling at his son in an effort to seem unconcerned.

'As you wish, sir,' Arthur replied carefully.

'What would you wish?'

After enduring a week's ban from Catalina's bed, with everyone remarking among themselves that no child had been made, Arthur felt embarrassed. He had not gone back to her bedroom and she had sent no message to invite him to resume his visits.

'She does not seem very merry,' Arthur observed.

'She's homesick,' his father said briskly. 'It's up to you to divert her. Take her to Ludlow with you. Buy her things. She's a girl like any other. Praise her beauty. Tell her jokes. Flirt with her.'

Arthur looked quite blank. 'In Latin?'

His father barked his harsh laugh. 'Lad. You can do it in Welsh if your eyes are smiling and your cock is hard.'

There was no answering brightness from his son. 'Yes, sir.'

'If you don't want her with you, you're not obliged to take her this year. You were supposed to marry and then spend the first year apart.'

'That was when I was fourteen.'

'Only a year ago.'

'Yes, but . . .'

'So you do want her with you?'

His son flushed. The father regarded the boy with sympathy. 'You want her, but you are afraid she will make a fool of you?' he suggested.

The blond head drooped, nodded. 'If she dislikes me . . .' he started, his voice very low.

Henry rested a heavy hand on his boy's shoulder. 'Oh, my son. It doesn't matter what she thinks of you,' he said. 'Perhaps your mother was not my choice, perhaps I was not hers. When a throne is involved the heart comes in second place if it ever matters at all. She knows what she has to do; and that is all that counts.'

'Oh, she knows all about it!' the boy burst out resentfully. 'She has no shame at all.'

Henry caught his breath. 'She is shameless? She is passionate?' He tried to keep the desire from his voice, a sudden lascivious picture of his daughter-in-law, naked and shameless, in his mind.

'No! She goes at it like a man harnessing a horse,' Arthur said miserably. 'A task to be done.'

Henry choked down a laugh. 'But at least she does it,' he said. 'You don't have to beg her, or persuade her. She knows what she has to do?'

Arthur turned from him to the window and looked out of the arrow slit to the cold River Thames below. 'I don't think she likes me.'

'My boy, she doesn't know what she thinks of you. The sooner you and she are alone together, the sooner you two will come to terms. You can take her with you to Ludlow and you can get acquainted.'

The boy nodded, but he did not look convinced. 'If it is your wish, sire,' he said formally.

'Shall I ask her if she wants to go?'

The colour flooded into the young man's cheeks. 'What if she says no?' he asked anxiously.

His father laughed. 'She won't,' he promised. 'You'll see.'

Henry was right. Catalina was too much of a princess to say either yes or no to a king. When he asked her if she would like to go to Ludlow with the prince she said that she would do whatever the king wished.

'Is Lady Margaret Pole still at the castle?' she asked nervously.

He scowled at her. Lady Margaret was now safely married to Sir Richard Pole, warden of Ludlow Castle. But Lady Margaret had been born Margaret Plantagenet, beloved daughter of the Duke of Clarence, cousin to King Edward and sister to the beheaded Edward of Warwick whose claim to the throne had been so much greater than Henry's own.

'You have no cause to avoid her,' he said gruffly. 'What was done, was done in my name, by my order. You don't bear any blame for it.'

She flushed as if they were talking of something shameful. 'I know.'

'I can't have anyone challenging my right to the throne,' he said abruptly. 'I can't have anyone claiming by their pretended right what I have won by conquest. And I won't have anyone else claiming by conquest either.'

'I thought you were the true king,' Catalina said hesitantly.

'I am now,' said Henry Tudor bluntly. 'And that's all that matters.'

'But you are of the royal line?'

'I have royal blood in my veins,' he said, his voice hard. 'No need to measure how much or how little. I picked up my crown off the battlefield, literally; it was at my feet in the mud. Everyone saw God give me the victory because I was his chosen king. The archbishop anointed me because he knew that too. That's an end to it.'

She bowed her head to the energy in his words. 'I know, sire.'

Her submissiveness, and the pride that was hidden behind it, fascinated him. He thought that there had never been a young woman whose smooth face could hide her thoughts like this one.

'Tell me! Would you like to go to Ludlow with Arthur, or would you rather stay here with me?'

She smiled faintly. 'You are the king,' she said quietly. 'I must do whatever you command.'

Henry knew he should not keep her at court beside him but he could not resist playing with the idea. He consulted her Spanish advisers, and found them hopelessly divided and squabbling among themselves. The Spanish ambassador insisted that the princess should go with her new husband. Her duenna, the formidable and difficult Doña Elvira, preferred not to leave London. She had heard that Wales was a hundred miles away, a mountainous and rocky land. If Catalina stayed in Baynard's Castle and the household was rid of Arthur, then she would rule the princess and the little Spanish court.

The queen volunteered her opinion that Catalina would find Wales too cold and lonely in mid-December and suggested that perhaps the young couple could stay together in London until spring.

'You just hope to keep Arthur with you, but he has to go,' Henry said brusquely to her. 'He has to learn the business of kingship and there is no better way to learn to rule England than to rule the Principality.'

'He's still young, and he is shy with her.'

'He has to learn to be a husband too.'

In the end, it was the king's mother who gave the decisive advice. 'Send her,' she said to her son. 'We need a child off her. She won't make one on her own in London. Send her with Arthur to Ludlow. They are married and they have to live together and make an heir.'

He shot her a swift smile. 'She is only just sixteen,' he said, 'and still missing her mother. You make no allowances for her youth, do you?'

'I was married at twelve years old, and gave birth to you in the same year. No one made any allowances for me. And yet I survived.'

'I doubt you were happy.'

'I was not. I doubt that she is. But that is the last thing that matters.'

We are to go to my castle at Ludlow,' Arthur remarked awkwardly to Catalina. They were seated side by side at dinner, the hall below them and the gallery above crowded with people who had come for the free entertainment of watching the court dine. She bowed her head but did not look at him. 'Is it your father's command?' she asked.

'Yes.'

'Then I shall be happy to go,' she said.

'We will be alone, but for the warden of the castle and his wife,' Arthur went on. He wanted to say that he hoped she would not be bored, or sad or—worst of all—angry with him.

She looked at him without a smile. 'And so?'

'I hope you will be content,' he stumbled.

'Whatever your father wishes,' she said steadily, as if to remind him that they were merely prince and princess and had no rights and no power at all.

He cleared his throat. 'I shall come to your room tonight,' he asserted.

'Whatever you wish,' she said in the same neutral tone.

He came when she was in bed and Doña Elvira admitted him to the room, her face like a stone, disapproval in every gesture. Catalina sat up in bed and watched as his groom of the bedchamber took his gown from his shoulders and went quietly out, closing the door behind him.

Awkwardly the young man came to the bed, turned back the sheets, got in beside her. She turned to look at him, and he knew he was blushing beneath her enquiring gaze. He blew out the candle so she could not see his discomfort. Arthur felt the bed move as she lay back and pulled her nightdress out of the way. He felt as if he were a thing to her, an object of no importance, something she had to endure in order to be Queen of England.

He threw back the covers and jumped from the bed. 'I'm not staying here. I'm going to my room,' he said tersely.

'What?'

'I shan't stay here. I'm not wanted.'

'Not wanted? I never said you were not—'

'It is obvious. The way you look . . .'

'It's pitch-black! How d'you know how I look? And anyway, you look as if someone forced you here!'

'I? It isn't me who sent a message that half the court heard, that I was not to come to your bed.'

He heard her gasp. 'I did not say you were not to come. I had to tell them to tell you—' She broke off in embarrassment. 'It was my time . . . you had to know . . .'

'Your duenna told my steward that I was not to come to your bed. How d'you think that looked to everyone?'

'How else was I to tell you?' she demanded.

'Tell me yourself!' he raged. 'Don't tell everyone else in the world.'

'How could I say such a thing? I should be so embarrassed!'

'Instead it is me who is made to look a fool!'

Catalina slipped out of bed and steadied herself, holding the tall carved bedpost. 'My lord, I apologise if I have offended you, I don't know how such things are done here . . . In future I will do as you wish.'

He said nothing.

She waited.

'I'm going,' he said and went to hammer on the door for his groom to come to him.

'Don't!' The cry was forced out of her.

'What?' He turned.

'Everyone will know,' she said desperately. 'Know that there is something wrong between us. What do you want people to think? That I disgust you, or that you are impotent?'

'Why not? If both are true?' He hammered on the door even louder.

She gasped in horror and fell back against the bedpost.

'Your Grace?' came a shout from the outer chamber and the door opened to reveal the groom of the bedchamber and a couple of pages, and behind them Doña Elvira and a lady-in-waiting.

Catalina stalked over to the window and turned her back to the room. Uncertainly, Arthur hesitated, glancing back at her for some indication that he could stay after all.

'For shame!' Doña Elvira exclaimed, pushing past Arthur and running to throw a gown round Catalina's shoulders. Once the woman was standing with her arm round Catalina, Arthur could not return to his bride; he stepped over the threshold and went to his own rooms.

I cannot bear him. I cannot bear this country. I cannot live here for the rest of my life. That he should say that I disgust him! That he should dare to speak to me so! Has he forgotten who I am? Has he forgotten himself?

I am crying with temper, it's not grief. I tuck my head into the pillow of my bed, so that no one can hear me and tell everyone else that the princess cried herself to sleep because her husband would not bed her.

After a little while I stop, I wipe my face, I sit up. I am a princess by birth and by marriage, I should not give way. I shall have some dignity even if he has none. He is a young man, a young English man at that—how should he know how to behave? I think of my home in the moonlight, of how the walls and the tracery gleam white and the yellow stone is bleached to cream. That is a palace, where people know how to behave with grace and dignity. I wish with all my heart that I were still there.

Oxford, Christmas 1501

They set off a few days before Christmas. The queen had asked that they might at least stay for the twelve-day feast but My Lady the King's Mother had ruled that they should take their Christmas at Oxford, it would give the country a chance to see the prince and the new Princess of Wales, and what the king's mother said was law.

Catalina travelled by litter, jolted mercilessly over the frozen roads, chilled to the bone however many rugs and furs they packed around her. The king's mother had ruled that she should not ride for fear of a fall. The unspoken hope was that Catalina was carrying a child. Catalina herself said nothing to confirm or deny the hope.

They had separate rooms on the road to Oxford, and separate rooms at Magdalen College when they arrived. The choristers were ready, the kitchens were ready, the extraordinarily rich hospitality of Oxford was ready to make merry; but the Prince and Princess of Wales were as cold and as dull as the weather.

They dined together, seated at the great table facing down the hall, and as many of the citizens of Oxford who could get into the gallery watched the princess put small morsels of food in her mouth, and turn her shoulder to her husband, while he looked around the hall for companions and conversation, as if he were dining alone.

They brought in dancers and tumblers, mummers and players. The princess sat alone, stiffly on her hard carved wooden chair, her head held high and a small, defiant smile on her lips while the prince walked around the room, affable and pleasant to the great men of the city. He spoke in English, all the time, and his Spanish-speaking bride had to wait for someone to talk to her in French or Latin, if they would.

At last it was midnight and the long evening could end. Catalina rose from her seat and watched the court sink into bows and curtsies. She dropped a low Spanish curtsy to her husband. 'I bid you good night, Your Grace,' said the princess in Latin.

'I shall come to your room,' he said. There was a little murmur of approval; the court wanted a lusty prince.

The colour rose in her cheeks at the very public announcement. There was nothing she could say. She could not refuse him; but the way she rose and left the room did not promise him a warm welcome when they were alone. The court smiled behind their hands at the high spirits of the bride.

Arthur came to her half an hour later, fired up by drink and resentment. He found her still dressed, waiting by the fire, her duenna at her side, her ladies still talking and playing cards as if it were the middle of the afternoon.

'Sire, good evening,' she said and rose and curtsied as he entered.

Arthur had to check his backwards step. He was in his nightgown with only a robe thrown over his shoulders and was acutely conscious of his bare legs and a chuckle of laughter from one of his men behind him.

'I expected you to be in bed,' he said.

'I was about to go to bed. It is very late,' she returned with glacial courtesy. 'But when you announced so publicly that you would visit me in my rooms I thought you must be planning to bring all the court with you. Why else announce it at the top of your voice so that everybody could hear?'

'I did not announce it at the top of my voice!'

She raised an eyebrow in wordless contradiction.

'I shall stay the night,' he said stubbornly. He marched to her bed-room door. 'These ladies can go to their beds.' He nodded to his men. 'Leave us.' He went into her room and closed the door behind him.

She followed him and closed the door behind her, shutting out the bright, scandalised faces of the ladies. Her back to the door, she watched him throw down his robe and gown and climb into her bed. He plumped up the pillows and leaned back, his arms crossed against his narrow bare chest, like a man awaiting an entertainment.

It was her turn to be discomforted. 'Your Grace . . .'

'You had better get undressed,' he taunted her.

She turned one way, and then the other. 'I shall send for Doña Elvira.'

'Do. Don't mind me, please.'

Catalina bit her lip. He could see her uncertainty. She could not bear to be stripped naked in front of him. She turned to the door and went out of the bedchamber.

There was a rattle of irritable Spanish from the room next door. Arthur grinned; he guessed that she was undressing out there. When she came back, he saw that he was right. She was wearing a white gown trimmed with exquisite lace and her hair was in a long plait down her back. She looked more like a little girl than the haughty princess she had been only moments before, and he felt his desire rise up with some other feeling: a tenderness.

She glanced at him, her face unfriendly. 'I will have to say my prayers,' she said. She went to the prie-dieu and knelt before it. He watched her bow her head over her clasped hands and start to whisper. For the first time he thought how hard it must be for her. Surely, his unease and fear must be nothing to hers: alone in a strange land, at the beck and call of a boy a few months younger than her, with no real friends and no family, far away from everything and everyone she knew.

The bed was warm. The wine he had drunk to give him courage now made him feel sleepy. He leaned back on the pillow. When she came to bed he thought he would take her with confidence but with gentleness. It was Christmas, he should be kind to her. Perhaps they would learn to give each other pleasure, perhaps he would make her happy. His breath-ing deepened, he gave a tiny little snuffly snore. He slept.

Catalina looked round from her prayers and smiled in pure triumph.

Then, absolutely silently, she crept into bed beside him and, carefully arranging herself so that not even the hem of her nightgown could touch him, she composed herself for sleep.

Arthur did not speak to her in the morning, his boy's high pride was utterly cut to the quick. She had shamed him at his father's court by denying him her rooms, and now she had shamed him in private. He rose up and went out in sullen silence. He went to Mass and did not meet her eyes, he went hunting and was gone all day. He did not speak to her at night. They watched a play, seated side by side, and not one word was exchanged all evening. A whole week they stayed at Oxford and they did not say more than a dozen words to each other every day.

When the morning came for them to move on to Ludlow the sky was grey with clouds, fat-bellied with snow. Catalina came out of the doorway of the college and recoiled as the icy, damp air hit her in the face. Arthur ignored her.

'Will it not be very cold?' she asked.

He turned a hard face to her. 'You will have to get used to the cold, you're not in Spain now.'

'So I see.'

She drew back the curtains of the litter. Inside there were rugs for her to wrap around herself and cushions for her to rest on, but it did not look very cosy.

'It gets far worse than this,' he said cheerfully. 'Far colder, it rains or sleets or snows, and it gets darker. In February we have only a couple of hours of daylight at best.'

She turned and looked up at him. 'Could we not set out another day?'

'You agreed to come,' he taunted her. 'I would have been happy to leave you at Greenwich.'

'I did as I was told.'

'It's your choice. Shall I leave you here?' he asked briskly.

'No,' she said. 'Of course not,' and climbed into the litter and pulled the rugs over her feet and up around her shoulders.

Arthur led the way out of Oxford, bowing and smiling at the people who had turned out to cheer him. Catalina drew the curtains of her litter against the cold wind and would not show her face.

They stopped for dinner at a great house on the way and Arthur went in to dine without even waiting to help her from the litter. The lady of the house, flustered, went out to the litter and found Catalina stumbling out, white-faced and with red eyes.

'Princess, are you all right?' the woman asked her.

'I am cold,' Catalina said miserably. 'I have never been so cold.'

She hardly ate any dinner. She looked ready to drop with exhaustion; but as soon as they had eaten Arthur wanted to push on, they had twenty more miles to go before the early dusk of winter.

'Can't you refuse?' Maria de Salinas asked her in a quick whisper.

'No,' the princess said. She rose from her seat without another word. But when they opened the great wooden door to go out into the courtyard, small flakes of snow swirled in around them.

'We cannot travel in this, it will soon be dark and we shall lose the road!' Catalina exclaimed.

'I shall not lose the road,' Arthur said, and strode out to his horse. 'You shall follow me.'

The lady of the house sent a servant flying for a heated stone to put in the litter at Catalina's feet. The princess climbed in, hunched the rugs around her shoulders, and tucked her hands in deep.

They left the warmth and lights of the great house and turned the horses' heads to the west, and to the white sun which was sinking low on the horizon. It was two hours past noon but the sky was so filled with snow clouds that there was an eerie grey glow over the rolling landscape. Arthur rode ahead, singing merrily, Catalina's litter laboured along behind. At every step the mules threw the litter to one side and then the other; she had to keep a hand on the edge to hold herself in place, and her fingers became blue from cold.

An hour passed, the mules walked down the road, their heads bowed low against the east wind that whirled flakes around their ears and into the litter. The snow was getting thicker now, drifting into the ruts of the lane. Catalina had hunched up under the covers, lying like a child, the rapidly cooling stone at her belly, her knees drawn up, her cold hands tucked in, her face ducked down, buried in the furs and rugs.

All around, outside the litter, she could hear men chattering about the cold, swearing that they would eat well when the train got into Burford. Their voices seemed to come from far away; Catalina drifted into a sleep from coldness and exhaustion.

Groggily, she woke when the litter bumped down to the ground and the curtains were swept back.

'Infanta?' Doña Elvira asked. The duenna had been riding her mule, the exercise had kept her warm. 'Thank God, at last we are here.'

Catalina would not lift her head.

'Infanta, they are waiting to greet you.'

Still Catalina would not look up.

'What's this?' It was Arthur's voice, he had seen the litter put down and the duenna bending over it. He saw that the heap of rugs made no movement. 'What's the matter?'

'It is nothing.' Doña Elvira straightened up and stood between the prince and his young wife, shielding Catalina as he jumped from his horse and came towards her. 'The princess has been asleep, she is composing herself.'

'I'll see her,' he said. He put the woman aside with one confident hand and knelt down beside the litter.

'Catalina?' he asked quietly.

'I am frozen with cold,' said a little thread of voice. She lifted her head and he saw that she was as white as the snow itself and her lips were blue. 'I am so c . . . cold that I shall die and then you will be happy.' She broke off into sobs.

'Catalina?' He was utterly bemused.

'I shall never see my m . . . mother again. But she will know that you killed me with your miserable country and your cruelty.'

'I have not been cruel!' he rejoined at once, quite blind to the gathering crowd of courtiers around them. 'By God, Catalina, it was not me!'

'You have been cruel.' She lifted her face from the rugs. 'You have been cruel because—'

It was her sad, white, tear-stained face that spoke to him far more than her words could ever have done. She looked like one of his sisters when their grandmother had bullied them into tears—and he realised that it was he who had bullied her. He had left her in the cold litter for all the afternoon while he had ridden on ahead and delighted in the thought of her discomfort.

He reached into the rugs and pulled out her icy hand. Her fingers were numb with cold. He knew he had done wrong. He took her blue fingertips to his mouth and kissed them, then he held them against his lips and blew his warm breath against them. 'God forgive me,' he said. 'I forgot I was a husband. I didn't realise that I could make you cry. I won't ever do so again.'

She blinked, her blue eyes swimming in unshed tears. 'What?'

'Let me take you inside and we will get warm and I shall tell you how sorry I am and I will never be unkind to you again.'

At once she struggled with her rugs and Arthur pulled them off her legs. She was so chilled that she stumbled when she tried to stand. Ignoring the muffled protests of her duenna, he swept her up into his arms and carried her like a bride across the threshold of the hall.

Gently he put her down before the roaring fire, gently he put back her hood, untied her cloak, chafed her hands. He waved away the servants, offered her wine. He made a little circle of peace and silence around them, and he watched the colour come back to her pale cheeks.

'I am sorry,' he said, sincere. 'I was very, very angry with you but I should not have taken you so far in such bad weather and I should never have let you get cold. It was wrong of me.'

'I forgive you,' she whispered, a little smile lighting her face.

'I didn't know that I had to take care of you. I didn't think. I have been like a child, an unkind child. But I know now, Catalina. I will never be unkind to you again.'

She nodded. 'And you too must forgive me,' she said. 'I have been unkind to you.'

'Have you?'

'At Oxford,' she whispered, very low.

He nodded. 'And what do you say to me?'

She stole a quick upwards glance at him. He was not making a play of offence. He was a boy still, with a boy's fierce sense of fairness. He needed a proper apology.

'I am very, very sorry,' she said, speaking nothing but the truth. 'I was sorry in the morning, but I could not tell you.'

'Shall we go to bed now?' he whispered to her, his mouth very close to her ear.

'Can we?'

'If I say that you are ill?'

She nodded, and said nothing more.

'The princess is unwell from the cold,' Arthur announced generally. 'Doña Elvira will take her to her room, and I shall dine there, alone with her, later.'

'But the people have come to see Your Grace . . .' his host pleaded. 'They have an entertainment for you, and some disputes they would like you to hear . . .'

'I shall see them all in the hall now, and we shall stay tomorrow also. But the princess must go to her room at once.'

'Of course.'

There was a flurry around the princess as her ladies, led by Doña Elvira, escorted her to her room. Catalina glanced back at Arthur. 'Please come to my room for dinner,' she said clearly enough for everyone to hear. 'I want to see you, Your Grace.'

It was everything to him: to hear her publicly avow her desire for him. He bowed at the compliment and then he went to the great hall and called for a cup of ale and dealt with the half-dozen men who had mustered to see him, and then he excused himself and went to her room.

53

Catalina was waiting for him, alone by the fireside. She had dismissed her women, her servants, there was no one to wait on them, they were quite alone. She had even dismissed her duenna. There was no one to see what she had done to her apartments, nor how she had set the dinner table.

She had swathed the plain wooden furniture in scarves of light cloth in vivid colours, she had even draped scarves from the tapestries to hide the cold walls, so the room was like a beautifully trimmed tent.

She had ordered her servants to saw the legs of the table down to stumps, so the table sat as low as a footstool, a most ridiculous piece of furniture. She had set big cushions at either end, as if they should recline like savages to eat. The dinner was set out on the table at knee level, drawn up to the warmth of the burning logs like some barbaric feast.

Arthur was about to complain at the wild extravagance of sawing up the furniture; but then he paused. This was, perhaps, not just some girlish folly; she was trying to show him something.

She was wearing a most extraordinary costume. On her head was a twist of the finest silk, turned and knotted like a coronet with a tail hanging down. Instead of a decent gown she wore a simple shift of the finest, lightest silk, smoky blue in colour, so fine that he could almost see through it, to glimpse the paleness of her skin underneath. He could feel his heartbeat thud when he realised she was naked beneath this wisp of silk. Beneath the chemise she was wearing a pair of hose—like men's hose—but nothing like men's hose, for they were billowy leggings which fell from her slim hips where they were tied with a drawstring of gold thread, to her feet where they were tied again, leaving her feet half bare in dainty crimson slippers. He found himself bereft of speech.

'You don't like my clothes,' Catalina said flatly, and he was too inexperienced to recognise the embarrassment that she was ready to feel.

'I've never seen anything like them before,' he stammered. 'Are they Arab clothes? Show me!'

She turned on the spot, watching him over her shoulder and then coming back to face him again. 'We all wear them in Spain,' she said. 'My mother too. They are more comfortable than gowns, and cleaner. Everything can be washed, not like velvets and damask.'

'They are . . . beautiful.' He nearly said 'barbaric' and was so glad that he had not, when her eyes lit up.

'Do you think so?'

'Yes.'

At once she raised her arms and twirled again to show him the flutter of the hose and the lightness of the chemise.

'You wear them to sleep in?'

She laughed. 'We wear them nearly all the time.'

'You cannot wear it here,' Arthur said. 'I am so sorry. But My Lady the King's Mother would object if she knew you even had them with you.'

She nodded. 'I know that. But I wanted something to remind me of my home and I thought I might keep them in my cupboard and tell nobody. Then tonight, I thought I might show you. Show you myself, and how I used to be.'

Catalina gestured to him that he should come to the table. He felt too big, too clumsy, and on an instinct, he stooped and shucked off his riding boots. She gave a little nod of approval and beckoned him to sit. He dropped to one of the gold-embroidered cushions.

Serenely, she sat opposite him and passed him a bowl of scented water, with a white napkin. He dipped his fingers and wiped them. She offered him a gold plate laid with food: roasted chicken legs, devilled kidneys, with white manchet bread; a proper English dinner. But she had made them serve only tiny portions on each individual plate. She had sliced apples served alongside the meat, and added some precious spiced meats next to sliced sugared plums. She had done everything she could to serve him a Spanish meal, with all the delicacy and luxury of the Moorish taste.

Arthur was shaken from his prejudice. 'This is . . . wonderful,' he said, seeking a word to describe it. He could not think of anything that he had ever seen that was like her. Then an image came to him. 'This is . . . like a picture. You are like a painting I once saw on a plate,' he said. 'A treasure of my mother's from Persia. You are like that. Strange, and most lovely.'

She glowed at his praise. 'I want you to understand,' she said, speaking carefully in Latin. 'I want you to understand what I am.'

'What you are?'

'I am your wife,' she assured him. 'I am the Princess of Wales, I will be Queen of England. I will be an Englishwoman. That is my destiny. But also, as well as this, I am the Infanta of Spain, of al Andalus.'

'I know.'

'You know; but you don't know. I want to explain myself to you. I am a princess of Spain. When we dine alone, we eat like this. When we are on campaign, we live in tents and sit before the braziers like this, and we were on campaign for every year of my life until I was seven.'

'But you are a Christian court,' he protested. 'You are a power in Christendom. You have chairs, proper chairs, you must eat your dinner off a proper table.'

'Only at banquets of state,' she said. 'When we are in our private

55

rooms we live like this, like Moors. Oh, we say grace; we thank the One God at the breaking of the bread. But we do not live as you live here in England. We have beautiful gardens filled with fountains and running water. We have bath houses with hot water to wash in and thick steam to fill the scented room, we have ice houses packed in winter with snow from the sierras so our fruit and our drinks are chilled in summer.'

The words were as seductive as the images. 'You make yourself sound so strange,' he said reluctantly. 'Like a fairy tale.'

'I am only just realising now how strange we are to each other,' Catalina said. 'I thought that your country would be like mine but it is quite different. Perhaps you thought that I would be a princess like your sisters, but I am quite, quite different.'

He nodded. 'I shall have to learn your ways,' he proposed tentatively. 'As you will have to learn mine.'

'I shall be Queen of England, I shall have to become English. But I want you to know what I was, when I was a girl.'

Arthur nodded. 'Were you very cold today?' he asked.

'Yes,' she said. 'I was very cold. And then I thought that I had been unkind to you and I was very unhappy. And then I thought that I was far away from my home and the sunshine and my mother and I was very homesick. It was a horrible day, today.'

He reached his hand out to her. 'Can I comfort you?'

Her fingertips met his. 'You did,' she said. 'When you brought me in to the fire and told me you were sorry. You do comfort me. I will learn to trust that you always will.'

He drew her to him; the cushions were soft and easy, he laid her beside him and he gently tugged at the silk that was wrapped around her head. It slipped off at once and the rich red tresses tumbled down. He touched them with his lips, then her sweet slightly trembling mouth, the lobes of her ears. Then he felt his desire rise and he kissed the hollow at the base of her throat, her thin collarbones, the warm, seductive flesh from neck to shoulder, the hollow of her elbow, the warmth of her palm, and then he drew her shift over her head and she was naked, in his arms, and she was his wife, and a loving wife, at last, indeed.

I love him. I did not think it possible, but I have fallen in love with him. I am a young woman in love with my husband. I am in love with the Prince of Wales, and we shall be King and Queen of England. Who can doubt now that I am chosen by God for His especial favour? He brought me from the dangers of war to safety and peace in the Alhambra Palace and now He has given me England and the love of the young man who will be its king.

LUDLOW CASTLE

1502

THE WINTER SUN was low and red over the rounded hills as they rattled through the great gate that pierced the stone wall around Ludlow. Arthur, who had been riding beside the litter, shouted to Catalina over the noise of the hoofs on the cobbles. 'This is Ludlow, at last!'

Catalina saw a town as pretty as a tapestry. The timbered second storeys of the crowded buildings overhung cobbled streets with prosperous little shops and working yards tucked cosily underneath them on the ground floor. From the upper storeys the glovers' girls and shoemakers' apprentices, the goldsmiths' boys and the spinsters leaned out and called her name. Catalina smiled, and waved back.

Catalina leaned forwards to see her castle as the gate was flung open. They went in, and found the greatest men of the town assembled to greet them: the mayor, the church elders, the leaders of the trades guilds.

Arthur pulled up his horse and listened politely to a long speech in Welsh and then in English.

'When do we eat?' Catalina whispered to him in Latin and saw his mouth quiver as he held back a smile.

'When do we go to bed?' she breathed, and had the satisfaction of seeing his hand tremble on the rein with desire. Finally the interminable speeches of welcome were finished and the royal party could ride on through the great gate of the castle to the inner bailey.

It was a neat castle, as sound as any border castle in Spain, but it was small, something a very minor lord of Spain would be proud to have as his home.

'Is this it?' she asked blankly, thinking of the city that was housed inside the walls of her home, of the gardens and the terraces, of the teeming life of the town centre, all inside defended walls.

At once he was aghast. 'What were you expecting?'

She would have caressed his anxious face, if there had not been hundreds of people watching. 'Oh, I was foolish. I was thinking of Richmond.' Nothing in the world would have made her say that she was thinking of the Alhambra.

He smiled, reassured. 'Oh, my love. Richmond is new-built, my father's great pride and joy. London is one of the greatest cities of Christendom, and the palace matches its size. Ludlow is only a town, a great town in Wales, for sure, but a town. But the hunting is good and the people are welcoming. You will be happy here.'

'I am sure of it,' said Catalina, smiling at him.

She looked around her and saw, in the centre of the inner bailey, a curious circular building like a squat tower.

'What's that?' she asked, struggling out of the litter as Arthur held her hand.

He glanced over his shoulder. 'It's our round chapel,' he said.

At once she recognised with delight the traditional shape of the mosque—designed and built in the round so that no worshipper was better placed than any others, because Allah is praised by the poor man as well as the rich. 'It's lovely.'

Arthur glanced at her in surprise. To him it was only a round tower built with the pretty plum-coloured local stone.

'Yes,' he said, hardly noticing it. 'Now this,' he indicated the great building facing them, with a handsome flight of steps up to the open doors, 'this is the great hall. To the left are the council chambers of Wales and, above them, my rooms. To the right are the guest bedrooms and chambers for the warden of the castle and his lady: Sir Richard and Lady Margaret Pole. Your rooms are above, on the top floor.'

He saw Catalina's swift reaction. 'She is here now?'

'She is away from the castle at the moment.'

She nodded.

'It is a busy place, merry,' he said. 'You will like it.'

'I am sure I will.' She smiled. 'And which are my rooms?'

He pointed to the highest windows. 'See up there? On the right-hand side, matching mine, but on the opposite side of the hall.'

'But how will you get to my rooms?' she asked quietly.

He took her hand and led her towards the grand stone stairs to the double doors of the great hall. There was a ripple of applause and their companions fell in behind them. 'As My Lady the King's Mother commanded me, four times a month I shall come to your room in a formal procession through the great hall,' he said. He led her up the steps.

'Oh.' She was dashed.

He smiled down at her. 'And all the other nights I shall come to you along the battlements,' he whispered. 'There is a private door that goes from your rooms to the battlements that run all around the castle. My rooms go onto them too. You can walk from your rooms to mine whenever you wish and nobody will know whether we are together or not.'

He loved how her face lit up. 'We can be together, whenever we want?' she asked.

'We will be happy here.'

It was night-time, past midnight. They were in bed, sleepy, but too desirous of each other for sleep.

'Tell me a story,' Arthur said.

'I have told you dozens of stories.'

'Tell me another,' he insisted. 'Tell me the one about Boabdil giving up the Alhambra Palace with the golden keys on a silk cushion and going away crying.'

'You know that one. I told it to you last night.'

'Then tell me the story about Yarfa and his horse that gnashed its teeth at Christians.'

'You are a child. And his name was Yarfe.'

'But you saw him killed?'

'I was there; but I didn't see him actually die.'

'How could you not watch it?'

'Well, partly because I was praying as my mother ordered me to, and because I was a girl and not a bloodthirsty, monstrous boy.'

Arthur tossed an embroidered cushion at her head. She caught it and threw it back at him. 'I shall tell you about my home,' she offered.

'All right.' He gathered the purple blanket around them both and waited.

'When you come through the first door to the Alhambra it looks like a little room. Your father would not stoop to enter a palace like that.'

'It's not grand?'

'It's the size of a little merchant's hall in the town here, nothing more.'

'And then?'

'And then you go into the courtyard and from there into the golden chamber.'

'A little better?'

'It is filled with colour, but still it is not much bigger.'

'And then, where shall we go today?'

'Today we shall turn right and go into the Court of the Myrtles.'

He closed his eyes, trying to remember her descriptions. 'A courtyard in the shape of a rectangle, surrounded by high buildings of gold.'

'With a huge, dark wooden doorway framed with beautiful tiles at the far end.'

'And a lake, a lake of a simple rectangle shape, and on either side of the water, a hedge of sweet-scented myrtle trees.'

'And the gateway at the end is reflected back in the water, and the arch around it, and the building that it is set in. So that the whole thing is mirrored in ripples at your feet. And the birds . . .'

'The birds?' he asked, surprised, for Catalina had not told him of them before.

She paused while she thought of the word. '*Apodes*?' she said in Latin.

'*Apodes*? Swifts?'

She nodded. 'They flow like a turbulent river of birds just above your head, round and round the narrow courtyard, screaming as they go, as fast as a cavalry charge, round and round, as long as the sun shines on the water they go round, all day. And at night—'

'At night?'

'At night they disappear, you never see them settle or nest. They just disappear—they set with the sun, but at dawn they are there again, like a river, like a flood.' She paused. 'It is hard to describe,' she said in a small voice. 'But I see it all the time.'

'You miss it,' he said flatly. 'However happy I may make you, you will always miss it.'

She made a little gesture. 'Of course. It is to be expected. But I never forget who I am. Who I was born to be.'

He smiled in reply and drew her closer to him; they lay back together.

'I knew I would marry you almost from the moment I was born,' he said reflectively.

'Lucky that I please you, now I am here.'

He put his finger under her chin and turned her face up towards him for a kiss. 'Even luckier, that I please you,' he said.

'I would have been a good wife anyway,' she insisted. 'Even without this joy.' She closed her eyes and lay back, waiting for his touch.

Their servants woke them at dawn and Arthur was ceremonially escorted from her bed. They saw each other again at Mass but they were seated at opposite sides of the round chapel, each with their own household, and could not speak.

After Mass the royal pair went to break their fast in their separate rooms, though they would rather have been together. Ludlow Castle was a small reproduction of the formality of the king's court. The king's mother had commanded that after breakfast Arthur must work with his tutor at his books or at sports as the weather allowed; and Catalina must work with her tutor, sew, or read.

In the afternoon they might ride out together to hunt in the woods around the castle. It was a rich countryside, the river fast-flowing through a wide valley with old thick woodlands on the sides of the hills.

They went out into the town once a week, to go to St Laurence's Church for Mass, or to a dinner organised by one of the guilds, or to see a cockfight, a bull-baiting, or players. Catalina was impressed by the neat prettiness of the town; the place had escaped the violence of the wars between York and Lancaster that had finally been ended by Henry Tudor.

'Peace is everything to a kingdom,' she observed to Arthur.

'The only thing that can threaten us now is the Scots,' he said. 'The Yorkist line are my forebears, the Lancasters too, so the rivalry ends with me. All we have to do is keep the north safe.'

'And your father thinks he has done that with Princess Margaret's marriage?'

'Pray God he is right, but they are a faithless lot. When I am king I shall keep the border strong. You shall advise me, we'll go out together and make sure the border castles are repaired.'

'I shall like that,' she said.

They dined together at dusk, and at last they could be close, seated side by side at the high table looking down the hall of the castle. Arthur always put Catalina on his left, closest to the fire, and she wore a cloak lined with fur, and had layer upon layer of linen shifts under her ornate gown. Even so, she was still cold. Her Spanish ladies, Maria de Salinas, her duenna Doña Elvira and a few others, were seated at one table, the English ladies who were supposed to be her companions at another. The great lords of Arthur's council, his warden of the castle, Sir Richard Pole, Bishop William Smith of Lincoln, his physician, Dr Bereworth, his treasurer, Sir Henry Vernon, the steward of his household, Sir Richard Croft, his groom of the privy chamber, Sir William Thomas of Carmarthen, and all the leading men of the Principality, were seated in the body of the hall. At the back and in the gallery every nosy parker in Wales could see the Spanish princess take her dinner, and speculate if she pleased the young prince or no.

There was no way to tell. Most of them thought that he had failed to bed her. For see! The Infanta sat like a stiff little doll. The Prince of Wales spoke to her as if by rote, every ten minutes. They scarcely even looked at each other. The gossips said that he went to her rooms, as ordered, but only once a week and never of his own choice. Perhaps the young couple did not please each other.

No one could tell that Catalina's hands were gripped tight in her lap to stop herself from touching her husband, nor that every half-hour or so he glanced at her, apparently indifferent, and whispered so low that only she could hear: 'I want you right now.'

After dinner there would be dancing and perhaps mummers or a story-teller, a Welsh bard or strolling players to watch. Sometimes the poets would tell strange tales in their own tongue that Arthur could follow only with difficulty, but which he would try to translate for Catalina.

> 'When the long yellow summer comes and victory comes to us,
> And the spreading of the sails of Brittany,
> And when the heat comes and when the fever is kindled
> There are portents that victory will be given to us.'

'What is that about?' she asked him.

'The long yellow summer is when my father decided to invade from Brittany. His road took him to Bosworth and victory. It was hot, that year, and the troops came with the Sweat, a new disease, which now curses England as it does Europe with the heat of every summer.'

When the fire burned low they would sing the old Welsh songs of magical doings in dark woods that no man could know. And they would tell stories of Arthur and Camelot, and Merlin the prince, and Guinevere: the queen who betrayed her husband for a guilty love.

'I should die if you took a lover,' he whispered to her as a page shielded them from the hall and poured wine.

'I can never even see anyone else when you are here,' she assured him. 'All I see is you.'

Every evening there was music or some entertainment for the Ludlow court. The king's mother had ruled that the prince should keep a merry house—it was a reward for the loyalty of Wales that had put her son Henry Tudor on an uncertain throne.

When the musicians played the slow formal dances of Spain, Catalina would dance with one of her ladies, conscious of Arthur's gaze on her, keeping her face prim, like a little mummer's mask of respectability; though she longed to twirl around and swing her hips like a Moorish slave girl dancing for a sultan. But My Lady the King's Mother's spies watched everything, even in Ludlow, and would be quick to report any indiscreet behaviour by the young princess.

Even after the music was over and the entertainers gone away, the young couple could not be alone. There were always men who sought council with Arthur, who wanted favours or land or influence, and they would approach him and talk low-voiced, in English, which Catalina did not yet fully understand, or in Welsh, which she thought no one could ever understand. The rule of law barely ran in the borderlands, each landowner was like a warlord in his own domain.

Arthur argued, and praised, and suggested that feuds should be forgiven, that trespasses should be made good, that the proud Welsh chieftains should work together to make their land as prosperous as their neighbour England, instead of wasting their time in envy.

Catalina would watch Arthur as he talked with one man and then another, and then, at a sign from Doña Elvira, she would curtsy to her husband and withdraw from the hall. She would read her evening prayers, change into her robe for the night, sit with her ladies, go to her bedroom and wait, and wait and wait.

As the castle settled for the night, she was ready for him. At last she would hear the quiet sound of his footfall at the outer door of her room, where it opened onto the battlements that ran between his tower and hers. She would fly to the door and unbolt it, he would be pink-cheeked from the cold, his cape thrown over his nightshirt as he tumbled in, the cold wind blowing in with him as she threw herself into his arms.

A messenger came from the king's court bringing the newlyweds some gifts: a pair of deer from the Windsor forest, a parcel of books for Catalina, letters from the queen, and orders from My Lady the King's Mother who had heard, though no one could imagine how, that the prince's hunt had broken down some hedges, and who commanded Arthur to make sure that they were restored and the landowner compensated.

He brought the letter to Catalina's room when he came at night. 'How can she know everything?' he demanded, shaking his head at the power of his grandmother.

'It's how you rule,' she said. 'Isn't it? You make sure that you know everything and that anyone with a trouble comes to you. Then they take the habit of obedience and you take the habit of command.'

He chuckled. 'I can see I have married another Margaret Beaufort.'

Catalina smiled. 'You should be warned,' she admitted. 'I am the daughter of a strong woman. Even my father does as he is bid by her.'

He put down the letter and gathered her to him. 'I have longed for you all day,' he said into the warm crook of her neck.

With one accord they moved to the bed.

'Tell me a story.'

'I am like Scheherazade, you want a thousand stories from me.'

'Oh yes!' he said. 'I will have a thousand and one stories. How many have you told me already?'

'I have told you a story every night since we were together, that first night, at Burford,' she said.

'Forty-nine days,' he said.

'Only forty-nine stories. If I was Scheherazade I would have nine hundred and fifty-two to go.'

He smiled at her. 'Do you know, Catalina, I have been happier in these forty-nine days than ever in my life before?'

She took his hand and put it to her lips. 'Pray God we have long years together,' she said. 'And we shall do the right thing by the country.'

'Yes,' he said. 'I have such plans for us when we come to the throne.'

'What shall we do?'

Arthur hesitated. 'You will think me a child, my head filled with stories from books.'

'No I shan't, tell me!'

'I should like to make a council, like the first Arthur did. A council of knights, one for each county. Not chosen by me but by their own county, as the best of men to represent them. And I should like them to come to the table and each of them should know what is happening in their own county, they should report. And so if a crop is going to fail and there is going to be hunger we should know in time and send food.'

Catalina sat up, interested. 'They would be our advisers. Our eyes and ears.'

'Yes. And I should like each of them to be responsible for building defences, especially the ones in the north and on the coasts.'

'And for mustering troops once a year, so we are always ready for attack,' she added. 'They will come, you know.'

'The Moors?'

She nodded. 'They are defeated in Spain for now, but they are as strong as ever in Africa, in the Holy Lands, in Turkey and the lands beyond. When they need more land they will move again into Christendom. They will come against us.'

'I want defences all along the south coast against France, and against the Moors,' Arthur said. 'A string of castles, and beacons behind them, so that when we come under attack in—say—Kent, we can know about it in London, and everyone can be warned.'

'You will need to build ships,' she said. 'My mother commissioned fighting ships from the dockyard in Venice.'

'We have our own dockyards,' he said. 'We can build our own ships.'

'How shall we raise the money for all these castles and ships?' Isabella's daughter asked the practical question.

'Partly from taxing the people,' he said. 'Partly from taxing the merchants and the people who use the ports. It is for their safety, they should pay. I know people hate the taxes but that is because they don't see what is done with the money.'

'We will need honest tax collectors,' Catalina said.

'Yes, but how d'you find men that you can trust? You need loyal servants who owe their salary and their obedience to the crown. Otherwise they work for themselves and they take bribes and all their families become overmighty.'

'The church could teach the sons of poor men,' Catalina suggested. 'Just as the imam teaches such boys for the Moors. If every parish church had a school attached to it, if every priest knew he had to teach reading and writing, then we could found new colleges at the universities, so that boys could go on and learn more.'

'Is it possible?' he asked. 'Not just a dream?'

She nodded. 'It could be real. To make a country is the most real thing anyone can do. We will make a kingdom that we can be proud of, just as my mother and father did in Spain. We can decide how it is to be, and we can make it happen.'

'Camelot,' he said simply.

'Camelot,' she repeated.

'I want to ask you to meet a lady who is a good friend of mine and is ready to be a friend of yours,' Arthur said, choosing his words with care.

Catalina's ladies-in-waiting, bored and listless on a cold afternoon with no entertainment, craned forwards to listen.

At once Catalina blanched as white as the linen she was embroidering. 'My lord?' she asked anxiously. He had said nothing of this in the early hours of the morning when they had woken and made love. She had not expected to see him until dinner. His arrival in her rooms signalled that something had happened.

'A lady? Who is she?'

'You may have heard of her from others, but I beg you to remember that she is eager to be your friend, and she has always been a good friend to me.'

Catalina's head flew up, she took a breath. For a moment, for a dreadful moment, she thought that he was introducing a former mistress into her court, begging a place among ladies-in-waiting for some woman who had been his lover, so that they might continue their affair.

If this is what he is doing, I know what part I must play. I have seen my mother haunted by the pretty girls that my father, God forgive him, could not resist. Each time my mother behaved as if she had noticed nothing, dowered the girl handsomely, married her off to an eligible courtier, and encouraged him to take his new bride far, far away.

I know that a sensible woman looks the other way and tries to bear her humiliation when her husband chooses to take another woman to his bed. What she must not do, is behave like my sister Juana, who shames herself and all of us by giving way to hysterical tears, and threats of revenge.

'It does no good,' my mother once told me. 'If a husband goes astray you will have to take him back into your life and into your bed, whatever he has done; there is no escape from marriage. If you are queen and he is king you have to deal together. If he forgets his duty to you, that is no reason to forget yours to him. However painful, you are always his queen and he is always your husband. Those whom God has joined together, no man can put asunder.'

Catalina summoned this bleak counsel and faced her young husband. 'I am always glad to meet a friend of yours, my lord,' she said levelly, hoping that her voice did not quaver at all. 'But, as you know, I have only a small household. Your father was very clear that I am not allowed any more companions than I have at present.'

'Oh no, you mistake me. It is not a friend who wants a place,' he said hastily. 'It is Lady Margaret Pole, who is waiting to meet you. She has come home here at last.'

Arthur saw her quick gesture of rejection. 'Please,' he said hurriedly. 'She has been away caring for her children or she would have been here with her husband to welcome you to the castle when we first arrived. She wants to greet you now. We all have to live together here.'

Catalina put out a shaking hand to him and at once he came closer, ignoring the fascinated attention of her ladies.

'I cannot meet her,' she whispered. 'Truly, I can't. I know that her brother was put to death for my sake. I know my parents insisted that there should be no doubt over your inheritance. I know they did. Edward Plantagenet's blood is on my head. Our marriage is under the curse of his death.'

Arthur recoiled, he had never before seen her so distressed. 'My God, Catalina, you cannot really think that we are accursed?'

'In this one thing.'

'No. You must know we are blessed.' He drew closer and said very quietly, so that no one else could hear, 'Every morning when you wake in my arms, do you feel accursed then?'

'No,' she said unwillingly. 'No, I don't.'

'We are not cursed,' he said firmly. 'We are blessed with God's favour. Catalina, my love, trust me. She has forgiven my father, she certainly would never blame you. I swear to you. She wants to meet you. Come with me and let me present her to you.'

'Alone then,' she said, still fearing some terrible scene.

'Alone. She is in the castle warden's rooms now. If you come at once, we can leave them all here, and go quietly by ourselves and see her.'

She rose from her seat and put her hand on the crook of his arm.

'I am walking alone with the princess,' Arthur said to her ladies. 'You can all stay here.'

They looked surprised to be excluded. Catalina went past them without looking up.

Once out of the door he preceded her down the tight spiral staircase, one hand on the central stone post, one on the wall. Catalina followed him, lingering at every deep-set slit window, looking down into the valley. It was cold, even for March in Wales, and Catalina shivered as if a stranger was walking on her grave.

They came to the floor below the princess's suite of rooms and without hesitation, Arthur tapped on the thick wooden door of the warden's apartments and went in.

The square room overlooking the valley was the match of Catalina's presence chamber upstairs, panelled with wood and hung with bright tapestries. There was a lady waiting for them, seated by the fireside, and when the door opened she rose. She was dressed in a pale grey gown with a grey hood on her hair. She was about thirty years of age; she looked at Catalina with friendly interest, and then she sank into a deep, respectful curtsy.

Disobeying the nip of his bride's fingers, Arthur withdrew his arm and stepped back as far as the doorway. Catalina looked back at him reproachfully and then bobbed a small curtsy to the older woman. They rose up together.

'I am so pleased to meet you,' Lady Pole said sweetly. 'And I am sorry not to have been here to greet you. But one of my children was ill and I went to make sure that he was well nursed.'

'Your husband has been very kind,' Catalina managed to say.

'I hope so, for I left him a long list of commandments; I so wanted your rooms to be warm and comfortable. I hope you will be very happy here with us,' she said.

'I hope to . . .' Catalina breathed. 'But I . . . I . . .'

'Yes?'

'I was very sorry to hear of the death of your brother.' Catalina dived in. Her face, which had been white with discomfort, now flushed scarlet. 'Indeed, I was very sorry. Very . . .'

'It was a great loss to me, and to mine,' the woman said steadily. 'But it is the way of the world.'

'I am afraid that my coming . . .'

'I never thought that it was any choice or any fault of yours, Princess. When our dear Prince Arthur was to be married his father was bound to make sure that his inheritance was secured. I know that my brother would never have threatened the peace of the Tudors, but they were not to know that. And he was ill advised by a mischievous young man, drawn into some foolish plot . . .' She broke off as her voice shook; but rapidly she recovered herself. 'Forgive me. It still grieves me. He was an innocent, my brother. There is no doubt in my mind that he is in God's keeping now, with all innocents.'

Catalina was listening intently. 'I know my mother and father wanted to be sure that the Tudor line was without challenge,' she breathed. 'I know that they told the king.' She felt as if she had to make sure that this woman knew the depth of her guilt.

'As I might have done if I had been them,' Lady Margaret said simply. 'Princess, I do not blame you, nor your mother or father. I do not blame our great king. Were I any one of them, I might have behaved just as they have done, and explained myself only to God.'

'I felt that I came to this country with his death on my conscience,' Catalina admitted in a sudden rush.

The older woman shook her head. 'His death is not on your conscience,' she said firmly. 'And it is wrong to blame yourself for another's doing. You need not take the blame for the sins of others.' Lady Pole smiled at Catalina and stretched out her hand. 'You see,' she said pleasantly, 'I was a Princess Royal myself once. I was the last Plantagenet princess, raised by King Richard in his nursery with his son. Of all the women in the world, I should know that there is more to life than a woman can ever control. There is the will of your husband, and of your parents, and of your king, and of your God. Nobody could blame a princess for the doings of a king. How could one ever challenge it? Our way has to be obedience.'

Catalina, her hand in the warm, firm grasp, felt wonderfully reassured. 'I am afraid I am not always very obedient,' she confessed.

The older woman laughed. 'Oh yes, for one would be a fool not to think for oneself,' she allowed. 'True obedience can only happen when you secretly think you know better, and you choose to bow your head. Anything short of that is just agreement, and any ninny-in-waiting can agree. Don't you think?'

And Catalina, giggling with an Englishwoman for the first time, laughed aloud and said, 'I never wanted to be a ninny-in-waiting.'

'Neither did I,' gleamed Margaret Pole.

I am so surprised to find that the woman whose presence I have dreaded is making the castle at Ludlow feel like a home for me. Lady Margaret Pole is a companion and friend to comfort me for the loss of my mother and sisters.

I have missed having an older woman to be my friend. Maria de Salinas is a girl as young and silly as I am, she is a companion, not a mentor. Doña Elvira was nominated by my mother the queen to stand in a mother's place for me; but she is not a woman I can warm to. She and her husband, who commands my household, want to make a little Spain in England. But I am certain that my way ahead in England is to become English.

Margaret Pole was educated as the niece of a king and is as fluent in Latin as I am. We speak French easily together, she is teaching me English, and when we come across a word we don't know in any of our shared languages, we compose great mimes that set us wailing with giggles.

With Margaret, Catalina raised the question of her future, and her father-in-law of whom she was frankly nervous. 'He was displeased before we came away,' she said. 'It is the question of the dowry.'

'Oh, yes?' Margaret replied. The two women were seated in a window, waiting for the men to come back from hunting. It was bitterly cold and damp outside; neither of them had wanted to go out. Margaret thought it better to volunteer nothing about the question of Catalina's dowry; she had already heard from her husband that the Spanish king had perfected the art of double-dealing. He had agreed a substantial dowry for the Infanta, but then sent her to England with only half the money. The rest, he suggested, could be made up with the plate and treasure that she brought as her household goods, which outraged King Henry.

Catalina was caught between the determination of two cold-hearted men. Margaret guessed that one of the reasons that Catalina had been sent to Ludlow Castle with her husband was to force her to use her own household goods and so diminish their value. If King Henry had kept her at court, she would have eaten off his plates and her father could have argued that the Spanish plate was as good as new, and must be taken as the dowry. But now, they ate from Catalina's gold plates and every scrape of a careless knife knocked a little off the value. King Ferdinand might be a hard man and a cunning negotiator but he had met his match in Henry Tudor of England.

'He said that I should be a daughter to him,' Catalina started carefully. 'But I cannot obey him as a daughter should, if I am to obey my own father. My father tells me not to use my plate and to give it to the king. But he won't accept it. And since the dowry is unpaid the king sends me away with no provision; he doesn't even pay my allowance.'

'Have you not asked the prince what you should do?'

Catalina hesitated. 'It is a matter between his father and my father,' she said cautiously. 'I didn't want to let it disturb us. He has paid for all my travelling expenses here. He is going to have to pay for my ladies' wages at midsummer, and soon I will need new gowns. I don't want to ask him for money. I don't want him to think me greedy.'

'You love him, don't you?' Margaret asked, smiling, and watched the younger woman's face light up.

'Oh yes,' the girl breathed. 'I do love him so.'

The older woman smiled. 'You are blessed,' she said gently. 'To be a princess and to find love with the husband you are ordered to marry. You are blessed, Catalina.'

'I know. I do think it is a sign of God's especial favour to me.'

'And do you have any signs?'

Catalina looked puzzled.

'Of a child coming? You do know what to look for?'

The young woman blushed. 'I do know. My mother told me. There are no signs yet.'

'It's early days,' Lady Margaret said comfortingly. 'But if you had a child on the way I think there would be no difficulty with a dowry.'

'Tell me a story.'

They were bathed in the dappled gold of candlelight and firelight. It was midnight and the castle was silent but for their low voices.

'What shall I tell you about?'

'Tell me a story about the Moors.'

'I will tell you a story about one of the sultanas,' she said. 'She was in the harem; you know that the women live apart from the men in their own rooms?'

He nodded, watching the candlelight flicker on her neck, on the hollow at her collarbone.

'She looked out of the window to where the poor children of the town were playing on the slipway for the boats. They had spread mud all around and they were slipping and sliding in the mud. She laughed while she watched them and she said to her ladies how she wished that she could play like that.'

'But she couldn't go out?'

'No. Her ladies told the eunuchs who guarded the harem and they told the Grand Vizier and he told the sultan, and when she left the window and went to her presence chamber, guess what?'

He shook his head, smiling. 'What?'

'Her presence chamber was a great marble hall. The floor was made of rose-veined marble. The sultan had ordered a thick paste of oil of rose petals and herbs and spread it, one foot thick, all across the floor of her presence chamber. The sultana and her ladies stripped to their chemises and slid and played in the mud, threw rosewater and petals and all the afternoon played like the mudlarks.'

He was entranced. 'How glorious.'

She smiled up at him. 'Now it is your turn. You tell me a story.'

'I have no stories like that. It is all fighting and winning.'

'Those are the stories you like best when I tell them,' she pointed out.

'I do. And now your father is going to war again.'

'He is?'

'Did you not know?'

Catalina shook her head. 'The Spanish ambassador sometimes sends me a note with the news, but he has told me nothing. Is it a crusade?'

'No, it is a far less heroic cause. Your father, rather surprisingly to us, has made an alliance with King Louis of France. Apparently they plan to invade Italy together and share the spoils.'

'King Louis?' she asked in surprise. 'Never! I had thought they would be enemies until death.'

'Well, it seems that the French king does not care who he allies with. But why would your father join with our enemy?'

'He has always wanted Naples,' she confided to him. 'Naples and Navarre. One way or another he will have them. King Louis may think he has an ally but there will be a high price to pay. I know him. He plays a long game but he usually gets his own way. Who sent you the news?'

'My father. I think he is vexed not to be in their counsel. He fears the French worse only than the Scots. It is a disappointment for us that your father would ally with them on anything.'

'On the contrary, your father should be pleased that my father is keeping the French busy in the south. Will your father not join with them?'

Arthur shook his head. 'His one great desire is to keep England at peace. My father says it is a terrible thing to see a country at war.'

'Your father only fought one big battle,' she said. 'Sometimes you have to fight. Sometimes you have to beat your enemy.'

'I wouldn't fight to gain land,' he said. 'But I would fight to defend our borders. And I think we will have to fight against the Scots unless my sister can change their very nature.'

'And is your father prepared for war?'

'He has the Howard family to keep the north for him,' he said. 'He has reinforced the castles and he keeps the Great North Road open so that he can get his soldiers up there if needs be.'

Catalina looked thoughtful. 'If he has to fight he would do better to invade them,' she said. 'Then he can choose the time and the place to fight and not be forced into defence.'

'Is that the better way?'

She nodded. 'My father would say so. It is everything to have your army moving forwards and confident, and you have the wealth of the country ahead of you, for your supplies.'

'You are a tactician,' he said. 'I wish to God I had your childhood and knew the things you know.'

'You do have,' she said sweetly. 'For everything I know is yours, and everything I am is yours. But now, I want you to tell me a story. Tell me about your mother and father.'

He thought for a moment. 'My father was born an heir to the Tudors, but there were dozens in line for the throne before him,' he said. 'His father wanted him called Owen, Owen Tudor, a good Welsh name, but his father died before his birth, in the war. My grandmother was only a child of twelve when he was born, but she had her way and called him Henry—a royal name. You can see what she was thinking even then.

'My father's fortunes soared up and down with every battle of the civil war. One time he was a son of the ruling family, the next they were on the run. His uncle Jasper Tudor kept faith with my father and with the Tudor cause, but there was a final battle and our cause was lost, and our king executed. Edward came to the throne and my father was the last of the line. He was in such danger that Uncle Jasper fled with him out of the country to Brittany.'

'The French didn't hand him back?'

Arthur laughed. 'They supported him. He was the greatest challenge to the peace of England, of course they encouraged him.'

She nodded, she was a child of a prince praised by Machiavelli himself. Any daughter of Ferdinand was born to double-dealing. 'And then?'

'Edward died young, in his prime, with only a young son to inherit. His brother Richard first held the throne in trust and then claimed it for himself and put his own nephews, Edward's sons, the little princes, in the Tower of London. They never came out again,' Arthur said bleakly. 'God bless their souls, no one knows what happened to them. The people turned against Richard, and summoned my father from France.'

'Yes?'

'My grandmother organised the great lords one after another, she was an arch-plotter. That's why my father honours her so highly: he owes her his throne. And he waited until he could get a message to my mother to tell her that he would marry her if he won the throne.'

'Because he loved her?' Catalina asked hopefully. 'She is so beautiful.'

'Not he. He hadn't even seen her. He had been in exile for most of his life, remember. It was a marriage cobbled together because his mother knew that if she could get those two married then everyone would see that the heir of York had married the heir of Lancaster and the war could be over.'

'He didn't love her?' She was disappointed.

Arthur smiled. 'No. It's not a romance. And she didn't love him. But they knew what they had to do. When my father marched in and beat Richard and picked the crown of England out of the wreckage of the battlefield, he knew that he would marry the princess, take the throne, and found a new line.'

'But wasn't she next heir to the throne anyway?' she asked, puzzled. 'Since it was her father who had been King Edward? And her uncle who had died in the battle, and her brothers were dead? Why didn't she claim the throne for herself?'

'Not in this country,' Arthur ruled. 'We don't have reigning queens in this England. Girls don't inherit. They cannot take the throne.'

'But if a king had only a daughter?'

He shrugged. 'Then it would be a tragedy for the country. You have to give me a boy, my love. Nothing else will do.'

'But if we only had a girl?'

'She would marry a prince and make him King Consort of England, and he would rule alongside her. England has to have a king.'

She drew away from him in indignation. 'I tell you this, if we have only one child and she is a girl then she will rule as queen and she will be a queen as good as any man can be king.'

'Well, she will be a novelty,' he said. 'We don't believe a woman can defend the country as a king needs to do.'

'A woman can fight,' she said instantly. 'You should see my mother in armour. Even I could defend the country. I have seen warfare, which is more than you have done. I could be as good a king as any man.'

He smiled at her, shaking his head. 'No English army would take orders from a woman,' he said. He saw by her stubborn face that she was not convinced.

'All that matters is that you win the battle,' she said. 'All that matters is that the country is defended. It doesn't matter who leads the army as long as they follow.'

'Well, at any rate, my mother had no thought of claiming the throne for herself. She married my father and became Queen of England through marriage. And because she was the York Princess and he was the Lancaster heir my grandmother's plan succeeded. My father may have won the throne by conquest; but we will have it by inheritance.'

Catalina nodded. 'What matters is not the winning but the keeping of it.'

'We shall keep it,' he said with certainty. 'I shall be king at my father's death. And at my death, my son will reign.'

'Shall we call him Arthur?' she asked. 'Or Henry for your father?'

'Arthur is a good name,' he said. 'A good name for a new royal family in Britain. Arthur for Camelot, and Arthur for me. We don't want another Henry; my brother is enough for anyone. Let's call him Arthur, and his older sister will be called Mary.'

'Mary? I wanted to call her Isabella, for my mother.'

'You can call the next girl Isabella. But I want our first-born to be called Mary.'

'Arthur must be first.'

He shook his head. 'First we will have Mary so that we learn how to do it all with a girl.'

'How to do it all?'

He gestured. 'The confinement, the birthing, the christening. My grandmother has written a great book to rule how it shall be done. It is dreadfully complicated. But if we have our Mary first then our nursery is all ready, and in your next confinement we shall put our son and heir into the cradle.'

She rose up and turned on him in mock indignation. 'You would practise being a father on my daughter!' she exclaimed.

'You wouldn't want to start with my son,' he protested. 'We shall make a great country for my son, you and me. We shall build roads and markets, churches and schools. We shall put defences around the coastline and build ships.'

'We shall create courts of justice as my mother and father have done in Spain,' she said, settling back into the pleasure of planning a future on which they could agree. 'So that every man knows that he can go to the court and have his case heard.'

He raised his glass to her. 'We should start writing this down,' he said. 'And we should start planning how it is to be done.'

'It will be years before we come to our thrones.'

'You never know. I don't wish it—God knows, I honour my father and my mother and I would want nothing before God's own time. But we will be King and Queen of England. We should know who we will have at our court, we should know what advisers we will choose, we should know how we are going to make this country truly great. If it is a dream, then we can talk of it together at night-time, as we do. But if it is a plan, we should write it in the daytime, take advice on it, think how we might do the things we want.'

Her face lit up. 'When we have finished our lessons for the day, perhaps we could do it then.'

'And we could start here, in Wales,' he said. 'I can do what I want here, within reason. We could make a college here, and build some schools. We could even commission a ship to be built here.'

She clapped her hands like the girl she was. 'We could start our reign!' she said.

'Hail Queen Katherine! Queen of England!' Arthur said playfully, but at the ring of the words he stopped and looked at her more seriously. 'You know, you will hear them say that, my love. Vivat! Vivat Catalina Regina, Queen Katherine, Queen of England.'

Catalina glowed. 'I shall be the best Queen of England that I can be,' she said. 'I shall care for the poor and assist the church, and if we are ever at war I shall ride out and fight for England just as my mother did for Spain.'

Planning for the future with Arthur, I forget my homesickness for Spain. Every day we think of some improvement we could make, of some law that should be changed. We talk about whether people can be trusted with their freedom, of whether a king should be a good tyrant or should step back from power. We talk about my home: of my parents' belief that you make a country by one church, one language, and one law. Or whether it could be possible to do as the Moors did: to make a country with one law but with many faiths and many languages, and assume that people are wise enough to choose the best.

We argue, we talk. Sometimes we break up in laughter, sometimes we disagree. Arthur is my lover always, my husband, undeniably. And now he is becoming my friend.

Catalina was in the little garden of Ludlow Castle, which was set along the east wall, in earnest conversation with one of the castle gardeners. In neat beds around her were the herbs that the cooks used, and some herbs and flowers with medicinal properties grown by Lady Margaret.

Arthur, seeing Catalina as he walked back from confession in the round chapel, glanced up to the great hall to check that no one would prevent him, and slipped off to be with her. As he drew up she was gesturing, trying to describe something. Arthur smiled.

'Princess,' he said formally in greeting.

She swept him a low curtsy. 'Sire.'

The gardener had dropped to his knees in the mud at the arrival of the prince. 'You can get up,' Arthur said pleasantly. 'I don't think you will find many pretty flowers at this time of year, Princess.'

'I was trying to talk to him about growing salad vegetables,' she said. 'But he speaks Welsh and English and I have tried Latin and French and we don't understand each other at all.'

'I think I am with him. I don't understand either. What is salad?'

'It is vegetables that grow in the ground and you eat them without cooking them,' she explained.

'You eat them raw? Without boiling?'

'Yes, why not?'

'Because you will be dreadfully ill, eating uncooked food.'

'Like fruit, like apples. You eat them raw.'

He was unconvinced. 'More often cooked, or preserved or dried. And anyway, that is a fruit and not leaves. But what sorts of vegetables do you want?'

'*Lactuca*,' she said.

'*Lactuca*?' he repeated. 'What is it, exactly? I have never heard of it.'

She sighed. 'I know. You none of you seem to know anything of vegetables. *Lactuca* is like . . .' She searched her mind for the truly terrible vegetable that she had been forced to eat, boiled into a pulp at one dinner at Greenwich. 'Samphire,' she said. 'But you eat *lactuca* without cooking and it is crisp and sweet.'

'Vegetables? Crisp?'

'Yes,' she said patiently.

'And you eat this in Spain?'

She nearly laughed at his appalled expression. 'Yes. You would like it.'

'And can we grow it here?'

'I think he is telling me: no. He has never heard of such a thing. He has no seeds. He does not think it would grow here.' She looked up at the blue sky with the scudding rain clouds. 'Perhaps he is right,' she said, a weariness in her voice. 'I am sure that it needs much sunshine.'

Arthur took Catalina's hand and tucked it in the crook of his arm. 'You know sometimes in summer, it is very hot here. Truly.'

She looked disbelievingly from the cold mud at her feet to the thickening clouds.

'Not now, I know; but in summer. I have leaned against this wall and found it warm to the touch. You know, we grow strawberries and raspberries and peaches. All the fruit that you grow in Spain.'

'Oranges?'

'Well, perhaps not oranges,' he conceded.

'Lemons? Olives?'

He bridled. 'Yes, indeed.'

She looked suspiciously at him. 'Dates?'

'In Cornwall,' he asserted, straight-faced. 'Of course it is warmer in Cornwall.'

'Sugar cane? Rice? Pineapples?'

He tried to say yes, but he could not repress the giggles and she crowed with laughter.

When they were steady again he said, 'I am sure we can grow your *lactuca*, whatever it is. All we need is a gardener who can bring the seeds and who has already grown the things you want. Why don't you write to the gardener at the Alhambra and ask him to send you someone?'

'Could I send for a gardener?' she asked incredulously.

'My love, you are going to be Queen of England. You can send for a regiment of gardeners.'

'But where should he garden? There is no room against the castle wall, and if we are to grow fruit as well as vegetables . . .'

'You are Princess of Wales! You can plant your garden wherever you please. You shall have all of Kent if you want it, my darling.'

'Kent?'

'We grow apples and hops there, I think we might try at *lactuca*.'

'I didn't think of sending for a gardener. If only I had brought one in the first place. I have all these useless ladies-in-waiting and I need a gardener.'

'You could swap him for Doña Elvira.'

She gurgled with laughter.

'Ah God, we are blessed,' he said simply. 'In each other and in our lives. You shall have anything you want, always. I swear it.'

'I will write to Juana,' she decided. 'In the Netherlands. She is in the north of Christendom like me. She must know what will grow in this weather. I shall write to her and see what she has done.'

'And we shall eat nothing but *lactuca*!' he said, kissing her fingers.

It is morning. I lie awake, it is dawn and I can hear the birds slowly starting to sing. The sun is coming up and through the lattice window I can see a glimpse of blue sky. Perhaps the summer is coming at last.

Beside me, Arthur is breathing quietly and steadily. I can feel my heart swell with love for him; I put my hand on the fair curls of his head and wonder if any woman has ever loved a man as I love him.

I hear the footsteps of the maid moving about in my presence chamber, bringing wood for the fire, raking up the embers. Still Arthur does not stir.

I put a gentle hand on his shoulder. 'Wake up, sleepyhead,' I say, my voice warm with love. 'The servants are outside, you must go.'

He is damp with sweat, the skin of his shoulder is cold and clammy.

'My love?' I ask. 'Are you well?'

He opens his eyes and smiles at me. 'Don't tell me it's morning already. I am so weary I could sleep for another day.'

'It is. And you will have to go now.'

Arthur holds me close, as if he cannot bear to let me go.

Suddenly, I am struck by the warmth of his body, the tangled heat of the sheets around us. 'You are so hot!'

'It is desire,' he says, smiling. 'I shall have to go to Mass to cool down.'

He gets out of bed and throws his gown around his shoulders. He gives a little stagger.

'Beloved, are you all right?' I ask.

'A little dizzy, nothing more,' he says.

I get up from bed, and unbolt the battlements door to let him out. He sways a little as he goes up the stone steps, then I see him straighten his shoulders to breathe in the fresh air. I close the door behind him, and then go back to my bed. I glance round the room; nobody could know that he has been here.

In the chapel they could do no more than exchange hidden smiles. After Mass, Arthur went riding and Catalina went to break her fast. After breakfast was her time to study with her chaplain.

Margaret Pole came in as Catalina was closing her book. 'The prince begs your attendance in his rooms,' she said.

Catalina rose to her feet. 'Has something happened?'

'I think he is unwell. He has sent away everyone but the grooms of the body and his servers.'

Catalina left at once, followed by Doña Elvira and Lady Margaret. The prince's rooms were crowded by the usual hangers-on of the little court: men seeking favour or attention, petitioners asking for justice. Catalina walked through them all to the double doors of Arthur's private chamber, and went in.

He was seated in a chair by the fire, his face very pale. Doña Elvira and Lady Margaret waited at the door as Catalina went quickly to him.

'Are you ill, my love?' she asked quickly.

He managed a smile but she saw it was an effort. 'I have taken a chill, I think,' he said. 'Come no closer, I don't want to pass it to you.'

'Are you hot?' she asked fearfully, thinking of the Sweat which came on like a fever and left a corpse.

'No, I feel cold.'

'Well, it is not surprising in this country where it either snows or rains all the time.'

He managed another smile.

Catalina looked around and saw Lady Margaret. 'Lady Margaret, we must call the prince's physician.'

'I sent my servants to find him already,' she said, coming forwards.

'I don't want a fuss made,' Arthur said irritably. 'I just wanted to tell you, Princess, that I cannot come to dinner.'

Her eyes went to his. 'How shall we be alone?' was the unspoken question.

There was a tap on the door and a voice called out, 'Dr Bereworth is here, Your Grace.'

Arthur raised his hand in permission, Doña Elvira opened the door and the man came into the room.

'The prince feels cold and tired.' Catalina went to him at once, speaking rapidly in French. 'Is he ill? I don't think he's ill. What do you think?'

The doctor bowed low to her and to the prince. He bowed to Lady Margaret and Doña Elvira.

'I am sorry, I don't understand,' he said uncomfortably in English to Lady Margaret. 'What is the princess saying?'

Catalina clapped her hands together in frustration. 'The prince . . .' she began in English.

Margaret Pole came to her side. 'His Grace is unwell,' she said.

'May I speak with him alone?' Dr Bereworth asked.

Arthur nodded. He tried to rise from the chair but he almost staggered. The doctor was at once at his side, supporting him, and led him into his bedchamber.

'He cannot be ill.' Catalina turned to Doña Elvira and spoke to her in Spanish. 'He is just overtired. He rode for a long time yesterday. And it was cold, there was a very cold wind. I noticed it myself.'

'A wind like this can kill a man,' Doña Elvira said gloomily. 'It blows so cold and so damp.'

'Stop it!' Catalina said, clapping her hands to her ears. 'I won't hear another word. He is just tired, overtired.'

Lady Margaret stepped forwards and gently took Catalina's hands. 'Be patient, Princess,' she counselled. 'Dr Bereworth is a very good doctor, and he has known the prince from childhood. We will soon have him well again.'

Catalina nodded, and turned to sit by the window and look out. It was raining again, the raindrops chasing down the small panes of glass. Catalina watched them. She tried to keep her mind from the death of her brother who had loved his wife so much, who had been looking forward to the birth of their son. Juan had died within days of taking sick, and no one had ever known what was wrong with him.

The physician seemed to take a long time and when he came out of the bedchamber, Arthur was not with him.

'I think his grooms of the body should prepare him for bed,' the doctor said. 'He is very weary. He would be better for rest.'

'Is he ill?' Catalina demanded, speaking slowly in Latin.

The doctor spread his hands. 'He has a fever,' he said cautiously in slow French.

'Do you know what it is?' Lady Margaret asked, her voice very low. 'It's not the Sweat, is it?'

'Please God it is not. And there are no other cases in the town, as far as I know. But he should be kept quiet and allowed to rest. I shall go and make up a draught and I will come back.'

The low-voiced English was incomprehensible to Catalina. 'What does he say? What did he say?' she demanded of Lady Margaret.

'Nothing more than you heard,' the older woman assured her. 'He has a fever and needs rest. Let me get his men to undress him and put him properly to bed.'

Lady Margaret opened the door and beckoned to the prince's chief gentlemen. She gave them their orders and then she drew the princess through the crowd to her own rooms. 'Come, Your Grace,' she said. 'Come for a walk in the inner bailey with me and then I shall go back to his rooms and see that everything is comfortable for him.'

'I shall go back now,' Catalina insisted. 'I shall watch over his sleep.'

Margaret glanced at Doña Elvira. 'You should stay away from his rooms in case he does have a fever,' she said, speaking slowly and clearly in French so that the duenna could understand her. 'Your health is most important, Princess. If you should be with child, we would not want you to take his fever.'

'But he will want to see me!'

'Depend upon it,' Lady Margaret smiled. 'When his fever has broken he will want to see you. You have to be patient.'

Catalina nodded. 'I must go to the chapel. I must pray,' she said.

Dearest God, spare Arthur, spare my darling husband, Arthur. He is only a boy, I am only a girl, we have had no time together, no time at all. You know what plans we have for this country, what a holy castle we will make from this land, how we shall defend this kingdom from the Scots. Dear God, in Your mercy spare Arthur and let him come back to me. We want to have our

children: Mary, who is to be the rose of the rose, and our son Arthur who will
be the third Holy Roman Catholic Tudor king for England. Let us do as we
have promised. Oh dear Lord, be merciful and spare him. It is I, Catalina,
who asks this, and I ask in the name of my mother, Queen Isabella, who has
worked all her life in Your service, who is the most Christian queen, who has
served on Your crusades. She is beloved of You, I am beloved of You. Do not, I
beg You, disappoint me.

It grew dark as Catalina prayed but she did not notice. It was late when
Doña Elvira touched her gently on the shoulder and said, 'Infanta, you
should have some dinner and go to bed.'

Catalina turned a white face to her duenna. 'What word?' she asked.

'They say he is worse.'

In the morning they said that he had passed a good night, but the
gossip among the servers of the body was that he was sinking. The fever
had reached such a height that he was wandering in his mind.

'I shall see him,' Catalina announced to Lady Margaret at noon.

'Princess, it may be the Sweat,' her ladyship said bluntly. 'I should be
failing in my duty if I let you go too close to him.'

'Your duty is to me!' Catalina snapped.

The woman, a princess herself, never wavered. 'My duty is to
England,' she said. 'And if you are carrying a Tudor heir then my duty is
to that child, as well as to you. Do not quarrel with me, please, Princess.
I cannot allow you to go closer than the foot of his bed.'

'Let me go there, then,' Catalina said, like a little girl.

Lady Margaret bowed her head and led the way to the royal chambers. The crowds in the presence chamber had swollen in numbers as
the word had gone around the town that their prince was fighting for
his life; but they were silent, silent as a crowd in mourning.

The double doors to the inner chamber were thrown open and
Catalina went in. A makeshift apothecary's room had been set up in the
prince's privy chamber: a trestle table with large glass jars of ingredients,
a pestle and mortar, a chopping board, and half a dozen men in the gab-
erdine gowns of physicians were gathered together. Catalina paused,
looking for Dr Bereworth.

'Doctor?'

He came towards her at once, and dropped to his knee. 'Princess.'

'What news of my husband?' she said, speaking slowly and clearly for
him in French.

'I am sorry, he is no better. *Il est très malade,*' he said simply.

Catalina heard the words but it was as if she had forgotten the language. She could not translate them. She turned to Lady Margaret. 'He says that he is better?' she asked.

'He says that he is worse,' Lady Margaret said honestly.

'But they will have something to give him?' She turned to the doctor. '*Vous avez un médicament?*'

He gestured at the table behind him, at the apothecary.

'Oh, if only we had a Moorish doctor!' Catalina cried out. 'They have the greatest skill, there is no one like them.'

'We are doing everything we can,' the doctor said stiffly.

Catalina tried to smile. 'I am sure,' she said. 'Can I see him?'

'I will see if he is awake,' he said, and went through the door.

Catalina waited. She could not believe that only yesterday morning Arthur had slipped from her bed. Now, he was so ill that she could not even touch his hand.

The doctor opened the door. 'You can come to the threshold, Princess,' he said. 'But for the sake of your own health, and for the health of any child you could be carrying, you should come no closer.'

Catalina stepped up quickly to the door. Lady Margaret pressed a pomander stuffed with cloves and herbs in her hand. Catalina held it to her nose. The acrid smell made her eyes water as she peered into the darkened room.

Arthur was sprawled on the bed, his face flushed with fever. His blond hair was dark with sweat, his face gaunt. He looked much older than his fifteen years. His eyes were sunk deep into his face, the skin beneath his eyes stained brown.

'Your wife is here,' the doctor said quietly to him.

Arthur's eyes fluttered open and she saw his blue eyes narrow as he tried to focus on the bright doorway and Catalina, standing before him, her face white with shock.

'My love,' he said. '*Amo te.*'

'*Amo te,*' she whispered. 'They say I cannot come closer.'

'Don't come closer,' he said, his voice a thread. 'I love you.'

'I love you too!' She could hear that her voice was strained with tears. 'You will be well?'

He shook his head, too weary to speak.

'Arthur?' she said, demandingly. 'You will get better?'

'I will try, beloved. I will try so hard. For you. For us.'

'Is there anything you want?' she asked. 'Anything I can get for you?' She glanced around. There was nothing that she could do for him. If she had brought a Moorish doctor with her, if her parents had not destroyed the learning of the Arab universities, if the church had allowed the study of medicine, and not called knowledge heresy . . .

'All I want is to live with you,' he said, his voice a thin thread.

She gave a little sob. 'And I you.'

'The prince should rest now, and you should not linger here.' The doctor stepped forwards.

'Please, let me stay!' she cried in a whisper. 'Please allow me. I beg you. Please let me be with him.'

Lady Margaret put a hand round her waist and drew her back. 'The prince needs to rest.'

'I shall come back,' Catalina called to him, and saw the little gesture of his hand which told her that he had heard her. 'I shall not fail you.'

Catalina went to the chapel to pray for him, but she could not pray. All she could do was think of him, his white face on the white pillows. They had been married only one hundred and forty days, they had been passionate lovers for only ninety-four nights. They had promised that they would have a lifetime together, she could not believe that she was on her knees now, praying for his life.

At dinner time she rose up, dipped her finger in the holy water, crossed herself, and with the water still wet on her forehead went back to his chambers, with Doña Elvira following, close behind.

The crowds in the halls outside the rooms made way for the princess without a word but a quiet murmur of blessings. Catalina went through them, looking neither to left nor right, through the presence chamber, past the apothecary bench, to the very door of his bedchamber.

They were bending over him on the bed. Catalina heard him cough, a thick cough as though his throat was bubbling with water.

'*Madre de Dios*,' she said softly. 'Holy Mother of God, keep Arthur safe.'

The doctor turned at her whisper. His face was pale. 'Keep back!' he said urgently. 'It is the Sweat.'

At that most feared word Doña Elvira stepped back and laid hold of Catalina's gown as if she would drag her from danger.

'Loose me!' Catalina snapped and tugged her gown from the duenna's hands. 'I will come no closer, but I have to speak with him.'

The doctor heard the resolution in her voice. 'Princess, he is too weak.'

'I have to speak to him. This is the business of the kingdom.'

One glance at her determined face told him that she would not be denied. He went past her with his head low, his assistants following behind. She made a little gesture with her hand and Doña Elvira retreated.

Catalina stepped over the threshold and pushed the door shut on them.

She saw Arthur stir in protest. 'I won't come any closer,' she assured him. 'I swear it. But I have to speak with you alone.'

His young round face when he turned it to her was shiny with sweat; he looked strained as the disease leached the life out of him.

'I am dying,' he said bleakly.

Catalina did not interrupt nor deny him. He saw her straighten a little, as if she had staggered beneath a mortal blow.

He took a rasping breath. 'But you must still be Queen of England.'

'What?'

He took a shaky breath. 'Love—you have sworn to obey me.'

'I will do anything.'

'Marry Harry. Be queen. Have our children.'

'What?' She was dizzy with shock.

'England needs a great queen,' he said. 'Especially with him. He's not fit for it. You must teach him. Build my forts. Build my navy. Defend against the Scots. Have my daughter Mary. Have my son Arthur. Let me keep England safe through you. Let me live through you.'

'I am your wife,' she said fiercely. 'Not his.'

He nodded. 'Tell them you are not.'

She staggered at that, and felt for the door to support her.

'Tell them I could not do it.' A hint of a smile came to his drained face. 'Tell them I was unmanned. Then marry Harry.'

'You hate Harry!' she burst out. 'You cannot want me to marry him. He is a child! And I love you.'

'He will be king,' he said desperately. 'So you will be queen. Marry him. Please. Beloved. For me.'

The door behind her opened a crack and Lady Margaret said quietly, 'You must not exhaust him, Princess.'

'I have to go,' Catalina said desperately to the still figure in the bed.

'Promise me . . .'

'I will come back. You will get better.'

'Please.'

Lady Margaret opened the door wider and took Catalina's hand. 'For his own good,' she said quietly. 'You have to leave him.'

Catalina turned away from the room, she looked back over her shoulder. Arthur lifted a hand a few inches from the rich coverlet. 'Promise,' he said. 'Please. For my sake. Promise. Promise me now, beloved.'

'I promise,' burst out of her.

His hand fell, she heard him give a little sigh of relief.

They were the last words they said to each other.

Ludlow, 2nd April 1502

At six o'clock, Vespers, Arthur's confessor, Dr Eldenham, administered extreme unction and Arthur died soon after. Catalina knelt on the threshold as the priest anointed her husband with the oil and bowed her head for the blessing. She did not rise until they told her that her boy-husband was dead and she was a widow at sixteen years old.

Lady Margaret on one side and Doña Elvira on the other half carried and half dragged Catalina to her bedchamber. Catalina slipped between the cold sheets of her bed and knew that however long she waited there, she would not hear Arthur's quiet footstep on the battlements outside her room, and his tap on the door.

'I cannot believe it,' she said brokenly.

'Drink this,' Lady Margaret said. 'The physician left it for you. It is a sleeping draught. I will wake you at noon.'

Catalina drank it down, ignoring the bitter taste. More than anything else she wanted to be asleep and never wake again.

They buried Arthur, Prince of Wales, on St George's Day, this first prince of all England, after a nightmare journey from Ludlow to Worcester, when the rain lashed down so hard that they could barely make way.

Hundreds turned out to see the miserable cortege go through the streets to Worcester Cathedral. Hundreds wept for the loss of the rose of England. After they lowered his coffin into the vault beneath the choir, the servants of his household broke their staffs of office and threw them into the grave with their lost master. It was over for them. Everything they had hoped for in the service of such a young and promising prince was finished. It was over for Arthur. It felt as if everything was over and could never be set right again.

For the first month of mourning Catalina stayed in her rooms. Lady Margaret and Doña Elvira gave out that she was ill, but not in danger. In truth they feared for her reason. She did not rail against fate or weep for her mother's comfort, she lay in utter silence, her face turned towards the wall. She knew she must not give way to weeping and madness, for if she once let go she would never be able to stop.

When they woke her in the morning she said she was tired. They did not know that she hardly dared to move for fear that she would moan aloud. After they had dressed her, she would sit on her chair like a stone. As soon as they allowed it, she would go back to bed, lie on her back, and look up at the brightly coloured tester that she had seen with eyes half-closed by love, and know that Arthur would never pull her into the crook of his arm again.

'I am afraid her mind is affected,' Lady Margaret said to Dr Bereworth. 'She does not speak, she does not even weep for him.'

'Will she eat?'

'If food is put before her and if she is reminded to eat.'

'Might she be with child?' he whispered. It was the only question that now mattered.

'I don't know,' she replied. 'She has said nothing.'

'She is mourning him,' he said. 'She is mourning like a young woman, for the young husband she has lost. We should let her grieve. She will have to rise up soon enough. Is she to go back to court?'

'The king commands it,' Lady Margaret said. 'The queen is sending her own litter.'

'Well, when it comes she will have to change her ways then,' he said comfortably. 'She will recover. The young have strong hearts. And it will help her to leave here, where she has such sad memories, poor child.'

But Catalina did not look like a poor child, Lady Margaret thought. She looked like a statue, like a stone princess carved from grief. Doña Elvira had dressed her in her new dark clothes of mourning, and persuaded her to sit in the window. The summer had come as Arthur had promised her that it would, it was warm as he had sworn it would be; but she was not walking by the river with him, greeting the swifts as they flew in from Spain. She was not planting salad vegetables in the gardens of the castle and persuading him to try them. The summer was here, the sun was here, Catalina was here, but Arthur was cold in the dark vault of Worcester Cathedral.

'Princess,' Lady Margaret started tentatively.

Slowly, the head under the heavy black hood turned towards her. 'Yes, Lady Margaret?' Her voice was hoarse.

'I have to ask you about your journey to London. The royal litter has arrived and you will have to leave here.'

'Can I not stay here?' Catalina asked.

'I understand the king has sent for you. I am sorry for it. They write that you may stay here until you are well enough to travel.'

'Why, what is to become of me?' Catalina asked, as if it was a matter of absolute indifference. 'When I get to London?'

'I am sorry. I do not know what is planned. My husband has been told nothing except to prepare for your journey to London.'

'Does a Princess of Wales have a house in London as well as here?' she asked. 'Shall I go back to Baynard's Castle?'

'You are not the Princess of Wales,' Lady Margaret started. She was going to explain but the look that Catalina turned on her was so darkly angry that she hesitated. 'I beg your pardon,' she said. 'I thought perhaps you did not understand . . .'

'Understand what?' Catalina's face was flushing pink with temper. 'I am the Princess of Wales. I have been the Princess of Wales all my life.'

'Now you are the Dowager Princess.'

Catalina clapped a hand over her mouth to hold back a cry of pain. 'I will never answer to it.'

'It is a title of respect. It is only the English word for widow.'

Catalina gritted her teeth and turned away from her friend to look out of the window.

The older woman hesitated. 'The queen writes to me. They want to know if you might be with child. If you are with child and that child is a boy then he will be the Prince of Wales, and then King of England, and you would be My Lady the King's Mother.'

'And if I am not with child?'

'Then you are the Dowager Princess, and Prince Harry is Prince of Wales.'

'And I?'

'You are the Infanta still. As you will always be.'

'And the next Queen of England?'

'Will be the wife of Prince Harry.'

The anger went out of Catalina; she walked to the fireplace. The little fire burning in the grate threw out no heat that she could feel through the thick black skirt of her mourning gown. She stared at the flames as if she would understand what had happened to her.

'I am become again what I was, when I was a child of three,' she said. 'The Infanta of Spain, not the Princess of Wales. Of no importance.'

Lady Margaret, whose own royal blood had been carefully diluted by a lowly marriage so that she could pose no threat to the Tudor throne of England, nodded. 'Princess, you take the position of your husband. It is always thus for all women. If you have no husband and no son, then you have no position. You have only what you were born to.'

Catalina said nothing, but the face that she showed to her friend was closed and cold.

'I will find a way to fulfil my destiny,' she said presently. 'I know what is my duty and what I have to do. I shall do as God wills, whatever the difficulties for me.'

I will tell no one what I promised. I will tell no one that in my heart I am still Princess of Wales, I will always be Princess of Wales until I see the wedding of my son and see my daughter-in-law crowned.

I have told no one whether or not I am with child. But I know, well enough. I had my course in April, there is no baby. There is no Princess Mary, there is no Prince Arthur. My love, my only love, is dead and there is nothing left of him for me, not even his unborn child.

I have to consider what I am to do, and how I am to claim the throne that Arthur wanted for me. I have to think how to keep my promise to him, how to tell the lie that he wanted me to tell. How I can make it convincing, how I can fool the king himself, and his sharp-witted, hard-eyed mother.

But I have made a promise, I do not retract my word. He dictated the lie I must tell, and I said 'yes'. I will not fail him.

Croydon, May 1502

The princess and her party arrived at Croydon Palace and Doña Elvira led Catalina to her private rooms. For once, the girl did not go to her bedchamber and close the door behind her, she stood in the sumptuous presence chamber, looking around her. 'A chamber fit for a princess,' she said.

'The Spanish ambassador is in attendance,' Doña Elvira told her. 'Shall I tell him that you will not see him?'

'I will see him,' Catalina said quietly. 'He may have word from my mother.'

The duenna bowed and went to find the ambassador. He was deep in conversation in the gallery outside the presence chamber with Father Alessandro Geraldini, the princess's chaplain.

'She could be with child?' the ambassador asked in a whisper. 'You are certain?'

'Pray God it is so. She is certainly in hopes of it,' the confessor told his countryman.

'Dr de Puebla!' the duenna snapped, disliking the confidential air between the two men. 'I shall take you to the princess now.'

De Puebla turned and smiled at the irritable woman. 'Certainly, Doña Elvira,' he said equably. 'At once.'

Dr de Puebla limped into the room, his richly trimmed black hat already in his hand, his small face wreathed in a smile that he meant to be reassuring, and saw her scrutinise him with no answering warmth in her face. She gave him her hand and then she sat in a straight-backed wooden chair before the fire.

'You may sit,' she said graciously, gesturing him to a lower chair, further away. 'Do you have any messages for me?'

'Of sympathy, from the king and Queen Elizabeth and from My Lady the King's Mother,' he replied, 'and from myself of course. They will invite you to court when you have recovered from your journey and are out of mourning.'

'How long am I to be in mourning?' Catalina enquired.

'My Lady the King's Mother has said that you should be in seclusion for a month after the burial. But since you were not at court during that time, she has ruled that you will stay here until she commands you to return to London. She is concerned for your health . . .'

He paused, hoping that she would volunteer whether or not she was with child, but she let the silence stretch.

'Do you have any letters from Spain?'

He bowed and gave her the letter he was carrying in the hidden pocket in his sleeve. She nodded her head in thanks and held it.

'Do you not want to open it now? Do you not want to reply?'

'When I have written my reply, I will send for you,' she said simply, asserting her power over him. 'I shall send for you when I want you.'

I open my mother's letter with hands that are trembling so much that I can hardly break the seals. The first thing I see is the shortness of the letter, only one page.

'Oh, Madre,' I breathe.

I read the short letter through once, and then, almost incredulously, I read it through again.

It is not a letter from a loving mother to her daughter. It is not a letter from a woman to her favourite child, and that child on the very edge of despair. Coldly, powerfully, she has written a letter from a queen to a princess. She writes of nothing but business.

She says that I am to stay in whatever house is provided for me until I have had my next course and I know that I am not with child. If that is the case I am to command Dr de Puebla to demand my jointure as Dowager Princess of Wales and as soon as I have the full money and not before (underlined so there can be no mistake), I am to take ship for Spain.

If, on the other hand, God is gracious, and I am with child, then I am to assure Dr de Puebla that the money for my dowry will be paid in cash and at once, he is to secure me my allowance as Dowager Princess of Wales, and I am to rest and hope for a boy.

I fold the letter carefully. I think that if she knew how very alone I am, how grieved I am, how much I miss him, she would not write to me of settlements and jointures and titles. If she knew how much I loved him and how I cannot bear to live without him she would write and tell me that she loves me, that I am to go home to her at once, without delay.

I tuck the letter into the pocket at my waist, and I stand up, as if reporting for duty. I am not a child any more. I will not cry for my mother, for she is not only a mother, she is Queen of Spain, and she has to ensure that she has a grandson, or failing a grandson, a watertight treaty. I am not just a young woman who has lost the man she loves. I am a Princess of Spain and I have to produce a grandson, or failing that a watertight treaty.

I am buying time, letting them think that I am with child. And while I say nothing they have to wait too. They will not send me home to Spain while they hope that I might still be My Lady the Mother of the Prince of Wales. They have to wait.

And while they wait I can plan what I shall say, and what I shall do. I have to be wise as my mother would be, and cunning as the fox, my father. I have to think how and when I shall start to tell this lie, Prince Arthur's great lie. If I can tell it so that it convinces everyone, if I can place myself so that I fulfil my destiny, then Arthur, beloved Arthur, can do as he wished. He can rule England through me, I can marry his brother and become queen. Arthur can live through the child I conceive with his brother, we can make the England we swore that we would make, despite misfortune, despite his brother's folly, despite my own despair.

I shall not give myself to heartbreak, I shall give myself to England. I shall keep my promise. I shall be constant to my husband and to my destiny. And I shall plan and plot and consider how I shall conquer this misfortune and be what I was born to be. The queen.

London, June 1502

Catalina had spent less than a month of seclusion at Croydon Palace, when her little court was moved to Durham House. She did not seem particularly pleased at the change of scene, though Durham House was a pretty palace with gardens running down to the river. The ambassador came to visit and found her in the gallery at the front of the house.

She let him stand before her.

'Her Grace, the queen your mother, is sending an emissary to escort you home as soon as your widow's jointure is paid. Since you have not told us that you are with child she is preparing for your journey.'

De Puebla saw her press her lips together as if to curb a hasty reply.

'How much does the king have to pay me, as his son's widow?'

'He has to pay you a third of the revenues of Wales, Cornwall and

Chester,' he said. 'And your parents are now asking, in addition, that King Henry return all of your dowry.'

Catalina looked aghast. 'He never will,' she said. 'Why should he repay the dowry and pay a jointure when he has nothing to gain from it?'

The ambassador shrugged his shoulders. 'It is in the contract.'

'So, too, was my allowance, and you failed to make him pay that,' she said sharply.

'You should have handed over your plate as soon as you arrived.'

'And eat off what?' she blazed out.

Insolently, he stood before her. He knew, as she did not yet understand, that she had no power. Every day that she failed to announce she was with child her importance diminished.

'Why did you ever agree to such a contract? He has to return the dowry that he has been paid, he cannot have my plate, and he owes me this jointure. Ambassador, you must know that he will never pay this much. And clearly he will never give me the rents of—where?—Wales and, and Cornwall?—for ever.'

'Only until you remarry,' he observed. 'And we must assume that you will remarry soon. I imagine that the emissary is coming to fetch you home just for that. Their Majesties probably have a marriage contract drawn up for you already.'

For one moment de Puebla saw the shock in her face then she turned abruptly from him to stare out of the window.

He watched the tightly stretched shoulders and the tense turn of her neck, and he was surprised that his shot at her second marriage had hit her so hard. Surely she must know that she would go home only to be married again?

Catalina let the silence grow as she watched the street beyond the Durham House gate. It was so unlike her home. There were no street sellers with rich piles of spices, no flower sellers staggering under small mountains of blooms. There were no herbalists, physicians, or astronomers, plying their trade as if knowledge could be freely available to anyone. Instead there was the bustle of one of the greatest cities in the world, the relentless, unstoppable buzz of prosperity and commerce, and the ringing of the bells of hundreds of churches.

'This is my home now,' she said. 'The king should not think that I will go home and remarry as if none of this has happened. My parents should not think that they can change my destiny. I was brought up to be Princess of Wales and Queen of England. I shall not be cast off like a bad debt.'

The ambassador smiled at her unseeing back. 'Of course it shall be as you wish,' he lied easily. 'I shall write to your father and mother and say that you prefer to wait here, in England, while your future is decided.'

Catalina rounded on him. 'No, I shall decide my future.'

He had to bite the inside of his cheeks to hide his smile. 'Of course you will, Infanta.'

'Dowager Princess.'

'Dowager Princess.'

'You may tell my father and mother, and you shall tell the king, that I am not with child.'

'Indeed,' he breathed. 'Thank you for informing us.'

'I shall write to my mother. But you are not to make arrangements for me to leave. It may be that I shall stay in England for a little while longer. If I am to be remarried, I could be remarried in England.'

'To whom?' he demanded.

She looked away from him, not yet ready to show him her full plan. 'How should I know? My parents and the king should decide.'

I have to find a way to put my marriage to Harry into the mind of the king. Now that he knows I am not with child surely it will occur to him that the resolution for all our difficulties is to marry me to Harry?

If I could get a letter to my mother without de Puebla seeing it then I could tell her of my plan, of Arthur's plan.

But I cannot. I am alone in this. I do feel so fearfully alone.

'They are going to name Prince Harry as the new Prince of Wales,' Doña Elvira said quietly to the princess as she was brushing her hair in the last week of June. 'He is to be Prince Harry, Prince of Wales.'

She expected the girl to break down at this last severing of her links with the past but Catalina did nothing but look around the room. 'Leave us,' she said to the maids who were turning down the bed.

They went out quietly and closed the door behind them. Catalina tossed back her hair and met Doña Elvira's eyes in the mirror.

'I want you to write to my parents and tell them that my marriage with Prince Arthur was not consummated,' she said, smoothly. 'I am a virgin as I was when I left Spain.'

Doña Elvira was stunned, the hairbrush suspended in midair, her mouth open. 'You were bedded in the sight of the whole court,' she said.

'He was impotent,' Catalina said, her face as hard as a diamond.

'You were together once a week.'

'With no effect,' she said, unwavering.

'Infanta, you never said anything. Why did you not tell me?'

THE CONSTANT PRINCESS

Catalina's eyes were veiled. 'What should I say? We were newly wed. He was very young. I thought it would come right in time.'

Doña Elvira did not even pretend to believe her. 'Princess, there is no need for you to say this. Being a widow is no obstacle to a good marriage. They will find someone for you. They will find a good match for you, you do not have to pretend—'

'I don't want "someone",' Catalina said fiercely. 'You should know that as well as me. I was born to be Princess of Wales and Queen of England. It was Arthur's greatest wish that I should be Queen of England.' She pulled herself back from thinking of him. 'I am a virgin untouched, now, as I was in Spain. You shall tell them that.'

Doña Elvira's eyes darted away; she was thinking furiously. 'No one would believe us if we say you are a virgin.'

'They would. You have to tell them. No one would dare to ask me. They will believe you because you are close to me, as close as a mother.'

'I have said nothing so far.'

'And that was right. But you will speak now, Doña Elvira.'

'Everyone saw that he was in love with you.'

'No, they didn't. Everyone saw that we were together, as a prince and princess. Everyone saw that he came to my bedroom only as he had been ordered. No more. No one can say what went on behind the bedroom door. No one but me. And I say that he was impotent.'

The older woman bowed her head to gain time. 'I can tell them what you wish. If you wish to say your husband was impotent and you are still a maid then I can say that. But how will this make you queen?'

'Since the marriage was not consummated, there can be no objection to me marrying Prince Arthur's brother Harry.'

Doña Elvira gasped with shock at this next stage.

Catalina pressed on. 'When this new emissary comes from Spain you may inform him that it is God's will and my desire that I be Princess of Wales again, as I always have been. He shall speak to the king. He shall negotiate, not my widow's jointure, but my next wedding.'

Doña Elvira gaped. 'You cannot make your own marriage!'

'I can,' Catalina said fiercely. 'I will, and you will help me.'

'You cannot think that they will let you marry Prince Harry?'

'Why should they not? The marriage with his brother was not consummated. I am a virgin. The dowry to the king is half-paid. He can keep the half he already has and we can give him the rest of it. He need not pay my jointure. The contract has been signed and sealed, they need only change the names, and here I am in England already. It is the best solution for everyone.'

PRINCESS-IN-WAITING
1503

KING HENRY AND HIS QUEEN, driven by the loss of their son, were expecting another child, and Catalina, hoping for their favour, was sewing an exquisite layette of baby clothes before a small fire in the smallest room of Durham House in the early days of February. Her ladies, hemming seams according to their abilities, were seated at a distance; Doña Elvira could speak privately.

'This should be your baby's layette,' the duenna said resentfully under her breath. 'A widow for a year, and no progress made. What is going to become of you?'

Catalina looked up from her delicate black-thread work. 'Peace, Doña Elvira. It will be as God and my parents and the king decide.'

'Seventeen, now,' Doña Elvira said, stubbornly. 'How long are we to stay in this godforsaken country, neither a bride nor a wife? Neither at court nor elsewhere? With bills mounting up and the jointure still not paid?'

'Doña Elvira, if you knew how much your words grieve me, I don't think you would say them,' Catalina said clearly.

The duenna said nothing more, Catalina did not have the energy to argue. She knew that during this year of mourning for Arthur, she had been steadily pushed to the margins of court life. Her claim to be a virgin had not produced a new betrothal as she had thought it would; it had made her yet more irrelevant. She was only summoned to court on the great occasions, and then she was dependent on the kindness of Queen Elizabeth.

The king's mother, Lady Margaret, had no interest in the impoverished Spanish princess. She had not proved readily fertile, she now said she had never even been bedded. She was of no use to the house of Tudor except as a bargaining counter with Spain. She might as well stay at her house in the Strand, as be summoned to court. Besides, My Lady the King's Mother did not like the way that the new Prince of Wales looked at his widowed sister-in-law with puppy-like devotion. My Lady the King's Mother had privately decided that she would keep them apart. She mistrusted Catalina. Why would the young widow encourage a brother-in-law who was nearly six years her junior? What did the

Spanish widow hope to achieve by sending him books, teaching him Spanish, laughing at his accent and watching him ride at the quintain, as if he were in training as her knight errant?

Nothing would come of it. But My Lady the King's Mother would allow no one to be intimate with Harry but herself, and she ruled that Catalina's visits to court were to be rare and brief.

'But what will happen?' Doña Elvira spoke again.

Catalina turned her head away. 'I don't know,' she said shortly.

There was a sharp rap at the door. 'Urgent message for the Dowager Princess of Wales!' the voice called out.

Catalina dropped her sewing and rose to her feet. Her ladies sprang up too. It was so unusual for anything to happen in the quiet court of Durham House that they were thrown into a flutter.

'Well, let him in!' Catalina exclaimed.

Maria de Salinas flung open the door and one of the royal grooms of the chamber came in and knelt before the princess. 'Grave news,' he said shortly. 'A son, a prince, has been born of the queen and has died. Her Grace the Queen has died too. God pray for His Grace in his kingly grief.'

'God save her soul,' Catalina replied correctly. 'God save the King.'

There was a great state funeral for Queen Elizabeth, and Catalina was in mourning black again. Through the dark lace of her mantilla she watched the orders of precedence, the arrangements for the service, she saw how everything was commanded by the great book of the king's mother. Even her own place was laid down, behind the princesses, but before all the other ladies of the court.

Lady Margaret, the king's mother, had written down all the procedures to be followed at the Tudor court, from birth chambers to lying in state, so that her son and the generations which she prayed would come after him would be prepared for every occasion, and so that every occasion, however distant in the future, would be commanded by her.

Now her first great funeral, for her unloved daughter-in-law, went off with the order and grace of a well-planned masque at court, and as the great manager of everything she stepped up visibly, unquestionably, to her place as the greatest lady at court.

After weeks spent alone, mourning for his wife, the king returned to the court at Whitehall Palace, and Catalina was invited to dine with the royal family and seated with the Princess Mary and the ladies of the court. The young Harry, Prince of Wales, was placed securely between his father and grandmother. He smiled at Catalina and she shot him a look that she hoped was discreetly warm, then cast down her eyes. When she glanced up, he was still looking at her and then he blushed red to be caught. A child. She shot a sideways little smile even as she silently criticised him. A child of eleven. All boasting and boyishness.

A woman could rule a boy like that, she thought. A woman could be a very great queen if she married such a boy. For the first ten years he would know nothing, and by then, perhaps he might be in such a habit of obedience that he would let his wife continue to rule. Or he might be, as Arthur told me, so lazy that he could be diverted by games and hunting and sports and amusements, so that the business of the kingdom could be done by his wife.

If they give him everything that he wants, perhaps he might be the one who chooses his bride, she thought. They are in the habit of indulging him. Perhaps he could beg to marry me and they would feel obliged to say 'yes'.

She held his gaze for a long moment, she took in a little breath and parted her lips as if to whisper a word to him. She saw his blue eyes focus on her mouth and darken with desire, and then, calculating the effect, she looked down. Stupid boy, she thought.

The king rose from the table and all the men and women on the crowded benches of the hall rose too, and bowed their heads.

'I give you thanks for coming to greet me,' King Henry said. 'But now forgive me, as I wish to be alone.'

He nodded to Harry, he offered his mother his hand, and the royal family went through the little doorway at the back of the great hall to their privy chamber.

'You should have stayed longer,' the king's mother remarked as they settled into chairs by the fire and the groom of the ewery brought them wine. 'It looks bad, to leave so promptly.'

'I was weary,' Henry said shortly. He looked over to where Catalina and the Princess Mary were sitting together. The younger girl was red-eyed, the loss of her mother had hit her hard. Catalina was—as usual—cool as a stream. He thought she had great power of self-containment. Even this loss of her only real friend at court, her last friend in England, did not seem to distress her.

'She can go back to Durham House tomorrow,' his mother remarked, following the direction of his gaze. 'It does no good for her to come to court. She has not earned her place here with an heir, and she has not paid for her place here with her dowry.'

'She is constant,' he said. 'She is constant in her attendance on you, and on me.'

'Constant like the plague,' his mother returned.

'You are hard on her.'

'It is a hard world,' she said simply. 'Why don't we send her home?'

'Do you not admire her at all?'

She was surprised by the question. 'What is there to admire in her?'

'Her courage, her dignity. She has beauty, of course, but she also has charm. She is educated, she is graceful. And she has borne herself, under this disappointment, like a queen.'

Catalina looked up and saw them watching her. She gave a small, controlled smile and inclined her head. Henry rose, went to a window bay on his own, and crooked his finger for her. She did not jump to come to him, as any of the women of court would have jumped. She looked at him, she raised an eyebrow as if she were considering whether or not to obey, and then she gracefully rose to her feet and strolled towards him.

'Good God, she is desirable,' he thought to himself. 'No more than seventeen. Utterly in my power, and yet still she walks across the room as if she were Queen of England crowned.'

'You will miss the queen, I dare say,' he said abruptly in French as she came up to him.

'I shall,' she replied clearly. 'I grieve for you in the loss of your wife.'

He nodded. 'We share a grief now,' he observed. 'You have lost your partner in life and I have lost mine.'

He saw her gaze sharpen. 'Indeed,' she said steadily. 'We do.'

'You must teach me the secret of your resignation,' he said.

'Oh, I don't think I resign myself.'

Henry was intrigued. 'You don't?'

'No. I think I trust in God that He knows what is right for all of us, and His will shall be done. I know my destiny,' Catalina said calmly. 'He has been gracious to reveal it to me. I am blessed.'

'And what is this great destiny that God has for you?' he said sarcastically. He hoped so much that she would say that she should be Queen of England, and then he could ask her, or draw close to her, or let her see what was in his mind.

'To do God's will, of course, and bring His kingdom to earth,' she said cleverly, and evaded him once more.

I speak very confidently of God's will, and I remind the king that I was raised to be Princess of Wales, but in truth God is silent to me. Since the day of Arthur's death I can have no genuine conviction that I am blessed. How can I call myself blessed when I have lost the one thing that made my life complete?

How can I be blessed when I do not think I will ever be happy again? I have to give the illusion of being sure of my destiny. I am the daughter of Isabella of Spain. My inheritance is certainty.

But in truth, of course, I am increasingly alone. There is nothing between me and despair but my promise to Arthur, and the thin thread, like gold wire in a carpet, of my own determination.

King Henry did not approach Catalina for one month for the sake of decency, but when he was out of his black jacket he made a formal visit to her at Durham House. He saw the signs of wear and tear in the curtains and rugs and hangings and congratulated himself on not making it easier for her in this last year. She should know by now that she was utterly in his power and her parents could do nothing to free her.

His herald threw open the double doors to her presence chamber and shouted, 'His Grace, King Henry of England . . .'

Henry waved aside the other titles and went in to his daughter-in-law.

She was wearing a dark-coloured gown with blue slashings on the sleeve, a richly embroidered stomacher and a dark blue hood. It brought out the amber in her hair and the blue in her eyes and he smiled in instinctive pleasure at the sight of her as she sank into a deep formal curtsy and rose up.

'Your Grace,' she said pleasantly. 'This is an honour indeed.'

He had to force himself not to stare at the creamy line of her neck, at the smooth, unlined face that looked back up at him. This was a girl who should be bedded. He checked himself at once, and thought he was part lecher, part lover to look on his dead son's child-bride with such desire.

'Can I offer you some refreshment?' she asked.

'Thank you. I will take a glass of wine.'

'I am afraid I have nothing fit to offer you,' she said smoothly. 'I have nothing left in my cellars at all, and I cannot afford to buy good wine.'

Henry did not show by so much as a flicker that he knew she had trapped him into hearing of her financial difficulties. 'I am sorry for that, I will have some barrels sent over,' he said. 'Your housekeeping must be very remiss.'

'It is very thin,' she said simply. 'Will you take a cup of ale? We brew our own ale very cheaply.'

'Thank you,' he said, biting his lip to hide a smile. The year of widowhood had brought out her courage, he thought.

'Is My Lady the King's Mother in good health and the Princess Mary well?' she asked.

'Yes, thank God,' he said. 'And you?'

She smiled and bowed her head. 'And no need to ask for your health,' she remarked. 'You never look any different.'

'Do I not?'

'Not since the very first time we met,' she said. 'When I had just landed in England and you rode to meet me.' It cost Catalina a good deal not to think of Arthur as he was on that evening. Determinedly she put her young lover from her mind and smiled at his father and said, 'I was so surprised by your coming, and so startled by you.'

He laughed. He saw that she had conjured the picture of when he first saw her, a virgin by her bed, and how he thought then that he had come upon her like a ravisher.

He turned and took a chair to cover his thoughts, gesturing that she should sit down too. Her duenna, the same sour-faced Spanish mule, he noticed irritably, stood at the back of the room with two other ladies.

Catalina sat perfectly composed, her white fingers interlaced in her lap, her back straight, her entire manner that of a young woman confident of her power to attract.

A servant came in with two cups of small ale. The king was served first and then Catalina took a cup. She took a tiny sip and set it down.

'D'you still not like ale?' He was startled at the intimacy in his voice.

'I drink it only when I am very thirsty,' she replied. 'But I don't like the taste it leaves in my mouth.' She put her hand to her mouth and touched her lower lip. Fascinated, he watched her fingertip brush the tip of her tongue.

'What did you drink in Spain?' He was still watching her soft mouth, shiny where her tongue had licked her lips.

'We could drink the water,' she said. 'In the Alhambra the Moors had piped clean water all the way from the mountains into the palace. And we drank juices from the fruits of course. We had wonderful fruits in summer, and ices, and sherbets and wines as well.'

'If you come on progress with me this summer we can go to places where you can drink the water,' he said. He thought he was sounding like a stupid boy, promising her a drink of water as a treat. Stubbornly, he persisted. 'If you come with me we can go hunting, we can go to Hampshire, beyond, to the New Forest. You remember the country around there? Near where we first met?'

'I should like that so much,' she said. 'If I am still here, of course.'

'Still here?' He was startled, he had almost forgotten that she was his hostage, she was supposed to go home by summer. 'I doubt your father and I will have agreed terms by then.'

'Why, how can it take so long?' she asked, her blue eyes wide with assumed surprise. 'Surely we can come to some agreement?'

It was so close to what he had been thinking that he rose to his feet, discomfited. At once she rose too. The top of her pretty blue hood only came to his shoulder; he thought he would have to bend his head to kiss her. He felt his face flush hot at the thought of it. 'Come here,' he said thickly and led her to the window embrasure where her ladies could not overhear them.

'I have been thinking what sort of arrangement we might come to,' he said. 'I should certainly like you to stay here.'

Catalina did not look up at him. If she had done so then, he would have been sure of her. But she kept her eyes down, her face downcast. 'Oh, certainly, if my parents agree,' she said.

He felt himself trapped. He felt he could not go forwards while she held her head so delicately to one side and showed him only the curve of her cheek and her eyelashes, and yet he could hardly go back when she had asked him outright if there was not another way to resolve the conflict between him and her parents.

'You will think me very old,' he burst out.

'Not at all,' she said levelly.

'I am old enough to be your father.'

She looked up at him. 'I never think of you like that,' she said.

Henry was silent. He felt utterly baffled by this slim young woman who seemed at one moment so deliciously encouraging and yet at another moment, quite opaque. 'What would you like to do?' he demanded of her.

At last she raised her head and smiled up at him, her lips curving up but no warmth in her eyes. 'Whatever you command,' she said. 'I should like most of all to obey you, Your Grace.'

What does he mean? What is he doing? I thought he was offering me Harry and I was about to say 'yes' when he said that I must think him very old, as old as my father. And of course he is, indeed, he looks far older than my father, that is why I never think of him like a father, a grandfather perhaps. I spoke only the truth when I said that I never see him like that.

But then he looked at me as if I had said something of great interest, and asked me what I wanted. I could not say to his face that I wanted him to overlook my marriage to his oldest son, and marry me anew to his youngest. So I said that I wanted to obey him. There can be nothing wrong with that. But somehow it was not what he wanted. And it did not get me to where I wanted.

Henry went back to Whitehall Palace, his face burning and his heart pounding, hammered between frustration and calculation. If he could persuade Catalina's parents to allow the wedding, he could claim the rest of her substantial dowry, be free of their claims for her jointure, reinforce the alliance with Spain at the very moment that he was looking to secure new alliances with Scotland and France, and perhaps, with such a young wife, get another son and heir on her. One daughter on the throne of Scotland, one daughter on the throne of France should lock both nations into peace for a lifetime. The Princess of Spain on the throne of England should keep the most Christian kings of Spain in alliance. England would be safe. Better yet, England's sons might inherit the kingdoms of France, of Scotland, of Spain. England might conceive its way into peace and greatness.

It made absolute sense to secure Catalina; he tried to focus on the political advantage and not think of the line of her neck nor the curve of her waist. He tried to steady his mind by thinking of the small fortune that would be saved by not having to provide her with a jointure nor with her keep, by not having to send a ship, several ships probably, to escort her home. But all he could think was that she had touched her soft mouth with her finger and at the thought of the tip of her tongue against her lips he groaned aloud.

'Your Grace?' someone asked him. 'Are you ill?'

'Bile,' the king said sourly. 'Something I have eaten.'

His chief groom of the body came to him. 'Shall I send for your physician, Your Grace?'

'No,' the king said. 'But send a couple of barrels of the best wine to the Dowager Princess. She has nothing in her cellar, and when I have to visit her I should like to drink wine and not ale.'

'Yes, Your Grace,' the man said, bowed, and went away. Henry continued to his rooms, which were crowded with people as usual: courtiers, petitioners, favour seekers, fortune hunters, some friends, some gentry, some noblemen attending on him for love or calculation. Henry regarded them all sourly.

'Where is my mother?' he asked one of them.

'In her rooms, Your Grace,' the man replied.

'I shall visit her,' he said. 'Let her know.'

He gave her a few moments to ready herself, and then he went to her chambers.

'I'll announce myself,' the king said to the guard at her door, and stepped in without ceremony.

Lady Margaret was seated at a table in the window, the household accounts spread before her, inspecting the costs of the royal court.

She looked up as he came in. 'My son.'

He knelt for her blessing as he always did when he first greeted her every day, and felt her fingers gently touch the top of his head.

'You look troubled,' she remarked.

'I am,' he said. 'I went to see the Dowager Princess.'

'Yes?' A faint expression of disdain crossed her face.

'We—' He broke off and then started again. 'We have to decide what is to become of her. She spoke of going home to Spain.'

'When they pay us what they owe,' she said at once. 'They know they have to pay the rest of her dowry before she can leave.'

'Yes, she knows that.'

There was a brief silence.

'She asked if there could not be another agreement,' he said.

'Ah, I've been waiting for them to show their hand,' Lady Margaret said exultantly. 'I knew that they were waiting for us to make the first move. Ha! That we have made them declare first!'

He raised his eyebrows. 'For what?'

'A proposal from us, of course,' she said. 'They knew that we would never let such a chance go. She was the right match then, and she is the right match now. Especially if they pay in full. And now she is more profitable than ever.'

His colour flushed as he beamed at her. 'You think so?'

'Of course. She is here, half her dowry already paid, the rest we have only to collect, the alliance is already working to our benefit—we would never have the respect of the French if they did not fear her parents, the Scots fear us too—she is still the best match in Christendom for us.'

His sense of relief was overwhelming. If his mother did not oppose the plan then he felt he could push on with it.

'And the difference in age?'

'It is what? Five, nearly six years? That is nothing for a prince.'

He recoiled as if she had slapped him in the face.

'And Harry is tall for his age and strong. They will not look mismatched,' she said.

'No,' he said flatly. 'No. Not Harry. I did not mean Harry. I was not speaking of Harry!'

Her gaze flashed across his face, reading him rapidly, as only she could. 'Not Harry?'

'I thought you were speaking of me.'

'Of you?' She quickly reconsidered the conversation. 'Of you for the Infanta?' she asked incredulously.

THE CONSTANT PRINCESS

He felt himself flush again. 'Yes.'

'Arthur's widow? Your own daughter-in-law?'

'Yes! Why not? He was too young. It was not consummated,' he said, repeating the words that the Spanish ambassador had learned from Doña Elvira, which had been spread throughout Christendom.

She looked at him, noting the colour in his cheeks and the trouble in his face. 'They are probably lying. We saw them wedded and bedded and there was no suggestion then that it had not been done.'

'That is their business. If they all tell the same lie and stick to it, then it is the same as the truth.'

'Only if we accept it.'

'We do,' he ruled.

She raised her eyebrows. 'It is your desire?'

'It is not a question of desire. I need a wife,' Henry said coolly, as though it could be anyone. 'And she is conveniently here, as you say.'

'She would be suitable by birth,' his mother conceded, 'but for her relationship to you. She is your daughter-in-law even if it was not con-summated. And she is very young.'

'She is seventeen,' he said. 'A good age for marriage.'

'The people won't like it,' she observed.

He shrugged. 'They will be glad enough if she gives me a son.'

'Oh yes, if she can do that. But she was barren with Arthur.'

'As we have agreed, Arthur was impotent.'

She pursed her lips but said nothing.

'And it gains us the dowry and removes the cost of the jointure,' he pointed out. 'And she is here already.'

'A most constant presence,' she said sourly.

'A constant princess,' he smiled.

'Do you really think her parents would agree?'

'It solves their dilemma as well as ours. And it maintains the alliance.' He found he was smiling, and tried to make his face stern, as normal. 'She herself would think it was her destiny. She believes herself born to be Queen of England.'

'Well then, she is a fool,' his mother remarked smartly.

'She was raised to be queen since she was a child.'

'But she will be a barren queen. No son of hers will be king; if she has one at all, he will come after Harry,' she reminded him. 'He will even come after Harry's sons. It's a far poorer alliance for her than marriage to a Prince of Wales. The Spanish won't like it.'

'Oh, Harry is still a child. His sons are a long way ahead. Years.'

'Even so. Her parents will prefer Prince Harry. That way, she is queen

103

and her son is king after her. Why would they agree to anything less?'

Henry hesitated. There was nothing he could say to fault her logic, except that he did not wish to follow it.

'Oh. I see. You want her,' she said flatly when the silence extended so long that she realised there was something he could not let himself say. 'It is a matter of your desire.'

He took the plunge. 'Yes,' he confirmed.

Lady Margaret looked at him with calculation in her gaze. He had been taken from her as little more than a baby for safekeeping. Since then she had planned his future as a man, she had defended his rights as a king but she had never known tenderness for him.

'That's very shocking,' she said coolly. 'She stands as a daughter to you. This desire is a carnal sin.'

'There is nothing wrong in honourable love,' he said. 'She is not my daughter. She is his widow. And it was not consummated.'

'You will need a dispensation, it is a sin.'

'But you do not advise me against it,' he said.

'It is a sin,' she repeated. 'But if you can get dispensation and her parents agree to it, then—' She pulled a sour face.

'I shall tell the Spanish ambassador to propose it to Their Majesties of Spain and I shall talk to her tomorrow.'

Henry saw that Dr de Puebla, the Spanish ambassador, was invited to Whitehall in time for dinner, given a seat at one of the top tables, and plied with the best wine. Some venison, hanged to perfection and cooked in a brandywine sauce, came to the king's table, he helped himself to a small portion and sent the dish to the Spanish ambassador. De Puebla, who had not experienced such favours since first negotiating the Infanta's marriage contract, loaded his plate and wondered quietly behind his avid smile what it might mean.

He was no fool, he knew that something would be required. But given the horror of the past year—when the hopes of Spain had been buried beneath the nave in Worcester Cathedral—at least these were straws in a good wind. Clearly, King Henry had a use for him again as something other than a whipping boy for the failure of the Spanish sovereigns to pay their debts.

De Puebla had tried to explain to Catalina that he could not make the English king pay a more generous allowance for the upkeep of her household, nor could he persuade the Spanish king to give his daughter financial support. Both kings were utterly stubborn, both quite determined to force the other into a weak position. Neither seemed to care that in the meantime Catalina, only seventeen, was forced to keep house with an extravagant entourage in a foreign land on next to no money.

Henry rose from the throne and gave the signal that the servers could clear the plates. They swept the board and cleared the trestle tables, and Henry strolled among the diners, pausing for a word here and there.

At length Henry completed his circuit and came to de Puebla's table. 'Ambassador,' he greeted him.

De Puebla bowed low. 'I thank you for your gift of the dish of venison,' he said. 'It was delicious.'

The king nodded. 'I would have a word with you.'

'Of course.'

'Privately.'

The two men strolled to a quieter corner of the hall while the musicians in the gallery struck a note and began to play.

'I have a proposal to resolve the issue of the Dowager Princess,' Henry said as drily as possible.

'Indeed?'

'I suggest that we forget the issue of the dowry,' Henry started. 'Her goods will be absorbed into my household. I shall pay her an appropriate allowance, as I did for the late Queen Elizabeth—God bless her. I shall marry the Infanta myself.'

De Puebla was almost too shocked to speak. 'You?'

'I. Is there any reason why not?'

The ambassador gulped, managed to say, 'No, no, at least . . . I suppose there could be an objection on the grounds of affinity.'

'I shall apply for a dispensation. I take it that you are certain that the marriage was not consummated?'

'Certain,' de Puebla gasped.

'You assured me of that on her word?'

'The duenna said . . .'

'Then it is nothing,' the king ruled. 'They were little more than promised to one another. Hardly man and wife.'

De Puebla could hardly speak for shock at the suggestion that this man, who had just buried his wife, should marry his dead son's bride. 'Of course. So, shall I tell Their Majesties that you are quite determined on this course? There is no other arrangement that we should consider? Your son, for instance?'

'My son is too young to be considered for marriage as yet,' Henry disposed of the suggestion with speed. 'He is eleven and his grandmother insists that we plan nothing for him for another four years. And by then, the Princess Dowager would be twenty-one.'

'Still young,' gasped de Puebla.

'I don't think Their Majesties would want their daughter to stay in England for another four years without husband or household of her own,' Henry said with unconcealed threat.

'If she could return to Spain to wait?' de Puebla hazarded.

'She can leave at once, if she will pay the full amount of her dowry, and find her own fortune elsewhere. Do you really think she can get a better offer than Queen of England? Take her away if you do!'

De Puebla knew he was beaten. 'I will write to Their Majesties tonight,' he said.

'The king is here again,' Doña Elvira said to Catalina, looking out of the window. 'He has ridden here with just two men. Not even a standard-bearer or guards.'

Catalina flew to the window and peered out. 'What can he want?' she wondered. 'Tell them to decant some of his wine.'

Doña Elvira went out of the room in a hurry. In the next moment Henry strolled in, unannounced. 'I thought I would call on you.'

Catalina sank into a deep curtsy. 'Your Grace does me much honour,' she said. 'And at least now I can offer you a glass of good wine.'

The two of them stood while Doña Elvira returned to the room with a Spanish maid-in-waiting carrying a tray of Morisco brassware with two Venetian glasses of red wine. Henry noted the fineness of the workmanship and assumed correctly that it was part of the dowry that the Spanish had withheld.

'Your health,' he said, holding up his glass to the princess.

To his surprise she did not simply raise her glass in return, she raised her eyes and gave him a long, thoughtful look. He felt himself tingle, like a boy, as his eyes met hers. 'Princess?' he said quietly.

'Your Grace?'

They both of them glanced towards Doña Elvira.

'You can leave us now,' the king said. 'I shall talk in private with my daughter-in-law.'

Doña Elvira curtsied and left.

Catalina smiled at the king. 'As you command,' she said.

He felt his pulse speed at her smile. 'Indeed, I do need to speak to you privately. I have a proposal to put to you. I have spoken to the Spanish ambassador and he has written to your parents.'

At last. This is it, Catalina thought. He has come to propose Harry for me. Thank God, who has brought me to this day. Arthur, beloved, this day you will see that I shall be faithful to my promise to you.

'I need to marry again,' Henry said. 'I am still young'—he thought he would not say his age of forty-six—'and it may be that I can have another child or two.'

Catalina nodded politely; but she was barely listening. She was waiting for him to ask her to marry Prince Harry.

'I have been thinking of all the princesses in Europe who would be suitable partners for me,' he said.

Still the princess before him said nothing.

Henry ploughed on. 'My choice has fallen on you,' he said bluntly, 'for these reasons. You are here in London already, you have become accustomed to living here. You were brought up to be Queen of England. The difficulties with the dowry can be put aside. You will have the same allowance that I paid to Queen Elizabeth. My mother agrees with this.'

At last his words penetrated her mind. She was so shocked that she could barely speak. She just stared at him. 'Me?'

'There is a slight objection on the grounds of affinity but I shall ask the Pope to grant a dispensation,' he went on. 'I understand that your marriage to Prince Arthur was never consummated. In that case, there is no real objection.'

'It was not consummated.' Catalina repeated the words by rote, as if she no longer understood them. The great lie had been part of a plot to take her to the altar with Prince Harry, not with his father.

'Then there should be no difficulty,' the king said. 'I take it that you do not object?'

He found that he could hardly breathe, waiting for her answer. Any thought that she had been leading him on, tempting him to this moment, had vanished when he looked into her shocked face.

He took her hand. 'Don't look so afraid,' he said, his voice low with tenderness. 'I won't hurt you. This is to resolve all your problems. I will be a good husband to you. I will care for you.'

She knew she had to reply. 'I am so surprised,' she said.

'Surely you must have known that I desired you?'

Catalina gave a little nod. She had known something—fool that she was—she had known something was happening; and praised her own diplomatic skills for being so clever as to lead the King of England by the nose.

'I desired you from the moment I first saw you,' he told her, his voice very low.

She looked up. 'You did?'

'Truly. When I came into your bedchamber at Dogmersfield.'

She remembered an old man, travel-stained, the father of the man she would marry. She remembered the sweaty male scent as he forced his way into her bedroom, she remembered thinking: what a clown, what a rough soldier to push in where he is not wanted. And then Arthur arrived, his blond hair tousled, and with the brightness of his shy smile.

'Oh yes,' she said. From somewhere deep inside her own resolution, she found a smile. 'I remember. I danced for you.'

Henry drew her a little closer and slid his arm round her waist. 'I watched you,' he said. 'I longed for you.'

'But you were married,' she said primly, forcing herself not to pull away.

'And now I am widowed and so are you,' he said. He felt the stiffness of her body through the hard boning of the stomacher and let her go. He would have to court her slowly, he thought. She might have flirted with him, but now she was startled by the turn that things had taken. He would have to give her time.

'I will leave you now,' he said. 'I will come again tomorrow.'

She nodded, and walked with him to the door of her privy chamber. There she hesitated. 'You mean it?' she asked him, her blue eyes suddenly anxious. 'You mean this as a proposal of marriage, not as a feint in a negotiation? You truly want to marry me? I will be queen?'

He nodded. 'I mean it.' The depth of her ambition began to dawn on him and he smiled as he slowly saw the way to her. 'Do you want to be queen so very much?'

Catalina nodded. 'I was brought up to it,' she said. 'I want nothing more. I was born to be a queen.'

He took her hand and bent over it. 'I shall make you Katherine of Aragon, Queen of England,' he promised her, and saw her blue eyes darken with desire at the title. 'We can marry as soon as we have the dispensation from the Pope.'

Doña Elvira waited until the princess's bedtime and until all the maids-in-waiting, the ladies and the grooms of the bedchamber had withdrawn. She closed the door on them all and then turned to the princess, who was seated in her bed, her pillows plumped behind her.

'What did the king want?' she demanded without ceremony.

'He proposed marriage to me,' Catalina replied bluntly. 'For himself.'

For a moment the duenna was too stunned to speak then she crossed herself, as a woman seeing something unclean. 'God save us,' was all she said. Then: 'God forgive him for even thinking it.'

'God forgive you,' Catalina replied smartly. 'I am considering it.'

'He is your father-in-law, and old enough to be your father.'

'His age doesn't matter,' Catalina said truly. 'If I go back to Spain they won't seek a young husband for me but an advantageous one.'

'But he is the father of your husband.'

Catalina nipped her lips together. 'My late husband,' she said bleakly. 'And the marriage was not consummated.'

Doña Elvira swallowed the lie; but her eyes flicked away, just once. 'Even so! Princess, you cannot want this?'

The princess's little face was bleak. 'He will not betroth me to Prince Harry,' she said. 'He says the boy is too young. So what can I do but marry the king? I was born to be Queen of England and mother of the next King of England. I have to fulfil my God-given destiny. I thought I would have to force myself to take Prince Harry. Now it seems I shall have to force myself to take the king. Perhaps this is God testing me. But my will is strong. I will be Queen of England, and the mother of the king.'

'I don't know what your mother will think,' the duenna said. 'I should not have left you alone with him, if I had known.'

Catalina nodded. 'Don't leave us alone again.' She paused. 'Unless I nod to you,' she said.

The duenna was shocked. 'He should not even see you before your wedding day. I shall tell the ambassador that he must tell the king that he cannot visit you at all now.'

Catalina shook her head. 'We are not in Spain now,' she said fiercely. 'D'you still not see it? We cannot leave this to the ambassador, not even my mother can say what shall happen. I shall have to make this happen. I alone have brought it so far, and I alone will make it happen.'

Catalina waited for the king to visit her as he had promised. He did not come the next day but Catalina was sure he would come the day after. When three days had elapsed she walked on her own by the river, chafing her hands in the shelter of her cloak. She had been so sure that he would come again that she had prepared herself to keep him interested, but under her control. She planned to lead him on, to keep him dancing at arm's length. When he did not come she realised that she was anxious to see him. Not for desire—she thought she would never feel desire again—but because he was her only way to the throne of England. When he did not come, she was afraid that he had had second thoughts, and would not come at all. Finally, she sent the king a message, hoping that he was well.

Henry, seeing her ambition as the key to her, had given the girl a few days to consider her position. He thought she might compare the life she led at Durham House, in seclusion with her little Spanish court, with the life she might lead as a young queen at the head of one of the richest courts in Europe. He thought she had the sense to think that through on her own. When he received a note from her, enquiring as to his health, he knew that he had been right; and the next day he rode down the Strand to visit her.

Her porter who kept the gate said that the princess was in the garden, walking with her ladies by the river. Henry went through the back door of the palace to the terrace, and down the steps through the garden. He saw her by the river, walking alone, ahead of her ladies, her head slightly bowed in thought, and he felt an old, familiar sensation in his belly at the sight of a woman he desired. It made him feel young again, that deep pang of lust.

His page, running ahead, announced him and he saw her head jerk up at his name and she looked across the lawn and saw him. He smiled, he was waiting for that moment of recognition between a woman and a man who loves her—the moment when their eyes meet and they both know that intense moment of joy.

Instead, like a dull blow, he saw at once that there was no leap of her heart at the sight of him. In the first moment of surprise, she was nothing more than startled. She looked up, she saw him—and he could tell at once that she did not love him. There was no shock of delight. Instead, chillingly, he saw a swift expression of calculation cross her face. This would be a marriage of convenience to her, whatever it was to him. And more than that, he knew that she had made up her mind to accept him.

He walked towards her and took her hand. 'Good day, Princess.'

Catalina curtsied. 'Your Grace.'

She turned her head to her ladies. 'You can go inside.' To Doña Elvira she said, 'See that there are refreshments for His Grace when we come in.' Then she turned back to him. 'Will you walk, sire?'

'You will make a very elegant Queen of England,' he said with a smile. 'You command very smoothly.'

'I still have many English ways to learn.'

'My mother will teach you,' he said easily. 'You will live at court in her rooms and under her supervision.'

Catalina checked a little in her stride. 'Surely I will have my own rooms, the queen's rooms?'

'My mother is occupying the queen's rooms,' he said. 'She moved in after the death of the late queen, God bless her. She thinks that you are too young as yet to have your own rooms and a separate court. You can live in my mother's rooms with her ladies and she can teach you how things are done.'

He could see that she was troubled, but trying hard not to show it.

'When do you think we will hear from the Pope?' she asked.

'I have sent an emissary to Rome to enquire,' Henry said. 'We shall have to apply jointly, your parents and myself. But it should be resolved very quickly. If we are all agreed, there can be no real objection.'

'Yes,' she said.

'And we are completely agreed on marriage?' he confirmed.

'Yes,' she said again.

He took her hand and tucked it into his arm. Catalina walked a little closer and let her head brush against his shoulder. She was not wearing a headdress, only the hood of her cape covered her hair, and the movement pushed it back. He could smell the essence of roses on her hair, he could feel the warmth of her head against his shoulder.

'Catalina,' he said, his voice very low and thick.

She stole a glance and saw desire in his face, and she did not step away. 'Yes, Your Grace?' she whispered.

He could not resist the invitation, he bent and kissed her on the lips. There was no shrinking, she took his kiss, her mouth yielded under his, he could taste her, his arms came around her, he pressed her towards him, he could feel his desire for her rising in him so strongly that he had to let her go, that minute, or disgrace himself. He could say nothing, for he knew his voice would tremble. Silently, he offered her his arm once more, and silently she took it.

'Our children will be your heirs?' she confirmed, her voice steady, following a train of thought very far from his own whirl of sensations.

He cleared his throat. 'Yes, yes, of course.'

'That is the English tradition?'

'Yes.'

'They will come before your other children?'

'Our son will inherit before the Princesses Margaret and Mary,' he said. 'But our daughters would come after them.'

She frowned a little. 'How so? Why would they not come before?'

'It is first on sex, and then on age,' he said. 'The first-born boy inherits, then other boys, then girls according to age. Please God there is always a prince to inherit. England has no tradition of ruling queens.'

'A ruling queen can command as well as a king,' said the daughter of Isabella of Castile.

'Not in England,' said Henry Tudor.

She left it at that. 'But our oldest son would be king when you died,' she pursued.

'No. The king after me will be Prince Harry, the Prince of Wales.'

She frowned. 'But if we have a son? Can you not make Harry king of your French dominions, or Ireland, and make our son King of England?'

Henry laughed shortly. 'No. For that would be to destroy my kingdom, which I have had some trouble to win and to keep together. Harry will have it all by right.' He saw she was disturbed. 'Catalina, you will be Queen of England, one of the finest kingdoms of Europe, the place your mother and father chose for you. Your sons and daughters will be princes and princesses of England. What more could you want?'

'I want my son to be king,' she answered him frankly. 'I had thought to be Queen of England and see my son on the throne,' she repeated. 'I had thought to be a power in the court, like your mother is. I had thought that there are castles to build and a navy to plan and schools and colleges to found. I want to defend against the Scots on our northern borders and against the Moors on our coasts. I want to be a ruling queen in England, these are things I have planned and hoped for.'

He could not help himself, he laughed aloud at the thought of this girl, this child, presuming to make plans for the ruling of his kingdom. 'You will find that I am before you,' he said bluntly. 'This kingdom is run as I command. I did not fight my way to the crown to hand it over to a girl young enough to be my daughter. Your task will be to fill the royal nurseries and your world will start and stop there.'

'But your mother . . .'

'You will find my mother guards her domains as I guard mine,' he said. 'She will command you as a daughter and you will obey. Make no mistake about it, Catalina. You will come into my court and obey me, you will live in my mother's rooms and obey her. You will be Queen of England and have the crown on your head. But you will be my wife, and I will have an obedient wife as I have always done.'

The ambassador, summoned to Durham House, found Catalina waiting for him in her privy chamber with only Doña Elvira in attendance.

'I spoke with the king yesterday and he repeated his proposal of marriage,' Catalina said, a little pride in her voice.

'Indeed.'

'But he told me that I would live at court in the rooms of his mother.'

'Oh.' The ambassador nodded.

'And he said that my sons would inherit only after Prince Harry.'

The ambassador nodded again.

'Can we not persuade him to overlook Prince Harry? Can we not draw up a marriage contract to set him aside in favour of my son?'

'It's not possible. The king's oldest son is always the Prince of Wales.

He always inherits the throne. This king, of all the kings in the world, is not going to make a pretender of his own legitimate heir.'

As always, Catalina flinched at the thought of the last pretender, Edward of Warwick, beheaded to make way for her.

'If my son is not to be king, then what is the point of me marrying a king?' Catalina demanded.

'You would be queen,' the ambassador pointed out.

'What sort of a queen would I be with My Lady the King's Mother ruling everything? The king would not let me have my way in the kingdom, and she would not let me have my way in the court.'

'You are very young,' he started, trying to soothe her.

'I am old enough to know my own mind,' Catalina stated. 'And I want to be queen in truth as well as in name. But he will never let me be that, will he?'

'No,' de Puebla admitted. 'You will never command while he is alive.'

'And when he is dead?' she demanded, without shrinking.

'Then you would be the Dowager Queen,' de Puebla offered.

'And Harry's wife would be Princess of Wales, and Harry's wife would be the new queen. And her sons would be Kings of England.'

'That is true.'

'Then I have to be Prince Harry's wife,' she said. 'I have to be.'

De Puebla was quite horrified. 'I understood you had agreed with the king to marry him! He gave me to believe that you were agreed.'

'I had agreed to be queen,' she said, white-faced with determination. 'Not some cat's-paw. We will break this promise and make another. I shall not marry the king, I shall marry another.'

'Who?' he asked numbly.

'Prince Harry, the Prince of Wales,' she said. 'So that when King Henry dies I shall be queen in deed as well as name.'

There was a short silence.

'Perhaps,' said de Puebla slowly. 'But who is going to tell the king?'

Ambassador Dr de Puebla found himself in the uncomfortable position of having to bring bad news to one of the most powerful and irascible kings in Christendom. He had firm letters of refusal from Their Majesties of Spain in his hand, and he had Catalina's determination to be Princess of Wales.

The king had chosen to see him in the stable yard of Whitehall Palace, where he was looking at a consignment of new Barbary horses, brought in to improve English stock.

'Your Grace,' de Puebla said, bowing low.

'De Puebla,' the king said shortly.

'I have a reply from Their Majesties of Spain to your most flattering proposal. The truth is . . .' de Puebla prepared to lie. 'They want their daughter home, and they cannot contemplate her marriage to you. The queen is particularly vehement in her refusal.'

'Because?' the king enquired.

'Because she wants to see her daughter, her youngest, sweetest daughter, matched to a prince of her own age. It is a woman's whim—' The diplomat made a little diffident gesture. 'But we have to recognise a mother's wishes, don't we? Your Grace?'

'Not necessarily,' the king said unhelpfully. 'But what does the Dowager Princess say? I thought that we had an understanding.' The king's eyes were on the Arab stallion, walking proud-headed round the yard, his ears flickering backwards and forwards, his tail held high, his neck arched like a bow. 'I imagine she can speak for herself.'

'She says that she will obey you, as ever, Your Grace,' de Puebla said tactfully.

'And?'

'But she has to obey her mother.' He fell back at the sudden hard glance that the king threw at him. 'She is a good daughter, Your Grace. She is an obedient daughter to her mother.'

'I have proposed marriage to her and she has indicated that she would accept.'

'She would never refuse a king such as you. How could she? But if her parents do not consent, they will not apply for dispensation. Without dispensation from the Pope, there can be no marriage.' De Puebla attempted a sympathetic smile. 'If the Queen of Spain will not apply for dispensation there is nothing that can be done.'

'I am not one of Spain's neighbours to be overrun in a spring campaign,' the king said shortly. 'I am no Granada. I am no Navarre. I do not fear her displeasure.'

'Which is why they long for your alliance,' de Puebla said smoothly.

'An alliance how?' the king asked coldly. 'I thought they were refusing me?'

'Perhaps we could avoid all this difficulty by celebrating another marriage,' the diplomat said carefully, watching Henry's dark face. 'A new marriage. To create the alliance we all want.'

'To whom?'

At the banked-down anger in the king's face de Puebla lost his words. 'Sire . . . I . . .'

'Who do they want for her now? Now that my son, the rose, is dead and buried? Now she is a poor widow with only half her dowry paid, living on my charity?'

'The prince,' de Puebla plunged in. 'She was brought to the kingdom to be Princess of Wales. She was brought here to be wife to the prince, and later—much later, please God—to be queen. Perhaps that is her destiny, Your Grace.'

'And we old men have to stand back, do we? She has told you of no preference, no particular liking for me?'

The ambassador heard the bitterness in the old man's voice. 'She is allowed no choice,' he reminded the king. 'She has to do as she is bidden by her parents.'

King Henry shrugged his shoulders and turned from the schooling ring. 'So it is over?' he asked coldly. 'She does not desire me, as I thought she did. She meant to be nothing but filial?' He laughed harshly at the thought of her kiss by the river. 'I must forget my desire for her?'

'She has to obey her parents as a Princess of Spain,' de Puebla reminded him. 'On her own account, I know there was a preference. She told me so herself.' He thought that Catalina's double-dealing could be covered by this. 'She is disappointed, to tell you the truth. But her mother is determined to have her daughter returned to Spain, or married to Prince Harry. She will brook no other suggestion.'

'So be it,' said the king, his voice like ice. 'I had a foolish dream, a desire. It can finish here.'

He turned and walked away from the stable yard, his pleasure in his horses soured.

'And the betrothal with Prince Harry?' the ambassador asked. 'May I assure Their Catholic Majesties that it will go ahead?'

'Oh, at once. I shall make it my first and foremost office.'

'I do hope there is no offence?' de Puebla called to the king's retreating back.

The king turned on his heel and faced the Spanish ambassador, his clenched fists on his hips, his shoulders square. 'She has tried to play me like a fool,' he said through thin lips. 'I don't thank her for it. Her parents have tried to lead me by the nose. I won't forget this. You Spaniards, you will not forget it either. And she will regret the day she tried to lead me on as if I were a lovesick boy, as I regret it now.'

'It is agreed,' de Puebla said flatly to Catalina.

'I am to marry Prince Harry,' she said in a tone as dull as his own. 'Has he signed anything?'

'He has agreed. He has to wait for a dispensation. But he has agreed.'

She looked up at him. 'Was he very angry?'

'I think he was even angrier than he showed me. And what he showed me was bad.'

'What will he do?' she asked.

He scrutinised her pale face. She was white but she was not fearful. She did not look like a damsel in distress, she looked like a woman trying to outwit a most dangerous protagonist.

'I don't know what he will do,' he said. 'His nature is vengeful. But we must give him no advantage. Your father will have to pay the dowry and pay you an allowance. We must give them no excuse to withdraw. If your dowry is not paid he will not marry you to the prince. Infanta, I must warn you, he will revel in your discomfort. He will prolong it.'

Catalina nodded. 'He is my enemy then.'

'I fear it.'

'It will happen, you know,' she said inconsequentially.

'What?'

'I will marry Harry. I will be queen.'

'Infanta, it is my dearest wish.'

'Princess,' she replied.

'You are to be betrothed to Catalina of Aragon,' the king told his son, thinking of the son who had gone before.

The blond boy flushed as pink as a girl. 'Yes, sire.'

'Don't think the marriage will happen,' the king warned him.

The boy's eyes flashed up in surprise. 'No?'

'No. They have taken advantage of our friendship, and now we will take advantage of their weakness.'

'Surely we are all friends?'

Henry grimaced, thinking of that scoundrel Ferdinand, and of his daughter, the cool beauty who had turned him down. 'Oh, yes,' he said. 'Loyal friends.'

'So I am to be betrothed and, when I am fifteen, we will be married?'

The boy had understood nothing. So be it. 'Say sixteen.'

'Arthur was fifteen.'

Henry bit down the reply that much good it had done Arthur. Besides, it did not matter since it would never happen. 'Oh, yes,' he said again. 'Fifteen, then.'

The boy knew that something was wrong. His smooth forehead was furrowed. 'We do mean this, don't we, Father? I would not mislead such a princess. It is a most solemn oath I will make?'

'Oh, yes,' the king said again.

THE CONSTANT PRINCESS

*The night before my betrothal to Prince Harry, I have a dream so lovely that I
do not want to wake. I am in the garden of the Alhambra, walking with my
hand in Arthur's, laughing up at him, and showing him the beauty around us:
the great sandstone wall that encircles the fort, the city of Granada below us
and the mountains capped with silvery snow on the horizon.*

*'I have won,' I say to him. 'I have done everything you wanted, everything
that we planned. I will be princess as you made me. I will be queen as you
wanted me to be. My mother's wishes are fulfilled, my own destiny will be
complete, your desire and God's will. Are you happy now, my love?'*

*He smiles down at me, his eyes warm, his face tender, a smile he has only
for me. 'I shall watch over you,' he whispers. 'All the time. Here in al-Yanna.'*

It was a bright, hot June day. Catalina was dressed in a new gown of
blue with a blue hood, the young boy opposite her was radiant with
excitement, dressed in cloth of gold.

They were before the Bishop of Salisbury with a small court present:
the king, his mother, the Princess Mary and a few other witnesses.
Catalina put her cold hand in the prince's warm palm and felt the
plumpness of childhood beneath her fingers.

Catalina looked beyond the flushed boy to his father's grave face. The
king had aged in the months since the death of his wife, and the lines in
his face were more deeply grooved, his eyes shadowed.

Catalina smiled at him shyly, but there was no echoing warmth from
the man who would be her father-in-law for the second time, but had
wanted her for his own. Now, seeing his cold look, she had a moment of
fear that perhaps this ceremony—even something as serious and sacred
as a betrothal—might perhaps be nothing more than a revenge by this
most cunning of kings.

Chilled, she turned away from him to listen to the bishop recite the
words of the marriage service and she repeated her part, making sure
not to think of when she had said the words before, only a year and a
half ago, when her hand had been cool in the grasp of the most handsome young man she had ever seen.

The young prince, who had been dazzled then by the beauty of his
sister-in-law the bride, was now the bridegroom. His beam was the bois-
terous joy of a young boy in the presence of a beautiful older girl. She
had been the bride of his older brother, she was the young woman he
had been proud to escort on her wedding day. He had looked at her at
her wedding feast and that night prayed that he too might have a
Spanish bride just like her.

When she had left the court with Arthur he had dreamed of her, he

117

had written poems and love songs, secretly dedicating them to her. He had heard of Arthur's death with a fierce joy that now she was free.

Now, not even two years on, she was before him, her hair brushed out bronze and golden over her shoulders signifying her virgin state, her blue lace mantilla veiling her face. Her hand was in his, her blue eyes were on him, her smile was only for him.

Harry's braggart boyish heart swelled so full in his chest that he could scarcely reply to his part of the service. Arthur was gone, and he was Prince of Wales. Arthur was gone, and Arthur's bride was his wife. He stood straight and proud and repeated his oaths in his clear treble voice. Arthur was gone, and there was only one Prince of Wales and one Princess: Prince Harry and Princess Katherine.

PRINCESS AGAIN

1504

I MAY THINK that I have won; but I have not. Harry reaches twelve, and they declare him Prince of Wales but they do not come for me, declare our betrothal or invest me as princess. I send for the ambassador and I ask him why I have not been invested as Princess of Wales alongside Harry and he does not know. He suggests that they are waiting for the payment of my dowry and without it, nothing can go ahead.

My mother the queen must know that I am desolate; but she has nothing to say to me. I fear that she is ashamed of me, as I wait at court like a supplicant for the prince to honour his promise. In November I am so filled with foreboding that she is ill or sad that I write to her and beg her to reply to me, to send me at least one word. That, as it happens, was the very day that she died and so she never had my letter and I never had my one word. She leaves me in death as she left me in life: to silence and a sense of her absence.

I knew that I would miss her when I left home. But it was a comfort to me to know that the sun still shone in the gardens of the Alhambra, and she was still there beside the green-trimmed pool. I did not know that the loss of her would make my situation in England so much worse. My father, having long refused to pay the second half of my dowry as part of his game with the King of England, now finds his play has become the bitter truth—he cannot pay. He has spent his life and his fortune in ceaseless crusade against the Moors and *there is no money left for anyone. The rich revenues of Castile are now paid to Juana, my mother's heir; and my father has nothing in the treasury of Aragon for my marriage. If the gossips are to be believed, Juana has run as mad as a rabid dog, tormented by love and her husband into insanity. Our family fortunes are cascading down like a house of cards without my mother's steady hand and watchful eye. There is nothing left for my father but despair; and I fear it is the same for me.*

I am only nineteen. Is my life over?

1509

I waited. *Incredibly, I waited for a total of six years. I knew then that King Henry's rage against me was bitter, and effective, and long-lasting. No princess in the world had ever been made to wait so long, or treated so harshly, or left in such despair. I am not exaggerating this, as a troubadour might do to make a better story—as I might have told you, beloved, in the dark hours of the night. No, it was not like a story, it was like being a hostage with no chance of redemption, it was loneliness, and the slow realisation that I had failed.*

Without the dowry payment from Spain I could not force the English to honour the betrothal. With the king's enmity I could force them to do nothing. Harry was a child of thirteen, I hardly ever saw him. I was powerless, neglected by the court and falling into shameful poverty.

Then Harry was fourteen years of age and our betrothal was still not made marriage, and that marriage not celebrated. I waited a year, he reached fifteen years, and nobody came for me. So Harry reached his sixteenth and then his seventeenth birthday, and still nobody came for me. Those years turned. I grew older. I waited. I was constant. It was all I could be.

News, always slow to reach the bedraggled Spaniards on the fringe of the royal court, filtered through that Harry's sister the Princess Mary was to be married, gloriously, to Prince Charles, son of King Philip and Queen Juana, grandson to both the Emperor Maximilian and King Ferdinand. Amazingly, at this of all moments, King Ferdinand at last found the money for Catalina's dowry, and packed it off to London.

'My God, we are freed. There can be a double wedding. I can marry him,' Catalina said, heartfelt, to the Spanish emissary, Don Gutierre Gomez de Fuensalida, who had now replaced Dr de Puebla.

He was pale with worry, his yellow teeth nipping at his lips. 'Oh, Infanta, I hardly know how to tell you. Even with this alliance, even with the dowry money—dear God, I fear it comes too late.'

'How can it be? Princess Mary's betrothal only deepens the alliance with my family.'

'What if . . .' He broke off. He could hardly speak of the danger that he foresaw. 'Princess, all the English know that the dowry money is coming, but they do not speak of your marriage. Oh, Princess, what if they betroth Prince Harry to Princess Eleanor, the sister of Charles?'

'They cannot, he is betrothed to me.'

'They may plan it as part of a great treaty. Your nephew Charles to marry Princess Mary, and your niece Eleanor for Prince Harry.'

'But what about me? Now that my dowry money is on its way at last?'

He was silent. It was painfully apparent that Catalina was excluded by these alliances, and no provision made for her.

'A true prince has to honour his promise,' she said passionately. 'We were betrothed by a bishop before witnesses, it is a solemn oath.'

The ambassador shrugged, hesitated. He could hardly make himself tell her the worst news of all. 'Your Grace, Princess, be brave. I am afraid he may withdraw his oath.'

'He cannot.'

'Indeed, I am afraid it is already withdrawn. He may have withdrawn it years ago.'

'What?' she asked sharply. 'How? How can such a thing be done?'

'An oath sworn before a bishop that he was not acting of his own free will would be enough to secure his release from his promise.'

'So all these years that I have been betrothed to him, and all these years that I have waited and waited and endured . . .' She could not finish. 'Are you telling me that for all these years, when I believed that we had them tied down, contracted, bound, he has been free?'

The ambassador nodded; her face was so stark and shocked that he could hardly find his voice.

'This is . . . a betrayal,' she said. 'A most terrible betrayal.'

He nodded again.

There was a long, painful silence. 'I am lost,' she said simply, her blue eyes horrified. 'I made a promise,' she continued, her voice harsh. 'I made a solemn and binding promise.'

'Your betrothal?'

She made a little gesture with her hand. 'Not that. I swore a promise. A deathbed promise. Now you tell me it has all been for nothing.'

He could say nothing, her pain was too raw for any soothing words.

After a few moments, she raised her head. 'My father will defend me from this . . . cruelty!' she burst out. 'They should have thought of that before they treated me so. There will be no treaties for England with Spain when he hears about this. He will take revenge for this abuse of me.'

He could say nothing, and in the still silent face that he turned to her she saw the worst truth.

'Oh. Oh. I see. Of course. He knows, of course he knows, doesn't he? My father? The dowry money is just another trick. He knows of the proposal to marry Prince Harry to Princess Eleanor. And so he knows that the prince has broken his oath to me? And is free to marry? I have failed him and he has cast me aside. I am indeed alone.'

'So shall I try to get us home now?' Fuensalida asked quietly. Truly, he thought, it had become the very pinnacle of his ambitions. If he could get this doomed princess home to her unhappy father and her increasingly deranged sister Juana, the newly widowed Queen of Castile, he would have done the best he could in a desperate situation. Nobody would marry Catalina of Spain now she was the daughter of a divided kingdom. Everyone could see that madness was coming out in her sister, who was on a crazed progress across Spain with her dead husband's coffin. Ferdinand's tricky diplomacy had rebounded on him and now everyone in Europe was his enemy. The best that this unlucky princess could expect was a scratch marriage to some Spanish grandee and retirement to the countryside. The worst was to remain trapped and in poverty in England, a forgotten hostage that no one would ransom.

'What shall I do?' Finally she accepted danger. He saw her take it in. He saw her, a queen in every inch, learn the depth of her defeat.

'We shall leave,' he said decisively. 'It is over for you and England. You have held on and faced humiliation and poverty, you have faced it like a princess, like a queen, like a saint. Your mother herself could not have shown more courage. But we are defeated, Infanta. You have lost. We have to get home as best we can. We have to run, before they catch us.'

'Catch us?'

'They could imprison us both as enemy spies and hold us to ransom,' he told her. 'They could impound whatever remains of your dowry goods and impound the rest when it arrives. God knows, they can make up a charge, and execute you, if they want to enough. We have to go.'

I know I have to leave England; Arthur would not want me to stay to face danger. I have a terror of the Tower and the block that would be fitting only if I were a traitor, and not a princess who has never done anything wrong but tell one great lie, and that for the best. It would be the jest of all time if I had to put my head down on Warwick's block and die, a Spanish pretender to the throne where he died a Plantagenet.

That must not happen. And I think the time to run away is now.

'You have done what?' Catalina demanded of her ambassador. The inventory in her hand trembled.

'I took it upon my own authority to move your father's treasure from the country. I could not risk . . .'

'My dowry.' She raised her voice.

'Your Grace, we both know it will not be needed for a wedding. He will never marry you.'

'It was my side of the bargain!' she shouted. 'I keep faith! Even if no one else does! I make a promise and I keep to it, whatever the cost!'

'The king would have used it to pay for soldiers to fight against your father. He would have fought against Spain with your father's own gold!' Fuensalida exclaimed miserably. 'I could not let it happen.'

'So you robbed me!'

He stumbled over the words. 'I took your treasure into safekeeping in the hopes that . . .'

'Go!' she said abruptly.

'Princess?'

'You have betrayed me, just as everyone always betrays me,' she said bitterly. 'You may leave me. I shall not send for you again. Ever. But I shall tell my father what you have done. I shall write to him at once and tell him that you have stolen my dowry monies, that you are a thief. You will never be received at the court in Spain.'

He bowed, trembling with emotion, and then he turned to leave, too proud to defend himself.

'You are nothing more than a traitor!' Catalina cried as he reached the door. 'And if I were a queen with the power of the queen I would have you hanged for treason.'

He stiffened. He turned, he bowed again, his voice when he spoke was ice.

'Infanta, you are badly mistaken. It was your own father who commanded me to return your dowry. I was obeying his direct order. It is he who wanted the dowry money returned because he has given up all hope of your marriage. He wanted the money kept safe and smuggled safely out of England.

'But I must tell you,' he added with weighty malice, 'he did not order me to make sure that you were safe. He gave no orders to smuggle you safely out of England. He thought of the treasure but not of you.'

As soon as the words were out of his mouth he wished he had not said them. The stricken look on her face was worse than anything he had ever seen before.

'He told you to send back the gold but to leave me behind?'

'I am sure . . .'

Blindly, she turned her back to him and walked to the window so that he could not see the horror on her face. 'Go,' she repeated. 'Just go.'

I am the sleeping princess in the story, a snow princess left in a cold land and forgetting the feel of the sun. This winter has been a long one, even for England. Even now, in April, when I walk outside on the icy grass, it crunches thickly under my feet and I can feel its chill through the thin soles of my boots. This summer, I know, will have all the mild sweetness of an English summer; but I long for the burning heat of Spain. I feel as if I have been cold for seven years, and if nothing comes to warm me soon I shall simply die of it. If the king is indeed dying, as the court rumour says, and Prince Harry comes to the throne and marries Eleanor, then I shall ask my father for permission to take the veil and retire to a convent. It could not be worse than here. It could not be poorer, colder or more lonely. My father has forgotten his love for me and given me up, just as if I had died with Arthur. Indeed, now, I acknowledge that every day I wish that I had died with Arthur.

I try to pray to God but I cannot hear Him. I fear He has forgotten me as everyone else has done. I no longer think I am His special child, chosen to be blessed. I think He has turned His face from me. I don't know why, but if my earthly father can forget me, and forget that I was his favourite child, as he has done, then I suppose my Heavenly Father can forget me too.

Each day, when I go to pray I look up at the crucified Christ and say: 'Your will be done'. That is each day for seven years, that is two thousand, five hundred and fifty-six times. This is the arithmetic of my pain. I say: 'Your will be done'; but what I mean is: 'make Your will on these wicked English councillors and this spiteful, unforgiving English king, and his old witch of a mother. Give me my rights. Make me queen. I must be queen, I must have a son, or I will become a princess of snow.'

21st April 1509

'The king is dead,' Fuensalida the ambassador wrote briefly to Catalina, knowing that she would not receive him in person, knowing that she would never forgive him for stealing her dowry and telling her that her father had abandoned her. 'I know you will not see me but I have to do my duty and warn you that on his deathbed the king told his son that he was free to marry whoever he chooses.'

Catalina scrunched the letter into her hand. She never trusted anyone with anything now. 'I am going for a walk,' she said.

Maria de Salinas stood up and put Catalina's patched cloak about her shoulders. It was the same cloak that she had worn in the winter cold when she and Arthur had left London for Ludlow, more than seven years earlier.

'Shall we come with you?' Maria de Salinas offered, without enthusiasm, glancing at the grey sky beyond the windows.

'No.'

As I pound alongside the river, I wonder if there is any chance that my luck might change, might be changing now. The king who wanted me, and then hated me for refusing him, is dead. Now he has gone. It will be the prince who decides.

I know the boy, Harry. I swear I know him. I have watched him and judged him. I know his strengths and his weaknesses, and I think I have faint, very faint, reason for hope.

Harry is vain, it is the sin of a young boy and I do not blame him for it, but he has it in abundance. On the one hand this might make him marry me, for he will want to be seen to be doing the right thing—honouring his promise, even rescuing me. But equally, his vanity could work against me. If they emphasise the wealth of Princess Eleanor, the influence of her Hapsburg family, the glory of the connection to the Holy Roman Emperor—he may be seduced.

But even if he wants to marry her, it still leaves him with the difficulty of what to do with me. He would look bad if he sent me home; surely he cannot have the gall to marry another woman with me still in attendance at court? I know that Harry would do anything rather than look foolish. If I can find a way to stay here until they have to consider his marriage, then I will be in a strong position indeed. I have to stay.

Fuensalida, summoned to the king's council, went in with his head held high, trying to seem unbowed, certain that they had sent for him to tell him to leave and take the unwanted Infanta with him. The new king's ministers were seated round the table; there was a place left empty for him in the centre.

'Perhaps I should start by explaining the condition of the Princess of Wales,' Fuensalida said diffidently. 'The dowry payment is safely stored, out of the country, and can be paid in . . .'

'The dowry does not matter,' one of the councillors said. 'The king is minded to be generous to his betrothed.'

There was a stunned silence from the ambassador. 'His betrothed?'

'Of the greatest importance now is the power of the King of France and the danger of his ambitions in Europe. The king is most anxious to restore the glory of England. English safety depends on a three-way alliance between Spain and England, and the emperor. The young king believes that his wedding with the Infanta will secure the support of the King of Aragon to this great cause. This is, presumably, the case?'

'Certainly,' said Fuensalida, his head reeling. 'But the plate . . .'

'The plate does not matter,' one of the councillors repeated.

'I shall have to tell her of this . . . change . . . in her fortunes.'

The Privy Council rose to their feet. 'Pray do.'

'I shall return when I have . . . er . . . seen her.' Pointless, Fuensalida thought, to tell them that he could not be sure that she would see him. Pointless to reveal that the last time he had seen her he had told her that her cause was lost and everyone had known it for years.

He staggered as much as walked from the room, and almost collided with the young prince. The youth, still not yet eighteen, was radiant.

'Ambassador!'

Fuensalida dropped to his knee. 'Your Grace! I must . . . condole with you on the death of . . .'

'Yes, yes.' He waved aside the sympathy. He could not make himself look grave. He was wreathed in smiles. 'You will wish to tell the princess that I propose that our marriage takes place as soon as possible.'

Fuensalida found he was stammering. 'Of course, sire.'

'I shall send a message to her for you,' the young man said generously. He giggled. 'I know that you are out of favour. I know that she has refused to see you, but I am sure that she will see you for my sake.'

'I thank you,' the ambassador said.

Catalina kept her ambassador waiting, but she admitted him within the hour. He had to admire the self-control that set her to watch the clock when the man who knew her destiny was waiting outside to tell her.

'Emissary,' she said levelly.

He bowed. 'Dowager Princess, I have been to the Privy Council. Our troubles are over. He wants to marry you.'

Fuensalida had thought she might cry with joy, or pitch into his arms, or fall to her knees and thank God. She did none of these things. Slowly, she inclined her head. The tarnished gold leaf on the hood caught the light. 'I am glad to hear it,' was all she said.

'They say that there is no issue about the plate.' He could not keep the jubilation from his voice.

She nodded again.

'The dowry will have to be paid. I shall get them to send the money back from Bruges. It has been in safekeeping, Your Grace. I have kept it safe for you.' His voice quavered, he could not help it.

Again she nodded.

He dropped to one knee.

'Princess, rejoice! You will be Queen of England.'

Her blue eyes when she turned them to him were hard, like sapphires. 'Emissary, I was always going to be Queen of England.'

I have done it. Good God, I have done it. After seven endless years of waiting, after hardship and humiliation, I have done it. I go into my bedchamber and kneel before my prie-dieu and close my eyes. But I speak to Arthur, not to the risen Lord.

'I have done it,' I tell him. 'Harry will marry me, I have done as you wished me to do.'

For a moment I can see his smile. Before me again is the brightness of his face, his eyes, the clear line of his profile. And more than anything else, the scent of him, the very perfume of my desire.

Even on my knees before a crucifix I give a little sigh of longing. 'Arthur, beloved. My only love. I shall marry your brother but I am always yours.'

GREENWICH PALACE

11th June 1509

I WAS DREADING the wedding, the moment when I would have to say the words of the marriage vows that I had said to Arthur. But in the end the service was so unlike that glorious day in St Paul's Cathedral that I could go through it with Harry before me, and Arthur locked away in the very back of my mind.

There was no great congregation in a cathedral, there were no watching ambassadors, or fountains flowing with wine. We were married within the walls of Greenwich Palace in the church of the Friars Observant, with only three witnesses and half a dozen people present.

There was no rich feasting or music or dancing, there was no drunkenness at court or rowdiness. There was no public bedding. I had been afraid of that—the ritual of putting to bed and then the public showing of the sheets in the morning; but the prince—the king, I now have to say—is as shy as me, and we dine quietly before the court and withdraw together. They drink our healths and let us go. His grandmother is there, her face like a mask, her eyes cold. There is no suggestion that I shall be living in her chambers under her supervision. On the contrary, she has moved out of her rooms for me. I am married to Harry. I am Queen of England and she is nothing more than the grandmother of a king.

My ladies undress me in silence, this is their triumph too, this is their escape from poverty as well as mine.

They leave me in one of my dozen exquisite new nightgowns and withdraw in silence. I wait for Harry, as long ago I used to wait for Arthur. The only difference is the utter absence of joy.

The men-at-arms and the gentleman of the bedchamber brought the young king to the queen's door, tapped on it and admitted him to her rooms. She was in her gown, seated by the fireside, a richly embroidered shawl thrown over her shoulders. The room was warm, welcoming. She rose as he came in and swept him a curtsy.

She saw that he was flush with embarrassment. 'Will you take a cup of wedding ale?' she invited him. She made sure that she did not think of Arthur bringing her a cup for courage.

'I will,' he said. His voice, still so young, was unsteady in its register. She turned away to pour the ale so he should not see her smile.

They lifted their cups to each other. 'I hope you did not find today too quiet for your taste,' he said uncertainly. 'I thought with my father newly dead we should not have too merry a wedding.'

She nodded but said nothing.

'I hope you are not disappointed,' he pressed on. 'Your first wedding was so very grand.'

Catalina smiled. 'I hardly remember it, it was so long ago.'

He looked pleased at her reply, she noted. 'It was, wasn't it? We were all little more than children.'

'Yes,' she said. 'Far too young to marry.'

He shifted in his seat. She knew that the enemies of Spain would have spoken against her. His own grandmother had advised against this wedding. This transparent young man was still anxious about his decision, however bold he might try to appear.

'Not that young; you were fifteen,' he reminded her.

'And Arthur was the same age,' she said, daring to name him. 'But he was never strong, I think. He could not be a husband to me.'

Harry was silent and she was afraid she had gone too far. But then she saw the glimpse of hope in his face.

'It is indeed true then, that the marriage was never consummated?' he asked, colouring up in embarrassment.

'Never,' she said calmly. 'He tried but he was not strong. He may even have bragged that he had done it, but it meant nothing.'

I shall do this for you,I say fiercely, in my mind, to my beloved. You wanted this lie. I shall do it thoroughly. If it is going to be done, it must be done with courage, conviction; and it must never be undone.

Aloud, Catalina said, 'We married in the November, you remember. December we spent most of the time travelling to Ludlow and were apart on the journey. He was not well after Christmas, and then he died in April. I was very sad for him.'

'He was never your lover?' Harry asked, desperate to be certain.

'How could he be?' She gave a pretty, deprecatory shrug that made the shawl slip off one creamy shoulder a little. She saw his eyes drawn to the exposed skin, she saw him swallow. 'He was like a stranger to me for all our marriage. We lived like children in a royal nursery. We were hardly even companions.'

He sighed as if he were free of a burden, the face he turned to her was bright. 'You know, I could not help but be afraid,' he said. 'My grandmother said . . .'

'Oh! Old women always gossip,' she said, smiling. She ignored his widened eyes at her casual disrespect. 'Thank God we are young and need pay no attention. You are king and I am queen and we shall make up our own minds. We hardly need her advice. Why—it is her advice that has kept us apart when we could have been together.'

It had not struck him before. 'Indeed,' he said, his face hardening. 'We have both been deprived. And all the time she hinted that you were Arthur's wife, wedded and bedded, and I should look elsewhere.'

'I am a virgin, as I was when I came to England,' she asserted boldly.

'You are kind to tell me,' he said. 'It is better to have these things in the light, so no one is uncertain. It would be terrible to sin.'

'We are young,' she said. 'We can be honest and straightforward together. We need not fear rumours and slanders. We need have no fear of sin.'

'It will be my first time too,' he admitted shyly. 'I hope you don't think the less of me?'

'Of course not,' she said sweetly.

Harry rose to his feet and held out his hand. 'So, we shall have to learn together,' he said.

Easily she moved into his arms, and felt his body stiffen at her touch. 'I have wanted you since I first saw you,' he said breathlessly. He stroked her hair, her neck, her naked shoulder, with a hurried touch, wanting all of her, at once. 'I dreamed that it was me that married you that day.' He was flushed, breathless.

Slowly, she untied the ribbons at the throat of her nightgown, letting the silky linen fall apart so that he could see her throat, her round, firm breasts, her waist, the dark shadow between her legs. Harry gave a little groan of desire at the sight of her.

He dropped his face into the warmth of her neck, she could feel his breath coming fast and urgent in her hair, his body was pushing against hers, Catalina felt herself respond. She remembered Arthur's touch and gently bit the tip of her tongue to remind herself never, never to say Arthur's name out loud. She let Harry push against her, force himself against her and then he was inside her. She gave a little rehearsed cry of pain but she knew at once that it was not enough. She had not cried out enough, her body had not resisted him enough. She had been too warm, too welcoming. It had been too easy. He did not know much, this callow boy; but he knew that it was not difficult enough.

He checked, even in the midst of his desire. He knew that something was not as it should be. He looked down at her.

'You *are* a virgin,' he said uncertainly. 'I hope that I do not hurt too much.'

But he knew that she was not. Deep down, he knew that she was no virgin. Somewhere in his mind, he knew that she was lying.

She looked up at him. 'I was a virgin until this moment,' she said, managing the smallest of smiles. 'But your potency has overcome me. You are my husband, you have taken your own.' She saw him forget his doubt in his rising desire. 'You have done what Arthur could not do,' she whispered.

They were the very words to trigger his desire. The young man gave a groan of pleasure and fell down onto her, his seed pumping into her, the deed undeniably done.

He doesn't question me again. He wants so much to believe me that he does not ask the question, fearing that he might get an answer he doesn't like. He is cowardly in this.

Partly, it is his desire to have me, partly it is to disprove everyone who warned him against the trap that I had set for him. But more than anything else: he envied my beloved Arthur and he wants me just because I was Arthur's bride, and—God forgive him for an envious, second son—he wants me to tell him that he can do something that Arthur could not do. Even though my beloved husband is cold under the nave of Worcester Cathedral, the child that wears his crown still wants to triumph over him. The greatest lie is not in telling Harry that I am a virgin. The greatest lie is in telling him that he is a better man, more of a man than his brother. And I did that too.

In the dawn, while he is still sleeping, I take my penknife and cut the sole of my foot, where he will not notice a scar, and drip blood on the sheet where we had lain, enough to pass muster for an inspection by My Lady the King's Grandmother. There is to be no showing of the sheets for a king and his bride; but I know that everyone will ask, and it is best that my ladies can say that they have all seen the smear of blood, and that I am complaining of the pain.

In the morning, I do everything that a bride should do. I say I am tired, and I rest for the morning. I smile with my eyes looking downwards as if I have discovered some sweet secret. I walk a little stiffly and I refuse to ride out to hunt for a week. I do everything to indicate that I am a young woman who has lost her virginity.

Harry woke in the night and his quiet stillness woke Catalina.

'My lord?' she asked.

'Go to sleep,' he said. 'It's not yet dawn.'

She slipped from the bed and lit a taper in the red embers of the fire, then lit a candle. She let him see her, nightgown half-open, her smooth flanks only half-hidden by the fall of the gown. 'Would you like some ale? Or some wine?'

'A glass of wine,' he said. 'You have one too.'

She put the candle in the silver holder and came back to the bed beside him with the wineglasses in her hands. She could not read his face, but suppressed her pang of irritation. With Arthur she had known in a second what he wanted, what he was thinking. But anything could distract Harry. He had been raised to be accustomed to sharing his thoughts, accustomed to guidance. He liked constant conversation. Catalina had to be everyone to him.

'I have been thinking about war,' he said.

'Oh.'

'King Louis thinks he can avoid us, but we will force war on him. They tell me he wants peace, but I will not have it. I am the King of England, the victors of Agincourt. He will find me a force to be reckoned with.'

She nodded. Her father had been clear that Harry should be encouraged in his warlike ambitions against the King of France. He had written to her in the warmest of terms as his dearest daughter, and advised her that the English should reconquer the region of Aquitaine. Spain would be in strong support. It would be an easy and glorious campaign.

'In the morning I am going to order a new suit of armour,' Harry said. 'Not a suit for jousting, I want heavy armour, for the battlefield.'

She was about to say that he could hardly go to war when there was so much to do in the country. The moment that an English army left for France, the Scots, even with an English bride on their throne, were certain to take advantage and invade the north. The whole tax system was riddled with greed and injustice and must be reformed, there were new plans for schools, for a king's council, for forts and a navy of ships to defend the coast. These were Arthur's plans for England, they should come before Harry's desire for a war.

'I shall make my grandmother regent when I go to war,' Harry said. 'She knows what has to be done.'

Catalina hesitated, marshalling her thoughts. 'Yes, indeed,' she said. 'But the poor lady is so old now. She has done so much already. Perhaps it might be too much of a burden for her?'

He smiled. 'Not her! I don't think anything would be too much for her as long as it kept us Tudors in power.'

'Yes,' Catalina said. 'And how well she has ruled you! She never let you out of her sight for a moment. When you were a boy, she never let you joust, she never let you gamble, she never let you have any friends. She dedicated herself to your safety and your well-being. She could not have kept you closer if you had been a princess.' She laughed. 'I think she thought you were a princess and not a lusty boy. Surely it is time that she had a rest? And you had some freedom?'

His swift, sulky look told her that she would win this.

'Besides,' she smiled, 'if you give her any power in the country she will be certain to tell the council that you will have to come home, that war is too dangerous for you.'

'She could hardly stop me going to war,' he bristled. 'I am the king.'

Catalina raised her eyebrows. 'Whatever you wish, my love. But I imagine she will stop your funds, if the war starts to go badly. You could find yourself betrayed at home—betrayed by her love, I mean—while you are attacked abroad. You might find that the old people stop you doing what you want. Like they always try to do.'

He was aghast. 'She would never work against me.'

'Never on purpose,' Catalina agreed with him. 'It is just that she will always think that she knows your business best. To her, you will always be a little boy.'

She saw him flush with annoyance. 'I shall not be limited by an old woman,' he swore.

'Your time is now,' Catalina agreed.

'D'you know what I shall do?' he demanded. 'I shall make you regent when I go to war! You shall rule the country for me while I am gone. You shall command our forces at home. We shall rule together. And you will support me as I require. D'you think you could do that?'

She smiled at him. 'I know I can. I won't fail,' she said. 'I was born to rule England. I shall keep the country safe while you are away.'

'That's what I need,' Harry said. 'And your mother was a great commander, wasn't she? She supported her husband. I always heard that he led the troops but she raised the money and raised the army?'

'Yes,' she said, a little surprised at his interest. 'Yes, she was always there. Behind the lines, planning his campaigns, raising funds and raising troops, and sometimes she was in the very forefront of the battles. She had her own armour, she would ride out with the army.'

'Tell me about her,' he said, settling himself down in the pillows. 'Tell me about Spain. About what it was like in the Alhambra?'

It was too close to what had been before. It was as if a shadow had stretched over her heart.

'Oh, I hardly remember it at all,' she said, smiling at his eager face. 'There's nothing to tell.'

'Go on. Tell me a story about it.'

'No. I can't tell you anything. D'you know, I have been an English princess for so long, I could not tell you anything about it at all.'

In the morning Harry was filled with energy, excited at the thought of ordering his suit of armour, wanting a reason to declare war at once. He woke her with kisses and was on her, like an eager boy, while she was waking. She held him close, welcomed his quick, selfish pleasure, and smiled when he was up and out of bed in a moment, hammering at the door and shouting for his guards to take him to his rooms.

'We must go hunting,' he ruled. 'It is too good weather not to take the dogs out. You will come, won't you?'

'I'll come,' she promised him, smiling at his exuberance. 'And shall we have a picnic?'

'You are the best of wives!' he exclaimed. 'A picnic would be wonderful. Will you tell them to get some musicians and we can dance? And bring ladies, bring all your ladies, and we shall all dance.'

She caught him before he went out of the door. 'Harry, may I send for Lady Margaret Pole? Can I have her as a lady-in-waiting?'

He stepped back into the room, caught her into his arms and kissed her heartily. 'You shall have whoever you want to serve you. Send for her at once. And appoint Lady Elizabeth Boleyn too. She is returning to court after her confinement. She has had another girl.'

'What will she call her?' Catalina asked, diverted.

'Mary, I think. Or Anne. I can't remember. Now, about our dance . . .'

She beamed at him. 'I shall get a troupe of musicians and dancers and if I can order soft-voice zephyrs I will do that too.' She laughed at the happiness in his face.

I married him for Arthur, for my mother, for God, for our cause, and for myself. But in a very little while I have come to love him. It is impossible not to love such a sweet-hearted, energetic, good-natured boy as Harry, in these first days of his reign. He wakes happy every morning, filled with the confident expectation of a happy day. And, since he is king, and surrounded by courtiers and flatterers, he always has a happy day. When work troubles him or people come to him with disagreeable complaints he looks around for someone to take the bother of it away from him. In the first few weeks it was his grandmother who commanded; slowly, I make sure that it is to me that he hands the burdens of ruling the kingdom.

Men seeking advantage, advocates seeking help, petitioners seeking justice, all learn that the quickest way to a fair, prompt decision is to call first at the queen's rooms and then wait for my introduction.

I never have to ask anyone to handle him with tact. Everyone knows that a request should come to him as it were fresh, for the first time. Everyone takes a warning from the case of his grandmother who is finding herself put gently and implacably to one side, because she openly advises him, because she takes decisions without him, because once—foolishly—she scolded him. Harry is a king so careless that he will hand over the keys of his kingdom to anyone he trusts. The trick for me is to make sure that he trusts only me.

Together with the men of the Privy Council I am bringing the kingdom into one powerful, peaceful country. We are starting to consider how to make the law run from one coast to another. We are starting to work on the defences of the coast. We are making a survey of the ships that could be commanded into a fighting navy, we are creating muster rolls for an army. I have taken the reins of the kingdom into my hands and found that I know how it is done.

Statecraft is my family business. I sat at my mother's feet in the throne room of the Alhambra Palace. I listened to my father in the beautiful golden Ambassadors' Hall. I learned the art and the craft of kingship as I had learned about beauty, music and the art of building, all in the same place, all in the same lessons. Becoming a Queen Regnant is like coming home. I am happy as Queen of England. I am where I was born and raised to be.

The king's grandmother lay in her ornate bed, curtains drawn close so that she was lulled by shadows, the soft murmur of prayers around her.

Catalina knelt at the foot of the bed, her head bowed, a rosary in her hands, praying silently. My Lady Margaret, confident of a hard-won place in heaven, was sliding away from her place on earth.

Outside, in her presence chamber, Harry waited for them to tell him that his grandmother was dead. The last link to his subordinate, junior childhood would be broken with her death. When she was dead he could be a man, on his own terms. There would be no one left who knew him as a boy. Although he was waiting, outwardly pious, for news of her death, inside he was longing to hear that she was gone, that he was at last truly independent, at last a man and a king. He had no idea that he still desperately needed her counsel.

'He must not go to war,' the king's grandmother said hoarsely from the bed.

Catalina rose to her feet. 'What did you say, my lady?'

'He must not go to war,' she repeated. 'Our way is to keep out of the endless wars of Europe, to keep behind the seas, to keep safe.'

'No,' Catalina said steadily. 'Our way is to take the crusade into the heart of Christendom and beyond. Our way is to make England a leader in establishing the church throughout Europe, throughout the Holy Land, to Africa, to the Turks, to the Saracens, to the edge of the world.'

'The Scots . . .'

'I shall defeat the Scots,' Catalina said firmly. 'I am well aware of the danger.'

'I did not let him marry you for you to lead us to war.' The dark eyes flared with fading resentment.

'You did not let him marry me at all. You opposed it from the first moment,' Catalina said bluntly. 'And I married him precisely so that he should mount a great crusade.'

'You will promise me that you will not let him go to war,' the old lady breathed. 'My dying promise, my deathbed promise. I lay it on you from my deathbed, as a sacred duty.'

'No.' Catalina shook her head. 'Not me. Not another. I made one deathbed promise and it has cost me dearly. I will not make another. Least of all to you. You have lived your life and made your world as you wished. Now it is my turn. I shall see my son as King of England and perhaps King of Spain. I shall see my husband lead a glorious crusade against the Moors and the Turks. I shall see my country, England, take its place in the world, where it should be. I shall see England at the heart of Europe, a leader of Europe. And I shall be the one that defends it and keeps it safe. I shall be the one that is Queen of England, as you never were.'

The old woman raised herself up, struggled for breath. 'You pray for me.' She laid the order on the younger woman almost as if it were a curse. 'I have done my duty to England, to the Tudor line. You see that my name is remembered as if I were a queen.'

Catalina hesitated. If this woman had not served herself, her son and her country, the Tudors would not be on the throne. 'I will pray for you,' she conceded grudgingly. 'And as long as there is a chantry in England, as long as the Holy Roman Catholic Church is in England, your name will be remembered.'

'For ever,' the old woman said, happy in her belief that some things could never change.

'For ever,' Catalina agreed.

Then, less than an hour later, she was dead; and I became queen, undeniably in command, without a rival, even before my coronation. No one knows what to do in the court, there is no one who can give a coherent order. Harry has never ordered a royal funeral, how should he know where to begin?

I summon my oldest friend in England, the Duke of Buckingham, who greeted me on my arrival all those years ago and is now Lord High Steward, and I ask for Lady Margaret Pole to come to me. My ladies bring me the great volume of ceremonial, The Royal Book, written by the king's dead grandmother herself, and I set about organising my first public English event.

It was a quiet ceremony of smooth dignity, and everyone knew that it had been commanded and ordered by the Spanish bride. Those who had not known before realised now that the girl who had been waiting for seven years to come to the throne of England had not wasted her time. She knew the temperament of the English people, she knew how to put on a show for them. And she knew, as a princess born, how to rule. In those days before her coronation, Catalina established herself as the undeniable queen, and those who had ignored her in her years of poverty now discovered in themselves tremendous affection and respect for the princess.

She accepted their admiration, just as she had accepted their neglect: with calm politeness. She knew that by ordering the funeral of the king's grandmother she established herself as the first woman of the new court, and the arbiter of all decisions of court life. She had, in one brilliant performance, established herself as the foremost leader of England.

We decide not to cancel our coronation, though My Lady the King's Grandmother's funeral preceded it. The arrangements are all in place, we judge that we should do nothing to mar the joy of the City or of the people who have come from all over England to see the boy Harry take his father's crown. We agree that the people are expecting a great celebration and we should not deny them.

In truth, it is Harry who cannot bear a disappointment. He had promised himself a great moment of glory and he would not miss it for the world. Certainly not for the death of a very old lady who spent the last years of her life preventing him from having his own way in anything.

24th June 1509

They carried Catalina from the Tower to Westminster as an English princess. She travelled in a litter made of cloth of gold, carried high by four white palfreys so everyone could see her. She wore a gown of white satin and a coronet set with pearls, her hair brushed out over her shoulders. Harry was crowned first and then Catalina bowed her head and took the holy oil of kingship on her head and breasts, stretched out her hand for the sceptre and the ivory wand, knew that, at last, she was a queen, as her mother had been: an anointed queen, a greater being than mere mortals, a step closer to the angels, appointed by God to rule His country, and under His especial protection. She knew that finally she had fulfilled the destiny that she had been born for, she had taken her place, as she had promised that she would.

She took a throne just a little lower than King Henry's, and the crowd that cheered for the handsome young king coming to his throne also cheered for her, the Spanish bride, who had been constant against the odds and was crowned Queen Katherine of England at last.

I have waited for this day for so long that when it comes it is like a dream, like another dream of longing for Arthur.

But this time it is real.

When we come out of the Abbey and I hear the crowd cheer for him, for me, I turn to look at my husband beside me. I am shocked then, a sudden shock like waking suddenly from a dream—that he is not Arthur. He is not my love. I had expected to be crowned beside Arthur and for us to take our thrones together. But instead of the handsome, thoughtful face of my husband, it is Harry's round, flushed beam. Instead of my husband's shy, coltish grace, it is Harry's exuberant swagger at my side.

I realise at that moment, that Arthur really is dead, really gone from me.

'Are you happy?' the boy asks me, shouting to make himself heard above the pealing of the bells and the cheering of the crowds. 'Are you happy, Catalina? Are you glad to be Queen of England?'

'I am very happy,' I promise him. 'And you must call me Katherine now.'

'Katherine?' he asks. 'Not Catalina any more?'

'I am Queen of England,' I say, thinking of Arthur saying these very words. 'I am Queen Katherine of England.'

'Oh, I say!' he exclaims, delighted at the idea of changing his name, as I have changed mine. 'That's good. We shall be King Henry, and Queen Katherine. They shall call me Henry too.'

KATHERINE, QUEEN OF ENGLAND

Summer 1509

THE COURT, DRUNK WITH JOY, with delight in its own youth, with freedom, took the summer for pleasure. The progress from one beautiful, welcoming house to another lasted for two long months when Henry and Katherine hunted, dined in the greenwood, danced until midnight, and spent money like water. The great lumbering carts of the royal household went along the dusty lanes of England so that the next house might shine with gold and be bright with tapestries, so that the royal bed—which they shared every night—would be rich with the best linen and the glossiest furs.

No business of any worth was transacted by Henry at all. The work for the king followed him in boxes from one beautiful parkland castle or mansion to another, and these were opened and read only by Katherine, Queen of England, who ordered the clerks to write her orders to the Privy Council, and sent them out herself over the king's signature.

Not until mid-September did the court return to Richmond and Henry at once declared that the party should go on. Why should they ever cease in pleasure? The weather was fair, they could have hunting and boating, archery and tennis contests, parties and masquings. The victors of Bosworth who had staked their lives and made their fortunes on the Tudor courage in great danger found themselves alongside newcomers who made their fortunes on nothing more than Tudor amusements.

Henry welcomed everyone with uncritical delight; anyone who was witty and well read, charming or a good sportsman could have a place at court. Katherine smiled on them all and set herself the task of keeping her teenage husband entertained all the day long. Slowly, but surely, she drew the management of the entertainments, then of the household, then of the king's business, then of the kingdom, into her hands.

Queen Katherine had the accounts for the royal court spread out before her, a clerk to one side, a comptroller of the household with his great book to another, the men who served as exchequers of the household standing behind her. She was checking the books of the great departments of the court: the kitchen, the cellar, the wardrobe, the servery, the payments for services, the stables, the musicians.

It was steady, unrelenting work, to keep the court running as a well-ordered centre for the country, and to keep the king's business under tight control. Queen Katherine, determined to understand her new country, did not begrudge the hours she spent reading letters, taking advice from Privy Councillors, inviting objections, taking opinions. She had seen her own mother dominate a country by persuasion. Isabella of Spain had brokered her country out of a collection of rival kingships and lordships by offering them a nationwide system of justice, an end to corruption and an infallible defence system. Her daughter saw at once that these advantages could be transferred to England.

But she was also following in the steps of her Tudor father-in-law, and the more she worked on his papers and read his letters, the more she admired the steadiness of his judgment. From his records she could see how he balanced the desire of the English lords to be independent, on their own lands, with his own need to bind them to the crown. Cunningly, he allowed the northern lords greater freedom and greater wealth and status than anyone, since they were his bulwark against the Scots. Katherine had maps of the northern lands pinned around the council chamber and saw how the border with Scotland was nothing more than a handful of disputed territories in difficult country. Such a border could never be made safe from a threatening neighbour. She thought that the Scots were England's Moors: the land could not be shared with them. They would have to be utterly defeated.

She shared her father-in-law's fears of overmighty English lords at court, and when Henry thought to give one man a handsome pension in an exuberant moment, it was Katherine who pointed out that he was a wealthy man already.

'Did your father never warn you about the Howards?' she asked as they stood together watching an archery contest. Henry, stripped down to his shirtsleeves, his bow in his hand, had the second-highest score and was waiting for his turn to go again.

'No,' he replied. 'Should he have done so?'

'Oh no,' she said swiftly. 'I did not mean to suggest that they would play you false in any way, they are love and loyalty personified, Thomas Howard has been a great friend to your family, keeping the north safe

138

for you, and Edward is my knight, my dearest knight of all. It is just that their wealth has increased so much, and their family alliances are so strong. I just wondered what your father thought of them.'

'I wouldn't know,' Henry said easily. 'I wouldn't have asked him. He wouldn't have told me anyway. He thought I wouldn't be king for years yet. He had not finished making me study my books. He had not yet let me out into the world.'

She shook her head. 'When we have a son we will make sure he is prepared for his kingdom from an early age.'

At once, his hand stole round her waist. 'Do you think it will be soon?' he asked.

'Please God,' she said sweetly, withholding her secret hope. 'Do you know, I have been thinking of a name for him?'

'Have you, sweetheart? Shall you call him Ferdinand for your father?'

'If you would like it, I thought we might call him Arthur,' she said carefully.

'For my brother?' His face darkened at once.

'No, Arthur for England,' she replied swiftly. 'When I look at you sometimes I think you are like King Arthur of the round table, and this is Camelot.'

'Do you think that, little dreamer?'

'I think you could be the greatest king England has ever known since Arthur of Camelot,' she said.

'Arthur it is, then,' he said, soothed as always by praise. 'Arthur Henry.'

'Yes.'

They called to him from the butts that it was his turn, and that he had a high score to beat, and he went with a kiss blown to her. Katherine made sure that she was watching as he drew his bow, and when he glanced over, as he always did, he could see that her attention was wholly on him. The muscles in his lean back rippled as he drew back the arrow, he was like a statue, beautifully poised, and then slowly, like a dancer, he released the string and the arrow flew—faster than sight— true to the very centre of the target.

'A winning hit!'

'Victory to the king!'

The prize was a golden arrow and Henry came bright-faced to his wife to kneel at her feet so that she could bend down and kiss him on both cheeks, and then, lovingly, on the mouth.

'I won for you,' he said. 'You, alone. You bring me luck. I never miss when you are watching me. You shall keep the winning arrow.'

'It is a Cupid's arrow,' she responded. 'I shall keep it to remind me of the one in my heart.'

'She loves me.' He rose to his feet and turned to his court, and there was a ripple of applause and laughter.

'Who could help but love you?' Lady Elizabeth Boleyn, one of the ladies-in-waiting, called out boldly. Henry glanced at her and then looked down from his great height to his petite wife.

'Who could help but love her?' he asked, smiling at her.

That night I kneel before my prie-dieu and clasp my hands over my belly. It is the second month that I have not bled, I am almost certain that I am with child.

'Arthur,' I whisper, my eyes closed. 'Arthur, my love. He says that I can call this boy Arthur Henry. So I will have fulfilled our hope—that I should give you a son called Arthur. And though I know you didn't like your brother, I will show him the respect that I owe to him; he is a good boy and I pray that he will grow to a good man. I shall call my boy Arthur Henry for you both.'

I feel no guilt for my growing affection for this boy Henry though he can never take the place of his brother, Arthur. It is right that I should love my husband and Henry is an endearing boy. He is selfish as a child, but he has a child's generosity and easy tenderness. He is vain, he is ambitious, to tell truth, he is as conceited as a player in a troupe, but he is quick to laughter and quick to tears, quick to compassion, quick to alleviate hardship. He will make a good man if he has good guides, if he can be taught to rein in his desires and learn service to his country and to God. It is my task and my duty to keep him from selfishness. Like any young man, he is a tyrant in the making. If I can love him, and hold him to love me, I can make a great king of him. And England needs a great king.

At night-time in October, after Katherine had refused to dance after midnight for the previous three weeks, and had insisted, instead, on watching Henry dance with her ladies, she told him that she was with child, and made him swear to keep it secret.

'I want to tell everyone!' he exclaimed. He had come to her room in his nightgown and they were seated either side of the warm fire.

'You can write to my father next month,' she specified. 'But I don't want everyone to know yet. They will all guess soon enough.'

'You must rest,' he said instantly. 'And should you have special things to eat? I can send someone for it at once, they can wake the cooks. Tell me, love, what would you like?'

'Nothing! Nothing!' she said, laughing. 'See, we have biscuits and wine. What more do I ever eat this late at night?'

'Oh, usually, yes! But now everything is different.'

'I shall ask the physicians in the morning,' she said. 'But I need nothing now. Truly, my love. I feel very well.'

'Not sick? That is a sign of a boy, I am sure.'

'I have been feeling a little sick in the mornings,' she said, and watched his beam of happiness. 'I feel certain that it is a boy. I hope this is our Arthur Henry.'

'And when do you think he will be born?'

'In early summer, I think.'

'It cannot take so long!' he exclaimed.

'My love, I think it does take that long.'

'I shall write to your father in the morning,' he said. 'I shall tell him to expect great news in the summer. Perhaps we shall be home after a great campaign against the French then. Perhaps I shall bring you a victory and you shall give me a son.'

Henry has sent his own physician, the most skilled man in London, to see me. The man stands at one side of the room while I sit on a chair at the other. He cannot examine me, of course—the body of the queen cannot be touched by anyone but the king. He cannot ask me if I am regular in my courses or in my bowels; they too are sacred. He is so paralysed with embarrassment at being called to see me that he keeps his eyes on the floor and asks me short questions in a quiet, clipped voice.

He asks me if I eat well, and if I have any sickness. I answer that I eat well enough but that I am sick of the smell and sight of cooked meats. He asks me if I know when I conceived. I say that I cannot say for certain, but that I know the date of my last course. He smiles as a learned man to a fool and tells me that this is little guide as to when a baby might be due. I have seen Moorish doctors calculate the date of a baby's birth with a special abacus. He says he has never heard of such things and such heathen devices would be unnatural and not wanted at the treatment of a Christian child.

He suggests that I rest. He asks me to send for him whenever I feel unwell and he will come to apply leeches. Then he bows and leaves.

I look blankly at Maria de Salinas, standing in the corner of the room for this mockery of a consultation. 'This is the best doctor in England?' I ask her. 'I wonder if we can get someone from Spain.'

'Your mother and father have all but cleared Spain of the learned men,' she says, and in that moment I feel almost ashamed of them.

'Their learning was heretical,' I say defensively. She shrugs.

'Can we not find someone?' I suggest. 'Not a heathen, of course. But someone who has learned from a Moorish physician? There must be some Christian

doctors who have knowledge. Some who know more than this one?'

'*I will ask the ambassador,' she says.*

'*He must be Christian,' I stipulate. I know that I will need a better doctor than this shy ignoramus, but I do not want to go against the authority of my mother and the Holy Church. If they say that such knowledge is sin, then, surely, I should embrace ignorance. It is my duty. I am no scholar and it is better if I am guided by the ruling of the Holy Church. But can God really want us to deny knowledge? And what if this ignorance costs me England's son and heir?*

Katherine watched the dancing at the Christmas festivities, applauded her husband when he twirled other ladies round the room, laughed at the mummers, and signed off the court's bills for enormous amounts of wine, ale, beef, and the rarest and finest of everything. She gave Henry a beautiful inlaid saddle for his Christmas gift, and some shirts that she had sewn and embroidered herself.

'I want all my shirts to be sewn by you,' he said, putting the fine linen against his cheek. 'I want to never wear anything that another woman has touched. Only your hands shall make my shirts.'

Katherine smiled and pulled his shoulder down to her height. He bent down like a grown boy, and she kissed his forehead. 'Always,' she promised him. 'I shall always sew your shirts for you.'

'And now, my gift to you,' he said. He pushed a large leather box towards her. Katherine opened it. There was a great set of magnificent jewels: a diadem, a necklace, two bracelets and matching rings.

'Oh, Henry!'

'Do you like them?'

'I love them,' she said.

'Will you wear them tonight?'

'I shall wear them tonight and at the Twelfth Night feast,' she promised.

The young queen shone in her happiness, this first Christmas of her reign. The full skirts of her gown could not conceal the curve of her belly; everywhere she went the young king would order a chair to be brought for her, she must not stand for a moment, she must never be wearied. He composed for her special songs that his musicians played, special dances and special masques were made up in her honour. The court, delighted with the young queen's fertility, with the health and strength of the young king, with itself, made merry late into the night and Katherine sat on her throne, her feet slightly spread to accommodate the curve of her belly, and smiled in her joy.

I wake in the night to pain, and a strange sensation. I dreamed that a tide was rising in the River Thames and that a fleet of black-sailed ships were coming upriver. I think that it must be the Moors, coming for me. In my distress I toss and turn in bed and I wake with a sense of dread and find that it is worse than any dream, my sheets are wet with blood, and there is a real pain in my belly.

I call out in terror, and my cry wakes Maria de Salinas, who is sleeping with me.

'What is it?' she asks, then she sees my face and calls out sharply to the maid at the foot of the bed and sends her running for my ladies and for the midwives, but somewhere in the back of my mind I know already that there is nothing that they can do.

By the time they arrive, I am on my knees on the floor like a sick dog, praying for the pain to pass and to leave me whole. I know that there is no point in praying for the safety of my child. I know that my child is lost. I can feel the tearing sensation in my belly as he slowly comes away.

After a long, bitter day, when Henry comes to the door again and again, and I send him away, calling out to him in a bright voice of reassurance, biting the palm of my hand so that I do not cry out, the baby is born, dead. The midwife shows her to me, a little girl, a white, limp little thing: poor baby, my poor baby. My only comfort is that it is not the boy I had promised Arthur I would bear for him. It is a girl, a dead girl, and then I twist my face in grief when I remember that he wanted a girl first, and she was to be called Mary.

I cannot face Henry and tell him myself. I cannot bear the thought of anyone telling the court, I cannot bring myself to write to my father and tell him that I have failed England, I have failed Henry, I have failed Spain, and worst of all—and this I could never tell anyone—I have failed Arthur.

The king's physician went to the king directly from the queen's apartments. 'Your Grace, I have good news for you.'

Henry turned a face to him that was as sour as a child's whose joy has been stolen. 'You have?'

'I have indeed.'

'The queen is better? In less pain? She will be well?'

'Even better than well,' the physician said. 'Although she lost one child, she has kept another. She was carrying twins, Your Grace. She has lost one child but her belly is still large and she is still with child.'

For a moment the young man could not understand the words. 'She still has a child?'

The physician smiled. 'Yes, Your Grace.'

Henry crossed himself. 'God is with us,' he said positively. 'This is the sign of His favour.' He paused. 'Can I see her?'

'Yes, she is as happy at this news as you.'

Henry bounded up the stairs to Katherine's rooms. He brushed through the crowd who whispered hushed blessings for him and the queen, strode through her privy chamber, where her women were sewing, and tapped on her bedroom door.

Maria de Salinas opened it and stepped back for the king. The queen was out of her bed, seated in the window seat, her book of prayers held up to the light.

'My love!' he exclaimed. 'Here is Dr Fielding come to me with the best of news.'

Her face was radiant. 'I told him to tell you privately.'

'He did. No one else knows. My love, I am so glad!'

Her eyes were wet with tears. 'It is like a redemption,' she said. 'I feel as if a cross has been lifted from my shoulders.'

'I shall go to Walsingham the moment our baby is born and thank Our Lady for her favour,' he promised. 'I shall endow the shrine with a fortune, if it is a boy.'

'Please God that He grants it,' she murmured.

It was Maria de Salinas, my true friend who had come with me from Spain, and stayed with me through our good months and our hard years, who found the Moor. He was attending on a wealthy merchant, travelling from Genoa to Paris; they had called in at London to value some gold.

'They say he can make barren women give birth,' she whispers to me.

I cross myself as if to avoid temptation. 'Then he must use black arts.'

'Princess, he is supposed to be a great physician. Trained by masters who were at the university of Toledo.'

'I will not see him.'

'Because you think he must use black arts?'

'Because he is my enemy and my mother's enemy. She knew that the Moors' knowledge was unlawfully gained, drawn from the devil, not from the revealed truth of God. She drove the Moors from Spain and their magical arts with them.'

'Your Grace, he may be the only doctor in England who knows anything about women.'

Maria took my refusal and let a few weeks go by and then I woke in the night with a deep pain in my belly, and slowly, felt the blood coming. She was quick and ready to call the maids with the towels and with a ewer to wash, and when I was back in bed again and we realised that it was my monthly courses returned, she came quietly and stood beside the head of the bed.

'Your Grace, please see this doctor.'

'He is a Moor.'

'Yes, but I think he is the only man in this country who will know what is happening. How can you have your courses if you are with child? You may be losing this second baby. You have to see a doctor that we can trust.'

'Maria, he is my enemy. He is my mother's enemy. She spent her life driving his people from Spain.'

'We lost their wisdom with them,' Maria says quietly.

I am in such pain that I cannot bear an argument. 'Oh, let him come then,' I say. 'But not while I am like this. He can come next week.'

She brings him by the hidden stairway that runs from the cellars through a servants' passage to the queen's private rooms at Richmond Palace. I grimace at the thought of what my mother would say at a man coming into my privy chamber. But I know, in my heart, that I have to see a doctor who can tell me how to get a son for England. And I know, if I am honest, that something is wrong with the baby they say I am carrying.

I know him for an unbeliever the moment I see him. He is black as ebony, his eyes as dark as jet, his face both merry and compassionate, all at the same time. The back of his hands are black, dark as his face, long-fingered, his nails rosy pink, the palms brown, the creases ingrained with his colour. I know him at once for a Moor and a Nubian; and I want to order him away from my rooms. But I know, at the same time, that he may be the only doctor in this country who has the knowledge I need.

'I am Catalina, Infanta of Spain and Queen Katherine of England,' I say bluntly, that he may know that he is dealing with a queen and the daughter of a queen who had defeated his people.

He inclines his head, as proud as a baron. 'I am Yusuf, son of Ismail,' he says.

'You are a slave?'

'I was born to a slave, but I am a free man.'

'My mother would not allow slavery,' I tell him. 'She said it was not allowed by our religion, our Christian religion.'

'Nevertheless, she sent my people into slavery,' he remarks.

'Since your people won't accept the salvation of God then it doesn't matter what happens to your earthly bodies.'

His face lights up with amusement, and he gives a delightful, irrepressible chuckle. 'It matters to us, I think,' he says. 'My nation allows slavery, but we don't justify it like that. And most importantly, you cannot inherit slavery with us. When you are born, whatever the condition of your mother, you are born free. That is the law, and I think it a very good one.'

'Well, it makes no difference what you think,' I say. 'Since you are wrong.'

Again he laughs aloud, in true merriment, as if I have said something very funny. 'How good it must be, always to know that you are right,' he says. 'Perhaps you will always be certain of your rightness. But I would suggest to you, Catalina of Spain and Katherine of England, that sometimes it is better to know the questions than the answers.'

I pause at that. 'But I want you only for answers,' I say. 'Do you know medicine? Whether a woman can conceive a son? If she is with child?'

'Sometimes it can be known,' he says. 'Sometimes it is in the hands of Allah, praise His holy name.'

I cross myself against the name of Allah, quick as an old woman spitting on a shadow. He smiles at my gesture, not in the least disturbed. 'What is it that you want to know?' he asks, his voice filled with kindness. 'What is it that you want to know so much that you have to send for an infidel to advise you? Poor queen, you must be very alone if you need help from your enemy.'

My eyes are filling with too-quick tears at the sympathy in his voice and I brush my hand against my face.

'I have lost a baby,' I say shortly. 'A daughter. My physician says that she was one of twins, and that there is another child still inside me, that there will be another birth.'

'Why should you doubt your own physician's opinion?'

I turn from his enquiring, honest gaze. 'I don't know,' I say evasively.

'I should think you do know, despite yourself,' he insists gently. 'Your body will tell you. I suppose your courses have not returned?'

'No, I have bled,' I admit unwillingly. 'Last week.'

'With pain?'

'Yes.'

'Your breasts are tender?'

'They were.'

'Are they fuller than usual?'

'No.'

'You can feel the child? He moves inside you?'

'I can't feel anything since I lost the girl.'

'You are in pain now?'

'Not any more. I feel . . .'

'Yes?'

'Nothing. I feel nothing.'

He says nothing, he sits quietly, he breathes so softly it is like sitting with a quietly sleeping black cat. He looks at Maria. 'May I touch her?'

'No,' she says curtly. 'She is the queen. Nobody can touch her. She has an anointed body.'

146

He smiles as if the holy truth is amusing. 'Well, I hope someone has touched her, or there cannot be a child at all,' he remarks.

'Her husband. An anointed king,' Maria says shortly. 'And take care of how you speak. These are sacred matters.'

'If I may not examine her, then she will have to make do with guesswork.' He turns to me. 'If you were an ordinary woman and not a queen, I would take your hands in mine now.'

'Why?'

'Because it is a hard word I have to tell you.'

Slowly, I stretch out my hands with the priceless rings on my fingers. He takes them gently, his dark hands as soft as the touch of a child. His dark eyes look into mine without fear, his face is tender, moved. 'If you are bleeding then it is most likely that your womb is empty,' he says. 'There is no child there. If your breasts are not full then they are not filling with milk, your body is not preparing to feed a child. If you do not feel a child move inside you in the sixth month, then either the child is dead, or there is no child there. If you feel nothing then that is most probably because there is nothing to feel.'

'My belly is still swollen. I look as I did before I lost the first baby.'

'It could be an infection,' he says consideringly. 'Or—pray Allah that it is not—it could be a growth, a swelling. Or it could be a miscarriage which you have not yet expelled.'

I draw my hands back. 'You are ill-wishing me!'

'Never,' he says. 'To me, here and now, you are not Catalina, Infanta of Spain, but simply a woman who has asked for my help. I am sorry for you.'

'Some help!' Maria de Salinas interrupts crossly.

'Anyway, I don't believe it,' I say. 'Yours is one opinion, Dr Fielding has another. Why should I believe you, rather than a good Christian?'

He looks at me for a long time, his face tender. 'I wish I could tell you a better opinion,' he says. 'But I imagine there are many who will tell you agreeable lies. I believe in telling the truth. I will pray for you.'

'I don't want your heathen prayers,' I say roughly. 'You can go, and take your bad opinion and your heresies with you.'

'Go with God, Infanta,' he says with dignity, as if I have not insulted him. He bows. 'And since you don't want my prayers to my God (praise be to His holy name), I shall hope instead that when you are in your time of trouble that your doctor is right, and your own God is with you.'

I let him leave, as silent as a dark cat down the hidden staircase, and when he is gone, quite gone, and the downstairs door is shut and I hear Maria de Salinas turn the key in the lock, then I find that I want to weep—not just because he has told me such bad news, but because one of the few people in the world who has ever told me the truth has gone.

Spring 1510

Katherine did not tell her young husband of the visit of the Moorish doctor, nor of the bad opinion that he had so honestly given her. She drew on her sense of destiny, on her pride, and on her faith that she was still especially favoured by God, and she continued with the pregnancy, not even allowing herself to doubt.

She had good reason. The English physician, Dr Fielding, remained confident, the midwives did not contradict him, the court behaved as if Katherine would be brought to bed of a child in March or April.

In February she attended the Shrove Tuesday feast and shone before the court and laughed. They saw the broad curve of her belly, they saw her confidence as they celebrated the start of Lent. They moved to Greenwich, certain that the baby would be born just after Easter.

We are going to Greenwich for the birth of my child, the rooms are prepared for me as laid down in My Lady the King's Grandmother's Royal Book—hung with tapestries, carpeted with rugs and strewn with fresh herbs. I hesitate at the doorway, behind me my friends raise their glasses of spiced wine. This is where I shall do my greatest work for England, this is my moment of destiny. I take a deep breath and go inside. The door closes behind me. I will not see my friends, the Duke of Buckingham, my dear knight Edward Howard, my confessor, the Spanish ambassador, until my baby is born.

My women come in with me. Lady Elizabeth Boleyn places a sweet-smelling pomander on my bedside table, Lady Elizabeth and Lady Anne, sisters to the Duke of Buckingham, straighten a tapestry, one at each corner, laughing over whether it leans to one side or the other. Maria de Salinas is smiling, standing by the great bed that is new-hung with dark curtains. Lady Margaret Pole is arranging the cradle for the baby at the foot of the bed. She looks up and smiles at me as I come in and I remember that she is a mother, she will know what is to be done.

'I shall want you to take charge of the royal nurseries,' I suddenly blurt out to her, my affection for her and my sense of needing the advice and comfort of an older woman is too much for me.

There is a little ripple of amusement among my women. They know that I am normally very formal, such an appointment should come through the head of my household after consultation with dozens of people.

Lady Margaret smiles at me. 'I have been counting on it,' she says.

'I know you will care for him as if he were your own son,' I whisper to her.

She takes my hand and helps me to the bed. I am heavy and ungainly, I have this constant pain in my belly that I try to hide.

Henry comes in to bid me farewell. His face is flushed with emotion and his mouth is working, he looks more like a boy than a king. I take his hands and I kiss him tenderly on the mouth. 'My love,' I say. 'Pray for me, I am sure everything will be well for us.'

'I shall go to Our Lady of Walsingham to give thanks,' he tells me again. 'The nuns are praying for you now, my love. They assure me that they are praying all the time.'

'God is good,' I say. I think briefly of the Moorish doctor who told me that I was not with child and I push his pagan folly from my mind. 'This is my destiny and it is my mother's wish and God's will,' I say.

'Can I get you anything?' he asks. 'Before I leave, can I fetch you anything?'

I do not laugh at the thought of Henry—who never knows where anything is—running errands for me at this late stage. 'I have everything I need,' I assure him. 'And my women will care for me.'

He straightens up, very kingly, and he looks around at them. 'Serve your mistress well,' he says firmly. To Lady Margaret he says, 'Please send for me at once if there is any news, at any time, day or night.' Then he kisses me farewell very tenderly, and when he goes out they close the door behind him and I am alone with my ladies, in the seclusion of my confinement.

I wait. All through March I wait. Nothing seems to be happening; not for my baby nor for me. The midwives ask me if I feel any pain, and I do not. Nothing more than the dull ache I have had for a long time. They ask if the baby has quickened, if I feel him kick me, but, to tell truth, I do not understand what they mean. They glance at one another and say over-emphatically that it is a very good sign, a quiet baby is a strong baby; he must be resting.

The unease that I have felt from the start of this second pregnancy, I put right away from me. But April comes and I can hear the patter of rain on the window, and then feel the heat of the sunshine, and still nothing happens.

My gowns that strained so tight across my belly through the winter feel looser in April. I send out all the women but Maria, and I unlace my gown and show her my belly and ask if she thinks I am losing my girth.

'I don't know,' she says; but I can tell by her aghast face that my belly is smaller, that it is obvious that there is no baby in there, ready to be born.

In another week it is obvious to everyone that my belly is going down, I am growing slim again. The midwives try to tell me that sometimes a woman's belly diminishes just before her baby is born, as her baby drops down to be born, or some such arcane knowledge. I look at them coldly, and I wish I could send for a decent physician who would tell me the truth.

'My belly is smaller and my course has come this very day,' I say to them flatly. 'I am bleeding. As you know, I have bled every month since I lost the girl. How can I be with child?'

They flutter their hands, and cannot say. They don't know. They tell me that these are questions for my husband's respected physician. It was he who had said that I was still with child in the first place, not them.

'But you saw me lose my baby. You saw my belly stay big. What could cause that if not another child?'

'God's will,' says one of them helplessly.

'Amen,' I say, and it costs me a good deal to say it.

'I want to see that physician again,' Katherine said quietly to Maria de Salinas. 'Find out if he is still in London. Don't tell anyone that it is I who have asked for him.'

Maria de Salinas looked at her mistress with sympathy. 'But you said that you did not want pagan knowledge. You said your mother was right to close the universities of the infidel.'

'My mother was wrong to turn her back on the learning of the Moors. She was mistaken. I have never thought that she was perfect, but I think the less of her now. She made a great mistake when she drove away their wise scholars along with their heretics.'

'The church itself said that their scholarship is heresy,' Maria observed. 'How could you have one without the other?'

'I am sure that you know nothing about it,' said Isabella's daughter, driven into a corner. 'It is not a fit subject for you to discuss and besides, I have told you what I want you to do.'

They brought the Moor to Katherine under cover of darkness, to the chamber where she was confined. She sent the women from the room at the appointed hour and told them that she wanted to be alone. She sat in her chair by the window, and the first thing he saw, as she rose when he came in, was her slim candlelit profile against the darkness of the window. She saw his little grimace of sympathy.

'No child.'

'No,' she said shortly. 'I shall come out of my confinement tomorrow.'

'You are in pain?'

'Nothing.'

'Well, I am glad of that. You are bleeding?'

'I had my normal course last week.'

He nodded. 'Then you may have had a disease which has passed. You will want to conceive a child as soon as possible,' he guessed.

'Yes.'

He thought for a moment, then spoke up again. 'Well, Infanta, since you have had one child, even if you did not bear it to full term, we know that you and your husband are fertile. That is good.'

'Yes,' she said, surprised by the thought. She had been so distressed by the miscarriage she had not thought that her fertility had been proven. 'But why do you speak of my husband's fertility?'

The Moor smiled gently. 'It takes both a man and a woman to conceive a child.'

'Here in England they think that it is only the woman.'

'Yes. But in this, as in so many other things, they are wrong.'

'They say that if a baby is lost, then the woman is at fault, perhaps she has committed a great sin.'

He frowned. 'It is possible,' he conceded. 'But not very likely. Otherwise how would murderesses ever give birth? I think we will learn in time that there are humours and infections that cause miscarriage. I do not blame the woman, it makes no sense to me.'

'They say that if a woman is barren it is because the marriage is not blessed by God.'

'He is your God,' he remarked reasonably. 'Would he persecute an unhappy woman in order to make a point?'

Katherine did not reply. 'They will blame me if I do not have a live child,' she observed very quietly.

'I know,' he said. 'But the truth of the matter is: having had one child and lost it, there is every reason to think that you might have another.'

'I must bear the next child to full term.'

'If I could examine you, I might know more.'

She shook her head. 'It is not possible.'

His glance at her was merry. 'Oh, you savages,' he said softly.

She gave a little gasp of amused shock. 'You forget yourself!'

'Then send me away.'

That stopped her. 'You can stay,' she said shortly. 'But you cannot examine me.'

'Then let us consider what might help you conceive and carry a child,' he said. 'Your body needs to be strong. Do you ride horses?'

'Yes.'

'Ride astride before you conceive and then take a litter thereafter. Walk every day, swim if you can. You will conceive a child about two weeks after the end of your course. Rest at those times, and make sure that you lie with your husband at those times. Try to eat moderately at every meal and drink as little of their accursed small ale as you can.'

Katherine smiled at the reflection of her own prejudices. 'Do you know Spain?'

'I was born there. My parents fled from Malaga when your mother brought in the Inquisition and they realised that they would be tormented to death.'

'I am sorry,' she said awkwardly.

'We will go back, it is written,' he said with confidence.

'I should warn you that you will not.'

'I know that we will. I have seen the prophecy myself.'

At once they fell silent again.

'Shall I tell you what I advise? Or shall I just leave now?' he asked, as if he did not much mind which it was to be.

'Tell me,' she said. 'And then I can pay you, and you can go. We were born to be enemies. I should not have summoned you.'

'We are both Spanish, we both love our country. We both serve our God. Perhaps we were born to be friends.'

'Perhaps,' she said gruffly, turning her head away. 'But I was brought up to hate your people and hate your faith.'

'I was brought up to hate no one,' he said gently. 'Perhaps that is what I should be teaching you before anything else.'

'Just teach me how to have a son,' she repeated.

'Very well. Drink water that has been boiled, eat as much fruit and fresh vegetables as you can get. Do you have salad vegetables here?'

For a moment I am back in the garden at Ludlow with his bright eyes on me. 'Lactuca? What is it, exactly?'

He saw the queen's face glow.

'What are you thinking of?'

'Of my first husband. He told me that I could send for gardeners to grow salad vegetables, but I never did.'

'I have seeds,' the Moor said surprisingly. 'I can give you some seeds and you can grow the vegetables you will need.'

'You would give me . . . you would sell them to me?'

'Yes. I would give them to you.'

For a moment she was silenced by his generosity. 'You are very kind.'

He smiled. 'We are both Spanish and a long way from our homes. Doesn't that matter more than the fact that I am black and you are white? That I worship my God facing Mecca and you worship yours facing west?'

'I am a child of the true religion and you are an infidel,' she said, but with less conviction than she had ever felt before.

'We are both people of faith,' he said quietly. 'Our enemies should be the people who have no faith, who bring cruelty into the world for no reason but their own power. There is enough sin and wickedness to fight, without taking up arms against people who believe in a forgiving God and who try to lead a good life.'

Katherine found that she could not reply. On the one hand was her mother's teaching, on the other was the simple goodness that radiated from this man. 'I don't know,' she said finally, and it was as if the very words set her free. 'I don't pretend to know.'

'Now, that is the very beginning of wisdom,' he said gently. 'I am sure of that, at least. Knowing that you do not know is to ask humbly, instead of tell arrogantly. That is the beginning of wisdom. Now, more importantly, I will go home and write you a list of things that you must not eat, and I will send you some medicine to strengthen your humours. Don't let them cup you, don't let them put leeches on you, and don't let them persuade you to take any poisons or potions. You are a young woman with a young husband. A baby will come.'

It was like a blessing. 'You are sure?' she said.

'I am sure,' he replied. 'And very soon.'

Greenwich, May 1510

I send for Henry, he should hear it first from me. He comes unwillingly. He does not like to come into a room that has been prepared for a confinement. Also, there is something else: a lack of warmth, I see it in his face, turned away from me. The way he does not meet my eyes. But I cannot challenge him about coolness towards me when I first have to tell him such hard news.

'Husband, I am sorry, I have sad news for us,' I say.

The face he turns to me is sulky. 'I knew it could not be good when Lady Margaret came for me.'

There is no point in my feeling irritation. 'I am not with child,' I say, plunging in. 'The doctor must have made a mistake. There was only one child and I lost it. This confinement has been a mistake. I shall return to court tomorrow.'

'How can he have mistaken such a thing?'

I give a little shrug of the shoulders. I want to say: because he is a pompous fool, and you surround yourself with people who only ever tell you the good news and are afraid to tell you bad. But instead I say neutrally: 'He must have been mistaken.'

'I shall look a fool!' he bursts out. 'You have been away for nearly three months and nothing to show for it.'

'No one will think anything at all,' I say firmly. 'If anything, they will say that it is I who am a fool to not know whether I am with child, or no. But at least we had a baby and that means we can have another.'

'It does?' he asks, immediately hopeful. 'But why should we lose her? Is God displeased with us?'

'My conscience is clear,' I say firmly.

'Mine too,' he says quickly, too quickly.

But my conscience is not clear. That night I go on my knees to the image of the crucified Lord and for once I truly pray, I do not dream of Arthur, or consult my memory of my mother. I close my eyes and I pray.

'Lord, it was a deathbed promise,' I say slowly. 'He demanded it of me. It was for the good of England. It was to guide the kingdom and the new king in the paths of the church. It was to protect England from the Moor and from sin. If it is sin, Lord, then show me now. If I should not be his wife, then tell me now. Because I believe that I did the right thing, and that I am doing the right thing. And I believe that You would not take my son from me in order to punish me for this. I believe that You are a merciful God. And I believe that I did the right thing for Arthur, for Henry, for England and for me.'

Lady Margaret Pole comes to sit with me this evening, my last evening in confinement, and she takes the stool on the opposite side of the fire, close enough so that we cannot easily be overheard. 'I have something to tell you,' she says.

I look at her face; she is so calm that I know at once something bad has happened. 'Tell me,' I say instantly.

She makes a little moue of distaste. 'I am sorry to bring you the tittle-tattle of the court.'

'Very well. Tell me.'

'It is the Duke of Buckingham's sister.'

'Elizabeth?' I ask.

'No, Anne.'

I nod, this is Elizabeth's younger sister, a girl with a roguish twinkle and a love of male company.

'What of her?'

'She has been seeing William Compton, without telling anyone. They have had assignations. Her brother is very upset. He has told her husband, and he is furious at her risking her reputation and his good name in a flirtation with the king's friend.'

I think for a moment. William Compton is one of Henry's wilder companions; the two of them are inseparable.

'It turns out that she has gone missing from a masque, once during dinner and once all day when the court was hunting. Her brother has complained to Compton and there has been a quarrel. The king has defended Compton.'

I press my lips together to prevent myself snapping out a criticism in my *irritation. The Duke of Buckingham is one of the oldest friends of the Tudor family, with massive lands and many retainers. He greeted me with Prince Harry all those years ago; he is now honoured by the king, the greatest man in the land. If Henry had any sense he would not have involved himself in this petty courtiers' quarrel.*

'Can I not leave the court for a moment without my ladies climbing out of their bedroom windows to run after young men?'

Lady Margaret leans forwards and pats my hand. 'It seems not. It is a foolish young court, Your Grace, and they need you to keep them steady. I am afraid that when you come out of your confinement Anne's husband will not allow her to wait on you, and then your honour is involved.' She pauses. 'I thought you should know now rather than be surprised by it all tomorrow morning. Though it goes against the grain to be a tale-bearer of such folly.'

'It is ridiculous,' I say. 'I shall deal with it tomorrow, when I come out of confinement. But really, what are they all thinking of? This is like a schoolyard!'

Queen Katherine came out of her confinement, without announcement, and returned to her usual rooms at Greenwich Palace. She came out without comment, as if she had suffered some secret, shameful illness, and everyone pretended that she had been gone for hours rather than nearly three months.

Her ladies-in-waiting, who had become accustomed to an idle pace of life with the queen in confinement, assembled at some speed in the queen's chambers.

Katherine caught several furtive glances among the ladies and assumed that they too had guilty consciences over misbehaviour in her absence; but then she realised that there was a whispered buzz of conversation that ceased whenever she raised her head. Clearly, something had happened that was more serious than Anne's disgrace; and, equally clearly, no one was telling her.

She beckoned one of her ladies, Lady Madge, to come to her side.

'Is Lady Elizabeth not joining us this morning?' she asked, as she could see no sign of the older Stafford sister.

The girl flushed scarlet to her ears. 'I don't know,' she stammered.

'Where is she?' Katherine asked.

The girl looked desperately round for help but all the other ladies in the room were suddenly taking an intense interest in their sewing, in their embroidery, or in their books.

'I think she has gone,' the girl said baldly.

'Gone?' Katherine looked around. 'Will someone please tell me what is happening?' she asked, her tone reasonable enough. 'Where has Lady

Elizabeth gone? And how can she have gone without my permission?'

The girl took a step back. At that moment, Lady Margaret Pole came into the room.

'Lady Margaret,' Katherine said pleasantly. 'Here is Madge telling me that Lady Elizabeth has left court without my permission and without bidding me farewell. What is happening?'

Katherine felt her amused smile freeze on her face when her old friend shook her head slightly, and Madge, relieved, dropped back to her seat. 'What is it?' Katherine asked more quietly.

'I believe the king and the Duke of Buckingham have had hard words,' Lady Margaret said smoothly. 'The duke has left court and taken both his sisters with him.'

'But they are my ladies-in-waiting. In service to me. They cannot leave without my permission.'

'It is very wrong of them, indeed,' Margaret said. Something in the way she folded her hands in her lap and looked so steadily and calmly warned Katherine not to probe.

'So what have you been doing in my absence?' Katherine turned to the ladies, trying to lighten the mood of the room.

At once they all looked sheepish. 'Have you learned any new songs? Have you danced in any masques?' Katherine asked.

'I know a new song,' one of the girls volunteered. 'Shall I sing it?'

Katherine nodded; at once one of the other women picked up a lute. It was as if everyone was quick to divert her. She knew, as a woman who had been born and raised in a court of conspirators, that something was very wrong indeed.

There was the sound of company approaching and Katherine's guards threw open the door to the king and his court. The ladies stood up, shook out their skirts, bit their lips to make them pink, and sparkled in anticipation. Henry strode in, still in his riding clothes, his friends around him, William Compton's arm in his.

At Katherine's sharp look Compton awkwardly disengaged himself. Henry greeted his wife without enthusiasm, he took her hand and then kissed her cheek, not her mouth.

'Are you well now?' he asked.

'Yes,' she said calmly. 'I am quite well now. And how are you, sire?'

'Oh,' he said carelessly. 'I am well. We had such a chase this morning. I wish you had been with us. We were halfway to Sussex, I do believe.'

'I shall come out tomorrow,' Katherine promised him.

'Will you be well enough?'

'I am quite well,' she repeated.

He looked relieved. 'I thought you would be ill for months,' he blurted out.

Smiling, she shook her head, wondering who had told him that.

'Let's break our fast,' he said. 'I am starving.'

He took her hand and led her to the great hall. The court fell in informally behind them. Katherine could hear the overexcited buzz of whispers. She leaned her head towards Henry so that no one could catch her words. 'I hear there have been some quarrels in court.'

'Oh! You have heard of our little storm already, have you?' he said. 'It is something and nothing. I have had a quarrel with your great friend, the Duke of Buckingham. He has left the court in a temper!' He laughed, glancing at her sideways to see if she was smiling, trying to judge if she already knew all about it.

'Indeed?' Katherine said coolly.

'He was insulting,' Henry said, gathering his sense of offence. 'He can stay away until he is ready to apologise. And his sour sister Elizabeth can go too.'

'She is a good lady-in-waiting and she and her sister are in my household,' she observed. 'I have the right to choose and dismiss my own ladies.'

She saw the quick flush of his childish temper. 'You will oblige me by sending them away from your household! Whatever your rights! I don't expect to hear talk of rights between us!'

The court behind them fell silent at once. Everyone wanted to hear the first royal quarrel.

Katherine released his hand and went round the high table to take her place. It gave her a moment to remind herself to be calm. When he came to his seat beside hers she smiled at him. 'As you wish,' she said evenly. 'I have no great preference in the matter. But how am I to run a well-ordered court if I send away young women of good family who have done nothing wrong?'

'You were not here, so you have no idea what she did or didn't do!' He waved the court to sit and dropped into his own chair. 'You locked yourself away for months. You should never have gone into confinement, there was no child, anyone could have seen that there would be no child.'

She was so taken aback that she could hardly speak. 'This is about my confinement?'

'It would hardly have happened without. But everyone could see there would be no child. It was wasted time.'

'Your own doctor . . .'

PHILIPPA GREGORY

'Doctors know nothing!' he suddenly burst out. 'They are always guided by the woman; everyone knows that. And a woman can say anything. Is there a baby, isn't there a baby? Is she a virgin, isn't she a virgin? Only the woman knows and the rest of us are fooled.'

Katherine felt her mind racing, trying to trace what had offended him, what she could say. 'I trusted your doctor,' she said. 'He was very certain. He assured me I was with child and so I went into confinement. Another time I will know better. I am truly sorry, my love. It has been a very great grief to me.'

'It just makes me look such a fool!' he said plaintively. 'It's no wonder that I . . .'

'That you? What?'

'Nothing,' said Henry, sulkily.

It is such a lovely afternoon, let us go for a walk,' I say pleasantly to my ladies. 'Lady Margaret will accompany me.'

We go outside. I breathe deeply, it is so good to be out of that room and to feel the sun on my face again that I hardly want to open the subject of Lady Anne.

'You must know what took place?' I say shortly.

'I know some gossip,' she says levelly. 'Nothing for certain.'

'What has angered the king so much?' I ask. 'He is upset about my confinement, he is angry with me. What is troubling him? Surely not the Stafford girl's flirtation with Compton?'

Lady Margaret's face is grave. 'The king is very attached to William Compton,' she said. 'He would not have him insulted.'

'It sounds as if all the insult is the other way,' I say. 'It is Lady Anne and her husband who are dishonoured. I would have thought the king would have been angry with William. Lady Anne is not a girl to tumble behind a wall.'

Lady Margaret shrugs. 'I don't know,' she says. 'You would think so. But if it is a flirtation, why would the duke be so very offended? Why quarrel with the king? Why would the girls not be laughing at Anne for getting caught?'

'And Compton remains in high favour?'

'They are inseparable.'

I speak the thought that is sitting cold in my heart. 'So do you think that Compton is the shield and the love affair is between the king, my husband, and Lady Anne?'

Lady Margaret's grave face tells me that my guess is her own fear. 'I don't know,' she says, honest as ever. 'The girls tell me nothing, and I have not asked anyone that question.'

'Because you think you will not like the answer?'

She nods. Slowly, I turn, and we walk back along the river in silence.

158

Katherine and Henry led the company into dinner in the grand hall and sat side by side under the gold canopy of state as they always did. There was a band of special singers that had come to England from the French court and they sang without instruments, very true to the note with a dozen different parts. It was complicated and beautiful and Henry was entranced by the music. When the singers paused, he applauded and asked them to repeat the song. They smiled at his enthusiasm, and sang again. He then sang the tenor line back to them: note perfect.

It was their turn to applaud him and they invited him to sing with them the part that he had learned so rapidly. Katherine, on her throne, smiled as her handsome husband sang in his clear young voice, and the ladies of the court clapped in appreciation.

When the musicians struck up and the court danced, Katherine came down from the raised platform of the high table and danced with Henry, her face bright with happiness and her smile warm. Henry, encouraged by her, danced like an Italian, with fast, dainty footwork and high leaps. Katherine clapped her hands in delight and called for another dance as if she had never had a moment's worry in her life. One of her ladies leaned towards another. 'He has fooled her. He has played her for a fool, and now he is fair game to any one of us. She has lost her hold on him.'

I wait till we are alone, and then I wait until he beds me with his eager joy, and then I slip from the bed and bring him a cup of small ale.

'So tell me, Henry,' I say to him simply. 'What is the truth of the quarrel between you and the Duke of Buckingham, and what were your dealings with his sister?'

His swift sideways glance tells me more than any words. He is about to lie to me. I hear the words he says: a story about a disguising and all of them in masks and the ladies dancing with them and Compton and Anne dancing together, and I know that he is lying.

It is an experience more painful than I thought I could have with him. We have been married for nearly a year, a year next month, and I have never heard anything but truth in his voice: boastfulness, certainly, the arrogance of a young man, but never this uncertain deceitful quaver.

I stop him, I truly cannot bear to hear it. 'Enough,' I say. 'I know enough at least to realise that this is not true. She was your lover, wasn't she? And Compton was your friend and shield?'

His mouth is trembling. He cannot bear to admit what he has done. 'I didn't mean to . . .'

'I know that you did not,' I say. 'I am sure you were sorely tempted.'

'You were away for so long . . .'

'I know.'

A dreadful silence falls. If Henry cannot remain faithful when I am in confinement with our child, our dearly needed child, then how shall he be faithful till death? How shall he obey his vow to forsake all others when he can be distracted so easily?

'Dear husband, this is very wrong,' I say sadly.

'It was because I had such doubts. I thought for a moment that we were not married,' he confesses.

'You forgot we were married?' I ask incredulously.

'No!' His head comes up, his blue eyes are filled with unshed tears. His face shines with contrition. 'I thought that since our marriage was not valid, I need not abide by it.'

I am quite amazed by him. 'Our marriage? Why would it not be valid?'

He shakes his head. He is too ashamed to speak. I press him. 'Why not?'

He kneels beside my bed and hides his face in the sheets. 'I liked her and I desired her and she said some things which made me think . . .'

'Think what?'

'What if you were not a virgin when I married you?'

At once I am alert. 'What do you mean?'

'She was a virgin . . .'

'Anne?'

'Yes. Sir George is impotent. Everyone knows that.'

'Do they?'

'Yes. So she was a virgin. And she was not like you. She . . .' He stumbles for words. 'She cried out in pain. She bled, I was afraid when I saw how much blood, really a lot . . .' He breaks off again. 'She could not go on, the first time. I had to stop. She cried, I held her. She was a virgin. That is what it is like to lie with a virgin, the first time. I was her first love. I could tell. Her first love.'

There is a long, cold silence.

'She fooled you,' I say cruelly, throwing away her reputation, and his tenderness for her, making her a whore and him a fool, for the greater good.

He looks up, shocked. 'She did?'

'She was pretending.' I shake my head at the sinfulness of young women. 'It is an old trick. She will have had a bladder of blood in her hand and broke it to give you a show of blood. She will have cried out. I expect she whimpered and said she could not bear the pain from the very beginning.'

Henry is amazed. 'She did.'

'She thought to make you feel that you had taken her virginity, her maidenhead, and that you owe her your protection.'

'That is what she said!'

'She tried to entrap you,' I said. 'She was not a virgin, she was acting the part of one. I was a virgin when I came to your bed and the first night that we were lovers was very simple and sweet. Do you remember?'

'Yes,' he says.

'There was no crying and wailing like players on a stage. It was quiet and loving. Take that as your benchmark,' I say. 'I was a true virgin. You and I were each other's first love. We had no need for play-acting and exaggeration. Hold to that truth of our love, Henry. You have been fooled by a counterfeit.'

'She said that you must have been Arthur's lover.' He stumbles before the white fierceness of my face. 'That you had lain with him, and that . . .'

'Not true. My marriage with Arthur was not consummated. I came to you a virgin. Would anyone dare to say to my face that I am not your first love, a virgin untouched, your true wedded wife, and Queen of England?'

'No,' he says.

'Not even you?'

'No.'

'It is to dishonour me,' I say furiously. 'And where will scandal stop? It insults me, but it threatens you. Scandal against the queen rocks the throne itself. Be warned, Henry.'

'She said it!' he exclaimed. 'Anne said that it was no sin for me to lie with her because I was not truly married!'

'She lied to you. She pretended to her virgin state and she traduced me.'

His face flushes red with anger. It is a relief to him to turn to rage. 'What a whore!' he exclaims crudely.

'You cannot trust young women,' I say quietly. 'Now that you are King of England you will have to be on your guard, my love. They will try to charm you and seduce you, but you have to be faithful to me. I was your virgin bride, I was your first love. I am your wife. Do not forsake me.'

He takes me into his arms. 'Forgive me,' he whispers brokenly.

'We will never ever speak of this again,' I say solemnly.

'No,' he says fervently. 'Before God. We will never speak of this nor allow any other to speak of it again.'

'I have good news for you,' Katherine said to Henry. They had thrown open the windows of her bedroom to let in the cooler night air. It was a warm night and for once, Henry had chosen to come to bed early.

'Tell me some good news,' he said. 'My horse went lame today, and I cannot ride him tomorrow. I would welcome some good news.'

'I think I am with child.'

He bounced up in the bed. 'You are?'

'I think so,' she said, smiling.

'God be praised. I shall go to Walsingham the minute you give birth to our son. I shall wear a suit of pure white. I shall give Our Lady pearls.'

'Our Lady has been gracious to us indeed.'

'And how potent they will all know that I am now! Out of confinement in the first week of May and pregnant by the end of the month. That will show them! That will prove that I am a husband indeed.'

'Indeed it will,' she said levelly.

'And you are certain?' He had no tact to phrase his anxiety in gentle words. 'You are certain this time?'

She nodded. 'I am certain. I have all the signs.'

'God be praised. I knew it would come. I knew that a marriage made in heaven would be blessed.'

Katherine nodded. Smiling.

'What a celebration we shall have when our baby is born. When will it be?'

'After Christmas,' Katherine said. 'In the New Year.'

Winter 1510

I should have been a soothsayer, I have proved to be so accurate with my prediction, even without a Moorish abacus. We are holding the Christmas feast at Richmond and the court is joyful in my happiness. The baby is big in my belly, and he kicks so hard that Henry can put his hand on me and feel the little heel thud out against his hand. There is no doubt that he is alive and strong, and his vitality brings joy to the whole court.

I pray for a boy but I do not expect one. A child for England, a child for Arthur, is all I want. If it is the daughter that he had wanted, then I will call her Mary as he asked.

Henry's desire for a son, and his love for me, has made him more thoughtful at last. He takes care of me in ways that he has never done before. I think he is growing up, the selfish boy is becoming a good man at last, and the fear that has haunted me since his affair with the Stafford girl is receding. Perhaps he will take lovers as kings always do, but perhaps he will resist falling in love with them and making promises that a man can make but a king must not.

I will have to go into confinement again but I leave it as late as I dare. Henry swears to me that there will be no other while I am confined, that he is mine, all mine. I leave it till the evening of the Christmas feast and then I go once more into the quietness of my bedroom.

In truth, I don't mind missing the dancing and the heavy drinking. I am tired, this baby is a weight to carry. I rise and then rest with the winter sun, and spend much time praying for a safe delivery, and for the health of the child that moves so strongly inside me.

Henry comes to see me, privately, most days. The Royal Book is clear that the queen should be in absolute isolation before the birth of her child; but the Royal Book was written by Henry's grandmother and I suggest that we can please ourselves. I don't see why she should command me from beyond the grave. Besides, I don't trust Henry on his own in court. On New Year's Eve he dines with me before going to the hall for the great feast, and brings me a gift of rubies. I put them round my neck and see his eyes darken with desire for me as they gleam on the plump whiteness of my breasts.

'Not long now,' I say, smiling; I know exactly what he is thinking.

'I shall go to Walsingham as soon as our child is born, and when I come back you will be churched,' he says.

'And then, I suppose you will want to make another baby,' I say with mock weariness.

'I will,' he says, his face bright with laughter.

He kisses me good night, wishes me joy of the new year and then goes out of the hidden door in my chamber to his own rooms, and from there to the feast. I tell them to bring the boiled water that I still drink in obedience to the Moor's advice, and then I sit before the fire sewing the tiniest little gown for my baby, while Maria de Salinas reads in Spanish to me.

Suddenly, it is as if my whole belly has turned over, as if I am falling from a great height. The pain is so thorough, so unlike anything I have ever known before, that the sewing drops from my hands and I grip the arms of my chair and let out a gasp. I know at once that the baby is coming. I am filled with joy and a holy terror. I know that the baby is coming and that he is strong, and that I am young, and that everything will be all right.

As soon as I tell the ladies, the chamber bursts into uproar. The midwives are summoned from the hall, they have gone off to make merry, gambling that they would not be needed on New Year's Eve. The physician cannot be found at all, and pages are sent running all over the palace looking for him.

Unbelievably, it is little more than six hours—though one of those hours lingers on for at least a day—and then there is a rush and a slither, and the midwife mutters 'God be praised!' quietly and then there is a loud, irritable cry, and I realise that this is a new voice in the room, that of my baby.

'A boy, God be praised, a boy,' the midwife says and Maria looks up at me and sees me radiant with joy.

'Really?' I demand. 'Let me see him!'

They cut the cord and pass him up to me, still naked, still bloody, his little mouth opened wide to shout, his eyes squeezed tight in anger, Henry's son.

'My son,' I whisper.

'England's son,' the midwife says. 'God be praised.'

I put my face down to his warm little head, still sticky, I sniff him like a cat sniffs her kittens. 'This is our boy,' I whisper to Arthur, who is so close at that moment that it is almost as if he is at my side. 'This is our son for England, and he will be king.'

1511

The whole of England went mad when they learned on New Year's Day that a boy had been born. Everyone called him Prince Henry at once, there was no other name possible. In the streets they roasted oxen and drank themselves into a stupor. In the country they rang the church bells and broke into the church ales to toast the health of the Tudor heir, the boy who would keep England at peace, who would keep England allied with Spain, who would protect England from her enemies and who would defeat the Scots once and for all.

Henry came in to see his son, disobeying the rules of confinement, tiptoeing carefully, as if his footstep might shake the room. He peered into the cradle, afraid almost to breathe near the sleeping boy.

'He is so small,' he said. 'How can he be so small?'

'The midwife says he is big and strong,' Katherine corrected him, instantly on the defence of her baby.

'I am sure. It is just that his hands are so . . . and look, he has finger-nails! Real fingernails!'

'He has toenails too,' she said.

The two of them stood side by side and looked down in amazement at the perfection that they had made together.

'Show me,' he said.

Gently, she pulled off the little silk shoes that the baby wore. 'There,' she said, her voice filled with tenderness.

Henry bent over the crib, and tenderly took the tiny foot in his big hand. 'My son,' he said wonderingly. 'God be praised, I have a son.'

I've never known such simple joy. When I doze I wake with my heart filled with delight, before I even know why. Then I remember. I have a son for England, for Arthur and for Henry; and I smile and turn my head, and whoever is watching over me answers the question before I have asked it: 'Yes, your son is well, Your Grace.'

Henry is excessively busy with the care of our son. He comes in and out to see me twenty times a day with questions and with news of the arrangements he has made. He has appointed a household of no less than forty people for this tiny baby, and already chosen his rooms in the Palace of Westminster for his council chamber when he is a young man. I smile, and say nothing. Henry is planning the greatest christening that has ever been seen in England, nothing is too good for this Henry who will be Henry IX. My son, the King of England.

His sponsors are carefully chosen: the daughter of the emperor, Margaret of Austria, and King Louis the Twelfth of France. So he is working already, this little Tudor, to cloud the French suspicion against us, to maintain our alliance with the Hapsburg family.

His godparents are Archbishop Warham, my dear and true friend Thomas Howard, Earl of Surrey, and the Earl and Countess of Devon. My dearest Lady Margaret is to run his nursery at Richmond. It is the newest and cleanest of all the palaces near London, and wherever we are, whether at Whitehall or Greenwich or Westminster, it will be easy for me to visit him.

I can hardly bear to let him go away, but it is better for him to be in the country than in the City. And I shall see him every week at the very least.

Henry went to the shrine of Our Lady at Walsingham, as he had promised, and Katherine asked him to tell the nuns who kept the shrine that she would come herself when she was next with child.

She gave him a heavy purse of gold. 'Will you give them this, from me, and ask them for their prayers?'

'They pray for the Queen of England as their duty,' he said.

'I want to remind them.'

Henry returned to court for the greatest tournament that England had ever seen, and Katherine was up and out of her bed to organise it for him. He had commissioned new armour before he went away and she had commanded her favourite, Edward Howard, to make sure that it would fit precisely to the slim young king's measurements, and that the workmanship was perfect. She had banners made, and tapestries hung, masques prepared with glorious themes, gold everywhere: cloth of gold banners and curtains, gold plates and gold cups, gold tips to the ornamental lances, gold-embossed shields, even gold on the king's saddlery.

'This will be the greatest tournament that England has ever seen,' Edward Howard said to her. 'English chivalry and Spanish elegance. It will be a thing of beauty.'

'It is the greatest celebration that we have ever had,' she said, smiling. 'For the greatest reason.'

I know I have made an outstanding showcase for Henry but when he rides into the tiltyard I catch my breath. It is the fashion that the knights who have come to joust choose a motto; sometimes they even compose a poem or play a part in a tableau before they ride. Henry has kept his motto a secret, and not told me what it is going to be. I truly have no idea what it will say until he bows before me in the royal box, the banner unfurls and his herald shouts out his title for the joust: 'Sir Loyal Heart'.

I rise to my feet and clasp my hands before my face to hide my trembling mouth. My eyes fill with tears, I cannot help it. He has called himself 'Sir Loyal Heart'—he has declared to the world the restoration of his devotion and love for me. Everywhere I look, at every corner of the jousting green, on every banner, on every post there are Ks and Hs together. He has used this great joust, the finest and richest that England has ever seen, to tell the world that he loves me, that he is mine, that his heart is mine and that it is a loyal heart.

I look around at my ladies-in-waiting and I am utterly triumphant. I run my eyes over them, the prettiest girls from the greatest families of England, and I know that every one of them secretly thinks that she could have my place. If she were to be lucky, if the king were to be seduced, if I were to die, she could have my throne.

But his banner tells them 'Not so.' His banner tells them, the gold Ks and Hs tell them, the herald's cry tells them that he is all mine, for ever. The will of my mother, my word to Arthur, the destiny given by God to England has brought me finally to this: a son and heir in England's cradle, the King of England publicly declaring his passion for me, and my initial twined with his in gold everywhere I look.

I touch my hand to my lips and smile at Henry as he drops his visor and his big glossy black horse trots slowly to the end of the lists, and I smile on the people of London who call out my name and shout 'God bless Queen Katherine!' and I smile to myself because I am doing as my mother wished, as God decreed, and Arthur is waiting for me in al-Yanna, the garden.

Ten days later, when she was at the height of her happiness, they brought to Queen Katherine the worst news of her life.

It is worse even than the death of my husband, Arthur. I had not thought there could be anything worse than that; but so it proves. It is worse than my years of widowhood and waiting. It is worse than hearing from Spain that my mother was dead. Worse than the worst days I have ever had.

My baby is dead. More than this, I cannot say, I cannot even hear. I think Henry is here, some of the time; and Maria de Salinas. I think Margaret Pole is here, and I see the stricken face of Thomas Howard at Henry's shoulder.

I go into my room and I order them to close the shutters and bolt the doors. But it is too late. They have already brought me the worst news of my life; closing the door will not keep it out. I hear a pageboy laugh in the garden near my window and I cannot understand how there can be any joy or gladness left in the world, now that my baby has gone.

And now the courage I have held on to, for all my life, turns out to be a thread, a spider-web, a nothing. In the shadows of my room I plunge deep into the darkness that my mother knew when she lost her son, that Juana could not escape when she lost her husband. I am no different after all. It has only been that, so far, I have never lost someone who was worth more than life itself to me. When Arthur died my heart was broken. But now that my baby is dead, I want nothing but that my heart should cease to beat.

I cannot understand a God who can take him from me. I cannot understand a world that can be so cruel. In the moment that they told me, 'Your Grace, be brave, we have bad news of the prince,' I lost my faith in God. I lost my desire to live. I lost even my ambition to rule England and keep my country safe.

Lady Margaret Pole, who had been in charge of the dead child's nursery, came into the room without knocking, without invitation, and knelt before Queen Katherine, who sat on her chair by the fire, among her ladies, seeing nothing and hearing nothing.

'I have come to beg your pardon though I did nothing wrong,' she said steadily.

Katherine raised her head from her hand. 'What?'

'Your baby died in my care. I have come to beg your pardon. I was not remiss, I swear it. But he is dead. Princess, I am sorry.'

'You are always here,' Katherine said with quiet dislike. 'In my darkest moments, you are always at my side, like bad luck.'

The older woman flinched. 'Indeed, but it is not my wish.'

For the first time in weeks Katherine sat up and looked into the face of another person, saw her eyes, saw the new lines around her mouth, realised that the loss of her baby was not her grief alone. 'Oh God, Margaret,' she said, and pitched forwards.

Margaret Pole caught her and held her. 'Oh God, Katherine,' she said into the queen's hair.

'How could we lose him?'

'God's will. We have to believe it. We have to bow beneath it.'

'But why?'

'Princess, no one knows why one is taken and another spared. D'you remember?' She felt from the shudder that the woman remembered the loss of her husband in this, the loss of her son.

'I never forget. Every day. But why?'

'It is God's will,' Lady Margaret repeated.

'I don't think I can bear it.' Katherine breathed so softly that none of her ladies could hear.

'Oh, Katherine. You will learn to bear it. You can rage or you can weep but in the end, you will learn to bear it.'

Slowly Katherine sat back on her chair; Margaret remained, with easy grace, kneeling on the floor at her feet, handclasped with her friend.

'You will have to teach me courage again,' Katherine whispered.

The older woman shook her head. 'You only have to learn it once,' she said. 'You know, you learned at Ludlow; you are not a woman to be destroyed by sorrow. You will grieve but you will live. You will love. You will conceive another child, this child will live, you will learn again to be happy.'

'I cannot see it,' Katherine said desolately.

'It will come.'

The battle that Katherine had waited for, for so long, came while she was still overshadowed with grief for her baby.

'Great news, the best news in the world!' wrote her father. Wearily, Katherine translated from the code they used in their correspondence and then from Spanish to English. 'I am to lead a crusade against the Moors in Africa. Send me the best of your knights—you who claim to be the new Camelot—and I shall take them to Africa and we will destroy the infidel kingdoms as holy Christian kings.'

Wearily, Katherine took the translated letter to Henry. He was coming off the tennis court, a napkin twisted round his neck, his face flushed. He beamed when he saw her, then at once his look of joy was wiped from his face by a grimace of guilt. At that fleeting expression, at that brief, betraying moment, she knew he had forgotten that their son was dead. He was playing tennis with his friends, he had won, he saw the wife he still loved, he was happy. Joy came as easily to the men of his family as sorrow to the women of hers. She felt a wave of hatred wash over her, so powerful that she could almost taste it in her mouth.

'I have a letter from my father,' she said.

'Oh?' He was all concern. He came towards her and took her arm. She gritted her teeth so that she did not scream: 'Don't touch me!'

'Did he tell you to have courage? Did he write comforting words?'

The clumsiness of the young man was unbearable. She summoned her most tolerant smile. 'No. It is not a personal letter. It is a letter about a crusade. He invites our noblemen and lords to raise regiments and go with him against the Moors.'

'Does he? Oh, does he? What a chance!'

'Not for you,' she said, quelling any idea that Henry might have that he could go to war when they had no son. 'It is just a little expedition.

But my father would welcome Englishmen, and I think they should go.'

'I should think he would.' Henry turned and shouted for his friends, who were hanging back like guilty schoolboys caught having fun.

'Hey! Anyone want to go to war against the Moors?'

A chorus of excited yells answered his holloa.

'I will go!'

'And I will go!'

'Show them how Englishmen fight!' Henry urged them. 'I, myself, will pay the costs of the expedition.'

'I will write to my father that you have eager volunteers,' Katherine said quietly. 'I will go and write to him now.' She turned away and walked quickly towards the doorway. She did not think she could bear to be with them for another moment. These were the men who would have taught her son to ride, who would have been his statesmen, his Privy Council.

In the event, the glorious crusade never happened. The English knights arrived at Cadiz but the crusade never set sail for the Holy Land. Katherine translated letters between Henry and her father in which her father explained that he had not yet raised his troops, that he was not yet ready to leave, and then, one day, she came to Henry with a letter in her hand and her face shocked out of its usual weariness.

'Father writes me the most terrible news.'

'What is happening?' Henry demanded, bewildered. 'See, here, I have just received a letter from an English merchant in Italy. He writes that the French and the Pope are at war.'

'It is true. This is from my father. He says the Pope has declared that the French armies must get out of Italy,' Katherine explained. 'And the Holy Father has put his own papal troops into the field against the French. King Louis has declared that the Pope shall no longer be Pope.'

'How dare he?' Henry demanded, shocked to his core.

'Father says we must forget the crusade and go at once to the aid of the Pope. We must form an alliance against France. King Louis cannot be allowed to take Rome. He must not advance into Italy.'

'He must be mad to think that I would allow it!' Henry exclaimed. 'Would I let the French take Rome? Would I allow a French puppet Pope? Has he forgotten what an English army can do? Does he want another Agincourt?'

'Shall I tell my father we will unite with him against France?' Katherine asked. 'I could write at once.'

He caught her hand and kissed it. For once she did not pull away and he drew her a little closer and put his arm around her waist. 'I'll come with you while you write and we can sign the letter from us both. Thank God that our troops are in Cadiz already,' Henry exclaimed as his good fortune struck him.

Katherine hesitated, a thought forming in her mind. 'It is . . . fortuitous.'

'Lucky,' Henry said buoyantly. 'We are blessed by God.'

'My father will want some benefit for Spain from this.' Katherine introduced the suspicion carefully as they went to her rooms.

'Of course, but you will guard our interests as you always do,' he said.

Slowly, the queen emerged from her grief and started to take an interest in the running of the court and country once more. London was buzzing with the news that Scottish privateers had attacked an English merchant ship. Everyone knew the name of the privateer: he was Andrew Barton, who sailed with letters of authority from King James of Scotland as if the two countries were already at war.

'He has to be stopped,' Katherine said to Henry.

'He does not dare to challenge me!' Henry exclaimed. 'James sends border raiders and pirates against me because he does not dare to face me himself. He is such a hypocrite to promise peace and marry Margaret on one hand and license these raids on the other! I shall write to Margaret and tell her to warn her husband that we cannot accept raids on our shipping. They should keep to their borders too.'

'Yes,' Katherine agreed. 'If we let the Scots rule the seas then we let them command us. This is an island; the seas must belong to us as much as the land or we have no safety.'

'My ships are ready and we sail at midday. I shall capture him alive,' Edward Howard, the Admiral of the Fleet, promised Katherine. She thought he looked very young, as boyish as Henry; but his flair and courage were unquestioned. The Howards traditionally held the post of Lord Admiral, but Edward was proving exceptional. 'If I cannot capture him alive, I shall sink his ship and bring him back dead.'

'For shame on you! A Christian enemy!' she said teasingly, holding out her hand for his kiss.

He looked up, serious for once. 'I promise you, Your Grace, that the Scots are a greater danger to the peace and wealth of this country than the Moors could ever be.'

He saw her wistful smile. 'You are not the first Englishman to tell me that,' she said. 'And I have seen it myself in these last years.'

'It has to be right,' he said. 'In Spain your father and mother never rested until they could dislodge the Moors from the mountains. For us in England, our closest enemy is the Scots. It is they who have to be suppressed and quelled if we are ever to be at peace.'

'Come home safely,' she urged.

Katherine spoke to Thomas Howard, Earl of Surrey, Edward Howard's father, at the end of the Privy Council meeting as the men came out of the king's rooms.

'My lord? Have you heard from Edward?'

The old man beamed at her. 'We had a report this day. He has captured the pirate Andrew Barton with two of his ships.'

'He is a hero!' Katherine said enthusiastically. 'England needs great sailors as much as we need soldiers. We need to rule the seas as the Saracens rule the deserts. We have to drive pirates from the seas and make English ships a constant presence. Is he on his way home?'

'He will bring his ships into London and the pirate in chains with him. We'll try him, and hang him on the quayside. But King James won't like it.'

'Do you think the Scots king means war?' Katherine asked him.

'This is the worst danger to the peace of the kingdom of any in my lifetime,' the older man said honestly. 'We have subdued the Welsh and brought peace to our borders in the west, now we will have to put down the Scots. After them we will have to settle the Irish.'

'They are a separate country, with their own kings and laws,' Katherine demurred.

'So were the Welsh till we defeated them,' he pointed out. 'This is too small a land for three kingdoms. The Scots will have to be yoked into our service.'

'The king thinks that their army would be small and easily defeated,' Katherine remarked.

Howard choked back a laugh. 'His Grace has never been to Scotland,' he said. 'He has never even been to war yet. The Scots are a formidable enemy, whether in pitched battle or a passing raid. They have no laws of chivalry, they fight to win and they fight to the death. We will need to send a powerful force under a skilled commander.'

'Could you do it?' Katherine asked.

'I could try,' he replied honestly. 'I am the best weapon to your hand at the moment, Your Grace.'

'Could the king do it?' she asked quietly.

He smiled at her. 'He's a young man,' he said. 'He lacks nothing for courage. And he is skilled on his horse. But he needs to be seasoned in a few battles before he fights the greatest war of his life—the war for his very kingdom. The king, even though a king, will have to learn.'

'But in the meantime, what can we do to limit the raids of the Scots? Should the border lords be reinforced?'

'Yes, but it is a long border, and hard to keep. King James does not fear an English army led by the king. He does not fear the border lords.'

'Who could make James fear us and keep him in Scotland while we reinforce the border and get ready for war? What could make him delay?'

'Nothing,' he declared, shaking his head. 'There is no one who could hold back James if he is set on war. Except perhaps only the Pope, if he would rule? But who could persuade His Holiness to intervene between two Christian monarchs quarrelling over a pirate's raid and a patch of land? And the Pope has his own worries with the French advancing. Why would His Holiness intervene for us?'

'I don't know what would make the Pope take our side,' said Katherine. 'If only he knew of our need! If only he would use his power to defend us!'

Richard Bainbridge, Cardinal Archbishop of York, happens to be at Rome and is a good friend of mine. I write to him that very night, a friendly letter as between one acquaintance to another far from home, telling him of the news from London, the weather, the prospects for the harvest and the price of wool. Then I tell him of the enmity of the Scottish king, of his wicked licensing of attacks on our shipping and—worst of all—his constant invasions of our northern lands. I tell him that I am so afraid that the king will be forced to defend his lands in the north that he will not be able to come to the aid of the Holy Father in his quarrel with the French king. It would be such a tragedy, I write, if the Pope was left exposed to attack and we could not come to his aid because of the wickedness of the Scots.

What could be more natural than that Richard, my brother in Christ, should take my letter to His Holiness the Pope and say how the whole alliance to save the Eternal City is threatened by this bad neighbourliness?

The Pope, reading my letter to Richard, reads it aright, and writes at once to King James and threatens to excommunicate him if he does not respect the peace and the justly agreed borders of another Christian king. King James, forced to accede to the Pope's wishes, forced to apologise for his incursions, writes a bitter letter to Henry saying that Henry had no right to go running behind his back to the Holy Father.

'I don't know what he is talking about,' Henry complained to Katherine, finding her in the garden playing at catch with her ladies-in-waiting.

'What is he saying? I have never appealed to the Pope. I did not report him. I am no tale-bearer!'

'No, you are not, and so you can tell him,' Katherine said serenely, slipping her hand in his arm and walking away from the women. 'I may have mentioned my concerns to the archbishop and he may have passed them on,' Katherine said casually. 'But you can hardly be blamed if your wife tells her spiritual adviser that she is anxious.'

'Exactly,' Henry said. 'I shall tell him so. And you should not be worried for a moment.'

'Yes. And the main thing is that James knows he cannot attack us with impunity, His Holiness has made a ruling.'

Henry hesitated. 'You did not mean Bainbridge to tell the Pope, did you?'

She peeped a little smile at him. 'Of course,' she said. 'But it still is not you who has complained of James to the Pope.'

'You are a redoubtable enemy. I hope we are never on opposing sides. I should be sure to lose.'

'We never will be,' she said sweetly. 'For I will never be anything but your loyal and faithful wife and queen.'

Spring 1512

It was hard for Henry not to embark in person when the fleet sailed to join King Ferdinand's campaign against the French. It was a glorious start: the ships went out flying the banners of the great houses of England, they were the best equipped, finest arrayed force that had left England in years. Katherine had been busy, supervising the endless work of provisioning the ships, stocking the armouries, equipping the soldiers.

She sent out an expeditionary fleet that was better organised than any that had gone from England before, and she was confident that under her father's command they would defend the Pope, beat the French, and establish the English as major landowners in France once more.

Then there was nothing to do but to wait. The English army were in Fuenterrabia, waiting for the Spanish to join with them for their invasion of southern France. The heat of the summer came on as they kicked their heels, ate badly and drank like thirsty madmen. Katherine alone of Henry's council knew that the heat of midsummer Spain could kill an army as they did nothing but wait for orders. She concealed her fears from Henry and from the council but privately she wrote to her father asking what his plans were.

Her father, riding with his own army, on the move, did not reply.

The summer wore on, Katherine did not write again. In a bitter moment, which she did not even acknowledge to herself, she saw that she was not her father's ally on the chessboard of Europe—she realised that she was nothing more than a pawn in his plan. She did not need to ask her father's strategy; once he had the English army in place and did not use them, she guessed it.

It grew colder in England, but it was still hot in Spain. At last Ferdinand had a use for his allies, but when he sent for them, and ordered that they should spend the winter season on campaign, they refused to answer his call. They mutinied against their own commanders and demanded to go home.

Winter 1512

It came as no surprise to Katherine, nor to the cynics on the council, when the English army came home in dishonoured tatters in December. Lord Dorset, despairing of ever receiving orders and reinforcements from King Ferdinand, confronted by mutinying troops, hungry, weary, and with 2,000 men lost to illness, straggled home in disgrace, as he had taken them out in glory.

'What can have gone wrong?' Henry rushed into Katherine's rooms and waved away her ladies-in-waiting. He could not believe that his force that had gone out so bravely should come home in such disarray. He had letters from his father-in-law complaining of the behaviour of the English allies, he had lost face in Spain, he had lost face with his enemy France. He fled to Katherine as the only person in the world who would share his shock and dismay.

I take his hands. I have been waiting for this since the first moment in the summer when there was no battle plan for the English troops. As soon as they arrived and were not deployed I knew that we had been misled by my father.

I am no fool. I know my father as a commander, and I know him as a man. When he did not fling the English into battle on the day that they arrived, I knew that he had another plan for them, and that plan was hidden from us. He always keeps his men moving, he always keeps them in work and out of mischief.

If the English were left to rot in camp it was because he had need of them just where they were—in camp. He did not care that they were getting sick and lazy. That made me look again at the map and I saw what he was doing. My father kept the English troops dancing on the spot in Fuenterrabia so that the French, alarmed by such a force on their flank, would place their army in defence. Guarding against the English they could not attack my father who, joyously alone and unencumbered, at the head of his troops, marched into the unprotected kingdom of Navarre and so picked up that which he had desired for so long at no expense or danger to himself.

'My dear, your soldiers were not tried and found wanting,' I say to my distressed young husband. 'There is no question as to the courage of the English.'

'He says . . .' He waves the letter at me.

'It doesn't matter what he says,' I say patiently. 'You have to look at what he does.'

The face he turns to me is so hurt that I cannot bring myself to tell him that my father has used him, played him for a fool, used his army, used even me, to win himself Navarre.

'My father has taken his fee before his work, that is all,' I say robustly. 'God forgive me for saying it, but my father is a masterly double-dealer. If we are going to make treaties with him we will have to learn to be as clever as him. He made a treaty with us and said he would be our partner in war against France, but all we have done is win him Navarre, by sending our army out and home again.'

'They have been shamed. I have been shamed.'

He cannot understand what I am trying to tell him. 'Your army has done exactly what my father wanted them to do. In that sense, it has been a most successful campaign.'

'They did nothing! He complains to me that they are good for nothing!'

'They pinned down the French with that nothing. Think of that! The French have lost Navarre.'

'I want to court-martial Dorset!'

'Yes, we can do so, if you wish. But the main thing is that we still have our army, we have lost only two thousand men, and my father is our ally. He owes us for this year. Next year you can go back to France and this time Father will fight for us; not us for him.'

'He says he will conquer Guienne for me, he says it as if I cannot do it myself! He speaks to me as a weakling with a useless force!'

'Good,' I say, surprising him. 'Let him conquer Guienne for us.'

'He wants us to pay him.'

'Let us pay for it. What does it matter as long as my father is on our side when we go to war with the French? If he wins Guienne for us then that is to our good; if he does not, but just distracts the French when we invade in the north from Calais, then that is all to the good as well.'

For a moment he gapes at me, his head spinning. Then he sees what I mean. 'He pins down the French for us, as we advance, just as we did for him?'

'Exactly.'

He is amazed. 'Did your father teach you how to do this—to plan ahead as if a campaign were a chessboard, and you have to move the pieces around?'

I shake my head. 'Not on purpose. But you cannot live with a man like my father without learning how a general thinks.'

'But what made you think of invading from Calais?'

'Oh, my dear, where else would England invade France? My father can fight in the south for us, and we will see if he can win us Guienne. You can be sure that he will do so if it is in his interest. And, at any rate, while he is doing that, the French will not be able to defend Normandy.'

Henry's confidence comes rushing back to him. 'I shall go myself,' he declares. 'Your father will not be able to criticise the command of the English army if I do it myself.'

For a moment I hesitate. Even playing at war is a dangerous game, and while we do not have an heir, Henry is precious beyond belief. But I will never keep my hold on him if I coop him up as his grandmother did. Henry will have to learn the nature of war, and I know that he will be safest in a campaign commanded by my father, who wants to keep me on my throne as much as I want it; and safer by far facing the chivalrous French than the murderous Scots. Besides, I have a plan that is a secret. And it requires him to be out of the country.

'Yes, you shall,' I say. 'And you shall have the best armour and strongest horse and handsomest guard of any king who takes the field.'

'Thomas Howard says that we should abandon our battle against France until we have suppressed the Scots.'

I shake my head. 'You shall fight in France in the alliance of the three kings,' I assure him. 'It will be a mighty war, one that everyone will remember. And if the Scots invade the north when you go to war, they are so unimportant that even I could command an expedition against them while you go to the real war in France.'

'You?' he asks.

'Why not? Are we not a king and queen come young to our thrones in our power? Who should deny us?'

'No one! I shall not be diverted,' Henry declares. 'I shall conquer in France and you shall guard us against the Scots.'

'I will,' I promise him. This is just what I want.

Spring 1513

The English preparations for the war against France went on briskly with Katherine and her assistant Thomas Wolsey working daily on the muster rolls for the towns, the gathering of provisions for the army, the forging of armour and the training of volunteers to march, prepare to attack, and retreat, on command. Wolsey observed that the queen had two muster rolls, almost as if she was preparing for two armies. 'Are you thinking we will have to fight the Scots as well as the French?' he asked her.

'I am sure of it.'

'The Scots will snap at us, as soon as our troops leave for France,' he said. 'We shall have to reinforce the borders.'

'I hope to do more than that,' was all she said.

'His Grace the king will not be distracted from his war with France,' he pointed out.

She did not confide in him, as he wanted her to do. 'I know. We must make sure he has a great force to take to Calais. He must not be distracted by anything.'

Handsome young Edward Howard, in a new cloak of dark sea-blue, came to take leave of Katherine as the fleet prepared to set sail with orders to blockade the French in port, or engage them if possible on the high seas.

'God bless you,' said the queen, and heard her voice a little shaken with emotion. 'God bless you, Edward Howard, and may your luck go with you as it always does.'

He bowed low. 'I have the luck of a man favoured by a great queen who serves a great country,' he said. 'It is an honour to serve my queen.'

Katherine smiled. All of Henry's friends shared a tendency to think themselves into the pages of a romance. Camelot was never very far away from their minds. Katherine had served as the lady of the courtly myth ever since she had been queen. She liked Edward Howard more than any of the other young men. His genuine gaiety and his open affection endeared him to everyone, and he had a passion for the navy and the ships under his command that commended him to Katherine, who saw the safety of England could only be assured by holding the seas.

'You are my knight, and I trust you to bring glory to your name and to mine,' she said to him, and saw the gleam of pleasure in his eyes as he dropped his dark head to kiss her hand.

'I shall bring you home some French ships,' he promised her. 'I have brought you Scots pirates, now you shall have French galleons.'

'I have need of them,' she said earnestly.

It is the feast of St George and we are still waiting for news from the English fleet, when a messenger comes in, his face grave. Henry is at my side as the young man tells us, at last, of the sea battle that Edward was so certain he should win, that we were so certain would prove the power of our ships over the French. With his father at my side I learn the fate of Edward, my knight Edward, who had been so sure that he would bring home a French galleon to the Pool of London.

He pinned down the French fleet in Brest and they did not dare to come out. He was too impatient to wait for them to make the next move, too young to play a long game. He went into battle like a boy who has no fear of death.

With the English fleet unable to go forwards and the French sitting snug in harbour, he took a handful of rowing boats and threw them in, under the French guns. Edward himself led the boarding party onto the flagship of the French admiral—an act of extraordinary daring—and almost at once his men failed him. They jumped down from the deck of the French ship into their own rowing boats, shot ringing around them like hailstones. They cast off, leaving him fighting like a madman, his back to the mast, hacking around him with his sword, hopelessly outnumbered. He made a dash to the side and if a boat had been there, he might have dropped down to it. But they had gone. He tore the gold whistle of his office from his neck and flung it far out into the sea, so that the French would not have it, and then he turned and fought them again. He went down, still fighting, a dozen swords stabbed him, he was still fighting as he slipped and fell, supporting himself with one arm, his sword still parrying. Then, a hungry blade slashed at his sword arm, and he was fighting no more. They could have stepped back and honoured his courage; but they did not.

They threw his body into the sea, they cared so little for him, these French soldiers, these so-called Christians. Then they realised that it was Edward Howard, my Edward Howard, the admiral of the English navy, and the son of one of the greatest men in England, and they were sorry that they had thrown him overboard like a dead dog. Not for honour—oh, not them—but because they could have ransomed him to his family and God knows we would have paid well to have sweet Edward restored to us. They sent the sailors out in boats with hooks to drag his body up again. They gutted his corpse like a carp, they cut out his heart, salted it down like cod, they stole his clothes for souvenirs and sent them to the French court. The butchered scraps that were left of him they sent home to his father and to me.

This savage story reminds me of Hernando Perez del Pulgar who led such a desperately daring raid into the Alhambra. If they had caught him they would have killed him, but I don't think even the Moors would have cut out his heart for their amusement. They would have acknowledged him as a great enemy, a man to be honoured. They would have returned his body to us with one of their grand chivalric gestures. They were Moors; but they had a grace that these Christians utterly lack. When I think of these Frenchmen it makes me ashamed to call the Moors 'barbarians'.

Summer 1513

The death of Edward Howard made Katherine work even harder for the preparations of the English army to leave for Calais. Henry might be going to play-act a war, but he would use real shot and cannon, swords and arrows, and she wanted them to be well made and their aim to be true. She had known the realities of war all her life, but with the death of Edward Howard, Henry now saw, for the first time, that it was not like in a storybook, it was not like a joust. A well-favoured, brilliant young man like Edward could go out in the sunshine and come home, butchered into pieces, in a cart. To his credit, Henry did not waver in his courage as this truth came home to him.

They sent the first part of the army to Calais in May, and Henry prepared to follow them with the second batch of troops in June. Katherine and Henry rode slowly through England from Greenwich to Dover for Henry's embarkation. The towns turned out to feast them and muster their men as they went through. Henry and Katherine had matching great white horses and Katherine rode astride, her long blue gown spread out all around. Henry, riding at her side, looked magnificent, taller than any other man in the ranks, stronger than most, golden-haired and smiling.

In the mornings when they rode out of a town they would both wear armour: matching suits of silver and gilt. Katherine wore only a breast-plate and a helmet, made from finely beaten metal and chased with gold patterns. Henry wore full armour from toes to fingertips every day, whatever the heat. He rode with his visor up and his blue eyes dancing, and a gold circlet round his helmet. The people shouted 'God Bless the King!' and 'God Bless the Queen!' When they left a town, with the troops marching behind them, and the bowmen before them, the towns-people would crowd the sides of the road to see them ride by, and they threw rose petals and rosebuds on the road in front of the horses.

They took nearly two weeks to get to Dover and the time was not wasted, for they gathered supplies and recruited troops in every village. Every man in the land wanted to be in the army to defend England against France. The whole country was united in wanting revenge against the French. And the whole country was confident that with the young king at the head of a young army, it could be done.

Thanks to Katherine and Thomas Wolsey the arrangements for the embarkation were timed to perfection. Henry's ships—400 of them, brightly painted, with pennants flying, sails ready-rigged—were waiting to take the troops to France. Henry's own ship, blazing in gold leaf with the red dragon flying at its stern, bobbed at the dock. His royal guard, superbly trained, their new livery of Tudor green and white, were paraded on the quay, his two suits of gold-inlaid armour were packed on board, his specially trained white horses were in their stalls. The preparations were as meticulous as those of the most elaborate of court masques and Katherine knew that for many of the young men, they were looking forward to war as they did to a court entertainment.

Everything was ready for Henry to embark and sail for France when in a simple ceremony, on the strand at Dover, he took the great seal of state and before them all invested Katherine as regent in his place, Governor of the Realm and Captain General of the English forces for home defence.

I make sure that my face is grave and solemn when he names me Regent of England, and I kiss his hand and then I kiss him full on the mouth to wish him God speed. But as his ship is taken in tow by the barges, crosses the bar of the harbour, and then unfurls her sails to catch the wind and sets out for France, I could sing aloud for joy. I am more than Princess of Wales, I am more than Queen of England, I am Governor of the Realm, I am Captain General of the army, this is my country indeed, and I am sole ruler.

And the first thing I will do—indeed, perhaps the only thing I will do with the power vested in me, the only thing that I must do with this God-given chance—is defeat the Scots.

As soon as Katherine arrived at Richmond Palace she gave Thomas Howard, Edward's younger brother, his orders to take the cannon from the armouries in the Tower and set sail with the whole English fleet, north to Newcastle to defend the borders against the Scots. He was not the admiral that his brother had been but he was a steady young man and she thought she could rely on him to do his part to deliver the vital weapons to the north.

Every day brought Katherine news from France by messengers that she had already posted along the way. Wolsey had strict instructions to report back to the queen the progress of the war. She knew that Henry would give her an optimistic account. It was not all good news. The English army had arrived in France, there was much excitement in Calais and feasting and celebrations. But the Emperor Maximilian failed to muster his own army to support the English. Instead, pleading poverty but swearing his enthusiasm to the cause, he came to the young prince to offer his sword and his service.

It was clearly a heady moment for Henry, who had not yet even heard a shot fired in anger, to have the Holy Roman Emperor offering his services, overwhelmed by the young prince.

On the advice of Maximilian, the English army laid siege to Therouanne—a town which the Holy Roman Emperor had long desired, but of no tactical value to England—and Henry, safely distanced from the short-range guns on the walls of the little town, walked alone through his camp at midnight, spoke comforting words to the soldiers on watch, and was allowed to fire his first cannon.

The Scots, who had been waiting only until England was defenceless with king and army in France, declared war against the English and started their own march south. Wolsey wrote with alarm to Katherine, asking her if she needed the return of some of Henry's troops to face this new threat. Katherine replied that she thought she could defend against a border skirmish, and started a fresh muster of troops from every town in the country, using the lists she had already prepared.

She commanded the assembly of the London militia and went out in her armour, on her white horse, to inspect them before they started their march north.

I draw a silent breath as I look at myself in the mirror. I look so like my mother in my armour that it could be her reflection, standing so still and proud, with her hair caught back from her face, and her eyes shining as bright as the burnished gilt on her breastplate; alive at the prospect of battle, gleaming with joy at her confidence in victory.

'Are you not afraid?' Maria de Salinas asks me quietly.

'No.' I speak the truth. 'I have spent all my life waiting for this moment. I am a queen, and the daughter of a queen who had to fight for her country. This is a time for a queen who has the heart and stomach of a man. I am that queen. I shall ride out with my army.'

There is a little flurry of dismay. 'Ride out? But isn't it dangerous?'

I reach for my helmet. 'I shall ride with them north to meet the Scots. And if the Scots break through I shall fight them. And when I take the field against them I shall be there until I defeat them.'

'But what about us?'

'Three of you will come with me to bear me company and the rest of you will stay here. Those who come with me will behave as soldiers in the field.'

There is an outburst of dismay, which I avoid by heading for the door.

The troops are drawn up before the palace. I ride slowly down the lines, letting my eyes rest on one face and then another. I have seen my father do this, and my mother. My father told me that every soldier should know that he is

valued, should feel himself to be an essential part of the body of the army.
When I have ridden past every single one of the five hundred, I go to the front
of the army and I take off my helmet so that they can see my face. I am not
like a Spanish princess now, with my hair hidden and my face veiled. I am a
bareheaded, barefaced English queen. I raise my voice so that every one of
them can hear me.

'Men of England,' I say. 'You and I will go together to fight the Scots, and
neither of us will falter nor fail. This is not a quarrel of our making, this is a
wicked invasion by James of Scotland; breaking his own treaty, insulting his
own English wife. An ungodly invasion condemned by the Pope himself. He
has planned this for years. He has waited, like a coward, thinking to find us
weak. But he is mistaken for we are powerful now. We will win. I can assure
you of this because I know God's will in this matter. He is with us.'

There is a great roar of approval and I turn and smile to one side and then
the other, so that they can all see my pleasure in their courage. So that they
can all see that I am not afraid.

'Good. Forward march,' I say simply to the commander at my side and the
army turns and marches out of the parade ground.

As Katherine's first army of defence marched north under the Earl of
Surrey, the messengers rode desperately south to London to bring her
the news she had been expecting. James's army had crossed the Scottish
border and was advancing through the border country, recruiting soldiers and stealing food as they went.

'A border raid?' Katherine asked, knowing it would not be.

The man shook his head. 'My lord told me to tell you that the French
king has promised the Scots king that he will recognise him if he wins
this battle against us.'

'Recognise him? As what?'

'As King of England.'

He expected her to cry out in indignation or in fear, but she merely
nodded, as if it were something else to consider.

'How many men?' Katherine demanded of the messenger.

He shook his head. 'I can't say for certain.'

'How many do you think?'

'I am afraid sixty thousand, Your Grace, perhaps more.'

'How many more? Perhaps?'

He paused. She rose from her chair and went to the window. 'Please,
tell me what you think,' she said. 'You do me no service if, thanks to
you, trying to spare me distress, I go out with an army and find before
me an enemy in greater force than I expected.'

'One hundred thousand, I would think,' he said quietly.

He expected her to gasp in horror but when he looked at her she was smiling. 'Oh, I'm not afraid of that.'

Katherine's men, all 40,000 of them, straggled along the road behind the royal guard, weighed down by their weapons and sacks of food in the late-summer sunshine. Katherine, at the head of the train, rode her white horse where everyone could see her, with the royal standard over her head, so that the men should know her now, on the march, and recognise her later, in battle. She kept monastic hours, rising at dawn to hear Mass, taking Communion at noon, and going to bed at dusk, waking at midnight to say her prayers for the safety of the realm, for the safety of the king, and for herself.

Messengers passed constantly between Katherine's army and the force commanded by Thomas Howard, Earl of Surrey. Their plan was that Surrey should engage with the Scots at the first chance, anything to stop their rapid and destructive advance southwards. If Surrey were defeated then the Scots would come on and Katherine would meet them with her force, and fling them into defence of the southern counties of England. If the Scots cut through them then Katherine and Surrey had a final plan for the defence of London. They would regroup, summon a citizen's army, throw up earthworks round the City and if all else failed, retreat to the Tower, which could be held for long enough for Henry to reinforce them from France.

We are sixty miles out of London, at Buckingham. This is good speed for an army on the march, they tell me it is tremendous speed for an English army; they are notorious for dawdling on the road. I am tired, but not exhausted. The excitement and—to be honest—the fear in each day is keeping me like a hound on a leash, always eager, straining to get ahead and start the hunt.

And now I have a secret. Each afternoon, when I dismount from my horse, I get down from the saddle and first thing, before anything else, I go into the necessary house, or tent, or wherever I can be alone, and I pull up my skirts and look at my linen. I am waiting for my monthly course, and it is the second month that it has failed to come. My hope, a strong, sweet hope, is that when Henry sailed to France he left me with child.

I will tell no one, not even my women. I can imagine the outcry if they knew I was riding every day, and preparing for battle when I am with child, or even in hopes of a child. I dare not tell them, for in all truth, I do not dare do anything that might tilt the balance in this campaign against us. Of course, nothing could be more important than a son for England—except this one thing:

holding England for that son to inherit. I have to grit my teeth on the risk I am taking, and take it anyway. I have to defeat the Scots, I have to be a great general. When that duty is done, I can be a woman again.

At night, I have news from Surrey that the Scots are encamped on a strong ridge, drawn up in battle order at a place called Flodden. He sends me a plan of the site, showing the Scots camped on high ground, commanding the view to the south. One glance at the map tells me that the English should not attack uphill against the heavily armed Scots. The Scots archers will be shooting downhill and then the Highlanders will charge down on our men. No army could face an attack like that.

'Tell your master he is to send out spies and find a way round the back of the Scots to come upon them from the north,' I say to the messenger, staring at the map. 'Tell him my advice is that he makes a feint, leaves enough men before the Scots to pin them down, but marches the rest away, as if he is heading north. If he is lucky, they will give chase and you will have them on open ground. Is it good ground? He has drawn a stream on this sketch.'

'It is boggy ground,' the man confirms. 'We may not be able to cross it.'

I bite my lip. 'It's the only way that I can see,' I say. 'Tell him this is my advice but not my command. He is commander in the field, he must make his own judgment.'

10th September 1513

'Your Grace!' a pageboy came dashing into Katherine's tent, bobbed a most inadequate, hurried bow. 'A messenger, with news of the battle! A messenger from Lord Surrey.'

Katherine whirled round. 'Send him in!'

The man was already in the room, the dirt of the battle still on him, but with the beam of a man bringing good news, great news.

'Yes?' Katherine demanded, breathless with hope.

'Your Grace has conquered,' he said. 'The King of Scotland lies dead, twenty Scottish lords lie with him, bishops, earls, and abbots too. It is a defeat they will never rise up from. Half of their great men have died in a single day.'

He saw the colour drain from her face and then she suddenly grew rosy. 'We have won?'

'You have won,' he confirmed. 'The earl said to tell you that your men, raised and trained and armed by you, have done what you ordered they should do. It is your victory, and you have made England safe.'

Her hand went at once to her belly, under the metal curve of the breastplate. 'We are safe,' she said.

He nodded. 'He sent you this . . .'

He held out for her a surcoat, terribly torn and slashed and stained with blood.

'This is?'

'The coat of the King of Scotland. He is dead, the Scots are defeated. You have done what no English king since Edward the First could do. You have made England safe from Scottish invasion.'

'Write out a report for me,' she said decisively. 'Dictate it to the clerk. Everything you know, and everything that my lord Surrey said. I must write to the king.'

'Lord Surrey asked . . .'

'Yes?'

'Should he advance into Scotland and lay it waste? We could destroy them, they are utterly at our mercy.'

'Of course,' she said at once, then she paused. It was the answer that any monarch in Europe would have given. A troublesome neighbour, an inveterate enemy lay weakened. Every king in Christendom would have advanced and taken revenge.

'No. No, wait a moment.'

She turned away from him and went to the doorway of her tent. Outside, the men were preparing for another night on the road, far from their homes. There were little cook-fires all around the camp, torches burning, the smell of cooking and dung and sweat in the air. It was the very scent of Katherine's childhood, a childhood spent for the first seven years in a state of constant warfare against an enemy who was driven backwards and backwards and finally into slavery, exile and death.

Think, I say to myself fiercely. Think with a hard brain, a soldier's brain. Think as a queen. My enemy is defeated, the country lies open before me, their king is dead, their queen is a young fool of a girl and my sister-in-law. I can cut this country into pieces. Any commander of any experience would destroy them now and leave them destroyed for a whole generation. My father would not hesitate; my mother would have given the order already.

I check myself. They were wrong, my mother and father. Finally, I say the unsayable, unthinkable thing. Soldiers of genius they may have been, convinced they certainly were, Christian kings they were called—but they were wrong. It has taken me all my life to learn this.

A state of constant warfare is a two-edged sword, it cuts both the victor and the defeated. If we pursue the Scots now, we will triumph, we can lay the country waste, we can destroy them for generations to come. But all that grows on waste are rats and pestilence. They would recover in time, they would come against us. Their children would come against my children and the savage battle would have to be fought all over again. Hatred breeds hatred. My mother and father drove the Moors overseas, but everyone knows that by doing so they won only one battle in a war that will never cease until Christians and Muslims are prepared to live side by side in peace. War does not answer war, war does not finish war. The only ending is peace.

'Get me a fresh messenger,' Katherine said over her shoulder, and waited till the man came. 'You are to go to my lord Surrey and tell him I give him thanks for this great news of a wonderful victory. You are to tell him that he is to let the Scots soldiers surrender their arms and they are to go in peace. I myself will write to the Scots queen and promise her peace if she will be our good sister and good neighbour. We are victorious, we shall be gracious. We shall make this victory a lasting peace, not a passing battle and an excuse for savagery.'

The man bowed and left. Katherine turned to the soldier. 'Go and get yourself some food,' she said. 'You can tell everyone that we have won a great battle and that we shall go back to our homes knowing that we can live at peace.'

She went to her little table and drew her writing box towards her. The ink was corked in a tiny glass bottle, the quill especially cut down to fit the small case. The paper and sealing wax were to hand. Katherine drew a sheet of paper towards her. She wrote a greeting to her husband, she told him she was sending him the coat of the dead Scots king.

I pause. With this great victory I can go back to London, rest and prepare for the birth of the child that I am sure I am carrying. I want to tell Henry that I am once again with child; but I want to write to him alone. This letter—like every letter between us—will be half-public. He never opens his own letters, he always gets a clerk to open them and read them for him, he rarely writes his own replies. Then I remember that I told him that if Our Lady ever blessed me with a child again I would go at once to her shrine at Walsingham to give thanks. If he remembers this, it can serve as our code. I shall have told him the secret, that we will have a child, that we may have a son. I smile and start to write, knowing that he will understand what I mean, knowing what joy this letter will bring him.

I make an end, praying God to send you home shortly, for without no joy can here be accomplished, and for the same I pray, and now go to Our Lady at Walsingham, that I promised so long ago to see.
Your humble wife and true servant, Katherine

OUR LADY OF WALSINGHAM

Autumn 1513

BELOVED, BELOVED, I have done it. I sent the coat of the Scots king to Henry and I made sure to emphasise that it is his victory, not mine. But it is yours. It is yours because when I came to you and to your country, my mind filled with fears about the Moors, it was you who taught me that the danger here was the Scots. Then life taught me a harder lesson, beloved: it is better to forgive an enemy than destroy him. If we had Moorish physicians, astronomers, mathematicians in this country we would be the better for it. The time may come when we also need the courage and the skills of the Scots. Perhaps my offer of peace will mean that they will forgive us for the battle of Flodden.

I have everything I ever wanted—except you. I have won a victory for this kingdom that will keep it safe for a generation. I have conceived a child and I feel certain that this baby will live. If he is a boy I shall call him Arthur for you. If she is a girl, I shall call her Mary. I am Queen of England, I have the love of the people and Henry will make a good husband and a good man.

I sit back on my heels and close my eyes so the tears should not run down my cheeks. 'The only thing I lack is you, beloved. Always you. Always you. Wait for me in the garden,' I whisper. 'I will come to you. I will come one day soon. In the garden, when my work here is done.'

BLACKFRIARS HALL

The Papal Legate sitting as a court to hear the King's Great Matter

June 1529

WORDS HAVE WEIGHT, something once said cannot be unsaid, meaning is like a stone dropped into a pool; the ripples will spread and you cannot know what bank they wash against.

I once said, 'I love you, I will love you for ever,' to a young man in the night. I once said, 'I promise.' That promise, made twenty-seven years ago to satisfy a *dying boy, to fulfil the will of God, to satisfy my mother and—to tell truth—my own ambition, that word comes back to me like ripples washing to the rim of a marble basin and then eddying back again to the centre.*

I knew I would have to answer for my lies before God. I never thought that I would have to answer to the world. I never thought that the world could interrogate me for something that I had promised for love, something whispered in secret. And so, in my pride, I never have answered for it. Instead, I held to it.

And so, I believe, would any woman in my position.

Henry's new lover, Elizabeth Boleyn's girl, my maid-in-waiting, turns out to be the one that I knew I had to fear: the one who has an ambition that is even greater than mine. She does not desire Henry as a man—I have seen his lovers come and go and I have learned to read them like an easy storybook. This one desires not my husband, but my throne. She has had much work to find her way to it, but she is persistent and determined. I think I knew, from the moment that she had his ear, his secrets, and his confidence, that in time she would find her way to my lie. And when she found it, she would feast on it.

The usher calls out, 'Katherine of Aragon, Queen of England, come into court'; and there is a token silence, for they expect no answer. There are no lawyers waiting to help me there, I have prepared no defence. I have made it clear that I do not recognise the court. They expect to go on without me. Indeed, the usher is just about to call the next witness . . .

But I answer.

My men throw open the double doors of the hall that I know so well and I walk in, my head up, as fearless as I have been all my life. The regal canopy is in gold, over at the far end of the hall with my husband, my betraying, unfaithful husband in his ill-fitting crown on his throne sitting beneath it.

On a stage below him are the two cardinals, also canopied with cloth of gold, seated in golden chairs with golden cushions. That betraying slave Wolsey, red-faced in his red cardinal's robe, failing to meet my eye, as well he might; and that false friend Campeggio. Their three faces, the king and his two procurers, are mirrors of utter dismay.

They thought they had so distressed and confused me, separated me from my friends and destroyed me, that I would not come. They thought I would sink into despair like my mother, or into madness like my sister. They are gambling on the fact that they have frightened me and threatened me and taken my child from me and done everything they can do to break my heart. They never dreamed that I have the courage to stalk in before them, and stand before them, shaking with righteousness, to face them all.

Fools, they forget who I am. They are advised by that Boleyn girl who has never seen me in armour, driven on by her who never knew my mother, did not know my father. She knows me as Katherine, the old Queen of England, devout, plump, dull. She has no idea that inside, I am still Catalina, the young Infanta of Spain. I am a princess born and trained to fight. I am a woman who has fought for every single thing I hold, and I will fight, and I will hold, and I will win.

They did not foresee what I would do to protect myself, and my daughter's inheritance. She is Mary, my Mary, named by Arthur: my beloved daughter, Mary. Would I let her be put aside for some bastard got on a Boleyn?

That is their first mistake.

I ignore the cardinals completely. I ignore the clerks on the benches before them, the scribes with their long rolls of parchment making the official record of this travesty. I ignore the court, the city, even the people who whisper my name with loving voices. Instead, I look at no one but Henry.

I know Henry, I know him better than anyone else in the world does. I studied him when he was a boy, when he was a child of ten who came to meet me and tried to persuade me to give him a Barbary stallion. I knew him through the eyes of his brother, who said—and rightly—that he was a child who had been spoilt by too much indulgence and would be a spoilt man, and a danger to us all. I knew him as a youth, and I won my throne by pandering to his vanity. I was the greatest prize he could desire and I let him win me. I knew him as a man as vain and greedy as a peacock when I gave to him the credit for my war: the greatest victory ever won by England.

At Arthur's request I told the greatest lie a woman has ever told, and I will tell it to the very grave. I am an Infanta of Spain, I do not give a promise and fail to keep it. Arthur, my beloved, asked me for an oath on his deathbed and I gave it to him. He asked me to say that we had never been lovers and he commanded me to marry his brother and be queen. I did everything I promised him, I was constant to my promise. Nothing in these years has shaken my faith that it is God's will that I should be Queen of England, and that I shall be Queen of England until I die. No one could have saved England from the Scots but me—Henry was too young and too inexperienced to take an army into the field. He would have lost the battle and died at Flodden and his sister Margaret would have been Queen of England in my place. It did not happen because I did not allow it to happen.

I do not regret the lie. I held to it, and I made everyone else hold to it, whatever doubts they may have had. As Henry learned more of women, as Henry learned more of me, he knew, as surely as he had known on our wedding night, that it was a lie, I was no virgin for him. But in all our twenty years of marriage together, he found the courage to challenge me only once, at the very beginning; and I walk into the court on the great gamble that he will never have the courage to challenge me again, not even now.

I walk into court with my entire case staked on his weakness. I believe that when I stand before him, and he is forced to meet my eyes, he will not dare to say that I was no virgin when I came to him, that I was Arthur's wife and Arthur's lover before I was ever his. His vanity will not allow him to say that I loved Arthur with a true passion and he loved me. That in truth, I will live and die as Arthur's wife and Arthur's lover, and thus Henry's marriage to me can be rightfully dissolved.

'Katherine of Aragon, Queen of England, come into court,' the usher repeats stupidly, as the echo of the doors banging behind me reverberates in the shocked courtroom, and everyone can see that I am already in court, standing like a stocky fighter before the throne.

It is me they call for, by this title. It was my dying husband's hope, my mother's wish and God's will that I should be Queen of England; and for them and for the country, I will be Queen of England until I die.

'Katherine of Aragon, Queen of England, come into court!'

This is me. This is my moment. This is my battle cry.

I step forwards.

PHILIPPA GREGORY

'I think that the reason for my devotion to history is my belief that my own life and the history of my family is partly determined by, and reflects, the historical events of our times,' says Philippa Gregory. 'I was writing *The Constant Princess* at a time of increased tension between Christian and Muslim during the Iraq War and it crystallised for me how history lives so powerfully in the modern world, and how we can learn from the past—but only if we know about it. My hope is that *The Constant Princess* will make readers think about the long struggle between these two religions, and how fundamentally similar they are in their humanity. We would not have our science, arts and civilisation if it were not for the Muslim scientists, artists and philosophers. Equally, they would not have established their societies without the Greeks. The Crusades, at the time of Katherine of Aragon's childhood, brought the end of the peace that the Muslim kings had established in Spain. Their vision had been that all the 'people of the book'; Jews, Christians and Muslims could live together in peace. Right now we are experiencing great difficulty with that vision, but I believe that the vision is right and that we can live together with mutual respect. Isabella of Spain would have disagreed, but I think her daughter Katherine of Aragon learned to love tolerance.'

Philippa Gregory is meticulous in her research and always visits the places she writes about. 'The Alhambra Palace, where Katherine was raised, is fabulous. The Palace is, in Moorish tradition, unassuming from the outside. The entrance door is small, the inner hall modest. The beauty of the place unfolds

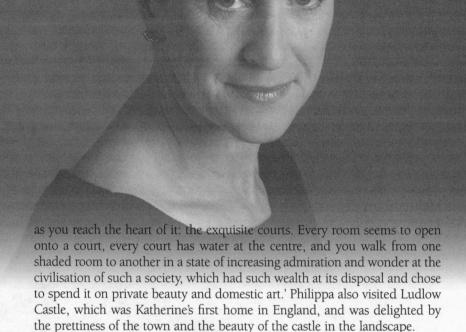

as you reach the heart of it: the exquisite courts. Every room seems to open onto a court, every court has water at the centre, and you walk from one shaded room to another in a state of increasing admiration and wonder at the civilisation of such a society, which had such wealth at its disposal and chose to spend it on private beauty and domestic art.' Philippa also visited Ludlow Castle, which was Katherine's first home in England, and was delighted by the prettiness of the town and the beauty of the castle in the landscape.

It was during one of her research trips to The Gambia for an earlier novel, *A Respectable Trade*, that Philippa donated £300 for a well to be built in a local school. Thus began Gardens for The Gambia, a charity that Philippa set up in 1993. 'The little project in The Gambia just keeps on going. It is one of my greatest joys and one of the things I am most proud of. In The Gambia we have now put wells into more than sixty very poor local primary schools and thousands of children have had a better education and been better fed because of the work they themselves have done in our gardens.'

So where next for Philippa Gregory? 'I'm just off on a three-week book tour in America and then on to the next book.' Will if feature the Tudors? I asked her. 'Oh, yes, I think so. Whenever I think I have finished with Henry VIII, I find other characters that I just have to explore!'

Jane Eastgate

Recipes for a Perfect Marriage

Kate Kerrigan

As Tressa learned to cook at her Irish

grandmother's elbow, and picked freshly

grown vegetables at her grandfather's side,

she would bask in the warmth of their love

for one another, and marvel at the effortless

devotion between them. To her it always seemed

they had the perfect marriage.

Only now, facing the prospect of tying

the knot herself and haunted by doubt,

does Tressa begin to discover more about

her grandparents' relationship.

Prologue

THE HEART OF A RECIPE, what makes it work, is a mystery. Taste is such a personal thing and yet the right recipe can open a person's senses to a food they thought they didn't like. Then again, you can put all the right ingredients together, follow the instructions exactly and still have a disaster on your hands.

That's how it has always been with me and my Grandma Bernadine's brown bread. I would do exactly as she showed me, but it would always come out a little too crumbly, or doughy, or hard.

'You're too fussy,' she'd say. 'Put some jam on and just eat it anyway. It'll be different again tomorrow.'

And it was always different. But it was never right.

Like my marriage to Dan.

They say you just *know* the man you are going to marry. That's how it's supposed to work. You date guys, sleep with them, live with them. Then one day you meet this man and you just know he is 'The One'. He's different from everyone else you have ever met. You feel happier, more special, more alive when you are with him. So you get married.

For two weeks you are Barbie and Ken. There's a big show-off wedding in the Plaza, and you wear a white meringue of a dress even though you are over thirty. You spend what should be the down payment for your first home on fourteen days in the Caribbean.

Then, when you get your 'Ken' home, you realise he was an impulse buy. You wanted the 'married' label so badly that you didn't think it through, and now he doesn't look as good as he did under the spangly lights of singledom. Although you convinced yourself he'd be suitable for

195

everyday use, you now find him irritating. Everything he does and everything he says makes you scream inside.

You are ashamed of having made such a terrible mistake. You know that this silent torture you are living with is entirely your own fault for marrying him when you didn't really love him. Now that you think back on it, did you ever love him at all or was it all just about you desperately wanting to get married? Because surely love is too strong to allow these petty everyday annoyances to turn into hatred? Love is bigger than this. Love doesn't make mistakes. Not real love. Not the kind of love that makes you marry someone.

By the seventh week the statistic that one in four marriages ends in divorce cheers you and you have decided that six months is a respectable amount of time to be seen to be trying to make it work.

Except that you know you haven't. Tried, that is. And you can't help thinking that perhaps you are just part of a generation of women who find marriage a challenging and difficult state of being.

Or perhaps there is no universal group. In which case I am just a woman who married the wrong guy and is trying to find a way out.

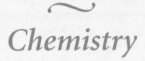

Chemistry

It either works or it doesn't work

Gooseberry Jam

Jam, in itself, is not difficult to make, but the quality of the fruit is important and key to this is when you pick it. Fruit contains its own thickening agent, pectin, which is only present in the fruit when it is just ripe. Too early and the fruit will thicken but taste sour; too late and the fruit will be sweet, but the jam runny and weak.

Gooseberries are ideal because they grow wild and in abundance in this part of the country. Add 4 lb sugar to 3 lb gooseberries and boil them hard in a metal pot with one pint of water. It is important not to turn the heat down; the fruit must keep boiling throughout the process, otherwise the jam will be no good. To check if the jam is ready, decant a spoonful onto a cold plate. As it starts to cool, gently push to one side with a spoon. If it wrinkles on the top, it is ready. Put into jars sterilised with boiling water and seal immediately.

Manhattan, New York: 2004

JAM IS SO SIMPLE to make—just fruit, sugar and water—yet the success of it hinges on chemistry, which is quite tricky to control. The jam has to be heated to a ferocious boil, then kept there for just the right amount of time, until it is ready to solidify.

If the heat is not right to start with, the thickening process will never kick off. If it over-boils, the jam becomes cloying and thick. Then sometimes you can have the best-quality ingredients, apply just the right amount of heat and, for some reason, the chemistry just never kicks in at all. Sound familiar?

Dan is an ordinary guy. I don't mean that badly; being an ordinary guy is a good thing. What I really mean is that he is ordinary to me and that is the problem.

Was I ever in love with him? I just don't know any more. I made the ultimate declaration of love on our wedding day and somehow, in the hugeness of the gesture, I lost the clarity of what love was. Lost faith in the feeling that made me say 'yes' to him in the first place.

Dan is great. Really. Just not for me.

I met him about a year and a half ago (if I loved him, I would be able to remember exactly), although I guess he had been knocking about on the edge of my life before then. He was the superintendent in my apartment building. 'Don't sleep with your building super!' I hear you cry. Basic rule of being a single woman in Manhattan. Your water pipe bursts: who are you going to call? It is one relationship you *don't* mess with. Unless you are so sad and desperate that you are afraid of turning into one of life's lonely: the lingering huggers, the abandoned wives who have begun actively to crave a human touch. The New York singles scene was tough.

There were the players: high-maintenance, competitive husband-hunters; manicured, buffed, styled-up peak performers. Then there were the rest of us, just bumbling through the bars forgetting to change out of our work shoes, knowing that we were never going to meet a man if we didn't start making an effort. All of us were trying to look as if we didn't care, pretending that what really mattered to us was each other. Maybe I'm cynical, but I always knew that, ultimately, I was an emotional stand-in for the man my girlfriends hadn't met yet. Men, marriage, children: as we buffed and polished and shone through our thirties this life cycle was turning from a birthright to a dream.

I was bad at pretending.

Reared in that liberal single-mom-by-choice way that never feels entirely sure of itself, my role models for love were my maternal grandparents. James, my grandfather, was the local schoolteacher in their small village and my grandmother Bernadine was a wonderful housekeeper and cook. I visited them for at least two summer months each year as a child and benefited from the warmth they so clearly felt towards me and each other. Their marriage provided my childhood with a structured, traditional environment so different from the permissive, unpredictable upbringing I had with my bohemian artist mother—their daughter, Niamh. The long summer days were taken up entirely with simple household chores: James tending to his vegetable garden; Bernadine baking bread and allowing me to dust her kitchen in flour. My grandparents were not physically demonstrative, but their love was obvious in all the little things they did for each other.

Bernadine and James were married for fifty years, and I remember as a teenager wondering at the miracle of love that would keep two people together for almost three of my lifetimes. My grandmother outlived my grandfather by eight years. The legacy they left in my heart was my ambition to find a man with whom to have a relationship like theirs. A romance so strong that it could last out half a century.

I always knew that I wanted to be married. I dated losers and bastards and nice-but-not-right guys. Marriage was too important a state to compromise on. I knew that much, and once or twice I fell in love and had to pull myself back from the brink of a big mistake. Although, looking back now, I realise it is always better to follow your heart than your head. In the end I married one of the nice-but-not-right ones because my head told my heart that this could be my last chance. Biology and bad luck conspired and conned me into a feeling like love. With Dan, it was never the real thing and it needs to be. Fake love won't last the course.

I was having one of those indulgent afternoons that you can have when you live alone. And I don't mean the pampering 'home-spa' type that you see in the magazines. I mean the phone-off-hook feeling sorry for yourself kind. It didn't happen often, but maybe once a year (often around my birthday) I'd take the day off work and stay in bed feeling miserable. Other girls did meditation and yoga. I took to my bed with a quart of Jack Daniel's and a six-pack of chocolate muffins. After twenty-four hours of watching off-peak TV, I would emerge longing to see my friends and generally more content with my lot in life.

Being self-employed meant that I could indulge myself. After a lucky break early on I had worked my way up the food-magazine ladder, from kitchen assistant to recipe tester and stylist's assistant to senior food writer and stylist. Somewhere around five years ago I became tired of the politics of publishing and took a chance that I would get work as a freelance and on my thirty-third birthday resigned my post as senior food editor on America's top-selling food magazine. Within days I was approached by an agent and have since published three moderately successful recipe books. I also design and test recipes for food companies and enjoy a peculiar but nonetheless lucrative sideline as a kitchen-design consultant for wealthy hostess wives. I have a good reputation in the food industry and my work is 'out there', which means I am always in the running for a big break; there is talk of TV.

So I was the typical child of the baby-boomer generation. Brilliant career—love life an unmitigated disaster. My decision to hibernate the day I met Dan had been triggered by the tail end of a hurt from yet another jerk. After fifteen years as a leading food writer, you would think I might have learned about the 'up-coming chefs and photographers' syndrome. Those men whose only 'talent' was getting unmarried thirty-something women into bed, which, in my own sullied experience, took little more than two Vodka Martinis and rather less charm than I could ever admit to.

Ronan, the chef, was a classic; we had sex, I thought he would call and he didn't. He turned up two weeks later at a launch with a model on his arm. I tried to be cynical, but when you get to a certain age bitter looks too ugly so you have to absorb the hurt. It had been a petty puncture, but I was feeling deflated and sad when Dan walked into my life.

'Fire drill, Ma'am . . .'

Our building supers changed every couple of years, largely because their allocated apartment was a dingy, windowless hole in the basement of our building. I had been away on a photo shoot when Dan had done his 'new-super' tour of the building. I guess he had been there a few weeks before I met him.

'Ma'am, I am going to have to ask you to participate in our fire drill.'

I hate to be called 'Ma'am'. It makes me sound old and cranky.

'Ma'am, it is for your own safety.'

So I become old and cranky.

And in this case also drunk.

I flung open the door: 'You expect me to stand out on the street dressed like *this*!'—and I waved my pyjama-clad arms at him. Then I slammed the door on the answer to my own rhetorical question: 'No? Well then, fuck off!'

As I was doing so it hit me that our new super was incredibly handsome. Not just those acceptable good looks that combined with personality can turn an average man into a real prospect. No, he had those ludicrous, chiselled, shaving-cream ad looks. The kind you grow out of as soon as you realise that male models are out of your league or gay.

Of course, an intelligent woman in her mid-thirties knows that looks are not important. Especially as she brushes the crumbs of her fourth chocolate muffin from her flannel nightgown. It is what's on the inside that counts, which in my case was apparently a lot of bourbon and gas.

I must have seen something in Dan's eyes during our few-second exchange, some germ of desire, because—for no apparent reason—I did a clean-up on myself. Not a full leg shave or anything as extreme as that, but through the drunken haze a bit of tooth and hair brushing went on and the nightgown got exchanged for something a bit sexier, which, let's face it, didn't have to be much more than a clean pair of sweats.

Dan came back an hour later when the drill was over and, while I was not surprised at him calling back, I remember being shocked that he really was as handsome as I had first thought. More shocking still was the way that these melting hazel eyes were gazing at me with some undisguised lust/admiration combo. Like I was the most beautiful woman on earth. Nobody had ever looked at me like that before and it made me feel like laughing. I invited him in.

Seducing Dan was the easiest thing I have ever done. Normally I sit back and wait to be asked. I don't take much persuading, but I have never taken the lead before. But this guy looked so nervous, so smitten, that it made me feel certain of myself. Confident.

The sex was fantastic and he loved every inch of my body in a way that astonished me. He was heartbreakingly handsome, and there was something comforting and safe about being with him right from the start. But while I was flattered, I knew, deep down in my gut, that Dan was not my type: I am attracted to intellects, not bodies, and we had nothing in common. When I look back on it now, I worry that I seduced Dan for no other reason than I felt dirty and drunk and lonely. Oh, and of course—because I could. A toxic combination that was eventually legitimised by our marriage.

Hardly grounds for a happy one.

That first afternoon of sex with Dan somehow rolled itself into the comfort of a relationship. Dan patched me up and made me feel better, but my feelings for him were always sullied by the bad guy before him. Even if the chef was a jerk, he still had the power to hurt me. There had been some chemistry, albeit of the poisonous kind. Dan didn't have that power over me. Although I knew he would never do anything to hurt me, sometimes I wished he would. Because surely it is better to feel hurt than to feel nothing at all.

Perhaps I am making things sounds worse than they are. I do have feelings for Dan, of course I do. And when I married him, I thought I loved him.

Dan made me feel good. He was great in bed; I had confidence in my body around him. He thought I was gorgeous, he desired me and, I'll be honest, that was something different for me. I love to cook and I love to eat, so I am no beach bunny. That's never been a problem for me, nonetheless Dan was the first guy whom I felt that I didn't have to hide my body from. He was always telling me how sexy, how smart I was, what a great cook I was, what a hot body I had. Dan Mullins was stone-mad crazy in love with me. He was so sure about marrying me, so clear and certain that he could make me happy that I believed him.

After just three months he said, 'Marry me.'

Not 'Will you?' or 'I think it would be a good idea if we got married.'

Just 'Marry me. I know I can make you happy.'

No one had ever asked me before and part of me knew that no one would again. I was thirty-eight and I wanted to believe in something: in happy ever after, in him. So I said yes.

I allowed myself to get caught up in the arrangements, even though I knew that they were not the point. The dress, the cake, the venue, the canapés: getting married was the biggest, most glamorous photographic shoot I was ever going to organise. If I was using details as distractions, at least I had that in common with every other bride-to-be. Doreen, my fashion editor best friend, had her whole fashion team on me and they went into meltdown.

'A European wedding—I mean, it'll be *so* this season.'

'She's Irish. It doesn't count.'

'Why? Ireland's in Europe. Isn't it?'

'Physically, yes. Style-wise? It's Canada.'

'Oh.'

I enjoyed playing the princess, all the fuss and frivolity. And it turned out to be, just like in the magazines, the happiest day of my life.

Part of that was due to the bonding I had experienced that day with my bohemian artist mother. Niamh (I have always called her by her first name) flew in from London to be there. I had always wanted a conventional cookie-baking mother, but Niamh tried to make me into a friend rather than a daughter. We had not clashed so much as inhabited parallel worlds. My mother and I had little in common. I was pragmatic and conventional, an inverted rebellion against her chaotic, promiscuous nature. After she moved to Europe there was a minor estrangement. We spoke every couple of months on the phone, but I never had the urge to go visit her and she always had the excuse of poverty to not come see me. Five years had managed to pass without our having seen each other.

I had almost considered not inviting her. My mother stridently disapproved of marriage, and often claimed her own parents were unhappily married. I disagreed with her, but it was an argument neither of us wanted to have. She was hurt, I think, that I appeared closer to her parents than to her, and I was nervous, always, of her crossing the boundaries of protective parent and telling me things I was not ready to hear.

That my mother came at all was a revelation in itself. The night before the wedding she met Dan, and after he had departed back to his apartment, she and I stayed up drinking in my suite at the Plaza.

'I like him,' she said late on when we were both tipsy enough to be honest, but not so drunk that we wouldn't remember, 'although I know it's not important what I think.'

I argued briefly before she said, 'Bernadine would have approved.'

I wondered if she was right or if she was just saying it because she sensed some uncertainty.

'He seems solid.'

It was a cop-out understatement. Safe sidekick to the big pre-wedding night question, 'Do you love him?' It was the wrong thing to say and the wrong time to say it, and while I knew Niamh meant well in that moment, I longed with a fresh grief for my grandmother. It had been ten years since she had died but my love felt so alive. I wanted her to be there, not just so that I could get her approval of Dan but because it did not feel right for me to be taking this big step without her.

Niamh seemed to sense that and said, 'I miss her too.' She went over to her suitcase and pulled something out of its front pocket. It was a large, tattered brown envelope. 'Open it,' she said.

Inside was a pile of dusty pink and grey copy-books. I recognised them instantly as being the type they sold at the post office in Achadh Mor. My first cookbook, compiled between the ages of ten and twenty, had been written in one of those notebooks; a sky-blue one entitled 'Grandma B's Recipes'. I still had it hidden in the bottom of a kitchen drawer.

My stomach was churning as I took one of the books out and flicked my eyes over the italic letters of my grandmother's confident hand.

'It's her life story—from her late teens onwards.'

'Have you read them?'

Niamh was surprised at the question. She was right. It was a stupid question, but I could not help feeling slightly annoyed that she had never told me about them before.

'Of course I've read them. I am her daughter.'

She had said 'I am' as if Bernadine were still alive.

'I never gave them to you before because . . .'

I tried to relax my face out of looking angry.

'. . . because—I guess I was waiting for the right time.'

I could feel a fight starting in my head, but I reined it in and, as I did, Niamh reached across and took my hand.

'She still loves you,' she said, 'and so do I.'

Niamh was into this afterlife stuff which I had always believed was nonsense. But the soft tone of her voice led me to do something that I can remember doing only rarely as a child. I laid my head on my mother's chest and waited there until everything dissolved but the comfort of being held by her. As Niamh stroked my face, I felt the generations of mothers before her seep through her hands. For a moment I believed the strong arms of Bernadine were embracing me again.

I don't know how long I lay there, but when I sat up I knew, ten years after her death, that I had finally accepted Bernadine was gone. I knew with certainty that my next project would be to adapt her recipes into a cookbook and that my mother was right; I could not have tackled reading Bernadine's story before now.

What I still did not feel certain of was my decision to marry Dan the following day. I told myself it was pre-wedding nerves.

We had a traditional Catholic service, and Niamh walked me down the aisle and gave me away. Doreen was my maid of honour. As I stood at the top of the aisle in my big dress, I was filled with the knowledge that this was what I had always wanted. At the same time, there was disbelief that it was really happening. It was the most overwhelming moment of my life so far. I was part of a fairy tale I thought I had left behind long ago and now realised had just been lying dormant inside me. Dan was the man who had made that happen for me.

Dan was sure he could make me happy, but he was wrong. You can't make another person happy: they have to make themselves happy. I believed that Dan loved me, but I know now that it isn't enough. I needed to love him back.

And let's face it—you can't force yourself to love somebody if the chemistry just isn't there.

Fal Iochtar, Parish of Achadh Mor, Co. Mayo, Ireland: 1932

When love is pure, it is easy. It comes as fast and hard as a shower of hail, and often passes as quickly. It fills your heart and when it's gone you feel as hollow as an empty cave.

Then there is the other kind of love. The one that comes so slowly that you think it isn't love at all. Each day it grows, but by such a small measure that you hardly notice. Once your heart is filled with this old love, it will never be empty again.

I have known both and still I would not like to choose one over the other. Although for the longest time I thought I had.

The moment my eyes fell on Michael Tuffy, every love and loyalty I had experienced up to that point was rendered meaningless. I could feel the heat of my own blood in just looking at him. The first time his eyes met mine they branded me; from then on I would be defined by my love for him. In all my life—which has been long and textured with the emotions of wife, mother, grandmother—I have never forgotten what it felt like to fall so immediately and so completely in love. I would have followed him to the other side of the world. It all but destroyed my youthful optimism when I realised that I couldn't.

That first meeting was at a spraoi, a party, in Kitty Conlan's house. Kitty had the knack of matching, and there was nothing to do in Achadh Mor back then—only work and wait. Bad, unyielding land, and a hard history blighted with famine and the messy, bloody politics of occupation, meant that emigration to England and America from our area was almost absolute. Those of us left behind were half a community, not knowing whether we were lucky to be still at home when the greater number of our family and neighbours were in New York or London. We waited for our men to return from summers potato picking in Yorkshire, adventure implied in their new jackets and affluence in their shiny brown wallets. In the meantime we had to draw whatever entertainment we could from looking at each other.

I didn't mind being looked at. I was brazen by nature. Some people thought me spoilt, even my own mother at times.

'She wants jam on everything!' I remember her saying to Aunt Ann the summer her sister returned from America.

'Nothing is good enough for her. She wants everything her own way. She has her head full of silly notions.'

Falling in love certainly came under the banner of 'silly notions'. People had romances all the time but they rarely ended in marriage. Marriage was about land and security and money. To marry for love was considered reckless. Looking back, I suppose my mother was worried that my idealism would lead to disappointment and eventually despair.

I was the only daughter among three brothers and my father drank. In those days nobody had anything. A woman was at the mercy of how hard her husband was willing to work. A lazy man, no matter how much land he had, would end you in the poorhouse. A drinker was worse again, for he might work hard and then spend every penny in the pub and believe himself entitled to do so. That is how it was with my father. And so my mother, in addition to running the house, worked like a slave on the farm. She reared pigs for a Ballyhaunis butcher and sold eggs to a grocer in Kilkelly. Both men were careful to have business dealings only with my mother. They understood what type my father was and that they were providing our only source of income. They were decent, and doubtless the good price they gave her reflected my mother's desperation. Hardship had made my mother bitter and she was a slouching, distant woman with barely the gumption to nag. She was unhappy. I could see the miserable circumstances that had turned her that way and I was determined to avoid them.

Mam's elder sister, Ann, was my saviour. A confirmed spinster, Ann had gone to America in 1910 and became a seamstress to a wealthy American socialite. She returned in the thirties a 'millionaire'—the description in our poverty-stricken times of someone who owned more than one coat.

My aunt told me stories of New York. She read books and had an easy life, with plenty of money and no men to look after. She was always glad of my company and often asked my mother if I might stay with her the night. In the evenings we could suit ourselves entirely. Making dainty potato cakes and spreading them with butter and my mother's tart gooseberry jam, then eating them greedily as we discussed the news of the neighbours in intricate detail. Ann told shocking stories of their relations in America: this one's son married a Jew; another was killed boxing bare-fisted in a bar. I embellished duller tales of arguments over field boundaries with gory details. To me, Ann's house was a palace filled with exotic and beautiful things—a vase made of heavy glass, an ermine stole, two red cushions with gold-braid trim. My relationship with this glamorous aunt elevated me above the hoi polloi of our village. In my own mind certainly, and in the minds of many of the lads round about, who considered me one of the finer-looking girls among the diminishing supply of would-be wives in our parish.

It suited me just fine to be placed high on a pedestal, with my long black curls and my delicate pointed nose stuck high in the air. Those brave enough to approach me soon found themselves withered by my indifference. I had the idea of leaving Achadh Mor when the summer had passed. Aunt Ann still had contact with all her friends in America and would surely pay my passage across. I was an adventurous young woman. I would not have emigrated for survival but, with Ann as my role model, for success. It would have happened had I not fallen in love.

Love changes everything, but it does not always change for the better.

Ann did not come with me to Kitty Conlan's party that night. She thought the widow a foolish woman, indulging the young people of the parish with silly matchmaking games. Also, the men were allowed drink even though the company was mixed, and Ann didn't like that at all. She was prudish in matters where drink and romance were concerned. Looking back as an older woman myself now, I believe Ann was less committed to her spinster status than she let on. Perhaps she had been let down by a sweetheart in her younger days. Certainly that would go some way to explain what happened between her and me.

Kitty's parlour was small and her fire roaring, and the crowd kept having to disperse into the cold outdoors so as not to roast themselves alive. Cousin Mae and I were giggling over some trivia when she prodded me in the ribs and nodded towards the door.

Then I found I was both floating and sinking. The room grew huge as crowds of people receded into the white walls and Michael alone walked towards me. With each step he took, I knew he was the braver, stronger, of us because I could not move. For a moment I thought perhaps he did not care for me at all, otherwise he would be paralysed as I was. He did not speak, only held his hand out to mine so he could take me to dance. When we touched, a thrilling heat shot through me.

We danced: him holding my eye all the time and not speaking at all. I, drained of my usual brazen huff, blushed scarlet throughout, so that every neighbour could carry back as far as Kilkelly, Knock and Kiltimagh news of our big romance. That Bernadine Morley of Fal Iochtar in the parish of Achadh Mor and a young American lad by the name of Michael Tuffy, whose mother had returned to claim the estate of her deceased husband, Michael Senior, who had tragically passed away in New York City some six years past, were doing a line.

People talked but, as I said, I never minded that. Gossip and truth feed off each other. If our romance was great, then it was made greater by talk. The fireside ruminations of a thousand old biddies added fuel to our burgeoning passion.

Michael and his mother were strangers to Achadh Mor, but we welcomed them in a way we rarely welcomed our own. Returned emigrants, like Aunt Ann, seemed to goad those left behind with what might have been. They were expected to keep a low profile, sink back into the grim boggy landscape as if they had never been away. The likes of Maureen Tuffy and her handsome son were different. They were the Real McCoy—they had American accents and had not been born to the drudgery of our land, but had come here from choice. We thought them marvellous for believing us worthy of their company.

I could not believe that Michael had chosen me to love and yet, when I was with him, I felt so beautiful that I might have been picked by royalty itself. My disbelief was tempered by a sense of having known him all my life, a certainty that I would be with him until the day I died.

What we did, where we went, what was said is as meaningless now as it was then. We walked fields, we took tea with my aunt, we attended the same Masses. We stood across from each other on either side of the main street in Kilkelly on market day; our view of each other interrupted by cows and carts, we each wondered at the miracle of our matched souls meeting in this squally corner of the world. We saw God in each other and perhaps that was our only sin. What we had was rare, and still, after all that has happened since, I believe that to be true. It was the love that fools wait their whole lives for, then die loveless and bitter when it evades them.

Perhaps that knowledge alone saved me in the end. Knowing that my love for Michael Tuffy could never be repeated.

We didn't marry, although it was fully intended.

Our parents met in a hotel in Ballyhaunis at the suggestion of his mother. My father, for all his shaving and washing, looked like a boiled ham in his suit. My mother was already nervous and taken aback when money was mentioned, although she could see herself the opportunity that was being offered her. It seemed a small price to pay for her daughter's eternal happiness. Mrs Tuffy was clearly a woman of means and it was only a token of respect she was asking for.

In any case, we all knew that Aunt Ann would be happy to provide whatever money was needed. She, of all people, would be thrilled for me to marry into such a respectable household—and for love. It was every dream she could have had for me.

Ann did not poor-mouth over declining to pay my dowry. We all knew she could well afford it. Her first insult was to refuse to offer the money herself and instead to wait for my mother to ask her. It was a humiliation my mother had never had to endure before; Ann had quietly provided for our family countless times in the past.

My mother didn't give me any explanation. She just said that there was no money and that therefore I could not marry Michael Tuffy.

I begged my mother to ask again, but she refused. I threatened to run away with him. Michael and I were destined, nothing could keep us apart.

When I turned around to plan our escape, he was gone. Back to America. I knew I would never see him again.

I howled and tore at my hair until my father and brothers were afraid of me. For months, I locked myself in the house with my mother and shredded potatoes until my fingers bled, scrubbed flagstones until my knees bruised black. I never spoke to my aunt again.

As the next five years passed, the pain softened. I came to understand that I had been privileged to experience such a rare love at all, yet cursed because it had ruined me for anything that would come after. As for marriage—the very idea of it became an insult. Although part of me knew it was inevitable, there was one thing I was certain of: no one or nothing would ever match my love for Michael Tuffy.

He was gone, but the memory of him had marked me forever.

Compromise

You can't always have as much sugar as you'd like

Rhubarb Tart

Head and tail the rhubarb and cut into small pieces, about a ¼ inch—your eye will tell you. When the rhubarb is young you can put it raw into the tart. In late August, when it is tougher, I put it into a pan of water with a little sugar and leave it to warm over the fire while I am making the pastry. Sift 10 oz flour with ½ teaspoon salt, then mix in 2 dessertspoons sugar. Chop 4 oz butter, then crumble into the flour with your fingers. Beat an egg into 2 tablespoons of milk and work the mixture into a dough. Line a well-floured pan with a ½-inch thickness of the pastry, then put in your rhubarb and as much sugar as suits. I like it sweet and could take up to 3 tablespoons. James prefers it sour, but I'd put in an extra spoon anyway so as not to poison him. Cover with a pastry lid, then put in a medium oven for up to 1 hour.

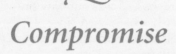

YOU CAN BUY ANYTHING in New York except rhubarb. Oh, you can buy the forced stuff all year round. Creamy-pink, firm, fat rods, but as far as this cook is concerned, they are a watery waste of time. What I want are the spindly sticks that used to grow wild in the field behind my grandparents' house. Bitter green leaves and a sore scarlet stalk gradually giving way to a white tip. They were shockingly sour, but with the addition of sugar they took on a unique, exotic flavour.

I have started reviving my grandmother's recipes. It is painful bringing all of her old dishes to life again and has made it clear that I am way off being ready to read those memoirs. As I work through my tatty old notebook, I can hear her talk me through the measurements and methods as if she were here. But she is only able to answer questions I already know the answers to, like how many ounces equals a cup of sugar. She is not here to give me the answer to the one question I really need to ask her, which is what she thinks of Dan. I wonder if Bernadine would have put Dan and me together, and when I am feeling unsure I long for her to be here. If I only knew her opinion, I think it might help. I guess I need someone else to feel certain on my behalf. I know that's not possible, and maybe that's why I have chosen to value the opinion of the one person who will, let's face it, never be able to give it to me.

Now that I have reorganised my apartment and sorted through the stored piles of junk I'd avoided for years, I need to get lost in this cookery project so that I can ignore the fact that Dan wants us to move to Yonkers.

The Hamptons? Of course. Brooklyn? Yes. The Bronx? Maybe. But Yonkers?

Dan owns a house there, which he has been renovating on and off for the past five years. I had never been to see it because, as far as I was concerned, it was just an investment. It was nice to know that I was marrying a guy who was a property owner, but it had never occurred to me that he intended for us to live there. It was a weekend building project he would scurry off to when I was away on press trips. Dan and I really did our own thing a lot. I didn't bring him to work functions and was good at avoiding socialising with his Irish-American buddies. If I had, I might have realised more definitely that we had nothing whatsoever in common.

Dan started this clumsy conversation about how Manhattan is getting 'real busy' and 'real crowded' and 'real dangerous' to try and ease me into his dumb idea of moving out of the city. I don't know which is worse. His wanting us to lose two prime apartments on Upper West Side, or the fact that he thought I would consider moving to Yonkers.

But then, that's just one of the 'things I hate about Dan'.

The list has been growing in my head so fast that I have found writing it down helps to lessen its power over me:

He wants to move to Yonkers.

His toenails are too long and they scratch me in bed.

He wears tartan shirts.

He keeps fishing catalogues in the bathroom.

He's too big and noisy—he lumbers around the apartment so that you always know he is there.

He shuffles and uses hillbilly words like 'real' when he gets nervous. Instant coffee. He *prefers* instant coffee? Explain!

He gets up before me in the mornings and wakes me with tea. It makes me feel guilty.

He forgets to put sugar in my tea.

He purses his lips just before he says something he thinks is clever.

Actually—that stuff about the list losing its power when it's written down? That's bullshit. The only power I have is in the list, which is hidden under my side of the bed. When Dan moves towards me in the night, or when he leans in to me in the morning, I know it's there. The list says more about what a bitch I am than anything else, which doesn't help me either. I hate everything about Dan. The only time I can look at him and not think, 'I hate you,' is the time when I look at him and think, 'What have I done?' Poison or panic. Take your pick because that's all that's on offer in my head right now.

Dan has been more or less resident in my apartment since we came together, but when we returned from honeymoon we had this ceremonial him-moving-his-stuff-in evening. There was a mountain of stuff I hadn't realised he owned: crates of old records, piles of cheap crockery, nasty acrylic navy pillow slips, back issues of magazines. As I watched it all piling up in the hall of my perfect minimalist palace, Dan happily hauling up another box of dusty videos, I honestly thought I was going to be sick. In the end, intuiting that I was unhappy with the mess, Dan moved most of it back down to the super's apartment again. But it can't stay there for ever and we both know it.

When we were dating, it was comforting to have him in my home. But now that Dan has the *right* to be here it feels wrong. I feel robbed of my privacy, and intimacy isn't supposed to feel intrusive, surely?

I can't tell anyone what is going on. My single friends will all say, 'Gasp! You don't love him! You must leave at once!' My married friends will say, 'Love? Get real, girl, this is *marriage*.'

This is not what I wanted when I got married to Dan. This is not who I thought I would turn into.

Virtually everything I say out loud these days is a petty complaint disguised as a question. 'Is the dishwasher still full?' 'Did you forget to buy toothpaste?'

Sometimes all I can do is make a statement. 'These are the wrong washing tabs.' 'I take one sugar in my tea.' 'This isn't whole milk.' Then he says he's sorry and I say, 'It's OK' in this clipped voice that makes it quite clear that it isn't OK at all. Without meaning to, I have joined the Passive Aggressive School of Non-Communication. All calm on the outside, I am a simmering concoction of hatreds that, sooner or later, will come spewing out of me in a shower of lethal bile.

My monster is tempered only by the knowledge that, boy, did Dan luck out the day he met *this* lady! I am scaring myself and I am scaring Dan. I can see him waiting for the row he knows is impending but cannot start because he hasn't the first idea what is wrong. His truth is: we are newlyweds and in love. And right now, my truth couldn't be more different.

I have never made rhubarb tart except with the vegetable grown from my grandmother's garden, and it's been ten years since I was last home in Kilkelly. Granddad Nolan had planted a single crown the year my mother was born. By the time I was a young adult, the single plant stretched out across a quarter of an acre, a mass of broad umbrella leaves hiding the scarlet underneath. It is an unremarkable and unruly-looking vegetable—yet when prepared right, it is truly delicious.

During my summer vacations in Ireland as a child I ate rhubarb tart every day. I returned to live full-time in Ireland as an English literature student at Galway University when I was eighteen. The memories I treasure from those three years of living in Ireland are not the late-night giggling staggers up cobbled bar-lined lanes, or losing my virginity to a beautiful but wild-haired philosophy student, or even the books I studied, but the time that I spent with my grandparents. I would carry one of my grandmother's rhubarb tarts all the way back on the bus from Kilkelly. Once back in my digs, I would have a slice of it with a cup of sweet tea before going to sleep. That daily ritual and my weekends in Kilkelly kept some order on my crazy student years and got me a first in English lit. Although I lived most of my life in America, rhubarb tart was the taste of home. Not the New York loft that my mother filled with Warhol prints and bummed-out boyfriends, but her parents' home in Kilkelly, which smelt of smouldering turf, beeswax and camphor. When I returned each summer I knew from their faces that they had been waiting ten months to see their only grandchild again. They adored me and they adored each other. I never heard a cross word pass between them; it was a marriage based wholly on love, it seemed to me.

From July to September I was the centre of their world, and rhubarb tart was always the first thing out of the oven. Tressa's favourite. So, if I cannot get the right type of rhubarb, I may have to leave Grandma Bernadine's tart as a fond memory rather than tarnish hers with a tasteless lookalike version. Sometimes, when you are really attached to an ideal, it is just not possible to compromise.

I had no interest in James Nolan. I respected him. We all did. He was a scholar from our area, but being between the ages of my brothers and my parents he had been unknown to me growing up. He had been away for a number of years and was thirty-five when he came back and took up the post of teacher at Fal Iochtar school. It was the fashion at that time to learn Irish, and on a Friday evening James opened the school and taught us local people the native language that had been beaten out of our grandparents. There was dancing and singing and great craic after the classes, and some nights we mightn't leave until after eleven.

James was a member of the Gaelic League, and along with that there were rumours that he had served us all in the Irish Republican Army. Nobody knew the whys and wherefores of his ten years away, but there was nothing unusual in that. The smart man knew how to keep his mouth shut. In any case, he had not been shirking because Kitty Conlan noted that his five sisters had been successfully dowered, two into the convent, and his brother had built a smart new house with a slate roof on the site next to their family home.

Mr J. Nolan was in danger of becoming something of a champion, except that he was local to our small, humble parish and would therefore never be allowed to consider himself anything other than unremarkable. Certainly his appearance gave nothing away about any heroics or romantic activity abroad. I barely remember the first time I saw James, except that I might have thought him ordinary beyond belief. More truthful is that I didn't think about him at all.

There had been some small speculation about who, among the women still available, might fancy him. He was respectable and kind with children by all accounts. There was the new house, which remained unoccupied—his brother and his wife having recently moved to England and the old mother refusing to budge from her old cottage—and a teacher's income, which was nothing to be sniffed at. He was, if you were pushing thirty, a good prospect. However, I was only twenty-one.

I might have had no interest myself, but there was some sport to be had watching the older women fall over themselves to get at him. Mae and I would be in kinks laughing at them, with their lipstick drawn on like clowns. The worst of them was Aine Grealy. She had a face as pale and plain as bread, but she had brains. She had won scholarship after scholarship and gone as far as university in Dublin. She was back that summer to decide what she was going to do with all her education. I didn't like her. Aine had made comments about Michael and they had got back to me.

My cousin Mae and I were the prettiest girls around the place. The two of us turned out in public like something you might see in a film. I had a yellow blouse and a matching yellow scarf; Mae had a pair of cream-coloured shoes with a leather bag to match. Aine was the type who would look down her nose on shows of glamour. She never spoke to us at the Irish classes and I knew she thought us stupid. I didn't mind as I thought it better, at that time, to be stupid and pretty than clever but plain. We were there for the dancing afterwards. Mae was on the look-out for romance, but I wasn't.

I only went after James Nolan to upset Aine Grealy.

It was childish and nasty, looking back, but Aine had riled me terribly. She had been talking away to James after Mass that Sunday and I had greeted them both in Irish as I passed by. Aine had corrected my pronunciation in reply. I thought it was a vile thing to do—and still do to this day—so I decided to put a halt to her gallop. Even if I broke his heart, I told myself, I was doing James a good turn. There was clearly an understanding developing between the two of them and I believed Aine to be ugly all through from the inside out. He seemed an easy-going type who would be happy for anyone who'd have him. James Nolan might be a scholar, but I had him down as a *ludarman*, an idiot, in matters of love.

I was wrong about that. It was the first and last time I was ever made to feel a fool in front of James, but it was the first time of many when I read his character wrongly.

The next Friday I was wearing a lavender cardigan, which I fully knew set off my long black curls to beautiful effect. The class was over and Aine had made a beeline for James before the last of his pupils had stood up. She was determined all right. But now she was up against Bernadine Morley. I might not have been good at Irish, but I knew something about love. At least I thought I did. I could look at any man and make his heart melt. It was cruel entertainment perhaps, but as far as I could see the men around me had it all their way. You had a few short years to tease them before you'd be darning their socks and tolerating their drunken abuse. That's how it was for my mother in any case. Except that I could see James was a harmless type.

All I did was look. I looked across the room at James in the way I had looked at Michael Tuffy some five years before when I had fallen in love. Except this was an imitation. When I had looked at Michael, my knees buckled and the colour rose in my cheeks in a fountain of pain and joy; this night I looked at our ordinary teacher and pretended. I cannot say how I did it, except that I stared hard at him until I knew he had noticed me. I knew, or believed back then, that I had something worth noticing.

He stayed by Aine's side that evening and walked her home as usual. I was irritated to have failed, but my resolve in the matter did not stretch to further action.

The following week Aine was not there and James asked me up for a dance. I was mortified as the other girls, including Mae, clapped us on as if there was something in it. As we were leaving, Mae nodded over to him, pointing out that he was loitering after us as if he had the intention of accompanying us. I scurried out quickly with her behind me.

I thought that was that, but before the week was up I would get the greatest shock of my life.

I came in from late Mass that Sunday and found James Nolan sitting in our kitchen. He was at the table with my father and there were papers in front of them. I was immediately confused; although my father was a brutish character, he could read and write. He wasn't like some of the unschooled who needed to get the teacher in to help them draft a letter.

Father nodded at the kettle for me to make them tea, then at a rhubarb tart I had made in a hurry the night before. I had left it aside because I had already put it in the oven before I realised that I had put no sugar in it. Rhubarb tart is bitter beyond belief without sugar, and so I made our guest tea and deliberately placed a slice of the rotten tart in front of him. My father took none as he was not in the habit of eating in front of anyone save his family. I thanked God for that, as my father would have thrashed me if he had found out what I had done.

James ate every last crumb and declared it the most delicious tart he had ever experienced. I was about to test his endurance and acting skills with another slice, when my father stood up and said, 'Take James and show him around the place, Bernadine.'

My father always called me Bernie.

James was quiet—sheepish, I think now with the benefit of hind-sight. I remember that he tried to take my hand and I pulled it away with the utmost rudeness to deter him. I must have had some inkling of what lay ahead. I gestured with my arms at the hens and the hay shed and we were back at the house within ten minutes. My parents had cleared out and I made busy around the kitchen, walloping pots to make it clear it was time for him to leave, which he did.

When my father came back in and found James gone he went mad—shouting that I was a useless strap. Still I didn't understand, until my mother ushered him out and sat me down at the table. Her voice was gentle, the sharp, busy tone gone out of it. She looked worried.

'Do you like James?' was all she said.

I knew then that they had come to an arrangement, although I could scarcely believe it of them—or, for that matter, of him.

The sordid details only came out later. How James had come calling with the intention of walking me out and my father had pinned him down to a marriage commitment there and then. After the family had shamed itself in not being able to dowry me to Michael Tuffy, the old bastard was afraid he would be stuck with me for ever. James and his mother took me on with no dowry, and they never told a soul or sinner in the parish to save my family name.

James had written and signed an informal contract with my father that afternoon, buying me like cattle, though no money changed hands. This man didn't love me, nor I him. My parents clearly did not love me, otherwise they would never have done such a terrible thing.

When Michael returned to America, I thought my heart had been torn asunder. My loving him, my missing him, that wrenching longing to see him came upon me again that day, and with terrible force.

I ran from the kitchen and walked fast across five fields and five ditches to a place we called Purple Mountain. It was a small hill, no more than a mound of heather, and below it on the other side was the 'lake'. In reality, this was a pond of water that changes from a large brown puddle to a deep pool depending on the rainfall. Beyond it stretched miles of black treacherous bog. There were plenty of stories of men who had tried to cut turf from it, and disappeared. To deter us from playing there, we were told they were dragged down to hell itself by the bony paws of the demons living beneath its surface.

I was full of sin and had gone past caring. Michael Tuffy and I had sinned ourselves senseless on several occasions. It was that, and the knowledge that I could not endure the rest of my life without him, that made the fact of our not getting married so terrible. We had been so certain of our fate together that we had enjoyed each other's bodies.

On the day of my father and James's arrangement, I stood on the top of that filthy mound of earth and thought about flinging myself in the lake. There had been heavy rainfall for weeks, so it was deep. I could not swim and I knew the demons would be ready for me after what I had done. I opened my arms and I swayed, but I could not do it.

So I thought about what I was left with.

I could flee, but I had nowhere to go. I could not stay at home, that much was clear. I realised I had no choice. I had to marry James.

As the weeks crept towards the wedding, I tried to keep up a front. It didn't help anyone for me to be surly and sad. My mother and Mae sold him hard to me and I took heed of them the best I could. James Nolan was clean, respectable and kind. He was not so old and I could do a lot worse. His mother was decent and we would have our own house. But

215

while I went along with them, every inch of me burned again for the young man who had gone to America five years before and taken with him my heart, my soul, my spirit: the tools I thought I needed to love.

On the morning of my wedding I put on the cream gown my mother had worn. It was silk and smelt of lavender. Cousin Mae put rouge on my cheeks and on my lips. As her fingers touched my mouth, she slipped her hand round the back of my neck and held my head so that I could weep. I shook into the silk of her shoulder and thought that nothing would ever be the same again.

When I had finished, I determined then that I would not cry again over any man. James Nolan was supposed to be good, but here he was dragging a young woman into a loveless marriage. So if he was happy with a wife who didn't love him, then that was exactly what he was going to get.

I smiled and charmed my way through the day of celebrations. I was, everyone agreed, the most beautiful bride Achadh Mor church had ever seen and James, being the popular teacher, drew out every neighbour in the vicinity to wish us well. It was gone ten before the last of them left the house and we settled into our first night alone together.

Two complete strangers—and I was determined that we should stay that way.

We went out to Yonkers today. Dan was great. He said that, if I didn't like it, then we didn't have to move there. He just wanted me to look as it was something that we had to decide about together. He is trying hard and has the patience of a saint, but the joint ownership thing hit me like a brick. Another complicated layer of commitment kicking in.

It's not that I have never been out of Manhattan, it's just that I prefer not to. I have lived on the Upper West Side most of my life, except for my university years in Galway. I found my apartment back in my twenties. Everyone was renting, but I had enough of my grandparents' Irish insecurity gene to push myself financially and purchase. And I have lived every which way in this two-bedroom apartment in a block built in the thirties on 77th. I lived with a single futon until my job as a magazine and cookery editor yielded enough for me to decorate in late eighties chrome and white leather, then Parisian purple and gold-leaf chic through the self-conscious stylish nineties until, after years of lobbying the board, I finally got to knock down a wall and get the huge minimalist kitchen/living space I'd been dreaming of for ever. My apartment is finally home. *My* home. First and only problem right there. I am not alone any more.

The superintendent's hole in the basement was never an option, so Dan has been more or less living in my apartment since we met. Out of pure necessity, I am paying lip service to the quaint 'what's mine is yours' principle. He puts his boots up on my original Eames chair and has terrorised my much-loved kitchen implements with his clumsy ham-sized hands. He put my Edwardian potato ricer in the dishwasher, where I found it rusting, devastated by the careless attack.

I don't know if I can accommodate Dan in my life for ever, but I do know I can't accommodate him in my apartment for much longer. I am beginning to think I would feel more in control renting it out and living elsewhere with my lumbering husband.

Almost as soon as we cross the Hudson, I feel the panic that descends when I move too far out of the city. There is this snobbery; nowhere else can quite match the cool island sanctum of New York City, but nowhere falls as glaringly short as the areas that surround it.

The roads yawn out from four lanes to eight, and the landscape makes that subtle shift. I start to see four-wheel drives, the occasional pickup, strip malls, aluminium sidings, and patches of grass that are not public parks but owned by individuals. To me, this has always been a place with more space yet less room to breathe; more churches but less soul; more light, more sky, yet less to look at.

All the while Dan is babbling on and on about the area and the friends he has there. He is painting truly awful pictures for me of barbecues on decked patios, with jumbo packages of chemically spiced meat.

His thought process is spoken out loud and along the lines of happily ever after in the suburban outback. Mine is a terrified implosion of panic. I know that all I have to do is look at the house, say 'I don't want this' and things will stay as they are. But this is what Dan wants. It's who he is—a man of simple tastes, conventional in that everyday, unremarkable way. I want something, some*one* different, a soulmate, and Dan isn't it. With the right person, I could share Yonkers in an ironic, postmodern way. But with Dan, clearly, that is not going to happen.

We were married one month yesterday. Dan bought me flowers. A mixed bunch in cellophane from a deli. It's the thought that counts—yet I just keep getting caught up in all these ways in which we are not right for each other. I don't need expensive flowers. I like simple but stylish. So buy me daisies from a florist, not roses from a deli. It's a small distinction, but a significant one to me. Shouldn't the right guy just know? Of course, it doesn't matter. It's a detail. Except now that I am wedded to this person a detail, barely discernible in the heady fog of our early romance, becomes intolerable once it has the weight of a lifetime attached. I know that it is hard adjusting to living with somebody else, but it just seems like there are too many things: plaid shirts, fishing catalogues, the wrong flowers. Then the basics, which I hadn't chosen to notice before. Every day I seem to become fixated on a different one. He blows his nose at the table. Once I have noted this, I can see nothing else; he appears to be blowing and wiping his nose continually. How had I never seen this before? I want to say something, but I don't. Because even though we are married, I don't have that right.

I don't love him. You have to love somebody before you can scream bloody murder at them for something as stupid as blowing their nose.

So I am living with this frenzied monologue in my head continually bleating on about all the irritating little things he does. He leaves the bathroom door open and talks to me while he pees. He leaves his knife in the open jam jar. He puts the butter back in the fridge so it's always hard. I am boring *myself* with my endless list of petty complaints.

Dan has no idea what is going on in my head. If he had, then it would undoubtedly be the end of our marriage. Maybe I am just not cut out for marriage at all. Unable to compromise or uncompromising. The former is bad, but isn't the latter a compliment? It means sticking with it, holding out for the real thing.

I wanted to be married. I wanted—want—children, or at least one child. I am a food editor and writer. I create a feeling of home in magazines that people aspire to. I wanted to create something special with somebody else. But you can't spin a lifestyle out of nothing. Otherwise it is just style with no life. You need love to build a home with conviction. And that crucial ingredient is missing for me.

I got married because I didn't want to be alone. Yet driving away from the city, my old life behind me and the possibility of a new one in front me, I never felt more alone in my life.

'This,' Dan says as we pull up at a small grocery store, 'is McClean Avenue.' He says it like we have finally arrived at our destination. Not in Yonkers, but in 'life'. McClean Avenue is where you can buy last Sunday's *Irish Independent*, enjoy a cup of Barry's Tea with your imported sausages and bacon, or get drunk on Irish beer in an Irish bar with people who also *wish* they were Irish—like Dan and some who lay greater claim to being Irish, like me.

In fact, Dan's whole 'Irish' angle really makes me crazy. It is the only thing we truly have in common, yet our perception of what it means to be Irish couldn't be more different. Although I wasn't born there, I spent some of my childhood and all my student years there. For me Ireland is the brooding brown boglands lit up a thousand shades of purple and gold by a temperamental sun. It is the sour smell of burning turf on a wet day and my grandmother's rhubarb tart. It is Joyce, Yeats, Behan—a complex, creative heritage too vast to attempt explanation.

For Dan? It is green beer and rubbery brack cake.

I know this because Dan comes back out of the shop with a carton of milk and a cellophane-wrapped package claiming to be 'genuine, original Irish Barm brack' made by a woman called Kitty. The sell-by date is next fall, and the list of ingredients a roll-call of chemicals.

'This is crap,' I say and he looks hurt. Like I wasn't just talking about the cake. There is an atmosphere building between us. He knows he is doing something wrong, but is afraid to ask me what it is. Then guilt kicks in, the arbiter of my honesty. As soon as things get close to the truth, guilt steps in to create a smokescreen.

'I'll bake you a better brack than this, baby. A real Irish porter cake.'

He leans over and kisses me even though he's driving, and I wonder how it's possible for me to turn myself into Doris Day so easily and that, more unbelievably, I have married a man who believes me when I do.

As we weave our way upward, the houses get more affluent. It seems that money can buy character and, the higher we go, the more interesting the houses become. My cynicism toward Yonkers is temporarily quieted by a three-storey red-brick with beautiful wrought-iron balconies. Dan stops the car and says, 'Here we are.'

I'm stunned. 'Here?'

'This is it, baby.'

'This? The red-brick?'

'You like it?' He's doing that thing that I cannot bear: wagging his tail with boyish enthusiasm, looking for my approval, my praise. 'I love you' by another name.

'It looks OK.'

Actually, I love it already. But I can't tell him that. Dan bought this house ten years ago as an investment. Not just financially, but in his belief that one day he would meet the right woman and have a proper home to put her in. If I say 'yes' to this house, I am saying 'yes' to so much more. It is idiotic to say that I do not feel ready to move into Dan's house when I have already agreed to spend the rest of my life with him. But as long as we have our separate apartments and a temporary à la carte living arrangement, I can still see my escape door.

There is no escape door in Longville Avenue. Inside the house are exposed beams, aged-oak floorboards, and a basement full of cranky bits of furniture that need polishing, upholstering, loving back to life. There is an original cast-iron bathtub languishing in a hallway and a dresser with an enamel worktop and broken hinges. A dozen rooms waiting to be cast in their roles as nursery, kitchen, living room, bedroom.

Dan is directly behind me shuffling, gawking, hoping. He starts, 'It's a real mess but . . .'

He wants me to finish his sentence. To tell him I can see what he sees: that with his work and my eye this house could be a wonderful family home. I can see his dream and I want to share it. Just not with him. The faded floral curtain over the back door shivers in a breeze and the sadness of my secret washes over me. I don't answer but walk towards the back door, rattle it open and step out into the garden. It is a wilderness.

I pick my way down a stone path that seems to go on for ever, then reach a bank of ivy and budding clematis that tells me I have reached the end. To my left are young, green nettles, which, I make mental note, would make excellent soup. To my right I can see a stone cherub peering at me from behind the weeds. As I brush them aside, the mossy figure falls with them. I lean down to rescue him and see that he has fallen onto a bed of voluminous frilly leaves sprung with narrow red stalks. It is rhubarb growing wild.

James and I favoured eleven o'clock Sunday Mass in the local village of Kilkelly. It was closer to us than our parish church of Achadh Mor and you did not have to cross fields to get to it. For that reason, it tended to be something of a fashion parade, attracting late risers and a less serious crowd than the dour farming stock of the country church. There were the poor who walked barefoot to Mass and put their shoes on behind the stile opposite the church, and there were the less poor who walked or cycled fully shod. It seemed, growing up, that they were from different planets and in marrying James Nolan I had joined the ranks of the latter. Through my connection with Aunt Ann, I already considered myself socially elevated, and being young and ignorant was able to draw some comfort from that.

I hated James that first year. I thought him arrogant for the way he carried himself in public, as if he were equal to everyone else. I felt I knew my place and I remember him introducing me to the doctor and his wife and being annoyed that he thought we were suitable for such grand company. The wife invited me round for tea and it irritated me even more that they both appeared to like James. I told her I didn't have time for such niceties as my husband worked me too hard. I could see she was shocked by my brashness, but James laughed at my attempt to embarrass him, as if I was the wittiest woman around.

He was always in his element showing me off. There was nothing I could say or do to deter him. If I wore a gaudy suit to Mass, he would declare I looked 'perfect'. When I said rude things, he believed I was joking. Everywhere we went he attracted people like a magnet, and the first thing he would always do was introduce me as his wife, his face flushed with pride, as if to say, 'Look what I've got.'

Although we both knew I did not belong to him. Not in any way that mattered.

Kilkelly church had a long aisle and was rather grand. James and I had a place in the second row, just under the pulpit, where, as teacher in the local school, James was expected to sit. As he ushered me into the church pew before him each Sunday, he would place the flat of his hand gently on the small of my back. And for the first full year of our marriage, that was the only way James touched me.

From the first night we spent together, I made it quite clear that if James Nolan wanted his marital rights, he was going to have to take them. I would not fight him off, my body was his property and it would be against God to deny him. But he knew how I felt. While I never said it, my dislike for him permeated our house. I made sure I was an exemplary wife in every way that was on show. Up at six every morning with the hens fed, fire lit and his shaving water warmed and waiting for him before he rose at eight. He ate hot porridge with cream and there was meat with two vegetables on the table at one o'clock each day. For tea there was always a choice of cake, tart, or bread and jam. His shirts were starched and pressed and every item from his socks to his felt trilby hat was darned and steamed until it was restored to a better condition than the day it was bought. The house was so clean that a visitor might feel awkward putting a boot on my shiny flagstones or hanging a dirty coat over one of my chairs. I was so scrupulous in my housekeeping that the very ashes in the grate held themselves in a tidy pyramid for fear of me.

If I worked hard, I knew that no person, not even God, could question my honour and respect for my husband. Only James and I knew that he did not want my honour or my respect.

He wanted my love, but I did not have the love in me to give to him. I had already given it all away to somebody else.

Only when our bedroom door closed at night did the truth of our loveless arrangement emerge. James continued to sleep on a settle at the side of our bed, which I had made up for him on our wedding night. I remember shaking with fear that first night in a stranger's bed, terrified that a man with whom I was barely acquainted would suddenly leap on me in the darkness. As the hours progressed, I almost wished his brutality upon me, so that it could be done with and the terrible waiting over.

It was only in the morning that I realised he had crept silently out of the room not one hour after lying down and spent the night sitting up in the kitchen reading. I was nearly angrier with him over that. I felt deceived in having expected this barbaric attack when my Viking ravager was adjusting his reading glasses over *The Capuchin Annual*. This I didn't understand.

Night reading was something James did often in that first year. He never asked, or suggested, or cajoled, or made any attempt on me whatsoever except in often telling me I looked beautiful. I was not grateful for the way my husband was managing his passions; in my ignorance, I thought him weak. I think now that if he had taken a firmer hand to me that first year, our marriage might have been a more balanced affair.

But then how quickly we become saints, willing to give all our hearts once we know our sacrifice is no longer needed.

Against all expectations, what helped me through that first year was James's mother, Ellie, who insisted from the first that I should call her by her Christian name. Widowed young, she had reared seven children, educating the older ones until they were old enough to help support the younger. She was a resourceful, extraordinary woman. Refusing to accept charity from her neighbours, she had farmed her children out to various relations while she spent several summers working in England alongside our local men. The fact that this had earned her respect and status among her neighbours, as opposed to scandalising them, was testament to the type of person she was. She was a hard-working, generous woman who did not care what people thought of her. And, in fairness to our community, she was thought of highly. I did not know about any of that when I found myself living next door to my new husband's invalid mother. All I knew was that, despite myself, I liked her and that she was kindly towards me, which she need not have been.

A routine developed quickly between us. After James had opened the school at nine o'clock, I would cross the short field with a tray for her breakfast. I would cook to please the old woman more quickly than I would for her son. I found his praise cloying and false, given the strained situation between us. Ellie's praise was always genuine, though she had no reason to give it. She confided that she was a poor cook and would go into ecstasies over my boxty pancakes, asking for the exact method, then laughing at the idea that she would ever make them. Ellie could afford to make jokes against herself as she was so very easy to love. Her house was higgledy-piggledy, and as I would start to fuss around the place cleaning, she would call out for me to sit and read to her. It felt decadent somehow to be reading novels at eleven o'clock in the morning when there was work to be done, but Ellie insisted we feed our minds as well as our bodies.

Her favourite was Sir Walter Scott's dramatic poem, *Marmion*. There was still plenty of fire in Ellie and she loved the bloody descriptions of combat on the Scottish Highlands.

I grieved for the women wailing for their perished loves, and while my voice quivered over some exaggerated declaration of love, I felt that Ellie knew I was thinking about Michael. She certainly knew about us in the way that everybody knew I had been doing a line with the Yank. I always felt Ellie knew more still—that I did not love her son, despite the fact that I would leap up from my seat before midday and rush back to prepare his dinner.

I believed Ellie loved James with the fierce, protective passion every mother has for her sons, but she befriended me anyway. She was in my life for such a short time and yet she had huge influence—perhaps because she made me feel that I was not so bad a wife as I pretended to be. Perhaps her unconditional approval made me less cruel than I might have been towards James, although I was still dismissive of him. Maybe this was her way of asking me to be a good wife to her son after she was gone. Or maybe she just liked me and was glad to have me related to her. I don't know—nor will I ever.

But this is what I believe: Ellie Nolan had more wisdom than I learned in the whole of my marriage, or ever will in the rest of my life. In losing her husband so young, she learned how little value we place on real love while we have it. The poetic passions of fiction are just that, a fiction. And the realities of love, the way it fades when you try to grab it, then clutches your guts with a painful squeeze of grief after you have lost it, reach so much further than a young girl's romantic dreams. Ellie struggled in the aftermath of her husband's death to feed, clothe and educate seven children on her own. She understood that poetry and passion were for reading by the fire, but a woman who could cook well and keep a clean house for her working son was a good enough start.

Ellie knew that the love that starts strongest often weakens with time, giving up before the race is ended. It is often the slowest to start that will finish the race. But this is not a lesson that anything other than time can teach you.

We were married one year to the day when Ellie died.

James had made a small fuss over our anniversary, presenting me with a brooch in the shape of a swallow. I thanked him politely, and then placed it to one side of my dressing table, not bothering to try it on. As I prepared Ellie's breakfast, my mind was occupied with my shiny new trinket. If I wore it, it would give James a message of love. If I left it aside for ever, perhaps he would not bother buying me another. I decided on a compromise. I would wear it across to Ellie's and show off what her son had given me. It would please her to see that James had made me happy.

It had taken me a full year to be willing to sacrifice a small corner of my pride for somebody else's happiness and it was too late.

When I found her, Ellie was lying on her back with her rosary beads in her hands. She had died peacefully in her sleep. She must have known she was going to die.

I wept over her cold body for one hour before fetching my husband. There are lies in tears. The ones we weep most loudly are usually for ourselves, yet how easily we can pass them off as grief. I was fond of the old woman, but I allowed her to turn cold while I contemplated my own troubles. Ellie had provided a distraction and now it was James and me alone. How was I going to cope?

Honesty, in my experience, is seldom an act of kindness; more often it is a brutal, selfish need to purge, thinly disguised as morality.

So I buried my face in Ellie's blanket and I wept for all my misfortunes. I told her I did not love her son, but I promised I would never stop trying. And, even as I said it, I knew that I had not tried to love him up to that point beyond keeping him and his house clean and tidy.

After I had cried myself dry, I went to the schoolhouse and I told James that his mother had passed away. He was stoical and kept the school open until lunchtime. Ellie was old and, once James had been seen leaving the school stony-faced, the neighbours had guessed at what had happened. The funeral began with barely an instruction from us.

The wake went on for three days and two nights. As was the custom, Ellie was laid out in her kitchen. The neighbours brought in their best crockery and laid out scones, sandwiches, tarts, cooked hams, chickens. Their message was clear: they had known and loved Ellie for all of her life and I was an interloper. For those few days the house belonged to them, and they came and went as they pleased. An obscene amount of food and five full bottles of whisky were consumed by a host of friends and strangers who came to pay their respects. James welcomed them all as if they had been as close to Ellie as he had been. He offered them food and drink as if they were as deserving of comfort as he.

I stayed by his side and together we accepted condolences until we could barely stand. It was the first thing in our marriage that I can truly say we did together. I had respected Ellie and for those few days I admired James for how he was handling his grief and for the generous way he received his guests.

For the burial I wore my fitted black coat and a smart woollen hat. On my lapel I wore the swallow James had given me. It was inappropriately decorative, but I didn't care. Neither did James and I felt Ellie would have been pleased at our small rebellion. I linked James's arm throughout the service as a public show of support. As the clay clattered down onto the coffin, I felt James's hand reach for mine and I did not move it one way or the other but let him hold me.

We arrived home, the two of us alone again as we had been on our wedding night, except our exhaustion from lack of sleep highlighted this even more. James was in the footless, disbelieving grief of the adult orphan. A mother draws a map for her child and places herself at the centre of it. Her death wipes that map clean. She leaves you knowing you must redraw it to survive and yet not knowing where to start.

I asked James if he wanted food and he declined. Although it was barely past four in the afternoon, I went into the bedroom, closed over the curtains and lay down in the bed. My eyes were like lead, but as sleep began to pull me down into its velvet blackness I suddenly felt something behind me. I leapt up automatically and called out in terror.

James had climbed into the bed next to me. I could see that his arms and shoulders were bare which I took to mean he was naked. The room was light and he was looking at me.

I supposed I had called out something awful and made attempts at a kind of an apology.

His eyes were stuck on my face. Love being too much to hope for, he was searching for the slenderest thread of feeling. Evidence to prove there could be some comfort in being married to me. He would not have expected much after the year we had had together. Just enough to get him through that night. He found nothing and I knew then that he had truly seen my disdain for him.

In that instant I witnessed the depth of his grief. His face crumpled in on itself and he turned his back to me. Our bed became a boat floating on the waves of his grief as it rocked in rhythm with his sobbing. I might have lost patience were these the petulant, self-pitying tears I was so familiar with in myself. But this was justified grief. He was a naked, rejected man unable physically to lift himself away from me, such was the power of his sorrow.

I was afraid, not of what James might do, but of what I could not do. Afraid of my own cold-heartedness. So afraid that I tried.

I reached over my hand and I touched the top of his head. His hair was wiry and this surprised me. I had looked at it often and wondered, yet never touched it before. I had expected his body to freeze, as if a single touch from me was enough to quell a mountain of passion. I was disappointed when he continued to cry. More than that I wanted him to stop. I did not feel I was strong enough to bear witness to such pain. So I leaned across his back and clumsily kissed the wet of his cheek.

He turned on me suddenly and kissed me hungrily on the mouth. I felt betrayed, as if he had tricked love out of me by weeping for his dead mother. I knew that was not how it was, but that was how it felt.

When you are young, feelings are your truth. Love is how you feel. The years have taught me that love is not an emotion that you feel about someone, but what you do for them. That night I gave James my body. I did not give it with the passion I had given to Michael Tuffy. But I gave.

In the years that came after I never told him I felt only pity in my heart for him that first night. That truth was hard and I knew it would hurt him, so I kept it to myself. I compromised my own truth for his.

Yet the truth is not always as it seems. Many years afterwards James told me that the person I had called out for in my fear had been him.

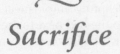

Sacrifice

In sacrificing something we believe,
we can be rewarded with something we love

Honey Cake
Although I always had a sweet tooth, I never liked honey until I ran clean out of sugar one day and tried this.

Mix 1 tablespoon cornflour and 2 teaspoons baking powder with 1lb flour and set aside. Cream together about 5oz butter with just short of a full jar of honey. Gradually add the dry ingredients along with 3 eggs beaten into ¼ pint milk until the mixture is smooth and creamy. You can add 1 teaspoon vanilla or cinnamon to taste—but I always preferred it plain. Turn into a greased loaf tin and cook in a medium/hot oven for up to 1½ hours.

REPLACING SUGAR WITH HONEY may seem like a straight swap, but it isn't as simple as that. Honey works best used with sugar, not instead of it. Of course, a lot depends on the honey—and as with all ingredients, some are better than others. Granddad kept bees, so the honey Grandma Bernadine used was unique and fresher than anything you could buy in a shop. I know. Westside Market stocks forty-six brands and I've tried them all. You can use a full jar of really expensive stuff and you still might not even be able to taste it. Generally, taking sugar out of a cake recipe for the sake of a little honey is a pointless sacrifice.

Dan's parents are Irish Catholics and he comes near the middle of eight children. He is the only one of the boys who wasn't married by age thirty, and the only one who does not attend Mass each Sunday. By his family's standards, he is wayward and unconventional. A real wild card.

Eileen, his mother, is a substantial woman who turns every question into a barked instruction: 'You'll have tea?'

She speaks with a flat Limerick accent distorted by a Yankee twang. Dan is a little afraid of his mother, which I find disconcerting. Her home is a shrine to marriage and children. It is crammed with trophies: china dolls, pictures of children in heart-shaped frames, frames with teddy-bear motifs. More cherubic faces are emblazoned on mugs, coasters and calendars. Every surface is groaning with wedding photographs. All of Dan's family are interconnected; they godparent each other's children, buy each other's cars, share ownership of ride-on mowers. They visit the mall in hair-sprayed, buggy-pushing gangs. They decorate each other's houses and feed each other's children. Reigning over this car-pooling, baby-sitting, meal-sharing, mall-mashing industry is Eileen Mullins. She cooks and co-ordinates, but mostly she just presides. Inscrutable, indestructible, in charge.

In contrast, Dan's father is a wiry, self-contained fellow who mostly just keeps out of everyone's way.

I'm with the father, hoping to stay on the outskirts, but it seems I'm not to get away with it.

Dan still has his superintendent's job on the apartment in Manhattan, so he has been commuting in and out of the city a lot. Finally he has appointed a deputy to cover his weekends and it is our first full Sunday in Longville Avenue. Dan says, 'You better get dressed, honey—we're due over for lunch at one.'

I'm confused. I have food in and this is a surprise. I don't like surprises, especially when it comes to food, and especially when I'm exhausted from unpacking boxes of junk in an effort to make our house home. 'What, have you booked somewhere?'

Dan raised his eyebrows quizzically, as if the answer was so obvious it didn't need stating. 'Mom's place, of course.'

Of course.

Ninety-eight per cent of Dan's extended family lives in or around Yonkers. An only child, I was raised in a loft with a mother who was trying to be bohemian and a series of her useless boyfriends. How was I to know that marriage was going to suck me into a vortex of relations? That saying 'I do' would initiate me into a tribe of women who rummage in each other's handbags for tissues?

'Sorry, Dan, but you should have told me earlier. I have things to do.'

The vastness of the understatement wasn't lost on him. We first visited this house just five weeks ago and already we have packed up my apartment and prepared it for rental. Dan has knocked a wall through from the front to the back of the house downstairs and is preparing the plumbing and electricity for my new kitchen. It's going to be pared-down Shaker style with open shelves and featuring an imported solid-fuel Waterford Stanley stove. Completely different from the high-tech state-of-the-art one in my apartment, it will be a grown-up working kitchen for serious hands-on cooking. I can get appliances in as and when I need them. But for the time being I want to keep my cooking as simple as possible. Perhaps because my head is swirling with complicated crap, my body craves the clarity of physical activity, the one-two-three order of mixing and beating and pouring. Only the sitting and waiting for it to bake disturbs me, so I have turned to the garden and have a vegetable patch cleared and ready to be planted.

Yesterday Dan joined me and, without asking if I needed his help, began to rake the soil while I remained on my knees crumbling it with my fingers. Mincing compost into the square metre of grey grit I had meticulously weeded the day before. He wittered on for a few minutes, asking me questions about what I was going to plant, then the two of us fell into a concentrated silence. We have worked well together in the past few weeks. Dan is physical, strong—and so, I have discovered, am I. We make a good team and I find myself appreciating the way we can pass tools, or make each other coffee, without the other having to ask. It is a kind of intimacy, an easing into our marriage. I keep busy because when I am working I am less aware of my guilt, the fear that all I am doing in creating this home is building more obstacles to hinder my eventual escape.

Next weekend it is the Symposium for Professional Food Writers in Chicago. It will be a break. It's bad to want a break from marriage after just two months, but it will give me time on my own to sort my head out.

Dan could have mentioned lunch at his mother's house while out in the garden yesterday, but he didn't. I need to draw the line. If I go with him today, then we will be expected to go every Sunday, something he'd always been expected to do before meeting me.

'We only need to go for an hour,' he says.

I am not attuned to the kind of emotional blackmail that Eileen can inflict on Dan. My mother has always been an independent woman. She does her thing and I do mine. My grandparents longed for my visits to Ireland, I knew that, but they never made me feel obliged and always celebrated my career successes even though they meant less frequent trips to see them. This pleading is alien territory to me.

'Please, Tressa.'

However, I do know about guilt. And I am learning real fast.

Dan is a good man. I now realise that's why I married him. And he is doing all the right things. He can plumb a toilet, fix a roof, wire a stove—he never says 'no'. He is staying up all night to put together kitchen units to my (exacting) specifications. He has accepted my lies about being exhausted from the stress of moving and has laid off me in bed. I can see how he is putting everything he has into this marriage and yet it is not enough. It will never be enough, because whatever it is *I* need to make me feel fulfilled, content, *sure*—that mysterious ingredient that just says, this is right—Dan does not have it. Not for me.

But because he is trying, I feel guilty. So I give in.

'OK, I'll get dressed. One hour, then we come home—right?'

He is beaming like a prize-winning schoolboy and it's making me nervous.

I am not in the house five minutes when I realise what a monumental aberration it is that I have managed to avoid this Sunday lunch gathering for so long. There are a lot of people here, maybe twenty including the children. It always alarms me when I see how many there are in Dan's family; names and ages start whirring and they seem to blur in front of my very eyes. Everyone is greeting me with the warmth one might reserve for somebody returned from the brink of death. Their relief is palpable, like *at last* Dan's wife has graced us. I realise that Dan's casual 'We'll pop in for an hour' invite had come after weeks of intense family pressure. So now there is this layer of knowledge: that I know that Dan knows that I don't like his family, even though I have never said anything to suggest it. And now *they* know that I don't like them because it has taken us so long to respond to this ongoing Sunday lunch summons.

Basically, it's one of those buttock-clenching, awkward moments.

Eileen grunts at me briefly, but that means nothing. She is from the generation before hugging was invented. Stern matriarchs who provide

shelter and food, but don't offer affection after your fifth birthday. No
wonder her kids are all grinning at me like frightened rabbits.

I ask, 'Can I help, Eileen?'

A sister-in-law, Shirley, catches my eye, and raises her brow a degree,
although I know that she doesn't mean her fellowship to comfort me.
Shirley is a cheap, competitive cow. She wore a white gauzy dress to our
wedding—and no underwear. Nipples in the chapel. Classy.

The twins leap up to help their mother. Kay and Meg are identical,
right down to their square straight teeth and their bubbly personalities.
They are mercilessly upbeat and friendly. You have to like them. They
seem much younger than their thirty years, and still live at home.

There is no order to the meal. Cutlery is thrown onto the centre of the
table along with an open packet of napkins. Kay hands out (unwarmed)
plates; men wander to get beer from the fridge and women take the
opportunity to call to them for a Sprite. Meg and Eileen start to carry out
platters of food, and guests haphazardly clear away newspapers, bills,
Walkmans, the miscellaneous stuff that gathers in every kitchen, to make
room on every crammed surface. The food is mostly fried meat—ribs,
drumsticks, steakhouse burgers—accompanied by man-made variations
of the potato—fries, waffles, wedges. Everyone grabs at it hungrily and
starts dipping into bowls full of various gloopy condiments.

Eileen picks up a plate of ribs and sticks it under my nose. I smile,
take one and she nods towards a bowl of sauce. She is going to police
my eating, check the fancy food writer's response to her cooking. I am
not, despite being a food snob, a fussy eater. But this pressure is making
me feel physically sick and the vinegary smell from the dripping meat
does not help. Dear God, I am going to hurl. I can feel the shocked faces
follow me onto the patio.

Dan comes straight out after me and when he lays his hand on my
shoulder it releases a breath I didn't know I had been holding. For no
specific reason I can determine I start to cry. He leads me to a corner of
the patio where nobody can see us and wraps himself round my head
and shoulders. He doesn't care that I am sobbing in the middle of what is
supposed to be a happy family gathering and he does not ask what is the
matter with me. This is just as well because I have not got the first clue
myself. It's a relief, briefly, to let myself go without thinking about it.

Dan holds me until I manage to gather myself back together, then he
takes my chin in his hand and wipes my wet cheek with his palm. I feel
about ten years old.

'I guess Mom's ribs are pretty bad, huh?'

I manage a smile and say, 'Thanks.'

'Thanks for Jack shit, baby—that's my job,' he says, then takes my hand and walks me back into the kitchen. In a funny way, I think he is pleased that I snapped; it showed I am human.

'Tressa's got a bug, folks. I'm taking her home.'

They are all concerned, though I can see Shirley smirking in the corner as if to say, 'Welcome to Ma Mullins's Sunday bonanza, bitch.'

As we are walking out the door, she calls, 'See you at the First Communion next weekend?' and I can feel Dan's hand weaken over mine.

Eight years passed and brought with them the inevitable intimacy of routine. I knew James's footsteps on the gravel of the road, I could trace the pattern of his body in our bed, I grew used to the smell of his skin, so that I found comfort in it. Still I would not let go of my ideal and not one single day passed when I did not think of Michael. Over those early years, especially, I remember walking out in the field at the back of our house late at night and looking up at the stars. I would say his name and imagine that he could hear me. *I still love you, Michael. I still love you.*

In saying it out loud, I was able to make it real again. So I was not an ordinary country schoolteacher's wife, but that passionate young woman again. A stream of whispers pouring out of me: *I still love you, I still love you,* over and over so that the words might make a line that would carry up and up across the galaxies and find him where he was. How many words would it take to get to America? How many to bring him back to me again? He would never forget me. Not Michael. Love like we had never dies. It never grows old or dulls with the bland, grey shades of familiarity. Love as vibrant as ours would live for ever.

In those early years I did grow fonder of James. I could not say that I loved him, but I came to understand that being married to him was not the disaster I had thought it would be. Although I did not fully appreciate it at the time, we had a good life. James, spurred on by my example, started to rise early and developed more of an interest in small farming, so we had a modest herd of cattle in addition to his teaching income. I kept hens and reared pigs for the slaughter as my mother had done, and James took up bee-keeping when war and sugar shortages threatened. Between us, we were virtually able to feed ourselves and sell on any surplus honey and eggs to a shopkeeper in Ballyhaunis. With the spare cash we made improvements to our house. We had running water in the scullery and a range built into the wall where the fire had been. I had the tailor Tarpey make me three suits a year and I bought fabric from him to make my own dresses. One year, we had a four-day holiday in Dublin. We stayed in great style at the Gresham Hotel and took tea in Bewley's Coffee House; I bought cinnamon and coriander and all kinds of spices from Findlaters on Harcourt Street; and we went to the cinema and saw *Random Harvest*, then walked up and down O'Connell Street into the late evening. I wore a lilac suit; James, a long trench coat with a trilby hat cocked over one eye. I remember feeling happy that day, thinking that life was close to perfect and wondering at my luck in being married to such an elegant man. Although I would always stop myself short, always pull back. I was afraid to let go and let myself love him. Afraid I would lose the bit of power I had if I didn't keep him at arm's length. During those few days in Dublin, though, I felt as if we had everything we could possibly want in life. And we did. Except for the one thing each of us wanted more than life itself.

For me it was Michael.

For James it was a child.

James knew I did not want children early on in our marriage, and being an educated, sensitive man, he went along with my wishes and took steps to avoid conception. There are ways that are not against nature or God, and we were lucky.

I was not maternal by nature. Babies and children left me cold. Some women who don't love their husbands have children so they can have somebody to love. I needed to love the man I was going to have children with, if I was going to sacrifice my body, my dignity, in that way. I was prepared to shrug off the snide comments as the years passed without our conceiving, the sideways looks in Mass when another infant was christened. Neighbours and James's sisters looked at me with disappointment, disbelief and latterly pity. I didn't care. I thought they were all fools. Babies, as far as I could see, were selfish, squawking parasites.

After eight years, without saying anything, James stopped withdrawing from me during lovemaking. He was over forty and I was edging ever closer towards thirty. I said nothing when he changed our routine. I just took myself from the bed immediately after we had made love, washed myself thoroughly and prayed.

The tension we had experienced in the first year came back into our marriage as if it had never been away. James had grown more sure of me, but I was still no pushover and we waged the second of our long-standing silent wars. I became physically elusive, which was my only weapon. James in turn started to behave out of character, which I found unsettling. When I scolded him (as I did every day) over some household trivia, I could see his chin set in anger and once or twice I feared he might rise up at me. He became irritable, criticising the priest and complaining about his job on a daily basis. One Sunday I caught sight of him as he looked up from his book to check the weather through the kitchen window. Pure sadness washed across his face, an expression of devastated loss like there had been after Ellie died. James had a long nose and delicate features that gave him an erudite, refined expression. When that confident, sophisticated face became sullied with anguish, the extremity of it tore at me.

I wanted to reach over as I had done the night we buried Ellie, except that this time I knew exactly what words would make his sorrow disappear. I couldn't speak them because I knew I was not prepared to follow them through. If I were a different, weaker kind of woman, I might have lied his pain away.

I did not love James but I was not cold-hearted and I could see that he was hurt. My mistake was in believing, after almost ten years of marriage, that I knew him. I thought that his pride was at stake. That it was his craving for convention, and the respect of his peers that was making him want a child. It was only after our daughter was born that I came to truly understand how James simply yearned to be a father.

Roseanne, my agent, rang this morning to see where she should send the tickets to Chicago. There was a sponsor interested in coming on board with my grandmother's recipes for TV, and Roseanne had heard back from the publishers who were excited already. It felt weird talking to her standing in the middle of the half-painted hallway in this wreck of a house. It was my voice, saying the same sort of stuff as usual, and even though it had only been the usual number of weeks since I got her bimonthly 'darling' call, it felt like I have been out of circulation for ever. Often I hide away, especially when I am working on developing recipes. But with the wedding, and the house move, and no kitchen to work in at the moment, it's like I've gone into hiding from myself.

I've lost who I was before I met Dan: Tressa Nolan, thirty-seven, Irish, single, successful food writer, living comfortably on the Upper West Side. My morning routine was a ten-minute walk in the park, followed by a mochaccino coffee from Starbucks, then a morning's work interrupted by my delivery guys arriving with fish, meat and organic dairy. I'd meet a girlfriend for lunch, then wander down to Citarella and splurge on chocolate or delicious olives, followed by a root around Westside Market's vegetables looking for ideas. All of the best ingredients I could possibly need were within a few blocks or could be ordered to the door.

I liked my life how it was and now I have lost it. Literally.

The house, Dan, his family, mall shopping, the two of us pushing a grocery cart around Farmers' Market with thousands of other Saturday supermarket couples—this is my life now. It doesn't feel like it belongs to me and I don't know that it ever will. I have to find new shops, new suppliers, and I am too set in my ways to be bothered. Truthfully—I don't know that I feel committed enough to this new life to start over.

I don't know what I was expecting from married life. Was the life I wanted just the life I had with the additional benefit of testosterone? The same of everything with somebody strong to put up shelves and demystify furniture instructions? Am I really that shallow? That cynical?

In some ways I wish I were.

The truth is the vision I had for myself is what I have now: a good man like Dan and a big old house to renovate, with enough of a plot out back for vegetables. But the important expectation, the only one that matters, was that I would be happy. And I'm not.

Happily ever after—so how does that work? Two months into my marriage and I'm miserable. It's just not working.

I wake up in the morning and the first thing I think is, 'I don't love Dan.' I work like a dog all day so that I don't have to think about it, then last thing at night it comes back, 'I don't love Dan.' I want to love him. I *need* to love him, but I just can't. Don't, can't, never will.

What the hell am I going to do? I can't stay married to a man that I don't love because it is not fair on either of us. Dan has it all there on paper. He is handsome, a listener, affectionate—he would make a wonderful father and a loyal husband. And he loves me. He really does.

So why can't I just love him back? I know I am married to a good man in my head, but my heart just isn't responding. It is a mystery that I can see all of Dan's good qualities but I still cannot drum up a feeling of love for him. But then falling and, more importantly, staying in love is a mysterious process. You just have to wait until it happens to you. Maybe I should have waited longer.

Maybes aside, Dan deserves better than this. He deserves a woman who adores the ground he walks on. A woman who would do anything for him. A woman who would give up the most important event in her work calendar to attend his niece's First Communion.

He dropped hints about it, but he wouldn't ask outright. Dan knew that this conference was really important to me. I told him that on Sunday, as soon as we left his mother's. After he had told me that his entire family was gathering at his Mom's for an informal reunion with some cousins from Ireland. His mother's brother, whom she hadn't seen for twenty years, would be there. It was kind of a historic event, really. Not just Deirdre's First Communion. He hadn't mentioned it before because he knew it clashed with my conference.

I told him that was really understanding of him and gave him a kiss.

The following day over breakfast Dan mentioned in a voice that was meant to sound casual, but didn't, that, actually, there would be quite a lot of people who weren't at our wedding coming to the First Communion. I looked forlorn and said that it truly was a terrible pity that the two things clashed. That if it had been any event other than this, I might have been able to change it. He shrugged and said it didn't really matter, but he looked as if he had just been run over by a bus.

The theme continued over supper with the revelation that it was a real shame I couldn't make it to the First Communion because his Uncle Patrick was kind of coming over from Ireland especially to meet me.

I kept my head. That was just awful, I said, but I felt sure I would get the chance to meet Uncle Patrick while he was here—perhaps your mother could bring him round for supper the following week? Not possible, unfortunately, said Dan, because Uncle Patrick was going to stay with his friend, the priest, in Los Angeles the day after the Communion, and this really was our only chance to meet him.

A tragedy, I conceded: if only somebody had taken the trouble to notify me when Uncle Patrick was booking his flights, then we might have arranged our lives around his trip. It was a last-minute thing, Dan rushed to inform me, he got a cheap deal. I was drawing breath on my final 'Oh well, never mind,' when Dan launched into a soliloquy about how his sister Kay had been really upset when he had broken the news that I might not be going. And poor little Deirdre, who had been telling all her friends that her new aunty would be at her party, was upset as well. Then he ended with the extraordinary information that his Mom hadn't made it clear how important this Sunday was to her because she didn't want to put us under any pressure.

So. No pressure then.

'What can I do, Dan?'

There was a pause. Checkmate. I didn't walk away because I had this terrible feeling that it wasn't over. It should have been. Important work event for his new wife versus dodgy lunch with ageing distant relative? No competition, surely.

Dan looked down at his feet and eventually said, 'You could cancel your trip.'

He said it really quietly and meekly. Like he knew he was wrong. More than that—like he was afraid.

I said nothing. I didn't know what to say. I had never seen him like this before. Vulnerable. Exposed. When he opened his eyes and looked up at me, his chin was shaking and he was looking at me in that I-don't-care, defensive male way. The look they put on before the inevitable rejection, so they save face.

In that moment I didn't care if Dan was afraid of his mother, or me, or his Uncle Patrick. I just knew that he had handed me something and was waiting for me to throw it back at him. I wasn't comfortable holding it; nobody had ever given me this kind of power before. Nobody had ever loved me enough to care if I turned up to some lousy family party.

Part of me wanted to find out the reason why he felt he needed me to be there so badly, then rationalise it away so he could go without me. Isn't that what you are supposed to do? Communicate, talk about your problems then reach an agreement about dealing with them? Except I knew that would have just been the scenic route to getting my own way.

I thought the party was less important than my work. But Dan wanted me to go. He needed me to be there. Sometimes why and how just doesn't matter. It was a straight yes or no.

'OK. I'll cancel Chicago and come to the Communion.'

I don't know what I was expecting—tears, declarations of heartfelt gratitude? An apparition of the Virgin Mary come to welcome me to the fellowship of eternal martyrs?

Dan just said, 'Thanks, baby,' and gave me a squeeze. Then he drained his coffee cup and switched on the TV.

I sacrifice an important work gig to make him happy and he flicks on the TV? Suddenly I feel very, very married.

When the time comes, because I feel I have given up so much to be at this party, I decide to dress up. I am not tall and I am curvy—and not *all* in the wrong places.

'What do you wear to a First Communion?'

Kay drops by often on her way home from work. She is a schoolteacher and has the sunny, smily disposition of the headgirl that makes you think it must have been an easy transition from student to teacher. Knowing how relentlessly downtrodden she is by her mother makes me believe she is tough behind that candy-girl personality.

The next three hours bear this out, as she bundles me into her car and marches me into a discount designer outlet on the outskirts of Yonkers. In and out of various pastel shades of awful suits later, we settle on a bias-cut calf-length dress in slate grey and a fuschia pink wrap. I am waiting for my card to go through at the register, when I look at Kay and suddenly I see Dan in her. The broad mouth, an imperceptible slant in the eyes, that wide-open expression. And it hits me: *This woman is my sister-in-law. I am married. To her brother. Dan.* There is a feeling of shock, like I am realising it for the first time. *Oh my God! I am related to this person. Married! For the rest of my life! What have I done?* I can't even say that it was a negative feeling. Only that it was a shock. Like waking up in hospital or winning the lottery. Shock is like that. Neither good nor bad. I had got over it by the time I signed my card, but I felt I had somehow shifted into a different gear.

Little Deirdre loved my sugar-pink iced cake with silver baubles laced around its edges, and her friends were duly impressed with it and the fifty-dollar Gap Kids gift voucher. For the adults, I made an understated honey cake, which I sliced, drizzled with lemon icing and set on two large trays covered with gingham napkins. Traditional, but not showy enough to intimidate Eileen, who grunted her acknowledgment and said she hoped I was feeling better. I saw her hand the tray round herself and nod in my direction once or twice.

Uncle Patrick sought me out. I think Dan had told him to, as he did not seem to have the first idea who I was and seemed a little over-whelmed to be there. He reminded me of the men my grandfather used to bring into our house in Mayo. Seemingly quiet, simple men, but once you got them talking, they had these enormous intellects. Living among nothing but fields and cattle, they became voracious readers of every-thing from great Russian literature to local newspapers.

'So you're Dave's wife.'

'Dan's.'

He ignored that. 'You made the honey cake?' He paused while I nodded. 'Eileen told me.'

His sing-song accent rolled around her name with real romance. The point was not that I had made the cake, but that his sister had told him about it. That was nice, and we sat for a moment and let the brief fantasy of Eileen being nice float over us.

'There was too much sugar in it for me, girl.'

I am used to this type of comment. Because I have a job that is creative and in the public domain, a certain breed of opinionated fool feels it is their 'duty' to criticise me. In the interests of improving my recipes, of course. I always have an answer.

'Oh really? There was no sugar in it, actually.'

And of all smart answers, I find that lies work the best.

'Well, you must have used really cheap honey, then.'

'Actually it was wild flower organic honey.'

'The label was maybe, but that honey was not wild.'

'And you know this because . . . ?'

Dan had left me sitting talking to a stream of dull relations for almost two hours. I was tired and bored and quietly seething. Dan had made out like this day was going to be really hard for him, then abandoned me almost as soon as we got here. He seemed to be coping perfectly well without his loyal wife to protect him from whatever abuses he had blackmailed me into protecting him from. I felt arbitrary and a little conned. All right—a lot conned. And Uncle Patrick was an easy target.

Except he wasn't.

'I have been keeping honey bees for over thirty years and I am telling you that is not good honey in that cake.'

Then he got up from his chair, disappeared upstairs and came back down two minutes later with a small brown paper package, which he thrust at me with an aggressive, 'There! *That's* wild honey—if you know the difference.'

The jar was sticky and as I prised open the jammed lid, part of a comb came with it. The scent of it passed through me, and the satin of unexpected memories brushed my skin. Granddad, in the swell of summer, bringing in the first batch of honey; the drama and fear of seeing my first swarm; how he called my grandmother 'honey girl' and kissed the wrinkled tissue of her aged hand. A vision of marriage that you don't know you've absorbed until you are married yourself and looking for answers to questions you are not supposed to ask.

'I know the difference,' I said.

Uncle Patrick was delighted. 'Eileen doesn't care for it. She says she'd prefer honey from the shop.'

I said nothing about that, but we both knew the other was horrified.

'How much have you got?'

'Six jars.'

'I'll buy them all.'

Patrick laughed. 'Tell you what, lady. Have these ones on the house and next time I'm over, then we'll talk.'

'You've been here before?'

He looked at me quizzically and said, 'I come once or twice a year.'

Great. Not only is my husband manipulative, but he's a liar too. Nice. A lifetime of joy and happiness right here. In a funny way, I approved.

The night was drawing in and I thought we would never get out of there. One of the kids had turned on the stereo and there was a terrible CD of disco hits banging away in the background. I had this horrible feeling that the party was just beginning, while I'd had enough.

Dan was talking animatedly to some cousin or other. I walked across

238

and took his hand and he continued talking, interlocking my fingers to let me know he knew I was there. Then this seventies love song came on and Dan grabbed me and started to dance.

> I would take the stars out of the sky for you
> Stop the rain from falling if you asked me to

I was really embarrassed, but Dan held me tight in his amateur sway as if we were the only ones there.

> I'd do anything for you
> Your wish is my command
> I could move a mountain when your hand is in my hand

'Thanks for coming today, baby.' He whispered it with the solemnity of a wedding vow, like it really had made all the difference to him.

And then I got it. Dan didn't need me to bake cakes, or dress up, or field his mother's expectations, or make his sisters feel important, or chit-chat to his relations. He just needed me to be there. Because when I was with him, it made it easier for him to be with his family. To be able to point across a room and say, 'She's with me', to his Uncle Patrick, his mother, his cousins, but most importantly, to himself. My being in his life—sitting, walking, breathing, talking in the background of his day— made it better. Made him look and feel like he was a better man.

Dan had lied to get me there that day because he believed that was what he needed to do to secure my presence. Only I knew that all he had to do was ask me straight and I would have said yes.

It felt good and in that moment I knew I had taken one step closer to being Dan's wife.

James was close to his brother Padraig, in age and appearance as much as anything else. We got along all right in the end, but we disapproved of each other for years. Padraig disliked the refined way of life I encouraged: trips to Dublin, elegant clothes, matching shoes and bags and their like. He found me ludicrous and shallow and I found him scruffy and too ardent in his politics. However, after eight years a grudging respect had developed.

'No china today, Bernie?'

'And have you break every piece on me?'

'That only happened once!'

'Yes—and it'll not happen again.'

'Such a strict mistress—James, I don't know how you put up with her silliness?'

'He likes my ways well enough because my husband is a gentleman.'

'Is that why he gets his tea in a china cup and I get mine in a tin mug?'

'Be grateful you're not drinking it out of a bucket with the dogs in the yard, Padraig.'

Then my brother-in-law would throw his head back and laugh.

Padraig was the only person apart from my father who dared shorten my name to the commonplace 'Bernie'. I didn't like it one little bit, but he was incorrigible so he got away with it. Though I would never have admitted it, I got a certain thrill from my brother-in-law's light-hearted abuse as I liked to suspect he did from mine.

Padraig and his wife Mary had seven children and had been married only a couple of years before us. I liked Mary and we should have been great friends, except that we had barely spoken a full sentence since the day we met. Children constantly surrounded her. At her breast, running around her feet, calling to her from another room. There was not a moment of her day when she was not feeding, answering, scolding or tending to one of them. Her house was a pigsty and horrified me at the time although, looking back on it now, it was just the home of seven children. Realising what an easy life I had by comparison, every week I would call in with a cake and offer to help with her chores. Often Mary would be sitting on the settle in the kitchen, surrounded by damp nappies and dirty dishes, reading to her children. It mystified me how she could be so calm in the midst of all this chaos; astonished me how she could be so patient as to play with her children, when there was so much work to be done in the house. She was an appalling housekeeper, there was no doubting that—but I admired her nonetheless because, in her shoes, I knew I would surely have dropped dead long ago from nerves.

Some days I would enjoy it. There was an adorable set of twin girls, Theresa and Katherine, who would call out 'Honey! Honey! It's honey aunty!' when they saw me walk up the driveway to their house. 'A kiss for a cake,' I would tease them and they would shower me with squealing kisses, their little hands grasping for my basket.

I enjoyed those moments, but they were always outbalanced by the bloody knees and the relentless bawling. I liked the twins because they paid me some attention, but mostly my nieces and nephews were a moving, messy blur of noise and neediness.

Mary and Padraig seemed happy in their life but the disorderly mess of their home was my most effective contraception.

Until the twins' First Communion.

I decided to host a party for the twin's First Communion. The weather was warm enough for the children to play outside and I enjoyed preparing the house for guests and baking. Hospitality was something that was generally offered in a casual drop-in way in those days, but entertaining James's family was a way I had of making up to him for how things were.

James loved people and took every opportunity to fill our house with them in all shapes and sizes. When we were first married, I scolded him constantly for bringing neighbours in, inviting his pupils' parents to call by, having an open-house policy with his siblings. My own parents had been ferociously protective of our privacy and nobody ever came into our home. But James, with his unfettered, popular ways, won out and I rose to the challenge of being as organised as a priest's housekeeper, with a selection of fresh cakes constantly at the ready. I grew to like the flow of visitors. It broke the day up and kept me on my toes. Taking my apron on and off, always having to have tidy hair and smart shoes by the scullery door to change into in case it was the priest or the doctor. It gave James and me something to talk about and stopped us from dwelling on ourselves. That was a trick I learned about marriage early on. Keeping myself busy.

Two of James's nephews were also having their First Communion that Sunday, but I took a particular interest in the twin girls and dug out special treasures for them both from my own collection. A pair of lace gloves for one and a set of mother-of-pearl rosary beads for the other. There would be in excess of eight adults on the day and so many children I didn't dare count them. On the Saturday James killed and prepared three chickens, then he went to Kilkelly and collected ham, jelly, oranges, custard powder, tinned peaches, chocolate, a bottle of sweet sherry and a bottle of Sandeman port. He spent four shillings on toffee so that each child would have a bag of sweets to go home with. It cost a small fortune, but neither of us cared. We had the money and it gave James pleasure to spend it on his family. With no children of our own, I saw my indulging him in this way as some small compensation.

Things had been cold between us for months, but in our joint preparations for the party a temporary truce had been called. When James found me still baking at seven o'clock in the evening he rolled up his sleeves to help. I felt relieved that my husband's dour mood seemed to be passing and so I insisted he don my frilliest apron, then instructed him in measuring, beating and mixing a honey cake. When I realised, in horror, that we had run out of sugar, James, in high spirits, tipped in nearly a full jar of the honey. He made an awful mess, trying to halt the sticky stream by turning the jar on its side, dripping cheeky wiggles all over the clean table. We laughed at his ineptitude at managing the honey and my dramatics over the sugar shortage. James finally declared that he would never complain about his job ever again as a woman's work was infinitely more complicated and the stress of it unmatched.

I don't remember there ever having been as much warmth between us as on that night. Although there was no reason for it, there was an air of anticipation before the party. As if, in our own separate worlds, we felt like something magical was about to happen.

James made love to me that night. As I rose from the bed as usual, I could feel his arms weighing down on my breast to try and hold me there. When I pulled myself away, he turned his body with a suddenness that indicated his annoyance.

The party was a success, although James had detached himself from me again. He did not comment on my outfit as we left for the church, which was his way of punishing me. While he laid his hand on my waist to guide me into the pew, all the life had gone out of his touch. I felt a pang of sadness at how quickly our rift had returned, and although I was busy making gallons of tea and slicing mountains of cake and keeping legions of children out of my parlour, I don't think the disappointment of that entirely left me.

The honey cake was a huge success and gone within minutes. People said it was the nicest cake they had ever eaten and asked what I had done differently to make it so special. I tried to find James and tell him of his victory, but he was deep in conversation. I had been feeding James's tolerance with these small shows of affection. But he had moved on to a different level now and I sensed that it was going to take more than a light-hearted compliment to bring him back.

Perhaps it was that realisation that made me see what I did. Or perhaps it was just a moment of clarity that comes to us all when we know that something is right.

It was a small thing.

I had just given Katherine the lace gloves. She was so excited she ran off, without thanking me, to show them to her mother. Mary was distractedly adjudicating some toddler scrap, and sent Katherine back to show her father. Padraig was sitting close to where I was standing, talking with James. Katherine put the glove on, her tiny hand swimming in it, and held it out for her father to look. As Padraig studied the lace glove, I watched his seven-year-old daughter's face and was taken aback by what I saw. Her eyelids were flickering in anticipation of what her father would think of the gloves, a look of such deep concern that you would not expect from a child. After less than a minute he said, 'They are beautiful, Katherine. You look like a real lady.' I could not take my eyes from young Katherine's face. Her eyes lit up with adoration for him. She was looking at Padraig the way I had looked at Michael Tuffy. With pure love.

I had never looked at my husband in that way and I knew I never would. But James was a good man, nonetheless, and he deserved to be loved in that same adoring way.

I knew then that I had to give him a child.

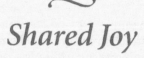

Shared Joy

There is love in watching other people love

Children's Fairy Cakes
This recipe makes just over a dozen.

Cream 4 oz margarine with 4 oz sugar then add 2 eggs. If you beat them gently first, it lessens the risk of curdling. Mix in 8 heaped tablespoons flour (about 10 oz) and ½ teaspoon baking soda. (This is your basic recipe, but it's fun to let a child mix in things at this stage for themselves. Your mother loved raisins, but I seem to remember one ten-year-old girl who made me mash in a banana. Imagine my surprise when it worked!)

Grease your bun tin generously, and cook in a medium/hot oven for up to 45 minutes. Leave to cool in the tin before turning out and leaving to cool on a rack. (Although if the little ones are around, they won't last that long!)

I AM *SO* ON A CREATIVE BUZZ with my new kitchen.

I have designed and built kitchens for myself, for magazines, for friends and for very rich people who want to pretend that they are going to cook in them. Kitchen companies employ me as a consultant; Tressa Nolan is— without wishing to sound egotistical about it—the living embodiment of the modern American kitchen. But the kitchen in Longville Avenue has taken my idea of the perfect cooking space to a new level.

It all started when I was flicking through some brochures trying to find the perfect Shaker look.

Dan looked over my shoulder and said, 'They look expensive.'

I told him all the companies would give me a deal and he said, 'Oh, right—it's just I thought you wanted to fix up these old things. There's this carpenter guy I know . . .'

As he trailed off, I looked round at all the broken-down stuff we had been living with for the past few weeks. There was the fifties larder unit with the tin worktop; an old sideboard we had been keeping the kettle on; and a small square table with turned legs and a peeling veneer top. All this scruffy old junk which, despite my craving for a pared-down Shaker-style kitchen, I had grown quite fond of. Did I want to throw it all on the scrap heap and replace it with brand-new stuff?

'Is he good?' I asked.

'Oh—he's good,' Dan said.

Dan knows that this kitchen is not only the most important room in the house, but a really important part of my working life. Still, I am not sure about going eclectic. But if it goes wrong, I can always call in the heavy guns. In my line of work, kitchens are frighteningly disposable.

So Dan makes a call to a guy, who makes a call to another guy, who gets his tattooed mute biker buddy to call round.

I take one look at him and my scepticism level soars.

'We don't need to save money on this, Dan, really,' I say, which is code for 'Get this Charles Manson lookalike freak out of my house!'

'Trust me, baby. Gerry won't save you money, but he's good. I know what you want from this kitchen and he's the best.'

He's going to cost us money? But I feel I have to give his friend Gerry a chance because—well, he is in my house and is, unbelievably, carrying a suitcase.

Two weeks on and it turns out this Gerry guy is a genius.

Gerry has waist-length grey hair and four teeth. He came here on a holiday visa from Ireland thirty years ago and has been working for cash ever since. He sleeps on the job or on friends' sofa beds and spends his money on bikes, dope and—I don't know—tattoos? He certainly doesn't spend it on clothes or dentistry, but I don't care because together, with Dan, we are building a unique kitchen more perfect than money can buy. Every shelf, every door, is different—hand-finished in a style fitting its job. The spice rack has ten pine shelves, each a different width to fit my higgledy-piggledy collection of jars. We have restored the original fifties cupboard and replaced the old tin worktop. I found original tin containers marked Flour and Sugar to place on it. His brief for the dresser was thirties Ireland. 'Got that,' he says and he goes to the garage and comes back five days later with, I swear, a replica of my grandparents' one in Fal Iochtar. I painted it buttermilk and pistachio and already it looks as if it has been there forever. There is nothing 'finished' or even describable about my kitchen. It will look like a place that has been cooked in by three generations of women. This time of year most of Dan's tenants are on vacation, so he is spending all the time he can at home helping Gerry.

I thought that having a stranger around the place was going to be a living hell, but in a strange way it has been good for us. All the awkward tension lying beneath the surface of our life since our honeymoon has completely gone. Dan has been showing me off to Gerry and I have found myself falling in with his game. It is like Gerry is our audience and we are playing our roles of happily married husband and wife in front of him. I find it safer to be physically affectionate towards Dan in front of other people and as a result he has been doing more than his usual amount of waist hugging and neck nuzzling. We bicker in a playful way to amuse Gerry and, ironically, I have felt an intimacy in behaving like a textbook wife. As if in acting like I am completely at ease with Dan, I have actually become more at ease with him. And myself.

The atmosphere in the house has been resolutely male; I'm allowed to do light work such as painting and polishing and, of course, providing refreshments without having a working oven. Yesterday I made a dozen fairy cakes in the microwave, with Dan and Gerry gawking at me open mouthed as if I had just performed a miracle. I split the buns and stuffed them with butter icing and white chocolate buttons for the pure amusement of turning two grown men into prepubescent schoolboys. As a joke, I gave Gerry the spatula and Dan the bowl to lick. They both regarded me with an adoring lust that made me laugh and feel like Playmate of the Month at the same time.

'Jesus, man,' Gerry said to Dan, raising his eyebrows, as he wrapped himself around a completed fairy cake and a home-made cappuccino.

'I know,' Dan said, glowing with pride.

Mother, master-chef, sex-goddess all rolled into one. Nobody ever made me feel quite that good before.

We took the rest of the afternoon off and Gerry cracked open a lethal bottle of tequila he had been carrying around. The three of us held an air-guitar contest. Gerry went hard core with Black Sabbath, Dan went for the middle-American vote with Springsteen, but in the end they let me win with Thin Lizzy's 'Whiskey in the Jar'. My trophy was the tequila bottle and Gerry presented it to me with great ceremony, then he decided that we needed a little smoke to finish the party properly and went off to score some. He was the kind of guy you knew you might not see again for a week and the second he was gone, Dan grabbed me with an uncharacteristic, 'C'mere you.'

We made love like casual, lazy lovers right there on the sofa and it was nice. It was like it had been in the beginning, except it was less exciting because I knew what to expect. For once that didn't feel like a problem. It was easy. Maybe it was all the tequila and tiredness, but easy felt good.

At five the next morning, I woke to go to the bathroom and saw Dan was gone. I found him in the kitchen, hand-sanding some skirting board. 'I have to work today, so I wanted to get these ready for you to paint,' he said.

I put on some coffee and, while it brewed, I watched him running the block of wood up and down along the bench. His face was set in concentration, although the job he was doing was pure manual, his arm muscles contracting and relaxing.

Without thinking I said, 'Thanks for building me this kitchen, Dan.'

'It's our kitchen, baby. This is as much for me as you.'

For once I didn't baulk at the 'we' reference. We were doing this together and I didn't mind. I liked it.

My happiness is as caught up with building my dream kitchen as it is with my husband—but it's still happiness, right? It still counts?

Enter Angelo and Jan Orlandi. Old friends, organic-food impresarios and officially New York State's most fabulous couple—according to *Vanity Fair* magazine.

An outline of their lives: Jan and Angelo met in college, married young and developed a mutual commitment to food, out of which they built successful careers as a food editor and chef respectively. They bought a huge house in Irvington before it became chic to do so and started up a small organic garden and wholesale sauces business. Now they own many thousands of acres of prime Californian farmland, supply all the big supermarket chains and have a dozen 'little cafes' and restaurants to their name, as well as a beachfront boutique hotel in the Caribbean. Add to that two beautiful children, a house worth featuring in *Vogue*—and the fact that they are still grounded enough to want to hang with an old friend even though they couldn't make her wedding—and the happiness goalposts start shifting. Put it like this, you'd want to be pretty secure in yourself to do a weekend in Irvington chez Orlandis.

I consider them good friends, but they haven't met Dan yet. They have always been my benchmark for a successful marriage.

This weekend is not just a test for Dan. It is a test for me. Things have been going so well, but I still need to be sure that marrying Dan was the right thing for me. I realise I've changed: now I want my marriage to work and hopefully this weekend I will get the answers I need to do that.

No change ever happened in me more absolutely or more immediately than that of motherhood.

I was crotchety and complaining all through the pregnancy. I dreaded the birth, the humiliation of it, with a horror I could barely name. Pregnancy did nothing to warm me to the idea. I did not like the feeling of my body being inhabited in that way. It felt intrusive and uncomfortable and, despite what everyone kept saying, completely unnatural.

Niamh was born in the early hours of a Monday morning after my waters had broken during Mass. It was an ordeal, from the embarrassment of stumbling with wet legs out of the church to the excruciating pain and the midwife's cruel pragmatism as she urged at me to 'push, push' and told me to 'offer my pain up for the souls in purgatory'. I thought it would never end.

Then Niamh was here, and in the split second that I heard her cry everything changed. I had carried her for nine months and yet she was a complete surprise. I could never have expected something so pure and so magnificent as this child. Immediately I held her a sob rose up through me, grief that I had left this joy so long to experience. She was tiny and frail, like a petal, yet as complex as nature itself. The earth, sun, moon, stars—all the continents of America and Africa and the galaxies beyond could not contain the love I felt. I wept, but with a joyful abandon. I wept in gratitude to God for her breath on my breast, and I wept because although I had made her, already I knew she did not belong to me and that one day I would have to let her go.

James must have been standing with his ear to the door because I heard him call out. The midwife told him that it was a girl and that we were not ready to see him, and I shocked myself by raising up from the bed and hollering at her to stop fussing around and let him in.

It was the first time I felt love in looking at James's face. Not pity, or concern, or grudging respect—but a passionate belonging. Almost ten years we had been together, yet I had always felt apart from him. I knew now that, as long as this child lived, we could not be parted. And in that moment I wanted to draw him to me. That the two of us should wrap ourselves around this new life to cherish, nourish and guide her. James looked from my face to the swaddled cocoon in my lap and his eyes shone with a symphony of emotion I had never seen before: terror, wonderment and a tender, tender love.

Watching something you love grow is both pleasure and pain. Each new phase—crawling, walking, talking—brings shouts of pride, but with each comes the mourning of the phase gone past. Never again the cluck of her chin as she fed on my breast; never again small enough to carry in one arm while I stirred soup or carried turf with the other; never again an infant lying in a muslin-covered basket in the top fields while we worked. The soft down of her scalp, fingers the size of beads, the mysterious whispers before words come: behind the joy in each new talent, I regretted the passing of the last. I had a secret longing to keep her small and precious and a part of me.

Time is impatient to take your child from you. So you learn that each moment is precious and that life is an inevitable clock. The pleasure of rearing a child is just a prelude to the pain of letting them go, and I anticipated that with an ache every day of her small life. I thought it would make it easier when she finally reached adulthood. But it didn't.

No matter what wisdom or tricks for happiness you learn, a mother worries every day of her life for her child. A wise one will pretend to let them go to keep them, but it's just a sweet and sensible lie. Motherhood is a sweet, sweet suffering; a joy today is marked by fear for tomorrow and a craving for yesterday.

The only cure is to have another child.

James was a wonderful father. Perhaps it was because he was a teacher, but he seemed to have a natural, easy way with Niamh that mystified me. How could you love somebody as completely and absolutely as we loved her and maintain such a detached fairness? I guess he was a more natural father than I was a mother. I had been surprised by my love for her, but as Niamh's personality developed my relationship with her became fraught. She was feisty—like myself—and we were both wilful and petulant. James became arbiter and confidant to us both. In those early years of our parenthood, I had the pleasure of feeling close to my husband. Often we would both lie down on our iron bed and hum our child to sleep at the tail end of a playful afternoon. Sunshine dappled across our lazy bodies, hypnotising us, and I would see what an extraordinary man he was to sing to his wife and child on a summer's afternoon when other men might be gathered in the pub to drink themselves daft.

When she was a small child Niamh and I often squabbled in the kitchen, as I taught her to make her favourite fairy cakes. Flour and butter would be everywhere, eggs dropped lethally on the polished flagstones. I would get frustrated when I realised that she was too young for instruction, but she was having too much fun for me to stop the lesson. James stood for a moment at the door watching me frantically wipe debris off the table, the floor, my face. And in his quietly observing me I would see myself as he saw me: in my everyday apron, dark hair wound to the back, a swirl of flour dashed across my cheek. I knew that I was more beautiful to him then, as mother to his child, than I had ever been in the beguiling days of my youth.

I knew also that James was just loving us both as he stood there. That in his teaching, his digging for potatoes, his tending the cattle, his reading, in everything James did, was hidden a eulogy to his two 'girls'. And I knew that I was a lucky woman to be able to take his protection and provision and paternal patronage for granted, and a blessed one for the luxury of all the little ways he found to love me.

At times like that I would believe that perhaps loving James as a father was as good as loving him as a man.

It all started to go wrong on the Thursday evening when Angelo rang and asked Dan if he wanted them to send us their driver.

Dan was furious. He thought Angelo was implying that we did not have a car. I tried to explain that when you are as enormously wealthy as the Orlandis you employ a full-time driver and that we would be doing them a favour in giving him something to do for the day. It was no big deal. Angelo had certainly not meant any offence and was just trying to be helpful.

Dan didn't buy it. I didn't really know how to deal with this sudden testosterone surge, but I knew right away that I had handled it wrong by defending Angelo. Dan then spent the rest of the day washing and waxing the car, and I overheard Gerry encouraging him to borrow a vintage Harley-Davidson from one of their mutual biker pals, a plan that, thankfully, did not make it past the plotting stage.

The journey was tense. While impressive by anyone's standards, their house in Irvington was homey enough—rambling rather than grand, unlike the mansion on their farm in California. I was relieved it was going to be an intimate affair, just them and us, as I really wanted them to get to know Dan.

'So what is this guy—an Italian?'

'Well, his parents are.'

'Yeah, right—a rich Italian. What is he—Mafia?'

'No, he is one of the most successful organic food producers in—'

'If these people are such good friends, how come they couldn't make it to the wedding?'

Dan was making it obvious that he did not want to go and I was getting irritated with his attitude. The Orlandis are fantastic hosts. *Anyone* would want to go and hang out with them for the weekend.

'They are incredibly busy people.'

'Hell—so are we!'

'I mean important—'

As soon as I said it I knew it was wrong.

'So we're not important?'

'That's not what I meant—'

'Making our wedding was not important enough for these important, incredibly busy people?'

One part of me wanted to bury a pickaxe in Dan's forehead, but another part was thinking, 'Wow! We are having a row—just like a normal couple.' It wasn't nice, but it felt like progress. Like we felt secure enough with each other to argue.

'At least they won't be feeding us frozen dog ribs.'

Oh dear. I knew I had taken a step too far. Dan's expression froze and his hands tightened on the wheel. I took it back immediately.

'I'm sorry, Dan. That was out of order.'

He waited before replying. I had just handed him a bag of ammo and he was figuring out how to use it.

'That is different, Tressa. That is family. These people are strangers.'

'Jan and Angelo are very good friends of mine—'

'So you keep saying.'

I wanted to tell him that no one on the planet felt stranger to me than his family and that the Orlandis were more my kind of people—educated, stylish, erudite—than any of the bonehead biker freaks he had introduced me to. But I thought I'd better keep that to myself. We had the weekend to get through and I could always save it for the next row.

To keep myself calm, I tried to get inside Dan's head and decided that he was simply feeling insecure. These people were wealthy, they knew me and considered me a peer. That must be very threatening for him and that was why he was acting all jealous and aggressive.

What he didn't know was that Angelo and I had had a brief fling before Jan and Angelo got married. My first job was as Jan's assistant. Although less than five years older than me, she was a food editor and I admired her hugely. I guess I had a kind of a crush on her. When she and Angelo split up after some time together, Jan hadn't seemed that upset. 'College boyfriends rarely stick—we've both changed,' she had said. She had seemed to shrug him off like a teenage denim jacket you still love, but know you've matured out of. Although I had only ever met Angelo with Jan, the New York food scene being as it was meant it was just a matter of weeks before I bumped into my boss's ex at the opening of a new bar. It seemed only polite to join him for a drink.

There was instant chemistry between us. It was as if our mutual relationships with Jan had been a barrier to what had always been there. We slept together that first night and sex was instant and easy and explosive all at the same time.

My instinct was to tell Jan right away—the next day. She might have felt weird about it, but I was convinced that she would get over it quickly once she realised how compatible Angelo and I were. Angelo persuaded me to stay quiet, saying it was best to be certain about each other first before hurting Jan. Being young and confident, I assumed things would continue; I thought relationships were that easy. I did get a shock when, a few days later, Jan came into work, beaming, and announced that she and Angelo were back together.

'We needed a break,' she said, but she looked relieved.

Angelo agonised with me over a hushed phone call from the office, but managed to convince me it was a close call.

I was shocked and hurt, but agreed to stay friends. After all, I was young and thought the world was bursting at the seams with Angelos. It was ten years before I realised that men that I could relate to intellectually *and* physically were thin on the ground.

Having said that, the affair itself was forever ago and was so very, very over that I forget about it myself most of the time. Although sometimes, I have to admit, I catch myself looking at Angelo and wondering, What if? It's ridiculous, and it doesn't mean anything, but deep in the pit of my stomach I knew that this weekend was about me lining Dan and Angelo up next to each other and hoping to pick Dan.

The Orlandis could not have been more welcoming when we arrived, although their housekeeper, Rosa, answered the door, which I could tell pissed Dan off. Dan is uncomfortable dealing with staff on this level. It comes from years of being staff himself.

We went up to our rooms to dress for dinner. We came straight back down and were slightly taken aback to see that there was a full dinner party awaiting us. Apart from our hosts, there was another food writer (whom I didn't really care for) with her lawyer husband, a food photographer I had booked once and never used again, and a publisher who was good friends with my agent. I felt 'networked' and responsible for Dan, who had been thrown headfirst into a clique of foodies.

The food was in season and unfussy. Perfectly prepared goes without saying. Halloumi with chilli oil, then chicken wrapped in Parma ham.

'Simplicity is *the* new style buzz,' the ghastly food writer blurted.

'Easy Entertaining?' Jan replied, her fingers flicking commas over the statement.

We all laughed at the allusion to the title of her cable TV show. Except Dan. He looked nervously at me waiting for me to explain the joke. I couldn't because actually, when I thought about it, it wasn't very funny.

The rest of the conversation didn't improve Dan's comfort zone much. It was centred on the dilemma of flying first or business class, restaurant reviews—as in where to eat next time you are on business in London—Martha Stewart (of course), and, awkwardly, agents and their percentages. All the time I was worrying that my husband has no interest in these subjects, so I said, 'Dan and I are building a new kitchen.'

'How fascinating! Who are you using?' the food writer asked Dan.

'We are doing it ourselves,' I answered for him.

Dan threw me a sharp look then, just to let me know I had blown my chance, and looked away from the table.

'Really? How do you mean?'

'Dan has a friend who is a wonderful bespoke carpenter, and we are customising and restoring everything to fit our needs.'

They were hanging on my every word, waiting for me to give an explanation other than saving money or fraternising with tradesmen.

'It's eclectic.'

And right when I said it I realised that I had managed to reduce the heart and the feeling of home that we had been creating for the last three weeks into a fashion statement.

When we eventually got to bed that night Dan just said, 'There's no need to talk for me, Tressa,' and turned away. I didn't reply, just lay there for hours between Egyptian cotton sheets sprayed with English lavender water and wondered how the hell I had got myself into this mess.

I thought these were my kind of people. I did not like all of them, but they were my peers and I could certainly hold my own among them. This kind of dinner party—networking, discussing food, wine, restaurants, and enjoying each other's stylish hospitality—was what I did. The language was ours—a peculiar foodie speak—yet it felt strange to be doing it with Dan. Wrong. Clearly it alienated him, but did I really want to give up this part of my life for him? Or was I destined to spend every weekend drinking beer and eating fried food with his family, stifling this part of my life and career?

I knew the next day was going to be hell, but I thought, He put me through the First Communion, he can cope with a day of macho insecurity bullshit with me and my 'fabulous' friends.

The publisher and photographer had gone, but the vile food writer and her drab husband were there for the whole weekend. She was all over Jan, doing an overpowering girl-buddy act in the kitchen. The lawyer was boring Angelo to death, but he was having no luck with Dan. My husband had taken to the great outdoors with Rosa and the two kids, who instantly adored him. He was avoiding everyone else, but especially me. By lunchtime everyone was drinking and picking on an over-the-top brunch buffet brought by the food writer. It was self-consciously casual: twice-baked leek and goat's cheese soufflés, sunblush roasted tomatoes in a balsamic jus. We knew the names because she had written them in gold italics on card in front of them. Tacky beyond comment.

I took a king prawn that would have looked overdressed at the Oscars and gazed out of the window at Dan. He had one child balancing on his shoulders while he swung the other round by his hands. Dan was like that: a big bear of a man. Maybe not a neat, educated college guy, but you wouldn't come to harm while he was around.

'Hey,' Angelo said in a dark, dangerous voice behind me, 'wanna see something?'

He had some special kind of arugula he wanted to show me in the greenhouse. So he said. He knew I particularly loved fresh herbs and salad. Freshness, flavour and simplicity itself.

It was one of those seductive film moments you can't resist. It hits you hard because you don't expect it. One minute you are fingering a fragrant herb, then your hands touch by accident. Next thing your eyes meet, they lock, then they pull you together into a kiss. You barely know you are doing it. It's an animal thing. An attraction you can't control. Chemistry.

I guess it had never gone away. That easy charm he has always had. The fact that we speak the same language; he always understood me.

We pulled away and didn't have a conversation about it. It was our little secret. We had kept our previous dalliance quiet for such a long time, anyway, and I'll admit it was thrilling to have the flame relit. Albeit briefly. It was a moment, a kiss. Something to remind us both that while we were married we were still capable of passion. We were still alive. No big deal. Nobody knows, nobody gets hurt.

The minute we got back to the house and I saw Dan's face, I felt sick. He had come inside to find me and this look flashed between us where he was querying and I was defensive. It was less than a second. I was a bit drunk and I can't even be sure I didn't imagine it.

Dan didn't drink for the rest of the day, which was his way of letting me know he intended to drive home that night. We stayed for dinner and just before dessert Angelo followed me into the bathroom. He was drunk, but I suspect he was acting more drunk than he was.

'Come on, Tressa—you know you want to. Let's live a little.'

'Are you crazy, Angelo? In the bathroom? With Dan and Jan down-stairs?' And the kids in the room next door, you disgusting dirt bag? But I kept that one to myself.

He looked at me hard and when he saw there was no persuading me he went instantly cold, shrugged his shoulders and said, 'Your loss.' Then he turned and left me standing there.

I was shaking and took a few seconds to calm myself down. In that moment I knew it was gone. Fifteen years of friendship over. I didn't want to be part of it any more. This glamorous, bullshit life where your seemingly doting husband tries to fuck your friend in a bathroom because he's rich and he thinks he can. Where you can't make it to your friend's wedding because you are too busy being fabulous. I had been part of this too. I had enjoyed the kiss, wanted it and now I felt cor-rupted. Now I had Dan.

I breathed in deeply and, in breathing out, I craved the simplicity of being sure again. Like I had been about my kitchen. Like I wanted to feel about my husband.

Jan was disappointed we had to leave, but Angelo brushed my cheek with his then gave me a nonchalant look as if he knew he'd never see me again and didn't care.

The drive home was quiet.

Gerry had left an empty pizza box with a note saying, *Gone drinkin*. He had left a small bag behind as evidence of his intended return but we both knew he might not be back for weeks, if ever.

Dan went straight upstairs for a shower, and I flicked the light on in the kitchen. I had been hoping the mood would lift when I got back to my project. But it didn't. I hadn't got the answers I wanted; in fact the weekend had just sent me away with more questions. Wretched ques-tions that had been haranguing me for almost four months now.

How could a few days have changed things so much? The last few weeks seemed as if they had been the halcyon days of a marriage that now felt all but over. I cursed myself for having broken the spell.

I realised that my joy was not in my dresser or the kooky antique kettle or the restored larder, it was in the people who built them.

Without the love and the spirit, they were just cupboards.

Perhaps the darkest secret I ever kept was also the most innocent. Deep in my heart I longed for a son. Perhaps because I imagined it would be a different kind of love from any I had felt before. Perhaps I would have called him Michael and poured all my dreams into him.

I will never know.

Month after month I waited, convinced that I had controlled my own destiny before by conceiving on demand and certain that I would do so again. As the months turned into a year and one year into two my despair deepened. Each time the bleeding started I felt my disappointment as a cold crater in the pit of my body, as if the child I did not conceive had been scooped out and taken from me.

Gradually it dawned on me that I had never been in charge of my own body in the way I had thought. I did not 'give' Niamh to James. God did. Now that I wanted a child, He was denying me. I was being punished.

So I prayed and I prayed. I said novenas, memorare to the Virgin Mary, went to Mass on the first Friday of every month and begged. I became obsessed—neglectful of Niamh and James, even my own appearance. Lovemaking became an ordeal—for both of us, I am sure.

James was worried for me, although he never judged. Once he tried to reassure me by saying that Niamh and I were enough for him. I bit his head off, screaming that he didn't understand, that he was an insensitive fool.

Such is the intimacy of marriage. The irony of its familiar, relentless kind of love was that, whenever I felt sad or afraid or alone the first person I always blamed was James. He was the most faultless, most attentive, most caring person I could have had to carry me through such a hardship and yet he became the focus of my anger.

I was too afraid to blame God, so I blamed my husband. His age, his body, his indifference. James knew that I was suffering, so he ignored me when he had to and forgave because he loved me. A man, when pushed to the limits of his patience, will usually show himself to be either stoical or violent. You will only discover which kind of man you have if you relentlessly prod and push, push, push. I was lucky, James was stoical. Still, if he had been hurt or disappointed about our not having another child, I wouldn't have noticed.

Eventually I lost my faith entirely. And as happens when a sadness is too deep to bear, it must find another, more familiar pain to distract from it.

I thought I saw Michael on the pier at Inniscrone.

The summer Niamh turned five, we took a taxi to the seaside village in Sligo and booked into a guest house on the main street for two weeks. James thought that the sea air would lift my spirits and Niamh was recovering from a spring fraught with childhood diseases: measles, mumps and chicken pox in immediate succession. Our fat little girl had turned slim and frail and needed the hot salty air to burn some colour into her cheeks. James and I needed to escape. Our bed was polluted by our failures, we felt defeated and my grief had turned our home into a prison. Although it was never said, I understood that this holiday was James drawing a line under my wish for another child. It was time to give up: go away, get over it and come back as I had been before.

For those of us who lived inland, the sea was a miraculous, incredible spectacle. James would disappear early to fish, and as Niamh collected shells I would sit on a blanket on the dunes and allow myself to become hypnotised by the sea—a glimmering mass of glass, the flat horizon turning into a gliding, moving hill until it lurched towards the land and dissolved clumsily into a sniggering mess in the sand. I'd imagine that there was nothing beyond the sea, no boats to carry off our neighbours, our families, to England and America. To take the boy I loved and place him beyond the Atlantic in New York or Boston.

I would look at the sun splashing the sky with a hundred shades of purple and gold, grey rain clouds hovering over Killala on the other side of the bay, while we briefly enjoyed the gift of sunshine. And I would think: God has created all this yet he won't give me another child. Sometimes I would succumb to my tears, let them mingle with the sea spray and allow myself the relief of weeping alongside nature. As the days went past, I felt the injustice of my not conceiving diminish, and my thoughts instead began to circle around an old grievance with new eyes.

Romance.

The gap in me where my imaginary son lived was the same place that was harbouring my unresolved yearning for passionate love. I could feel the sea breeze whisper across my neck, and the hem of my cotton skirt flicker on my knee, but I could no longer feel the touch of my husband, nor hear his voice, nor really see him. He had become an object, like furniture or bread. So my longing for a child was replaced by my longing for the thrill of that first forbidden kiss.

It was a more familiar pain. But it was still pain.

I was sitting on the rocks when I thought I saw him walking along the pier. He wore a brown suit, his black hair licking his collar in glossy waves. He was the same in that way that young love never gets the chance to age. I didn't see his face, but I knew it was Michael.

The shock did not paralyse me as it does in dreams, but propelled me towards the pier. My feet slid across the rocks; I did not even stop to think of taking the proper path up. That would have meant turning my back to him and I could not let him out of my sight. I did not call out or think of what I might have said when I reached him. Barefoot and perspiring, I was driven towards him in a straight line.

When I heard Niamh cry out from a rock pool behind me, I am ashamed to admit I was torn.

I went back, of course, and rescued my child. I comforted her about the jellyfish sting and carried her back to the boarding house, bathed her in salt, and cajoled and placated her. But my head was on a wild swivel searching for a glimpse of him again. I was irritable for the few days left of our break, but in a way that I know comforted James, in that he could see my deeper sadness had dissipated.

The sea had taken one dream and carried it away, sending me back a more familiar one. For weeks afterwards I dreamed of him. What might have happened when we met. What we might have said. How our eyes would have searched the other's face for unlocked memories, a habit of love reborn in our eyes. How we might have brushed cheeks when we said goodbye.

We always said goodbye.

Michael meant everything to me still: I burned for him and would always, even as a wretched old woman. James was my husband: I hated him for it, reviled him often. But fourteen years and a child had glued us together. Time and nature had bonded me to James against my will, beyond what I wanted, what I felt. Although I often wanted to escape, I knew I never could.

Wife. Mother. The words had become webbed into the fabric of my soul.

Many years later, when Niamh left for college, I realised that another child would not have been the answer. It would have been double the joy, but also double the pain of letting them go.

I was a good mother, but I was not a selfless one. I gave and, while I never asked, I was always waiting for something back. I craved those moments of surety a child's love gives you, was always ready for Niamh's reassurance and admiration and always disappointed when it didn't come on cue.

I was not destined to have more than one child. I know that now. I think my desire for another was just greed for the easy joy I had felt with James when Niamh was born.

Joy did not come naturally to me. I always grabbed so hard that I crushed it, examined it until I found a flaw, or tried to make it more than it was. It would always turn too quickly to disappointment. I found that, when happy, I held my breath and waited for it to fly away.

I waited all my life for joy to come and kidnap me as it had when I met Michael. The one place I never bothered looking for it was inside myself.

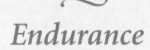

Endurance

When it feels difficult to give, give more

Everyday Bread

It seems foolish to be writing a recipe for bread because it is just something that has to be done every day, like peeling potatoes or cleaning the range. Every woman finds her own way of doing it, and the ingredients are certainly never measured, except in the cook's eye of what looks right. As for method, it is so ingrained in my fingers I would not know how to describe it. All I know is that as I get older, my bread has improved in texture and become more consistent. I nearly poisoned your poor grandfather, your mother only barely survived and you—my wee Tressa—got the best of it! If you really want to master an Irish soda bread, make it every day until it becomes as automatic as walking. There is no escaping its boring drudgery and only you can decide if it's worth it.

If you want to try, the basic ingredients are around 1lb flour—brown or white—1 teaspoon bread soda and as much buttermilk as will make a wet dough, but not so wet that you can't handle it. To this you can optionally add 1 tablespoon butter or any cooking fat, dried fruit, up to a dessertspoonful of honey or sugar, a pinch of salt, wheatmeal, porridge oats—use your imagination. Cook in a hot oven for up to 1 hour then tap the bottom, listening for a hollow sound to see if it's cooked. Wrap immediately in a clean tea towel to stop it going hard on you and let sit for a good half-hour before cutting.

WHEN YOU'RE AROUND something every day you stop seeing it. I can't make bread like my grandmother's and it drives me crazy. How many hours did I stand at the kitchen table in Fal Iochtar watching her make bread? She would do it every weekday, with the last loaf of the week baked on Saturday night, so that she would have the pleasure of rising late on Sunday morning with no other task but to prettify herself for eleven o'clock Mass.

For years now I have tried to draw up details in my mind's eye of how she made it, but my bread still falls so short of hers that I have all but given up. I can remember the yeasty smell of the buttermilk on a summer's day as the heat from the range steamed the windows of their cottage, then opening the back door to feel the freshness of the misty rain on my bare skin. I can remember waiting by her side, my chin barely reaching the tabletop, as she unfurled a linen tea towel from the fresh loaf; I can remember her favourite knife with the scorched yellow handle, the blade concave from years of sharpening, slicing through the fleshy crumble, then the fresh butter melting to a salty dribble. I remember how the sweet jam mingled with its sour flavour and burst my baby taste buds.

But I cannot remember anything that will help me make the damn stuff! How she handled the dough or any of the little tricks she must have shown me. One thing I do recall is how, when she was finished, her fingers sped across the Formica tabletop picking up every last shred of errant dough to add to the loaf.

'Waste not, want not,' she used to say.

I have already wasted a veritable mountain of flour and gallons of expensive buttermilk trying to replicate my grandmother's bread.

For punishment as much as anything else I am bringing my latest effort over to Ma Mullins this afternoon.

Yes. We are going there for Sunday lunch. Again.

Part of me cannot believe this is still going on.

The first Sunday lunch was dreadful for us both and I felt sure we had reached an understanding: me and your mother just don't mix—so don't mix us; little Deirdre's First Communion was a one-off.

But then it was some nephew's birthday, an anniversary, the first good barbecue day this month. One time he begged me to go, saying his mother was 'lonely' after the twins had left for a six-week vacation. I put together a special hamper to cheer up this lonesome old lady and found the house full of the usual horde of relations. With one thing and another, today will be the *seventh* time that we have Sunday lunched chez Ma Mullins. It has got so that going is the norm and not going is a big treat. It should be the other way around.

Oh, and are we going to be treated to organic lamb, rack-roasted with rosemary and cracked black pepper and served on a bed of wilted spinach? Are we talking pot-roasted chicken with pistachio-buttered baby carrots and new potatoes?

No.

There will be what there is every week: the usual revolting platters of fried bite-sized bowel blockers with some ready-made supermarket salads drenched in synthetic mayo.

And I'm worried about my bread not being good enough?

259

The really scary part about this is that I think I might be getting used to it. Extended exposure to the awfulness of these family get-togethers has upped my tolerance levels. Last week I skipped breakfast so I'd have enough of an appetite to be seen eating.

Dan is getting complacent and starting to assume that we'll go each week and I am getting lazy about objecting. I don't like going, but I can stand it. Once you don't notice that a family is dysfunctional any more, it means you have become a part of it.

I always thought that my background was really messed up: wanna-be artist weirdo for a mom and no dad. But now I realise that it was just unconventional. There's a difference. I knew I was loved, my grandfather was a stable father figure in my life and, although my mother had her faults, I could always talk to her. A mother can commit worse crimes than making you call her by her Christian name and having a propensity to tie-dye your wardrobe.

Dan's family make good small talk, but there is a poisonous under-current that I can't put my finger on. OK, yes, I *can* put my finger on it.

It's Eileen. She's cold, she's critical; all she does for her kids is get on to them about coming over, then shoves garbage food into them and glowers disapprovingly at their spouses. Hostess with the mostest, huh?

Dan's father is the non-event in the corner. The twins are cute, but they're on vacation (otherwise known as Escape from Alcatraz). Dan's younger brother Joe runs a car-parts shop, and his wife Anne is a small, plump, smiling woman who is nice, but won't commit herself, just nods and agrees with everything you say. Tom is in real estate—he's just a year older than Dan and his body double. A fact that appears to confuse his wife—bra-less Shirley—whom I have seen literally lick her lips when the two of them stand together. Shirley's age is blurred by collagen use and a body stuffed into the wardrobe of a teenage girl. I could rant about Shirley ad infinitum, but briefly? She gives me a pain.

On our way over in the car, I decide to give it my best shot and have one more go at getting my point across.

However, it is a ten-minute journey and I take five minutes to work out what I am going to say. Which gives me two minutes to say it, a minute for Dan to think about how to respond and two minutes to dis-cuss and resolve the whole issue.

I take the self-help guide approach and say something rehearsed and diplomatic along the lines of, 'I feel really uncomfortable with the number of Sundays we are spending at your mother's house.'

'Why?'

He is just being aggressively obtuse. We have had this conversation before and so he is goading me into saying what I really think, which is, I hate your mother!

'It's not that I dislike your mother Dan, but . . .'

Whoa. But. Not a good word on the end of a mother sentence.

Dan's face tightens into a worried scowl and I am starting to back-pedal when suddenly it hits me like a brick: Fuck you and your mother. That miserable cow has been vile to me. She summons us to her house every Sunday, then spends three hours ignoring me. She puts on this twisted, sarcastic face when I hand her the cakes and canapés, and generally goes out of her way to make me feel worthless. I hate her and I hate you—you weak, stupid, hapless ape—for not standing up to her, but most of all I hate myself for having married into this awful woman's family!

But before I get the chance to edit my anger into a more palatable version that I can actually say out loud, Dan pulls up to his mother's house.

'But what?' he says.

Bastard! I am boiling inside, but there is nothing I can do about it. I can't explode here, in the car, outside his mother's house. I just have to keep it together, get inside, get through the next few hours—then go home and say it like it is. Because—I am never, ever, *ever* going to put myself through the purgatory of this pretend happy family fiasco again.

I plaster an unconvincing smile across my face, and sing, 'Nothing!'

Then I unclick the seatbelt, spin myself out of the car and let him follow me up the path.

Shirley opens the door. 'Hi, folks!' she says, all curly eyelashes and cleavage. Then she looks sideways at my husband and says, 'Hi, Dan.'

Dan looks delighted and my rage rises another notch when I see how easily he is distracted from the fight we almost just had.

They are all there, sitting in silence round the TV. As well as family, there is a middle-aged couple that nobody bothers to introduce me to, and a woman in glitter Capri pants with dyed orange hair who can only be a friend of Shirley's.

'This is Candice.' Shirley flicks her nails in Candice's general direction. 'Her husband just left her for her sister.'

Candice spits, 'Slut', but I take it she means her sister and not me.

At this moment I do not want to be there. I don't think I can take it. The key is to keep busy and not sit down.

So I go straight out to the kitchen to prepare some food that I have brought with me. It's one of my tricks to tolerating these events: preparing food, working. Infiltrating Eileen's kitchen is never easy and she gives me her customary sideways grimace and shrugs when I say cheerily, 'Brought some nibbles, Eileen—do you mind?'

I work as slowly as I can. There is sport on the TV and I can hear the men calling out occasional shouts of encouragement or abuse.

I take forty-five minutes to pile the soda bread with tomato chutney, shredded Parma ham, crumbled goat's cheese and a drizzle of aged balsamic dressing. Eileen doesn't turn to me once while I am working. She just keeps shaking her bags of frozen titbits onto foil trays.

Holding on to my forced good humour as hard as I can, I start to work the room. Dan grabs one and stuffs it into his mouth without moving his eyes from the TV, Candice giggles a profuse 'Thank you' but looks uncertain how to handle this strange food. But—surprise, surprise—it is Shirley who finally causes me to snap.

'Oh, no,' she says, pushing me away with her palm as if I am a waitress, 'I hate that lumpy Irish bread.'

If I was looking for a person to bury in my displaced anger, I could not have found a more deserving candidate than Shirley Mullins.

It was as if every slight I had ever received in my lifetime, from the cool girls at school laughing at my tie-dyed pants to a bad review three years ago, had all pooled together with my doubts about Dan and my reservations about his family. I let rip.

I can't remember exactly what I said (I have wiped it from my memory), but I can make a fairly accurate guess based on what had been simmering away in my head all afternoon. The starting point was calling Shirley a stupid slut and accusing her of coming on to Dan. I do not know where that came from; I certainly hadn't thought it was something that bothered me sufficiently to lose my cool like that. I threw the tray of canapés on the floor, declaring the assembled group 'unappreciative ignoramuses'. When I caught sight of myself losing the plot in front of relative strangers and three actual ones, I grabbed my bag from the table and stormed out of the house.

Shaking, I rummaged in my bag praying that Dan had slipped the car keys in there like he always did. As I started the engine and drove home in five minutes flat, I knew it was over and I thought, 'Good riddance you shower of messed-up freaks.'

But by the time I got home, the shaking anger had given way to the awful realisation of what I had done.

I lay on our bed and bawled like a petulant child into the pillow.

Marriage was supposed to be the answer to everything: the blossoming of a mature love. It was supposed to be dignified, civilised, supportive, nurturing. Marriage wasn't easy, but surely it shouldn't be this hard.

That afternoon I realised I didn't know what marriage was supposed to be like at all. But I was pretty sure it wasn't supposed to be like this.

Life can be hard, but then we make it even harder by the way we look at it.

My mother walked across two fields to a well twice daily for water and she cooked on an open stove; the hem of her long skirt was blackened with soot, her arms muscled with the strain of lifting pots.

I didn't notice my mother's hardship because I was never called upon to do so. Suffering was ingrained in her—servile, solemn suffering. I never knew her any other way. Life was a slow penance, buying her time in the hereafter; it was not meant for enjoying, it was meant for serving. Life was a sentence. The harder it was and the quieter your forbearance, the more assured you were of eternal life.

My father often said cruel things to her when he was drunk, but she only ever took one beating from him that I know of. It was while she was pregnant with me, and her four brothers found him in our back field the following day and thrashed him with sticks to within an inch of his life. She told me this herself one day after he had hit my brother Patrick, sent him crashing to the floor during supper for some supposed slight. Patrick was extremely clever and this annoyed my father. He had won a scholarship to the local boys' school, but my father had refused to let him go on the grounds that we could not afford the uniform and books. The priest had been sent round to persuade him to change his mind and had said that the Church would provide any money needed to finish the boy's education. Patrick was devout and sensitive. My mother believed he could have been a priest. My father had refused out of pure stubbornness, saying that fourteen was time enough to leave school for any man and that he was needed on the farm. My mother saw her chance to have a priest for a son fly out of the window, and while she remained respectful of my father to his face she took up the habit of raging against him to me. She told me shocking stories of his brutality, embellishing them at times lest I should have any doubt of the kind of Godless animal my father was.

It was a small community and she had nobody else to talk to but her own daughter. At least her pride wouldn't be dented by talking to me. In any case, there was nothing she could do about her circumstances. By talking to me she found some release and she needed that to survive. Walking away from a marriage, no matter what indignities you suffered, was not possible. Complaining was weak and sinful and my mother wanted to be seen as neither.

When my mother told me about her brothers beating my father, her eyes glittered with pride. She defended the beating by explaining that my father would have killed me in the womb if they hadn't put the fear of God into him. It gave me a worse fear of my father than I had of him already, as well as a dread of any private contact with my mother. As the years went on, my mother's confidences stripped me of any loyalty I had to either of them.

My brothers all left Achadh Mor—Declan and Brian to Birmingham, where they both founds wives and started families, and Patrick to London. We never saw Patrick again. Ten years ago I got a letter from the Metropolitan Police in London to inform me that Patrick had died in a hostel in Camden Town. They had found my name and address on a piece of paper he had carried around in his pocket. Perhaps to remind him that he had a family, or perhaps in preparation for his death. Who knows? His was a wasted life. He could have been a doctor or a teacher if my father had given him the chance of an education. In the end all my father gave him was bad genes that drove him to drink.

My married brothers returned twice in twenty years. Their wives were strangers to us and their children had English accents. We welcomed them, but it was an uncomfortable reunion. They had been away too long and the gruff young men I had wrestled with as a girl had disappeared. They were overly polite, which is the worst insult a brother can pay you.

When my mother died only Brian came home. He said he was representing the Birmingham contingent. They could not find Patrick, which was the first sign that he was missing. It was an embarrassment to have such a small number of our immediate family present. My mother had suffered for us, but suffering does not buy you love. All it buys you is more suffering.

I had a dread of turning into my mother. It was why I had wanted to escape to America and why I had fallen so hard for the idea of falling in love. I never wanted to be trapped in the poverty of a loveless union. Even today, as I draw a picture of her in my mind, all I can see is my mother's long, sad face. Mouth turned down at the edges, deep lines etched down her cheeks—her face a map of everyday misery. My poor mother, I think, but I cannot conjure the same warmth as I felt for James's mother, who I knew for less than a year, or even for Ann, the aunt who betrayed me.

Knowledge is not enough, however, to stop a woman from turning into her mother. I heard myself moaning over nothing at all: crumbs on the carpet, a broken cup. I was married to a hard-working man who loved me, who would never let any harm come to me, yet I did not seem able to silence the nagging.

My need for constant improvement in our standard of living was as much to do with boredom as anything else. I loved my child, I had grown used to my husband, I knew I had a good life, and yet part of me always felt cheated of the dreams I had had as a young woman. As I got older, the fantasies I had nurtured seemed more and more ludicrous and reluctantly I had to let them go. My young man wasn't coming back; I was never going to work as housekeeper to a Hollywood starlet or twirl round a lamp post on Park Avenue in a pink satin skirt.

All my life I had been able to cut myself off and escape into the world of my imagination, where I was eternally smiling into a warm sun, Michael's arms closing round my waist. Sometime in my early forties I lost my ability to daydream. The clouds that used to carry me off had dissipated; when I closed my eyes to conjure an escape all I saw was my own stern face looking back at me, telling me not to be such a stupid fool. Perhaps it is our dreams that keep us young. Older women who cling on to youth may look ghoulish, but perhaps they are happier than those of us who grow old and crotchety before our time. Whatever the case, the routine of life grated on me, wearing me down and ageing me before my very eyes. I longed for something to shake me out of it. We took trips to Dublin, changed the wallpaper, moved the furniture round in the parlour, had electric lights put in, tiled the fire surround. Always wanting more, more, more—desperate for distraction.

Truthfully, I was bored beyond belief. This really was how it was going to be for the rest of my life. In this house with this man. The only thing I wanted to stay the same was Niamh and she was the one thing sure to change and leave. I could see it stretching on for ever, the rituals of our lives. Housework, marking exam papers, meeting parents, meal-times, Mass, bread-making every day except Sunday: comfortable, cosy commitment. Marriage—forever and ever world without end, amen.

I remember looking at James over the supper table one evening and thinking that I was so thoroughly sick of the sight of him—day in, day out—that I wanted to scream. I felt like hurling a plate at him for no other reason than to crash through his fog of contentment, which was suffocating me. If Niamh had not been around, I might well have thrown the plate. Who can say what difference such an unreasonable outburst of passion might have made? I decided to paint the hen house instead.

My wish for dramatic change did come true shortly after, but in a way that was to test my tolerance further still.

Waiting for Dan to get back from his mother's house was insufferable. The longest and most dreadful half-hour of my life. When I heard the front door bang, I thought I had been up in the bedroom for hours.

He came straight upstairs and found me lying face down on the bed. Gently, he put his hand on my shoulder. 'Are you OK, babe?'

Call me a raving psychopath who doesn't know when to stop, but I turned from a weak, weeping kitten into a possessed mad woman as soon as I felt his touch. 'Where have you been?'

'I came home as quick as I could—I had to get a lift off Tom.'

'Yeah, I bet that bitch Shirley had something to say about me.'

'She didn't say anything. We were all just really worried about you.'

That finished me off. 'Worried about *me*?!'

Dan was looking right at me and I saw his benign expression flicker for a second. I was still angry, but instinct made me draw back from ranting about his family and I finished with a frustrated, 'Huh!'

Dan turned to go. 'I'll go down and make us some coffee.'

'I don't want coffee!'

He spun back round, looked at me straight and said, 'Well then, what *do* you want, Tressa, because I am sure wearing myself out here trying to guess.' He wasn't shouting, but he was calling me out: eye-balling me in this calm you-better-start-talking way.

And I did not like it one little bit, not least because the answer was, 'I want to bury you and your family under twenty tons of shit, set light to it, then transport the ashes to outer space.'

'I just want the two of us to spend more time alone together.'

Where did that come from?

OK. I have this fear of the truth. Not the obvious truth like Dan's family are weird, or even the next layer under that, which is that his mother gives me the creeps, but the next floor down. Otherwise known as gut level: the underlying truth. Why do I find his family such hard work? Why do I find doing what I don't want to do for him so intolerable? If I loved him I could endure the unendurable. If we were meant to be together, I would gladly suffer boredom, indignities, awkwardness as part of my commitment to this marriage.

Within the confines of my own head, I can obsess about whether I really love Dan enough to be married to him and sometimes dream of escape. But as soon as I am given the chance to tackle this most fundamental of questions, an opportunity to speak my truth and thus put my hand on the handle of the 'out' door, I instantly teleport myself into a state of unswerving marital devotion.

Dan walked straight over and folded me in a suffocating hug.

He said, 'I have been so selfish, Tressa, putting my family before us.' Then he launched into this story about how his mother had had a stroke when they were all very young, how nobody had explained to them all why their mother couldn't speak properly and how the experience had made them all very protective of her. I wondered why he hadn't told me before, but was too self-absorbed to care. Too busy searching for the exit door on this dead-end alley of fake devotion. If it was there, it was blocked by my shame.

And so it was that I found myself standing at the front door of the house of a woman I loathed with a bunch of flowers in my hands, a rehearsed apology on my lips, and a heart that was thumping so hard it felt like it might jump out of my body and bite her.

Eileen wasn't going to make this easy, but knowing that didn't make it any more pleasant when she opened the door. She greeted me with expressionless silence, then walked straight back into her kitchen where she continued her chores as if I wasn't there.

I put the flowers down on the counter and said my piece. 'Eileen, I owe you an apology.' It was unreserved, featured no 'buts', offered no line of defence and was a textbook, perfect apology to which the only possible response was a counter-apology.

When no response of any kind was forthcoming, I started to flail about with explanations and excuses. Eventually I tripped across something that got her attention. 'Eileen, I love your son and . . .'

I hadn't had a chance to finish whatever thoughtless platitude was on its way out when the old woman turned to me, and her eyes were raging. 'You don't love my son.'

It was like a bolt had gone through me. I didn't know where to start with it. This sudden show of passion from a woman I thought was an impervious lump; then there was the whole ghastly element of it being true. 'Eileen! How could you say such a thing?'

'Because it's true!'

I was taken aback. We were heading for a showdown very different from the muted, grudging acceptance of apology I was prepared for. I was going to have to tread carefully if I wanted to stop my mother-in-law from beating me. 'I am not even going to comment on that, Eileen. Why would I have married your son if I didn't love him?'

'Because you are nearly forty and afraid of missing the boat . . .'

Thirty-eight, actually, but otherwise—good call.

267

Before I had the chance to formulate a response I was afraid I could not find, she added aggressively, '. . . *and* your brown bread is rubbish.'

Was this an escape route she was offering me? A side turning off the truth route perhaps neither of us was ready for right now?

Whatever. Nobody criticised my cooking and got away with it and I guess the old lady knew that.

'Oh, really? And what's wrong with it?'

'It's too dry. You need to use butter.'

'I always use butter.' Which was a lie.

'And an egg—'

'You don't put eggs in bread.'

'Well, maybe you should try, and a spoon of sugar might stop it tasting of cotton wool . . .'

'Thanks for your opinion, Eileen, but . . .' I stopped as I realised there was no but. She was right; my bread was shit. Then I saw what was really going on. We were two stubborn, self-righteous bitches standing in a kitchen arguing over how to make bread. It had been a long time since anyone had been anything other than deferential towards my cooking, so for chutzpah alone I decided to rise to her challenge.

'Well, show me how it's done, Eileen. I am all eyes and ears.'

She looked nervous—as well she might, the old cow. 'I don't have the ingredients.'

'Oh, I'm sure we can come up with something,' I said, stridently starting to open cupboard doors. I didn't care now. The old lady despised me anyway, so I may as well trample all over her boundaries and be done with it. I had nothing to lose.

I found flour, bread soda and sugar, then went to the fridge and removed a pat of butter, milk and rather pointedly placed a single egg on the worktop in front of her. Eileen looked stunned and for a second I felt sorry for her.

'We have no buttermilk. It's not the same without the buttermilk.'

She was trying to cop out.

'It'll do,' I said.

Eileen gave me one of her unnerving stares, then she emptied the sink of dirty dishes, rinsed out the blue plastic dish pan, dried it with a cloth and placed it on the work counter. She rooted in a cupboard under the sink and came out with a sieve, into which she roughly threw handfuls of the flour and a large unmeasured pinch of bread soda. As she shook the flour into fine downy peaks, the memories came flooding back. Grandma Bernadine's bowl was bright green and her sieve stainless steel not plastic, but otherwise they could have been the same. I don't know that their methods were identical; all I know is that as I watched Eileen's worn, plump fingers swiftly churn the milk and flour into an airy dough ball, I was transported back to my grandmother's side. Like a child, I was transfixed by the speed with which the expert hands hoovered up every crumb and placed the perfect, crossed dome onto a floured baking tray and into the oven.

When it was over, Eileen was flustered and could not untie her apron strings. I went and helped her and it was the first time that I had been that close to her physically. She smelt of sour milk and poverty, of an ordinary old woman who never bothered with pretty things. I felt a snap of pity, but knew this was no time to let down my guard.

'I'm impressed, Eileen,' then, by way of an olive branch, 'you make bread like my grandmother.'

She gave me a cursory 'Thanks', then disappeared into the living room. Just as I was wondering if I was meant to follow her, she came back and thrust a silver framed photograph at me.

The image was a black and white photograph of a kindly looking older woman with her hair swept back in a bun and small round glasses. 'She taught me.'

'Your mother?' I asked.

'Ha!' she said strongly. 'My grandmother.'

Over the next forty-five minutes, I dragged Eileen's story out of her. Her mother had become pregnant, then run away to America, leaving the baby Eileen in the care of her grandparents, whom she assumed to be her mother and father. Her grandparents sheltered her from the truth for as long as they could, but when she was seventeen her grandfather died and a neighbour let slip her parentage at his funeral. Grief-stricken and furious, Eileen bullied her mother's address out of her grandmother and started to write to her, but her mother never replied. Finally, when she was twenty-three, her grandmother managed to scrape together Eileen's passage to America and she went and found her mother living in Yonkers, only to be rejected in person. She had met and married a wealthy older man, who knew nothing of Eileen's existence. With no family and no money, Eileen presented herself at the presbytery of the first Catholic Church she could find and was given a job as assistant to their housekeeper. Dan's father was the housekeeper's younger brother and that was how they met.

All of this was delivered in matter-of-fact single sentences. Not a shred of embellishment or self-pity, just shrugging, that's-the-way-it-was pragmatism. When she had finished, I wanted to embrace her—this motherless burdened woman.

'The bread!'

We saved it just in time. I wanted to ask if she saw her grandmother or her mother again after that, but thought it best to let her finish reminiscing another day. There would, I knew, be other days to fill.

As I stood at the door, she handed me the loaf.

'Now,' she said, 'I hope it's up to your standards.'

She gave me one of her sarcastic lopsided looks.

I looked into her eyes and saw they were soft with affection.

With horror I remembered the stroke and realised that Eileen had been smiling at me all along.

I cannot say that what I felt for my father was love. I was afraid of him, yet worse than the fear was the way that I understood him. Whether he was silent and sullen or loud and abusive, I always sensed that it fell on me to make him better.

In his worst drunken moods I seemed to be the only person he could have around him. My mother could never fully understand my father because she did not have his blood running through her veins. So, while his maudlin ramblings enraged my brothers, calming and placating my father out of a drunken frenzy became my job. They all ran like rats out of the house when they saw him coming, my mother wailing and wringing her hands in a way I knew would anger him even more.

He always professed a passionate love for my mother and claimed that her cold-heartedness was killing him. But my father did not want to be loved. He wanted someone to run alongside him and witness his pain; someone to drown in his anguish with him. So he would sit at the kitchen table and start to list his grievances: his brother getting the farm, the bad price of cattle, some bastard this, some bastard that—working up to the climax of my mother's brothers giving him a beating. The betrayal of it! The humiliation! Then the fists would come down on the table and I knew it was nearly over and he was ready for some food.

I preferred my father angry because I could distract myself by staying safe. Once the fight had gone out of him, he was just a vulnerable mountain of man. As a small child it terrified me to see my father cry; as I grew older it broke my heart. I spent my childhood wishing my father's pain away. As a young woman I assumed that treacherous trickery of fear and guilt, that compulsion to cure, was love.

By the time my mother died I was a woman in my forties and I had learned different. Or at least I thought I had.

When I saw my father help carry my mother's coffin up the aisle, I knew that he was not going to survive on his own. His ferocious frame was confined in the black suit I had bought for him the day before; he shuffled his feet as if the ground was burning them. He had a look of anguish on his face, like an actor frozen mid-speech. It was as if my mother's death had been flung at him by an adversary. God. Punishment for all the bad things he had done.

When I looked at him, pathetic and broken like that, my heart disintegrated to dust. That was how it had always been. His anger always dwarfed the feelings of the people around him. My mother's funeral became not about her, but about how my father would cope without her.

After years of marriage to a decent man, I came to believe that perhaps my father was not a lost soul deserving of my tolerance and pity, but an evil, cunning man. But it takes more than believing something to reverse the habits of a devoted daughter.

My mother was sixty-seven when she died unexpectedly. She had waited on my father hand and foot. He knew how to light the fire and he knew where the well was, but he could not boil a pan of water and he did not know how many spoons of sugar he took in his tea. My family home was half an hour's bicycle ride from our house, and I thought I would manage my father's meals and look after him sufficiently without having to move him in with us. As the weeks after she died progressed, however, I realised that it wasn't going to be possible. A neighbour was supplying Daddy with alcohol, cheap poteen, and he wasn't bothering to eat the food I was leaving for him or to light the fire. Twice I found him asleep in the chair having soiled himself. The second time I thought he was dead and, I confess, I felt a flicker of relief. It's over, I thought.

It was perhaps only the shock and guilt I felt when he opened his eyes that made me bring him home with me.

That and James. My husband had been insistent from the first. 'Your father needs the comfort of his family.'

'Let one of my brothers take him back to England.'

'Oh, Bernadine . . .'

His voice moved across my name in that disappointed tone he always used whenever I said something nasty; as if cruel words were so unlike the kind-hearted Bernadine that he knew me to be.

James was a pioneer—a non-drinker. As a young woman, I had thought his refusal of alcohol patronising and unattractive. A man who did not drink was not a real man—no craic. As time went on, I began to realise that the only good thing my father ever gave me was a husband who didn't drink.

James occupied himself with his reading and always had plenty to keep him interested around the house, growing vegetables and keeping bees. He had more interest in Niamh than most men had in their children. As he got older, he sought out the company of other men, but through the more gentlemanly pursuits of fishing and shooting. The pub was somewhere he went to pay his respects after a funeral, or perhaps to buy his wife a bar of chocolate on his way home from town.

So I felt that James was innocent of the indignities and vulgarities of the drinking man. To him my father was just the person who had given me to him. He knew that Daddy drank, but he had never witnessed anything to make him believe that my father was different from any other man. The idea of my refined husband being exposed to the coarse treachery of my father's drunken tongue terrified me.

I was not afraid of my father himself, but of who I became when I was with him. All my adult sense told me that Daddy was a drunken old fool not worth taking heed of. But in my heart I was still a frightened child, eager to make everything better. James had seen me tired and grieving, but he had never seen me weak.

Mother died in mid-August and my father had moved in with us by early September. I was relieved at the timing as it was the beginning of the autumn term, so James and Niamh would be at school all day and I would be left to deal with my father on my own.

Daddy was seventy and should not have lived past sixty the way he abused himself. He was heavy and grew out of breath after even the shortest walk, but he was still a strong man.

For the first few months it looked as if everything was going to be fine. Daddy had got a fright when I found him passed out for the second time and promised his drinking days were well and truly behind him. He was still in shock having lost my mother, but seemed to accept that a holiday in our house was a good idea. He was more outgoing than I had ever seen him before, declaring James a charming man and saying that this not-drinking thing was very good indeed and that he wished he had taken his pledge more seriously as a youth. Niamh, who barely knew her grandfather, and was used to living in the exclusive company of her parents, adapted quickly to having him around. They both revelled in the novelty of each other's company and after supper would sit by the fire in a conspiratorial huddle, playing old maid or snakes and ladders, while I cleaned the scullery and James tended the vegetable garden.

Those evenings, watching them from the scullery door, I could not help feeling that my family had finally taken shape. Three generations under the same roof: there was such warmth in seeing how the old man was with my child. As if the complications of parenthood had disappeared with a generation, and all that was left was his paternal love. If my own childhood had been fraught, then perhaps this idyll was my reward.

While my husband and child were at school, a cheerful working relationship opened up between my father and me. He cleaned the fires and I even had him polishing furniture and cleaning windows. He seemed proud of finishing each task and we argued playfully over his reward.

'That'll be apple tart and cream on the menu tonight, young lady.'

'You'll have stewed gooseberries like the rest of us and be glad of them.'

'What about a few blackberries then?'

'You'll have to pick them first, Mister.'

I had never enjoyed a light banter with my father before and it was wonderful. He praised my cooking, and for the first time in my life I had the feeling of being my daddy's little girl. I began to understand the carefree confidence that James gave to Niamh. This late blossoming of affection was my reward for enduring a childhood of confusion and hardship. Compensation, perhaps, for losing the great love of my life and being married off heartlessly to the safest, cheapest option.

Although I was sorry my mother was dead, I was sorrier for the fact that, rather than her, I was enjoying the benefits of my father's sobriety. Meanwhile a little demon princess was whispering that perhaps I had some power over him that my mother had never had. Perhaps I had the secret to stopping my daddy drinking, after all, and all the wishes I had wished and all the prayers I had prayed had finally come true.

But then the day you believe you have found the answers is the day life tells you that you know nothing at all.

My father had terrorised his family for the best part of fifty years and been forgiven, forgiven, forgiven. But with men like my father, it isn't over until they draw their final breath. And even then you will carry them around for ever like a stone in your heart.

One day I came downstairs to find my father sitting by last night's fire. His back was to me and his head was as still as a statue.

'I didn't light the range for you this morning, Bernadine.'

His voice delivered the words deliberately as if he had been rehearsing them. Dread lurched up through my stomach. I knew from his inflection that my father had been drinking. He hadn't had much, maybe only a sniff of whiskey, but I could hear trouble in his tone.

'I am missing your mother today.'

'I miss her too, but we have to get on with our work.'

I was operating on a wing and a prayer, using the same harsh, pragmatic tone I used on my husband. As if it were the same thing, as if my everyday honest words would not antagonise him into a rage.

I had not lived under my father's roof for almost twenty years. This was my home. I had my own family; I was no longer a part of his world, but he of mine. He was staying in another man's house, and I was another man's wife. My father would not dare abuse me in my husband's house.

His voice was barely audible. 'You evil bitch.'

I had heard him say it to my mother. Mutter an atrocity so quietly that you might think the devil himself was whispering inside your head.

'Pardon?' The request to repeat it came out automatically.

'I said, you evil bitch.'

My hands were shaking as I scooped handfuls of flour into my basin and I repeated to myself: *Give us this day our daily bread, give us this day our daily bread.*

'Did you hear me, Bernadine? Are you going to reply to your father?' *Our Father, Who art in Heaven.*

I realised in that moment that I had no special skills for dealing with such a bully. No innate understanding running through my veins. What had protected me in the past was not my status as his blood relation or his child, but my mother. Suddenly I realised that she had been strong. Now she was gone he needed another victim to pour his rage into. Another 'cold-hearted' woman to justify his bitterness and depression. A reason he could give himself to explain the lump of pain inside and help dilute it into something more digestible—like hate.

'Look at you—standing there making bread. My daughter, the cold-hearted, evil bitch. Your mother lies in her grave and you are standing there. Making bread. You don't give a shit about anyone or anything.'

He had never spoken to me like that before, but when he had spoken in that way to my mother, I had always been terrified because I knew it presaged something bad. And as he spoke I knew I should be feeling afraid, but I wasn't.

I got angry.

I can't say exactly what I said, but a stream of obscenities I did not know I understood flew out of me and I threw the basin of flour across the room, narrowly missing my father's head.

Flour scattered around the fireplace, a cloud of it catching him on the side of the face in a ghostly sheath.

We both stood for a few seconds, shocked.

Then he came at me. Silently, his mouth opening around a half-formed insult, drugged by his own anger, he flung his arm at my head and swiped me to the ground. It was a blow as heavy as if he had been holding a brick. As if he were a big man and I still a little child.

I fell like a weighted cushion and, as my shoulder hit the flagstones, I surrendered. My anger vanished in the impact; defeat was instant and absolute. As my father lifted his leg to kick me, there was a shout.

'Bernadine!' James was at the door. The sound of his voice pushed my body into a foetal curl.

Everyone is capable of hate, of wanting to hurt, even kill another person. But when those hatreds manifest themselves out of the mind and into real life, a line is crossed. The line between human and animal.

'Get out of my house, John Morley, or, so help me God, I will kill you.'

My father stepped away from me and turned to James. For a moment I thought he might hit him and I cried out, 'No!'

As my father walked towards him, James put his hand to the back of the door and in one discreet motion took his hunting gun in his hand.

'I won't speak freely, John, but I know what kind of man you are. If you ever show such disrespect to my wife or lay a hand on her again, I will kill you. Now get out of my house.'

My father looked back at me, and his parting shot was a look of pathos. As if he were the slighted one. As if I were the only person who could understand that it was himself not me who was the victim.

That night I woke under the bedclothes with my head buried in the soft flesh of James's stomach, sobbing, 'Daddy, Daddy.'

James drew me up and held me in a protective knot, and I allowed the boundaries of father and husband to blur as he wiped my tears and kissed the top of my head. I cried without shame, and the schoolmaster comforted the brave girl who had reared him a daughter and grown grey hairs at her temples.

I never needed my husband's love as much as I did that night. It was as a replacement for someone else's, but he gave it willingly nonetheless.

Recovery from childhood traumas was unrecognised by my generation. They were not fashionable as they are now, but we felt them no less deeply. James was a perceptive man, ahead of his time in many ways.

'You know that your father can come back and stay here at any time, Bernadine. You only have to say the word.'

He was big enough to play second best, to a brutal alcoholic. He would always walk two steps behind if he thought it would make me happy.

It took a few weeks for the ice to thaw, but I continued to visit my father and tend to his needs twice a week. That day was never mentioned again.

Within a year the mild arthritis my father had been suffering from turned chronic. He became virtually chairbound and reluctantly came to live with us again. He remained with us for the rest of his life, another nine years. He drank when he had the energy to get alcohol himself, but there were no more ogre-like scenes.

Daddy was not an easy patient, nor always a polite one. I cannot look back on the nine years he was with us and pinpoint moments of joy or familial revelation or intimacy. Even his playmate, Niamh, in time withdrew from him. My father had a way of pushing people away, especially those who loved him. In his lifetime I had watched him come to despise those who loved him as much as he despised himself, as if their love wasn't genuine but a cruel joke they used to taunt him. He grew weak and quiet, but I would never say he mellowed. Mellow would be too kind a description for the silence he gradually applied to his anger.

I was never afraid of my father again after that day. When you have known real fear, to live without it can be a luxury. But you have to *know* when you are one of the lucky ones. That suffering is the destiny of some and the birthright of many.

I was spared my mother's suffering and that could be said to be down to one thing only: my marriage to James.

Respect

Complacency is the enemy of love

Porter Cake

I have been making this porter cake for as far back as I can remember. It's heavy with fruit and makes an ideal Christmas cake. Take 1lb flour and mix in a bowl with 1 teaspoon baking soda and whatever spices you have to hand—nutmeg, cinnamon, mixed spice—adding a flat teaspoon of each. Set aside. Mix up 4 eggs in a bowl and set aside also. In a heavy saucepan put the following: 1 bottle Guinness, 1lb rich brown sugar, 1lb each raisins and sultanas, 4 oz mixed peel and ½lb margarine. Allow it to boil for 5 minutes, then turn to a low simmer for a further 10. Five minutes into the simmer, add 4 oz glacé cherries. Leave to cool until a good deal cooler than lukewarm. To the cooled mixture add your flour and then the eggs—gradually and with great caution to avoid curdling. Pour the mixture into a 9-inch tin, which has been lined with greaseproof paper. Cook in a slow oven for 2½–3 hours.

YOU SHOULD NEVER take old favourites for granted in cooking. About the time a recipe becomes automatic and fail-safe is when it will let you down in front of an audience.

You've got to feel for these people who get dragged in as studio audiences. The sun is shining outside, yet they have been lured by the hollow promise of 'entertainment' into a windowless, cavernous space with uncomfortable tiered seating, to watch a nervous food writer panicking over a sunken fruit cake.

'I don't know what's happened.'

'Did you put in the raising agent?'

Great—my director bakes.

I did not dignify him with a reply, just said, 'We'll have to do it again.'

'I can't keep these people here any longer. They've already sat through two broken flans and a goose-giblet spillage this afternoon. They'll riot.'

And charming too.

This recipe was so simple—I had been doing it since I was, literally, seven years old. I had learned how to count—one, two, three, four eggs; four, five, six pounds of flour—measuring the ingredients out for my grandmother.

When my agents had rung and said I had been selected to screen-test for a show on a new cookery cable channel, I was pretty excited. Books and television work fed off each other. Getting screen-tested in itself meant that you were enough of a name in the book field to warrant a tryout and, if it worked out, that meant I could sell a lot more books and get more TV work and—well, suffice to say this was something I had hoped for a long time was on the cards and, finally, I seemed to be getting my moment in the sun.

Except I hadn't banked on the possibility that television might not be quite the glamorous easy ride I was expecting.

The whole thing felt like an experiment in Z-list celebrity humiliation. I had been plonked in front of a tired rented audience, who for their ten-dollar pay cheque and free lunch had already endured three hours of 'oohing' and 'ahhing' in front of Shelly—'the nail-care systems expert'—before being subjected to me splitting two custard flans and almost causing fatal injury to a cameraman, thanks to his sliding on a goose's undiscovered giblet.

It had not been my finest hour.

I was terrified of failing at this and had chosen Grandma's traditional Christmas cake because it is magnificent in an earthy, old-fashioned way. Fruitcake is substantial, no delicate confection liable to deflate with the slightest breeze through the oven door. So the collapse of it was a humiliation. People will forgive a deflated soufflé, but I could see them looking at me and thinking, 'How the hell did she do that?'

The director was not sympathetic to my being a nervous novice. This was a man who had been shooting pilots and screen tests for too long and was obviously being paid a set rate to finish the job, so he wasn't running over on hours.

'I'm sending this crowd home. There's a fresh lot due into Studio Four at seven and they are finishing early. We can prep now then film in there when the real chef is done.'

Like I said. He was a charmer. I wanted this day to be over.

In twelve hours I had gone from believing I was on the cusp of an exciting career breakthrough to the shattering realisation that I was a lousy TV cook. Lousy cook full stop was what the director's face said.

The cake was finished by seven and came out perfect, but the day wasn't over. Just as I was finishing up, who did I see out of the corner of my eye but the 'chef': the one I had been seeing just before I met Dan, the one who had passed me over for a model, the arsehole not worth naming? Well, his name is Ronan Robertson and though I had my eyes firmly trained on the camera, I could feel his eyes burning the back of my neck.

I somehow managed to close the show in one take and if the audience was pleased, and the director relieved, I didn't notice. As I turned and saw him still standing there, staring, this rush ran through me. Something bad was going to happen and there was nothing I could do to stop it.

'Ronan.'

I walked over to him and I could feel my limbs start to weaken. It was as if my body had gone into recall about how much I had wanted him that one night we had slept together. My physical senses were anticipating reaquainting myself with him without the permission of my brain.

'Tressa.'

He was looking at me in a quizzical, intense way and—oooh—the deep, grumbling voice. That was how he had got me into bed. That and a lot of alcohol.

'I need a drink,' I said. 'How about you?'

It was OK—safe to flirt. I was an old married lady after all, despite what my body was signalling. Just glad of the opportunity to let this egotistical arse know what he had missed out on.

It was all so different from how I thought it would be. Ronan was really subdued, not the consummate charmer who had seduced and then dumped me. I had truly fallen for him and he had left me bereft. I suggested we go uptown and called a cab. He shrugged, 'Whatever,' and there was an awkward silence in the cab that I broke with, 'Are you sure you want this drink, Ronan? You're very quiet.'

He shook his head and gave me a strange look.

'You are some piece of work, Tressa Nolan.'

Though curious, I didn't ask what he meant because the mystery of his statement felt good. For the first time since we had got into the cab I looked at him properly and instantly regretted it. Ronan is no pin-up, not nearly as conventionally handsome as Dan, but there is a quality about him that I find hard to resist. I cannot pinpoint it in what we said, or his sense of humour, or what we have in common, although educated, erudite, witty chef just about sums up his credentials for me. But Ronan feels familiar, almost a soulmate. I slept with him more or less a few hours after we first met and it didn't feel sluttish or wrong—it felt destined. As if he had always been there.

We had made love like we were in love. Afterwards, while I lay folded around his body, I remembered a night of understated emotion, of comfort in just being with him, like hearing a sad song for the first time and feeling like it was written about you.

Then he didn't call and started publicly dating a model, so I pegged him as an arrogant pig.

I didn't think back to the night we had had together, or how special it had felt, or how 'different' or how 'meant to be' it had all seemed. Betrayal is too painful a concept. 'All men are bastards' may be an old cliché, but sometimes you just need a line that works.

So here we were again.

His shirt was a faded blue, the same shade as his eyes by happy accident; his hands were scrubbed like a good chef's should be.

'You never called.'

Him not me. I couldn't believe my ears.

'You never called *me*,' I blurted out.

'You said *you* would call *me*, Tressa. You were like—don't call us, we'll call you.'

'That is just not true, Ronan. You said you would call me.'

'Other way around.'

Then he gave me this big broad grin and shook his head again. His eyes were sparking, he was suddenly filled with light and somehow I knew I had done that to him.

'What's going on here, Tressa? We are like, I don't know—'

'A couple of bickering kids?'

He leaned his elbow on the cab window, put his fingers to his forehead

279

and shook his head some more. Then he looked up from under his palm, his eyes full of happy mischief, and said, 'More than that, Tressa. I don't know what's going on with us. It's crazy, I just feel like—I don't know.'

I didn't know either. Except, of course, I did. I just didn't want to say it. I was married now, so I said, 'I need a drink.'

We stopped the cab around SoHo and went to the nearest bar. I ordered tequila slammers, although I rarely drink spirits. I guess I was trying to pretend I was someone else. Someone who was free to fall in love, helping to raise the stakes on the already intoxicating blend of adrenalin and emotion I was experiencing. Or perhaps it was just to help me forget I was married.

We spent an hour clearing the ground. He told me how he was sick of screwing models. He made a very convincing case (even though it takes very little to convince a slightly drunk woman in her late thirties that men prefer 'real women'), and when he talked about having screwed up by not pursuing me more assertively, there was genuine resignation in his voice.

'So, you're married, Tressa. How did that happen, hey?'

I shrugged. Honestly, I'd had three slammers at that stage.

'Yeah,' I said, beaming at all this adulation. 'I'm really happy.'

As soon as I said it, I knew it wasn't true. I wasn't really happy with Dan. If I was, I wouldn't be sitting here wobbling on a bar stool lying about it to this very special guy as he paused, looked deep into my eyes in a way that only he could and said, 'I've thought about you a lot.'

He faltered over the words as if he had more to say, but couldn't. We were both holding back—Ronan because it was too crazy for him to say out loud, and me because I was afraid it was too late.

I wasn't just afraid it was too late. It actually *was* too late. I was married. I had Dan.

I had to linger in the moment because it felt too good to let go, and so I allowed the inevitable to happen. We leaned; we kissed.

It was soft and slow and perfect. I was instantly sobered with the shock of how right it felt. With Angelo the emotion had been strong, but it had felt wrong.

I had thought I was safe with Dan, but that was before I knew what *sure* felt like. Now I knew. I can't describe it except that there was a deep, deep knowing.

They say there is one man for every woman and mine, I felt more certain than I had ever felt of anything in my life before now, was Ronan Robertson. And I had married somebody else.

It was tragic.

So I ordered another slammer, drank it down and realised that subconsciously I had noticed the bar we were in had rooms. The tariff was hanging behind the bar, so I called to the barman and said, a little too loudly, 'We want a room.'

'No, no. No way!' Ronan was up off the stool. 'This is too much Tressa, you're married and—'

I could see the longing in his eyes. We were playing out a scene from our own movie. 'And what?'

I could feel that my face was flushed, and wondered vaguely if I looked as beautiful as I felt. He certainly seemed to think so as his face collapsed in defeat.

'And I want you.' And that was it.

The room we entered was small, orange, irrelevant except for one detail—us. We attacked each other in a passionate frenzy, separating briefly for Ronan to tear his shirt off and, as he did, I caught sight of myself in a wall mirror I hadn't previously noticed. My face was devoid of make-up and slanted with drink. Briefly, I didn't recognise myself and thought I was looking at a window into another room.

It gave me a jolt.

This *wasn't* me in a hotel room about to commit adultery. Immediately I tried to turn it round. I wasn't doing anything wrong, just following my heart. Passions this strong cannot be ignored. Movies, love songs—irresistible, certain, destined love at first sight. It must mean something that I felt this way.

Dan would understand, wouldn't he?

And in the millisecond that my husband's smiling honest face flashed through my mind, my uncontrollable ardour disappeared.

'I have to go.' I buttoned my blouse and grabbed my bag. 'I'll pay for the room on my way out.'

Ronan was very upset. 'Tressa. You can't leave me like this.'

I let my eyes flick across him with a brief apology. I was afraid to look at him properly in case I changed my mind.

'This isn't right, Ronan. Call me.'

'I don't have your number, please, not like this. I'm begging you . . .'

As I was waiting for the lift, I gave in to the impulse to go back and leave my cellphone number with him. When I reached the room I held my ear to the door and listened. Ronan was talking on the phone to somebody. I took a business card out of my bag and quietly slipped it under the door.

When big things in our life start changing, we rely more heavily on small certainties to make us feel secure.

My body changed early. In my late forties it began to act against me like a rebellious teenager. I started to heat up like a furnace at irregular, unpredictable times. My palms became sweaty, my skin erupted in blotches and spots; it felt like there was some energy anxious to escape through the ends of my fingers and toes, so that I would sew and knit and run around frantically all morning, then collapse in the mid-afternoon exhausted. Often, I felt like weeping for no reason and that was possibly the hardest thing of all. I was never given to easy displays of emotion. When I cried, it meant that there was something powerful and terrible going on. I considered the misty-eyed sentiment of older women to be a weakness. Now here I was leaking emotion against my will and I did not like it. It made me bad-tempered. So I flung myself into the certainty of my proficiency as a housekeeper.

My house already being run with great efficiency, I sought out new ways to express myself as an exemplary home-maker. I took every tired or unworn piece of knitwear in the house—from old hats to holed socks and threadbare jumpers—then unpicked and reknitted them into a dreadful hodgepodge of multicoloured jumpers and cardigans, which my husband wore without demur.

I crocheted antimacassars and doilies, until all the surfaces in the house were covered in lace, and then invented new things to cheer the place up. Among the more ludicrous of them was a monogrammed linen wallet for James's daily newspaper and several decorative sacks to hold his gloves, hat and shooting scarf.

I made tea cosies and drawer tidies. I took every unused item in the house and turned it into something else; old mackintoshes into gardening aprons, felt hats into kettle holders. On one frustrated afternoon, I attacked the baby clothes that I had lovingly kept and cut them up into tiny triangles for cushion stuffing. When I saw the decimated pile, I wept with sentimental longing to have them back.

It was about then that I developed the habit of using a different cloth to polish every surface in the house. In later years Niamh called it my 'rag habit', as I was never able to let go of it fully. Cotton for cleaning; silk and nylon for polishing. Each rag then developed a special purpose in the house: this one for washing cups and everyday crockery, this one for china only and another again for wiping and another for drying. This one reserved for saucepans and this one for floors. If I inadvertently used the wrong rag on the wrong surface, I would have to go back and start again.

This neurosis developed in tandem with the disintegration of my ageing body. As I watched my childbearing years vanish behind me, I tried to fill the barren void with pointless fripperies. I had no purpose in life and was frantically searching for one. In another age I might have studied for a university degree. As it was, my legacy from that period was drawers full of doilies and a kitchen full of rags.

It was a terrible time. Just when you start to look forward to the wisdom of your maturing years, nature suddenly turns the clock back on your common sense and forward on your body.

It's unsettling and makes you do things that you would never normally do. Like insult a bishop.

As chairman of the board of management in James's school, the local priest was James's boss. And the bishop was *his* boss.

You had to kowtow to priests, that was a given. A bishop expected any manner of response, but only as long as it came within certain boundaries. These ranged from the standard respectful kissing of his outstretched hand to barely contained, simpering grovelling. For most of us the local bishop was the closest we could get to God without actually dying.

James thought their pomp and petty rules ridiculous because he was too political and too educated to believe otherwise. But his school was run, like every school in Ireland, by the Catholic Church, so he had no choice but to go along with the system.

James did not grovel because he did not have to. His education, reputation and standing in the community evened the ground between himself and the high-ranking religious. He treated the clergy with a quiet respect.

Needless to say, I was expected to do the same.

Every year Bishop Dunne honoured Kilkelly with his presence when he came to confirm the young people of our parish into the Catholic Church. As a local schoolteacher's wife, I was expected to tag along with my husband and contribute refreshments to the reception afterwards in the parish hall.

This particular year I decided to pull out all the stops and make the confirmation reception a special event, for no other reason than to make extra work to occupy myself. The trestle tables were covered with linen tablecloths, some of my own crockery was added to the humble parish stock and I prepared a veritable banquet.

I went into a cleaning frenzy, scrubbing and polishing the rough wooden floors of the parish hall and running a knife along the edges of the Formica table trimmings, scraping out years' worth of crumbs and gunk. I scrubbed the toilets and polished the taps and swept the front steps so that the place was, truly, fit for a bishop.

I barely slept the night before. James was confused as to why I was going to all this trouble, but he said nothing. Which was just as well because I did not know myself.

Secretly, I feared I might be losing my mind. And so, in the way that madness perpetuates itself, I woke on the morning of the confirmation and dressed myself as if I were going to meet the queen. I rarely wore make-up, excepting a little lipstick on a Sunday, but on this day, for reasons I am still at a loss to explain, I applied rouge to my cheeks and some blue eyeshadow (which was still new in its box). I agonised over what to wear—for so long that I ended up in a purple two-piece which was slightly too small for me and I had to wear the jacket open.

When I arrived at the hall to finish the preparations, I thought the other women working were looking at me strangely. When I went to check that the bathroom was as I had left it the night before, I saw in the mirror that rivers of sweat had run down my cheeks and made stripes of my rouge, which is what they would have been staring at. I wanted to weep, but girded myself instead with a terrible determination.

I was so angry that afternoon. Angry at having gone to all of this trouble; angry at the way I imagined the other ladies were excluding me from their talk. Angry at my runny rouge, my incurable symptoms and my uncontrollable, incontinent emotions.

But mostly I was angry with the bishop.

Every year he swanned in here in full dress regalia like some shrunken, aged bride. Not bothering to talk to the parents or thank the fawning ladies of the parish for all their hard work. When he arrived nervous children were swept aside in the triangular magnificence of his train, while he glided up to the refreshments table and gave me a haughty nod of the head to indicate he was ready for his tea and cake.

Odious man.

I cut him a slice of my rich fruit cake, from the recipe I normally keep in reserve for Christmas. It was always my speciality and he didn't deserve it, but I handed it over anyway.

Well. He looked me up and down with the disdain that seemed to be his permanent expression, then picked a corner of the cake and shoved it into his mouth. 'Eugh,' he said, 'this cake is dry.'

Bishop Dunne was famed for these rude, thoughtless outbursts. He had great trouble keeping a housekeeper for that reason.

But I wasn't his housekeeper. I wasn't his servant any more than this ignorant, greedy gremlin of a man was God's. And my cake was *not* dry.

'Perhaps it's *your* mouth that's dry, Father.'

His Lordship was flummoxed with horror at the implication that he was a dry-mouthed old bastard, but most of all at my not using his proper title. Bishop Dunne put down the plate and in a silent but incandescent rage he walked out of the parish hall.

In the second he turned his back I felt absolute terror wash over me as I realised what I had done. But as the last of his skirt disappeared out of the door, the relief in the room was palpable. There was sense that at any moment, there would be a round of applause. Bridie Malone actually came up behind me and said, 'He's had that coming for years—well done, Bernadine!' In that moment, then, I felt proud and a smile was about to break on my lips when I saw James standing in the kitchen doorway. There was a look of angry disapproval on his face.

'Dan, there's something I need to tell you.'

If he felt even a tenth of the dread in listening to that statement as I did in saying it, that was bad enough.

'You're leaving me.'

I was taken aback. Did he know?

'No, I'm not leaving you.'

'Then phew for that . . .' he said, laughing at his own joke. 'Gotcha! Say, what time is it, baby? Gerry said he'd be here round about two o'clock to help me fix up the bike.'

This was going to be harder than I thought.

It had been forty-eight hours of hell. My blood was poisoned by my own adrenalin.

After twenty-four hours I had more or less decided that perhaps Ronan Robertson was not my soulmate after all. I tried to recall the lust and longing I had felt—keep the image of us together as something special alive in my mind and put some romantic spin on it that would make it feel right—but guilt kept tapping me on the shoulder, tut-tutting my infatuation away.

I knew I had to tell Dan. It wouldn't be easy, but I couldn't carry it around with me any longer. I figured out my story and bit the bullet.

'I'm serious, Dan. We need to talk.'

He was covered in grease, fiddling around with some Harley bike parts on the table, making a mess.

'I'm sorry, Tressa, I'll clean this all up later. Once Gerry gets here . . .'

I coughed. 'I *nearly* had an affair.'

I looked him straight in the eye. Just like I promised myself I would. I thought he would be shocked, hurt. I was ready for tears.

'What do you mean "nearly"?'

He looked angry in a way I hadn't seen before. I faltered.

'I don't know. I—'

'What do you mean "nearly" had an affair, Tressa?' he repeated, wanting an answer.

'It was this guy at the shoot that I used to go out with and we went out and had a few drinks and then—'

'Did you sleep with him?'

'No.'

'Did you *want* to sleep with him?'

'Yes, no, yes . . . I don't know . . .'

'Did you kiss him?'

'Yes—sort of—I can't remember.'

'Don't bullshit me, Tressa—did you kiss him?'

'Ye-es!' I half-screamed, half-wailed it, like the drama queen I never knew I was. This was a scene I was not enjoying playing out.

'Did you enjoy it?' He said it in this cold way that was not one bit like Dan at all. He went on. 'Was it—I don't know—sexy? Fun?'

I was afraid of the way he was being. Nasty, spiteful. I responded with surprise, not at his anger but at his reaction and my fear.

'You don't get it, Dan.'

'Don't get *what*, Tressa? That my wife is out there having a "nearly" affair—kissing, maybe fucking other men? What's not to "*get*"?'

'Stop it! Stop talking like that. Be yourself.'

'What does that mean, Tressa? Myself? Slushy Dan, the big uneducated ape, who's too stupid to see what's going on under his nose? The gentle giant who'll forgive anything—'

'Stop it! Stop it!'

'What do you want me to do, Tressa? Do you want me to get down on my knees and beg you not to leave me?'

'I'm not leaving you Dan—'

'Do you want me to do this?'

And he picked up a coffee cup and hurled it towards the back window.

I screamed and that shocked him into silence. He stood in front of me, his lips curling into the beginning of a tight snarl, hands shivering with rage, eyes huge and sad and terrified. For a split second they seemed to be pleading.

'You are clearly not happy in this marriage, and you know what? You are making me really miserable too. Maybe we should call it a day. Whatever. I'm outta here.'

Then my devoted husband walked out of our house, slamming the door dramatically behind him.

I was shaking, shocked. I had never seen Dan angry before and I realised, to my own horror, that he was right. I did think he was a big soft fool who'd roll over and take anything. What I was taking in, more than anything, was the possibility that Dan would leave *me*. After all my uncertainty, all my humming and hawing, he was holding the cards.

After maybe ten minutes, I heard Gerry knock at the door.

There was no point in hiding from Gerry. He knew he was expected. He walked straight through the kitchen towards the back door.

'Is he out in the garage?'

'He's not here.'

'Oh, right—' and he started to rearrange the parts on the table.

'What's cooking, Tress?' Gerry always sniffed the air when he came into my kitchen like a homeless dog.

'We had a row. I think he's left me.'

'Shit no. Coffee'd be good.'

I hadn't thought that I needed to talk, especially not to Gerry, but sometimes you don't know you need to do something until you need to do it.

Gerry sensed he was expected to sing for his supper so he said, 'What happened?'

'I told him I nearly had an affair.'

'Whoa!' He took a step back and started waving his arms like landing crew warning off a crashing plane. 'Not my business, Tress, don't wanna know.'

But I was bringing this baby down. Dan wouldn't listen, so I was going to make sure I got my message across to his friend. 'I met this guy I'd known before, I thought we had something and then I realised he was *nothing* next to Dan. My love was challenged and I chose Dan.'

I felt triumphant. That sounded so good. No harm done; a dilemma sorted. Excellent work. Gerry let out a half laugh and raised his eyes to heaven. He looked at me with a mixture of pity and amusement.

'You already made your choice, Tressa. You're not in the market for those kind of decisions any more.'

Then he picked up a greasy carburettor from the kitchen table and headed out to the garage to wait for his betrayed friend.

Reality is just an interpretation. Some people believe only God really knows what's going on; we mortals just make up our own versions of it.

Reality One in my interpreted world was that Ronan and I were soul-mates whose love was thwarted by misunderstanding, bad timing and ultimately my marriage to somebody else. We met each other again and, in knowing that we could not be together, our souls found the freedom to express themselves honestly. We'd fallen in love—maybe. He was devastated when I didn't come through for him and spent the rest of the evening on the phone to his therapist.

Reality Two is that Ronan, on a day off from the live-in model, bumped into a vulnerable ex and, having overdosed on twenty-year-old beauties, fancied an evening of earthy no-strings sex with somebody else's wife. He is the type of man who would say anything to get a woman into bed, hence all the faltering soul-searching bullshit, which he figured (correctly) I needed to hear. There is also the ugly possibility that, having got the room paid for by yours truly, I had caught him in the act of rifling through his address book looking for a last-minute replacement, so the bed didn't go to waste.

The real truth is I will never really know.

The only thing that I feel absolutely certain of right now is that I have hurt Dan in the worst way possible. Sometimes, you can hurt another person by being true to yourself, but in the longterm you are doing both of you a favour. You can also hurt them by just being a selfish bitch and there is no excuse for that. Sometimes it is quite difficult to tell the two situations apart.

I guess it's like the sunken Christmas cake. If you take goodwill for granted and get sloppy, you might get away with it once or twice, but you won't get away with it for ever. You should always treat the things that treat you good with respect, because otherwise you will suffer for it.

More important than that is the fact that it's just the right thing to do.

James had never shown anger towards me before.

Twenty years is a long time to set a habit, and I knew my husband as a placid, mild-mannered man. He had never raised his voice or, God forbid, his hand, to any human or animal that I had ever seen. I knew he had been a captain in the IRA before we met and, although I was occasionally curious about the part he had played in our cruel war, I was mostly content to think of my husband as a harmless soul.

Even though I knew of the way other women were treated at the hands of bullying husbands, I never saw their misfortune reflected as my own good fortune.

Perhaps that is the way it is when women marry men who they have not chosen themselves. They had no hand in making the match so they never consider themselves lucky. The accident of two people meeting and falling in love gives marriage a romantic cachet the organised match does not have. Perhaps those who choose their partners can see the other's qualities more clearly and therefore forgive their faults more easily. Although I wonder if twenty years might erode such idealisms. Perhaps it is better not to fall for a person's characteristics in the first place rather than have time expose them as hollow charms.

I will never know because I was never given the choice. Now I think that romantic love should always stay the way I knew it. Locked away, like a precious jewel in a chest in the attic, to be opened occasionally when distraction is needed, so you can marvel at its beauty, but never expose it to the harsh light of day. Perhaps romantic love is too delicate, too beautiful, to withstand such ordinariness.

James never looked more plain, more unlovably ordinary than the afternoon we got back from the confirmation. Yet the disappointment with which he looked at me was unfamiliar.

'You upset the bishop, Bernadine.'

I knew I had done wrong, that I had put my husband's reputation, our very livelihood, at stake. I knew that had I been in full control of my senses, I would never have let such a thoughtless insult spill out of me without considering the consequences. I knew I should have bitten my lip, smiled with silent decorum and offered my intolerance up to a decent saint, who might see to it that the miserable weasel burned in hell for all eternity. I knew I was entirely at fault and that just made it all the worse. I had married a man I had not chosen and clambered hard all of my married life to make sure I stayed one inch above him on the moral high ground. I was not an affectionate wife, but I was always hard-working and diligent about my responsibilities. I was respectful. I did not love him in the way that he wanted me to, but when push came to shove I had never failed him. Until now.

'You upset the bishop, Bernadine.'

James said it in a patronising, schoolmasterly tone that irritated me. But my anger was truly rooted in my own failure as a wife.

'If you weren't such a weak man, you would have said it yourself.'

'That is not fair, Bernadine.'

If he was raging, I did not notice. Anger was not something I had to watch out for in James. There was no reason ever to be alert to it. If his voice shook over the words, I did not think that any reason to hold back. Twenty years is a long time. Long enough to know what to expect. I had started now and I could not find a way of stopping, nor did I think there was a good reason to.

'How dare you speak to me like that? I have sacrificed twenty years of my life to be your dutiful servant.' And then I said it, the unforgivable, 'We both know I was destined for greater things than the dull life of a schoolteacher's wife.'

The devil darted out of his eyes and at me in a pin-sharp flash. 'Greater things?'

Still, I did not believe there was anything to be afraid of. I stuck my chin in the air, although probably a fraction too high, as I was beginning to feel unsure. 'Yes. A certain Michael Tuffy that I was doing a line with? We were matched.'

'Oh, I see. And that match never came to fruition because?'

There was a nasty slant to his face. A tight look to his mouth, such as you might see on a bitter old woman. I had turned my gentle James into a monster. But I was no quitter. I had to see this through.

'Don't you try and torture me, James Nolan. You know very well my parents did not have the money for that match. If they had had a penny, they would never have settled on you . . .'

'But your Aunt Ann had the money.'

This sick dread descended on me like red mist. I had to make him stop. I had one more rage in me, a cruelty that I spat out. 'You will never be *half* the man Michael Tuffy was . . .' Even as I said it, I knew it was my last stand. Tears were already streaming down my face, my veins coursing with the heat of my confession. 'Michael was *my world*.' Perhaps if I had not hurt him so badly with the awful truth, James might have let it go. But I was *his* world, and he couldn't stop himself. James knew I loved Michael over him and he had found a way to live with that. It was the telling of it that he could not bear.

So he punished me by telling me the truth about Michael Tuffy.

Maureen Tuffy was, indeed, the widowed wife of Michael Tuffy Senior from Achadh Mor, but it seemed that was the only true thing that could be said about her. She never made legal claim to her husband's land; people assumed it was of no great value to her. But the truth was that the land had never been her husband's, but was his brother's, who was living in Chicago. The brother got wind of her scheme to cheat him out of his inheritance.

Arguments over land rights at that time were forgivable, but bigamy was not and Maureen Tuffy's greed had made a bigamist of her son. He had already married one other young woman, who was from a wealthy New Orleans Catholic family. The girl had run away to New York at the age of eighteen to seek her fortune and immediately she arrived in Grand Central Station she had met and fallen in love with Michael Tuffy.

He took the girl back home to meet Maureen, who got the measure of the girl's wealth and contacted her parents. Relieved that their daughter was safe and in respectable company, they rewarded Mrs Tuffy with a generous allowance to cover rent and board. Within months the girl was pregnant and a marriage was quickly arranged and dowry negotiated. However, as time went on, the girl began to miss the trappings of her wealthy Southern life. Weeks before the child was due to be born, she had said she was homesick for her parents and tried to persuade Michael to go back to New Orleans with her. By this time, it seemed, Michael had tired of her rich-girl whinings and told his mother he did not want to leave New York. The girl was put on a train back to New Orleans, her dowry was pocketed by the Tuffys and no mention was ever made of divorce.

In any case, state divorce was meaningless to our generation. You married once and for life as far as the Catholic Church was concerned, and that was the only kind of marriage there was.

When Maureen Tuffy came to Achadh Mor to claim her brother-in-law's land, she quickly discovered that there might be a bigger fish worth hooking in my Aunt Ann, and set out after her cash.

I was the bait.

Ann was suspicious of the Tuffys from the first, and had her vast network of New York biddies check them out. It only took a return telegram to warn her off.

Ann told my mother and was punished for being the bearer of bad news by my parents' estrangement from her. Catholic shame cut a strange path through the conscience in those days; my mother would have blamed Ann for bringing the information and herself just for receiving it. My parents never told me and I understood later that their silence had been a misguided testament to their love for me. As my future husband, they would have felt duty-bound to tell James. He was well connected and if he had ever found out about Michael Tuffy it would have broken their moral contract with him. After all, he had agreed to take on their daughter with no dowry. His silence on the subject up to that was testament to his tolerance.

I don't know what hurt most of all: the fact of Michael's betrayal, or James's in keeping this information from me for all these years.

The truth came out of James in a short, angry stream. How my parents had virtually fallen to their knees with relief when he had approached them, their relief when he had been dismissive of my shocking history. My mother had sold me to him as a hard-working, gentle prospect. Even as he said those words, I heard his voice break with regret at having hurt me. He paused, then added gently, 'And you have been that.'

James's fury crumbled away into the dry air, but I would not wet it with tears and went about my business.

Late that night I walked out to the back field and I looked up at the stars and I tried to make myself believe that my husband might have lied. I wanted to hate him, but I couldn't. I knew him too well and a lifetime of courtesy and affectionate kindness in the face of my cruel indifference would always set the balance in his favour.

I wanted my Michael back. Not the man—he was so distant that he might be dead—but the dream of him. The daring, handsome young lover with the furious blue eyes and the black, black curls. I wanted to close my eyes and be able to see myself in a soft lavender dress spread out on a pea-green hill and my lover spinning in the breeze ahead of me—his eyes against the sun flashing sapphire splinters that would cut a girl's heart asunder. I wanted the fresh, vivid colours of youth my dreams of love had brought me.

Soon I was going to be old and everything seemed so grey.

Acceptance

Acceptance is the first step to unconditional love

Boxty Pancakes

Peel and finely grate some large potatoes, then put the mush into a sieve and squeeze out most of the excess water, but not so much as to leave them bone dry. To each cupful of grated potato add 1 level teaspoon salt and ¼–½ cup flour. I favour less as I don't like a doughy consistency, but the flour binds, so the less you use the harder the mix is to manage in the cooking, since these pancakes have a terrible tendency to stick. Add sufficient milk to make a stiff pancake mixture—one that will drop from a spoon rather than pour. Heat lard or bacon dripping in an iron pan to smoking point, then fry until darker than golden brown on both sides.

I NEARLY BURNT the house down making those bloody boxty pancakes last night. Bacon dripping in an iron pan—hello? Is there any more dangerous kitchen feat I could perform late at night, while feeling as on edge and nervous as I am now? What does a girl cook when her husband of eight months has threatened to leave her?

I tell myself it's just for work, but in some old-fashioned part of me I was hoping that the smell of my crispy cakes frying in bacon fat would bring him puttering down the stairs for a late-night tasting session. It was what he always did—lumber into the kitchen in his jocks and grab a titbit from the top of a carefully prepared pile. Dan treated my cooking as if it were just for him and, while he had that in common with every single person who has ever come into my working kitchen, it annoyed the hell out of me. At least, I thought it did. Tonight I wasn't so sure.

It reminded me of the stray kitten I had once rescued from the street outside the apartment. We weren't supposed to keep animals, so I called Pet Rescue to come and take her. After they had gone, I missed the little thing and wondered why I hadn't made a case for keeping her. For months afterwards I felt this vague guilt, but one day passing a pet shop I realised it wasn't guilt at all. It was simply that I would have liked a kitten for myself. I was lonely.

This was much bigger, obviously, but the principle was the same. Now that Dan was threatening to leave, I decided that I wanted my marriage to work.

The brief encounter with Ronan had sorted out a lot of the nonsense in my head and made me clearer about my husband. Excitement, drama, that heart-pumping, skin-tingling desire was not for me after all. It had led me down too many relationship side roads in my life and was no more than a temporary, unsettling dynamic. When your emotions are being squeezed, you are filled with this passionate certainty. Something that is so powerful that it affects your body. Your stomach churns, you heat up and you think: what is this if it's not love?

Newsflash, Tressa—it's a little thing called sex.

It can dress itself up as passion, but when you come right down to the nuts and bolts of it, it's just sex looking for its own way.

That ten-second revelation had taken me from the idealistic fantasy of wild passion to the sometimes dull but always safe love of the married woman. A ten-second revelation that it had taken me thirty-eight years to get to.

Maybe I had paid a price in settling for one without the other.

Or maybe, just maybe, you had to choose. In which case, I chose Dan. Dan was the safe option, the easy option. He was honest, reliable and would never let me down. Dan made me feel good in a manageable, everyday way. I might not have always felt good about him, but I always felt good about *myself* when I was with him. This was what I needed, after all. This was right.

And now I had screwed it up in my silly quest to be 'sure'.

I didn't go up to bed last night. I stayed up cooking, then lay down on the sofa with a throw around me. I must have slept because I was woken by Dan moving round the kitchen.

Dan is a tall, broad man—heavy with muscle. His noise is usually soft and muted like tomorrow's thunder. This morning he was clattering—the stressed sound of metal on metal, doors slamming. He was defiantly preparing a cooked breakfast, even though it was unlikely he was hungry. Even though it was my kitchen and he hadn't a clue where anything was. The thought of that forced a smile out of me and a slither of fondness. If I held on to that, perhaps everything would be all right. Perhaps I could ride through this disaster on a chariot of love.

OK, who was I kidding with the chariot? A skateboard then—but it was worth a try.

I caught him picking a potato cake from the top of my pile. I kept my voice light and sunny and said, 'Hey, buddy—hands off.'

He gave me a look that said it was gone. The innocent, affable, harmless husband I thought I had was no more. The one I assumed I could afford not to love because he was this bottomless source of innocent adoration. That meant he would forgive everything, right? I was the complicated, passionate one. He was what? Earth to Tressa—reality check. What *did* you think Dan was—a stupid, worthless fool?

That's how I had treated him. And his look said that he knew it.

He dropped the golden sphere as if it was a turd and went back to the pan.

I had the nerve to feel hurt. 'There's no need to be like that.'

He stared up at me from under his bed-head hair. His eyes were hard and mean. Impenetrable. He looked like he hadn't slept all night. Alarm and lust fizzled through me simultaneously.

'To be like what?'

Dan was being openly confrontational. I had tried to break the ice by being playful and light. Working through this unpleasantness in a gentle, jovial way. And now he was responding with anger.

That was not very mature, I thought, not very helpful. Not very—'moving on'. I didn't like this game and I wasn't going to play it.

'Forget it.'

'Forget what, Tressa? Forget that you slept with somebody else or forget the marriage?'

He was being unreasonable now. Making me out to be a slut.

'I did *not* sleep with him. I could have slept with him and I didn't. I chose you.'

'You *chose* me?'

'Yes.' And very stupidly mistaking his tone for a positive one, despite Gerry's sage advice, despite knowing I was in the wrong, I added with gravitas, as if there was no need to say thanks for the great favour I had done us both, 'Yes. I chose you.'

He raised his chin and said, 'Fuck you, Tressa.'

Then he walked out of the room.

The pan was smoking on the stove, so I leaned over and switched it off. My head felt heavy on my neck and I realised I was exhausted. My mouth tasted like there was a dead mouse living under my tongue, and when I reached up to move my hair out of my eyes it was matted and dishevelled.

I looked and smelt a mess. At age thirty-old-enough-to-know-better I had been a bit unfaithful less than a year into my marriage. And I had chosen my husband.

Lucky Dan.

There was a patch of grease on the hob from last night's frying, so I went to the sink to wet a cloth. As I was there, I thought, What the hell am I doing worrying about a patch of grease when my marriage is falling apart? My face turned into my chest in a silent grimace; a line of fat tears dropped straight into the sink. A wedge of self-pity dislodged itself from my throat, and as it made its escape I realised I hadn't even said that I was sorry.

I could not let go of Niamh.

When she was twenty-five she announced that she was moving to America. It was 1964.

She didn't ask or consult or defer to us in any way. She just announced it as if our feelings didn't matter. As if she wasn't ripping out our hearts; as if, now that she had taken everything we had to give her—a good upbringing, endless love, an education, money, clothes, a car—she was quite happy to leave us behind and go on about another life. I could scarcely believe her capable of such selfishness.

I was furious. And you would be right to assume that I wasted no time in telling her so.

Of course, I knew that I was being completely unreasonable, but I was not able to stop myself. I was afraid. Afraid that the miles would forge a distance between us, even though I had evidence to the contrary because it was only after Niamh had moved away from Achadh Mor and up to Dublin that we had become friends.

I held on to her too tightly while she was growing up. All through her childhood and adolescence we fought. She was free-spirited and feisty. I saw myself in her and tried to contain her, to keep her safe. By the time she left for university to study English, I was exhausted from fighting with her. We disagreed on everything—her clothes, her hairstyle, her boyfriends. When she went into Swinford to the cinema with her friends, I would shake with fear until she came home again. James always offered a voice of reason. 'She'll be fine, Bernadine. She's an intelligent, sensible girl.' His attitude infuriated me. Sometimes I wished he would be more authoritarian, keep Niamh prisoner and scold her like other fathers did. Then I could be the gentle, easy-going parent and she and I could out-number him, instead of it always being the other way around.

Niamh had thick wavy hair like mine, and curves like a woman from the age of thirteen. Her bones were delicate and refined, like James's, but she had my large blue eyes. They were such windows on her innocence, her fear, her unsullied delight, her awakenings that I often found it hard to look into them.

Niamh was artistic: messy, emotional, expressive. She was beautiful but uninterested in the way she looked; she was bewildered when people admired her—she had inherited humility from her father. She laughed readily and her body was always open and stretched out in friendship. Her voice was loud and hearty, and her open passion gave voice to how I had felt all my life, but had never been able to express.

Sometimes she looked so perfect that I could scarcely believe she was a part of me, and my heart would collapse with fear that somebody might carry her away and hurt her.

At other times, when she was being stubborn or spiteful, she reminded me too much of myself and I would struggle not to hit her.

In a corner of my mind I was jealous of her joy, but my heart was hers completely. During the three years she was at university, I worried myself sick. It felt unnatural that I did not know where she was, or what she was doing every minute of the day and night. I remember grating potatoes for boxty one afternoon and becoming so lost in a terrified reverie of what tragedy might have befallen her that I tore off the side of my thumb. Later that night she telephoned and her father mentioned my accident to her.

'You should be more careful, Mam,' she scolded. I wanted to tell her how worried I was about her, and ask what exactly she had been doing all day and who she had been with. But I didn't dare. I had learned that my instinct to smother her made her run from me.

So I waited for her to offer me information on the details of her life, greedily snatching each new fact and squirrelling it away to help me build a picture in my mind of how she lived. A vision that would help me know that she was safe, which would make me feel more involved in her life. In those years that she was away in Dublin, I learned to pretend that I thought she was a capable adult. I gave Niamh her independence, but in name only. I never believed in her ability away from me. Reality told me she was an adult woman with a strong young body and a determined will. But if perception is truth, she was still an infant clinging to my breast; protected and warm in the cave of my soft arms.

Through pretending not to care too much, I was rewarded over the coming years with my daughter's friendship.

Niamh got a place teaching English in a school in Galway. She came home every other weekend through choice, and those were the best times we ever had together. She became the best friend I ever had, telling me almost every detail about her life, but omitting things that might hurt or distress me.

We began to love one another again. She started to paint and I was astonished by her work. Powerful splashes of nothing in particular, but I loved them and I told her so. She started to bring home friends. Sunny, friendly young people who admired my cooking and appeared interested in my opinions. One was an English boy with hair down to his shoulders who was studying law and said his wealthy mother had never cooked him a meal in her life. There was a girl from Dublin with a pale, terrified face, who sang like an angel and entertained us after supper each night. James and I welcomed them as if they were our own children because they brought our daughter with them. Niamh was delighted that we liked her friends, but more delighted, I think, that they liked us.

James cleared out one of our old cowsheds, and put a skylight in the roof to make a studio for Niamh to paint in; it was after she had been painting there every weekend for about six months that she announced she was moving to New York.

I was devastated and I reacted badly. But, ultimately, I knew I had to let her go. A short time before she left we rented a caravan in Inniscrone and all three of us went there for a week to say our goodbyes. I sat on the dunes one windless day as James and Niamh walked the strand arm in arm, like lovers. She teased him into rolling up his trousers and taking off his shoes. As I watched them jump the shredded lace of the tiny waves, I felt my heart tear open that this chapter of our lives would soon be closing. We were family, we three, and I thought we had arrived. I hoped that our family might grow, if Niamh married, but had trusted that we would always be together, like this. It seemed unlikely, unfair to be adjusting again in the autumn of our lives.

A gentle breeze blew across the dull, muggy day—a whisper from the sea flapped through from one ear to the other and made me feel hollow. Once again, I stared out at the Atlantic in search of a shadow from the other side. But there was only flat grey silk spread out in front of me and then sky, sky, sky. Perhaps it was true and there was no such place as America after all, and Niamh would never come back. Perhaps Michael had fallen over the edge of the world. The end of the world.

Later that evening Niamh and I made boxty, and she gently coaxed the grater from me as she saw me grate the potatoes too close to my hand.

We had only a few days and I wanted to say so much. That she had started her life as everything I had ever wanted and then become so much more than that again. That I would miss seeing her every other week, that I wished I had looked at her harder, listened more intently to her worries: that I was sorry for the years I scolded her; for not having shown her enough love, and for loving her too much.

'I'm only going to America, Mam.' She took my hand and held it until I loosened my grip, then she hugged me—taller, finer than I was now, or had ever been—and I cried for her. With her long arms wrapped round me, she told me not to be afraid, that America was only round the corner and that we would always be friends. I dabbed my eyes with a tea towel and felt it to be an old matronly act.

'Thanks, Mam,' she said.

'For what?' I asked.

'For not asking me to stay.'

When I realised I had not said sorry it was a great revelation to me.

I waited for Dan to get dressed and come back downstairs, then I ambushed him with my apology. 'Dan, I am really, *really* sorry about what happened.'

He ignored the apology and walked out of the door, saying, 'I don't know what time I'll be home. Don't bother cooking.' It took me the whole morning to talk myself through the rage.

God, I hated him. The arrogant, selfish shit. He was milking this for sure. Not accepting an apology? How low could you get? All I had done was kiss Ronan—hardly more than a handshake in this day and age and at least I had been honest about it. What did Dan think? I was a virgin before I met him? It's not like Ronan was a complete stranger, but an old flame. These things are complicated. If he couldn't be bothered to work this out—well, we might as well forget it.

The parting shot—'Don't bother cooking'—that *really* finished me off.

Fact. I cooked for him every single night, the lucky bastard.

Fact. The way he threw it away—'Don't bother'—as if I never went to any trouble over a meal, anyway.

Fact. He was living in the fifties, a woman cooking a hot meal for him every night and him not even noticing, the mollycoddled, mammy-dependent, unappreciative ass. He *so* did not deserve me. Apologise? To him? He should be apologising to *me* for taking me for granted. I'd be gone when he got back. Packed. I'd move back to the apartment. There were plenty of people I could stay with while the tenant's lease ran its course. No dinner? I'd give him no dinner—*ever again*! Let him come home every night to an empty house and see how he likes it. To this fabulous kitchen, *my* kitchen, empty, unloved, unlived in.

Somewhere round that point—in my thinking about the empty, unloved kitchen—I managed to turn back round. Having whipped myself up into a frenzy of justified fury, I slowed the blades down to mill gently around the horrible truth again. This was my fault. Dan felt hurt and betrayed, and he was bound to snap.

What I had to do was take control of this situation and create a solution. I had to make it clear to him that I knew how wrong I had been and how very sorry I was. No excuses, no 'buts'—just an unreserved apology. Dan *would* forgive me, and everything would be all right. We could get back to how things had been before, except that this time I would appreciate Dan properly because I had learned an important lesson about commitment, fidelity and marriage.

Through those brief flings, I had been looking for an answer and now I had found it.

Wisdom. What a fantastic thing it is when it finally hits home.

So I went and bought the ingredients for a shepherd's pie—Dan's favourite. And, significantly, I made another batch of boxty cakes. I could tell that he had been almost fatally attracted to them, which was why I had taken his final rejection of them so personally.

I kept my spirits up for the rest of the day. In between preparing dinner I got round to weeding a ferocious patch of tangles near the lettuces, which I'd been avoiding, and painted a few plant pots. I did some ironing, potted some seeds and lined the kitchen drawers in gingham oilcloth: jolly, housewifely tasks that made me feel virtuous and homey.

I set the table with a posy of garden flowers delicately drooping from a glass tumbler, and used retro mint-green plastic-handled cutlery for a Doris-Day-pleasing-her-man style.

The potato cakes were for nibbling while the Cheddar-cheese crust was toasting on the shepherd's pie. Normally, I would do a light dessert with such a heavy main, but tonight was Dan's night, so there was a comfort-food dessert of apple tart and—the ultimate compromise—raspberry-ripple ice cream from the shop.

I am not one of nature's pampering females, so styling my hair and applying make-up is usually an either/or decision. This evening I did both, and pushed the boat out by putting on a print dress I had worn on honeymoon. I dusted my arms with a glittery powder my fashion-editor friend Doreen had given me for my wedding day.

Seven o'clock came, eight, and there was no sign of Dan. It was OK, I told myself. He has to come home sometime. It doesn't matter how late. I'll be waiting; I'll be ready for him.

At eight thirty he came in. My heart was thumping ten to the dozen. I was all excited and shaky, and in a weird way it was like I was falling in love: a powerful, messy feeling, where I didn't know if I was terrified or elated. It was anticipation, I suppose. Knowing that soon, one way or another, this mess would be resolved.

'I told you not to cook,' he said and went straight out to the garage.

I stood there, momentarily paralysed with shock. I was a satirical photo still from a 1950s advert with my perfect dinner, my twee table setting, dress and lipstick. An image on a spoof postcard. I looked down at my arms and they were glittering ludicrously—like I was an alien life form. Then it hit me. I was being an alien. What was I doing grovelling like this? All I had done was try to be true to myself. Life was a journey, marriage a learning process and this incident with Ronan had just been part of that. Dan would just have to get over it.

I followed him out to the garage. 'Don't you walk away from me like that,' I snapped. 'I have been slaving all day, trying to make things better, trying to say "sorry" and you are just going to walk away from me.'

He didn't look up. 'Whatever, I told you not to cook.'

My day's efforts, frustration, disappointment all tumbled out and I shouted. 'I cooked because I love you!'

Dan looked up from the bench, and for a second I thought he was going to fold me in his arms and make everything better. Then I saw his eyes were flat and cold.

'No, Tressa. You cooked because it's what you do. I'm just the excuse.'

His hands were gripping the bench and his chin was shaking with fury. I felt very afraid suddenly and fell into a childish sobbing.

'How can you say that? How can you be so cruel?'

I knew he was right. I always cooked my way through crises. Apologised with a batch of iced buns or a pile of buttery potato cakes. I was an expert in comfort food.

When Dan had told me not to cook he had meant that it was going to take more than a batch of boxty to ferry me out of this fix. So it was time to beg. 'Please, Dan—I can't stand this. I am so sorry. Please say you forgive me. Look at me.'

He stopped working, but would not look up. His arms made a straight triangle with the bench and his eyes were closed. He was trying not to cry. I thought I might be getting somewhere.

'Please, Dan. Look at me.'

He looked up and his eyes flew across me briefly then back down again. 'I can't, Tressa. I can't look at you.'

It wasn't until that moment that I truly realised what I had done. I had planted a picture in Dan's head of me with another man. It was making him crazy. Dan didn't hate me. He loved me, but he couldn't stand what I had done and that was all that he could see when he looked at me. Me having sex with another guy.

'I didn't sleep with him, Dan.'

'You kissed him.'

'Yes. But I didn't sleep with him. I swear I didn't.'

I stared hard at the top of his head as his face was stuck firmly on his boots. He looked up briefly.

'You have to believe me, Dan. I did not have sex with Ronan.'

Finally, he turned away in disgust. 'Jesus, Tressa.'

It was the first time I had used Ronan's name. The guy I hadn't slept with now had a name. I had to be firm, so I didn't back away. I had to keep talking. I wasn't going anywhere until this barrier between us had been dismantled. 'We have to get past this, Dan.'

He shook his head, and now it was his turn to be sorry as he looked up at me, and his eyes were filled with tears. 'I don't know if I can, Tressa . . .'

'But it was just a kiss . . .' the petulant wail came out of me before I had the chance to stop it.

Dan shook his head and busied himself again to indicate the discussion was over.

He went out. He did not say where, but I think he went to his mother's house. And I was alone in the kitchen we had made together, wondering if I had ruined our marriage for good. When he wanted it, I was unsure. Now that I was sure he had moved away from me and all because of my stupidity.

But there are no easy answers and maybe no answers at all. All I could do was wait, and waiting is the worst thing. Waiting is just doing nothing, and I am a doer. I wanted to make things better. I wanted to make things work. Yet it seemed that I couldn't do either of those things without Dan. It takes two to make a marriage work. Making a marriage work is something you do together.

Isn't it?

I had no choice now. I had to accept that I had hurt Dan and I couldn't undo what I had done and I couldn't make it better. I might have had the power to hurt him, but that didn't mean I had the power to take that hurt away. I couldn't wrestle the bad feeling from him.

Like he said, I couldn't cook my way out of this one.

But I can still cook. And I guess that's just what I realised I had to do. Keep going. Keep doing my thing—just accepting the way things were for the moment.

Do what my Grandma used to do when something bugged her: throw her hands in the air and offer it up to God.

Niamh left us in the morning. She insisted that we not go to the airport to wave her off, but left it as a normal goodbye. As if we would see each other again soon. As I watched her back—bag hooked over her shoulders, legs marching in her strong, confident stride—I felt angry again that she was leaving. For the rest of the day I was irritable. James went swimming and brought his wet clothes into the caravan. Then he put muddy wellingtons on the clean floor. As I was starting to prepare supper, he decided he wanted a drink and I tripped over him as he reached for the icebox. I had a vegetable knife in my hand and it sliced his shoulder by pure accident.

'You stupid, stupid old man!' I shouted, in fear of having hurt him.

I pushed him down on the corduroy cushions of the bench and opened the cabinet above him to get the first-aid box. The short sleeve of his T-shirt was wet with blood, and I lifted it up and applied an antiseptic cloth to the small wound. James blanched and I looked at his face. Long and ghostly white, his eyes staring at me like saucers. They were full of sadness and fear.

Time and proximity had carved such knowledge of each other's faces that we didn't need words. We looked and each of us was thinking that all we had left now was the other: he with a woman who seemed barely able to tolerate him even after all these years; I with a man who looked delicate and old and whom I had never cared to love.

Yet James was the only person who could ever equal my love for Niamh. The sadness was his grief that she was gone. The fear was that I would no longer need him; that my reason for loving him was gone.

Old and fragile as he was, I did need him. I had thought that I neither wanted nor truly loved him, but knew now that we had grown to be a part of each other. I had no choice but to be with him. Like trees, whose roots and branches have intertwined; who have seen rain, sun and storms together, yet remain resolutely separate.

I was stuck with him and had no choice but to accept it.

Loyalty

The most expensive gift a man can give you is his pride

Slow-roasted Clove Ham

To get the salt out of a good ham and a delicate flavour into it takes time and patience, but a decent joint will then last you a few days.

Take your 3–4 lb joint and soak it in cold water for up to 24 hours. If I was cooking a ham for Sunday dinner, I would put it in to soak on the Saturday afternoon. Keep changing the water every few hours.

Next day, put your joint in fresh water and bring to the boil. After that first boil, change the water again, add a bay leaf and a slither of onion to it and allow the joint to boil slowly for 3/4 of an hour. While the joint is on its second boil, prepare a roasting dish by lining with tinfoil. In a teacup mix 2 teaspoons ground cloves, 1 dessertspoon honey and a pinch of brown sugar. Add boiling water to the top of the cup and stir until everything is dissolved. Put your boiled ham on the foil and cover it in the best mustard you can afford. Then pour your cupful of mixture over it, seal the foil around it and bake in a medium to hot oven for about an hour. For the last 1/2 hour of cooking time unwrap the foil, baste the joint in its own fat, spear with a dozen or so whole cloves and leave to crisp. Serve hot with boiled potatoes and cabbage, or cold as you like it.

KATE KERRIGAN

WHEN THINGS IN MY LIFE are uncertain, I fall back on the food of my youth. My grandmother's baked ham is wonderful for that. A huge hunk of meat, slowly simmered, then basted with honey, pricked with cloves and roasted in a hot oven until it is crisp and tender. A joint of bacon is not fast food, but it will last for days. Two of you will get one hot meal, a lunch and suppertime sandwiches out of it. Proving that sometimes putting your time into something will pay dividends.

Doreen had been my friend now for fifteen years and, though I hadn't seen her since our wedding day, she had remained a constant. An eternally forty-one-year-old fashion editor. Stick thin and irrepressibly stylish, with a tongue as sharp as her silk-wrapped nails, she is possibly the very last person I would have picked as a best friend. Yet Doreen got me my very first break as a food writer after she discovered me working in a diner local to her magazine offices. I was floating through my post-college early twenties, looking for a career path, and she was careering towards middle age, trying to stay thin. To the distress of her couturier, Doreen developed a lunchtime taste for my clove-roasted ham on rye, and felt compelled to call me out on it.

'I've gained nearly four pounds,' she squawked over the counter at me, then observing my generous bust and correctly assuming I wouldn't care, added, 'and I'm Jewish!'

I knew who she was. Doreen Frankes was a high-profile columnist and her style musings on everything from shoes to restaurants were legendary. So I told her I wanted to be a food writer and we struck a deal. She talked me up to her food-editor contact—Jan—and I left the diner.

Over the coming years I was to become responsible for a colossal two-inch addition to her waistline, but then Doreen only ever ate when I cooked for her.

People were often surprised by our friendship. Doreen was older than me and reputed to be an unscrupulous bitch. But that was never my experience with her. Doreen was cutting, but I found her humorous with it. Her unassailable wit and dramatic delivery could be exhausting, but she was always entertaining. As our friendship spilled into years, I discovered that the icy fashion queen had a warm heart that she took great pains to disguise.

We had some things in common. Where Doreen is an appalling style snob, I reserve my snobbery for food, 'although,' as she has often said, '*how* you can differentiate between one type of pasta and another is beyond me.'

'That's because you don't eat enough of it.'

'Enough? Honey, I haven't eaten pasta since *1977*.'

Doreen spoke in italics, and her minions copied her mannerisms as well as her clothes. So did half of New York, apart from me. I kept wearing my Levis and 'classic' John Smedley fine-knit sweaters bought mail order from England, despite Doreen's pleading.

'I am so bored, looking at you in those what-do-you-call-them?'

'Jumpers.' I always used my mother's Irish term for this particular item of clothing.

'Well, it's making me want to jump off the Empire State. This is a new one right? What *is* this colour? It's like something you'd see leaking from a child's nose.'

'Pea green.'

'Green is something you *eat*, darling, not wear.'

'But I'm Irish.'

'*Especially* if you're Irish. God, do you know nothing?'

For my part, I derided Doreen for disappearing when she stood sideways, and inspiring eating disorders in the nation's youth.

Doreen is a relationship-phobe. Married briefly in her early twenties, she had long since declared the concept of sharing one's life with another person to be overrated. 'Honey, I can barely stand to share a plate of sushi—but a bathroom? Eugh!' She nonetheless prevented me from going down the path of confirmed spinsterhood. 'Cardigans and cutting your own hair—that's where you're heading if you don't pull yourself together. You're not stylish enough to get away with being old and single and, besides, you can cook. You *have* to get married!'

Doreen kept me trying. She was deeply unimpressed when I first started seeing Dan. 'Slept with your building superintendent? Have you gone *mad*?'

'It had been so long, Doreen.'

'So, now all of a sudden you're a sex maniac . . .'

'I don't know what came over me.'

'I know it's tempting, Tressa. They're male, they're on hand . . .'

'I think I like him.'

'Oh Christ—you've done it more than once.'

'Last night.'

'*At night!* He's a building superintendent, Tressa. You stay friendly, and at Christmas you tip. If you must have sex with them, you do it in the afternoons in the laundry room and you only do it once.'

'Well, he makes me feel good.'

'You're just desperate, that's all. You're lonely. Whatever. Put an end to it now. It will end in tears. Believe me.'

It ended in marriage and, of course, I would be lying if I said there was not some ongoing friction between Dan and Doreen. Bluntly, Doreen did not think that Dan was good enough for me. If I had been a hundred per cent sure myself, none of her doubts would have been an issue.

Doreen had called me out on my decision to marry Dan in her own unique way. 'You've been seeing him *what*? Five months?'

'Nine.'

'Well that's a lie, honey. March, I was dragging you off to the D&G party. Then you start this "convenience-fuck" thing with your super . . .'

It was going to be an impossible conversation because Doreen knew me inside out. She could smell I wasn't entirely convinced about Dan and she was going to run with it. But though I wasn't sure marrying him was the right thing, I was less sure that it was the wrong thing.

As Doreen herself had once said, 'Being divorced is not the same thing as being terminally single. At least you *know* being married is not such a big deal.'

It would have been too easy for Doreen to assure me that somebody better than Dan was only round the corner. So I eyeballed her and told her I was totally sure. 'I love him,' I said. It's the last line of defence. The Holy Grail of the single girl. 'We're getting married. I love him.'

It was a mystery solved; job done; the end of the line. The question, solution, resolution all rolled into one.

I hoped that if I said it often enough it would come true.

Doreen couldn't argue with that, although she didn't for one second believe me. But she sat back and smiled. 'I suppose you'll want me floating up the aisle after you in green chiffon?'

She helped me organise the wedding and was the perfect companion on the day. She found a way of being nice about Dan—largely focused on how he looked, which made him blush like an embarrassed schoolgirl and me feel like I was marrying a Chippendale, but nevertheless I swallowed it. That was just Doreen's way, I told myself. She had a wicked sense of humour and I had enjoyed it long enough at other people's expense, so I could hardly be precious about it when it was pointed at myself and my new husband.

I guess since I moved out of the city Doreen and I had been busy building new lives. But while I had found a husband, I suspected Doreen was feeling left behind. She did not want, or need, a man—but she had become dependent on me for the small emotional sustenance she did need. Since my wedding she had fallen back on her gay fashion friends, and every time I rang her she appeared to be recovering from one party or on her way to another. I sensed she was protesting too much and could not find the words to tell me she missed me.

But since things came to a head with Dan, I found myself missing her.

Doreen and I have seen off several presidents, day-glo jewellery, shoulder pads, nouvelle cuisine, cigarettes and many boyfriends together. We have reviewed restaurants, 'done' Florence, danced to Diana Ross. We have hosted each other's birthday dinners, schmoozed each other's mothers, and interviewed each other's latest flames.

She makes me laugh like nobody else and, more than anything right then, I needed to laugh. I needed to break the bad spell poisoning my home and there is no witch better than Doreen for cutting through the shit and telling it like it is. So that afternoon I emailed her and invited her to slum it out in Yonkers for the weekend.

In the summer of 1979 I saw Michael Tuffy again.

I also saw the Pope.

If the apparition of the Virgin Mary in 1879 was the first miracle at Knock, the Pope's visit in 1979 felt like the Second Coming. The whole of Ireland, and much of the world, was looking at us. Emigrants flocked home in their thousands, Americans with the vaguest family connections rang ahead looking for beds. We were at the centre of the universe, where it was all happening. It was a magical time.

Achadh Mor, our sparsely populated sprawling parish, is invisible. Tourists take a wrong turn and think they are adventuring into the back of beyond, yet the truth is they rarely venture off the main roads onto the winding boreens, where our small farming communities are carved into the landscape. Cheery new bungalows perch hopefully on the edge of ancient bleak bog. Old homes beside them, no more than stone sheds. The melancholy is broken in the summer when the sun shines. When the hedgerows are heavy with fuchsia and cheeky hollyhocks, there is nowhere more beautiful. Yet while we now enjoy all the modern conveniences, Fal Iochtar is still an outback. There are still women between my mother's generation and mine who refuse to get in electricity. We are still a hidden people; not hiding but living in an older part of Ireland that many of our countrymen would sooner forget.

The Pope's visit gave us our moment in the spotlight.

The shrine had been there all of my life and most of my mother's too. The Virgin Mary had appeared to fifteen local people against the gable wall of the church of St John the Baptist in 1879.

Pilgrims travelled to the church from all over Ireland, and talk of miracle cures was commonplace in our homes: 'He was carried there on the back of a cart and he walked home to Limerick!' or 'He crawled on his belly to kiss the gable wall, then sprang up like a frog!'

If you were living in Ireland and looking for a miracle, Knock town was the place all right, but it had few benefits for those of us who lived in the area, bar keeping us entertained.

Until Father Horan came along. James Horan was an energetic priest who had previously served in our neighbouring village where he had built a huge parish hall. Dances were held there and many a Mayo marriage was made in St Mary's Hall, Tooreen, throughout the fifties. When Father Horan was sent to Knock in 1963 the shrine was simple: a few statues and offerings of weathered crutches of the formerly afflicted left as mementos against the gable wall.

Over the next ten years Horan built the place up to colossal proportions. Raising enormous sums of money, he had the gable wall encased in a glass chapel with giant marble statues depicting the scene of the apparition. He built a huge church to accommodate a crowd of thousands, which sat at the centre of rolling lawns like a well-appointed spaceship. A modern feat of mismatching architecture incongruous against our barren, rural backdrop. I was a bit cynical and secretly wondered how many of the miracles were a result of the spiritual mania the Blessed Virgin seemed to inspire in my guilt-ridden peers. But nobody could deny the energy or commitment of Father Horan. Even the atheists were quieted by his achievements as the centenary of the apparition in Knock drew in and the pontiff announced he was coming.

The woman who had first set her cap at James, Aine Grealy, was around at that time, having come back to Fal Iochtar in 1972. She was unmarried and clearly unhappy about the fact, because she made it her business to flick moments of misery in my direction whenever she could.

'Michael Tuffy is home—you'll be wanting to see him.'

I am a country woman, I don't mind gossip. In fact, liking gossip is a prerequisite for living in a small community. You gossip about your neighbours and they gossip about you, but there is a code. Good gossip requires subtlety. A story is made all the more interesting with a gradual, reluctant release. But there should always be a particular gentleness when you impart information that directly relates. You give all the information you can without assuming anything or searching the other's face for a reaction. Aine was always smart when it came to academic matters and pure thick in dealing with people.

It was a few days before His Holiness arrived, and our small church was thronged with irregular churchgoers hungry for news from the altar. There were shuttle buses to the basilica, picking up at the local shop, Roger, on the morning of Sunday, September 30, and people were being discouraged from keeping vigil in the surrounding fields overnight. For any of the older generation who were disinclined to brave the weather, St Mary's Hall in Tooreen would provide television coverage and light refreshments all day.

After Mass, Aine pushed her way over to me at the door and made her statement within earshot of everyone, beadily scanning my face for evidence of a reaction.

I ignored her, as if I hadn't heard, and she would have surely repeated her statement more loudly if James had not hurried me outside.

In actual fact, I did not ignore her deliberately, rather she had propelled me into a state of shock. James had not heard what she said, or at least if he had he passed no comment, but was irritated by my distractedness as we took off in the car. 'For God's sake, Bernadine, are you listening to me at all? I've volunteered to work in St Mary's for the day. The crowds will be terrible at the shrine itself, and Father Kenny has asked me to give a talk on the stories of the fifteen.'

I caught my reflection in the wing mirror, and felt sadness wash over me. Sadness that here I was in my sixties, yet so easily overcome by romantic reverie; that the decades had robbed my beauty and forged lines of wisdom on my face, yet my stomach was fluttering like a silly schoolgirl's.

James went on: 'I've put you down for serving refreshments between eleven and two in St Mary's. You can do later if you like, but . . .'

'No.'

For over forty years I had held my love for Michael Tuffy as sacred. He had abandoned me, tried to embezzle from my family and had dishonoured my name. But, as sure as a part of me had died when I learned the truth about him, another came alive at the thought I might see him again. Aine had harboured her grudge all this time and got to me.

Michael would be here to see the Pope, and the Pope would not be appearing at St Mary's Hall in Tooreen.

'I want to go to Knock.'

'But the crowds will be terrible, Bernadine, and I've already said . . .'

'I'll go alone, then.'

'No, no—if that's what you want, I can cancel.'

But this was something I had to do without James.

'I'll go on the bus. Cousin Mae is going with the Ballyhaunis ICA. I'll go along with them.'

'No, it's fine. I'll just tell Father Kenny that we've changed our minds and . . .'

'No, you go to Tooreen. It's important. I'll be grand with Mae.'

There was a moment's stand-off while James interpreted my protes-tation. The Pope's visit was history in the making, and it was an event that husband and wife should experience together. Yet his wife wanted, for some reason, to go without him.

James was hurt, but I couldn't care less. True love had beckoned and I had no choice but to follow.

Waiting for somebody to forgive you is slow emotional torture. It had been three weeks since the 'Ronan' business and things were far from resolved. Dan moved back into our bedroom, but would lie next to me like a frigid schoolgirl, terrified I might touch him after I made a couple of aborted attempts to seduce him. I tried to be patient, but after a few days playing the reformed, ashamed hooker, I snapped, 'Jesus, Dan— I've said I'm sorry!' He gazed through me with a look of anguish to illus-trate that I would never know or understand the depths of his pain.

I didn't know why I was still there.

Why *was* I?

Maybe it was because I knew there are two ways to get salt out of bacon. The first is to do what Bernadine did and leave it to soak, let the salt release itself slowly, then rinse it clean and soak again. Rinse clean and soak as often as you can, for as much time as you can spare, and the salt will eventually out. The second is to boil it really fast in Coca-Cola.

Both methods work, but I think the first one tastes better because you have to wait for it. My belligerent self would argue it should taste exactly the same, but the point is I always take the hard option when it comes to food and the easy option when it comes to relationships. So now I was trying to do it the other way around.

Every time Dan and I had a brief toxic exchange, I rinsed it off and started again. Maybe I was imagining it, but things did seem to be thaw-ing. On the other hand, maybe my thermometer was just adjusting to the cold. Or maybe I only want something when I think I can't have it.

Now that Dan has withdrawn his love from me, I miss it. The irony is that now that I have finally grown up I have managed to turn the gentlest, nicest man in Manhattan into a hardened cynic.

Either way, Dan made no fuss when I announced Doreen would be coming for the weekend.

'That'll be nice,' he said flatly, then lied. 'I like Doreen.'

Dan claims to like everybody. Actually Doreen makes him feel uncomfortable. Why *had* I invited Doreen up for the weekend while Dan and I were experiencing marital frostiness?

In fairness, it had to be done sometime. Doreen was my best woman, after all, and Dan was, despite appearances to the contrary, my husband. If nothing else, perhaps she would give Dan and me some distraction. Gerry proved an unwitting mediator while we were building the kitchen, and perhaps Doreen would fill the same role. The way things were at that moment, it seemed like a straw worth clinging on to.

The house was really taking shape, just as our relationship seemed to be falling apart. The irony of that was not lost on me, although I would feel like a much nicer person if it had been.

As I prepared the place for Doreen's visit, the experience was made all the more pleasurable by the fact that Doreen was a fussy bitch who would clock in and check off every detail with her in-built style radar. It was a challenge that I enjoyed rising to. Especially as I needed a challenge I could control like did the scented candle in the guest bedroom co-ordinate with the hand soap in the guest bathroom? Now I had no control over my husband's feelings, I was catching my attention up in meaningless details: feathering the edges of cotton napkins, arranging Moroccan glasses by bedside tables, hoping that the bigger things like unfinished paintwork wouldn't be noticed. The same tactic went for Dan as I tried to convince myself that the ludicrous minutiae of good housewifery—like ironing his boxers—would eventually add up to heal what had happened. And I felt resentful when he didn't notice my unasked-for efforts, as if he believed ironed underpants were his birthright. Ultimately, I'd been looking for reasons to hang my anger on: something outside of myself to blame for all this frustration and shame.

Doreen arrived in the early evening and it was awkward. Not between herself and Dan, but strangely between her and me.

'This is all rather cute,' was the first thing she said when she entered the kitchen and picked up a floral milk jug I had rescued from Eileen's vast and largely ghastly collection.

'The jug or the kitchen?' I asked, not really wanting the answer.

'Is there a correct answer to that question?'

We gave each other a sardonic smile, but mine lacked commitment and hers lacked humour. Cruel wit had once been our intimate language; that we could take it from each other was an illustration of how close we were. Suddenly, I felt like the wit was missing and only the cruelty was left. Maybe I was having a crisis of confidence. I didn't want my house to be 'cute', but I wasn't confident enough to defend it against Doreen's cutting-style review.

So I didn't ask again and got on with preparing our supper, a ludicrously fattening carbonara with roasted garlic and Parma ham and a salad fresh from the garden. Dan was puttering in and out of the kitchen and at one point rewarded me with, 'That smells good, honey.'

Doreen raised her eyes to heaven and I was immediately conscious of our folksy homeliness, even though the pleasant communication was a minor breakthrough for us. Aside from that brief moment, Dan kept out of our way for the first few hours as Doreen entertained me with gossip about friends and colleagues. As Dan joined us for the meal, Doreen threw in a couple of unnecessarily graphic sexual anecdotes designed to shoo him away from the table in embarrassment. Which they did.

'Married bliss?' she quipped, after Dan had excused himself to go and meet Gerry for a beer.

I hadn't realised I needed to talk until I had my old friend in front of me, asking. It all came tumbling out: my lack of certainty about Dan, kissing Angelo and Ronan and how I had ruined everything and just wanted things to be OK with my marriage. It felt good to get it all out in the open, and I realised how much I had been carrying around in my head for the past few months. Doreen nodded sagely for the time it took me to get everything off my chest, and her face was full of genuine concern. She opened another bottle of wine while I was talking and kept our glasses filled. I always took responsibility for our food, she for our drink. It felt old and familiar. Safe.

When I had finished, Doreen reached over and took my hand.

'Do you want to know what I think, Tressa?'

The relief of my confession over, I suddenly saw how drunk Doreen was. I had been talking and she had been drinking. Now it was her turn to reveal. And instinctively I knew: this was a confession I did not want to hear. Before I had time to come to my senses and shout, 'No!', she said, 'You have to leave him.'

I recoiled swiftly, but not physically. She squeezed my hands with drunken zeal and said what she had wanted to say since the day I had told her I was marrying Dan. Everything I didn't want to hear. Everything I had myself feared was true.

Dan wasn't good enough for me. He wasn't 'The One'. I should never have had doubts. Doubts were bad; they meant you had made the wrong choice. I shouldn't be 'settling'. That there was no need to compromise; I should have more respect for myself. That I wasn't even forty yet, there was plenty of time. I should follow my gut instinct and leave now. So Ronan was a shit, but there were other Ronans out there who would make my heart beat and my stomach somersault. I deserved that.

I was a passionate woman blah, blah . . . deserved to have *all* my needs
met blah, blah . . . madly-in-love soulmates . . . blah, blah, blah.

When she started, I was scared. I thought: I can't listen to this, it's too
close to the bone. But as she went on I realised there was no nerve being
hit. And then I thought, Actually, Doreen, this is bullshit. Dan *is* what I
need; he *is* what I want, what I deserve. Because suddenly I saw that life,
love and marriage are actually a whole lot simpler than this nit-picking,
navel-gazing quest for the perfect man. I want, need, deserve to be
loved. Doesn't everybody? And Dan loves me. He deserves me to love
him back and I am endeavouring to do just that.

It wasn't always easy because I seem to be naturally attracted to flaky,
unavailable arseholes, but suddenly knowing the love of a good man,
and then coming so close to losing it, was curing me of that particular
obsession. Maybe my natural predilection for dangerous men was
changing, or maybe this was what mature love felt like. And how much
self-respect would I have if I traded in a perfectly nice man to go stand
back in a bar in Manhattan waiting for some Hollywood cupid to throw
arrows at me?

After all, Mr Right only feels right until he does something wrong.

I let Doreen finish, then disappointed her by saying I was tired and it
was time to go to bed. No dramatic bag-packing exits for me. She
drained her glass and patted my arm, as if to say, 'You sleep on it, girl—
I know you'll do the right thing.'

Dan came in late and stumbled into bed. He was drunk and for once
forgot that he hated me, so we made tired, sloppy, ordinary love. He
curled away from me afterwards and put his arm out to pull me in, but I
settled it back onto his belly, then hung back and watched his broad,
muscled shoulders slow into the heavy rhythm of sleep.

'I love you,' he said as he finally dropped off.

'I love you too.'

He always said it first. I always thought that was a negative reflection
on me. Now I think maybe that's just the way we are.

On Saturday lunchtime the weather was nice, so Doreen and I took
Pimms into the back garden. Dan was drinking beer and was hot so had
taken his shirt off. Doreen had realised I wasn't going to take her advice
and had returned to her 'stupid but cute' attitude to him.

'I mean, Dan, how can you *say* you have never read William
Faulkner. That's *ludicrous*! Still, who needs literature with muscles like
those?' And she leaned over to give his biceps a squeeze.

Dan was mortified, but went along with her. Sometimes an act of love
is not what you say, but what you don't say and Dan was saying nothing.

In life loyalty is something that you earn and Doreen had more than earned my loyalty over the years. But marriage is a rogue state with its own rules, and one of them is pledging your loyalty to somebody before you can be fully sure that they deserve it, so you stand their ground. You mess with him? You mess with me. That's the new rule. A husband is instant family. He gets the loyalty of a blood tie without doing any of the work. Except poor Dan was working for it too.

'Oh yessss—you bagged yourself a regular Hemingway here, Tressa.'

'Hemingway?'

God, I really wish Dan hadn't said that.

Doreen laughed and patted him on the cheek with one hand, while the other reached for her cigarettes.

Doreen had been really bitchy all day, but I knew it was her own insecurity at play. She could see that, despite everything I'd told her, we were on our way to being settled. And it unsettled her for some reason. It was what she had wanted for me, but, now that she saw me with it, it felt alien to her.

I was in the midst of a marriage crisis, just keeping myself afloat by trying to second-guess my husband's emotions and keep my own in check, and I didn't have time for self-obsessed and, let's face it, just plain mean girlfriends any more. So did Doreen have my best interests at heart here? No, I didn't believe so.

Was she flexible enough to make the adaptation necessary to be a supportive friend to Tressa, the married woman? Seemingly not.

Oh, and plus? She was pissing me off with her bad-mannered attempts at humour.

'Don't talk to my husband like that, Doreen.'

'Like what?' She raised her eyebrows in me, falsely incredulous.

'In that patronising tone—he's not a child.'

Dan talked over me with, 'Hey, wait a minute, honey. It's OK . . .'

I was irritated with him butting in, but at the same time, I heard his old softness in the word 'honey' and I knew I couldn't back down.

'No, Dan, it's not . . .'

In a show of emotional intelligence my husband said, 'I'll make coffee' and bolted at full speed towards the kitchen door.

'I can hear what you are trying to do, Doreen,' I said, 'and it is *not* OK.'

Doreen does not operate within boundaries, at least not those set by other people. 'You are a fool, Tressa, and I am not going to be spoken to like this,' she said simply and walked towards the door. On reaching it she turned, rather grandly, saying, 'I'll send a car later for my things.' In that stylish gesture I realised, Yes, I am going to miss this woman, this friend in my life, but the hard truth is that fifteen years of friendship can be flushed when the stake is a marriage.

Even a short, shaky one like mine.

'I'm off now, Bernadine,' James shouted from the door. 'There'll be a bus leaving the Church of the Apparition at five o'clock, if you want to leave early and come on down to Tooreen.' Then, on my giving no reply, he repeated, 'Bernadine?' He came into the bedroom and found me fussing through my wardrobe, looking for a coat. 'What are you doing? Mae will be here in a few minutes.'

It was nearly noon and my husband was full of excitement. He had been watching the pontiff's visit live on television that morning.

'Come and watch, Bernadine. Bishop Eamon Casey is on,' he had called earlier. 'Jesus, but he's a great man altogether—such confidence. Come on, Bernadine—you're missing it all!'

I could not bear to watch. The day before I had seen, with disbelief and despair, the size of the crowds in Dublin and Drogheda: tens of thousands of people stretched across miles; jubilant, hymn-singing faithful, sure that they would get a good view of St Peter's successor as he whirred through the clouds in his helicopter. The TV cameras caught him up close, his hands raised in greeting and benediction—but that proximity was a false promise. If the pontiff himself was just a white dot to the thousands there, in reality what hope had I of finding Michael Tuffy in the crowd?

For the full week before I had been trying to talk myself out of seeing the Pope's visit as a backdrop to my own childish fantasy. That Michael and I would be the two whom fate would mysteriously draw together through the crowded fields. We had spent a lifetime apart, yet the greater part of me still wondered if Michael and I were destined to be together. With the Pope there, God was sure to be in attendance. And 'fate' was very much God's remit.

'What coat should I wear?' I said to James, holding aloft a navy rain mac, and a hooded cardigan that Niamh had posted me from New York.

'Wear the mac,' James said. 'It looks like rain.'

He was right, of course, but I decided to wear my daughter's gift from New York. For luck.

At 3 p.m., as the pontiff's helicopter landed to one side of the basilica, the crowd let out a welcoming cheer. Four hundred and fifty thousand individual bodies seemed to merge into one giant mass of devout delight. Exultation.

Four hundred and fifty thousand—and me. I have never felt so alone in my life.

Utterly underestimating the sheer vastness of the crowd, I had left Mae and the others at the coach park and wandered ignorantly into the masses to search for Michael. I walked and walked, expecting the crowd to thin out, but it grew thicker the further in I walked. Within moments I was lost in a forest of bodies. The familiar landscape of Knock was gone, and all I could see was the grass under my feet and people crushed around me on all sides. The grey sky seemed to descend on us. It was one of those days that struggle to overcome dawn and turn to twilight soon after lunch. My cardigan was pulling down on me from a damp hem. The early beginnings of my arthritis (a condition I associated with old age and was therefore in denial about) began to tug at my knees. I wanted to sit down.

As if by magic, a hush went over the crowd when we heard the clack of helicopter wings overhead. Silence ruled for a second while we took it in: was it really—could it be? Then everyone was whooping and shouting. The noise was deafening. Four hundred and fifty thousand people cheering in our special guest, welcoming a new dawn of hope for the future, celebrating the newfound prestige of our country, our county, the blessed, holy townland of Knock.

Four hundred and forty-nine thousand, nine hundred and ninety-nine people—and I wasn't one of them.

I pushed my way angrily through the thick soup of people. I thought I would never escape. The rain was a soft, damp mist that made it hard to breathe. I don't know how long I walked, but it was further than it had taken me to get in. Eventually, weeping with frustration and fear, I grabbed a stranger and said, 'Which is the way out?'

He signalled me to grab his coat and dragged me through the final thicket of hopeful head strainers.

The road outside was cordoned off, but I must have looked dreadful because the man put me in the care of a steward. He found a stool and put me sitting by the door of St John's to wait for the Tooreen bus.

It was a four-hour wait.

They say there is no fool like an old fool and through those four hours there was no one felt more of a fool than I—drenched to the skin, my knees stabbing at me, my bones creaking with damp. I remember thinking what a stupid old woman I was and what a cruel thing love is when it robs you of your good sense, your propriety, your dignity. That it can hibernate inside you for ever, then a smell, a name, a memory, can prod the peaceful sleeping beast and make it howl with hunger. I thought of the bag of baked ham sandwiches I had packed that morning and left with Mae so that if I met Michael Tuffy I would not be carrying an old plastic bag with me. She, and all the ICA, would be enjoying them now with their flasks, cosy in their rain proofs and sensible wellington boots. Other women our age were watching us all from the comfort of their homes, or in the hall in Tooreen with friends. I was here, alone in a cardigan, my feet frozen in a pair of flimsy fabric shoes, looking for an old sweetheart in a crowd of nearly half a million.

Eventually the bus came and the crowd that had gathered around me all struggled on board, anxious to escape the rain and get stuck into a nice hot cup of tea in St Mary's.

'Wasn't he fantastic, though!'

'"The goal of my journey", that's what he called us.'

'He came as a pilgrim, like the rest of us, that's what he said.'

'Ah, but sure, he has great humility.'

Everyone was buzzing, and I smiled weakly back as they bantered and recalled the Mass in every euphoric detail.

I had not achieved the goal of my journey.

I took a window seat and looked out as the bus crawled its way past the knick-knack shops and hotels promising soup and sandwiches for under a pound. The hunger had gone off me. I was beyond it.

I wondered then, Would I ever recover from my true love's broken promise, no matter what age I got to be?

I didn't even bother looking for James when I got to St Mary's Hall, because I knew he would be caught up with some responsibility or other. So I was surprised when I found him waiting for me at the door. The hall was not as packed as I had expected it to be. There were chairs along the walls, not all of them taken, and there were tables dotted across its vast dance floor. Four large television sets sat on trestle tables on the stage. It was a predictable crowd, our neighbours in age and locality were largely here.

I looked around to see who I might sit with. Rather, in the humour I was in, who I might *not* sit with. I spotted Aine Grealy right away. She looked across and waved me over enthusiastically. She was up to no good and it was only then that I saw who she was sitting with.

Michael.

I lost my balance, but James, who had appeared beside me, caught my arm. 'Would you like some tea, dear?'

James spoke into the muted murmur of village curiosity. The room had quietened by half; the polite pretended to talk while others openly stared. There was not a sinner in the whole place who did not know the connection between Michael Tuffy and me. And if there were any gaps, Aine Grealy had had all day to fill them in.

James and I were the floor show.

I started to shake and gripped on to James's steady arm. He did not let me go, but glided me across the floor towards his lifetime rival.

'Aine,' he said, 'I wonder if I might ask you to help me prepare my talk. There's a few translations that could use your expert opinion.'

He gave her no choice but to peel herself away, although she no doubt consoled herself with spending an hour alone sharing her brilliant brain with my husband.

It was all I could do to keep my breath from exploding out of my mouth. If I opened it to smile at him, it would surely draw back over my cheeks in a shocked sob and then everyone would know. Even him. Especially him.

I had never in my mind's eye envisioned Michael as an old man. The last time I had seen him we had both been young and full of vigour. I had watched myself age and, with the evidence of getting older, I had pushed my handsome young Michael further into my memory. As decades passed, I let him rest in the place of dreams where the young stay beautiful for ever. As the years moved on, I stopped wondering.

Now he was here. He was wearing a brown suit that was out of fashion and a blue shirt that did not go well with it. Much of his hair was gone and his face was lined. The blue eyes remained.

He was my own Michael. The same as that first night we had seen each other in Kitty Conlan's parlour and I had known we were meant to be together. The years had passed like a moment, as if he had turned to pick a flower for my hair and now I was sixty. I knew from his eyes he didn't care. I knew I looked the same to him now as I had then. We had aged, yet each other's beauty had simply matured, like exquisite wine.

Eventually I said, 'Michael Tuffy.'

He smiled at me. Broad, brave mischief. 'You look the same,' he said.

I shrugged and looked away. I was afraid to hold his eye for too long.

We sat looking forward for a moment, not needing words but locked together in our world as we had always been. I had questions to ask, but there was time enough for that.

He leaned over to me and I could feel his breath next to my ear. Like the warm breeze on the beach in Inniscrone the day I dreamed I saw him.

'Do you remember how we were, Bernadine Morley? Do you remember how it was then?'

I went to close my eyes to conjure up my most treasured, most private summer-meadow daydream that I might share it with Michael

Tuffy, but as my lids folded down I saw James across the room.

He was shuffling his feet, half talking to Aine and half looking back at me. His agitation broke my spell but then, for one second, I caught my husband's eye. He looked tired and nervous. No sparkling shots of blue, no grand desires, no dreams, no jokes, no promises of passionate delights. Just worn, worried, everyday husbandhood.

And I knew I had to get up from my chair and walk over to him. Because however much I loved Michael Tuffy, still and for ever, a promise is a promise. James had kept his promise to me and been a good husband. If I answered Michael Tuffy's question, I would be making a choice. And, whatever my heart told me, I had to be loyal to my husband.

He deserved my love, but I owed him my loyalty.

I took one last look at my one true love. My hands held tightly in my lap as I scanned his face in goodbye.

'No, Michael Tuffy,' I said. 'I barely remember it at all.'

I stood and walked across to James. His face crumpled in relief and he took my hand and held me by him for the rest of that afternoon.

Michael, I saw, left shortly afterwards. I believe he returned to America, although I never heard of him again.

Trust

You don't have to feel love to give it

Pobs

Your mother was a fussy eater when she was a child, and on days when she would not trust to my cooking I would feed her a slice of bread mashed into a cup of warm milk, with a sprinkle of sugar on top. As her tastes developed and changed, she would always return to a cup of 'pobs' as comfort food. It was the only recipe I could ever get your mother to master, and I know you were virtually reared on it yourself.

Sometimes we can only stomach the simplest of things. This is food for the very young and the very old. As it is only at the very beginning and the very end of our lives that we have answers, I have come around to thinking that, with all of the fuss we make over food, perhaps all any of us really needs is bread, milk and a little sugar to sweeten it at times.

I AM STAYING in a hotel on Palm Beach, Miami. Everything is warm and candy coloured, even the women in their bikinis. I am speaking at a conference here and the manager upgraded me to a suite overlooking the beach. Somewhere behind the clamour of the *Vogue* fashion teams ordering breakfast on the patio beneath my balcony I sense I can hear the sea.

I miss Dan.

I didn't think I would and I am not sure why I do.

It's just that in the past year my new husband has grown on me. I notice when he isn't here with his clumsy, lumbering ways and doing those things I hate: blowing his nose, using hillbilly words and drinking instant coffee. I don't feel madly in love with him. But a small, slow miracle has occurred inside me so that he no longer annoys me as much as he used to. Maybe that counts for something, or maybe my standards have dropped and I should be worried. But I have found a kind of freedom in shrugging stuff off, and I'm going to stick with it. Tolerance is an unfashionable quality, but I have found that being irritated wastes an awful lot more energy than you think.

Dan is kind of over the Ronan thing. Kind of.

He didn't exactly dance a jig when I said I'd been invited to Miami for work for a few days. I asked him rather than told him, although I don't know what I would have said if he had said 'no', which, of course, he would never have done. He said something much worse which was, 'I trust you.'

There was a menu of potential rows to choose from.

For starters: 'Well, gee, *thanks*, honey for allowing me to go work and earn money.'

Then a meaty entrée: 'Can we *please* put the "my wife's a slut" card to the back of the pack now?'

And for dessert that old family favourite: 'I never should have married you in the first place!'

The thing that really drives me crazy is that *I* completely trust Dan.

Trust is nothing when you have it. It's bread and milk. Basic. There's no glamour, no emotion, no drama—you just trust and that's it. Trusting someone is boring. It's a non-event. But take it away—try living without trust and suddenly your relationship is plunged into a living hellhole. I've been there, and I have seen my friends live with men they didn't trust: men who lie. Not little 'no, you haven't gained weight' lies, but terrifying 'working late while really I am banging my secretary' lies.

I always thought you had to be really crazy about somebody not to trust them. Actually, you just have to be with somebody who is untrustworthy. Like somebody who really *would* feel up your friend under a dinner party table. Or somebody who never says 'I love you' first.

Dan deserves my trust. I don't deserve his. I'd like it. It would make my inner life easier and make me feel like I was a nicer person. But I don't have it. Not all of it, or not yet. Dan has always known that he loves me that bit more than I love him. When I betrayed him, it shifted the balance too far in my direction.

'I trust you,' was my punishment for the past and my challenge for a future.

So I am standing in front of two hundred food industry executives about to deliver my wisdom on memory and food when the shithead Angelo Orlandi walks right up to the front of the theatre and plonks himself down in front of the podium. He is minus Jan and wearing dark glasses, so I can't see his eyes. He starts to look round the room as I talk, like I am boring him. It unnerves me and I stumble over a couple of sentences.

When I am finished, he walks over to the side of the stage, standing almost directly beneath me. I am sorely tempted to bury my heel in the top of his head. Not for the first time I wish I had worn stilettos to work.

'Hi, Tressa.'

I hate men. Behind me I have a smug husband saying 'I trust you' when he so does not, and in front of me I have a lecherous manipulative ex who probably wants a fuck and may be just crude enough to ask me straight out for one.

'You free for dinner?'

Same thing.

'Where's Jan?'

'She's not here.'

Then he gives me this thoroughly delighted with himself grin.

I cannot be bothered with this man any more. He is an insult to the principle of marital trust. I find him so appalling that he can no longer tempt me.

So I look at one of the richest, cleverest, most admired men in the food industry in America and I think: What is it that I hate about you so much? Then I see it, clear as the blue Miami sky. Angelo lacks integrity. And the reason I can see it with such clarity is because I am married to a man who *has* got integrity, so I know when it is missing and it is missing in Angelo Orlandi in spades.

And I realise, in that moment, that integrity of that sort is the only kind that counts. Or rather, it's the only kind that counts for me. Great men, good men, humane, heroic, brilliant, history-making men shit on their own doorsteps all the time.

And that's fine. I just don't want to be married to one of them and, thankfully, I am not.

So Dan won. He won the stupid test I had set him before the Orlandi weekend. That it had taken me this long to figure it out was no credit to me, yet it was so simple. You make a promise and you keep it.

Not until you don't feel like keeping it any more, not until you get bored, or restless, or someone more exciting, more interesting, comes along. You say you are going to do something and then you do it.

Like living with the same person, day in and day out for the rest of your life because you said that you would. And that, I realised, is how love grows.

'Go home to Jan,' I said.

Angelo looked at me like, 'What is *that* supposed to mean?'

And I hoped that I would never be so detached from the reality of my own marriage that I would not at least know when it was in trouble.

I didn't switch my cell back on, but went straight upstairs to phone Dan. I had a compulsion to tell him that I loved him. Say it first. Without analysis, or thinking about whether I really, *really* meant it or not. I just wanted him to hear it. I wanted to give him that.

I tripped over an envelope that had been pushed under my door and opened it hurriedly, assuming it would be some PR itinerary.

It was a typed hotel memo.

'Gerry rang. There has been an accident. Please phone him urgently.'

There are so many things about marriage that are never spoken of either within or outside it.

Although nobody ever said it, it was understood that the death of a first wife in childbirth could be the making of a man. He was free to marry again and often the second wife's dowry made his fortune.

Then, there were those families with a dozen children. In a two-room cottage there is no privacy for a wife to object to her husband's advances. Some women would send their husbands to the pub with the week's housekeeping, praying that he would get so drunk that he might fall and hit his head on a rock and be found dead in a ditch in the morning. There would be weeping and wailing and genuine grief. But there would also be a widow's pension that would see the older children through school and the younger ones fed properly.

I never suffered hunger or indignity at the hands of my husband and yet, at times, I had wished him dead. In the early years of our marriage I fantasised about it. What would happen if some tragedy should befall him? Then Michael would come back and marry me, the young widow.

I could have been forgiven for my youth and the circumstances under which we were married, but as the years went on I continued to harbour the occasional petty death wish over a pompous comment, or a query as to how I had prepared the ham, as it was not as much to his liking as usual. Right up to my fifties, when I was fit and strong and still perceived myself as an attractive woman, at times I would look at James and think that if he were to die, I might still have ten good years left to make another life for myself entirely.

You might assume that contentment is the right of the elderly, but you'd be wrong. Peace of mind does not come with time or age or routine. It masquerades as luck and personality, but in fact serenity is hard won through prayer and perseverance, and intelligent understanding of hardship. For some people hardship is a husband who beats them, the death of a child. Others will search for and find hardship in an everyday rain cloud.

The trick to contentment is knowing when hardship has passed and appreciating its absence for every moment that it is not there. I was never content with James because I was determined not to be. I looked at him and saw what he was not. What he never could be.

When the doctor told me James was dying, the shock was harder for me having wished him dead. It was my first indication that what we feel is an irrelevance. It is only what is, what exists, that is important. To feel that you want somebody dead is a luxury you can only enjoy when they are wholeheartedly alive. When they are dying, suddenly nothing exists except keeping them alive. You do not think about whether you love them, how you will grieve for them; you are stripped of the privacies of petty hatred and resentment as all your time and energy is swallowed up in caring for them.

There is so much you can say about a person dying, yet there is so little worth saying. We get caught up in the language of disease, use it to distract ourselves from the truth of what is happening; we become experts in diagnosis, in treatments, yet cannot say the only thing worth saying, which is that soon this person will not be with us any more.

James had a heart condition and bowel cancer. He was seventy-eight; the doctor talked about cell growth, and breathing patterns and blood pressure. In the year he was sick I learned to use a syringe; I cleaned and fed him like a small child and, towards the end, like a baby. I would not let a nurse into the house, or see him suffer the indignity of being fed or washed by anyone but his own wife.

When Niamh came to stay during that time we fought. She wanted to tend him and I would not let her. Niamh called me a 'stubborn old bitch'. I never told her then that James thought he was her hero. He could not have borne his daughter seeing him as reduced as he was.

'Read to him,' I said.

Niamh never saw James untidy or in pain. I wonder now if I was right to have protected her from the truth. Perhaps I should have trusted to the depth of what existed between them, in her strength of character and the natural order of a child watching their parent die.

They say that it is not until you lose both parents that you finally mature into an adult. But a life partner dying brings home the inevitability of your own death. There is nothing that can prepare you.

James kept saying it: 'I am dying, I am dying,' and I kept swatting him back like a kitchen bluebottle.

'I'm not afraid,' he said, 'I've made my peace. I just want to know that you'll be all right. Bernadine . . .'

To the end, even in the sweet relief of his morphine-induced dementia, James said my name, 'Bernadine . . .' as if I were an answer to his prayer. The great love of his life.

We lived a year like that: me watching him so closely that I could not see him any more. I saw only individual details like the fine membrane of his skin as I changed his drip; rheumy eyes that needed cleaning; a mouth peeled back in a noiseless scream, as the morphine wore off. I shaved him, washed him, trimmed his hair and nails. I changed his sheets every two days, his pyjamas every day. When people came, I put a shirt and a tie on him and covered the bed in Foxford tweed rugs, to take the bare, bedridden look off him. I aired his room and filled it with flowers and I banished the smell of death from our house.

You can study death, you can talk about it, you can know it is going to happen, but nothing can prepare you. So you tell yourself you may as well stay unprepared.

When you care for the dying, you don't absorb the things you so desperately want to remember after they have died: their voice in whispered prayer, a hand that grips, eyes that move across you, a chest moving up and down with breath. Life to the end is a series of small miracles you can only see someone perform after they are gone. The instant the miracles cease, you wish you had looked harder, treasured the gift of life itself; the ability to communicate, to see, simply to breathe.

You wish you hadn't wasted so much time wanting more.

RECIPES FOR A PERFECT MARRIAGE

Bloody Gerry.

I couldn't get hold of him. The psycho old hippie has a cellphone but he doesn't know how to use it. There was no reply from Longville Avenue, Dan's cell was off, and the only flight I could get back was on a tinpot airline with no phone.

I was in such a panic that it did not even occur to me to call his mother. I had no idea what had happened. I did not know if Dan was dead or alive. I went through every possibility in my head. He had come off that cursed bike, perhaps he had decided to refelt the garage roof like he had been threatening to do for weeks, or—dear God—there had been major electrical work going on at his work. Please don't let him have got himself electrocuted.

What did 'accident' mean, anyway? It could mean he was dead. 'There has been an accident,' is what they say in the films. No. 'There has been a terrible accident' is what they say when someone has died. He wasn't dead—was he? No—surely Gerry would have said. Or not. It's not the sort of thing you leave with a hotel receptionist: 'Husband dead. Please phone home.'

If it was really serious, Gerry would have told the hotel and they would have interrupted my talk.

I flagged a steward and ordered three whiskies. I threw them down back to back and slept my way out of my panic.

I was nudged awake five minutes after landing to an almost empty plane. My head was thumping as I made it to the cab rank, and my heart joined in with it as the queue snailed along and I wondered whether to faint my way to the top of it. Once in the cab, I didn't know where to go. A hospital, but which one? Did this accident happen at home or in Manhattan? I decided to go home first anyway.

My hands were trembling so hard I could hardly get my key in the lock. I fell in the door, weak with dread, and made my way towards the back of the house. If there was a note, it would be on the kitchen table. There was the faint noise of conversation to my left, so I opened the door to the living room and walked in.

The TV was on and Dan was asleep on the sofa. His head was leaned back, his mouth was open and there was a perfectly healthy man's snore emanating from it. He had one of my good patchwork quilts tucked in under his neck, which looked out of place with the surrounding bachelor debris: three Domino's Pizza boxes, and a pile of Budweiser tins.

Some kind of unholy rage rose up in me.

'What the fuck is going on?' I shouted.

Dan leapt up in shock when he saw me, then recoiled in pain. As the

325

blanket fell aside, I saw that his arm was in a sling. 'Ouch!'

'I thought you were *dead!*'

He looked kind of annoyed himself, cradling his hurt arm. 'Sorry to disappoint you!'

I sensed Gerry loitering behind me and I swirled on him like a dervish before he had the chance to retreat. 'And you've got some bloody explaining to do—'

'I'm sorry, Tress, I swear—I tried calling you again, but the booth at the hospital was bust and my cellphone was dead and . . .'

I had never felt so angry in my life. My extremities were fizzing.

'Don't blame Gerry, babe, it was my fault. I took my eye off the road for a second and there was this piece of wood or something—'

'Next thing—wham, he goes down and I'm right behind and I go "shit!"'

'And I came off—right there on my side and next thing I remember I'm—'

'*Shut up the pair of you!*' I didn't recognise my own voice, it came out in such a roar. 'You are both in so much fucking trouble.'

I caught Dan giving Gerry a cheeky schoolboy wink and realised, for the first time since I came in, that they were both more than a little drunk. That sent me right over the edge. I can't remember what I said next, but it was a boiling stream of consciousness and contained references to the fact that I was not his mother, that they were both like children, that I was a very important person who did not appreciate being dragged across the country for no good reason, and that I had always said that that bike was a death trap and he was never going out on it again. Never. *Ever.*

Dan was nodding and trying to look contrite, but I saw his eyes flick across Gerry, who was standing behind me, and the beginnings of a smile form on his lips.

Hateful bastards. Laughing at me.

'Is that arm broken, Dan?' I needed to assess the seriousness of his injury in order to calculate whether I could reasonably add to it.

'No it's . . .'

'. . . fractured. Just hairline,' his partner in crime butted in.

I stood there, literally hopping from foot to foot I was so mad. I didn't know what to do with myself. I wanted to bang their two heads together.

Then I had an idea. 'Right,' I said. 'That's *it!*'

They followed me out to the garage, where I picked up a large hammer from Dan's tool shelf and swung it in an arc at the side of the bike, tearing a huge lump down one side. There was a joint, horrified gasp from behind me.

I didn't care. This was a revelation—violence felt good.

So I swung again. The two men shouted, 'No!' and Dan grabbed the hammer, while Gerry threw himself at his beloved Kawasaki and begged its forgiveness for having put it in the path of a madwoman.

I turned and accidentally belted Dan's bad arm.

'Ow!' he yelped.

'*I thought you were dead!*' I screamed, then I caught sight of my collapsing, angry face in his eyes. We stood for a moment, our eyes glued to the other's in the shock of strong emotion. I was brought back to that first afternoon we slept together, my disbelief that this handsome stranger desired me, the unthinking, simple way that Dan fell instantly in love with me and his solid willingness to follow through on it.

If you ask a girl like me 'What more could you ask for?' I will always think of something.

But I didn't want to lose him and I hadn't realised I cared so much.

Neither had he.

Dan put his good arm round me. Even with one arm, he was strong. 'You can trust me, baby—I wouldn't go dying on you. Not yet anyway.'

When he said that I realised that while I had virtually no trust in my *own* judgment, I had always, and could always, totally trust Dan.

I knew then that he was the only man in my life I would ever believe in that completely. My husband.

James died on a Tuesday. I remember it because I had been studying the weather, looking for hardship in rain clouds. The summer had been swinging between terrible slashing storms that would make you afraid to leave the house and glorious sunshine that made the humble hedgerows vigorous and colourful. This day was neither. It felt airless and flat: a plain day where everything looked like itself. No beauty, no pain—just as it is.

And I remember thinking nothing in particular, only what an ordinary day it was, and noting that no day could be more ordinary than a Tuesday, which falls neither at the beginning, middle or end of the week.

James looked so sleepy that morning that I decided to forgo the day's toilet routine and let him doze. I gave him his painkillers in the mid-morning and fussed around the room chatting about something stupid—the Munnellys' vegetable-digging cat, I think it was. It was one of the new things I did when James got ill. I became chatty; I poured out a constant stream of pointless tittle-tattle to fill the space left by his weak silence. Sometimes he raised his hand to indicate I was annoying him. But this particular day I could tell he was enjoying listening to me. Not to the words surely, but just to the sound of my voice.

For lunch I had mashed some potatoes through with bacon and cabbage. James was barely eating now, but I was determined about producing a balanced diet for him. Every day I cooked him proper food—worried and nagged when he didn't eat it. I would not give in.

On this Tuesday I gave in to him. He asked me to prepare warm milk and bread for his lunch. He said the single word 'Pobs' as a child would.

As I fed him, I talked my tittle-tattle. My silly verbal nonsense balanced out his physical disability; as distraction from the humiliation of napkins and spoons and liquidised food I would turn myself into a mindless gossip.

'So I said to Mary—start again and this time I want details. Tell me what did he say to you? Then what did you say to him . . .'

I wiped James's mouth and, as I did, he raised his hand and took my wrist. I raised my eyes to heaven to indicate that I understood him telling me to stop the story before he lost his mind and I half stood up.

James shook his head and tried to grip my wrist harder, failed, and his hand slid down my arm, but he did not let go. He wanted to speak, but seemed unable.

'What is it?' I said, then started to work down my list, 'Apple jelly? Tea? The paper? Do you want me to read the paper? The television? '

James shook his head as if he could not speak, but his face was alive and I could tell there was energy in him. I got irritated.

'Speak up, you silly old fool. Tell me what you want.'

James rested his head back on the pillow, shut his eyes and spoke. It was barely above a whisper, but I heard him clearly.

'Tell me you love me.'

I was stunned.

James had broken the understanding that had existed between us for fifty years: our unspoken contract. He was my husband, but my heart had always belonged to another man. James knew that. The night his mother died James told me he loved me. I had never said it back. It was understood from that day on, when I didn't say it to comfort him then, that I was never going to say it.

Now he was dying and it felt like a manipulation more than a request.

James's eyes were still closed as he repeated his request to me: quieter still, almost as if to himself. Beyond meek, beyond hopeful, in the face of my silence: 'Tell me you love me, my only Bernadine.'

I knew he was waiting for me. Of all of the things I had done for

James, this was the only thing he had ever wanted. Perhaps because it was the one thing he knew he could never have.

The alarm on the bedside cabinet went off to indicate it was time for his drugs. We both started, but before I stood up to busy myself I had a sense that I should stay sitting for one moment longer: a feeling outside myself, like I was being held in the chair.

I looked at this man I had known nearly all my life. This man I did not love, whom I had lived with for longer than my mother, my father, my child. This man whom I had married, a stranger, yet who had become my oldest friend. The person I had tried to keep myself hidden from and yet who knew me better than anyone.

I did not go and fetch his tablets, but sat instead and noticed, for the first time how frail and withered he was. James was barely in the room. The robust, elegant schoolteacher, soldier, father and husband was gone. All that was left was this barely breathing slither of soul, asking for love. Not asking me if I loved him, or had I ever loved him, but just to say the words 'I love you' to him.

Once. That once would be enough to set him free.

In that moment, what had been impossible all my life now seemed so simple. I did not have to love James to tell him I loved him.

I just had to say the words.

'I love you.'

Briefly James opened his eyes and his mouth closed around my name for the last time.

In the moment he was gone there was a revelation.

As I said the words 'I love you' to my husband for the first time, I realised they were true.

I held him for one hour and I said the words, 'I love you, I love you, I love you' over and over into our empty room. And I imagined them carrying his soul in a stream of words out through the window and way up to Heaven—how many words does it take to carry a soul to Heaven? How many 'I love you's'?

It should have felt like I was saying it too late. But it didn't and that was the greatest revelation of all.

James had been the love of my life.

Not what I had wished for, not what I had dreamt of—but wishes and dreams don't live in the real world.

James had been my life. My reality.

Love can live in your mind and your heart, and it can be anything you want it to be. My love for Michael Tuffy, bar that first glorious summer, was a fantasy. What I shared with James was what truly belonged to me.

Love that lives in the world, that has to sacrifice, compromise, share, endure—tangible, tough, tender love—this is the real thing. Love you can touch, which can comfort and hold and protect you; love that smells and tastes familiar, if not always sweet. Love that is no more than skin and breath can become, in time, as essential as water.

The legacy James left me was his trust. He never faulted me as a wife, a lover or a mother—although I was lacking as all three. He had faith in my love for him, even though it remained unspoken for all of our life together. James saw love in my sense of duty towards him and, although I had never dared admit it, he was right. I looked at the shooting bag I embroidered with his initials and the antimacassar I crocheted for his chair imprinted with the shape of his sleeping skull and I thought that each thing I made him—each scone I baked, each crust I cut, each lettuce I grew—contained perhaps no more than a pinprick of love. But it was enough.

James had gathered each gesture and banked it away so that, at the end of his life, I knew he felt loved by me.

He just needed me to say it before he went. Although I believe he knew that I needed to say it too.

James had been the love of my life because I had shared my life with him. It was no more mysterious than that.

My husband had been my bread and butter, my sustenance. And Michael? Well, he was just jam.

They say there is no such thing as a perfect marriage, but there is. A perfect marriage is one where two people live together for most of their lives until death separates them. What there is no such thing as is an easy marriage. And when it comes to love, we somehow believe it should happen with ease.

The differences between men and women are what set our hearts alight, but the similarities are the fuel that keeps us going: warmth, companionship, bearing witness to another's grief, the original joy and pain of being human. Married love is the gold at the centre of the rubble after the fire has gone out. It can take years to find the hidden treasure, but the search is what is important and when treasure is too easily found how can you be sure it isn't fool's gold?

What my marriage taught me is that real love is only what you give. That's all. Love is not 'out there', waiting for you. It is in you. In your own heart: in what you are willing to give of it. We are all capable of love, but few of us have the courage to do it properly. We are afraid to give more in case the other won't give it back.

You can take a person's love and waste it. But you are the fool. When you give love, it grows and flowers inside you like a carefully pruned rose. Love is joy. Those who love, no matter what indignities, what burdens they carry, are always full of joy.

James was happy in our marriage because he gave me his love.

So in the end, despite myself, I realised I had loved my husband. Reluctantly and never absolutely.

But what in life is ever absolute?

Except death.

Commitment

You can make a commitment to love,
but you cannot truly love without commitment

Irish Stew

This is not my grandmother's recipe, but my own. Because sometimes, no matter how much pleasure you get from somebody else's work, there is no replacement for a recipe that you have developed yourself.

SERVES TWO

YOU WILL NEED:

rack of lamb (around 6 cutlets)
3–4 shallots, chopped
1 clove garlic, finely chopped
2 handfuls tiny new potatoes
8 small whole baby carrots
1½ cups lamb stock
2–3 sprigs rosemary, chopped
red wine

METHOD:

Brown the rack of lamb for 3 minutes on each side in a little oil in a hot ridged frying pan. Remove from the pan and throw in your shallots and garlic for one minute, then remove. Pour the hot stock into a saucepan and add the potatoes, carrots, garlic, shallots and rosemary, then bring to the boil.

Place the rack of lamb on top, cover and simmer for 15 minutes (rare) or 20 minutes (medium rare).

Transfer the rack of lamb and the vegetables with a slotted spoon into a shallow casserole dish. Cover with a tea towel and leave to rest for 5 minutes. In that time reduce the liquid by a third (on a high heat for 2–3 minutes). Once reduced, add a good slug of red wine and leave on high heat for another 2 minutes. Take off the heat and cover with a lid to keep gravy hot.

Slice the lamb into 6 cutlets, place 3 on each plate, and spoon the potatoes and carrots round them. Add the red-wine sauce just before serving.

Accompany with buttered, wilted white cabbage sprinkled with thyme. (Finely chop a ¼ head of white cabbage, simmer over a very low heat with 2 knobs of butter for 10 minutes, adding a little of the red wine. Add thyme 2 minutes before removing from the heat.)

THE FIRST YEAR of my marriage didn't work out quite how I had planned it, in all sorts of ways. My career as a food writer ground to a—temporary, I hope—halt. The TV pilot was unremarkable to say the least and my book *Recipes of an Irish Grandmother* was pre-empted by two weeks by *Recipes from an Irish Kitchen* written by a traitorous little cow who used to be my assistant. Dan kept saying, 'Things will work out,' until I thought I would kill him. Luckily for him, things *did* work out, only not in a way either of us could have predicted.

The photographs of our kitchen, which *N.Y. Interiors* magazine had shot months beforehand (and we had more or less forgotten about), hit the shops. The response to our customised cupboards was astounding and I was suddenly overwhelmed with requests to design kitchens. Except that everyone wanted a one-off 'original' like ours. Dan had an idea. He called Gerry and the two of them started calling in favours. They borrowed some muscle, big wheels, and started trawling around salvage yards and building suppliers. Before I had time to really figure out what was happening, the three of us were running a kitchen design and manufacturing company called, of all things, Eclectic Kitchens. Dan quit his job and we sold the apartment in Manhattan, trading it for the lease on a showroom. Less than three months' trading later and we have already been shortlisted for a new business award; it has been the craziest, busiest, most profitable, most scary, experience of my life. Dan and I spent our first wedding anniversary in a tiling factory briefing them on our new range of retro colours. And here's the craziest thing of all: *I loved it.*

It was the perfect end to the first year of what continues to be the biggest adventure of my life: marriage.

I found the first year hard because I ask too many questions. Questions are the sign of an active, intelligent mind: a filter you rinse your ideas through before you make a decision. But sometimes the filter gets clogged and then it becomes a barrier to the truth.

The truth is that while I was busy wondering if I loved Dan enough, measuring him up against ex-boyfriends, being attracted to other men, sweating, deliberating, agonising about my decision to spend the rest of my life with him, our marriage was just marching on anyway.

We moved home, we renovated a house, we negotiated around family, we built a kitchen, we entertained new and old friends. We lived, ate, slept together. Dan was busy just being my husband and, despite myself, I had been a wife to him.

An adoring, generous-spirited wife?

No.

The words 'grudging' and 'duty' spring to mind, but I guess it's a start.

I thought that you could not make a commitment until you were truly in love. What I know now is that you cannot love truly until you have made a commitment.

I like to have all the answers upfront before I decide if a risk is worth taking. But with relationships it just doesn't work like that. Being in love has a shorter guarantee than a kettle and in the long run can be a lot less use in a marriage. Better to be armed with a dose of blind faith so that when the love runs out you can believe it will be back again. Because it will. What I have learned this year is that married love is never complete or finite. It has to be elastic, adjustable. If you become too attached to a way of loving—the beautiful buzz, the thrill—you'll have no way of replacing it when it's gone.

Marriages (like our fabulous kitchens!) are custom made: you just jiggle them around until you find a way to make them fit.

They say the heart rules the head, but sometimes it works the other way round. I was a grown woman when I married Dan. I married him because his heart was big and brave enough to take me on. It needed to be, as I discovered that my own heart was small and wretchedly weak. Luckily for me, Dan's heart wouldn't let me go. He told me once that he loved me enough for the both of us. It frightened me at the time and I comforted myself with the fact that it was just a figure of speech.

But it wasn't—and I sure am glad that it was true.

Do I love him now?

'Yes,' but don't ask me to put a hundred per cent tag on it because I don't know if that mysterious gap that craves certainty will ever be filled.

In my most self-punishing moments, I still wonder if I married Dan just not to be alone. I wonder then if marriage is about love at all. Perhaps it is just the dance two people make when they move quietly about the same house. Perhaps it is not how I feel about Dan's little foibles that matters, but the fact that I know about them at all. Perhaps intimacy is not just loving everything about him, but knowing everything about him—and staying anyway.

This is my last chance at love—not because I am too old to meet anyone else, but because it is just time to stop. Stop running, chasing the moving target I call happiness and get happy with what I have got.

Dan is not the right guy, or the wrong guy. He is just my guy. My husband. The one I chose on the day I chose him and, right now, I plan to go on choosing him for the rest of my life.

In the meantime, I am going to keep another promise and read my grandmother's memoirs. Maybe I will discover what it was that kept Bernadine and James together for so long and perhaps my marriage to Dan will be different from theirs, but just as good. Like my Irish stew.

KATE KERRIGAN

For many years Kate Kerrigan worked as a journalist on several young women's magazines in London, including *More!* and *Just Seventeen*, but in 1990, deciding that she wanted to live in her parents homeland, she moved to Dublin to relaunch *Irish Tatler*. Later, after her son was born, she and her husband left Dublin for a small fishing village in County Mayo so that Leo could enjoy a country childhood.

At the time I contacted Kate for an interview, by chance she was coming to London to be questioned on Radio 4's *Woman's Hour* about the influence our grandmothers have on our lives—one of the themes that runs through *Recipes for a Perfect Marriage*. As we ordered lunch in Chez Gerrard's ('any restaurant with *"chez"* in the name is OK with me,' Kate had emailed, 'as we don't have any restaurants in my village!'), I quickly found myself caught up in a thought-provoking debate about the nature of modern marriage. 'I think that it is very difficult to be married these days,' Kate began. 'One of the reasons for this is that we have come to idolise the idea of falling in love, and being in love with somebody. It's been turned from a pleasant side effect into the whole point of marriage. And when the reality of marriage starts to kick in, when you start to realise that your partner has feet of clay, which we all do, it's actually quite a difficult thing to cope with because there is nothing in our modern culture to say, "actually, girl, you've just got to suck it up and get on with it." We live in a throw-away world and the proffered wisdom today is that when that initial passion and spark goes away, the marriage is over.'

In *Recipes for a Perfect Marriage*, Kate also wanted to find out more about what marriage was like for our grandparents' generation. 'How did they stay married for a lifetime? What did they expect from marriage? And what actually happened? And the best way to answer all of those questions, for me, has always been through fiction.'

Kate had many of her beloved grandmother's recipes and also poached others from her friends and family. 'Once I had the recipes in place, and had mapped out the areas of a marriage that I wanted to explore, such as trust, compromise, sacrifice and so on, I had the basic structure and could then write freely within it.' I asked Kate if she had tested the recipes herself and was she a good cook? 'I am now,' she laughed. 'I can cook those ten recipes really, really well. Although there were two dishes that I struggled with. The first is my mother-in-law's slow-roasted clove ham, which she upstages me with every Christmas, but now that I know how much work goes into it, I'm happy to take second billing. And the other is my sister's lamb stew. It's very modern and takes skill and timing that I just don't have. But the best recipe in the book is the porter cake. It is so easy to make and absolutely delicious. That was the easiest one but I recommend everyone to try out the recipes.'

So does Kate plan to continue examining relationships in her next novel? 'Oh, yes. I love writing about emotion. It probably stems from my favourite occupation of sitting around kitchen tables in pyjamas, chatting about everything and nothing with my mother, sisters and girlfriends. My next book is about mothers and daughters—and I can't wait to get started.'

Jane Eastgate

335

ALICE PETERSON

LOOK THE WORLD
IN THE EYE

❦

Katie Fletcher has everything a girl could

wish for—she's pretty, owns a successful

fashion boutique and lives in trendy

Notting Hill with her handsome boyfriend, Sam.

Yet all it takes to rock Katie's perfect world

is one phone call from her father, asking her to look

after her sister Bells for two weeks.

The trouble is that she has never told Sam

that she even has a sister—let alone the

fact that Bells is . . . well, different.

❦

CHAPTER ONE

'MORNING, EDDIE.' I hand him a white paper bag with a croissant inside.

'The usual, Katie?' He turns to start operating the cappuccino machine. 'You've been away, haven't you?'

'Well, I was in Paris two weeks ago on business. Catwalk shows . . .'

'Paris and models? Sounds like a holiday to me.'

'And racking through three thousand designers' clothes. After a while it's not much fun, I promise! It was like a cattle market.'

'One cappuccino, with organic chocolate on the top.'

'Wonderful.'

'Busy day ahead?'

'Yes, very. Rush, rush, rush. It never stops, does it?'

'You've changed your hair colour again,' he notes.

I smile excitedly. 'I've got my fashion show tonight.' I rummage in my purse, trying to find the right change. 'Got to run, see you tomorrow.'

'Five minutes to go!' I call out to the models. The dressing room has an overpowering smell of hair spray and styling solutions. I pace the corridor. Where is Sam? I punch in his number on my mobile.

'Katie, I'm on my way, promise,' he says. 'In a cab right now.' He starts to make car noises. 'Yes, left here, mate.'

'Sam! I can hear the phone in the background. You're still in the office, aren't you?'

'Half an hour, tops,' he tells me firmly.

'Sam, I really need you here.' I hang up, take a deep breath and walk back into the dressing room. Henrietta, one of the models, sits in the corner, stroking a strand of her blonde hair. 'Hen, five minutes,' I say.

339

I look at the chaos of high-heeled shoes and the racks of black clothes waiting to be modelled. I own a shop in Turnham Green Terrace called FIB, which stands for Female In Black, and tonight is the summer fashion show. The clothes are mainly black, of course, except for the odd accessory and the occasional burst of colour. I have started to organise fashion shows twice a year and this one is being held at a house in Chiswick, owned by a client of Sam's. The owners have gone for the minimal look: stripped floorboards, white walls, spotlights, large modern paintings and gilded mirrors. It is almost a clone of Sam's house, except his is half the size.

I can hear the audience taking their seats, there is that familiar sound of scraping chairs. This is the point when my nerves start to kick in. I pick up a half-full glass of champagne. 'Is your glass half-full or half-empty?' was the first thing Sam ever said to me when we met in a bar, followed by, 'Allow me to get you a refill,' and finished off with a wink.

If he had been bald with bad breath I probably would have politely refused. Instead, I was looking at a tall, attractive, dark-haired man. I had to look round to make sure he was talking to me.

Eve, who works at FIB with me, tells me the photographer wants a quick word before we start. 'Good luck, girls,' I say. 'Look the part, feel the part and you *are* the part.' Was one of the models rolling her eyes at me? I ask myself as I walk out of the room.

Quick look in the mirror. I am wearing one of the outfits we are showing tonight: a black halter-neck with a panel of silver beading around the neckline and bust. It is cut low at the back and fastened with small sparkling silver buttons and my outfit is finished off with slip-on silver heels. My dark brown hair has been dyed black especially for tonight and is pinned with a white rose.

The show begins with . . . 'It Started With a Kiss', by Hot Chocolate as the first model strides out in a black satin top and slim-fitting black hipster skirt, offset by a handcrafted black-and-silver beaded belt that shimmers under the lights. In one hand she clutches a black satin bag with a small silver clasp. She glides up to the fireplace, mushroom-coloured smoke weaving its way across the wooden floorboards at her feet. The audience marvels at it and claps as the model leaves the room. I see Emma, my old schoolfriend, taking a seat at the back. You can never miss her entry into a room. She's nearly six foot tall and always played Keeper in school netball classes.

Sophie Ellis-Bextor's 'Murder on the Dancefloor', plays as Henrietta walks on, her hair scraped back into a ponytail, high heels echoing on the floorboards. Her mother is in the front row, watching adoringly. She is lame but loaded, and after you have sat her down in the corner of my shop on the chaise longue, plied her with a few drinks and treated her like royalty, she buys her darling daughter Henrietta almost my entire stock. Sam often asks me if the 'old soak in the corner' came by.

The next girl waltzes out in a zebra-printed evening dress worn with a scarlet wrap. This is one of my favourite outfits. Her hair is dyed jet black with a sharp fringe, very *Chicago*-style. 'Superstition' by Stevie Wonder is on the turntable. This song always reminds me of when I was a child at home. 'Turn that blasted noise off!' I can hear from Mum's studio when Stevie Wonder's, 'I Just Called To Say I Love You' is played over and over again from my sister's bedroom. Another world now.

But I do think about Bells. I can still see her letter slipped into my leather diary, that neat familiar handwriting. I haven't even opened it. I didn't have time this morning. I feel guilty receiving letters from her because I don't write back. I intend to and then one thing after another gets in the way. 'How long does it take to write one letter?' Dad nags me. 'She really would love to hear from you.' Stevie Wonder fizzles out and fresh clouds of smoke magic their way down the catwalk.

The photographer from *Tatler* takes one last picture of all the models standing together. 'Lastly, and most importantly, I would like to thank Mr Todhunter for allowing me to use his fabulous home for the event, especially at such short notice,' I announce. Everyone applauds as I shake his hand. 'Please do stay on for a drink, and thank you all once again for coming tonight.' The crowd claps one last time and then starts to break up.

I feel a warm arm slide round my waist and turn round. 'Sam.'

'Congratulations, babe, it was sensational.' He kisses me, his baby-soft skin brushing against my cheek.

'You missed half of it.' But I smile, my earlier agitation melting at the sight of him.

'I saw the better half.'

'Sorry for snapping earlier, Sam. I was having my usual panic attack before the show.' I pull a silly frantic face at him.

'It's cool, don't worry about it.' He loosens his tie and then leans towards me and whispers, 'Is the old soak in the corner here?'

Emma makes her way towards me, dressed in sensible black working trousers and a turquoise cardigan. She's a doctor and has probably come straight from the hospital. But before we manage to say hello: 'Katie darling, that was the best show yet,' says Antonia, one of my customers who lives round the corner from the shop. 'I need to get rid of my post-birth stomach though before I can even think of purchasing some of those slinky outfits.' She laughs at herself, waiting for one of us to say she looks fabulous considering.

'You've got your figure back so quickly, Antonia,' I reassure her, 'you could get away with wearing any of my clothes.'

'Really?' She blushes. 'Well, I may pop by tomorrow and have a trying-on session. I have a very smart engagement party to go to.'

'Well, I'm sure FIB can sort you out. How's the new baby?' I ask.

'I might take it back to the store,' she chuckles at her own joke, 'and ask for a refund. Just a few nights' sleep would be nice.'

Sam, Emma and I make understanding noises although we do not really have a clue. Emma is the nearest of us to having children as she is engaged to Jonnie. 'Antonia, this is Emma, an old school and family friend, and Sam, my'—Partner? No.—'my boyfriend,' I finish.

'Well, I strongly advise that you two take precautions.' She nods at Sam and me, laughing again at her own humour. 'It is *exhausting*. If I'm honest, I never wanted to have more than one child, but my husband says it's selfish to have only one child. They always say only children are spoilt brats, don't they?'

'I'm an only child,' chips in Sam. I see him wink at Emma.

Antonia reddens. 'Do you have family, Katie? I'm sure they're so proud of you and what you've achieved.' She glances round the room. 'Your parents must be here tonight?'

'No, sadly they couldn't make it.' I look at Emma and Sam, hoping they might change the subject. Instead Sam asks me where the loos are and excuses himself.

'That's a shame. Do you have brothers? Sisters?' she asks inquisitively. I look around. Sam is out of earshot. 'No, it's just me. Little old me.' Emma gives me a long hard look. It's funny how just one small question can have an instantly sobering effect.

'Oh,' Antonia says hollowly. 'Well, never mind. It's OK to be an only child, I mean, like I said, I would have stopped at one.'

'Emma, don't.' I pull a warning face as we move away from Antonia.

'It's up to you,' she says in a spiky tone that makes me feel uneasy.

'It's just easier, then I get no awkward questions.'

'It's fine,' Emma says, but her tone is no more forgiving. 'If you think it's best, you carry on. Don't worry about it.'

The drinks come round again and we each take a glass.

'Right, back to business,' I say, making my way over to Hen's mother with a glass of champagne.

Sam turns the key and we walk inside. He and I have been going out for nine months and I moved in with him after only three. Sam works in the City. He used to be a currency trader, that's how he made his money. Now he works in mergers and acquisitions and lives in Notting Hill, a stone's throw from Portobello Market. It was an impulsive move on my part, but neither of us could see the point of being apart because I was staying with him almost every night. I can hop on a number 94 bus in the mornings, which takes me directly to Turnham Green. I used to live in Clapham with my last boyfriend, and that was more of a trek. Also, Sam has a wide-screen television in every room, and even a steam room on the top floor. How could I say no when he asked me to move in?

Mum was immediately suspicious, firing questions at me. 'Who is this man, Katie? You jump from one relationship to another like there's no tomorrow.' Her reaction didn't altogether surprise me but it made me want to move in with him even more.

Sam picks up the mail from the floor, which is mostly junk. 'Nothing that can't wait here,' he says, chucking it onto the table in the hallway. He wraps his arms round me. 'You are a fashion goddess, my darling.'

I kiss him. 'Thanks so much for helping me organise this evening.' I know Sam went out of his way to ask Mr Todhunter if we could use his house for the show. 'I couldn't have done it without you, you know.'

Sam's face burns with pride. 'It was my pleasure. We're a team, you and me. The best.'

I look over his shoulder. The red answering-machine light is flashing. I feel certain the message is for me.

'How about a liqueur? Cognac?' Sam starts to hum as he skips down-stairs to the kitchen.

'Yes, I'd love one.' I look at the machine again. Why do I feel I ought to see who called? I take off my high heels and decide that I might as well see who left a message.

'A steam?' Sam suggests before I press the button. He is holding two glasses and a bottle of Cognac. 'Leave it till tomorrow. It'll only be Maguire. He said he'd call tonight.' He takes my hand and grins. 'I've got a surprise for you, come on.'

'Really?' I laugh and turn away to follow him upstairs.

After a quick early-morning run to blow away the hangover, I arrive at the shop with my usual cappuccino and croissant, and a *pain au chocolat* for Eve, who is addicted to chocolate. I find her studying the books to see how last night went. 'We have many orders, especially for the French lace dresses, and many people for the mailing list,' she says, looking even more delighted when I hand her the pastry.

'That's wonderful! Last night went even better than I expected. Eve, I have to tell you,' I continue passionately, 'Sam is taking me skiing this Christmas, to Meribel! It was a surprise, he left the tickets on my pillow.'

'He is a dream,' she sighs. 'Hector and I, we do not get on very well at the moment.' Hector is her boyfriend. 'You two are very serious, *non?*' Eve is French. When I advertised for a new shop assistant six months ago, she was a league ahead of anyone else, wearing a black ribbed polo neck with a camel suede skirt, her long honey-blonde hair scooped into an immaculate ponytail.

'I guess we are serious. I'm such a lucky girl.'

'And he is lucky too. Perhaps he is "the one", Katie?'

'Perhaps.' I smile back at her.

It's late in the evening and I am about to lock up for the night. There is a tap on the shop window and I see Sam outside wearing his shades, holding a bottle of wine wrapped in tissue paper and a bunch of lilies.

I open the door and he kisses me and hands me the flowers. 'Thought I'd pick you up from work today. I finished early for a change.'

'What are these for?' I grin. 'Skiing and now flowers *and* a chauffeur. If you keep this up, I'll never want to leave you, so you'd better watch out.'

'That's the whole idea, Kitty-kins,' he says, as he kisses me again. It's a hot summer's evening and friends are meeting in restaurants after work, talking and drinking in the last of the sun. 'Remember, we're going out tonight,' Sam reminds me as he opens the front door.

'Are we? What are we doing?'

'I wrote it down in our social calendar, Katie. Dinner with Maguire and his new lady.' Sam breaks out into a little tap dance when he says 'lady'. 'He said he was going to get the barbecue going.'

'Great. Sorry, it slipped my mind. It's been hectic today, Eve and I didn't have a moment off.' I walk over to the answering machine and press PLAY. 'Can you fix us a drink, Sam? A nice glass of wine?' I add.

'Katie, it's your father,' says the familiar voice in a serious tone.

I stand rooted to the spot. This must be the message from last night. I knew something was up. I could feel it.

'I need to talk to you. It's'—he coughs—'it's really quite urgent.'

I swallow hard. Oh my God, something has happened to Mum. Or maybe Bells. He must wonder why I haven't called him back.

Sam looks at me curiously. 'Your old man never calls here.'

Sam is right. Dad always calls me at the shop. Why didn't he call me there today if it is so urgent?

'It's your mother, she's been working herself into the ground,' Dad continues. 'You know what she's like. We went to the doctor's and he strongly recommended a break. We haven't had a proper holiday for years. I'm taking her away. *So*,' he lingers on the word, 'we need to talk about who is going to look after Bells.'

Bells. Don't say anything more, Dad, please. Ask me to call you back and hang up.

'Who's Bells? Is that your dog?' Sam looks at me.

I nod. 'Sam, that glass of wine?' I say, praying he will go downstairs to the kitchen.

'Katie, you know I hate pets.'

I wrinkle my forehead at him. 'Drink?'

'Your mother and I are going to France for two weeks,' Dad continues, 'and Bells will need someone when we go away, we can't leave her on her own.'

'I've just bought those new leather sofas too,' Sam protests.

'Go and run me a bath,' I demand now, feeling myself burning under my skin.

'I need to talk to you, to make a plan,' Dad continues. 'I'm out all day tomorrow so can you call me back tonight?' There is a lengthy pause.

I want to say, *Dad, hang up, please, otherwise I will never forgive you*, but I am unable to utter a word. Besides, I cannot say anything when Sam is next to me. His presence feels like a loaded gun.

Dad draws in breath again, a habit I have inherited from him.

Sam laughs. 'He sounds so serious. It's only a dog, isn't it, Katie? Anyone would think he was talking about the future of the euro.'

My agitation reaches boiling point. 'Sam, go and run me a bath, *please*.'

He pushes past me. 'OK, OK. "Run me a bath, make me a drink",' he mimics.

'If I don't hear from you, I'll call you back later,' Dad finishes.

I feel as if I can breathe again when I hear the machine indicate the end of the call, followed by 'You have no new messages'.

'Sorry, Sam,' I say when he comes back with a drink and I can hear the bath water running strongly. 'I didn't mean to get snappy. It's Dad, he's such a worrier. I'd better call him. You go up, get ready for tonight.'

'No dog, Katie. Sorry.' Sam shakes his head as he goes upstairs. 'You can live here but no dog. End of story. *Capisce*?'

It's two o'clock in the morning and I cannot find my cigarettes. Sam would never have known I wasn't enjoying myself, but the evening was dismal for me because I could not stop thinking about Bells. Why did it have to happen now, when things are running so smoothly? And where has Sam hidden those cigarettes? There is nothing in Sam's kitchen. All the surfaces are kept carefully bare except for this art sculpture made out of what look like coloured milk bottles. Sam tells me it reflects the mood of the modern world.

I open one of the cupboards and run my eyes over the shelves. Then I stand on tiptoe and run my hand along the top of the cupboards. I could kill him. If I want a cigarette, why shouldn't I smoke one? I open each drawer impatiently, slamming it shut when no cigarettes are revealed. In my mind I replay my call to Dad earlier this evening.

'Katie, we know it's a lot to ask, but I need you to help,' he'd said.

'This is all so sudden, why didn't you tell me how tired Mum's been? How is she now?' I asked, biting my lip.

'She'll be fine, as long as she has a break and we take some time off.'

'Right,' I acknowledged. 'I know you need a holiday, but I'm not sure I can look after Bells. It's such short notice.'

'It's all booked,' Dad said firmly.

It is so unlike him to go ahead without asking me. I might be going on holiday too, or abroad on business. 'Couldn't you ask Aunt Agnes. She'd love to have Bells.'

'Bells wants to stay with you.'

'Why?' My voice was a loud whisper. 'I can't have her to stay here.'

Dad's patience snapped like a wafer. 'Can't or won't?'

'What about my shop? I can't drop everything. I'm sorry.'

'Now listen here, Katie. Your mother and I need this time together and Bells specifically asked if she could be with you in London. I told her she must write to ask you yourself. Didn't you get her letter?'

Dad sounded so stern I daren't say I had not opened it. 'It must have got lost in the post, it's so unreliable these days.'

'Oh, Katie.' He raised his voice in exasperation. 'Why won't you write to her? She's always asking after you. "How's Katie? Never see Katie."'

I could almost hear Bells saying that and my heart melted for a split second. Back to reality. 'Dad, two weeks is a long time. It's not as though I'm in my own home.'

'I understand you would have to ask Sam. We would help towards costs and—'

'No, the cost isn't the issue.' Sam came downstairs in his towel at this point and asked why I was taking so long. The bath was ready. A thought came to me. I could persuade him to go on a golfing weekend with Maguire. He would never know. 'I could have her for a weekend?'

'And where is she going to stay for the rest of the time then?'

'Can't she stay in Wales?' was my desperate last attempt.

'Well, she could, but that's miserable, quite frankly,' he said, his voice loaded with frustration.

'I'm sorry, Dad. I really can't. If I had my own apartment—'

He cut me short. 'That's not the real reason, is it, Katie?'

'What do you mean?'

'Isn't it high time you shared some responsibility for your sister? Are you going to pretend she doesn't exist for the rest of your life? You can't always leave it up to your mother and me. What would you do if something happened to us? Have you ever—'

'What do you mean, something happened to you? Like what? Everything is OK, Dad, isn't it?'

'All I meant was, your mother and I aren't always going to be here for Bells. You will have to take over some day, be her guardian. Katie, I'm not trying to scare you, but it is something you need to think about. Anyway, if you won't have Bells to stay, you call her and tell her yourself.' Dad's voice was trembling with anger now.

'All right, I'll have her to stay,' I told him reluctantly.

There was this great sigh of relief. 'Thank you,' Dad said.

Now, frustrated in my search for cigarettes, I put the kettle on to make myself a cup of tea. Is it unfair to expect Sam to have Bells to stay for two weeks? If it were my home, well, that'd be different, I reason to myself. Oh, God, who am I fooling? Yet I am furious that my parents have put me in this position.

I massage my forehead, desperately trying to think of an alternative. I can't go back up to bed, I won't be able to sleep. The kettle boils in the background. How am I going to cope with my sister? How will I introduce her to my friends? To Eve? To Sam?

Should I phone Aunt Agnes? Bells would have a much nicer time staying with her. I used to love my holidays there. I dig into my handbag to find my diary. In it is Bells's letter. I open it. The address, date and time are neatly underlined in the right-hand corner.

To my sister Katie Fletcher

Mum and Dad to stay in France and it would be very kind you have me to stay in summer holidays. To stay with Aunt Agnes, Suffolk too far, would be very loveley to stay with Katie in London please. Its very Longtime, since I saw you.

Love, Bells

I fold the letter and tuck it back into my diary. How can I say no?

347

1982

I am seven years old. I like staying with Aunt Agnes who lives in Suffolk, near the sea. She is very pretty and wears glasses, attached to small brown beads like a necklace, and a long checked apron when she is cooking. She makes the best Black Forest gâteau with flakes of real dark chocolate, and she cooks homemade chips with real potatoes in a large deep pan. She has these pointed shoes which look like witch's shoes and a train set that I play with in her large garden.

Her husband is funny. Uncle Roger. Once he sat back in his chair and the whole thing collapsed. I think their house is spooky. Uncle Roger swears to me that he has seen the ghost of his father at the top of the stairs. At night I run as fast as I can up those haunted stairs and into my bedroom. 'She is only a little girl but I think she's going to crash right through them,' I overheard Uncle Roger say once.

I am staying with my uncle and aunt while Mum has her baby. Mum finds being pregnant difficult. She has had three miscarriages—Dad explained to me what they were—and during this last pregnancy she has been in bed most of the time. Now it's time for me to go back home. 'Your mother has had a baby girl,' Aunt Agnes tells me. 'You'll need to help your mum a lot. She will be very tired.' She isn't smiling and keeps on glancing sideways at Uncle Roger who is shrugging his shoulders.

Aunt Agnes has been so excited all the time I have been staying, constantly showing me baby knitwear patterns and asking me whether she should make the booties pink for a girl, or perhaps 'sit tight' in case it is a boy. Aunt Agnes can't have children, Mum and Dad told me. That's why they like to pack me off to her in the holidays. Now Aunt Agnes looks as if she doesn't know what to say about the new arrival. It's as if this is bad news.

She hugs me on the platform and tells me to be brave. I cannot understand it. I am seven years old and I travel on my own to and from Suffolk. There is nothing to be brave about. The train trundles back to my parents' home, and I go to the buffet car and pick out a marshmallow biscuit with strawberry filling and a packet of cheese and onion crisps. In between mouthfuls I try to imagine what my baby sister will look like.

Dad meets me at the station as usual, wearing his dark-rimmed glasses and looking even thinner and longer than he usually does. My dad is over six foot two inches. Today he is wearing his scruffy jeans which he normally only wears around the house and his knitted chunky grey jumper that matches his hair. He always complains that he turned grey too early in life. On the way home I want to ask lots of questions about the new baby. Yet I feel as if I have a marble stuck in my throat which makes it impossible to ask. Instead, we drive home in silence. Eventually Dad says something. 'Your mother is tired,' he tells me, just as Aunt Agnes did. He tells me I must be a good girl. He is gripping the steering wheel so hard I can see his knuckles turning white.

'We're back,' Dad calls loudly. Everything is quiet in the house. Normally, when I return home from school or whatever I have been doing, I hear Mum in her studio with classical music playing in the background. Today we walk upstairs, towards my parents' bedroom with their big double bed covered with a quilted bedspread Mum made out of her wedding dress.

Mum is sitting on her bedside chair with her old bed jacket on. I kiss her on the cheek but she doesn't move, just sits there quietly. There is something wrong about Mum being so quiet. It is unlike her.

The crib stands in the middle of the room. It looks lonely and no noise comes from it. Mum looks over to Dad, who seems to be making some kind of secret sign at her. Her eyes look red and puffy.

'Before you see your new sister . . .' Dad starts slowly. I know then that something is wrong and I am scared. Immediately I walk over to the crib and look down.

CHAPTER TWO

'DID YOU REALLY BELIEVE Sam would never meet her?' asks Emma. She grinds some pepper onto our hummous. We are eating at a local Greek restaurant. It is our regular Tuesday night out. Emma and I go to a yoga class followed by a drink and supper. Sam plays poker on Tuesdays with Maguire and a few of his other workmates.

Emma tilts her head sideways, her forehead furrowed in concentration. Emma and I know almost everything about each other as we have been friends for twenty-five years. She was once my next-door neighbour. We went to school together, ballet classes together. She's tall and willowy now, but when she was little she was 'partridge-shaped' as my dad used to say.

We used to have a dressing-up box at home and we would put on my mother's old fur coats and stilettos and strut down to the shops together with Peggy, Mum's dog. I spent most of my time at Emma's house. When things at home were difficult, or if Mum and Dad were at the hospital visiting Bells, I stayed with Emma. I worshipped Emma's sister, Berry, because she was so pretty and everything I wanted to be. Emma is the only person I can talk to about Bells as she grew up with both of us.

'I knew Sam would meet her some day, if we were serious,' I finally reply.

'*Are* you serious?' She dips her pitta into the hummous.

'Yes, I think we are.'

'Then this is the perfect opportunity to tell him. It's given you the push you need. Otherwise, when will you?' she asks, almost accusingly.

'It has never been a conscious decision not to tell him about Bells,' I fight my own corner. 'He knows I have a sister, I just haven't told him much about her, that's all. Sam's not a curious person. He has never asked me what my sister does, hasn't even met my parents. I've never met his, come to that.'

Since going out with Sam I have discovered that his father worked overseas when he was young, leaving Sam and his mother behind most of the time. 'Mum and I were fine,' he insisted when I asked him once if he'd missed his father. 'We had a great time. Mum had a ball, in fact, when Dad left. Used to take me to all the parties. Think she got sloshed half the time,' he recalled with a short, dry laugh. 'Yeah, we had a grand time, Mum and I.' Sam doesn't like admitting anything is wrong. 'Life is for living, not for dwelling on, Katie,' he always says.

I know it's not really as simple as Sam makes it sound. Yet I've never felt able to tell him about my family; about how much I hated not seeing more of Mum after Bells arrived. Anyway, it doesn't matter because Sam doesn't ask. I don't need to explain anything.

'Eat some of this,' Emma demands, pushing the plate of hummous and pitta bread in my direction. 'You haven't touched your food.'

I look at the plate dispassionately. 'I'm not hungry.' Instead I pour myself another glass of wine.

'I think you're overreacting to the whole situation,' she says directly. 'You're not the only one to go through something like this, you know. Dad did exactly the same thing with Mum.'

'Really?' I look up.

'Yes.' Emma nods authoritatively. 'He didn't introduce her to his eccentric brother. You know, Uncle Spencer? Big ears, plays the piano very badly, rides a motorbike and wears dodgy purple ties?'

'I know Uncle Spencer.' I smile. 'He's the one who can tell you what day of the week you were born from the date of your birthday.'

'Exactly.' Emma laughs. 'He's wonderful, but he lives on another planet. Dad thought Mum might call off the engagement if she met him, so he was very wily and Mum met Uncle Spencer for the first time at the wedding. Apparently, he arrived on his motorbike wearing an extraordinary black shirt with a gold tiger on it.' She wrinkles her nose.

'Well, there you go!' I beam triumphantly, topping up my glass of wine. 'Your dad would understand then. *You* should too.'

'I do understand. But I asked Mum if it would have made any difference had she met Uncle Spencer before they married, and she said no. She was adamant. She would have married Dad anyway. He was a silly old fool who worried too much.'

'Ems, I do see what you're saying, I just feel Sam has to seriously fall in love with me before I introduce him to Bells. It's only been nine months and they have been fantastic. I'm happy. I don't want to risk Bells meeting him and whacking him hard in the balls.'

Emma's face dissolves into a smile. 'She doesn't do that any more though, does she? Come off it, that was when we were . . . what? Fourteen? Fifteen? And we are talking Toby, the prick who wore tight leather jackets and thought he was in *Grease*. And Ben who drew phallic diagrams all over his pencil cases. Bells did you a favour,' she laughs.

'I know,' I concede. 'Actually Ben got on quite well with her. But, Emma, it's two whole weeks. It's not a weekend, a few days, it's a whole fortnight. That's three hundred and thirty six hours. That's twenty—'

Emma stops me. 'Katie, this is ridiculous. You've got to stop worrying so much. Bells is not your average sister, but so what? She wants you to be a part of her life. Just this evening I had to see a young girl with leukaemia, for God's sake. You need to put it in perspective.'

The waiter takes our plates away. 'I know you're right,' I say, hanging my head with shame. 'I'm sorry, Emma, your job must be very difficult.'

She shrugs her shoulders. 'Bells gets on with it. You need to as well. When did you last see her? I mean, properly?'

'Last Christmas. I went home for a night.'

'You need to spend more time with her. You never know, you might actually enjoy her company. Things always come along to test us,' Emma continues. 'Life never stays on a nice even keel, it doesn't work like that.'

As she is saying this half of me wants to reply, 'What's ever tested you?' Emma's life is so utterly perfect. She gets on with her family, her brother is an architect, she has a close relationship with her parents,

Jonnie adores her. It's unfair though I would never say so. But it doesn't stop me thinking it occasionally.

'You don't see enough of your mum either, Katie. You might regret it one day.' She waits for my response. 'What's wrong? There's something else, isn't there?' she probes. 'Is it your mother?'

I tell Emma about my conversation with Dad. 'It seems a bit sudden, that's all. I can't help wondering if he's keeping something from me.'

'Your dad wouldn't lie,' Emma says with conviction. 'Look, I think they just want you to start making more of an effort with Bells.'

'Mum didn't even ring to ask me how my show went,' I tell her.

'OK, but did you ask her to be there?' Emma's patience is running out.

'No. Oh,' I wave a hand dismissively, 'I know. I'm nearly thirty, not sixteen. It shouldn't get to me like this.' I sink back into my chair and try to relax. 'I just wish I had told Sam straight away about Bells.'

'Tell him your sister's coming to stay. Describe her so he won't be too surprised, and I bet you he'll be fine about it. Tell him tonight. Don't put it off any longer.'

1982

'Katie,' Dad says sternly, 'don't upset your mother.'

I can't help it. I peer down into the cot again. 'But what's wrong with her?' I turn to look at Mum and Dad. 'Why hasn't my sister got a proper nose? It's all squashed down. And what's that funny hole between her nose and lip?' Mum is crying now, and Dad crouches down beside her, stroking her arm gently.

'Why does she look so funny?' I ask again. I can't look at the baby any more. It's scaring me.

'Katie,' Dad begins, 'this is the way she was born. I am afraid not all children are lucky enough to be born perfect.'

'Why?'

Dad takes off his glasses and wipes his eyes. 'Just because. We're going to have to help her. Your sister will have to see a doctor who will make her face better. It's going to be all right. We're—'

'Stop!' Mum sobs. 'Nothing's all right. How are we going to cope?'

'We'll manage. We'll make sure we do,' Dad reassures her. 'Katie will help us, won't you, darling?' He looks at me as if to say, Don't just stand there, come over and give your mother a hug.

Was this what Aunt Agnes meant by being brave? I walk over to Mum and put my arms round her.

The doctor is here and I am listening at the kitchen door. I am supposed to be doing my homework in my room.

'There is an excellent local team of specialists in facial-oral problems. They're very experienced in treating children born with a cleft of the lip and palate,' he is saying reassuringly. 'One child in approximately seven hundred and fifty births has this problem. We will also consult a plastic surgeon for advice. He will talk us through the reconstructive surgical procedures. With a series of operations, we can repair your daughter's lip and palate.'

'When can we start?' Dad asks.

'While she is still a baby but a bit bigger and able to cope with the surgery.'

'I don't understand why this happened. I felt fine during the pregnancy, I had plenty of rest . . .' Mum pleads for an explanation.

'It's not your fault,' Dad immediately tells her.

The doctor agrees. 'There is no known cause. Is there any family history, do you know?'

'No, not that I'm aware. I was sure I had done everything right,' Mum continues oblivious. 'But I should have had a scan. I should have—'

'Stop it,' Dad raises his voice. 'Don't continually blame yourself.'

'The specialists will go through everything with you. I know it's hard to take in, but we are very experienced in this field.' The doctor clears his throat. I can feel a terrible silence stretching out before he adds, 'I am afraid there is a further problem. She could be brain-damaged, though to what extent precisely we do not know at the moment.'

'Brain-damaged?' Mum says numbly.

'Yes. We'll carry out more tests but she will need a lot of your time and attention to begin with . . .'

'Her name is Isabel,' Dad cuts in. 'We've always loved that name.'

'Isabel, right. You have another girl too, don't you?' the doctor enquires.

'Yes, Katie. But there's no way I can manage the two of them on my own,' Mum says. 'We need help. I mean, how will I feed Isabel? How will I . . . my baby's really brain-damaged?'

Poor Mum. This is so unfair. I will help. Let me help.

'We'll be fine.' Dad speaks softly to her. 'We'll get through this together.'

I hear the doctor stand up to leave. I rush away from the door and run upstairs to my bedroom.

Mum doesn't come upstairs to say good night to me like she usually does. Dad comes instead. It seems dark and cold in my bedroom and I feel very alone as I hear his heavy footsteps walk away from me.

CHAPTER THREE

I PICK UP THE PICTURE of Sam in the silver frame by my bedside. He is wearing the white cotton shirt with the pale blue stripe that I bought him for his birthday, and his dark sunglasses are perched on the top of his head. He is looking directly at the camera with a confident smile. Sam is handsome and he knows it. Virtually every feature is symmetrical except for one of his nostrils which is not as open as the other—he puts that down to his mother smoking when she was pregnant with him.

I still have not told him about Bells. I have put it off for a week now and she is arriving tomorrow. I am picking her up from Paddington. I don't know why I believe the problem might go away if I don't talk about it. The phone rings. It's Dad. They are leaving tomorrow. 'Who are you staying with in France?' I ask.

'The Walters.'

I don't recognise the name. 'Who are they?'

'Old friends. He used to work with me at Sotheby's. They moved to France when you were about two.' Dad changes the subject quickly. 'Now, you've got my mobile . . .'

'Actually, could I take down the Wallers' number?' I ask.

'Walters,' he corrects.

'Can I have their number?'

'No, you won't need it.'

'Well, you never know.'

'We'll call you.'

'I think I ought to have it.' Our conversation is like a fast game of ping-pong.

'Just ring us on the mobile.'

'What if there's an emergency?'

'There won't be an emergency.'

'Why can't I have their number? Why are you being so funny about it?'

'Darling,' Dad finally slows the pace of his answers, 'it's simply easier if you ring us on the mobile. That way you can call at any time of day.'

I agree to this, unwillingly. 'Remember to turn it on then,' I say.

Dad always says he bought the mobile 'for emergency use only', but fails utterly to understand it is useless if he doesn't first switch it on.

'Yes, don't worry,' he protests.

'So, what will you be doing with the Walters?'

'Swimming, eating, sleeping, reading books. Darling, I have to go now. Will you thank Sam very much?' he finishes.

I put the phone down feeling uneasy. I am going to have to tell Sam about Bells tonight. I rang him from the shop a little earlier, saying he mustn't work late, that I am cooking him his favourite meal—steak with homemade chips, just like Aunt Agnes's. I have even made him a pudding: orange ice-cream cake with dark chocolate sauce. 'What have I done to deserve this, Katie?' I could hear his chair swivelling round. 'Are you feeling guilty about shagging someone behind my back?' And then he crowed with incredulity. Sam has enough arrogance to bottle and sell internationally, yet that is what I find most attractive about him. I always thought I would end up falling for an academic or maybe a writer. I never thought I would go for someone like Sam. Then again, I fancy Simon Cowell off X-Factor, which just about says it all.

I put the photograph frame back down on the bedside table, then open the sliding doors to our wardrobe and look at my clothes, neatly folded into different compartments, and the dresses, trousers and skirts hanging up. What shall I wear? I go for the dark red lace top with the velvet trim around the neck. I'll wear my black lacy bra underneath. Bottom half will be my Diesel jeans worn with black pointed boots. Sam likes this outfit. I look at myself in the long mirror. My hair, now dyed back to its original dark brown, hangs loose around my face. I pin it up with a clip. I have my father's fine hair. In fact, I have inherited most of my features from Dad; the long Fletcher nose, the high cheekbones, the wide mouth and my dimple.

I open one of the mirrored cupboards in our bathroom to find some cotton-wool pads and cleanser. Sam gets infuriated with me if I leave my toothpaste or cotton-wool pads lying around in the bathroom; everything has to be packed neatly into the mirrored cupboards.

I wipe the day's make-up off my face. From Mum I've inherited a splattering of freckles across my nose and cheeks, and my olive-green eyes. Dad always says he fell for her eyes straight away. When I first met Sam he told me I had 'come-to-bed eyes'. Wait till he sees Bells's eyes which are far more beautiful. They're a vivid green with no sludgy grey in them at all. I sit on the edge of the bath and start to run the water. I pour in a large capful of neroli oil and step into the sweet-scented water.

Tonight will be fine. I will tell Sam, he will be cool with it, everything will be OK, I reassure myself for what must be the hundredth time.

Later I light the dark red candle in its glass candlestick and finish laying the table. I open the fridge and pour myself a second glass of white wine. Sam should be here any minute now. I hear a key turn in the front door and something jolts sharply inside me. I breathe deeply, I think about Emma's advice to come clean.

'Hi, honey,' I call. I hear him coming downstairs, taking the steps two by two. The room smells of chips frying in golden oil. Dido is playing softly in the background. Sam likes her. He walks up to me and hands me a large bunch of scarlet and orange tulips: my favourite. I thank him with a kiss and he wraps his arms round my waist, pulling me close to him. 'Kitty-kins.' He rubs his nose against mine. 'I'm a lucky boy. I raced home. Not too late, am I?'

'Perfect timing. Good day?'

'Great day in the markets. Fabulous. Wham, bam, thank you, ma'am.' He winks. 'And now I'm all yours. Smells fab, I am starving.'

'Sit down,' I instruct, leading him to a chair. He sits down and it is me rubbing his shoulders this time. 'Relax and I'll get you a drink first.'

'Are you softening me up?' Sam murmurs with pleasure.

'Can't a girl just spoil her boy?' I run a hand over his back. 'Right, what do you want to drink? Beer or wine?'

I still have not told him and we have just finished our first course. What is wrong with me? I cannot say a word. I open the fridge. When I put the orange pudding on the table I am going to tell him. The trick lies in saying the first part: 'Sam, my sister is coming to stay tomorrow, is that OK? She's not quite what you'd expect . . .' I am going to scare the living daylights out of him, aren't I?

The pudding sits in front of him. Sam rubs his stomach and smiles. 'I could get used to this star treatment.' He slices the orange pudding and cream seeps out, making patterns in the chocolate sauce.

'Sam, I have to tell you . . . I should have asked you before . . . but my sister is coming to London . . .' I start.

'Really?' He eats a spoonful. 'Yum,' he moans appreciatively. 'Delicioso.'

'I was hoping she could stay with us? My sister Isabel?' I remind him.

'Sure, for how long? I'd like to meet her.'

'Two weeks.'

'Right.' Sam mulls this over, looking surprised that it's for so long. 'No, that's OK, see no reason why not. Isabel's younger than you, isn't she? I could set Maguire up, he needs a new bird.'

'But he had a new "lady" only days ago.'

'Nah, that didn't work out,' Sam says. 'Maguire likes it short and sweet. So Isabel's coming up for two weeks? *Perfecto*. Does she look like you?' he goes on. 'Just a younger, more wrinkle-free version?'

'Sam,' I say with some irritation. 'Is that all you think about? Image?'

'Yep,' he says simply. 'Well, it helps if she's not a complete moose. Come on, girls are just the same. Blokes are more honest, that's all.'

I pick up my plate and walk over to the sink.

He holds up his hands in a gesture of apology. 'How old is she then?'

'Twenty-two.' I sit back down, stare at the candle I lit so hopefully. Pudding is over and I still have not told him the whole truth. By the time it burns out he will know everything about Bells, I vow.

'What does she do? Is she a lap dancer?'

'Oh, Sam,' I sigh.

'Don't tell me . . . she works for MI5 or something exciting like that? Seriously, why don't I get Maguire over here one night and introduce them? Do you reckon she'd go for someone like him?'

Bill Maguire. Tall, with very blond hair the colour of an egg yolk, and eyebrows and lashes to match. A predator when it comes to women and loves to tell dirty jokes. 'Um, I mean, Bill is great, but . . .'

'Is she single?'

'Yes. Sam, there's something I need to tell you about her, though.' I watch the candle flame glowing in the dark. I remember as a child running my finger through one and Mum telling me off. 'Don't play with fire, it's dangerous.' Sam comes over to me.

'I'm looking forward to meeting her, babe. She's coming to stay tomorrow? Great, she can sleep in the white bedroom. What else is there to say?' He starts kissing my neck. 'I love this top,' he tells me. 'Why are you so tense, babe?' He pulls me to my feet and we start to dance. We love dancing in the kitchen. It's our time together, just Sam and me. He spins me around, singing softly in my ear, and it tickles. We both laugh together.

Why does my family have to be different? I curse quietly to myself as Sam holds me. Wouldn't it be wonderful to be able to say, 'My sister's a lawyer'? Or an architect, philosopher, psychologist, artist, writer, charity worker. Why do I care so much? Surely I should be past this stage? Shouldn't I be mature enough to tell Sam?

Finally we stop dancing. 'Thanks for the lovely evening, Katie. You know how to spoil me.' He takes my hand, kissing each finger in turn.

I don't want to tell him, it doesn't feel right to tell him now.

Sam blows the candle out, still holding onto my hand. The smoke evaporates into nothing.

1984

As I walk across the school playground I can see my mother standing apart from a cluster of parents waiting by the iron gates. Bells is with her in the pushchair. What is she doing here? A mixture of panic and anger jabs at my chest. Mum never picks me up. What normally happens is I go to Mr Stubbington's corner shop to buy some sherbet dips and marshmallows and then walk home for tea with Emma, my next-door neighbour, where we toast our marshmallows by the fire.

Mum is wearing her grubby apron with paint and oil stains down the front, her bright red shoes which look more like clogs, and her auburn hair is still pulled back tightly in one of her cotton head scarves. All the other mothers wear long navy skirts and frilly blouses with pearls, and their hair is curled. Why does my mum have to look so different? Why did she have to bring Bells?

'Katie, what is it?' Emma asks impatiently. 'I'm hungry. Come on.'

'Mum's here, with Bells.' I pull her back.

'So?' Emma shrugs. 'I want to go home.'

I haven't told anyone in my class about Bells, they wouldn't understand. Emma is the only one who has seen her from the beginning. Bells's face looks so strange. They laugh at anything that looks weird. Has Mum seen me? I dart behind the boys' outside loo, but almost choke because it smells. I can hear the parents talking. My mother's voice is louder than any of the others, I think crossly. 'Just *go* then,' I tell Emma, waving her away. 'Tell Mum I had to stay behind in class . . .'

I can hear people walking off, engines being turned on, prams being pushed, dogs barking. I wait with my fingers clipped firmly to my nose.

'Hello,' I can hear Mum saying, trying to be friendly. 'Don't look so worried, she won't bite you. Her name's Isabel. We call her Bells.'

Who's Mum talking to? I poke my head round the wall. It's Imogen, from the year below, with her mother.

'What's wrong with her?' Imogen asks, unable to take her eyes away from the baby in the pram. 'What's that big hole in her face?'

'Imogen, don't be rude,' the mother interrupts, turning the colour of beetroot. 'It's the inside that counts after all, isn't it?' she says to Mum.

Mum says nothing.

Imogen still stands rooted to the spot. Piss off, I want to shout. Her mother eventually pulls her away.

I wait until it is quiet and safe to come out. I have to get the timing right. After roughly ten minutes I poke my head round the wall. Mum is bending down talking to Bells. There is no one else around. I bolt side-ways and then stroll forward as if I have come out of school.

'Hi, Mum. I had to tidy up the paints . . . and stuff,' I falter.

Mum eyes me suspiciously. 'Emma said you were showing your needlework to the headmistress.'

We start to walk, my head hung low.

'Are your feet suddenly fascinating?' Mum asks.

'Nope.' I shrug.

'I had a call today,' she says, as we walk on briskly, the pushchair rat-tling against the tarmac pavement. 'From Mr Stubbington.'

My whole body freezes.

'Katie, I am ashamed of you. I leave you to walk home on your own because I think you're old enough. Then I find you have been going into his shop and stealing from the charity bag. What has got into you lately?' Mum stops walking and turns to look at me.

Mr Stubbington has banned me from the shop for a week because he caught me trying to steal coins from the charity stocking. When he turned away to put some apples into a paper bag one afternoon, I could not resist plunging my hand into the stocking to try to get a fifty-pence piece from the netting of the toe. 'This money goes to help the aged,' he rebuked me furiously when he turned back and saw what I was doing.

I can offer her no explanation.

'Unless you promise to stop stealing, I will collect you every day,' Mum threatens. 'With Bells,' she adds.

Does she know how I'm feeling? 'I promise I won't do it again, Mum.' Two girls are walking towards us. They stop and gawk when they see Bells. 'What's wrong with it?' one of them asks. I am focusing on a crack in the pavement. If I step on this line it will bring me bad luck.

'"It" is my daughter, Isabel. She was born with a cleft lip and palate, and your staring doesn't help,' Mum says brusquely, walking past them. I turn to look at them and they are still standing there staring. 'What the hell is a cleft lip?' one of them asks the other.

'I'm sorry, Mum,' I say.

'It's all right, but please don't steal again. I have enough to do, just looking after this one,' she says wearily.

After that, Mum and I walk home quietly. 'Hello, Bells,' I say behind the closed door, stroking her hair. 'I'll give her her tea tonight,' I tell Mum because I know she is tired. I like mushing up Bells's food. 'How are you today? Have you had a good day?' I push her into the kitchen. The guilty lump in my stomach is growing.

CHAPTER FOUR

'I'LL MEET YOU at the station,' Sam suggests, cramming in a mouthful of toast and marmalade. 'What time does Isabel's train get in?'

'Don't worry, we'll meet you back home.' I don't know why I think delaying the meeting is going to help. At some point the bomb will go off.

'You know, I'm really looking forward to meeting her. I'm quite curious to know what a Fletcher sister will be like.'

'Sam, she is very different.' This is the perfect time to tell him. 'I haven't told you everything about her,' I say. 'When she was born . . .'

He pulls a face. 'Can it wait till tonight? I'm running late already.' He plants a kiss on my lips, picks up his briefcase, opens the front door. 'What's the plan for *ce soir*, by the way? Because I thought you, me, a few of the boys'—he winks at me—'could take Isabel out for a drink tonight, get her embroiled in London night life, maybe go to a club for a bit of cheeky dancing?'

I can't take this any more, I should have told him straight away, just as Emma advised. My chest feels so tight that there is no room for further pretence. I know that if I do not tell him now I shall explode. Emma did warn me that the longer it took to tell him, the harder it would get. 'Sam, Isabel isn't going to be what you think.'

'What?' He looks puzzled. 'What do you mean?'

'She was born with a cleft lip and palate. It's quite a common thing,' I add when I see his alarmed expression. 'But there was an added complication because Bells was brain-damaged at birth. She lives in a community in Wales and it's her summer holidays, that's why she's coming to stay.' I feel as if I can breathe again. I wait for a reaction.

'Bells? This was what you were talking to your dad about?' Sam is thinking out loud. 'You let me believe she was your dog.'

'I never actually said that. Bells . . . Isabel.' I shrug my shoulders. 'We call her Bells for short.'

'Right.' He slowly scratches his head. 'Right, I should have clicked. Well, that's OK. No, hang on,' his voice rises, 'why didn't you *tell* me any of this?'

'I don't know. I'm sorry. I thought you might hate the idea of her staying.

And I have no choice, she has nowhere else to go. Mum and Dad are in France. My mother's not well,' I explain, hoping this will make him a little more sympathetic.

'Well, it looks like I have no choice either.' He frowns. 'Katie, I don't know what to say. I'm lost for words. See you later.'

'Don't go, Sam.' I grab his arm. 'We need to talk.'

'We had all week to talk, Katie. I'll see you later.' He pulls his arm away and I close the door after him. I feel terrible. Sick to my stomach. I feel so guilty. I have been lying to myself, to Sam, to Bells. Why am I such a coward? Why didn't I say anything to Sam before?

'I hope her train is early, touching wood,' Eve says in her smoky French accent, tapping my desk.

For a moment I think about correcting her English but then I think I prefer it the way she says it. 'Thanks, Eve, if you can lock up . . .'

'Yes, yes, do not worry. I look forward to meeting your sister *demain*.' She unpins her honey-coloured hair. I have never seen such long hair. 'Where are you picking up Isabel?' she asks, tying it back up into a bun and sticking in a long hairpin.

'Paddington.'

A customer comes in looking for a wedding outfit. It's an evening do and she wants to wear a black dress with a coloured shawl which she has already bought. 'Can I leave you to it?' I ask Eve.

'Yes, yes, I see you tomorrow. Please, come this way,' she says to the customer. 'I think we have just the thing for you.'

As I drive to Paddington in Sam's BMW, I make a mental list of the things I still need to do. I went to Sainsbury's in my lunch hour to buy some fish and chips for tonight. When I agreed to have Bells I called home to get an idea of what I needed to plan for the two weeks. For the first time in years Mum's classical music wasn't on in the background.

'In Wales they have a Mexican night on a Monday, she loves chillies and hot spicy food, and they're always given fish and chips on a Friday with mushy peas. I get her the tinned peas, disgusting, I know, but Bells likes them. If you don't have time to cook at lunch she enjoys vegetable samosas. On Wednesdays I think they have their Indian nights. Or is it their organic night? I can't remember.' Mum's voice trailed off.

As I listened, I knew I wouldn't be able to cater for Bells every single night of the week. I rarely cook at Sam's. Most nights we eat out, and if we want to drink Sam pays for a cab home with his company card. 'I don't like cooking, I hate the mess, all the surfaces get gooey and sticky.

'I think Tuesday is organic night. Bells likes her routine, it's very important to her. They eat lunch on the dot of twelve thirty.'

'I'll do my best, Mum, but she has to fit in with what I'm doing too.'

Mum sniffed. 'She likes her Coke too, but buy her the Diet Coca-Cola or her teeth will rot. And do let her choose ingredients and cook for herself as well. She always prepares the meals at home.'

'That's fine. Is that all?' My patience was running out rapidly.

'Yes, make sure she always carries her inhaler. Her asthma is much better but we can't afford to take any risks.'

'I'll definitely make sure she carries her inhaler.'

'Thank you, darling.' Mum seemed tired, I could feel it in her voice.

'Mum, nothing's wrong, is it?'

'Wrong? What do you mean? Just because we're taking ourselves off on holiday does something have to be wrong?'

'Oh, forget it!' I was twisting the phone cable, knotting it around my finger so tightly that it was turning purple. Why was she so defensive? 'I didn't mean that. It's about time you and Dad had a holiday,' I acknowledged. 'I hope you have a lovely time. I'll see you when you get back.'

'Katie?'

'Yes?'

She cleared her throat. 'Thank you for helping out. It means a lot to your father and me.'

I sensed she wanted to say something else so I waited for a moment, but she said nothing more. ''Bye, Mum. Love to Dad.'

''Bye, my darling.'

The train pulls in to the platform. The doors are opened and passengers step out in a heaving mass, each person pushing past me, staring ahead purposefully. The men wear grey flannel suits and carry briefcases. Some of them have taken their jackets off in this heat and loosened their ties. A pregnant woman walks past in a blue cotton shirt and pair of loose-fitting trousers, a girl totters by in high heels and a short sundress.

The crowds are filtering away, leaving a dull, lifeless platform. Where is she? She can't have missed the train. I start to walk down the platform, looking into each carriage, but there is no sign of anyone. Then I hear a door open. I see a small figure stepping out of the train. She is wearing a denim jacket with lots of badges on it, a round embroidered hat that looks more like a doily over her head, and a red football scarf. She carries a large purple zip bag and a couple of plastic bags.

'Bells!' I say, quickening my pace towards her.

'Hello, Katie. How're you?' I am so relieved she has arrived that I almost hug her. Instead, I take her purple zip bag. 'Well done, you made it,' I say. We walk away from the platform, past the guard at the entrance. There is a heavy silence as we drive away.

When we arrive back at Sam's, I show Bells round the house. The kitchen is in the basement; on the ground floor is a large airy room with Sam's new black leather sofas and a fireplace that is controlled by slick silver controls; he has a dark mahogany bookcase filled with glossy hardback books that he hasn't touched. On the first floor are the bedrooms, and a cosy room with leather beanbags. If we are in, we pretty much live in this room. On the top floor is the luxury steam room with the big old-fashioned bath. 'This is my favourite room, Bells,' I tell her.

'Sam rich?' she asks.

'Yes, he is. He works very hard.' I take her back downstairs to her room, a large bedroom with a double bed, wardrobe, a long mirror whose frame I gilded and one small bedside table with an orange and white stained-glass lamp on it. More or less everything in this room is white. The only other piece of colour is the rug with great big orange and red circles on it. Bells sits on the bed. It is hard to know what she makes of Sam's house.

'What's your room like in Wales?' I ask, sitting down next to her.

'Not big like this,' says Bells. 'Have small bed and television and lots of posters. Room looks out on garden and sea. In my plot of land, I grow carrots and potatoes. We grow strawberries this year too.'

'We don't have a garden here,' I say apologetically. 'But you've got your own television in here, so that's something, isn't it?' I point to the big silver TV in the corner of her room. 'You can watch the tennis. Who do you think is going to win Wimbledon this year?'

'Agassi.'

'You cannot be serious,' I say, imitating John McEnroe very badly.

She looks at me with no hint of a smile.

'Shall we unpack?' I open her zip bag and out comes a medley of junk and clothes. 'Why have you got Mary Veronica's jumper?' I ask, showing Bells the nametag in the jumper. 'Is this all you packed? Odd jumpers, a few T-shirts and a pair of dungarees? Oh, hang on, you have one frilly pink blouse here that says it belongs to Jessica Hall. I think I'm going to have to get you some summer clothes,' I say, talking to myself rather than to her. 'You put all this away while I put the fish and chips on. Deal? You like chips on Fridays, don't you?'

'You have crinkle chips, like ones Mum makes?'

'I'm going to make homemade ones, like Aunt Agnes's.'

'Oh,' she acknowledges, and it's hard to tell whether she is pleased or not. 'How's Aunt Agnes?'

'I think she's fine,' I reply.

'Uncle Roger? He died. Poor Uncle Roger.'

'I know. Poor Aunt Agnes too. I think she gets quite lonely.'

'Poor Aunt Agnes. How's Mum?'

'Well, you know she's on holiday.'

'How's Dad?'

'He's on holiday too. Aren't they lucky? They're in France.'

'In France, that's right. How's Granny Norfolk?'

Our mother's mother, Granny, lives in Norfolk, hence the name. I don't know how she is, I haven't spoken to her in months. 'Fine, I think,' I say. 'Look, you've got your own music system too,' I tell her, trying to stop the tirade of questions about the Fletcher family. 'Come downstairs to the kitchen when you've finished. You'll meet Sam soon.'

I can hear my voice but it's not me. I can't seem to stop talking to her as if she were ten years old.

'He's really looking forward to meeting you. You'll be good, won't you?' I can't help adding. 'No dramas in front of Sam. We are going to have a really nice two weeks, aren't we?'

'No dramas,' she repeats.

'Good. Come down when you're ready.'

I am onto my second vodka. The chips are frying. First hurdle is over. Bells is here, we are getting on fine, I think. The second major hurdle is Bells meeting Sam.

Stevie Wonder starts to blast out of Bells's bedroom. I run upstairs and open her bedroom door. Bells is on the bed, pinning up a poster of David Beckham, his diamond earrings sparkling.

The lovely white room is now covered in football badges and stickers and a Beatles poster is stuck to the door, **SEX, DRUGS AND ROCK 'N' ROLL** written in big black letters at the bottom. It reminds me of Bells's bedroom in our parents' home. She had the master bedroom with the basin that I was envious of, and wallpaper with flowery borders. Bells did not like the wallpaper, though, so she drew pictures of animals and pinned up posters of her favourite pop singers, Stevie Wonder, David Bowie and the Beatles. Mum did not mind her ruining the wallpaper. She wasn't strict in that sense.

Top of the Pops is on the television and the entire floor is covered with clothes, joined by a sketchpad, a small wooden case of oil paints, a collection of CDs and a photograph album. I take a deep breath and bend down to pick the mess off the floor. 'Bells!' I shout. 'Turn it down!' I climb onto the bed. 'What are you sticking the posters down with?

You're not putting pins in the walls, are you? Sam doesn't like that.' Oh, God, she is. 'Bells, don't put pins in the walls,' I shout at her.

'Why?'

'It leaves a hole.'

She continues to push a pin into the white paint.

'Bells, hey! Don't do that. What did I just say?'

'We do in Wales. Mum lets me too.'

I look down at the bedspread. 'I don't care what you do in Wales, you're staying with Sam and me now.'

'Katie bossy,' she says.

I shrug. 'Bells, can you take your boots off? Sam likes you to take your shoes off when you come into the house.'

'Why?' she asks, and then starts to use the bed as a trampoline.

'What is going on? What's all the flipping noise?' I hear from behind.

I spin round on the bed and almost lose my balance. 'Bells, keep still! Stop it.'

'Hello,' Bells says, extending her small hand. 'You handsome.'

Sam looks at her strangely. 'What did she just say to me? Katie, what is going ON? What's with the TV and the music?' He looks around. 'This room is a pigsty.'

Bells starts to make piglike noises and I want to disappear under the floorboards.

'Is this your . . .' He can hardly get the words out.

'This is my sister Isabel. Bells.'

'Hello, you Sam?' she says again, still offering her small pale hand.

He shakes it limply. 'This is Bells?' He looks around the room again, despair written over his face. 'How has she put the posters up? She hasn't put drawing pins in the wall? Tell me she hasn't, Katie?'

'I'm sorry, I'll deal with it, honey, I promise,' I tell him.

Sam puts his head into his hands. I jump off the bed.

'What's that burning smell?' he shouts above the noise, then marches over to the stereo and turns off the music, followed by the television.

'No like Sam,' Bells says.

'Bells! Don't be rude.' Thankfully I don't think he understood what she just said. He's still sniffing the air with a look of disgust. 'Oh, shit, it's the chips,' I yelp, and dart out of the room.

The chips were burnt and Sam hated the mushy peas. He attempted to ask Bells a few questions about the train journey but couldn't understand what she was replying.

'I haven't got a clue what she just said,' he kept on repeating when

Bells was staring at him for a response. She started to hit the kitchen table with her fork in frustration, repeating her questions in vain.

I know Sam is still angry with me for not telling him about Bells and I can't say I blame him. He has gone out for a few drinks with Maguire. No doubt he is telling his friend what a 'mare' he is having. I try to read but I can't even focus on one line. I turn off the light and close my eyes.

Some time later, I wake with a feeling of panic. I feel disorientated as I turn on the light and look at my watch. It's only midnight. I shiver. The house is deathly quiet. When we were children, Bells used to sleepwalk and Mum had to put white bars over her bedroom window. I step out of bed and walk down the corridor, to Bells's room. I open the door and find the light glaring out at me. Mum had told me Bells still hates sleeping in the dark and that I must keep a small light on in her bedroom.

I can hear her deep breathing as she turns over in the large double bed. She is so tiny, just under five foot tall. She looks young for her age because of her height. She could also be mistaken for a boy from behind because of her short auburn hair. Dad says he never wants Bells to grow her hair. 'You must never hide behind your hair,' he told her when she started to be a self-conscious teenager. 'You look the world in the eye.'

I kneel down by her bed and watch her as she sleeps, absorbing each line and movement of her face. There is the familiar scar over her upper lip which crosses like two letter Cs. Her hand pokes out from the duvet. I gently touch it. It feels as soft as melting butter.

We tidied her room after Sam went out and put the snowy owl that Mum made for her on the bedside table. Bells loves owls. She has placed her inhaler on the bedside table, along with her photograph album, which she has covered with David Beckham stickers. Mum told me she takes her album everywhere when she is away from home, it is like her comfort blanket. I pick it up and quietly leaf through the pages.

By each photograph, inscribed on a small white sticker, is a precise date, time, location and description of the person photographed. There is a picture of Mum in her studio; a terrible picture of Dad with red eyes reading the newspaper; there is a picture of the water meadows where we used to walk as children. My parents live in St Cross, Winchester. We used to walk by the lake and feed the ducks and avoid getting too close to the swans. There's a picture of a man wearing a purple track suit and football sweatshirt, holding onto a parrot. I don't know who he is so I read the sticker. *Ted, 1990, St David's, in the garden, summertime.*

She opens her eyes and looks straight into me. I panic, thinking I should not be here, but then she shuts them again. I wonder what she dreams about when she goes to bed at night? When she was little she used to have nightmares. Dad said Bells was terrified of the dark as a result of all the surgery she had to go through as a young child.

I stand up to leave, the stillness of the room contrasting strongly with the chaos earlier in the evening. I stop when I hear her muffled voice.

'Nothing around me?' she says groggily.

'Nothing around you,' I whisper back, just as Mum used to reply.

'Promise?'

'I promise.'

1989

I climb the three steps into Mum's chalky-aired studio. Her classical music is on in the background, just as it always is. Mum's studio is like a play zoo with the parrots, a pair of cockatoos, a zebra, a giraffe, a tiger, a lioness and a few monkeys perched on shelves, some half-finished. Mum's a sculptor. She makes different kinds of animals out of clay. Her last project was a camel on bended knee.

'How are you, darling?' she asks, her neck craned over her work. Her auburn hair is tied back in a navy and white dotted scarf and she is wearing large silver hoop earrings. She looks like a Gipsy.

I realise the only time I get to see or talk to Mum is either when she is cooking or when she is in the studio.

'Good day at school?' she mutters, continuing with her work and humming along to the background music. I can see her hands are sticky from the clay. Mum, turn round, I think. Instead I walk in front of her.

'Good day?' she repeats distractedly.

I drop my satchel onto the floor. I don't tell her that I got told off yet again for wearing mascara. 'Go and wash that black goo off your face,' my boring maths teacher says again and again. Last weekend I was caught stealing a black eyeliner, mascara and a block of spot cover-up from Boots, and the police came by the house to talk to Mum and Dad. It has been suggested that we need family counselling.

'Not bad. What are you listening to?'

'Classic FM. Puccini, *Madam Butterfly*.'

'What are you working on? Who's that for?'

'It's a cheetah.' She sits back and admires it. 'My mother took us to a wildlife orphanage in Africa when we were little. I remember this cheetah rolling on its back for me like a big tame cat. Did you know, the name "cheetah" comes from a Hindi word meaning "spotted one"?'

I shake my head. 'What are those dark lines by its eyes? Has your paint run?'

'Run? No! You are funny. Those are tear lines.' Finally she looks at me. 'Do you like him?'

'Oh, I love him. I think he is beautiful. He doesn't look as if he would want to harm anyone.'

'Here, have him, he's all finished.'

'Really?' I smile. 'But who were you making it for?'

'That doesn't matter.' She ruffles my hair and smiles. 'He's yours now.'

CHAPTER FIVE

I WAKE UP feeling disorientated again. I feel sure I was back at home, in Mum's studio. I can even smell the white spirit. Since the news that Bells was coming to stay I have been thinking a lot about home, particularly about Mum. Sam is still fast asleep. He must have crawled into bed at about four this morning. I slip my feet into my stripy zebra slippers and put on my silk dressing gown. I walk into Bells's bedroom but she is not there. She must be downstairs. I find her at the kitchen table poking the milk-bottle sculpture. She is wearing grey baggy track-suit bottoms and her red Oxford University T-shirt. Where did she get that?

'Careful, Bells.'

'What's this?'

'Do you like it?'

'No.'

I half smile. 'Don't say that to Sam. It's his favourite piece of art.'

'Don't like Sam.' She withdraws her hand from the sculpture immediately, as if she is touching something dirty.

'You don't know Sam,' I point out firmly. 'You mustn't judge so quickly. You be nice to him, OK?'

'Don't like him,' she states coldly.

'Bells, this is Sam's house. He has been kind enough to have you to stay. You need to get to know him. Do you want some breakfast?'

'In Wales have muesli for breakfast. Make it ourselves.'

'We need to go to Sainsbury's. Do you want to come with me?'

As we walk into the supermarket, I watch us on the CCTV screen. Bells is now wearing Jessica Hall's pink frilly blouse underneath a pair of denim dungarees, plus purple pixie boots and embroidered hat. I am wearing an orange skirt which clings to my hips, with a yellow Whistles top and orange beaded sandals. Bells tells me I look like a satsuma.

There is a delicious smell of fresh bread that makes me feel hungry. 'Hello, how're you?' Bells asks an old lady on a light blue scooter which has a black shopping basket at the front. 'How old are you?' She stares at the scooter which has 'Bluebird 2' painted on the back.

'Excuse me,' the lady says, avoiding eye contact and reaching across to grab an avocado.

Bells comes back to me with two lemons. 'I wouldn't say hello to everyone,' I tell her quietly. 'And, funnily enough, people aren't that happy to declare their age.'

Swiftly I push our trolley on. Bells fills it with everything organic. The only vegetable that isn't organic is the tin of mushy peas. That's the only thing she likes in a tin, she tells me. She is picking out packets of dried prunes, apricots, sultanas, figs and rolled oats for her muesli. Next she puts ingredients I have never even used into the trolley. She chooses dried porcini, coconut milk, chillies, coriander, bay leaves, stuffed olives, sesame seed oil and fresh ginger.

'You cook a lot in Wales, don't you?' I ask her. 'I bet they love you cooking for them.'

'Yes, they call me Queen of Kitchen.'

I feel relieved when we finally make it to the checkout desk. The queue is long and we stand behind a tall man with light brown tousled hair. Among the shopping in his trolley are a packet of crumpets, runny honey, a ready-made lasagne for two, mini Magnums and a bottle of red wine. Bells taps him hard on the arm. 'Hello.'

I look down at my feet.

He turns round. 'Hi,' I hear him say, and look up. He's wearing glasses, a white T-shirt and dark jeans.

'I'm sorry,' I say, drawing in breath.

'Hello.' Bells whacks him hard on the arm now and then holds out her hand.

'Bells! Don't punch so hard. I'm sorry,' I say, wincing in sympathy. He manages a pained smile as he rubs his arm and stretches out his own hand to Bells.

'You like Beckham?'

I am sure he is wondering if he heard right and I subtly nod. If you can imagine talking without being able to touch the roof of your mouth with your tongue, that's what Bells sounds like. It's easy for me because I have learned her language since I was a little girl.

'Yes, I think Beckham's great, and Posh Spice too. I can see you love him,' he intimates, looking at the football badges on her dungarees.

'You have children?' she goes on. Oh, please, stop talking.

I can tell he did not understand from the way he laughs. 'Really?'

'You have children?' she asks, urgently now.

He watches her intently, trying to work out what she just said. 'No, I don't have children,' he replies confidently, and I nod, as if to say, Well done, you got it right. 'Well, I hope not.' He pulls a crooked smile.

'How old?'

'Bells!' I say, exasperated. I want to blindfold her and put a scarf around her mouth too.

'It's OK,' the man says, starting to pack his food. 'I'm twenty-nine.'

'My sister, Katie.' She thumps my arm. 'I staying in London.'

He tells her that that sounds like fun. As he speaks I can't help thinking that if he brushed his hair, took off his glasses, fattened up a little, he could be quite attractive.

'You want cash back?' the assistant asks him.

'No, thanks.'

'Nectar card?'

He digs into his pocket which I can hear is full of change and produces a few cards. As he hands the right one to the girl he turns to look at me again. It's strange but I feel like we have met before. He signs his receipt, but I can't make out his name.

''Bye,' he says, finally.

'Yeah, 'bye,' I say, still trying to put a name to his face.

''Bye,' Bells adds.

The man turns round once more and looks in our direction. 'By the way, I'm really thirty-four! I find it hard facing up to my age first time round.' I laugh as I watch him walk away.

Bells asks the woman serving us how old she is. I suppose it is better than asking her how much she weighs, I think desperately.

'Excuse me?' she says.

'Bells, stop it!' I demand, before she has time to ask again. I tell her once more not to ask strangers personal questions, especially their age. Sometimes I think she does it deliberately to embarrass me. 'I'm sorry,' I apologise to the checkout girl.

'It's fine,' she says.

I push the trolley brusquely towards the exit door and out to the car park beyond.

I unlock the boot of the car and unload the shopping with Bells's help, then we both get inside. I put the keys in the ignition and breathe a sigh of relief. 'This is only day one, I can cope with this, I can cope,' I mutter to myself.

1988

I am thirteen years old. 'How did you meet Dad?' I ask Mum in the car. She is taking Bells and me to watch Dad conduct an auction. It's one of the first times we have all gone out together. A trip to London! Normally we don't do anything.

'Well, my mother had given me an Impressionist painting so I went to Sotheby's to see if it was worth anything. It was a bit of a mystery as it wasn't signed but it looked like a Pisarro,' says Mum.

'And was it worth anything?'

'It was worth a free dinner,' she laughs. 'I met your father and he asked me out. I knew he was going to be a part of my life the moment I met him. Sometimes you can't explain it, it's just a feeling.'

'Like love at first sight?' I ask.

'Yes, I suppose it is. He was an assistant back then. He was unbelievably attractive, the sort of man who could get away with anything. I remember thinking what a big nose he had. But it didn't matter, it went with his long thin face. And his eyes were so mischievous and flirtatious.' She was getting carried away now. 'He only had to smile and his eyes were chatting you up. You'll know what I mean when you're older. I remember him giving me his business card. Christopher Fletcher. I liked that name. Marianne Fletcher, I said to myself.'

'Mum, that's sad,' I sigh heavily. I cannot imagine wanting to marry anyone.

The auction room is dark with lots of people coming in and out. I am sitting next to a man with such a large moustache he looks like a walrus. Mum was too mean to buy us a catalogue each so I try to lean over and look at Walrus's. I can see lots of stars scribbled on each page.

Over breakfast Dad explained how it all worked, his eyes alight as he talked about the auction. 'There is an estimate for each painting and then a reserve price, which means I can't sell below that figure. I'm proud my girls are going to be watching me today,' he added as he ate his last mouthful of toast.

The Walrus peers over at me and I sit straight in my chair. He twirls a pen in his fingers and eyes me curiously. 'You want to have a look?'

he says in a heavy accent. He is a French walrus.

This feels exciting. Like when you go to the cinema and everyone is waiting for the main film to start. Everyone is waiting for my dad.

Finally he enters the auction room in his polished shoes, smart suit and tie. 'That's my dad,' I whisper loudly to my French neighbour.

'Good afternoon, we have a feast of paintings here today so let's get started.' He coughs to clear his throat and I watch him intently. 'Lot number one. Sketch by Matisse of a lady's face. Who's going to start the bidding at twenty-five thousand pounds . . .?'

The Walrus holds up what looks like a ping-pong bat.

Suddenly the bidding is fast and furious. As the auction heats up, Mum is growing redder in the face from trying to stop Bells putting up her hand to confuse the bidding. 'Hello, Dad!' she calls out. I can hear people tut-tutting behind us and whispering, 'Why bring a child to a place like this? It's quite ridiculous.'

I feel Mum's hand tug at mine. 'We're going,' she mutters. 'Excuse me,' she asks the person next to her. Chairs are shifted, legs are tucked in to allow us to pass. I don't want to go. I was having a good time. I can feel everyone's eyes on us and two old ladies nudge each other triumphantly. 'Whatever happened to being seen but not heard?' I turn round and stick two fingers up at them. The two ladies gasp and my father looks directly at me, disappointment in his eyes. ''Bye, Dad,' Bells is shouting.

In the car on the way home I scream, 'Why can't you be normal? You're so embarrassing! We can't go anywhere with you.'

Mum brakes suddenly and swerves into the side of the road. 'Now you listen to me, Katie. If you ever say that about your sister again, I mean *ever*, you forfeit your pocket money for weeks.' She grips the steering wheel tightly. 'It's *not* Bells's fault.'

'You always take her side,' I protest.

'You are very lucky you—'

'—don't have a cleft lip,' I finish for her like a robot. If I am difficult, Mum and Dad's invariable response is to tell me how lucky I am not to have been born with something wrong.

'Well, you are,' Mum says.

I don't think I'm lucky. 'You love her more than me,' I tell Mum.

'I do not,' she says wearily. 'That is absolutely not true. All I'm saying is you are the fortunate one and should be more of a role model.'

I shrug.

'All I wanted to do was watch your father today with no dramas but I see that's impossible. No more outings, that's it,' she tells us with finality.

Back to doing nothing.

If Bells hadn't been naughty none of this would have happened. I can feel my chin wobbling but I am determined not to cry. Instead I shrug and turn to face the window again. I can feel a few tears trickle down my cheek but no one can see them. They are my own secret tears. Why am I getting the blame? I wasn't the one causing trouble. I might as well be the naughty one, though. At least that way I get to have some fun.

CHAPTER SIX

'WHAT AM I DOING now?' Mr Vickers rubs his large hands together, thinking up his next trick. We are in my shop and Mr Vickers and Bells have been playing this charade game for about five minutes. Already I am finding it tiring having Bells around. She likes to ask customers how rich they are. 'How much money you have?' she asked a tall willowy girl in a lime-green sundress. The girl pretended not to hear. And now . . . who is this man with hands the colour of a purple cabbage? His circulation is so poor that his feet, squashed into old beige shoes, are also a mottled purple.

I sent Bells off to buy a baguette for lunch, and somehow she managed to pick up this man along the way and bring him back here. 'Sorry, who are you?' I asked him as he walked into the shop. 'Who is this?' I looked sharply at Bells. I don't want weirdos in my shop.

'I, er, don't want to intrude,' he started.

'I'm sorry, who are you?' I asked again.

I finally discovered that he is called Mr Vickers and he works at the local library. He has grey hair and wears mustard-coloured trousers. What's peculiar about him is that he has a bump about the size of a golf ball in the middle of his forehead.

'Why funny lump on head?' Bells immediately attacked.

'Oh, my goodness,' Eve said. 'Bells, it might be personal.'

Our visitor looked at me for a translation. 'She asked you what the, um, lump was on your forehead?' My voice rose at the end.

'I was, er, born with it,' he replied. 'I'm not quite sure, er, what it is . . . soft tissue or something like that.' He didn't seem embarrassed.

'What am I, er, doing now?' he asks Bells again. He holds his hand in midair, fingers clenched as if he is holding onto something, and starts rocking backwards and forwards, making strange noises.

'You are riding a horse?' Eve has joined in and is guessing seriously, her finger resting on her lip as if she is trying to solve an important crime. Then shakes her head. 'No, that does not explain the hand.'

I glance at the door. Don't come in, don't come in, walk on by, I say to myself when I see a couple of women going past.

'Shall I, er, do it again?' he asks enthusiastically, his eyes widening. 'I'll give you, um, another clue,' he adds generously.

Bells starts rocking like Mr Vickers. It's the first time I have seen her enjoying herself since she arrived. He still makes those odd noises as he rocks. 'Mind the gap,' he announces sporadically. 'That is,' he pauses, 'er, the clue,' and he smiles at Bells and Eve.

'*Bien sûr!* You are on a train!' Eve claps her hands together.

Bells starts to clap too. 'Choo-choo train!'

'I am on the, er, underground at Waterloo.' He talks slowly, emphasising every word, in between his stammering. 'I could not get a seat so I am er . . . er . . .'

SPIT IT OUT! I want to shout. Is it only me who thinks this is insane?

'I am holding onto the, er, strap.'

He is about to do another role-play and I have to say something now, I am at breaking point. 'I'm sorry, Mr Vickers, we're busy.' Eve, Bells and Mr Vickers look round the empty shop. 'Would you mind—' I don't have to finish the sentence. He says he has to go anyway.

'Er, nice to meet you, Isabel, Eve.' He looks at me and nods.

'You come back?' Bells calls after him.

When he has gone, Eve looks at me disapprovingly and I shrug my shoulders. This is my shop, it is not a local community centre.

'I'm sorry, honey, I didn't realise it was your turn to host the poker night,' I apologise again. Sam watches me as I throw down my handbag, newspaper and the house keys on the sofa. Today felt about a week long. No visit from Mr Vickers but the thing that makes me seriously draw in breath is when Bells touches the clothes with her gummy fingers. No one wants sticky grains of sugar on their dresses. Eve took her up to the tiny box-room off the first floor, where I keep a kettle, coffee, a small make-up bag and my delivery boxes. She said she would help Bells wash her hands. 'Hot soapy water,' I could hear my sister saying.

'You bite your nails? You should eat raw jelly,' I overheard Eve suggest. 'I will treat you to a French manicure. You would like?' I wonder what I would do without Eve. That manicure gave me enough time to refold all the clothes.

Now Bells sits down on the sofa and opens her Magnum ice cream wrapper, oblivious to my conversation with Sam. I can see him eyeing the sticky chocolate wrapper, which is precariously close to his cream-coloured cushion. 'I don't understand why you plonk your crap on the sofa when there's a perfectly good table next to it.' He frowns. 'Isabel, give me that wrapper.'

'You like Stevie Wonder?' Bells asks him seriously, holding the CD towards him, ice lolly wobbling in the other hand.

'Not a fan,' he says dismissively. 'What I really don't like, though, is junk lying around the place. It's my home so if you could respect the rules? Good girl,' he says, avoiding eye contact. 'Wrapper, please.'

She hands it to him and he marches off downstairs to the kitchen. I follow him. I can hear the television being turned on upstairs.

'I can't go out tonight, Sam, I really need to get my accounts done.'

'Katie, it's strictly a boys' night,' he tells me bluntly, lifting the bin lid, throwing the wrapper in and slamming it shut. 'I thought Tuesday night was your girls' night with Emma?'

'I had to cancel.' I open the fridge and look inside. Potatoes for baking are in the bottom drawer, as well as a head of organic broccoli and a bag of organic carrots. 'Bells can stay with me in our bedroom,' I tell Sam. 'Oh, shit, what does she cook on a Tuesday?'

'What do you mean, "on a Tuesday"? Get a takeaway.'

'I'll have to microwave a potato.'

'I do not believe this!' He watches me slit the potatoes across the top. 'The boys will be here in an hour. It's so unfair. This is my house!'

I run a hand over my face now and squeeze my eyes shut. I am so tired. 'You sound like a spoilt brat.'

'You're ruining my boys' night.'

'Er, hello, I am saying I won't make any noise. You won't even know Bells and I are here.' He still looks furious. 'Is this really about her? If it were just me, would you mind?' I ask him.

Sam ignores me. 'If you have to bloody well be here, can you go to the upstairs room? I don't want you next door to us.'

'Sam, as scintillating as it might be listening to you boys, I promise I won't eavesdrop. I've got work to do anyway.'

He makes a disgruntled noise. 'You really promise?'

'Promise.'

Bells sits on the edge of our double bed eating her baked potato. She was cross with Sam because he wouldn't let her cook. 'There's no time,' he shouted at her, and then at me.

I watch her as she eats. She doesn't look impressed by the soggy-skinned potato. 'Try not to get anything on the duvet,' I whisper to her.

'Sam kill me if I make a mess,' she says.

'Shh! Yes, he will. Bells, you can sit more on the bed if you like.'

She slides a bit closer to me but still doesn't look relaxed. 'Do you want to read a magazine? Look, I bought a *Tatler*.' I hold it up towards her. 'My shop is going to be in this next month, I had a fashion show.'

Bells shows no interest. She looks so bored.

'Or you can watch the tennis but with the volume off?' Bells is staring absently at the walls. Mum and Dad told me, before they left, that she did get easily fed up when she was staying with them and often wanted to go back to Wales.

'I know it's boring,' I say, hearing a loud knock on the front door.

Bells puts her plate on the floor. 'We've got to be quiet now,' I tell her.

'Bossy Katie. You like traffic warden,' she says. 'Where's Sam?'

'Sam's here, it's his boys' night.' I'm smiling at that image of me.

'Who's at door?'

Oh God, I think to myself. Perhaps it was a bad idea staying in.

'Davey, mate,' I hear Sam bellow, followed by a few manly slaps.

'Who Davey?' Bells asks loudly.

'Bells, remember, whisper. Davey works in the City with Sam. I told you, they play poker each week.'

'Lakemore,' Davey returns in a ringing tone. 'Am I the first here?'

'Yep, you are *numero uno*,' Sam trills. 'No one else here,' he emphasises loudly. 'Come on in. Looking sharp, mate.' I can imagine him winking at Davey now. Sam always follows a compliment with a wink.

'New Paul Smith shoes. They're the business, aren't they?' Davey says.

'Very nice. How about this for style?' Sam challenges him.

I imagine he is pointing to his new purple silk shirt.

'Sharp. I like it, Lakemore. Bet the girls like it too.'

'Saw it down the Fulham Road. Look the part, feel the part . . .'

'. . . and you *are* the part,' they both finish together. 'Pour yourself a whisky, Davey.'

'Cheers.'

The door knocker again.

'Crispin, me old diamond geezer.'

'Lakemore.' Another thump. I can hear their shoes clicking across the wooden floor. Sam has put out the card table with the polished casino chips in the sitting room. 'Weh-hey, Gravy Daveyeeeeeee!'

'Crisps! How goes it?'

'Who Crisps?' Bells asks me in an even louder voice. Perhaps she is unable to whisper? I never thought of that.

The door knocks again.

'MAGUIRE!' shouts Sam. The door crashes open.

'LAKEMORE!' he shouts back.

'They all deaf?' Bells asks me, putting her fingers into her ears.

'Good question,' I tell her. 'You'd think so, wouldn't you?'

'Davey mate . . .'

'Maguire, what you up to?'

'Crispin, you diamond!'

I start to laugh quietly to myself. They all sound the same.

'You OK, Bells?' She is doodling on my newspaper. 'Give us a clue,' I suggest and put my files down. Sam has been playing poker for about an hour now, and I don't know why he worried about me listening to their conversations. Boys together are about as interesting as a night out in Slough.

'I'm gonna raise you twenty quid,' I can hear one of them say.

The chips go into the pot.

'I'll play,' one of them says, more chips going in.

'Are we all on for Ibiza this summer?'

'Absolutely,' one of them says.

'Yeah, yeah, yeah, absolutely,' echoes another.

'Tobes isn't coming this year, his wife has put the mockers on it.'

'D'you think he played away?'

''Course he did,' one of them guffaws.

'I wonder how she found out? Pub rules. What goes on tour, stays on tour,' someone says authoritatively.

Bells and I look at each other. I pull a silly face at her and she suddenly laughs. I am taken aback by just how pleased I am to hear that.

'Stupid boys,' I mouth at her, hoping to hear her laugh again.

'Very stupid,' she repeats, rocking forward with her thumb up.

I move closer to her. 'Boring, aren't they?' I whisper into her ear.

'Ha-ha!' she grunts, and almost laughs again. 'Very boring.'

'She was a right moose too,' one of them carries on. 'I said to Tobes, "Mate, you could have done better than that." Sam, who was that bird you got friendly with last year?'

I put down my file and go to stand by the door.

'Can we go now?' Bells asks impatiently. 'I'm bored.'

I put a finger over my lips.

'Need loo,' she says, getting up.

'Boys, can you keep the noise down?' I hear Sam asking.

'What's got into you, Lakemore? You've turned a bit quiet. He must be holding seriously bad cards. Where's your poker face gone?'

'I could be bluffing, Maguire.'

'You're coming to Ibiza, aren't you, Lakemore?'

'Yep,' he says punchily.

'What was that girl's name?'

'Er, I don't know. Cigar, anyone?'

'Scared the missus will find out?' They all laugh.

'I wasn't going out with Katie then,' Sam reminds them. 'I would never cheat on her,' he says loudly, rather overdoing it. 'Music, anyone?'

Stevie Wonder starts to play 'I Just Called To Say I Love You'.

They start to laugh and the music abruptly stops. 'What the . . .?' Sam is clearly ejecting the CD. 'Must be one of Katie's,' he says, trying to keep his composure.

I put a hand over my mouth to try and stifle a nervous giggle when Chris de Burgh comes on next.

'Blimey, mate. What's happened to your taste in music?' Maguire starts to roar with laughter. 'Next you'll be playing Celine bloody Dion!'

'Katie drives me mad,' Sam mutters.

I can hear Bells now, laughing in the loo, and then there is a flushing sound. Oh my God! I turn round and lean against the door. Bells! How could I have forgotten to remind her not to flush the loo? Sam will kill me. He will kill us both. She comes out of our bathroom.

'Lakemore? What's that sound? Have you got someone here?'

I can feel my heart beating hard. I pull Bells back inside and hold her arm firmly as we lean against the bathroom door. 'We're in serious trouble,' I whisper.

'Serious trouble. Not funny, Katie.'

'No, it's not funny.'

'Lakemore, who are you hiding? Someone just flushed the loo,' one of the boys says incredulously.

I find myself laughing now and Bells copies me. This situation is so ridiculous. Sam has just got to come clean. Tell them we're here.

'No one is here, boys. Can we just get on with the game?' he insists.

'Come off it!' I can hear a chair scrape back and the click of heels across the floor.

I frown. Yes, come off it! 'Are we *that* embarrassing?' I ask out loud.

'Come off it!' Bells says, stamping her feet.

'Maguire, it must be the neighbours. You can hear everything, and I mean, *everything*. Sit down and finish the game.'

The neighbours? Oh, for God's sake, Sam. Bells is getting restless and wants to leave the room but I hold her arm firmly. I want to see if Sam is eventually going to confess that we are here. But Bells manages to escape.

'Too tight, not funny, Katie,' she says now at the top of her voice, wrestling to open the bathroom door.

'Lakemore, someone *is* in your house.'

Another door is flung open and Bells disappears from the bedroom. I can see her rushing past the sitting room, her arms flailing in the air. This should be interesting . . .

'Who the fuck was that little person with the funny boots?' one of them bursts out. 'Sam, the game's up. Confess all.'

'I told Katie it was poker night,' Sam shouts, banging his fist against the table. 'She's here,' he admits crossly.

'But that wasn't Katie,' Maguire exclaims. 'Unless she's shrunk.'

I put my shoes on and run past them and down the stairs. 'Hi, sorry, got to go,' I say, unable to turn round and face them.

'Thanks, Katie,' Sam shouts with heavy sarcasm.

'Lakemore,' Maguire now says, clearly wanting an explanation. 'What the fuck is going on?'

It is the morning following the disastrous poker evening. I find Bells in the kitchen. She is listening to one of her Beatles CDs, wearing her embroidered hat and dungarees again. They must be glued to her body.

'How are you, Bells?' I ask, opening the cupboard that houses the mugs and cereal bowls.

'Bored,' she says blankly.

I shake my head, flicking the kettle switch on. 'If you want to go back home, you would say, wouldn't you?' I ask her, feeling ashamed that if she said she wanted to go, I would be relieved. Sam and I have barely spoken since Bells arrived. We are more like ships passing in the night.

'If you want to go home, if you're unsettled . . .' I try again. She hasn't been here a week yet. Why am I such a bad sister? Shouldn't I want to spend some time with her?

She nods halfheartedly, chopping dried apricots and figs on the table. 'Bells, use a proper chopping board,' I tell her. 'You're marking the table.' I find her a small board. 'And remember to say sorry to Sam when he comes downstairs.'

'Why?' She bangs the knife into the board angrily.

'Careful, please. You know why,' I tell her again. 'You must say sorry for fiddling around with his music. Bells, please. It's really important.'

Sam comes into the kitchen and heads for the coffee machine. His hair is dark and damp after his shower.

'Hello, Sam,' Bells says, looking up at him.

'Hi,' he manages, briefly looking sideways at her.

There is a long awkward silence. 'Wasn't there something you wanted to say, Bells?' I look at her and then at Sam. Still she says nothing. 'You wanted to say something to Sam?' I prompt strongly.

'Sorry, Sam.'

'No problem,' he says. 'Don't do it again, OK?'

That was simple enough, I think with relief. I watch him making his coffee in the shiny silver machine. Sam has hardly touched me since Bells arrived. We have gone from nine months of barely being able to keep our hands off each other almost to taking a vow of chastity.

I watch Bells eating her homemade muesli and drinking her sage tea. She starts to cough. I think she might be coming down with a cold.

'What are you going to do today?' Sam asks her awkwardly, his head still down.

'Don't know,' she replies.

'You're staying here while I go to my yoga class,' I tell her. I cannot face Bells coming with me. 'And then we're going to my shop.'

'Oh, great,' Sam says, but I know he is not listening. His mind is still firmly focused on his disastrous poker evening. I should think all he wants to know is exactly what date and time Bells's train is leaving and if she wants a lift. 'Well, it's a nice day out there,' he carries on painfully. I look outside and it's drizzling.

The telephone rings and Sam sees this as the perfect opportunity to go. 'I'll see you this evening.' He takes his car keys off the breakfast counter and is away before I even have time to say goodbye.

After my yoga class, Bells and I catch the bus to the shop. The one good thing that came out of Mum rarely taking Bells and me shopping to buy clothes was that I learned to sew.

'Where did you get that material from?' she asked me suspiciously as I had already been caught for shoplifting. It was one morning in the school holidays and I was sitting on the sofa hacking up an old red curtain that I'd found. I had made myself a pattern out of tracing paper and found Mum's black Singer sewing machine with the foot pedal.

'I'm making a skirt,' I announced proudly.

She peered at it, did her famous disparaging sniff and then turned away, muttering, 'Well, always good to have a hobby. I'll get you some more material.' I think she was delighted that I had found something to do in the school holidays that would keep me quiet and away from the shops, and meant she could carry on working undisturbed in her studio.

Needlework and textiles were the only subjects for which I received glowing praise in my school reports. None of the other girls in my class were interested and I was the one who was asked to show her work to the headmistress.

I started to make all my own clothes as my interest in fashion grew. I liked touching all the different fabrics in the upmarket material shops and imagining what I could transform the exquisite rolls of silk into, but my pocket money took me to the local markets. There I searched for leathers to make jackets and skirts. I became good at my bargaining skills, negotiating prices for beads, zips, feathers and fabric off-cuts.

The cheapest and quickest things to make were beaded chokers and belts out of sparkling black and gold beads, which I sold to school-friends. I created a small factory in my bedroom, the sewing machine kept permanently in the corner by the window, and all the money I made went into a tin that I kept hidden under the bed. I dreamed about leaving home and starting up my own business, and longed to be in control of my own life.

I did not want to be financially dependent on my parents, so I left home when I was eighteen to live with my electrician boyfriend to whom Mum had taken an immediate dislike because his arms were covered in tattoos. But I was determined to start my own life and make a success of it, with or without my parents.

'No touching the clothes,' I tell Bells as I hand her a blueberry muffin wrapped in a white napkin. I'd popped into Eddie's deli to grab us some breakfast. My plan from now on is to stay out of Sam's way.

'No touching clothes.' She coughs again.

'Good.' I sit down behind my large wooden desk, which is angled diagonally across one corner of the shop. The desktop has a panel of glass covering black and white photographs of our latest fashion show. 'Don't touch the Visa-card machine. And no asking customers how rich or how old they are, OK?'

'Yes, Katie, that's right.' Bells nods to me.

I carry on: 'No commenting on what people are wearing or what they look like. Or saying hello to customers three times. It's embarrassing for them.'

'Embarrassing for them.' She starts to rock on her feet, something she does when she is nervous or overexcited.

'What did I just say?' I test her, to make sure she was listening rather than merely repeating. Things do not necessarily compute with her, or if they do, she deletes them immediately.

ALICE PETERSON

'No saying hello, Katie.' Bells starts to wave frantically.

'Who are you waving at?' I ask, my voice loaded with despair, and turn round. Mr Vickers is outside the shop, peering through the window. He is carrying a black umbrella with a duck-shaped handle.

'Hello, Mr Vickers,' Bells calls. He waves tentatively.

I grab her arm in an attempt to stop her from opening the door. 'Bells, I don't want him hanging around the shop.'

She pulls away from me. 'Like Mr Vickers.'

'Bells,' I raise my voice now, 'please don't make me cross.'

She watches him walk away.

'Poor Mr Vickers. Mr Vickers nice man.'

'I know, but I have a shop to run.' I can see through the window Henrietta and her mother approaching and quickly turn to Bells. 'Why don't you go upstairs and start unpacking the delivery boxes? That would be so helpful,' I tell her, pushing her upstairs ahead of me. 'Clean your hands first,' I say, leading her to the basin. 'The boxes are here. These are black T-shirts.' I point to four brown boxes. 'Scissors are in the drawer. If you could unpack them all before you come back down . . . Thank you.' I don't even wait for an answer.

The simple truth is I don't want Bells putting off my customers.

I have made some good sales this morning. Henrietta bought two dresses and three tops while her mother sat on the chaise longue drinking cups of coffee, spiked with Bailey's from a small bottle that she produced from her bag.

Bells has been extraordinarily quiet, I think happily to myself. Perhaps I will treat her to a quick lunch. I find her sitting on the floor, the T-shirts heaped around her in a muddle.

'Bells, what have you done?' I cry out, kneeling down next to her and picking up one of the black shirts with a small red heart printed on the breast line. I'd thought I could trust her with cotton T-shirts. I mean, how wrong can you go?

'Unpacking shirts,' she says with surprisingly little interest, followed by a cough. Isn't it obvious how angry I am? I open my mouth to speak but nothing comes out. Finally, 'What were you thinking of?' I whisper in despair, picking up the labels she's cut out that look more like silk raffle tickets strewn over the floor. 'People buy these shirts *because* of the labels.' I can't look at her otherwise I might hit her.

Bells stands up.

'Don't touch anything else, you hear me?'

'Help Katie. You said unpack everything?'

'No! Leave everything alone. If you touch one more I will be really angry. Did I tell you to cut out the labels? You stupid, *stupid* girl!' I scream at her, almost in tears. I cannot cope any more.

'Not stupid, Katie. *Not* stupid.' Bells runs down the stairs.

I stand looking at the muddle of T-shirts, too paralysed to do anything constructive. All I can do is stare, willing the labels magically to return to where they belong. I hear a door shut on the floor below, so I go downstairs, trying to compose myself for the next customer.

'Hello,' I say, walking towards a tall slim man.

'Hi, I'm looking for a present, I wonder if you can help me?'

'Where's Bells?' I say out loud.

'Sorry?' he says, looking puzzled. 'Who's Bells?'

'My sister. Did you see someone running out of the shop?' I can hear the tone of my voice rising in anger and fear.

'No, no one.' He shakes his head.

'Can you come back later?' I start pushing him towards the door.

'Hey!' he protests, hanging back. 'I came here especially to buy my cousin a present. Her birthday's tomorrow,' he starts to explain then looks straight at me. 'Hang on, haven't we met before? In Sainsbury's?'

'Oh, have we? Right,' I say agitatedly. 'Look, my sister . . .'

'The one who kept on asking me my age? I remember her.'

'Yes, she's run off and I've got to find her.' I shut the door behind me and then realise I need the keys to lock up. 'Oh God, oh God,' I say, going back inside and grabbing my handbag from behind my desk. I plunge into it as if it were a lucky dip, hoping to pick out the right keys. Instead I can feel Bells's inhaler, which I throw onto the shop floor. My powder compact is chucked after it in frustration. Why do I always pick out everything from my bag except my shop keys? Why can't I have one with practical inside pockets? My hand is shaking uncontrollably.

'Look, let me help you find her,' the man is saying. 'Where do you think she might be?'

I let out a frustrated yelp. 'I don't know, she could be anywhere.' Finally I find the right keys. Oh, why did Eve have to be sick today? I scribble on a piece of paper *Back in half an hour* and pin it to the door.

'OK, here's what we do,' the man says authoritatively. 'You go across the park, I'll go on the main road, and we both head for the tube station and the shops. If you find her, whistle like this.' He puts his hand to his mouth and belts out a loud whistle. 'It works in the classroom,' he adds.

I breathe deeply. 'I can't do that.'

'Well, use a real whistle then. I'm a teacher,' he quickly explains. 'Always keep one on me for emergencies.' He digs into his black rucksack and pulls out a red plastic whistle attached to a piece of string, which he places round my neck. 'We'll find her, she can't be far away.'

'What's your name?' I ask, as we turn in different directions.

'Mark.'

'Thanks, Mark,' I call after him.

It's damp and overcast and the park is almost deserted. 'Bells,' I shout. 'Bells, where are you?'

I see a couple ahead of me. The girl has her hand tucked into the back pocket of her boyfriend's jeans. 'Um, hello . . . hey, you.' I run after them. They turn round in surprise. 'I'm sorry, I've lost my sister. She's short, have you seen her?'

'She's short? That doesn't give us much to go on.' The boy smirks.

'What's she wearing?' the girl asks.

What's she wearing? Good question. 'She's wearing a Chinese embroidered hat and dungarees,' I describe breathlessly. When I get no response, I add, 'And some sort of football shirt with stickers on.'

'You're having me on.' The boy smiles at me. 'Is this some kind of joke? We're on some funny game show, right? *Graham Norton*?' He starts darting his head around looking for the hidden cameras.

I stare at him hard and pin my hopes on the girl. She chews gum thoughtfully and then shrugs her shoulders. 'We've only just got here. Good luck finding her, though.' As I watch them walk on, I fumble in my handbag for my mobile phone. I stab in the numbers and wait for Sam to answer.

'I'm in a meeting. I'll call later, I promise. Remember, I'm out tonight,' he finishes helpfully.

'She's run away,' I say, my eyes staring ahead. 'What am I going to do?'

'Katie, I'm sorry, but what can I do stuck behind my desk? Do you want me to leave the office and come and help you look for her?' He chuckles as if the idea is absurd.

'No, Sam. That would make you a nice person.' I hang up abruptly. I don't even know why I called him. I start keying in my father's mobile number, although I know it's crazy. What can he do when he's not even in the country? I listen to the ringing tone but there is no answer.

'I've lost my sister. Have you seen my little sister?' I ask a lady sitting on a bench reading a newspaper. The familiar sound of the train rattles in the background. What if Bells is on it?

'What does she look like, darling?' She's American.

I am about to repeat everything I have said before but find myself starting to cry. It's awful but I cannot stop. My chin is wobbling uncontrollably. I put my head in my hands. What have I done? Bells, I'm so sorry, please forgive me for shouting at you. She could be run over and dead by now for all I know, and it's my fault. I look up and the stranger smiles sympathetically as she hands me a tissue from her handbag.

'What does she look like?' she asks softly again. 'Come on, we'll find her. She can't be far away.'

I smile gratefully at her. 'If you've seen someone who doesn't blend into the crowd, well,' I sniffle, 'that's her.'

She makes me sit down for a few moments to compose myself. I tell her about our argument. I tell her about Bells. It's surprisingly easy telling a stranger about our family. 'I'm sorry for crying,' I add.

'No, don't be. You're going through a traumatic time, you're allowed to be emotional.' I look up at her and smile. 'What is that whistling noise?' The woman looks around.

I can see Mark running towards us, pulling Bells along with him. 'Thank God,' I leap up from the bench and start clapping my hands together.

'I think you should thank that nice young man,' the American remarks.

As they approach I can tell something's seriously wrong. 'She needs her inhaler,' Mark shouts.

I try to find it in my bag, and then remember where it is.

Bells is fighting for breath. 'Her inhaler,' Mark says again. 'Where is it?'

'It's in the shop. OK, sit down,' I tell Bells, guiding her to the bench. The American lady stands up to give her room. I can feel the tightness in Bells's chest as she gasps for breath. 'Put your hands on your knees . . . Don't let her lie down, Mark. She has to sit up and try to relax.' He sits with her while I run as fast as I can across the park to the shop. I unlock the door with trembling hands and rush to pick up the inhaler. I slam the door shut and just about remember to lock it behind me.

Bells takes the inhaler immediately. We watch and wait.

'How's she doing?' the American lady asks.

'If the inhaler doesn't work we'll have to call an ambulance,' I say. I draw in my breath, waiting to see if the inhaler helps Bells.

'I'm all right,' she finally says.

I can feel her breathing becoming more even as I continue to stroke her back. 'You're really all right?' I say nervously. 'Oh God, Bells, don't ever . . . I mean *ever* . . . scare me like that again.'

Mark tells me not to shout, that she's safe, that's all that matters.

'Oh, Bells.' I reach out and pull her close to me. 'I'm sorry. I'm so sorry for shouting at you. It'll never happen again.' I feel her arms clutching the small of my back and hold her even more tightly. 'Mark's right. You're OK, that's all that counts.'

I pull the duvet over her.

'Tired,' Bells says, turning onto her side.

'Get some rest. Come down for supper later. I'm going to make you your favourite supper.'

'Why you hate me?' she asks.

'What?' Should I pretend I didn't hear that? I draw her curtains.

'You hate me,' she states simply.

'Why do you say that? I don't hate you.' I turn off the main light and shut the door behind me. Outside I lean against it. I feel winded by her question. Bells is no fool. I can't keep on talking to her as if she's ten years old.

Bells screams then. 'Too dark,' she cries out.

I rush back in and turn on the light. Dad once explained to me why Bells hated the darkness so much. After the surgery she developed a phobia about anaesthetics and would scream before each injection. She didn't know what anaesthesia was, but she knew exactly what it meant. Blackness. Dad was good at explaining. He was naturally gentle.

I kneel down beside her and make my voice like his. 'I'm sorry, Bells. I forgot. That was stupid of me.'

'That's right, Katie. You don't write me,' she says. 'Mum writes me. Dad writes me. You don't.'

I am about to say something along the lines of no one writes letters any more, only Mum and Dad's generation, but then I realise how pathetic that would sound. She's right.

'You don't visit me.'

'No, I don't,' I say.

'Why?'

'I don't know,' I reply simply. 'I don't know, Bells.' I try to explain, but I don't know where to start. 'I don't hate you, but I hated watching you in the park. I was so scared. If anything had happened to you, I would never have forgiven myself. I do care. I'm sorry for shouting, and—'

'In Wales cut labels,' she mutters.

'Oh God, I don't care about the labels any more. It doesn't matter. And I will start writing to you, I'd like to.' I realise as I say this that I can't make an empty promise. Bells deserves more than that.

'Mark's nice man. Nice man.'

I smile. 'He is very nice, I am so sorry, Bells.' Without thinking I kiss her forehead and softly touch her cheek. I want to tell her that I love her but I don't feel I deserve to say it. Instead I stand up and switch on the small stained-glass lamp in the corner of her room, before turning off the overhead light.

386

'Nothing around me?' she asks.
'Nothing around you,' I say.
'Promise.'
'I promise.'

'Thank you, Mark. Thank you so much for everything you did today. You don't know me, know us, you didn't have to help,' I tell him as I make us both a hot drink in the kitchen. I asked him back to Sam's place as I felt it was the least I could do. Also I wanted to ask him how he had found Bells, and to talk to him without her listening. I'd thought he would say no, that he had to get on with his day, but he agreed.

'Is she all right?' he asks, obviously concerned, turning away from the milk-bottle sculpture.

'Yes, I think so. She's lying down.'

Mark tells me he found Bells waiting at a bus shelter. She was clearly in an agitated condition but no one at the stop was doing anything.

I feel such a failure as I listen to him recall the drama, realising Bells is having a miserable time with me. She wanted to see the bright lights of London and the most gripping thing we have done together is go to Sainsbury's. Now I know where I met Mark before. 'That's right, of course,' I tell him. 'You're thirty-four.'

'Yes. But you can forget that bit.' He laughs for the first time today.

I sigh. 'If you hadn't been there anything could have happened.'

He looks at his shoes sheepishly. 'I did nothing special. Where does Bells live? I mean, I hadn't seen her around before that day in Sainsbury's, and I think I'd remember if I had.'

'She lives in a community in Wales. My parents are on holiday so I'm having her to stay for two weeks.'

'Is this your place?' Mark asks, glancing around the bare kitchen. 'I like this . . . um . . . sculpture,' he finishes lamely.

'It's Sam's.'

'Oh, right,' he acknowledges. 'He's your boyfriend?'

'Yes.'

'What happened to Bells? I mean, what . . .'

'What makes her different?' I suggest, sitting down opposite him.

'Yes, exactly.'

I tell him she was born with a cleft lip and palate. 'She was also brain-damaged at birth, though a large part of her brain still works. If you tap into a subject she knows a lot about, then you're OK. But she's never been able to lead a fully independent life.'

'Is she aware that she's different?'

'Yes and no. I think she is comfortable with herself now, but as a teenager she hated the way she looked. Well, that's what Dad said,' I add. 'You see, I didn't really see that side of Bells because I left home when I was eighteen and she was only eleven.'

'It must have been tough for your parents.'

'Yes, it was,' I say, wondering if I have ever told them how good they were, and still are, with Bells. No, I know I haven't. I've spent too much time feeling left out of the family and resenting all the energy they put into her. 'To be honest, I've never had Bells to stay with me in London before and I'm finding it pathetically hard. I mean, look what happened today.' Suddenly I feel overwhelmed by the events of the day and in desperate need of relief. 'Shall we have a drink? I could really do with one.'

After a couple of drinks, to lighten the conversation I decide to tell him about the ruined poker night and the switched CDs. He is clearly trying hard not to laugh.

'It's OK, laugh away. It is quite funny.' I tell him how Bells had asked a customer's husband why he had no hair. 'I felt so sorry for that man but Bells wasn't being mean, it's just her way. She says what she thinks. If she doesn't like someone she says so. She might tell them they're boring or stuffy.' I decide not to tell Mark that Bells definitely does not like Sam.

'How old is she?'

'Twenty-two. The thing is, you can't put a mental age on Bells. Some things she's very good at, like gardening and cooking. But if you ask her to visualise something abstract it means nothing to her at all. When my Uncle Roger died, Bells bought some flowers and wrote in the card: "Dear Uncle Roger, I am sorry to hear you are dead".' The words are flowing effortlessly and I am surprised by how easy it is to talk to Mark. I look at him and hope he is not too bored.

'It's getting late,' Mark says. 'I ought to be . . .'

'No, have another drink. Stay and have some pizza with Bells and me. I'll order some from up the road. You don't live far away, do you?'

'I live near your shop actually, in Chapel Road.'

'No way! That's where Emma lives. She's a really old friend,' I add when I see Mark's blank expression. 'What number?'

'One.'

'She's twenty-nine.'

'My first fake age.' He smiles.

'Exactly. Come on, stay.' The truth is I don't want to be left on my own. 'What do you feel like?' I open the fridge.

'I think I'd better be on my way.' He scrapes his chair back.

'Another beer? How about some wine?' I continue.

'Hey,' Mark says, walking towards me. 'Look, it's been a shitty day, it's not surprising you're feeling like this.' He lays a hand on my shoulder.

I'm thinking about Bells and what she said to me earlier. 'Why do you hate me? Why don't you write me?' I start to cry and he holds me.

CHAPTER SEVEN

'BELLS! STOP!' I scream.

Mum's footsteps hurtle down the corridor. '*Stop her!*' she shouts at me.

Bells is towering over Mum's dog Peggy, clutching a chunky pair of black jagged-edged scissors. Everything turns to slow motion as I watch my sister. She holds the scissors near one of Peggy's ears and smiles as she opens the handles. Peggy looks up at her innocently. I have to stop Bells from hurting her, but my feet won't move.

'Stop her!' Mum shouts again.

'*MOVE!*' I shout. '*MOVE!*'

I wake up in a sweat, gasping for breath. Was that me screaming? I take a look around the dark room. It was only a bad dream. Calm down. Deep breaths, Katie. Let it all go. It's all right. I sit up and hug my knees tightly under the duvet. Our bed is empty. Sam is not back yet. Where is he? Why didn't he even call? The room feels black and cold. What's the time? I lean over to the bedside table, turn on the lamp and hold up my watch. It's nearly three o'clock.

When I go to bed alone I keep my mobile on the bedside table. I pick it up now and ring Sam. It's his voicemail. I turn off the lamp and lie down again in the darkness. When I was a child I hated the darkness, just as Bells did, but I did not admit it to Mum. I was terrified there was a crocodile under my bed, a witch behind my door or demons lurking under the window seat. Now I shut my eyes and try to think of something nice to dream about.

'Nothing around me,' I whisper to myself.

'Nothing around you,' I can hear my mother's voice say.

I hear a creaking noise and quickly open my eyes again. I lie in bed, rigid. Someone is in the house. I am going to be strangled in my bed!

I decide it is pointless trying to get to sleep. I put my dressing gown on and walk past Bells's room. I look in and see she is breathing heavily, fast asleep. Quietly I shut her door and walk downstairs. I pray Sam has not hidden the cigarettes in too hard a place this time. Thankfully I find a packet in the cutlery drawer.

I sit and think about home again. After Bells's birth I felt this over-whelming sense that I had to look after Mum. It wasn't because she was falling apart, I simply felt responsible for her. I started to plan what I could do to help. I can remember going shopping with her and how I would slip packets of orange Club biscuits and salt and vinegar crisps into the bags without being caught. I knew we didn't have a lot of money because I'd heard Mum and Dad talking about it. Mum no longer had time to work in her studio and Dad was earning a pretty meagre salary in the auction house. I told Mum she did not have to give me any pocket money and she seemed touched. I said I would raise money at school by selling horse chestnuts in the playground. I wanted to help on the practical side too. I helped Mum feed Bells and dress her. I was very protective of Bells. I knew she was vulnerable, not the same as other small children; my sister was different.

I started to withdraw from Mum when she spent so much time at the hospital. Bells was about two years old then and I was nine. By this stage she needed a series of operations to start healing her face. It was rather like a puzzle. Piece by piece, the doctors slowly rebuilt the gap between her nose and lip.

In the school holidays, when Dad was at work and Mum was at the hospital, I spent most of my time with Emma's family. Berry, her sister, was seventeen then and I can remember thinking how grown-up she was. Berry was tall and willowy, with long black hair which she dyed with purple streaks. She wore Gothic clothes and her eyelashes were coated in thick layers of black mascara.

When Emma's family was away, Miss Grimes, our local baby sitter, filled in. I hated my mother for making me put up with her. Miss Grimes wore the same brown tweed skirt the colour of mud every time I saw her, and boring brown lace-up shoes. She wore steel-framed glasses perched on the end of her nose. It was hard to believe she lived only three doors away from us. She looked as if she came from another coun-try. One where all they ate was cabbage.

'She is very nice, poppet,' Mum told me when I wrinkled my nose in disapproval. 'The main thing is I won't have to worry about leaving you.'

I will never forget the time she came to look after me for an entire night. Mum and Dad had taken Bells to hospital the day before her next operation. 'You always have your nose in a book,' Miss Grimes scolded me, leaning over to see what I was reading. She was knitting a sludgy green jumper the colour of damp moss. 'You're far too young for a book like this,' she said, and swiped Jilly Cooper's *Riders* away from me.

I tried to grab it back, clutching the air. 'Give it back!' I shouted.

'You'll amount to nothing,' she said to the click of her knitting needles. 'You're just a little piece of fluff. Your sister has a lot more problems than you but she will be a proper little person.'

I shrugged my shoulders and muttered, 'Piss off.'

She lurched forward and hit me hard on the knuckles with her grey knitting needles. 'I beg your pardon?' When she was cross or excited her eyes started to roll so all I could see was their whites.

I held in my breath, I did not want her to see that hurt. 'You look like a mad blind lady!' I told her, smiling to cover up the pain.

Before I knew it, I was being dragged upstairs and into the spare room. She pushed me inside and I could hear her turning the key in the lock and saying *that* would teach me. I banged on the door, I screamed and shouted, 'Let me out,' but she ignored me.

Miss Grimes unlocked the door the following morning and told me she was sorry. I told her she was a sad lonely old spinster woman. When Mum and Dad returned I described what had happened. Mum told me to stop lying; she said she knew how much I hated Miss Grimes and that I would do anything to get rid of her. I looked at Dad, who was so often my ally, but he told me not to harass Mum. Couldn't I see how drained and tired she was? Miss Grimes continued to babysit for us, despite my telling Mum I was no longer a child. She carried on locking me in the bedroom. I never forgave them for not believing me. They closed their ears and eyes to it because they had too much else to think about.

When my father finally became an auctioneer, his salary increased and we could afford to have someone coming in during the day to look after Bells. This was when Mum started to work in her studio again. She started working round the clock in between looking after Bells. I think it took her mind off the family problems. It felt like she was not interested in me any more and we started to grow even further apart.

Bells was, 'Mum's girl'. Bells was the 'artistic one'; Mum encouraged her to draw, paint, write, cook—all the things she loved as a child and still loves. Katie was the 'rebellious one'.

'What have you *done* to yourself, Katie!' I can still hear Mum cry in that familiar despairing tone. 'How could you have been so stupid?'

I had dyed my hair blue and pink, like an exotic bird. I was copying Berry who changed her hair colour as often as Madonna.

I can feel Mum's arm pulling mine. 'Which godforsaken hairdresser did this to you?' she is shouting. 'It looks like you have pink and blue worms crawling in your hair. Why do you deliberately try to upset me all the time? Katie, what's happened to you?'

Wasn't it obvious? Did I have to get my tongue pierced next to get her attention?

When I think about it now, it seems almost trivial; people go through much worse things. It wasn't Bells's fault, I know she never set out to be the golden child in Mum's eyes, and I know how much she has gone through, but there is still a part of me that blames her for needing Mum so much. Bells had speech-therapy classes every week, or her eyesight had to be tested, or her hearing aid needed to be fitted. I suppose I have never confronted Bells about it because Mum always instilled in me how lucky I was not to have the same affliction. How dare I be angry or cross when I had my whole life ahead of me?

In many ways my childhood helped me. It made me strive to be independent. Yet I'm still not truly independent, am I? Look at the way I move in with every man I meet. I want to feel loved; I want to feel needed. I blame my parents, especially my mother, for not loving me the way she loves Bells. I have this gaping hole inside me which I have tried to ignore for years, yet it will never go away. When I hear Bells talking about Mum so freely all that old anger and jealousy return, as if they have never gone away. Well, they haven't.

There was closeness once, there was tenderness between Mum and me, so how did it all go wrong?

'Sam, a fat lot of use you were.'

'What are you talking about, babe?' He was shaving and I was talking to his reflection in the mirror.

'Yesterday!' I shout in exasperation as I pull on my work jeans. 'Bells went missing and you didn't even call.'

'Had she run off then?' he remarks, without a flicker of concern.

I hurl a trainer at him. It hits him on the back and thuds to the floor.

'Jesus, Katie, what was that for? Damn, I've cut myself now.'

'You could at least try to pretend you're interested.'

'Well, you found her, didn't you?' He turns to me impatiently. 'Katie, I haven't got time for this, I'm seeing my personal trainer in half an hour.'

I throw the other trainer at him. This one hits him bang in the face.

'What has got into you?' Sam yells, touching his cheek. 'Great, I'm going to have a socking big bruise on my face. Thanks, Katie.'

'Yesterday was awful,' I say, lowering my voice but making sure it doesn't lose its angry edge. 'If it hadn't been for Mark . . .'

'Who's Mark?' There is a slight twitch of interest, at last.

'He is a very nice man,' I point out emphatically. 'He found Bells yesterday. He came home for pizza too.'

'For pizza?' This piece of information has done the trick. At last Sam pays attention. 'Why did you have to invite the guy back for pizza?'

'To say thank you,' I say simply. 'If he hadn't found her, I don't know what would have happened. She had an asthma attack.'

'Why did Bells run away in the first place?' Sam asks, sitting down on the bed and putting his trainers on.

'Because that is what she does when she gets upset,' I explain to him, as if he really ought to know. 'It used to happen a lot at home.' I tell him about the labels, relieved to find that Sam might in fact care a little.

'Well, if you hadn't shouted at her in the first place,' he says smugly, 'then none of this would have happened, would it?' He stands up in his jogging trousers, tight T-shirt and trainers. 'I'm late for my PT. I haven't got time for all this.' He pauses at the door, then turns back and puts one hand against the wall. 'But you've had your say, now it's my turn. You never told me about Isabel and now, all of a sudden,' he raises his eyebrows, 'I am supposed to be deeply concerned about her welfare? Katie, I didn't know that she runs off when she's upset. I still don't know a thing about her. I don't feel comfortable around her because *you* haven't made me feel comfortable.'

I sit down on the bed.

'Did you think I would go off you because of her . . . you know, the way she is?' he finishes. 'It's your own hang-up, Katie. If you hadn't been so ashamed to tell me about her . . .'

Bells is standing behind him now in her cotton pyjamas and football slippers and I desperately try to signal to Sam to shut up, but he is paying no attention.

'If you hadn't been so ashamed of your own sister,' he stresses, 'things might have got off to a better start. OK, she's different, but so what? I was on the tube the other day and there was this woman sitting opposite me barking like a dog. There are lots of Isabels around, she's not unique.'

Bells looks at me and I put my head in my hands. She walks back to her bedroom and shuts the door loudly. Sam glances round, finally realising he wasn't talking just to me. 'I couldn't do anything when you called because I was about to go into a meeting. I *am* to blame for not calling you back, and I'm sorry. But don't blame it all on me. Perhaps you should take a good hard look at yourself too, Katie Fletcher,' he says firmly before slamming the door behind him.

I lie back on the bed and stare up into the ceiling. Bells is now playing Stevie Wonder. Stevie Wonder is probably the only constant thing she has in her world at the moment. It is her comfort food.

The closeness we shared yesterday, the affection—well, it has all been undone in one swift blow and I am taken aback by just how much I care. I can't let Bells think she isn't important to me.

'And even though Sam did eventually apologise for not calling to see if I had found Bells, he actually told me it was *my* fault because I hadn't told him enough about the way she is,' I end in an outraged voice down the phone to Emma. It is later that morning and I am in the shop, while Eve and Bells have popped out to buy some croissants and cappuccinos.

Emma is now painfully quiet. Please tell me that Sam is in the wrong, I think. Yet deep down I know that there is a lot of truth in what he said. I should have told him all about Bells. Thankfully she doesn't say, 'I told you so'.

'Is Bells all right?' she asks. 'Do you want me to take a look at her? Her asthma hasn't flared up again?'

'Thanks, Emma. I think she's OK but she has been a bit quiet,' I admit. 'I know she heard what Sam said but I haven't mentioned it to her yet. I've really mucked up, Emma. Bells is miserable.'

'It's not too late,' she says comfortingly. 'Look, I'm not doing much today,' she continues, 'so why don't I fill in for you at the shop and you can take Bells out? Give her a good time, try to make up for it?'

'I would love to,' I say. 'She gets so bored in the shop. Are you sure?'

'Yes. Jonnie is being boring and spinning records at home so I'm free. Take Bells shopping. Spend some proper time together.'

'I could get her something to wear for your wedding!'

'Yes, great idea. I haven't even got my own dress yet,' she adds.

'I'll help you. Thanks, Ems, I'd really like to do that.'

'How about this?' I suggest to Bells, holding up a pale green skirt and a contrasting embroidered silk jacket. I peer at the label on the skirt: size 12. I will have to take it up a good five inches.

'I like it.' She takes the jacket and skirt from me, without really looking at them. She pulls the curtain of the changing room. 'No come in.'

I can hear her stamping her feet in her big black DM boots. She is giving the purple pixie boots a rest today. I turn to apologise to the shop assistant who says nothing. Instead she looks away. Why did I bother to say sorry? What am I actually saying sorry for? I open the curtain slightly. 'Please let me come in,' I ask. 'Please.'

'All right, Katie,' Bells says.

I sit down on a stool in the corner. 'Do you need a hand?'

'No, can do it on own. Can dress myself.'

'I know, I'm sorry.' I don't seem to be able to do anything right. 'What's that funny thing you have in your hand?' I ask, desperately trying to break the ice between us.

She shrugs.

'Please show me. What is it?'

She holds out her hand. 'You shake hand,' she says impatiently. I place my hand in hers and something vibrates loudly against my palm; it makes the kind of sound you hear when contestants press their buzzers on a game show. 'What's that?' I shriek, withdrawing my hand and shaking it free. 'Do it again!' I giggle once more. Bells laughs with me for the first time this morning. She said nothing on the bus; she didn't even say hello to the other passengers.

I watch with fascination as Bells starts to take off her clothes. My sister's style is what you'd call the 'bag lady' look. She takes off her denim jacket, covered in yet more football badges and stickers. Under this is her bright red Oxford University T-shirt.

'On the catwalk, Isabel Fletcher now models a grubby football shirt covered in more Manchester United badges and stickers.' I smile as I lean back against the wall. 'Aren't you boiling?' I ask as yet another layer comes off. She is like a Russian doll. I am surprised she can even walk. 'Bells, it's the summer. You're dressed for a day in Siberia.'

'Feel cold,' she mutters, extracting the next top, a holey and faintly smelly tank vest. It is followed by another stringy vest with more holes.

I do a bit of fake snoring.

'Ha, ha, very funny, Katie,' she repeats, rocking forward with a smile.

I can see the shop girl's pointed toes. She peers round the curtain and immediately shuts it again when she sees me attempting to get the jacket onto Bells. It is too tight over her bosom. Bells has a heavy chest considering she's only four foot ten. Nature over-compensated. If only we could do a swap. I could give her some of my height—I am five foot nine and a half; and she could give me some of her bosom. I instinctively start to unbutton the jacket. It reminds me of dressing and undressing Bells when she was little. 'Oh, Bells, sorry,' I say, pulling away quickly. 'Sorry.'

'All right, Katie. You help me,' she says, nodding her head. 'You are Fashion Queen,' she adds.

I break into a big smile. 'Well, I think that jacket is too small. Do you want me to see if they have a size fourteen for you? And shall we try another colour for fun?'

'No, we don't, I'm afraid,' the shop girl whispers loudly through the curtain. I step out and she is hovering over our changing room, not wanting to let us out. If this shop had a box-room that is where we would have ended up. She wants to boot us out of here as soon as possible so that we do not put off customers. How sad. And I realise, too, that I have behaved in the same way as this girl. How truly pathetic I am.

'Sorry? You don't what?' I ask.

'It only comes in that colour, the colour she's in.'

'Really? But I'm sure I saw it in another colour.' I step out of the changing room and walk over to the rails. Sure enough, the jacket does come in a different colour. In fact it comes in about four different shades. I take another one off its hanger and walk back into the changing room. 'Bells, try it on in a different colour,' I say loudly.

I hear more customers coming in. 'Can I help you or are you just browsing?' a sugar-sweet voice asks them.

This jacket buttons up smoothly. I stand back and tell Bells to come out. 'You look lovely, come on,' I encourage her. We stand outside, behind a girl with honey-blonde hair who is posing in front of the mirror, holding up a black dress. Bells shuffles forward, trying to catch a glimpse of herself. The girl moves out of the way and I thank her. Bells's skirt trails on the ground like a train. The jacket and skirt are matching and the colour brings out the green of her eyes. Bells takes another step and then I hear a rip. Immediately I push her back into the changing room and examine the skirt. There's a large rip above the hem. 'Bugger,' I mutter, 'bugger.'

'Bugger,' Bells repeats loudly.

'Shh!' I say. 'Get dressed quickly.' I look at the pile of clothes. Once Bells is ready we walk out to the shop desk. I am ready to tell the girl what happened and buy the skirt. I can mend it at home.

'Are you going to take that?' she enquires, straining to be polite.

'You married?' Bells asks her. 'You have children?' She steps forward to shake the girl's hand. I can see she has her little electrical device ready. I am about to stop her, but when I see the expression on the girl's face I change my mind.

'Oh my God!' she yells and recoils as the device goes off, withdrawing her hand in horror. Bells rocks forward in delight and I smile. The girl glares at us both with nothing but disdain now. 'What happened to her?' she spits, now looking directly at me. 'Is she mad or something?'

'"She",' I emphasise, 'is called Bells. If you have a question, why don't you ask her?'

'Born with poorly brain and a cleft lip and palate,' Bells says, just as Mum used to tell her.

'If someone asks, you tell them straight. You have nothing to be ashamed of,' I can hear Mum saying.

'Will you be taking the skirt?' the assistant demands.

'I am afraid it has a rip in it so, no, we will not be taking it,' I say, hardly believing that these words are coming out of my mouth. 'We are not interested in damaged goods,' I carry on, relishing every word now.

The shop girl claws the outfit away. 'I'm sure there was nothing wrong with it earlier . . .'

'You not very nice lady,' Bells says to her. I walk out, holding onto my sister's arm. 'Not very nice lady, Katie,' she repeats, shaking her head.

'No, not nice at all.'

I take Bells out for lunch. 'No more shops, Katie,' she'd said. I order a glass of wine and a Coca-Cola. I watch Bells as she looks at the menu. She still has not mentioned anything to me about that conversation with Sam. I wonder how she feels now? She looked so hurt earlier this morning, so vulnerable, shoulders hunched as she walked back to her room.

Why didn't I tell Sam about her? I suppose the reason is simple. We tell friends about the things we feel comfortable with, proud of. I like the glossy world we have created together. Sam the hotshot guy in the City; Katie who runs her own business. Talking about Bells brings back a lot of memories I would rather erase. But I realise none of this makes it forgivable. Sam was right.

'Bells, about what you heard earlier . . .'

'You ashamed,' she says quickly.

When I hear her say it out loud it makes me feel even lousier about myself. 'I am really sorry. Can we make a fresh start? You have one more week with me in London and I'd like to make it up to you. It was wrong of me not to tell Sam about you. It was just one of those things you do and then wish you could rewind time.'

Bells doesn't say anything.

'Where's the thingy that vibrates?' I laugh nervously as I take her hand. 'Friends,' I tell her firmly, but still do not feel I have said sorry properly. I think of all the times when people asked me at parties, 'Do you have brothers or sisters?' and I replied I was an only child because I could not face the follow-on questions: Where does she live? What does she do?

I look at Bells who is drinking her Coke so quickly that she starts to make loud slurping noises through her straw. Without thinking, I glance around to see if anyone is staring, but no one is looking at us. They are too interested in their own drinks and food. 'Bells, the thing

Sam said about being ashamed of you . . .' I start again.

'It's all right, Katie,' she says, looking at the framed poster on the wall.

'No, it's not all right. The person I am really ashamed of is myself.'

'Why?'

'Sometimes I find it hard . . .' I don't know how to end my sentence so I start again. 'To be honest, I was dreading you coming to stay.' I don't look at her because I am scared I am hurting her. 'You remind me of everything I don't have.'

'Don't understand,' she says.

'I don't feel part of our family, I feel like an outsider. Look at your photo album. No pictures of me. It's my fault, I'm the one who distances myself. I'm not blaming you, but you, Mum and Dad are so close. When you were young I was palmed off to Aunt Agnes, or stayed with Granny Norfolk, or some horrible baby sitter looked after me. You needed their help. Mum and Dad had no choice, I know that, but I didn't cope with it very well. I . . . Do you understand what I'm trying to say?'

'Sort of. Difficult for Katie too.'

'Yes. I feel so guilty for feeling like this, I don't want to feel this way.'

'That's right. You jealous?'

'Yes,' I reply, realising how perceptive she is. 'I was jealous of you for having all the attention. But I know it wasn't your fault.'

'You blame Mum?' Bells asks.

'I guess I do. Dad and I have always been closer. Shall we make a pact?'

'Yes, pact.'

'That we make a fresh start?'

'Friends.' She holds out her hand, with her short little fingers and bitten nails.

'Yes, friends,' I tell her, clutching that tiny hand.

It's nearly six o'clock and I am making fresh price tags with black velvet ribbon. Eve has just left, picked up by Hector who was not at all what I'd expected: short and oily like a sardine.

Eve bought a baby chandelier for the shop today, with shimmering cut-glass drops. She also found some ivory silk cushions trimmed with black lace to decorate the cream chaise longue in the corner of the shop. Very *Moulin Rouge*. We work well together because she has a real flair for design and enjoys making the shop look lavishly aesthetic.

'Where's Mark?' Bells mentions again.

'Since five minutes ago, I still don't know,' I reply. I can see she is getting restless. 'We'll be going home soon. Draw me something,' I suggest, handing her my notepad. I have a papier-mâché pot on my desk with pens and pencils in it. 'Take one,' I say.

'Mark married?' she asks, stopping the pacing for a second.

'No, I don't think so. In fact, I'm sure not,' I add.

'Girlfriend?'

'I don't know.'

'Pets? He have a dog?'

'Bells! I don't know. You should have asked him.'

I wonder if Bells misses 'going out' with men, not being able to have a relationship. Does it even occur to her? This is when I feel guilty about envying her. There is so much she cannot have which I take for granted.

'Mark nice man.'

I can see she is not going to let him slip from her mind. 'Draw me a picture of him,' I say, pleased that she looks interested in that idea. She takes the pad and a pencil and sits down on the wooden stair. 'We going to see Mark again?' she asks as she draws earnestly.

'Maybe.' Mark scribbled down his phone number just before he left. The piece of paper is still in my handbag. He told me he was around if I needed him as it was the school summer holiday. I could call him. We could go out. Sam doesn't need to know. Mark is Bells's friend after all.

I have thought a lot about Mark and our pizza evening together. It has been a ray of light in the last few days. 'I have a friend who has a brother,' he told me, after the tears. 'I had never met the brother until I went to their sister's wedding. I was the very informal photographer,' he added with a modest cough. 'I was in the kitchen with the brother whose name was Ben, and he seemed normal to me, sitting there in his jacket and tie, until he asked his father if he could have a Scotch egg.' Mark smiled slightly. 'I thought it was strange,' he furrowed his eyebrows, 'a man of thirty-something asking his father if he could have a Scotch egg, but then I thought nothing more of it until he turned to me, quite randomly, and said that their dog should be put down.'

I laugh out loud, remembering. 'What so funny?' Bells asks as she walks over to my desk clutching the pad.

'Something Mark told me.'

'Mark nice man, isn't he?'

'He *is* a very nice man,' I echo. 'Back to your portrait.' And I am surprised when she sits down obediently and carries on drawing.

'I was amazed my friend had never told me much about him,' Mark continued. 'Baffling, really. I had known him for six years. Been to university with him,' he uttered incredulously.

I smile, thinking about that word 'baffling'.

Then came the awful question that all of us ask though we wish we didn't. 'And what do you do?' I was focusing on the large hole Mark had in the elbow of his navy jumper.

'I'm a teacher, English and drama.'

There is something romantic about being a drama teacher, I think now, tapping my red Biro against the desk.

'Really?' I asked. Why do we say, 'Really?' Did I expect Mark to stick his tongue out and say, 'No, only joking'? 'What age?' I continued.

'Teenagers. I like a challenge.' He smiled wryly. 'Holidays are great too.'

With his tousled dark brown hair which has no parting whatsoever, the small mole on the right side of his face, even the nerdy round glasses he wears, I reckon a lot of the girls would have a crush on Mark.

'Where have you been today then?' I asked Mark, still looking at his holey jumper.

'The library. I took the day off. I'm trying to write a book,' he said. 'I find it difficult working from home, too many distractions like daytime television. There's Wimbledon, too. If Henman's playing I have to leave the house, my nerves can't cope.'

He asked me about my shop. I told him about my time at art college and working for a West End theatre, designing and making costumes, followed by working for a fashion designer for three years. Bells had come downstairs then in her pyjamas, clutching her photograph album. He turned his attention to her as I made a salad to go with our pizzas. They talked about the tennis and Mark asked her about football. I couldn't help noticing the ease between them.

Mark looked at all her pictures slowly. 'Who are they?' he asked.

'Mary Veronica, Ted, in Paris,' Bells said proudly. I went over to have a look. Mary Veronica and Bells were standing outside a café with their thumbs up. Ted was in the middle with his arms crossed.

'And who is this? She is very beautiful.'

'My mum,' Bells said. 'That's my dad. That's Budge, he plays for my football team.'

'Katie, how come there are no pictures of you?' Mark asked.

I start to clear my desk. It's late and I want to go home. What have we got to eat tonight? Only today I popped out of the shop to post some letters and found myself hoping I might bump into Mark. Well, he knows where I am. He knows where the shop is too. If he wants to see us, I am sure he will pass by. 'Let's go, Bells. What are we going to do tonight?'

'Sainsbury's? Cook tonight, organic night.'

I pull a face. 'Let's just get a video and takeaway.'

'Mark likes Sainsbury's.'

Good point. 'OK, actually yes, I do need some vodka.'

Bells and I are sitting like plum puddings on the sofa, sharing a tub of toffee ice cream with a slice of chocolate biscuit cake and watching the old black and white film *Titanic*. Earlier Bells cooked us a wild mushroom and aubergine risotto. She showed me how to prepare the aubergines, slicing them and sprinkling them with salt, telling me we had to leave them for half an hour before cooking them.

There was no sign of Mark at Sainsbury's.

Bells tells me she has watched this movie at least one hundred times, it is the favourite film in Wales.

'About to hit iceberg.' She claps as she leans forward and laughs outrageously. 'The wallies! It's coming, it's coming!'

I sit forward too.

'Rewind,' she says. I pick up the controls and rewind. I hear the front door shut and Sam coming upstairs.

'SMACK!' Bells cries out. Sam stands at the door, shakes his head disapprovingly and walks out. I follow him downstairs to the kitchen. 'Sam, hello, good evening, nice to see you, did you have a good day? What is this silent treatment?'

He sits down at the kitchen table which is covered with a baking tray, a greasy butter wrapper, tin of cocoa, biscuits and a bag of sultanas.

'Sorry,' I say, quickly beginning to clear the mess. 'Bells and I made a chocolate biscuit cake for our pudding. I thought we'd have time to clear up before you got home.' I walk past him and put the dirty bowl, licked wooden spoon and tray in the sink.

'Katie, I'm sorry. I'm behaving like an idiot.'

I turn round and lean against the oven. 'Yes, you are. We both are. I'm sorry too. I was scared when Bells ran off. I feel responsible for her, but I shouldn't have taken it out on you.' I sit down next to him and Sam slides his fingers in between mine. 'We are OK, aren't we?' I ask.

'I think so. 'Course we are. Come here.'

'Katie!' I hear Bells shouting.

I pull away from him. 'Where are you going?' he asks.

'To watch the rest of the movie. Coming?'

'No,' he says awkwardly. 'I'm going to make myself something to eat and clear up this mess.'

'Sam, Bells won't bite.'

'I've seen *Titanic*.'

'Doesn't matter, so have I. Bells has seen it a thousand times!' I laugh, wanting him to change his mind. 'Come on, Sam, please come. Bells will clear this up later, she loves washing up.'

'No!' Sam shouts at me. 'I will clear it up *now*.'

All the tension between us returns but I don't want another argument. I leave him in the kitchen.

'Katie,' he calls after me.

'About to hit iceberg, Katie,' Bells tells me again. 'Katie, watch.'

I sit down with her. 'The wallies! What do you call them, Bells?'

'Wallies.' She laughs hysterically, in short sharp infectious trills. I watch her face light up as she stares at the screen.

'*Smack!*' we both laugh together. 'Rewind.'

CHAPTER EIGHT

I HAD THE STRANGEST DREAM that I was singing 'Purple Rain' in front of Simon Cowell, dressed only in a purple feather boa. He told me that I wasn't quite what he had in mind. I clearly did not have the X-factor. I smile to myself as I flick the kettle on. Sam has already escaped from the house. His alarm clock went off so early that I thought it was still the middle of the night.

'Morning, how are you, Bells?' I yawn widely. 'Sleep well?'

'Bored.' She is sitting at the kitchen table, eating chopped apricots and figs. She stops for a moment to open a can of Diet Coke.

'You're bored? What do you expect to be doing at seven thirty in the morning?'

She shrugs. She is wearing a grey track suit with her red Oxford University T-shirt which now has chocolate stains down the front. 'I need to put some washing on,' I say flatly, still trying to wake up.

I open the blind and squeeze my eyes shut. The sun streams through the window. I stretch my arms out above my head and let out a great big sigh. Bells continues to eat quietly, occasionally prodding the milk-bottle sculpture.

I am going to skip my run this morning. I am going to make myself a bacon sandwich for breakfast with lots of tomato ketchup. Go on, Katie, be wild! I make an even bolder step by deciding I will take two days off in a row. I think Eve likes being in charge. 'We are going out today,' I tell Bells, already planning the day in my mind.

'Where? The shop?'

'No, it's a surprise, you'll see,' I say, trying to hide my own excitement. 'Get dressed quickly. Look at the sun, Bells. It's a beautiful day. Your dungarees are in the airing cupboard, I washed them for you, and it's hot today so wear something cool. Don't wear five smelly vests!'

'Where we going?'

'It's a surprise.'

'Can Mark come?'

'Yes! Brilliant idea.' I dig into my handbag and give her the crumpled piece of paper with his number on it. 'Ring him,' I say.

I feel a tiny twinge of guilt for not being at work again, but it disappears when I see Bells tapping her hands together excitedly. After queuing for an hour and a half at the London Eye, we are standing in our glass capsule, propelled high into the air and surrounded by tourists. Mark wasn't at home, but it's nice to spend time with Bells, just the two of us.

'Not moving?' Bells jitters. 'Broken down, broken down!'

'We are moving, I promise. Apparently we're moving about one quarter of a metre per second,' I tell her, putting Sam's binoculars round her neck. 'Take a look.' I stand close behind her. She smells of Persil and lime after her shower. 'You can see all of London from here, Bells,' I say, pointing to different landmarks. 'Doesn't that make you feel tiny? Like an ant.' She is breathing deeply. 'There's Big Ben . . . the Houses of Parliament . . . look, you can see Buckingham Palace where the Queen lives. Isn't it incredible?'

'Yes, Katie, yes.'

A Japanese couple are taking pictures of one another at every possible opportunity with their Polaroid camera. 'Ah,' they sigh repeatedly as they look at the pictures. They ask me if I will take a picture of them both and link arms as the flash goes off. Bells rushes over to me and they offer to take a picture of us. Bells is clapping her hands against her thighs now, then she runs to the side of the capsule and calls to me, 'Look, Katie, look! London. Where Sam's house?'

'Turn round for a second,' I say. She swings round and I signal to the Japanese man to take our picture quickly before she runs off again.

Later that morning, Bells and I are lying on a pale yellow checked rug in St James's Park, looking up into the clear blue sky. We have just finished eating our picnic: vegetable samosas and a Diet Coke for Bells, a Pimm's and a packet of Marks & Spencer sushi for me.

'There are no clouds, Bells. Just clear blue sky like the sea.'

'No fluffy clouds,' she echoes. 'In Wales we have sea.'

'Do you miss Wales?'

'Yes.' She tilts her head. 'No. A bit.'

'What do you miss?'

'Miss Ted.'

'Who's Ted?'

'My friend.' She laughs mischievously, restlessly kicking her legs.

I lean on my elbow and look at her. 'Really? So Ted's the lucky man. You've kept that very quiet. You're a dark horse, Bells.'

'A dark horse,' she laughs back at me. 'Ted just friend, my friend.'

'Are you happy there?'

'Yes, Katie, yes. Sometimes sad,' she adds.

'Why sad?'

'Miss home, miss Mum, Dad.'

I notice she does not add me. Why would she? Still, it surprises me how much I want to be added to the list. 'I'm sure they miss you too,' I tell her. 'Let's give them a call now, tell them we've been up in the sky.'

I take the mobile out of my bag and punch in the numbers. Their phone is switched off. I knew this would happen. They are hopeless. 'Not there,' I tell Bells. 'How often do they call you in Wales?'

'One time a week.'

Well, they've called twice since she has been staying with me, yet each time have sounded oddly distanced. 'Tell me more about Wales. What do you do all day?'

'Go to college Monday.'

'What do you do there?'

'Learn respect.'

'Respect?'

'Towards other people,' she tells me. 'Learn health and safety too. In kitchen. Fire rules and safety.'

'Oh, right. That's important when you're Queen of the Kitchen.'

'That's right. Me the queen.'

'Do you enjoy college?'

'Yes, love college.'

'What else do you do?'

'I go to football club each week, watch my team play. Watch Budge play. Budge very handsome. I cook. Ted and I make stuff, weave and paint, we watch football videos. Clean room, make beds.'

'Are you on a rota system? You clean and make the beds one week, Ted the next?'

'Yes, that's right, Katie, that's right. Rota.'

I realise how little I know about Bells's life. I know a tiny fragment from her childhood and that's about it. I've never wanted to be involved, but now . . . 'I can see why you get bored with me.'

'Sometimes bored, that's right, Katie.' She laughs. 'You marry Sam?'

I dodge the question. 'How did you learn to cook so well, Bells?'

'You marry Sam?' she asks again, quite insistently.

'I can't see myself marrying anyone, not yet anyway. Bells, you're not burning, are you? We'd better put some cream on, just in case.' I dig into my basket for a tube of sunblock, then apply it gently to her forehead and cheeks. She doesn't flinch. Her skin is as pale as a china doll's.

'What you looking at?'

'You,' I say, as I dab a large blob of cream on her nose and laugh.

'Not funny, Katie.'

'I think it is *very* funny,' I say to her as I start to pack up our things.

Bells and I sit on the bus and it's rush hour, the traffic is as slow as a slug. After our picnic we went shopping along the King's Road. In a charity shop we found her a pair of red shoes with clover-shaped patterns embroidered onto them. If there was no one helpful in any of the shops I simply 'threw in the towel', as Sam would say. Why should they see my Visa card? In the end, with the help of a lovely shop assistant, we found a dark red-and-gold Chinese dress with a jacket for Bells. 'You like it?' she asked the girl.

'I love it.' The girl beamed at her, kneeling down and adjusting the hem. 'I think it's dead stylish, you are going to be the belle of the ball.' I thought my heart might burst as I watched Bells looking proudly at herself in the mirror, her outfit finished off with the red shoes. When Bells was out of earshot I thanked the girl. 'For what?' She looked almost put out. 'I've had more fun today than during my whole time here,' she said. 'And I've been here for over a year.'

'Pull my finger,' Bells says. I turn and look at her dubiously. The moment I pull it she sticks out her tongue and starts to roar with laughter. The grey-haired woman sitting opposite stares at us strangely and then returns to her paperback.

'Pull mine.' I hold out one long tapered finger. I am wearing the three-band silver ring Sam gave to me and have painted my fingernails a pale pink. Bells leans forward to touch my finger.

'Bad luck, missed,' I exclaim, quickly withdrawing my hand.

She laughs and the woman opposite stares directly at Bells with cold blue eyes. I want to tell her to stop staring. I myself am guilty of wanting to hide my sister for fear of being embarrassed by her, yet I am surprised by how much it still angers me when people are rude or stare. Who are they to judge anyone? I shift in my seat. She is still looking at us. It

405

makes me feel uncomfortable but at least Bells doesn't appear to notice. Mum and Dad used to tell strangers what was wrong with her. Dad always explained to me, 'It puts them at their ease. It's normally fear or ignorance that makes people stare. You have to work hard to reassure them. It shouldn't be like that, but that's the way it is.'

'Oh, dear.' I shake my head solemnly at Bells. 'Too slow, miss a go.'

'Not funny, Katie!' she cries excitedly, clapping her hands.

'Pull my finger, come on.' She misses again. 'Sorry, if you snooze, you lose.' That's an expression of Sam's. I doubt he meant it to be used in exactly the same context, however. 'Shit, this is our stop!' I grab our bags and Bells follows. 'Mind the step.'

I wish I had said something, I think to myself, as the sour-faced lady bristles and looks down at her book dismissively.

Bells points animatedly to each tray behind the counter—couscous with pine nuts and peppers, carrot cake with a whipped orange and butter icing, warm ciabatta bread with olives or spinach, rice cakes with garlic. We buy some ginger to make a sticky ginger pudding 'like the one Mum makes', she tells me. I buy some pistachio nuts, fresh bread and olives. Emma's coming over tonight especially to see Bells.

'I am not going near those chillies,' I tell her when she asks Eddie for three red ones. She wants to make a chilli sauce to go over her vegetarian sausages. 'The last time I chopped them I forgot to wash my hands, picked my nose, and boy, did it kill!' I laugh.

'Not funny, Katie.' She comes forward and touches me briefly on the shoulder.

'No, it wasn't!' I carry on, still glowing from her touch. It is the first time she has initiated affection and it makes me feel as if someone has wrapped a warm soft towel around me.

'That's disgusting, Katie,' says Eddie. 'Is that all, girls?' I had forgotten Eddie was standing there. He is wearing a short blue apron which shows off his hairy legs, finished off with brown sandals and socks.

'You wearing anything under that?' Bells asks him.

'Wouldn't you like to know?' he replies and winks at her. 'How much longer are you here for, Bells?'

'Two day.'

'You make sure you come and say goodbye, won't you?' he says.

'No, I'd prefer the table in the corner, please . . . um, say about seven thirty . . . thanks.' Sam puts down the phone as Bells and I come into the kitchen. 'I am going to take you and Isabel out tomorrow evening, for

406

her last night in London,' he announces proudly.

'Are you?' I look at him, wondering what has brought this on.

'I am,' he declares, and looks at Bells for a response.

'Where are you taking us, then? Bells, did you hear that? Sam's taking you and me out on the town.'

She nods.

Sam looks disappointed. 'We're going to my favourite restaurant. They have the best wine list in town and serve top-quality steak . . .'

'Bells doesn't drink,' I can't help adding.

'Don't eat meat,' she finishes.

I feel bad for sounding ungrateful. 'Sam, that's a lovely idea, thanks.'

'Thank you,' Bells murmurs, turning Stevie Wonder on.

Sam and I go upstairs. 'I have had one of the nicest days,' I tell him, sitting down on our bed and kicking my shoes off.

'Really? At work?' He lies down next to me.

'No, with Bells. We went on the London Eye, had a picnic, went shopping and Bells bought an outfit for Emma's wedding. I really feel I'm getting to know her.'

'What d'you mean, getting to know her? She's your sister.'

'What I mean is—'

'I'm going to the gym tonight, want to come?' he asks.

'No.' I shake my head. 'You go.'

'I need to buy a new pair of trainers,' he's muttering. 'Remember, we're going away for the weekend when Bells leaves.' There is a book on hip hotels on his side of the bed which he now picks up, turning to the marked page. 'I booked the Moroccan Suite, Katie. Look at it, it's beautiful. Next weekend, honey, we need to get away. *Look* at this place.'

The hotel bedroom seems like a mini-paradise. A four-poster bed with white linen sheets, pale blue shutters, and creamy blue tiles with ornate patterns in the bathroom. 'It looks nice . . .'

'Nice? I don't do "nice", Katie. I do "amazing". The place is at its most beautiful now, in the summer when all the roses are out. This hotel ticks *all* the boxes. I mean, even Madonna has stayed there,' Sam boasts, 'so if Madonna has stayed, I think we can be sure it's going to be a classy joint. I asked if we could have the same suite she stayed in and they said they would see what they could do.'

I smile. 'You are . . .' I am about to say 'a sad name-dropper', but then I stop myself. Sam's mouth and eyes have not flickered at all. Normally, am I impressed by all of this? Yes, I suppose I am. All I want to say to him now is, Who cares?

'Sam, I had forgotten about our weekend away,' I say hesitantly.

'That doesn't matter.' Finally he finds his trainers in his gym bag that he takes to work. 'It's all booked. Done and dusted. All you have to do is enjoy it. There's a spa and beauty room. Right, I've got to run.'

He stands in front of the mirror to make last-minute adjustments to his hair. 'I'm looking forward to having this place to ourselves again.'

'Um . . . me too.'

'No offence to your sister, but, well, you know what I mean.'

She touched my arm today and it felt wonderful, I want to shout. You should have seen her expression when I took her on the London Eye. It was one of pure joy, and I was responsible for that. We played silly games on the bus and it was fun fooling around with her. Today made me feel alive. I want to tell all of this to Sam, I am aching to tell someone; but I don't think it will mean anything to him.

I will tell Emma all about it when she comes over this evening. I can't wait to tell her how well Bells and I are getting on.

Sam kisses me, bringing me back to reality. 'In a few days it's back to just you and me, babe.' As I kiss him, all I can think is that I should be feeling relieved that the two weeks are nearly up, shouldn't I?

CHAPTER NINE

'WHEN ARE YOU, er, going home, Isabel?' asks Mr Vickers. He was walking past the shop after work and Bells had rushed out to greet him.

'Tomorrow, catch train from Paddington. Do your funny thing,' Bells demands.

He looks at me nervously. I clear my throat. 'Mr Vickers, would you like to stay for a cup of tea?'

This question sets him in a spin. 'Er, er . . .' He looks at Bells.

'Stay, Mr Vickers,' she insists.

'How very, er, kind, er, of you. You are so very kind. Yes, please.'

I leave them downstairs while I go upstairs to the box-room. Eve nipped out to get some milk, she'll be back in a minute. I make the tea and take it downstairs, only to find Mr Vickers parading about in front of Bells. He appears to transform himself into a confident comedian when he is performing in front of an audience. 'Who is, er, this?' He clears his throat, puckers his lips and places his large hands behind his back. 'These plants look very interesting, well worth talking to.'

'Don't know. Who?' Bells punches his arm for an answer.

'Hello, Mr Vickers,' Eve says as she returns with the milk.

I hand him a mug of tea and a custard cream.

'Thank you so much,' he repeats. 'Do you, er, know who it is?' He looks at each of us in turn.

'I did not see you do it properly,' Eve says. 'Can you do it once more?'

He looks flattered by the attention and prepares himself again. 'These plants look very interesting, well worth talking to.'

'Oh, my goodness,' Eve says, jumping up and down. 'I know who you are, I know this voice.'

'So do I! Prince Charles,' I leap in before her.

Mr Vickers's face breaks into a smile and I find myself smiling back at him. His eyes are sunken and look weary, but when he smiles his entire face changes. 'Er, yes, you are right, er . . .'

'Katie. Call me Katie,' I tell him.

'Another one!' Bells demands just as Henrietta and her mother walk into the shop. They gawp at the strange party around my desk drinking tea. 'Do stay, Mr Vickers, and finish your tea.' I smile politely at him. 'My bank manager came round,' I tell Hen and her mother, signalling to Mr Vickers. 'It was so kind of you to come and see me personally,' I add, smiling at him.

Bells, Sam and I sit in the corner of the restaurant looking at the menus. I take another sip of my vodka and tonic, and start to crunch a large piece of ice.

'Don't do that, Katie. It's bad for your teeth,' Sam says twitchily.

'Hello, Katie.' Bells holds my hand and I can see she has the funny toy in her palm. As we touch the vibration goes off loudly. We both laugh.

'What *is* that?' Sam furrows his brow. Bells holds out her hand towards him. 'The waiter's coming over, do it later, yeah?' he mutters.

'I'd like the chicken, please,' I tell the smooth-haired waiter when he stands at our table with his pad poised.

'Chicken?' I feel someone kick me under the table.

'Sam, that hurt.'

'Katie, I'm here to spoil you and Bells. We can eat chicken any old day. Be a bit more adventurous.' He closes his menu smoothly. 'I think I'll go for the beef *en croûte*, please.'

'Certainly, sir, a popular choice,' the waiter affirms. 'How would you like it cooked?'

'Rare, please. You can't beat top-class beef.' Sam looks at me again. 'Choose something different, Katie.'

'But I love chicken, Sam.' I don't like the sound of my voice, a whimpering pathetic little sound.

He smiles at me as he touches his chin. 'Kitty-kins, you're a funny little mouse sometimes, a creature of habit.' He scans the menu for me. 'How about the scallops instead?'

'Yes, you're right,' I say firmly. 'The scallops would be lovely.'

'How about you, Isabel?' he asks.

Bells looks awkward. 'You have chips?' she asks the waiter.

Sam's face drops and now I kick him under the table. 'Yes, I'm sure you have chips, don't you?' I ask the waiter.

'Of course.'

'Why don't you have the homemade beef burger with chips?' Sam says.

'Bells is a vegetarian,' I say yet again. Does he never listen?

He raises his hands in a gesture of apology. 'Sorry I spoke.'

'Bells, why don't you have the vegetarian lasagne, with chips on the side?'

'Can choose my own food,' she shouts, banging her elbow against the table. 'Would like risotto,' she states boldly.

'You order the wine, Sam.' I push my chair back and it hits the wall. 'There's no space,' I exclaim irritably, 'is this the only table they had?' It feels like we have the children's table in the dark corner.

'I'm afraid so.'

'Really? But there are tables outside. It's warm tonight.'

He starts to rub his nose. 'Let's stay here, shall we?' His mouth starts to twitch too. 'So, what have you two been up to today? Your last night, hey, Isabel. Bet you're dying to get home.'

I know Sam is trying but he just irritates me.

'Mr Vickers said goodbye. I like Mr Vickers, nice man.'

'Mr Vickers? Who is he now? I'll just check I ordered the right wine,' Sam swiftly changes the subject. I look ahead and see a vaguely familiar man joining the group in front of us. Sam is now lifting the menu to shield his face. His mobile rings. Still holding on to the menu with one hand, he picks his phone up with the other. I start to talk to Bells and Sam excuses himself, darting through the doors that lead downstairs.

After five minutes he still hasn't returned. 'Bells.' I touch her arm. 'Be back in a minute.'

'All right,' she says flatly.

I pull the door and then see a great PUSH sign in front of me.

410

'Oh, mate, this is a nightmare.' I stand at the top of the stairs, then quietly tiptoe down a couple and lean over the banister just far enough to allow me to see him. Sam is by the cigarette machine, his back to me, one hand leaning against the wall. He starts laughing loudly. I think he is talking to Maguire. 'It's Isabel's last night and I seriously, I mean seriously, mate, need to get back in the good books with Katie. I've avoided them for a fortnight.' Sam is silent; he must be listening to something very profound. 'Too right, Maguire, hopefully more action between the sheets when she's gone. It's been like the Gobi Desert!'

I open my mouth and close it again.

'I tell you, mate, when she told me her sister was coming to stay I didn't expect this.' He pauses as he listens. 'Yeah, yeah, yeah . . . absolutely.' He starts pacing the floor. 'Too right, Maguire. This isn't what I signed up for.'

I don't know what to think.

'Yeah, I'll see how it goes. I mean, I do love her. At least, I think I do, and I know she's crazyeeee about me.'

Sharp intake of breath. Who does he think he is?

'Look, mate, better go and butter them up . . . Back to my post, yeah, you know how it is.'

The food still hasn't arrived when Sam returns. 'Sorry about that,' he says, 'a client, I had to take the call.'

On the surface I remain calm, but the pit of my stomach is a seething knot of fury. 'Really? Who was it?'

'No one you'd know, babes. All very boring stuff.'

'What did they want?' I ask casually.

'What's with all the questions? Crikey, Isabel, your sister can be a pain, can't she?' He laughs, hoping Bells will follow.

I watch Sam and can tell he is still preoccupied with the group in front of us. He is drinking quickly.

'Do you know those people, Sam? You keep on looking over?' I ask expectantly.

'No, I don't believe I do. Why don't we eat outside? You're right, it is warm tonight.' He gets up and takes his jacket.

'No, let's stay here.' I smile sweetly at him. 'Look, our food is arriving.'

Sam grimaces as he sits down again.

'Lakemore?' a man calls across to him then. 'It *is* you!' he bellows.

'Hi,' Sam says, trying to sound surprised, and puts up his hand, his cheeks burning with colour. The stout man with glasses comes over to our table. I smile at him and wait for Sam to introduce us. After a second-too-long gap I do it myself. 'Hello, I'm Katie.'

'Yes, sorry, this is Katie. Katie, Colin Lucker.'

'Hello, Katie, wonderful to meet you.'

'Hi, Colin.'

'Hello,' Bells says, holding out her hand.

'Hello, er . . .? Now who might you be?'

'This is my sister, Isabel,' I tell him.

'I'm Bells,' she corrects me.

'Hello, Bells.' Colin shakes her hand. 'Oh, my, what was that?' he laughs nervously.

I am about to tell him when Sam starts to laugh outrageously. 'Isn't it hilarious, Colin? She's a funny one is our Isabel.'

'Better be getting back to my table.' He shuffles back a few steps. 'Nice to see you again, Sammy boy. We must catch up soon.'

'Who was that, Sam?'

'Just my old boss,' he says, taking another large gulp of wine.

'Really? What a coincidence. We could join them for coffee.' The knot is unravelling in its own way. 'Mr Lucker?' I call out loudly.

Sam now kicks me so hard I don't dare to continue. 'Sorry, Colin, we'll leave you to your dinner, please ignore us,' Sam says cheerfully. He turns back to face me. 'What is your problem?' he asks in a low whisper.

'You,' I reply. I didn't want to say anything, not on Bells's last night, but I can't help it. I lean closer towards him. 'I heard everything you said on the phone just now. Everything.'

Sam runs a sweaty hand through his hair. 'What?' he finally says.

'This isn't what you signed up for, is it?' I try to look discreetly at Bells.

'Don't know what you're on about,' he mutters. 'I was talking to a client.'

'Don't lie!'

'Don't lie!' Bells repeats.

'You were talking to Maguire!'

'To Maguire.'

'What is your sister going on about?' he says to Bells, trying to keep his composure.

'Sam. I heard.'

'Well, you shouldn't have been fucking eavesdropping.'

'OK,' I say, drawing in breath. 'Let's not go into it now.'

'Sam said F word,' Bells laughs.

'Bells!' both Sam and I say together.

'You having pudding?' she asks.

'I'm pretty stuffed. Let's get the bill, shall we?' Sam turns to get the waiter's attention.

'I want a pudding.'

He allows Bells a quick chocolate brownie. While she is still eating he grabs his jacket from the back of the chair, tells me he is going to pay the bill and that we need to be ready, by the door, in five minutes. Sharp.

I stand on Bells's bed and take down her Stevie Wonder poster. The Beatles poster is pulled off the door. I open her wardrobe and take out her Chinese wedding outfit.

We fold her baggy jumpers, shirts and holey vests together. They go into the zip bag along with the medley of junk, including the buzzing device, her CDs, notepad, photograph album, box of paints and the football badges. 'Do you want to wear these . . . or these?' I hold up her large black boots and the purple pixie pair. Today she is wearing a black T-shirt I gave her from the shop with a little silver star in the middle, which is sadly hidden by her dungarees on top. She decides to go for the pixie boots.

Her large purple zip bag is finally packed; there is only one Stevie Wonder CD we cannot find. 'I'll send it on to you, promise.'

Bells doesn't appear too bothered. She tells me she will take the sheets off the bed, like they do at home.

''Bye, Isabel. It was great to meet you, and come and see us again,' Sam says, standing at her bedroom door in his jeans and leather jacket. It's funny how people are so nice to you when you are leaving.

'Thank you, Sam.' She goes forward and shakes his hand.

'No problemo.' He looks pleased that she thanked him without any prompting. 'Katie, I'll see you later.' Sam and I didn't say a word to each other last night. By the time I had said good night to Bells he was asleep on the sofa so I left him there. Now he walks away and minutes later I hear the door shut.

Bells says goodbye to her bedroom.

I take her bag and shut the door behind us.

'Passengers going to Haverfordwest need to change at Swansea,' says the loudspeaker. People are bustling past while Bells and I stand at the information desk waiting for Fiona, one of the staff in Wales, to meet us. She is going to accompany Bells back home. She is late and the train leaves in ten minutes.

'What does Fiona look like?' I am scanning the crowds. Perhaps we are in the wrong place?

'She's fat.'

'Bells!' I laugh at her.

'Like partridge.'

'Eddie and Eve would love to see you again, you'll come back, won't you?' I would love to see you again, that is what I should be telling her.

'Very nice people. Would like to see Mark again.'

'Me too.' I still think about Mark and what he did for us. We didn't manage to meet up again, and now that Bells is going, I have no excuse to ring him.

'Here's Fiona,' Bells says, her hands in a flutter. I am not sure if she is nervous or excited. Fiona is waddling towards us in a checked cotton skirt and white blouse with a frilly collar.

'Hello, I'm Katie.' I shake her hand.

'Hello,' she says. 'Hi, Bells. How are you?' Her voice warms up. 'How was your holiday? Mary Veronica has really missed you, she got back yesterday.' She takes Bells's bag and I walk behind them. 'We'd better be quick, I'm running late. I thought we were meeting at the ticket desk?'

'No, I'm sure we said . . .'

'Never mind, Katie, all is well. Was it fun, Bells?' she continues.

'Yes, fun,' Bells says. Fiona marches us onto the correct platform where the train waits. I am not going to have time to say anything now, I panic to myself, my feet pattering along to keep up. I have had all of this morning to tell Bells that I would like to visit her, that I have enjoyed the last few days so much, but I haven't said anything.

'Went on London Eye,' Bells continues. 'Saw all London.'

'How marvellous,' Fiona says. 'It sounds like you've had a smashing time.' She turns to me. 'Thank you, Katie. We'd better get on, the train leaves at nine twenty-one. Two minutes.' She steps up onto the train. Bells follows her. 'Say goodbye to your sister, Bells.'

NO! I want to shout. This is not how I imagined it would be. I want to say goodbye properly. Leave us be.

''Bye, Katie, 'bye.' Bells stops on the step and tries to turn round.

'Stand away from the door,' the guard instructs as Fiona is stowing Bells's bag in the luggage rack.

'Isabel, be careful. Mind the gap. Get right inside,' Fiona orders.

''Bye, Bells,' I call pathetically to her back. She turns and waves at me. ''Bye, Katie. Thank you for having me.' I watch her and Fiona taking their seats. Bells sits by the window, Fiona next to her. Bells looks out of the window and waves again. She hits her hand against the glass. The guard blows his whistle.

'No, hang on, don't go!' I push past the guard and press the red button to open the automatic doors into their carriage. Fiona is about to say something to me but I don't let her. 'I just want to say goodbye to my sister, properly,' I say, swallowing hard.

'Hello, Katie,' Bells says.

'Hi, Bells,' I say, my eyes beginning to fill. 'I . . .' Don't lose it now. The other passengers start to sigh and heavy-breathe around us.

'Excuse me.' The guard has followed me on board. 'We need to go. Unless you are travelling to Swansea, will you please get off the train?'

'Get a move on!' a boy jeers, pelting a tennis ball at me. It hits Fiona in the forehead and Bells starts to laugh inappropriately.

I wince. 'Fiona, I'm sorry, did that hurt?'

'Well, it did, rather.' She smiles at me now. 'Come on, quickly, say goodbye,' she urges.

I lean across and kiss Bells clumsily on the top of her embroidered hat. 'I'll come and see you, and I'll write, I promise. Will you come back to London too?'

'Yes, Katie, yes.'

I dare to make one final move before I am hurled off the train. I kiss her on the cheek. ''Bye, Bells. I've loved having you to stay.' I dig into my bag and find the photograph the Japanese couple took of us on the London Eye. I made a copy for myself on Sam's computer. 'Keep it carefully, show your friends in Wales. Put it in your album.'

'Yes, Katie, I will. Loverley photo. Thank you, Katie. Thank you.'

The guard rolls his eyes at me as he finally blows his whistle. I jog along the platform to keep up with the moving train. Bells waves at me and I wave back, tears running down my cheeks. ''Bye, Bells. 'Bye.'

The house feels so quiet as I walk inside. I go downstairs to the kitchen and give the milk-bottle sculpture a prod for Bells. I want to see some of her clutter in the room, instead the kitchen table is smooth and clean. It is eerily quiet without Stevie Wonder playing in the background. I walk upstairs and then up the further flight to our bedroom. I can't help looking into Bells's bedroom once more. I want to make sure she really has gone. The room is now a stark white again. It doesn't take long, does it?

I take a long shower. I didn't have time this morning. As the hot water blasts against my face I turn my mind to Sam. What am I going to do? Is it time to call it quits? I wash my hair, the shampoo lathering in my hands. If Sam and I split up, I lose this place, lose the convenience of living so near to my shop. I will miss the steam room, too. I mean, who else has a steam room in London?

I start to laugh. Come on, Katie, those aren't real reasons to stay with someone. What about love, commitment, having fun with someone? I did enjoy being with Sam until two weeks ago. Whatever his faults, he has his good points too. He is confident, successful, he can be charming. I love our secret dances in the kitchen and the way he sings Chris de Burgh songs to me. He is supportive of my work. Look at the way he organised my fashion show at his client's house. He has gone out of his way to book this weekend for us. He is taking me skiing this Christmas.

Maybe we just need to talk, I mean *really* talk about *real* things. If we stand a chance of staying together we have to be honest with one another and share more. I know I am very much to blame as I started the whole charade off by not telling him about Bells.

If we break up I will miss our lifestyle. Sam is handsome, he has money, a stylish house in Notting Hill, a good job. And he has chosen me. What's that terrible phrase: 'You could do a lot worse'? Surely the easiest thing is to do nothing, carry on as normal. Isn't it?

But is that enough for me any more?

That evening, I lock up the shop, but I don't want to go home. I find myself going to the bar across the road. I order a bottle of wine and buy a packet of cigarettes, too, since I don't have to put up with Sam telling me not to smoke. A bottle of wine and an hour later my mobile rings and Sam's number appears in the box. I sit staring at it. He tries to call again but I let it ring.

I pick up my mobile and am about to ring Emma. Then I put it down. Sam isn't exactly one of her favourite people and, anyway, I know what she would tell me. She always says it is better not to be in a relationship than to be in a dead one that is going nowhere. Better to go alone than be badly accompanied, she says. Of course I know what I have to do.

It's late by the time I get back home to Sam's. He's sitting on the sofa reading the *FT*.

'We need to talk,' I say, walking over to the window.

He puts the paper down. 'If it's about last night, let's just leave it, hey? I'm sorry you overheard me, it was just a load of bravado, Katie. You know what I'm like with the lads. I didn't mean any of it.'

I think about what he said to Maguire but I don't feel any anger or betrayal. I don't feel a thing. 'I've been thinking about this weekend . . . maybe we should cancel it. I think we've got a few things to sort out.'

'Sorry?'

'The weekend? I don't want to go,' I say, slowly and deliberately.

'Katie, you're joking, right?' He slams his glass onto the table. 'I'm not going to be able to get a refund at such short notice.'

He is unreal. 'Don't you want to know *why* I don't want to go?' I blurt out. 'Sam, this can't go on.' I start pacing the room.

'What can't go on? What has got into you? Is this about last night?'

'Yes,' I tilt my head, 'and no. You probably did mean what you said. This isn't what you signed up for. When we started going out, you knew nothing about my family. Well, now you do. I come with Bells. Also, I know nothing about yours. Why won't you tell me about your father?'

'There's nothing to tell,' he says, exasperated. 'He's a workaholic, I never see the guy, what else do you want to know?'

I frown with frustration. 'Where do you see us going?'

'I don't know what you're talking about.' Sam shakes his head. 'I thought we were having a great time, having some fun. Clearly,' he huffs, 'I was under the wrong impression.'

'We can go out, go to nice hotels and expensive restaurants, go skiing this Christmas, we can do all of that for another year or so, and then what?' I raise my voice. 'What next?'

'We wait and see. Jesus!' He stands up and faces me. 'What's your problem? What do you want?' His eyes open wide and he laughs sarcastically. 'A ring on your finger?'

'No way.'

'Well, what then? I thought we were happy the way we were.'

'But what about the future? If we're not right for each other we're wasting our time. I'm nearly thirty, you're thirty-six.'

Sam ignores me. 'We're going to that hotel, it's all booked,' he says, his tone overbearing. 'We need this time together. Can I have the nice fun Katie back, please? Where has she gone?'

'Sam, I know you meant what you said last night. You couldn't hack Bells, and the two weeks were pretty much a disaster.'

'It wasn't that bad, was it? I'm not used to someone like her, that's all. I thought we got on OK. Anyway, she's gone now, *c'est la vie*, move on.'

'No! Sam, I am not getting through to you at all, am I?' I shout. 'What on earth do you care about?'

'Look, you're not my shrink. What is it with this third degree? You've changed, Katie. Ever since Bells came to stay everything has changed.'

'Yes, it has, and that's no bad thing. I need a lot more than this.' I am about to say that it is not working any more, we are not right for each other and I am leaving him. 'You're a good friend, Sam,' I say, then realise he is not even that. Once we part I cannot imagine just meeting him for coffee. 'We've had some good times, but . . .'

'No way,' he says, cutting me off. 'Uh-oh, no way, I'm not listening to this. I think you should go,' he states coldly and walks past me. 'You can stay tonight, but I want you out by tomorrow. It's over between us, Katie.' I hear him go downstairs.

'Good!' I shout after him. 'I'm glad!'

I hear the front door slam shut, then sit down on the sofa and stare out of the window. I do not feel a thing. Sam gave nothing of himself to me, and I realise I gave nothing of myself to him.

I pick up his gin and tonic and drink it in one go. *C'est la vie*, Katie. Move on.

I key in the number and Dad answers immediately. They are due to come home in two days.

'Bells left today,' I tell him.

'You had a good time?' he asks, catching his breath.

'Yes, we went on the London Eye, and we bought Bells an outfit for Emma's wedding. May I have a word with Mum?'

'Katie, we have to go . . .'

'No, don't. How are you both? What have you been doing? You haven't been in touch for ages, I tried to call you the other day—'

'Katie, I can't talk right now,' he cuts me off. 'I'll call you later.'

I key in the number again but the phone's switched off now.

I sit staring at the telephone. Something is clearly wrong, why can't he tell me? Why are we such a dysfunctional family? Why can't we talk?

CHAPTER TEN

I FIND SAM'S CAR KEYS in his jacket pocket. I walk downstairs and out of the house. I find myself unlocking his BMW and turning the engine on. Who does Dad think he is fooling? Something is wrong.

As I drive down the grey motorway, I have this surreal feeling that I am looking down on myself, that it's not really me driving. I tap the steering wheel hard to reassure myself that I am in control.

I pull into our driveway. Mum and Dad's car isn't there and I instantly feel relieved. They aren't here. I shut the car door and take my house keys out of my bag. I bend down to open the bottom lock but the key won't turn. It doesn't need to be unlocked. The door creaks open as I turn the key in the other lock. Why hasn't Dad double-locked the door? He never forgets. They are here.

'Hello,' I call out, my voice echoing in the hallway. There is a lot of mail on the floor. I pick it up and put it on the hall table. I turn on a light and put my handbag down at the foot of the stairs. The curtains are drawn in the sitting room. The answering machine is on but it isn't flashing. That's strange. Surely someone has rung them since they've been away? I called once, but didn't leave a message.

My heart is racing as I walk into the kitchen. There are two dirty mugs in the sink. I touch the kettle but it's stone cold. I open the fridge. There's a packet of chicken, sitting in its blue polystyrene tray. There's a box of eggs, butter and mayonnaise on the top shelf. I shut the door.

I start walking upstairs but my pace quickens and then I'm running up them and down the landing into Mum and Dad's bedroom. The bed hasn't been made, Mum's wedding-dress quilt lies haphazardly across the sheets. Mum's moisturising cream sits on her dressing table, along with her hairbrush and tortoiseshell hair comb. I walk into their bath-room. There are Mum's and Dad's toothbrushes standing in a china pot in the shape of a fish. How dare they lie to me? Where are they? I stand, looking round the room, unable to comprehend what is going on. Then I hear the front door opening and wait to hear voices.

I can hear footsteps but no one is talking. The only immediate noise I can hear is my own breathing. 'Katie,' my father says in shock when he sees me at the top of the stairs. Mum stands next to him, her pale face vivid against her auburn hair.

My panic and fear turns to anger. 'You've been lying to me. Why are you here? Why aren't you in France?' Dad looks at Mum but neither of them say anything. 'Can someone tell me exactly what is going on?' Mum walks past Dad and into the kitchen. 'Dad?' I try.

He collapses in a heap on the bottom stair, his face buried in his hands. 'Dad, what is it?' I rush downstairs and kneel down in front of him. 'Dad, please tell me what's wrong.'

'I don't know where to start,' he finally mutters.

'Mum,' I call, my voice splintered with fear. 'Mum . . .' I lift my hand off Dad's knee and run into the kitchen. She's opened the drawer at the end of the kitchen table, where she keeps old letters. She's ripping them into shreds. She doesn't even acknowledge that I am standing there. 'What are you doing? Mum, please.' I start to shake her shoulders. 'Stop it,' I now shout. 'Please, will somebody tell me what's going on?'

'I don't know how to tell you,' she says, sitting down at last.

'Well, just try. Whatever it is, it can't make me feel much worse than what I'm feeling now. I'm terrified. Why is Dad crying?'

'Because I've just been told I have a brain tumour,' she states simply.

I watch Dad guiding Mum down the hallway. His arm is round her waist, and she moves one of her hands behind her back so that it gently touches his and their fingers interlock perfectly, like a puzzle.

I walk back into the kitchen and sit down. 'This can't be happening, it's not true. Tell me it's not true,' I say over and over again.

'I can't,' Dad says as he finally sits down at the kitchen table. 'We never thought we'd find ourselves in this position. Our GP told us it was nothing to worry about when your mother had an epileptic fit six months ago.'

'An epileptic fit?' I repeat mechanically. 'Why didn't you—'

Dad stops me. 'We didn't tell you because when we went to see the GP he dismissed it as a thing people sometimes get at our age. He told us not to worry about it.' Dad stands up and goes over to the drinks cabinet. He pours a whisky and swallows the lot. 'Then she had another one when she was in the kitchen cooking supper. She was standing right in this spot.' He slams his glass down. 'And then she had another and another, at monthly intervals, like clockwork. I insisted she saw a neurologist. When I called you to ask if you could have Bells to stay, we were due to see the neurologist two days later. I just couldn't cope with Bells and this at the same time.'

'No, I understand, but why didn't you tell me then?'

'Because we were still desperately hoping it was nothing, that the fits could be controlled with medication. She had the EEG and it showed nothing untoward. Then the neurologist suggested doing an MRI and we got the results at the hospital today.' Dad collapses back down in a chair. 'There's a tumour growing and the epileptic fits were caused by increased pressure on the brain. It may have been there for years.'

I don't know what to say.

'Believe me, Katie, I wanted to tell you so much, but she wouldn't hear of it. She felt there was no point in worrying you until we knew for sure what we were up against.'

'Can't she have an operation? Have it taken out?'

'Katie, please stop asking questions.' Dad raises his voice. 'Stop it.' He is shaking his head helplessly. Suddenly he stands up and pushes the chair away. I have never seen my father cry. I move forward to hold him, tears streaming down my own face now. He clings onto the back of my top, twisting and pulling the fabric. His face is pressed against my shoulder, and I can feel my top grow damp with his tears.

'I can't live without her, Katie. I can't live without her.'

I sit on the old dressing-up box which has now been turned into a window seat in my bedroom. I light a cigarette and blow a large smoke ring into the dark sky. I can hear happy voices in the street. Maybe they have just returned home from the pub. Do they realise that something might happen to them tomorrow that could change their lives? Of course they don't. They are just like I was a few weeks ago, thinking that it was a catastrophe when my father asked me to have Bells to stay; thinking it was the end of the world when she cut the labels out of my T-shirts. My mobile rings yet again and finally I take it out of my bag. It tells me I have three new voice messages. I dial 901 to listen to them.

'Where are you, and where's my fucking car?' Sam screams down the phone. 'Can today get any worse? Call me at once.' I switch it off and walk down the dark corridor, past Bells's old bedroom. How are we going to tell her about Mum?

I walk into the bathroom and bend over the sink, feeling sick. I stand up, open the mirrored cabinet door and stare at the various bottles and potions. Are there any sleeping pills? I pick up all the bottles in turn. There are so many, but none to help me sleep. 'God, help me,' I shout as I hurl them into the sink.

I stand in front of the mirror, the one where I used to stand and pray to God as a little girl to give me blonde hair and blue eyes. 'I know we aren't close, but I want her back.' My voice comes out jerkily. 'Dad needs her. Bells needs her. I need her. Oh, dear God, make Mum better.'

'Katie.' I hear Dad's voice, calm now. He strokes my back.

'I can't sleep, Dad. I—'

'Shh,' he hushes me. He puts an arm round my shoulders and walks me back to my bedroom.

'I can't sleep,' I repeat, walking past the bed and sitting back down on the window seat. I light another cigarette. Dad hates me smoking but he doesn't say anything. He sits down on the other end of the window seat.

I inhale deeply. 'How's Mum?'

'She's fast asleep.'

'Good. I still can't believe this is happening.'

'Nor can I.' He takes off his black-rimmed glasses and rubs his eyes. 'Oh, Katie, what are we going to do?'

'I wish I knew.'

We sit quietly, staring out into the dark sky.

'Dad,' I start cautiously. 'I think we should call Bells tomorrow. We need to tell her that Mum is unwell and that she should come home. Bells must be involved. Mum can't go on trying to protect her, or thinking she won't be able to cope, because it only excludes her and makes her feel like she's not normal and—'

'Katie,' Dad stops me abruptly, 'you're right, we agree. We want Bells here with us,' he states firmly. 'She's more precious to us than anything. You both are,' he adds quickly.

'Good, because that's right,' I say.

He stares at me quizzically. 'A few weeks ago you wanted nothing to do with Bells. You've changed. You're fighting for her.'

'I want to make up for being such a lousy sister. Since she came to stay, well, we're good friends. She's worth fighting for.'

Dad leans towards me and kisses my cheek. He reaches out for my hand and grips it tightly. 'I'm so proud of you, Katie,' he says.

I wake up from a disturbed sleep. Where am I? It takes me a minute to recollect and when I do my body feels heavy as I struggle to get up.

I find Mum in the kitchen. More letters are on the table, torn to pieces. She turns to me, a look of total calm on her face. 'Morning, Katie, did you sleep well?'

Confused more than anything, I tell her, 'Not bad. Mum, why are you tearing up your precious letters?'

'I don't want you and your father worrying about any of my business. The more I can get rid of now, the better.' She goes out of the kitchen, down the corridor, and climbs the two steps into her studio. 'What am I going to do with all these unfinished animals?' she asks herself.

'Mum . . .' I pull a chair back and sit at her worktable. 'One of us *has* to tell Bells. She has to know, today.'

She nods. 'OK. Can you arrange for her to come home?'

'I'll call her. If she gets a mid-morning train I can pick her up later.'

'I'd do it, but . . .' Her voice tails off. 'I can't even drive,' she says. 'I feel so useless, your father chauffeuring me around everywhere.'

I look at her. She is pencil thin, her eyes large and haunting. 'It's all right. I can do it, Mum. Don't be so hard on yourself.'

'How am I going to tell darling Bells?'

'Dad and I will be here. It'll be OK. We just need to tell her everything. Mum,' I start again, 'what did the neurologist say, exactly?'

'He told me I would be in charge of my pain control,' she replies, her voice once again as calm as still water as she sits down with me. 'He said we should see a neurosurgeon in Southampton. He's arranging an appointment, but . . .'

'But what?' A tiny flicker of hope presents itself. 'We will see him.'

'Katie, the neurologist thinks it could well be malignant. I'm not sure I can stand any more tests only to be told exactly the same thing. I can deal with this. I don't feel ill. In fact, it's hard to believe anything is actually wrong with me. I need to prepare myself, organise things, that's all. I just want to enjoy the time I have left.'

I shake my head. 'Mum, you need to see the surgeon.'

I don't think she is listening to me as she says, 'I want to go on holiday with your father. We always promised ourselves we'd go on a trip down the Nile, or else go back to Paris again. Or visit our old friends in France whom we haven't seen for fifteen years.'

'The ones you just pretended to be visiting,' I can't help adding.

'I'm sorry. I shouldn't have made your father lie. We were wrong about that. I would love to see them,' she insists.

'You can go, you can do anything you want, but I think we should follow the doctor's advice and see the surgeon.' I lean closer towards her, my elbows pressed hard against her worktable. 'I can't live with the knowledge that we didn't even try.'

'Nor can I,' Dad says as he walks into Mum's studio. He sits down at the table looking more positive this morning. 'I was going to say exactly the same thing.' He's holding the piece of paper with the surgeon's name and number on it.

Dad, Mum, Bells and I are sitting round the kitchen table. Dad has made a pot of tea but no one has touched their cup yet.

How are we going to tell Bells? I had told her on the telephone that Mum wasn't well and that she needed to come home.

Mum is wearing linen trousers with a white cotton shirt, her hair pulled back into her tortoiseshell clip. 'Bells, would you like some of your sage tea?' she asks, handing her a plate of chocolate digestives.

Here we are, trying to be a normal family having tea, when everything is falling apart. So I begin because I cannot bear the heavy silence. 'Bells, Mum and Dad wanted you to come home because—'

Mum stops me. 'Katie, can I?'

I nod. 'I'm sorry.'

'Darling,' Mum starts, looking directly at Bells, 'I wanted you to be here because I have something to tell you. I'm so sorry,' she says, reaching out to hold Bells's hand. But Bells won't let her take it.

'Why?' she asks.

'I have a brain tumour,' Mum states in one bold sentence.

We all wait for Bells to say something. Anything. The room is utterly silent except for Bells's heavy breathing. 'You going to die like Uncle Roger?' she finally asks, rocking backwards and forwards in her chair.

'Yes, I'll be joining Uncle Roger,' Mum says, her eyes looking upward as if to heaven. 'We'll have whisky and cherry-cake parties.'

Bells stands up to leave the kitchen. 'Going to watch *Titanic*,' she says.

Mum sits back with a look of relief, as if she has done the hard part.

'I'll talk to her again when she's ready. We'll let her watch *Titanic*.'

Dad nods and finally takes a gulp of tea. Mum takes a digestive biscuit. 'Well done, darling, you bought the dark chocolate ones.'

'No!' I shout, slamming my cup onto the table. 'You talk to her now. You tell her that we're going to see the surgeon, that we're waiting for the scans to be sent to him and that when they are'—I have to take a deep breath because I feel I am suffocating—'we are seeing him.'

Mum and Dad stare at me.

'Bells doesn't want jokes about Uncle Roger, for Christ's sake. She needs to understand. I am fed up with none of us talking, bottling everything up and pretending everything is OK, when it *isn't*.'

'Katie? Are you quite finished?' Mum asks.

We can hear the theme music to *Titanic* playing in the background.

'No, not quite,' I reply simply. 'I don't care if the boat's about to hit the iceberg. You go in there and turn *Titanic* off. You tell her now.'

I am eavesdropping outside the sitting room door. 'You scared?' Bells asks Mum.

'Yes, but I've got all my family around me.'

There's another long silence. I think Mum is comforting her. Suddenly the door opens and I quickly move away, but it's obvious I've been listening. 'I'm sorry . . . for shouting earlier,' I say to Mum.

'You were right. Now, I need to be on my own. I'm tired.' She touches my shoulder gently before walking upstairs. I hear her bedroom door shut before I go into the sitting room to join my sister.

CHAPTER ELEVEN

IT IS THE MORNING of Mum's operation.

'I think we can do something about this,' the surgeon had said, holding the MRI scan. 'I think the tumour could be benign. It may have a clear margin to cut round, so I would strongly advise you to have an operation. I can't be absolutely sure it isn't malign, but if we do nothing we shall never know.'

Was I dreaming? We had been expecting confirmation, not a different assessment altogether. I wanted to hug him, to get down on bended knee and pray to God but I tried to control myself. Dad held Mum's hand so tightly that I thought her bones might crack from the pressure.

'Thank you very much,' she said at last, as if he had just told her she could have pickle with her cheese. 'When can you slot me in?'

Now Dad sits awkwardly in the light blue armchair next to Mum's bed. I know he hates hospitals despite being so used to them. 'It never gets any easier,' he'd confided in me. Bells is sitting next to him. She hasn't said a word this morning.

'How are you feeling?' I ask Mum.

'I'm OK.' She clutches my hand. Besides her hospital gown, she is only wearing her gold wedding band and the plastic hospital wristband with her name and date of birth on it. Everything about her looks bare; stripped down. 'I'm ready to face it.' She breathes deeply. 'I'm so glad you're all here with me.'

Bells starts banging her forehead with her fist. She stands up, sits down, stands up again and then starts circling the bed. 'Sweetheart, will you sit down?' Mum pleads, clearly upset.

Bells grabs her inhaler from her pocket.

'I'm really thirsty. Can you get me a drink?' I ask in desperation. Dad immediately takes Bells off 'on a coffee run'.

I look at Mum. It is the first time we have been on our own today. 'Tell me about Sam,' she starts. Anything to fill the silence. 'Why did you break up? Was it because of Bells?'

'In a way. I think I would still be going out with him had it not been for her staying with us,' I admit.

Mum raises her eyebrows inquisitively. 'What do you mean? Did she hit him in the balls?' A small smile lights up her face.

'No, Bells has replaced whacking men hard in the balls with swapping their CDs around.'

'Your father hates me not putting the CDs back into their boxes.' Mum smiles. 'It's his biggest fetish.'

I smile back because I know he hates it too. 'Sam wasn't nasty to her,' I continue. 'He did take us out for a meal once, but he was so embarrassed because we met his old boss at the next table. Some of it's my fault. I never told him about her properly.'

'Oh, rubbish, Katie. I don't know Sam, but all I will say is that when we had Bells it sifted the good friends from the bad instantly. Some of them disappeared overnight. Will-o'-the-wisps,' she finishes neatly.

'You're right. Sam is a will-o'-the-wisp.' I have this image of him disappearing from my life like a plume of smoke evaporating into nothing.

He came to collect his car, told me how sorry he was to hear about Mum, handed me my mail, and then he was gone.

'Sometimes you find out about people the hard way,' Mum says. 'It sounds to me like Sam was pretty mediocre. Not good enough for you, Katie.'

'We just weren't right for each other.'

'No, he wasn't good enough for my Katie.' Her voice is starting to crack. She looks tired. I can see her trying to compose herself, not allow herself to cry. 'Tell me more about Bells's visit,' Mum continues.

I decide to tell her about Bells running away that wet afternoon. I tell her about my saviours, Mark and the American lady in the park. 'I was terrified. I would never have forgiven myself if something had happened to her. I shouldn't have got so angry.'

'It's easy to lose your rag.' Mum looks directly at me now.

'I didn't realise what a full-time job it is,' I run on. 'I had to watch Bells all the time and my patience did wear out.' Then I tell her about the poker night and Mum laughs so loudly that the other people in the ward cannot help but look our way.

'And we went on the London Eye. Mum, it was wonderful. Bells and I did bond, we got to know one another again. I want you to know that.' I reach into my bag and take out a letter she wrote to me.

'"Dear Katie Fletcher",' I start. 'I love the way she writes my surname,' I add, smiling. Very kind you to have me to stay in London. Very nice bedroom, lots of white. Nice house. You do that remember going to London Eye. I loved to go, saw all London and very loverley time with you on London Eye. Mark a very loverley man. You seen Mark? Mr Vickers too a very nice man. I am sorry I had to go, very kind you to invite me to come to London. Wonderful you. Hope not very Longtime to see you again. Nice you, very kind you, please send you my love. Thank you. Love, Bells. Ps Please RSVP me soon."'

Mum rests her head back against the pillow. 'Your father knew it would be good for you to spend time together. He's a wise old thing.'

'When you're better, we'll go on the Eye. You are going to come up to London and we'll go out for lunch and do fun things. Pact?'

I wait for her to answer.

'Katie, if I die . . .'

'You won't, you're going to be fine.'

'If I die,' she continues calmly, 'you'll take care of Bells and your father, won't you?'

'Mum, don't . . .'

'Listen. You were the one who made me realise that we must be honest now and say what we really feel.'

'Yeah, OK,' I acknowledge.

'I need to say it while they're not here. They'll be back in a minute.' She adjusts her position in the bed. 'Your father and I were going to redecorate the house and . . . well, he wouldn't have a clue,' she whispers, leaning closer towards me. 'You'll help him?'

'OK,' I say, feeling my bottom lip quiver.

'And you'll be there for Bells? You'll go to her open days and visit her?'

'Yes, I promise I will,' I say.

Mum looks like she is gearing herself up to say more. 'But who will look out for Katie?' she says, taking my hand again.

At that moment Dad and Bells return. Dad is holding a plastic tray with two cups of coffee on it. He sits down at the end of the bed.

'How're you, Mum?' Bells asks, rocking forward.

A nurse comes to the bedside. 'They're ready for you now,' she says.

Then they will shave Mum's hair, I can't help thinking.

Bells walks away. 'Don't like it here . . . not nice here.'

'Bells!' Mum cries out. 'Please come back. Will you go and get her?' she urges Dad.

Dad brings Bells back, trying to reassure her that nothing bad is going to happen.

'Say goodbye to your mother,' the nurse says impatiently to Bells.

I give her a hard, accusing look. How dare she make it sound so final?

Bells is rubbing her head and breathing heavily. ''Bye, Mum,' she finally says, throwing an arm over Mum's stomach and resting her head against the theatre gown. ''Bye, Mum.'

Mum strokes her hair. 'I love you. I'll see you later,' she says.

Dad is furiously writing lists at the kitchen table. I'm not sure what he's writing but it seems to help him take his mind off the operation. Bells is watching *Titanic* but she doesn't make any sound when it's about to hit the iceberg. I don't know what to do with myself. All I can do is look at the clock and watch the seconds tick by. Slowly.

Eventually the telephone rings and Dad and I move to it like lightning. 'You take it,' I say. I can hear Bells switching off the television.

Dad picks up the receiver. 'She's conscious,' he is saying, clearly repeating what the surgeon is telling him. 'It certainly looked benign.'

'Bells!' I scream, jumping up and down. 'Bells! Mum's OK!'

'Mum going to be all right,' Bells says, joining us. 'Mum all right.'

Dad flaps his hand furiously to shut us up.

'Can we visit her now?' he says. 'OK, we'll be there right away.'

427

'Go home,' Mum insists again, after I have given her some more water. 'You look even worse than me.'

I look at her. Her skin is so pale that she is almost camouflaged by the white pillow and sheets. Nothing covers her head except for a fine stubble of hair and a scar on the left-hand side of her face, curved like a question mark. It is two weeks after the operation. It was a success in that the tumour was benign and was taken out; but the surgery left her very weak and with virtually no movement on her right-hand side. She couldn't even turn herself over in bed. Everything had to be done for her and she slept a lot of the time.

Thankfully the physiotherapy is already helping her to regain strength and mobility. She has just started to get up and walk very slowly, up and down the ward. It is a miracle.

'Please, Katie, go home, darling. Take the awkward squad home too.' She is referring to Dad who is talking to one of the doctors. She thinks he fusses too much over her. She shuts her eyes. 'I need to get some sleep. And you do too,' she adds.

Mum's right. I do need some sleep. I haven't slept properly for days. Dad drives us home. We don't say much.

When I walk into the house it's very quiet. No Stevie Wonder. No Beatles. I find Bells in the kitchen again, wearing Mum's denim apron, her small hands encased in red spotted oven gloves. Yesterday Dad and I returned home and she had made us the most delicious cauliflower cheese I have ever tasted. The day before that she cooked a courgette and asparagus quiche. She chose not to come to the hospital today. In fact she hasn't been since the morning of Mum's operation. All she says is, 'Tell Mum get better.'

'Hello, how's Mum?' she asks immediately, putting a large white dish into the oven and then turning to face me. 'Mum all right?'

'She's OK, a bit grumpy and tired. She sends lots of love. Bells, wow, what are you cooking?'

'Stuffed pancakes with ricotta and spinach.' Suddenly the smell makes me ravenous. 'Made strawberry fool too. You like strawberries?'

'I love them. You are a star,' I tell her, collapsing into a chair.

'How's Mum?' she asks again, yet I know she is not expecting another answer. 'Make you drink,' she says, opening the cupboard. The bottle of vodka is laid out for me; Dad's whisky is ready for him.

She hands me my vodka. 'Bells, you really are amazing.'

Dad walks into the kitchen. 'Bells has made pancakes for supper and fixed us a drink,' I tell him and he smiles.

'How delicious,' he says. 'Thank you, Bells.'

'Sit down, Dad,' Bells insists, guiding him to a chair. 'Sit.'

'I might take my drink up with me, have a bath,' I say, prising my heavy body from my seat. I walk upstairs and into my bedroom. Bells has left a small bowl of lavender on my bedside table.

I find myself walking into Mum and Dad's bedroom. I notice she has placed the photograph of Mum and Dad's wedding by Dad's bedside light, along with another small bowl of lavender. I sit down on the bed and pick up the photograph.

I don't even hear Bells sitting down next to me. 'Mum all right?' she presses again.

'She's fine. She wants to come home though. She hates hospitals.' As I say it I quickly turn to Bells. That wasn't the most sensitive thing to say in front of her. 'Sorry, you more than anyone know what I mean.' I put my head into my hands.

'What wrong?'

'I'm tired.'

'How's Sam?'

'We're not going out any more,' I tell her. I've told her before, she must have forgotten.

'Not nice, Sam.'

'He was all right.' I hold the wedding picture in front of both of us.

'Beautiful Mum,' Bells says.

'Very.' I put the photograph back on the table. 'Thank you for my lovely lavender.'

'Lavender smells nice.'

'Thank you. You've done so much these last few weeks. Dad and I, well, we're really grateful.'

Bells rocks forward, scratching her forehead. She doesn't blush but I don't think she knows what to say or do when someone compliments her. 'In Wales, have cleaning rota,' she tells me. 'Clean Ted's room. Ted my friend.'

I smile at her. 'Ted's lucky. I just want someone to make things better, Bells. For you, Dad, for me, and for Mum, particularly Mum.'

'Mum didn't die like Uncle Roger,' she says.

She's right. I know I should be feeling fortunate. Mum is going to be all right. Yet, now that we know she's going to get better, I can't help thinking about everything else. I have no home. I'm worried for Dad. I'm worried about Mum and how we are going to cope when she comes home. It's no wonder I can't sleep. Bells is the one ray of light. Dad and I would have been lost without her.

'Do you get lonely, Bells?'

'At times.'

'When?'

'Night-time.'

'Me too. Why at night?'

'Dark. Don't like dark.'

'I just want everything to go back to normal. I want . . . hey, where are you going?' Bells has just walked off without listening to me. She's bored of me. I stare up into the ceiling. Minutes later Bells stands in front of me with the telephone.

'Who is it? I didn't hear it ring,' I say.

'Someone on phone for you.'

'Who?' I repeat, not wanting to take it until I know who it is. 'Is it Emma?' She rings every evening, around this time. It must be her.

'Mark,' she says simply.

'*Mark?*' I utter incredulously. 'Mark called?'

'No.'

'What?' I whisper.

'Katie?' I can hear in the distance. 'Hello. Katie?'

It's a man's voice. 'Who is this?'

'It's Mark.'

'Mark nice man. Mark nice. Mark helps.'

'Bells!' I say, holding my hand across the mouthpiece. 'Why did you call him? How did you get his number?'

'Mark nice man. Asked him to see us.'

'I know he's nice but . . . Oh, bugger . . .' I take my hand away from the mouthpiece. 'Hi, Mark,' I try to say casually.

'Katie, I'm so sorry to hear about your mum.'

Just hearing his voice makes me want to cry. 'It's OK, it's fine.'

'Bells asked me if I'd visit. I know this is weird, I hardly know you, but I'd like to. I mean, if there is anything I can do to help, or . . .'

'Bells would love to see you.' I can't believe he is on the phone. I tell him Mum is still in hospital and that she will be there for one more week. 'Maybe you could come when she's home?' I suggest.

'Fine. Just call me.'

'That would be great,' I say, realising how much I would like to see him too. 'Really great. I'll be in touch.'

After our conversation Bells claps her hands. 'Mark coming!'

'How did you get his number?' I ask again.

'Took it from bag. Had it in London. Kept it.'

I can't stop smiling. Mark is coming to see us! This is so random, so unexpected. Yet, at the same time, nothing feels more normal.

Bells and I are at the station, waiting for Mark to arrive. Mum has been at home for two days. It is fantastic having her back.

'Three minutes,' Bells says, looking at the flashing sign hanging above the platform.

'Two minutes . . . One minute . . . Mark!' Bells waves.

He walks towards us. His hair looks unbrushed and he is wearing the round glasses that make him look like a professor.

Bells hits his arm. 'Hello, Mark.'

'Hi, Bells.' He shakes her hand affectionately. Then he turns to me. It's that awkward moment when we don't know how to greet one another. Hug? Kiss? Hold hands? I lean towards him, ready to kiss formally on the cheek, but he puts his arms round me. 'I couldn't believe it when I heard the news. I'm so sorry.'

'Thank you for coming,' I say, not wanting to let him go.

When I open the front door Mum calls, 'Darling, we're in the kitchen.' She is longing to meet Mark. 'Is this the nice chap who helped you find Bells?' she'd asked me. 'Is he a boyfriend?'

'No,' I insisted. 'I've only met him a couple of times, Mum. He's Bells's friend as much as mine.'

Now Mark, Bells and I walk into the kitchen and are confronted by the sight of Mum, Dad and a very plump man standing behind a trolley stacked high with wigs.

'Hello, Mark,' gushes Mum, holding out a hand. She pats her head nervously. Her hair hasn't grown back apart from a few wisps. Dad tells her she looks like a fluffy chick. 'Katie, Bells, Mark,' she says, examining him closely again to see if he could be potential husband material, 'this is Mr Marshall, the wig man.'

He extends one thick hairy arm and shakes our hands. 'Isn't your mother doing well?' he beams. 'All we need to do now is fit her up with a nice wig and then she'll be the talk of the town!'

He bends down and takes a wig from his trolley. He holds up something that is ginger and cabbage-shaped, and I am dangerously close to laughing out loud. I know Mark is too, I can feel the vibes coming from him. Mum looks horrified. Dad is speechless. Bells roars with laughter. 'Very funny,' she says. 'Ha-ha, very funny!'

Mr Marshall looks puzzled but gamely carries on. 'This is a close match to your original colour. Shall we give it a go?'

He places it carefully on Mum's head, smoothing it over and making sure there is not a single hair out of place. He proceeds to stand back in admiration. Mum looks at Dad, waiting for a reaction. Dad looks at me. I look at Mark. Mark turns to Bells.

'You need a mirror,' Mr Marshall says when none of us utters a word. He holds up a square mirror in front of Mum. 'It looks super on you.'

Mum shrieks with dismay. 'But I had auburn hair, like my daughter, Isabel.' She glances at herself again and then quickly averts her eyes. 'I don't want to wear this. It looks like I have a satsuma on my head.'

'Mum, we can buy you some really pretty silk scarves,' I suggest. 'You don't have to wear a wig.'

We all agree, except for Mr Marshall who looks crestfallen as Dad and I show him out with his trolley of untouched wigs.

'Thank you for coming anyway,' Dad says quietly. 'I'm sorry if we sounded rude or ungrateful, but I don't think a wig's the answer.'

'No problem,' Mr Marshall says, 'but don't hesitate to ring me if you change your mind.' He bustles his trolley out of the front door.

When we walk back into the kitchen Mum is talking to Mark.

'I think you made the right choice,' Mark now assures her. 'A silk scarf would suit you much better.'

I smile gratefully at him. I am so glad he's here. Dad steps forward and kisses the top of her head. 'I love you, no matter what. You don't ever need to hide behind your hair. What was it we always said to you, Bells?'

'You look world in the eye,' she says.

'That's right,' Dad confirms. 'You look the world in the eye.'

Mum and I are watching an old black and white film on television. She is making a new tapestry cushion. She can never sit still and do nothing. Her colour is returning and her mobility improving each day.

She looks pretty in her rose-patterned scarf and the large dangling earrings that I bought for her. When Mark came down for the day, Bells and I took him shopping. 'They look like chandeliers,' he said, when I held the earrings up to my face. It was lovely seeing Mark, even though we had no time on our own. Mum and Bells monopolised him.

'Katie, you need to think about going back to London,' Mum says to me out of the blue. 'You need to go home.'

'I can't go, not yet.' I don't want to go. The idea fills me with horror.

'I feel guilty, keeping you from your friends and your life.'

'That doesn't matter. Nothing matters except you getting better.'

Mum puts her needle down and turns to me. 'You've been wonderful but you can't stay here for ever.'

'But who's going to make you breakfast in bed and cook? Dad can't cook. No, we can't leave you, not yet.'

'I'm getting better all the time and your father is a good nurse. It's time you and Bells went home.'

'I'm not sure,' I say nervously.

'I'm sure. You need to start thinking about where you are going to live,' she says with concern.

'I don't know . . .'

'Katie,' Mum puts her sewing on the table, 'I can't thank you enough for everything you've done.'

'I haven't done much.'

'You have, Katie,' Mum says. 'But I've been a dreadful mother.'

I feel a rush of blood coming to the surface.

Yes, you have. You were too wrapped up in your work, you distanced yourself from me and put all your time into Bells, saving only a crumb for me. I felt invisible most of the time. It felt like you didn't want to be involved in my life. That's what I would have said to her six weeks ago. Yet none of it really matters now.

'Mum, don't—'

'No!' She stops me abruptly. 'I want to. Let me. I've never been any good at saying how I feel. No better than you in fact.' She laughs painfully. 'If I can't say it now, I'll never be able to.'

'OK, tell me.'

'I've never let myself accept that I didn't give you enough time, that you needed me as much as Bells, just in a different way. I should never have said how lucky you were not to have her problems, it was the easy way out. I didn't applaud you in your own right. I've missed out on such a large chunk of your life and I want to make up for it. I know I retreated into my own world. My work became everything because it took me away from the everyday grind. Then you left home and suddenly you didn't need us any more. and look at you now. A beautiful, successful woman.'

'I'm not.'

'You are.' Mum stands up and walks slowly out of the room. 'I've got something for you,' she says. 'Stay there.'

She returns, holding a small gift wrapped in white tissue paper. She sits next to me as I unwrap the present. It is an oval silver box with an inlay of tortoiseshell and inside is her precious tortoiseshell comb. 'My mother gave the comb and the box to me as a wedding present.'

'I love this box, it's beautiful. And your comb . . . you always wear it.'

'Well, it seemed perfect timing,' she says, adjusting her scarf. 'Besides, I want you to have them. It's a thank-you for all you've done.'

I put the box down and hug Mum.

'Why did it take us so long to talk? Why did it have to take this to bring us together?' she asks, holding me close. 'I'm so sorry.'

433

CHAPTER TWELVE

BACK TO NORMALITY. Back to stocktaking, ordering from suppliers, organising the next fashion show. Back to yoga and swimming, going out again and socialising. Back to the daily grind of London.

I have moved in with Emma and Jonnie. They have a small house with a garden near Turnham Green Terrace, and Emma insisted I stay in their spare room until the New Year, just before they get married. Being with her has made the move far less daunting and it's ideal when they live so close to my shop and so near to Mark. I need to call him soon to let him know we are temporary neighbours.

This evening I am going to Jonnie's parents' home near Lisson Grove for supper. Since being back in London I haven't seen that many people. Last week, I went over to Sam's to pick up my sewing machine. It was the last thing I had to collect. I still have keys so I went in my lunch hour when he was at work. His house looked just the same. Everything spotless and in the appropriate place. It didn't look like I had ever been there. I put the keys through the door. "Bye, Sam,' I said.

As I wait in the sitting room for the taxi, I look at Emma and Jonnie's engagement photos taken in Battersea Park. They are in black and gilt cardboard folding frames. I pick one up off the mantelpiece. They remind me of those cards I used to take home with the end-of-year school photographs. Just thinking about home makes me miss it. It's ironic. All I wanted to do was leave home when I was a teenager. Now, it's the only place I want to be. I felt safe there. I felt needed.

The day I left, Dad and I stood quietly on the platform waiting for my train to arrive, both locked in our own thoughts. I was thinking about being a child again, climbing onto the train with my red suitcase to see Aunt Agnes, and Dad waving goodbye as the train started to move.

'I don't want to, I'm not going,' I said as the train approached.

Dad smiled as he brushed a strand of hair away from my eyes and tucked it behind my ear, like he used to do when I was young. 'You have to go.' He opened the door and helped me in with my luggage. 'Mum and I will be fine on our own.'

Bells had left the day before. 'One down, one to go,' Dad had said.

She was happy to go back. She missed college, her friends, her football and her normal routine. I hadn't missed anything and that scared me. 'Who's going to cook for you, Dad?' I called out as the train slowly started pulling away.

He waved his hand at me. 'I'll manage without Bells, don't worry.'

We blew kisses to each other. It was like a contest to see who stopped first. Dad's figure quickly faded into the distance. He was the only person left standing on the platform.

I open one of the photographs again. Emma is sitting down, Jonnie behind her with his arms wrapped around her shoulders. She's wearing a red dress that contrasts with her cropped dark brown hair and brown eyes. He's wearing a pale blue shirt to go with his blue eyes. It's all very colour-coordinated and very grown up. The doorbell finally rings and I put the photograph back in its place.

Emma hands me a large glass of wine. It's a solid, wide-brimmed glass that can hold almost a quarter of a bottle. Perfect. Jonnie leads me into the sitting room. 'You must meet my parents,' he says. They are standing expectantly by the fireplace. 'Mum, Dad, meet Katie.'

'Call me Will.' He is a big beefy man so it's forgiven that I nearly laugh out loud when I hear his soprano voice.

'Call me Hermione.' Jonnie's mother steps forward to shake my hand. She must come up to about my waist. She looks like a hamster and is wearing these peculiar multicoloured pointed shoes which curl up at the toes like the end of a gondola. She looks the way Will sounds.

'What do you do, Katie?' he enquires, wide-eyed and smiling. I am still trying to keep a straight face. Why didn't Emma warn me about that voice? She must have known how I'd react.

'I own a clothes shop,' I tell him.

'Oh, how interesting,' he squeaks, touching his navy V-neck jumper with both hands. It reminds me of the jumpers golfers wear.

'What's it called?' Hermione chirps enthusiastically.

'Well,' I cough, 'it's called FIB.'

'Fib?'

'It stands for Female In Black,' I tell her.

'Oh,' she says, her voice heavy with disappointment. 'I think black is so dreary, all you young things wear it,' she comments, scanning my outfit. I am wearing a soft black rounded-neck jumper with sequins edging the cuffs. 'So, you're living with Jonnie and Emma, I gather?' Hermione has lost all interest in my career, then.

'Yes, that's right,' I say, and then add, 'until I find my own place.'

435

'You're not married then, Katie?' Both Will and Hermione look at me expectantly, like Little and Large. I gulp down some more wine. 'No,' I say, and feel compelled to add, 'not yet.'

Hermione's mouth shrivels like a prune. She really does look like a hamster. 'You young people wait for so long. I married Will when I was just twenty. I had three children by the time I was your age.'

I am tempted to say she probably had to marry her husband quickly before he changed his mind and did a runner.

'Do you have any brothers or sisters?' the hamster enquires hopefully.

I take one more glug of wine to brace myself for the question which I know is coming next.

'I have a sister.'

'Is she married?'

'No.'

'Mum! Stop being so nosy,' Jonnie calls from the kitchen. 'Mum thinks everyone over twenty-one should be married,' he warns me.

'Oh. What does she do?'

Of course she was going to ask that. Asking people what they do is a kind of nervous tic with the middle classes. I cough even though I don't need to and draw in a deep breath. 'Well, Bells is a slightly unusual case. Er . . . she . . .'

'Bells? Is that what she's called?'

'Sorry. Bells—Isabel. We've always called her Bells for short. She lives in a kind of community, it sounds like a farm but it's not,' I add.

'She works on a farm?' Hermione creases her forehead in confusion. 'Is she a volunteer?'

'No, she's not a volunteer,' I say, twisting the silver ring on my finger. 'She lives there. It's a special home for . . . people with disabilities.'

If Hermione was in one of those hamster wheels she'd be spinning out of control by now. 'You mean, she's mentally handicapped?'

'Yes, I suppose if you put it that way,' I say stiffly, 'she is.'

'Oh dear, what a shame,' Will pipes up. 'Poor, poor thing.'

'She's not a poor thing,' I voice defiantly. 'She's wonderful. She's a very good cook, loves music and football. She has a magical sense of humour, too. Bells is her own person, and if you told her she was a poor thing she would hit you hard in the balls.' I want to take back the last bit but it's too late. Jonnie roars with laughter; Emma lets out a snort. I look at Will and Hermione but their expressions are still pitying. They're not listening. I let out a desperate, 'Do you need a hand?' to Emma and Jonnie in the kitchen.

'No, we're fine,' Emma calls back and I can hear the smile in her voice. Jonnie sympathetically tops up my glass.

'What's a pretty girl like you doing on her own tonight?' my taxi driver asks as he turns on the engine. Emma bundled me into the cab because she is staying with Jonnie and his parents tonight. 'Do you have a boyfriend?'

This cab driver is very forward, isn't he? 'I have one, thanks,' I hiccup, deciding it's much more fun to lie. 'I'm afraid I can't talk too much about it, though,' I say, crouching forward into the space between his seat and the front passenger one. 'A bit complicated. Wouldn't want it making headline news. We have to leave separately, too risky otherwise with the paparazzi.' I sink back into the seat and hiccup once more. 'Oops, sorry.'

'I don't believe you, man,' he laughs.

'OK,' I concede. 'I'm on my own. I've just split up.'

'I knew it,' he exclaims. 'I can sense things. Oh, that's sad. Too bad. I missed my wife when we split, you know what I mean?'

'I'm a bad picker of men. My last boyfriend was shallow and said silly things.'

'You pick the vermin?'

'What?'

'Vermin. That's what I call all those people who aren't any good. There are a lot of them out there, you know what I mean?'

'Vermin! I like that. I have this picture of rat-like people scurrying around with red flashing lights to show they are hazardous.'

'Yeah, rodents, man,' he laughs with me.

'Whoah, slow down, stop here,' I say, sitting forward again. I want to buy another bottle of wine from the off-licence.

I clamber out and pay him through the front passenger window. He smiles at me. 'You stay away from the vermin,' he says.

As he pulls away, I head into the off-licence and stare at the bottles of wine in front of me. In the end I take any old one and totter to the till. 'Thank you,' I say, clutching the carrier bag. 'Have a good day.'

'Katie?' I hear.

I stop and turn round. I know that voice. I tilt my head at him. He's holding a bottle of water and a large packet of barbecue-flavour crisps.

'Mark.' I smile, unable to conceal my delight at seeing him.

'What are you doing here?'

'I live here.' I explain I am staying with Emma temporarily.

'That's great. How are you? And how's your mother?'

'She's not here.' Why did I just say that?

Mark looks at me strangely. 'I have to pay for this, hang on a sec. Don't go anywhere.' He delves into his pocket to find some change.

I tell him I'll wait outside and do a quick drunken skip on the pavement. This is turning out to be a much better evening than I thought.

Hallelujah! I love Mark! We start to walk home, me cursing that we will be there in thirty seconds. Why can't we live at least a mile away?

'I've been waiting for you to call. When did you get back?' he asks.

'Five days ago. I would have called but I've had so much to do.'

'Don't worry, I understand. Well, this is me,' he says, stopping outside a black door with two steps leading up to it. 'But I'll walk you back to Emma's.'

I don't budge an inch. I can't let him go. I like him. I wanted to call him but I lost my nerve without Bells as an excuse. I need to pluck up the courage now. What have I got to lose any more? 'Can I come in? Let's crack open this bottle of wine.' I start walking up the steps.

He takes an arm to steady me. 'Don't you think you've had enough?' he asks, amusement in his tone.

I frown at him disapprovingly.

He gives in.

Mark's flat is small. His bike leans against the corridor wall. We go into the sitting room and I collapse into a soft sofa.

'I'm going to put the kettle on,' he tells me as he walks out of the room. 'Do you want a coffee?'

'What do you do?' I start talking to myself. 'What do you dooooo?' I can hear Mark laughing in the kitchen. Five minutes later he comes back with two mugs. I peer into my coffee as if I don't know what it is. 'It's Saturday night. I've been terrorised all evening by Jonnie's parents. Believe me, I need a proper drink.' I kick a wineglass on the floor at my feet. 'Oops! What are all these wineglasses doing?'

'Doing?' Mark grins. 'They're having a party.'

There's an open bottle of white wine on the coffee table in front of me. I pour some into the nearest glass, spilling a little. Mark picks up another glass that is precariously close to being kicked over. I can smell his aftershave. I suddenly want to nuzzle into his shoulder and have a hug. 'This place is a real tip, isn't it? Did you have a party tonight?'

'I had a few friends over.'

'You had a few friends over,' I repeat seriously, followed by a large gulp of wine. 'You know, Mark, it really is dandy to see you.'

'Dandy?' he laughs. 'I like that word.'

'You English teacher, you. D'you think it's fate, Mark, the way we bump into one another? There I am, at the off-licence, and—poof! We bump into one another, just like that. Or you living so close to Emma and me moving here, right next door to you. It's meant to be. Has to be.'

Mark raises one eyebrow.

'I've always wanted to do that!' I peer at him, my mouth hanging open. 'D'you know, I think it might be destiny, Mark. D'you believe in destiny?' He looks unsure. I lift myself up off the sofa to walk over to his music machine and look through his CDs. '*My Fair Lady*? Oh my God, you're gay. Haah!' I sigh deeply. 'It makes sense.'

Mark looks bewildered now. 'I am not gay, it's a school CD. We're putting on a production this year.'

'What's all this paper?'

Mark stands up abruptly and takes the bundle from me, putting it back on the desk. 'It's my book.'

'Oh. Shall we dance?' I twist round and Mark catches me, releases the glass of wine from my hand and holds me still. He could let go of me now, I think. Eventually he does and I collapse back onto his sofa.

'Look, I think you need your bed. Do you want me to take you home?'

'Do you want me to go home?' I ask coyly, trying to be seductive. 'You know, you're very attractive, Mark. Come a bit closer.' He edges nearer to me. 'Don't look so worried, Mark.' I close my eyes for a second, in anticipation of a kiss.

'Katie.' I feel a hand shaking my arm. 'Oh, shit, Katie. Wake up, Katie, please.' The words are echoing around me as I fall into a deep blackness.

I wake up the following morning on a soft sofa with a rug over me. I attempt to move. My head! I start to groan. I hold it heavily in my hands. I swallow. My mouth feels like a sewer. I summon all my strength to sit up, pulling the rug with me. Where am I? There is a glass of wine on the table in front of me and the smell of it makes me feel sick. I'm still wearing my clothes from last night. This is a bad dream. My head hits the pillow again. The last thing I remember vaguely was drinking stewed coffee. I shut my eyes and go back to sleep.

Later, I am woken by cramp in my arm. Quickly, I fling off the hairy tartan rug and stand up and start to shake my arm about. The wineglasses have gone. I look around me once more, trying to piece together the events of last night. Papers and books overflow from a desk and a tall silver lamp with long spidery legs stands to one side of a computer. There's a white-painted shelf holding even more books and a small television in the corner of the room. Sam would have a breakdown if his place looked like this. I pick up a glass of water from the floor and drink it steadily in one go. Next to the glass is a packet of white pills. There's a scrap of paper on the floor with a torn-off ring binder edge. *I've gone for a run, will be back soon, Mark. PS. These are for the sore head.*

Mark . . . I saw Mark last night! Of course I did. Where did I think I was? I start pacing the floor, knocking over a white plastic bowl. This is embarrassing. Did he think I was so drunk I was going to be sick in this during the night? Obviously he did.

He'll be back soon. How come I stayed here? I remember meeting him, but staying the night? Try to remember, Katie . . . My head feels cobwebby. What I could do is run back to Emma's and Jonnie's, have a shower, get myself looking decent and return to say thank you for . . . what? I'll figure that out later. Desperately I try to kick myself into action but nothing happens. I hear the distant bang of a door followed by a key turning nearby. My heart jumps again at the thought of seeing him.

Mark comes into the room clutching a carrier bag and a newspaper. His face looks fresh and squeaky clean. 'Good morning.' He smiles as if he has won a premium bond. 'How are you feeling?'

'Fine!' I lie. I wait for any clue as to why I found myself on his sofa.

'Really? You look terrible,' he says.

I laugh and admit, 'I feel dreadful. Worse than I look.'

'I bought us some breakfast. Well, lunch really. Stay for brunch, shall we say? I'm not going to take no for an answer so come into the kitchen when you're ready. Have a shower, if you like.'

My God, he is offering me a shower. Next he will be offering me his toothbrush. How has this happened? 'Mark,' I call, making my way to the kitchen. I find him at the stove frying bacon. I love the smell of bacon and toast. I sit down, suddenly starving. 'Mark, what were we talking about last night?' I ask tentatively.

'Nothing much.'

'I wasn't talking crud?'

'Crud? I love your turn of phrase. I particularly like "dandy".'

'Dandy? What was I saying last night?'

'I can't really remember,' he says, the corners of his mouth turning slightly upwards as he pretends to be absorbed in cooking.

'Come on,' I gently encourage. 'You can remember, I can tell.'

'All right then. You said it was dandy seeing me, and then conked out.'

I put a hand over my mouth. 'I'm so sorry. Was I really so drunk I couldn't make it five steps back home?'

'Yes, pig drunk.'

'Pig drunk?'

'I tried to lift you . . .'

'I am definitely going to start swimming,' I promise virtuously.

'Katie, I didn't mean that. Look at you, you're stick thin.'

'I eat like a horse but I run on my nerves. I've got my mum's genes.' Mum. I must ring today and see how she is. 'She's thin too but we both have round curvy bottoms,' I add proudly.

Mark raises an eyebrow as he scoops the bacon from the pan and puts it on some kitchen roll. He turns to me with the spatula in his hand. His pale blue shirt collar is sticking up rigidly and he is wearing that navy jumper with holes in the elbow again.

As we eat our bacon sandwiches and drink coffee, Mark asks me about Sam and why I am not living with him any more. I censor the story. I don't tell him exactly why; I don't mention what Sam said in the restaurant; all I say is that the relationship had run its course. Mark nods thoughtfully. 'I'm sorry. Is there a chance you can get back together?'

I shake my head adamantly. 'There is nothing left to say. I pick rodents.' I start to smile, slowly remembering the cab drive home.

'What?' Mark has that baffled look again.

'Never mind. What are you doing today?'

'I've got to finish my book. Deadline is tomorrow.' Mark looks at his watch. 'In fact, I must go soon.'

I feel a sharp twinge of disappointment. 'Don't you write from home?'

'Sometimes. I've just rented out this tiny office space because I find it easier writing away from here.'

'That sounds like a good idea. What's the book about?' I now feel I have to keep the conversation steered away from last night. Flashbacks are appearing in front of me like warning lights. *Do you think it's fate, Mark, the way we bump into one another?* I sink further into my seat.

The doorbell rings.

Mark picks up the entryphone. 'What a surprise,' he exclaims. 'I thought you weren't coming down until tonight?'

Oh my God, you're gay. I don't know when to stop, do I? Oh, well, what does it *really* matter? I try to convince myself.

'Are you going to let me in?' I hear from outside the flat.

'Sorry.' He presses the entry button.

'Who is it?' I ask casually.

'My girlfriend. She lives in Edinburgh.'

'Oh, right, that's nice.' A deep thud of disappointment hits the bottom of my stomach. 'Right, I should go,' I say.

A tall girl with light brown hair held loosely in a ponytail walks into the kitchen. She's wearing jeans and a fitted white shirt with small black dots on it. She steps forward to give Mark a kiss. 'Hello, you,' she says and they briefly hug. 'Surprise! I decided to catch an earlier train.'

Mark coughs. 'Jess, I'd like you to meet Katie.'

'Oh, hello.' She swings round in surprise. She smiles uncertainly at me and I can tell she is trying to work out why I am in Mark's kitchen, dressed in a black evening top, with smudged black-ringed eyes.

'Right, I'd better be off,' I say.

'Mark, sorry, but who . . . I mean, what's going on?'

'Nothing is going on,' he states firmly. 'I've told you about Katie,' he assures her. Then he looks at me. 'Sorry, but I told Jess about your mother, I hope you don't mind?'

'Oh, you're Katie,' she exclaims with some relief. Then bites her lip and looks at me closely again. 'How is your mother?' she asks slowly.

'She's much better, thanks.'

But Jess isn't listening. 'What exactly is going on?' She stares at Mark hard, then turns back to me. 'Did you stay the night?' she asks me coolly.

'Yes, I did stay, but definitely not in the way you think I did.'

'Jess, this is ridiculous,' Mark says. He makes her sit down at the table next to me, and pulls up a chair for himself. 'Katie and I bumped into one another last night at the off-licence. I walked her home, I wanted to find out how her mother was. She came in for a drink—and you were so tired, weren't you?' He gestures towards me. 'Then she fell straight to sleep on the sofa,' he finishes earnestly.

'I'm sorry, Jess, Mark was just being a good friend. I was really tired.'

'So nothing happened,' she says.

'Nothing,' Mark and I say together.

'Look, Katie slept next door.' He leads her into the sitting room.

'Mark, if you're lying to me, I couldn't bear it,' I can hear Jess saying quietly to him as she knows I am only a room away.

'You know I wouldn't lie to you,' he reassures her. This is the perfect time to make my escape. I edge my chair back, trying not to disturb them, and open the front door. 'I know it might look suspicious but I swear nothing happened. Come on, Jess,' Mark is saying.

Gently I shut the door behind me and start walking home, taking each step very slowly. The shock of Jess's arrival is now replaced with a nagging sense of disappointment that Mark has a girlfriend. *You know, you're very attractive, Mark. Come a bit closer. Don't look so worried . . .* I have made a complete fool of myself.

'Hey, why did you go without saying goodbye?' I hear. I turn round and see Mark racing towards me on his bike, his typescript balanced between the handlebars. He comes to an abrupt halt and the script flies onto the road and scatters into a hundred sheets.

'Shit!' Mark curses on his hands and knees. 'I knew I should have put it in a bag.' He is desperately grabbing sheets of paper. One floats off into the middle of the road and I bend down, trying to retrieve it. 'You weren't going to say goodbye?' he mutters.

'I need to go home, get out of these smoky clothes and have a bath.'

I smile at him. 'Shouldn't you be with Jess?'

'I have to get this work done, it won't take long,' he says. 'It's fine,' he reassures me.

'We know nothing happened so we have nothing to feel guilty about.'

'Exactly.' He stands up and I stand up with him. I start walking. He grabs his bike and follows me. 'Well, this is me.' I stand outside a red door with bits of paint flaking off it. 'Thanks, Mark, I'll see you soon.'

'Dandy.'

'Dandy,' I repeat. Mark doesn't say anything now. ''Bye then.' I start to turn the key in the door, aware that he still hasn't gone.

'Katie? I feel I should have told you—about Jess, I mean.'

'It doesn't matter,' I say, an octave too high.

This time he makes no reference to Bells. 'I'd like to see you again. There's no harm in us meeting for a . . .'

'Coffee?'

'And a sticky bun?' He pulls that funny crooked face.

'You know where I am.'

'Great. Friends?'

Ouch! That's painful. Did he think he had to say it so I wouldn't make a pass at him again?

'Friends,' I say.

CHAPTER THIRTEEN

THE HOUSE IS MODERN, down a very steep drive. Mum warned me how steep it was and that I must leave the car in gear. I have bought my own second-hand car and I love it. It's small, silver, shiny and fast. The next thing I need to do is buy a flat. I have saved enough now to put down a decent deposit. What am I waiting for?

My legs are stiff and aching from the long journey. I should have arrived at least half an hour ago had it not been for getting lost along the endless winding narrow roads. There are no signs outside Bells's house, it really was a stroke of luck I suddenly came upon it. I spotted a tall man wearing a track suit, with a bright blue jumper and an identity card around his neck, motioning me into the drive. I recognised him immediately from Bells's photograph album.

'Hello, I'm Ted,' he says, holding out a large hand which I shake. He has curly brown hair, the colour of a conker, and bright blue eyes.

'Hi, Ted. I'm Katie, Bells's sister.'

'Hello, Bells's sister. Welcome to Wales.'

A tall man with dark hair walks out and says hello too, asking me how my journey was. His name's Robert. He is one of Bells's 'key workers'. He leads me inside, down a long corridor, past a pinboard which gives details of the events of the month, and into the kitchen. 'Isn't the weather remarkable today?' Ted says, following closely behind. 'They said there would be lots of rain, but we haven't had a single drop.'

'Ted is fascinated by the weather,' Robert tells me. 'There's nothing he doesn't know about weather fronts across the country.'

The kitchen's the colour of primroses, and kept immaculately clean. I like the feel of the place immediately. Behind the long wooden kitchen table there are glass doors that open out onto a terrace and garden. 'What a lovely house,' I acknowledge, looking round the room.

'We like it,' Ted says proudly.

'Bells will be down in a minute, she heard your car arrive. Would you like a tea? Coffee?' Robert stands ready at the kettle.

'I'd love a tea, please.'

Above the larder fridge is a black and white photograph of Bells wearing her dungarees, standing over a wheelbarrow filled with cooking apples. She's smiling with her thumbs up. Robert can tell I'm looking at it.

'She's a great girl, Bells,' he comments. 'She's always doing something. She can't sit still, can she, Ted?'

'Never,' he says with authority. 'Bells and I go to college together. We learn all kinds of stuff, like art and writing, and I'm learning to dance.'

'Really? What kind of dancing?'

'Ballroom dancing.'

There's another photograph, on the other side of the room, to which Ted leads me. 'Guess where I am?' he says. I peer at the photograph. I can see Bells dressed in an Elvis outfit, strumming a tennis racquet as a guitar. Ted is just behind her, wearing what looks like a shiny all-in-one outfit, with fake sideburns. He's playing the drums.

'There you are!' I say, pointing.

'Groovy, huh?' He starts to laugh. 'It was my birthday party. Everyone had to dress up as Elvis Presley.'

'Really groovy.' I smile back.

I'm dying to see Bells so I ask if I can go upstairs, but then she walks into the kitchen. She's wearing her red football slippers, a pair of track-suit bottoms and the black T-shirt I gave her with the silver star on it. 'She's wearing it in your honour,' Robert says, winking at Bells.

'Hi, Bells.' She walks towards me. I'd like to hug her but Bells doesn't really do hugs. Instead we shake hands and then she hits me affectionately on the arm and I hit her back. 'That's right,' she says.

I pick up my bag. 'I brought you some olives and some cheese biscuits, and Eddie asked me to give you this ginger cake.'

'Eddie at deli.' She takes the bag. 'Thanks, Katie.'

After drinking our tea, Bells leads me upstairs. There is a large DO NOT DISTURB sign stuck to her door, along with lots of peeling off football stickers. Her room is small, with a single bed in the corner, and there is no wall space that hasn't been filled with paintings, stickers, posters, CDs and newspaper cuttings. There's the familiar poster of Bob Marley smoking a joint, and the one of the Beatles.

'How's Mum?' she asks. Her chest is wheezing. She picks up her inhaler from her bedside table.

'She's much better.'

I walk over to her window and catch a glimpse of the sea. 'Bells, wow!' I sigh. 'What a view you have. It's beautiful.'

She stands just behind me, breathing heavily. 'You like sea?' she asks, clearly pleased that I am impressed.

'I love the sea,' I say, turning to her. 'Come on, let's go for a walk.'

It's warm, but there are some dark threatening clouds hanging over us. We walk across the pale sand. I bend down and pick up a handful, letting it sift through my fingers like grains of sugar. Bells walks ahead of me. 'Do you swim in the summer?' I ask, catching up with her.

'No, too cold.'

I ask her if we can sit down for a minute. We have walked a long stretch of the beach. It's so peaceful here. There is not another soul in sight and the only sounds we can hear are from the seagulls.

'How's Dad?'

'He's all right. A bit tired from Mum bossing him around.' I gently nudge Bells.

'That's right.' She nods thoughtfully. 'Poor Dad. How're you?'

'I'm back in London, staying with Emma.'

'How's Emma?'

'She's fine. Getting ready for her wedding.'

'How's Sam?'

'I don't know. I haven't seen him. Did you get my last letter?'

'Yes. How's Aunt Agnes?'

After Bells and I have discussed every friend and member of our family, we start walking back. She continues to show me round her home and I can tell how proud she is by the way she points out everything. The sitting room has a piano. 'Ted plays piano,' she tells me. 'Poor Ted,' she adds, striking a key.

'Why poor Ted?'

'Very lonely, has no family.'

'No one visits Ted,' Robert says. He stands resting one hand on the door handle. He must have overheard us. 'I've worked here for twelve years and Ted hasn't had one visitor in that time,' he reflects. 'Everyone here loves Ted; he looks after us all.'

'Ted champion on trampoline,' Bells adds. She is looking at the collection of videos next to the television.

I turn to Robert. 'So you've worked here for twelve years?'

'Yep, and I love it. My father worked here, so it runs in the family. I don't know what else I'd do.'

'You seen *Trading Places*?' Bells asks me.

'I love that film,' I exclaim. Robert and I walk over to join Bells, and I look over her shoulder at the videos. 'Oh, *Tootsie*, that's my favourite!'

'Very funny, *Tootsie*,' Bells agrees.

In the afternoon, I drive us to the local football club, where Bells's team are playing a match. She is now wearing a football shirt and her red Manchester United scarf. When we enter the clubhouse, there are a couple of men sitting at the bar.

'Hello, Budge,' Bells calls out. 'He's captain,' she quickly tells me, her breathing intensifying. 'Hello, Paul. Hello, Budge.' She punches each one in turn. They turn round and hold up their hands to give her a high five. Bells's hand barely covers the palms of theirs.

'My sister Katie,' she tells them. They look at me briefly and say hello.

Budge is very good-looking. He has dark brown hair and dark eyes. 'Hi,' I say back, but I can see I have lost his attention already.

'Bells, you're going to watch the match today, aren't you?' Budge asks, pulling at her scarf. He starts to uncoil it. She laughs furiously, saying it's tickling her. I can see her blushing.

''Course she is,' says the other one. Another army of men walk into the clubhouse. They take it in turns clapping Bells on the back.

'How you doing, Bells?'

'How's our favourite mascot?'

'Bells, good to see you.'

I'm about to say something when a beefy man sweeps in from behind and gathers her up in his arms. They all cheer and I start to join in. He puts her onto his shoulders. Bells is laughing and clapping her hands.

446

'Come on, St David's,' they are starting to chant like a tribe. I have never seen her look so happy, nor so at home anywhere. She fits in here like the missing piece of a jigsaw. No one else will do but Bells. I stand back, letting them pass me. They're filing out now and onto the playing field. 'Katie,' I can hear her call, looking over her shoulder. 'You coming?'

I drive back to London early the following morning feeling happy. Bells's team won, 2–0. After the match, I drove Bells home and found a crowd of people in the kitchen. I met Mary Veronica, a girl called Jane, another man called Alex, and Ted was still in the kitchen, looking after everybody. Bells made a vegetable roulade and chocolate mousse.

I can now put faces to names; I can imagine what Bells does on a Saturday afternoon. I can see her being picked up like a trophy and carried onto the football pitch. I can hear her laughing and clapping.

It didn't feel sad leaving because I know Bells is in the right place. It's not perfect, nothing is, but it's her home. We've made a pact that I'll see her once a month and phone her every Monday and Friday night.

'Promise?' she said as I left.

'I promise.'

I am sitting at the kitchen table flicking through one of Emma's many *Brides* magazines. Brides with flashing white smiles and pearls the size of quail's eggs stare out of the pages at me. Emma will look nothing like them, I hope. I can overhear Jonnie and her next door talking about the wedding. They are getting married at St John's Church, Hyde Park.

I put my head into my hands. Why do I feel so flat? It's been two weeks now since I saw Mark. For some reason I'd imagined he might pass by my door . . . well, Emma and Jonnie's door . . . but nothing. I realise how much I want to buy my own flat. I need my own place.

I march into my bedroom and pick up my sketchbook. Since splitting up with Sam I have had more free time and I want to make the most of it. With renewed enthusiasm, I decide to go for a Sunday walk with my sketchpad. I want to start sewing again and I need to get ideas about what people want to wear. It's cold outside, but the autumn sun is warm. I put on my blue and red poncho over my dark jeans.

Jonnie looks relieved when I walk into the room. 'Where are you off to, cowgirl?'

'A walk.'

'Who are you hoping to bump into?' he asks with a naughty smile.

'Jonnie, we have to carry on with the wedding list,' Emma insists, her face crumpled with despair.

Jonnie pulls a desperate face. 'See you later.'

After a brisk stroll in the park, I walk into a café, order a cappuccino and sit down by the window. A girl walks past in a long dark brown skirt with ruffles round the bottom. She wears brown boots and a cream-coloured wrap-around cardigan. Tassels and fringes are back in, I notice, when I see yet another young girl walk past in a hippy layered skirt and a belt with a large golden buckle.

I start sketching but my mind keeps wandering. I think I would rather write to Bells. Ten minutes later I have written nearly two pages.

I loved visiting you last weekend and seeing your home. It meant a lot to me, Bells. I'm only sorry I haven't visited before. I still think about the view from your bedroom window. You are so lucky to be able to look out onto the sea every morning. That would put me in a good mood.

I thought Ted was lovely. Tell him I look forward to seeing him dance at your open day. I also loved the football. I forgot to tell you, but Mark asked after you. I saw him the other night. In fact, I made a fool of myself and drank too much, and then told him how much I liked him. I feel a real idiot now because he has a girlfriend. Anyway, it doesn't matter because we are still friends. Next time you come to London I am sure we can all meet up for . . .

I stop writing for a second, and think about what Mark said to me. I can still see him standing at Emma's front door.

I pick up my mobile and call him. 'Just wondered if you wanted to meet up for that coffee and sticky bun?'

My pen flies across the page as someone taps me from behind. A large smudgy ink mark splatters against the last sentence. 'Damn. Don't ever creep up on me like that again! You frightened me.'

'Sorry, Katie.' Mark smiles, leaning over me. Is he trying to read my letter? 'I was waving at you from outside but you looked so serious. You're not writing your will, are you?'

'Mark!' I cover the page, the way I used to if I thought someone at school was trying to cheat and steal my answers.

'Who are you writing to?'

'Bells.'

'May I add something?' He sits down next to me.

'No!' I shut my sketchpad firmly now. 'You can write your own letter.'

'Sorry,' he says again. 'I'm glad you called.'

Mark has this disarming way of being polite and formal with a naughty streak too, all at the same time. I begin to relax now that the letter is well and truly out of sight. 'Any news on the book yet?'

He lets out a long frustrated sigh. 'No. My agent says it needs more work. If you want instant gratification, don't be a writer.'

'You never told me what you are writing?'

'Just a fantasy adventure story,' he says modestly. 'It's for children and adults. I'm trying to be the next J.K. Rowling,' he confesses. 'My grand-mother used to read me *The Adventures of Uncle Lubin*. It's a book I've never forgotten. I'd love to be able to write something as good.'

'I don't know it. What's it about?'

'You don't know it?' he exclaims in disbelief. 'You must read it. Uncle Lubin looks after his young nephew Peter, but one day a great Bagbird swoops down,' Mark does the actions, 'and whisks the child away. Uncle Lubin has to find him. He travels around the world and up to the moon in his floppy hat and striped stockings. Uncle Lubin has a dream that he sees Peter under the sea, flanked by mermaids, and he's safe. When he wakes up he is distraught to find himself alone. Uncle Lubin never gives up, though, and in the end . . .'

'Don't tell me!' I bang my hand against the table. 'He rescues Peter?'

'Yes, sure.' Mark looks disappointed by my reaction. 'But it's more than that. It's about the human spirit and enduring love. It's about never giving up hope. I wish I still had that book, I don't know how Mum could have lost it.'

'Have you read *The Old Woman in the Vinegar Bottle*?'

Mark shakes his head.

'It's about this woman who lives in a vinegar bottle. She has a little ladder to go in and out by,' I wiggle my fingers as if climbing an imagi-nary ladder, 'but she grows discontented.'

Mark grins. 'I'm not surprised. Living in a vinegar bottle doesn't exactly sound enthralling.'

I smile. '"Tis a shame, 'tis a shame," she grumbles, and pictures her-self in a little white house with roses and honeysuckle growing over it, pink curtains, a pig in the sty. A fairy passing by feels sorry for her. "Well, never you mind," she says. She tells the old woman to go up to bed and turn around three times in her bottle. "When you wake up in the morning, you'll see what you will see!" When the old woman wakes she's in a room with pink curtains and she can hear a pig grunting out-side.' I do the sound effects. 'What's wrong?' Mark is looking at me in a strange way.

'Come on, tell me what happens next,' he insists.

'Well, the old woman is delighted but it never crosses her mind to *thank* the fairy. The fairy goes east and west, north and south, and then

449

comes back to the old woman, knowing how pleased she will be in her little white house. "Oh! 'tis a shame, so it is, 'tis a shame. Why should I live in a pokey little cottage? I want to live in a red townhouse and have a little maid to wait on me." "Well, never you mind," the fairy says.'

'"When you wake up in the morning, you'll see what you will see,"' Mark finishes for me.

'Next she wants to live in a house with white steps and men and maids waiting on her. Then she wants to live in a palace. "Look at the Queen. Why shouldn't *I* sit on a gold throne with a gold crown on my head?" The fairy grants her wish, but when she returns to hear the old woman complaining that the crown is too heavy for her head, she gives up. "Why can't I have a home to suit me?" the old woman moans. "Oh, very well, if all you want is just a home to suit you . . ." the fairy says wearily. The old woman wakes up and finds herself back in the vinegar bottle, where she stays *for the rest of her life.*'

'Serves the old woman right.'

'I remember that story so well, Mum read it to Bells and me. What about your family?' I ask. 'I've been so wrapped up in my own dramas that I know nothing about you. Are you close to your parents?'

'We've had our moments. I felt I'd let my father down when I told him I didn't want to be a lawyer. My brother emigrated to New Zealand and became a sheep farmer. Law is in Dad's blood. His father was a lawyer. Jess is a lawyer too so that helps.' He laughs drily.

'That must give her Brownie points?'

'Yes, they really like her. Jess is like family.'

So not only is she good-looking and bright, she is also like family. Bugger. 'How did you two meet?' I ask casually.

'At school, funnily enough. In Edinburgh.'

'Why were you in Edinburgh?'

'One of my father's first jobs was there and my parents loved the place so much they decided to move permanently.'

'So you've been going out with her for how long?'

'Only six months, but it feels like longer,' he adds, and I can't tell whether that's a good or a bad thing.

'How come it took you that long to start going out?'

'I don't know,' he says, his voice clipped and considered. 'We kind of fell into it. We went on holiday with a group of friends and that was it.'

Fell into it? That was it? Mark's vocabulary lacks a certain passion. Where's the romance? Where are the fireworks?

'Are you happy?'

'Am I happy? Well, that's a difficult question.'

'With Jess, not in general,' I say, hoping that I am not being too nosy. 'She's one of my closest friends . . . how did we get onto Jess?'

'We were talking about your father wanting you to be a lawyer.'

'Oh, yes. It's all about approval, isn't it? You want your parents to be proud, whatever you do.'

We sit quietly for a few minutes watching people go by. It doesn't feel awkward saying nothing. It feels peaceful.

Eventually I break the silence. 'Do you have any unusual characters in your family?'

'How about a grandmother who kept a lion under her bed?'

I laugh. 'Well, I'm glad it's not just our family then.'

From the corner of my eye I can see a girl walking by outside, wearing a baseball cap on back to front, a black bra, black vest, a black mini skirt, a small backpack and black knee-length platform boots. A group of girls walk past and I hear them laugh at her mockingly.

'You see that girl?' Mark says.

'You can hardly miss her, can you?'

'She looks a bit weird, but she's far more interesting than the other girls. They just look like clones of each other.'

I look at the backs of the three girls, each with dyed blonde hair and all wearing baggy trousers, skin-tight tops and trainers.

'Eccentric, unusual, out-of-the-ordinary characters make the world go round,' Mark says. 'God, life would be boring without them.'

When Mark left, I finished my letter to Bells and then went to the newsagent's to buy copies of *Vogue*, *Tatler*, *Harpers & Queen* and *Glamour*.

Two weeks later I have made myself a suede coat with panels on the front and a soft lining. I have also been working on my designs and compiled a small portfolio. I would like to have my own label in the future; it's something to work towards. 'I've bought a Katie Fletcher top,' I can hear someone saying excitedly. I've been people-watching constantly, looking around various shops in my lunch hour and seeing what's out there. I have been working late in the evenings after I close the shop too. It was time to change my image as well so I went to Ariel's, my Spanish hairdresser's, and he made me 'feel like a different woman', as he put it. He cut and layered my hair in the front. I like pulling it back into a short blunt ponytail. It feels symbolic of a new start.

And, even more impressive, I have bought a pair of luminous purple goggles and a black costume and have been swimming before work. I have even stopped smoking.

I like the new Katie Fletcher.

CHAPTER FOURTEEN

'Jonnie, who was on the phone?' I call. It's Monday evening and I'm about to go to bed.

'I don't know, he hung up again.' I walk into the sitting room. Emma is sitting next to him doing the crossword.

'He?'

'Well, the only person I can think of is Sam,' Jonnie suggests. 'D'you think he might want to get back in touch?'

'Possibly,' I say. Sam has called me a few times. He keeps on saying he wants to meet up, we need to talk, but I cannot see the point.

Jonnie studies my expression. 'Is it safe to talk about Sam now?'

'Quite safe.'

'Well, I always thought he was a bit of a tosser,' Jonnie comments.

'Jonnie!' Emma puts the crossword down.

'It's fine, honestly.' I shrug. 'If you look the part, you feel the part . . .'

'And you *are* the part,' we all finish, and start to laugh. I sink down on a corner of the sofa.

'I always thought you could do a lot better,' Emma admits, and then pauses as if she is not sure whether to say whatever is on her mind next. 'Like this Mark person?' she finishes, trying desperately to sound casual. 'I mean, you've been spending quite a lot of time with him.'

'Uh-oh, no, I want to be on my own. Anyway, he has a girlfriend.' I change the subject. 'I'm going to put the rubbish out, it's bin day tomorrow, isn't it?'

'It is,' Jonnie confirms. 'Bin day. What an exciting, fast-paced world we live in.'

I haven't smoked for a month now, no ash and stubs in the bin this time. I wobble out of the front door with two large black bags in my hands. I am tempted to go for an evening walk, I might bump into Mark. Since that Sunday morning, nearly a month ago, he and I have been out many times. I often go round to his place after work and we have a drink together.

It's a Monday night, he should be in. It's only ten o'clock. Just as I knock on the door to his flat I hear his bike outside and now he is coming through the front entrance. His face looks pink from the cold night air and he's wearing a bright yellow strap across his coat. 'Hi.' He rubs his hands together. 'How are you?'

'I'm fine. I was just putting the rubbish out then I thought about you.'

'Charming! Do you want to come in for a drink?'

'Would love to. Where have you been?'

'School. God, I'm tired,' he says as he walks into the kitchen. I follow him. 'We're rehearsing for *My Fair Lady* and there's so much work to do. Lines to be learned. Singing classes. Dancing.'

'Sit down,' I order. 'Tell me where everything is and I will make you something to eat and drink. My turn to fuss over you.'

'Wonderful,' he sighs, taking off his boots and bicycle clips.

I make two cups of coffee and Mark eats some toast with Marmite.

'Katie, I have a big favour to ask. Jess can't come to *My Fair Lady*. Obviously Edinburgh's a bit too far to come just for a school play. Also, she fell into her mother's flowerbed and sprained her ankle.'

I burst out laughing and Mark looks at me strangely. 'Oh, Mark, sorry, it's just the way you put it.'

'She was trying to find the house key under the flowerpot, you know the way parents think that's such a clever place to leave keys? Well, she picked up the pot, lost her balance, and fell into the rosebush.'

'Stop it!' I say, bending over double, unable to control my laughter. 'Is she going to sue the rosebush?'

'I can't think why you find it so funny,' he says, but I know he is smiling without even looking at him. 'Anyway, I was wondering if you would come with me instead?'

'Have you asked Jess?'

'I will, but I'm sure she won't mind. She knows that we're just friends.'

'All right, I'd love to come then. When is it?'

'Friday night.'

For a moment I long to have something else on to make him think I have a hectic and exciting social life. 'Right, fine, see you Friday. I'm going. I've had enough of you for one night.'

I am singing loudly in the street, pretending to be Eliza Doolittle.

'Shh!' Mark laughs, holding me back from swinging round the next lamppost. 'We're getting some really strange stares.'

'I've spent far too much time caring about what others think,' I tell him. 'It's a waste of time.' I turn to him. 'I really enjoyed tonight. I think your class are wonderful.'

'They sang their hearts out, didn't they?' he says proudly. 'Helen really belted it out.' Helen played Audrey Hepburn's part, Eliza. I don't want to tell Mark she nearly deafened the audience and that I wished I had taken my earplugs. Mark stayed so intent on the performance that I didn't dare breathe in case he missed a note or a word. I couldn't help watching him more than the musical. He clearly had a passionate interest in these children. His changing expressions told the whole story.

The best part, however, was the end. Everyone stood and applauded for what seemed like five minutes. The headmaster called Mark up onto the stage and he bowed together with the cast, who bunched round him. One actor hit his arm affectionately, another did a high five. Mark was congratulating them all. 'Who's that babe with you?' one of the boys asked loudly, pointing at me. I almost burst with pride. Nearly thirty and called a babe! I blushed furiously and had to pretend I needed something in my handbag. When I looked up Mark was smiling at me.

'Taxi!' Mark shouts as we see a black cab with its yellow light lit up.

He and I sink back into the seat. I break out into another *My Fair Lady* song and Mark joins in. The cab driver is shaking his head at us.

'What's your favourite thing in the world?' I ask. 'Apart from porn.'

Mark scratches his chin playfully. 'If it can't be porn, it has to be . . . um . . . marshmallow biscuits.'

'Don't overexcite yourself.'

'Come on, you then?'

'The smell of fresh coffee and bread.'

'Skiing on a beautiful day with fresh-powder snow.'

'Going to bed.'

Mark raises an eyebrow. 'With anyone in particular or on your own?'

'On my own and having the duvet all to myself.'

'Wow, aren't we a wild pair? OK, what do you hate most in the world?' he quickly moves on.

'Rude and narrow-minded people.'

'Traffic wardens,' the cab driver shouts through. 'And people who tell me which route I should take—that gets me, that does.'

'Ooh, I've got one! Christmas starting in August.'

'I like this game. People who trump you,' Mark goes on. 'I tell someone I went to Vienna and they tell me the place I ought to go to is Budapest.'

'Oh, yes,' I agree. 'Nothing more annoying. Vermin, that's the new name for people we don't like. Rodents, man.' We laugh.

'If you could change anything about yourself, what would it be?' I start again.

Mark wrinkles his nose as he is thinking this one through.

'I'll start,' I suggest. 'I wish I wasn't so stubborn.'

'I love the way you say what you think.'

'I don't, Mark, not always. Look how long it took Mum and me to start talking properly. I bottle things up, let myself stew over problems.'

'I'm too soft. I wear my heart on my sleeve. I even cried reading *Bridges of Madison County*.'

'You're a wimp. But I cried too,' I add.

'So did I.' The cab driver is still eavesdropping. 'Now, is it left here?'

Our legs gently brush. 'Mark.' I lean closer towards him. 'I've never noticed your eyes before.' One is tinged with brown, the other is blue. We look at each other for a second too long. I turn away first.

'Oh,' he says, 'a freak accident. I was about to score for a cricket match and was spinning a pencil between the guy ropes that hold up the practice nets when it spiralled out of my hand. The likelihood of that pencil hitting me was a million to one, but'—he gestures to his eyes—'I had to have three stitches. That's why I need the glasses.'

'You can barely tell. I mean, it's really subtle.'

'You're shivering. Here, have my jacket.'

He places it round my shoulders and I feel acutely aware of the warmth of his touch. 'You're such a gentleman,' I say.

'What is it with you two lovebirds? Is this some kind of mutual admiration society?' says the cab driver.

His intervention breaks the tension. We both smile. 'Lovebirds?' I start to laugh ironically. 'Have you ever had your palm read, Mark?'

'No way, I don't believe in any of that.'

I take his hand and turn it over. 'You have a very long lifeline,' I tell him, 'but your loveline is very poor. You haven't got much going on in *that* department. You have a very small . . .'

He pulls his hand away abruptly and takes mine. 'OK, Katie Fletcher, let's see what's in store for you.'

He circles my palm. 'Oh, no,' he starts saying. 'Oh dear. You are going to come back as a'—he's thinking—'centipede in the next lifetime.'

'Mark, you are mad.' I nudge him in the stomach. 'If I come back, I am going to be a pop idol and frolic in front of Simon Cowell.'

'I don't understand the attraction. Jess likes him too . . . It's right here, thanks,' Mark tells the cab driver. 'Do we really want to go home yet? Do you want to go somewhere for a drink?' he says with unusual urgency in his voice. 'Shall we tell him to go around the block while we decide?'

'Emma and Jonnie aren't in tonight. Why don't you come over to my place?'

'Yes, sounds good . . . So stop here, would you?'

Mark takes my hand as I step out of the cab. 'M'lady,' he says. 'By the way, I never said it but you looked beautiful tonight.'

'Why, thank you, sir.' We stand holding hands, neither of us moving. 'My place, then?' I say, finally letting go.

'Whose place?' Sam is waiting outside Emma and Jonnie's front door. He starts walking towards us. I can see his hands are trembling and he hasn't shaved properly. I feel almost sorry for him, alone in the cold.

'What are you doing here?' I ask him.

'More to the point, what are you two doing together? Looks cosyeee.'

'Sam, it's none of your business.'

His eyes narrow as he looks at Mark. 'Who are you?' he demands.

'Mark.'

'Well, hello, Mark. Where have you just taken Katie?'

'Look, it's got nothing to do—'

Mark stops me. 'I took her to see *My Fair Lady*.'

'But Katie hates musicals.'

'I do not,' I cut in. 'I loved *Mama Mia*.'

'Well, even nicer of her to come along then,' says Mark calmly.

'Mark who loves gay musicals, and my ex-girlfriend who's turned into a nun. Acts like she's wearing a habit and a chastity belt. So are you two together? Probably not, I'd guess.'

I don't feel so sorry for him any more. 'Sam, you're drunk.'

'Well, as her modesty's ensured, I'm surprised you had to come and check on such an unthreatening situation,' Mark says, taking my hand.

Sam pulls our hands apart.

'Sam, it's late, I think you should go home,' I tell him.

'It's not even midnight, Sister Fletcher.'

Mark and I continue to walk on without him. 'Do you want me to call a cab for him?' Mark asks quietly.

'I miss you,' Sam cries out. Mark and I stop and look back. 'I miss you. Katie, you can't go out with someone, live with them, and then never want to see them again,' Sam protests. 'I'm not going to leave until you talk to me.'

I tell Mark to go on without me, that I'll call him when Sam has gone.

'If you're sure?' He looks at me intently.

'I can't leave him out here. Honestly, go on.'

'All right,' he says. 'Come over later.'

'Make this quick, Sam,' I say as we step inside.

He sits down on the sofa. 'I've been an idiot, you were right. We need to start talking about you and me,' he says, moving his arm towards me and then letting it drop. 'Everything you said that night, I've been thinking about it.' He pats the space on the sofa. 'And you've been through so much since then. Come and sit next to me, Kitty-kins, come on.'

I pull up Jonnie's leather chair and sit opposite him. 'I'm comfortable over here, thanks.'

'Kitty-kins,' he tries again, putting on a silly baby voice.

'Sam, what do you want?'

He looks at me with surprise. 'OK, well, here goes. Nothing makes sense to me if you're not around. I want you to come back. We used to have fun together. Come on, what d'you say?'

'Sam, too much has happened, I don't think it would work.'

'Well, we can only find out for sure if we give it another go, can't we? I think you and me are worth fighting for.'

'Why, Sam? You didn't call me once when Mum was so ill.' I can't keep the hurt out of my voice.

'I know,' he says quickly. 'I'm sorry.'

'She could have died, Sam. You didn't even call me as a friend. That's what it's all about, getting through the hard times as well as having fun together. We're great when everything's going well, but we fall at the first hurdle when life throws us a challenge. What does that say about us?'

'Haven't I said I'm sorry a thousand times? I'm no good at dealing with stuff like that . . . illness, you know, I don't know what to say. Your mum's all right now, isn't she? What do you want? More sympathy?'

'You don't need to do anything. It's over,' I say. I realise I haven't missed him at all.

Sam starts telling me that if I don't go back to him his life will fall apart, he cannot live without me. 'I'll even marry you, I'll do whatever it takes,' he says, gambling that this last pledge of commitment will work. 'Katie, I'll do anything.'

'Sam, please stop,' I cry out. 'I don't know how to say this,' I start. 'I wish I didn't have to. I don't love you.'

'I know I was angry, I shouldn't have made you leave like that. I should have called you, been more supportive,' he says, choosing not to hear what I have just said.

'Look, it's OK,' I reassure him. 'Let's just move on.'

'It's not because of Mark, is it? Katie, you can do better than that. I mean, who is he? You can't be serious, picking him over me.'

I should have known he'd say that. I start to feel sorry for Sam and then he goes and says something like that. 'For your information, I like Mark. He's a friend. He's the same Mark who helped me when Bells went missing. Remember?'

'Did we split up because of Bells? We were happy before she came along. I know I didn't hit it off with her, but we can work on that.'

Has he listened to a word I have said? 'No, we can't. You can't change who you are. I'm tired, Sam. It's late. I'm going to call you a cab.' I walk over to the small table by the sofa and pick up the phone. I start to punch in the number of the local cab firm.

Sam snatches the phone from me and hangs up. 'I'm not going.'

I pick up the phone again. 'Well, you're not staying here.'

He grabs it from me, and the glass lamp base on the table crashes to the floor. 'Look what you've done now,' I shout. 'Emma loves this.' I bend down to pick up the shattered pieces of glass. 'Just go, please.' I can smell stale alcohol on his breath. He bends down and I think he is going to help me pick up the glass. Instead he tries to kiss me. 'Get off!' I pull away. 'Please go.'

'I'm not going till we sort this out,' he says relentlessly.

There's a knock on the door. Quickly I stand up and put the broken pieces of lamp on the table. 'Katie, are you all right?' I hear Mark calling. I open the door.

'Look who it is,' Sam sneers. 'Your knight in shining fucking armour!'

Mark pushes past him. 'I was worried.' He touches my shoulder. 'Are you all right?'

'Fine. He won't leave.'

Mark turns to Sam. 'I think you should go.'

'I don't give a fuck what you think.'

I actually feel embarrassed that I went out with this person. Mark opens the front door and stands there holding it.

Sam grabs his jacket and walks towards him. 'All right, I'll go,' he mutters. Mark and I briefly exchange relieved looks, but then, just as Sam is about to leave, he turns round and punches Mark in the face. Mark staggers backwards and his glasses fall to the ground.

'Sam, stop it!' I scream as he is about to have a second go at Mark. I plunge forward and grab his arm. Sam pulls away from me and proceeds to step on Mark's glasses. 'It's like a lion fighting a flea,' he says, grinding them into the ground. 'No contest.'

'Sam?' I hear Mark saying in a quiet flea-like voice.

Sam turns his head. 'Did that hurt?' He puts on his baby-like voice.

'Not as much as this.' Mark belts him in the stomach.

Sam holds himself steady and starts to laugh scornfully. 'You can do better than that, can't you?'

'That is enough!' I shout at them both, stepping between them. 'Go home,' I plead with Sam. 'And Mark, just leave it, OK?'

I watch Sam stagger down the steps. I never wanted it to end this way. 'Sam!' I call out.

He doesn't even turn round now. 'Shut up, Katie, I've had about enough of you. I'll leave you and lover-boy to it.'

Mark lies with his head on my lap and I rest the packet of frozen peas against his chin. 'How's the hand?'

'Painful. I feel like a loser. If you hadn't stepped between us he would have mashed me to a pulp.'

I adjust the position of the peas. 'I don't know what I would have done if you hadn't come. How does it feel now?'

'Not good. Carry on.'

'It's funny, but I was terrified of losing Sam. Before Bells came to stay, I didn't tell him about her. He had no idea what she'd be like. I was so nervous he'd do a runner, that he wouldn't want to know me.'

Mark sits up and turns to me. 'I remember you telling me this when we first met. That was so stupid, Katie.' His tone is uncomfortable. 'What did you ever see in that man?'

'There is a good side to him, I promise. I know he was behaving like an idiot tonight, but he's got no one, Mark. No support from his family. No real friends to confide in, only lads like Maguire. He does have a good side,' I repeat again. 'At least he doesn't pretend to be anything he isn't. I could learn from him there. I mean, who was I trying to be?'

Mark's tone softens. 'You shouldn't have to pretend to be anything. He shouldn't have made you feel like that. You wouldn't put yourself through all that again, would you, with the next man you meet?'

'No way,' I say. 'I've learned my lesson. Thanks for coming round tonight. No one's done anything like that for me before, Mark. You're a real mate. I owe you.'

'Well, you could get me some new glasses.'

We look at Mark's glasses, smashed to smithereens, and start to laugh. 'It's the least I can do,' I agree.

It's a Thursday, late afternoon, and Mark has asked me over for supper. I left the shop early as Eve and my new assistant, Jackie, were able to manage without me. I sit on the stool behind the breakfast counter in Mark's kitchen. There's a pile of paperwork in front of me, his red pen scrawled across the sheets. Essays on *The Mayor of Casterbridge* with that dreaded underlined word at the end of the assignment: 'Discuss'.

Mark opens the fridge. 'No bloody milk. What do you feel like eating tonight?'

'Why don't we go out?' I suggest. Mark and I have never 'gone out' apart from that one evening when we watched the school play. Normally he cooks me supper but I'm getting a little bored of spaghetti Bolognese.

'Go out? Do you think our friendship has reached that stage?' he asks, laughing.

'I think we're ready. Did I tell you, I've seen a flat I love?'

'You're moving?' he asks, and then wonders why he is surprised. 'I forget you're living with Emma and Jonnie sometimes.'

Emma and Jonnie haven't met Mark yet. 'You have mentionitis . . .' Emma said to me the other day while we were shopping for her wedding dress.

'Mention what?' I threw her a funny look.

'Mentionitis. You talk about Mark all the time. I'd like to meet him,' Emma told me as I helped her out of the dress. 'Are you scared of introducing him properly to us?'

This might sound ridiculous, as if I am in a school playground, but I don't want to share Mark yet.

'Katie?' I hear him say now. 'You do that a lot, you know.'

'Sorry? What?'

'Retreat into your own world, develop this kind of glazed expression. So where's the new flat?' Mark asks me.

'Ravenscourt Park.'

'Renting or buying?'

'Buying. I'm finally taking the plunge. I'm looking forward to living on my own.'

He leans against the counter. He's wearing the new pair of glasses that we bought together, almost exactly the same model as the broken ones, with black rims. I also persuaded him to buy a pale blue round-necked jumper without holes in the elbow.

'Calling Katie? Where is Katie?' Mark prods me again. 'Sounds perfect. When are you moving?'

'Just before Christmas.'

'That's less than a month away.'

'I know. Emma and Jonnie are throwing me a Christmas-stroke-leaving party in two weeks, Bells is coming down to stay and you'd better be around too, I'd like you to come.'

'I'll try and fit it in,' he says, and I throw his red marker pen at him.

'And Jess, is she around?'

'I'll ask her.'

'Why don't you live together?'

'What, besides the fact that she lives in Edinburgh? Anyway, I hate the idea. You live together and then you just merge into a married blob. We both lead quite independent lives and I like it that way.'

'How's her ankle?' I don't really care how it is but I know I ought to acknowledge she is around.

'It's fine,' he says. 'Right, tea?'

'That would be great.'

'You put the kettle on, I'll go out and get the milk and the biscuits.' He picks up his house keys and walks out of the room.

Mark's mobile starts to vibrate against the table. 'Can you get that for me?' he calls. I can hear him putting on his coat. The front door shuts.

I pick up the phone tentatively. I don't like taking calls for other people. 'Hello, Mark's phone,' I say in my best secretarial voice.

'Who's that?' a voice says abruptly. Is this Jess?

'It's just Katie.'

'Just Katie, this is Sasha Fox. Is Mark there?'

'Not right this minute.' She sounds terrifying.

'It's his agent, can you get him to call me back?' she says.

I put the phone down and start to walk around Mark's flat. I wonder if she has news on the book? She must have. I am about to walk back into the kitchen when I decide to take a quick detour into Mark's bedroom. Along the corridor, past the bathroom, and then three steps down and I'm there.

It's a large airy room with a large double bed with a carved oak headboard. Mark has shutters instead of curtains and there's a newspaper lying on the duvet. On his bedside table is a silver-framed photograph. Jess is sitting on a boat wearing denim shorts and a bikini, and Mark stands next to her proudly holding a barracuda. She's annoyingly pretty. I press my fingers to my temples. I don't think I have been myself lately.

I hear a door shut and run back up the stairs, tripping on the last step. I decide to go into the bathroom, slam the door shut and flush the chain. Then I open the door casually and walk back to the kitchen.

'Who was it?' Mark asks, clutching the bottle of milk.

'Your agent.'

'Sasha Fox? Really?' He sits down on the stool next to me and starts twisting his hands together. 'What did she say?'

'You've got to call her back. Call her now, she must have news on your book.'

'Did she sound in a good mood? Could you tell?' he presses me.

'She was a bit abrupt,' I confess. 'Go on,' I say, pushing the phone towards him. 'Ring her.'

'What if it's bad news? Rejections from every publisher she has approached, saying I'm a useless writer?' He sits forward and puts his head in his hands. 'Katie, I've had scripts rejected before. I've worked so hard on this book. If it's a no, I'll be miserable.' He stands up, paces the room and then sits down again. 'I'm feeling a bit nervous actually.'

'I can tell,' I say, longing to hug him for his insecurity. 'Look, your agent must believe in you. I think she would have e-mailed you if it was bad news,' I suggest.

'Good point. Although she didn't before.'

'Do you want me to go?' Please say no.

'No, stay,' he urges, taking the phone. 'Forget the tea, can you get me a proper drink?' He stands up and starts to pace around the room. He walks into the sitting room and I follow him. He opens his desk drawer.

'Mark, slow down. What are you looking for?'

He waves a packet of cigarettes at me. 'For emergencies. OK, wish me luck,' he says, punching in the number.

I walk into the kitchen to make vodka and tonics. I have butterflies in my stomach. I'm thinking of ways to console Mark. 'It's their loss,' or, 'Did you know J.K. Rowling had masses of rejections, and look at her now!' No, that's a lame thing to say.

Mark stands in front of me looking as if he's just been given a parking ticket. He slams the mobile onto the table. I wait for him to say something. When he says nothing I tell him I am sorry and hand him a neat vodka.

'Sorry for what?' He takes a large gulp. 'Penguin are going to publish it. I can't be bothered to cook supper. We are going out to celebrate!' He picks me up off the ground, and twirls me around. 'I am going to be published, Katie, can you believe it?'

'Hurray!' I shout, wrapping my arms round him and laughing at the same time. He puts me down and then opens the fridge. 'We need a drink. No champagne, bugger.'

'I'll go and get some, my treat.'

'Deal. I can't believe it,' he repeats incredulously, circling the kitchen as if he is drunk.

'Calm down.' I smile at him. 'I'll be back in a sec.' I find myself skipping along the road like an excited toddler.

'You look like a cat who's stolen the cream, and eaten it too,' the man at the off-licence says.

'My friend's just got a book deal.'

'Wow,' he acknowledges, taking my money. 'Tell him congratulations.'

Aren't people nice? Why do people say the British are chippy, that they don't like people fulfilling their dreams? There's not a chip in sight today.

When I return, I hear Mark talking in the kitchen. I stand in the hall and listen before joining him. 'We can celebrate when you get back . . . you don't have to do that. OK, we'll see . . . What am I doing tonight? Well, I think I'll have a few celebratory drinks.' I notice he doesn't say who with. 'Yes, I will have one on you, J.' He's listening to her and now his voice turns softer. 'I know, I wish you were here too,' he finishes.

Of course she is the first person he wants to ring with the news. This has to be one of the biggest, proudest moments in his life and he ought to be with her, not me. Why do I feel like second best? It only takes one phone call from Jess and—bam! Back to being Katie the good friend, someone to have a laugh with. I can't stand feeling like this.

'Love you too,' I hear him say.

That's it, enough dreaming, Katie. Mark and you have a great friend-ship, but that's as far as it goes. I need to go back into the kitchen, have one drink and then go home. I must accept this for what it is. I clutch the bottle of champagne and brace myself as I walk into the kitchen.

'Why do you have to go now?' Mark asks after we have had one glass of champagne together. 'I want to celebrate. Come on, have another.' He starts to refill my glass. 'Let's go out dancing.'

I push my glass aside. 'Sorry, Mark, I think I might be coming down with something,' I say vaguely. 'Emma had this twenty-four-hour sick bug. It hit her out of the blue.'

Mark whacks himself hard. 'It's come on, just like that? You were fine half an hour ago. Is something wrong?'

'I think I need to lie down.' I don't want to stay. I can't stay.

Mark feels my forehead. 'You *are* quite warm.' He lifts my chin and holds my face up to his. 'But this is my night, I don't want you to go.'

'I'm sorry.' I put my hand over his and gently remove it. I kiss him on the cheek. 'Well done, Mark. I'm so proud of you, author *extraordinaire*.' I pick up my bag.

He follows me to the door and then I feel him clutching at my hand. 'Why are you really going? I'm trying to figure out if I've done some-thing wrong, said something, in the space of ten minutes? I don't want you to go.'

'You've done nothing wrong, honestly. 'Bye, Mark.' I kiss him on the cheek one more time.

I haven't seen him for a fortnight. Now Mark stands at the front door, trailing his bike behind him. He left a message on my mobile but I didn't ring back or go round to his flat. However, I had to make contact when Bells arrived so I asked him if he wanted to go to the cinema with us tonight. Bells is staying for the weekend and will be around for Jonnie and Emma's Christmas party tomorrow evening. She wouldn't forgive me if she didn't see Mark.

His hands are covered in grime and his left cheek is smudged with oil too. His hair is even more all over the place.

'Did you fall, are you OK?' I ask. What's he doing here? It's only two o'clock.

'Nearly. The chain came off.' He grimaces. 'Clunk, in the middle of the street.'

'Hello, Mark.' Bells rushes up to him and claps him on the back.

'Hi, Bells! How are you?'

'You have car like Sam?' she asks.

'No,' he admits, almost in apology.

'Why?'

'Because I don't. Anyway, how are you?'

They hold hands and her little device vibrates. 'I should have known,' he laughs. Bells is rocking forward and clapping her hands together.

'Come in,' I tell him. He chains his bicycle to the gate and follows us indoors. His mobile rings and he quickly takes the call.

'That was Jess, she can come tomorrow,' he tells me, putting his phone back in his rucksack.

'Great!' I reply. 'It'll be good to meet her properly,' I continue in a horrible cheery tone that I don't recognise as my own.

'That your girlfriend?' Bells asks.

Mark nods.

'You gonna get married?'

He looks at me and I titter cheerfully. 'Bells, don't be so nosy.' I can't get rid of this merry persona—ironic when I feel anything but. We go into the kitchen and I put the kettle on. Bells hands round some fig rolls. 'Shut eyes,' she says as she holds something towards Mark. He looks at me, then back at Bells. I'm still smiling like a clown. 'Go on, don't worry, it's not a toad,' I laugh. 'Well, I don't know actually. I suppose it could be.'

'OK,' Mark whimpers. 'But I want a fig roll.' He squeezes his eyes shut.

Bells plants a square of mouldy cheese into his hand. It has fur all over it. From the way her shoulders are heaving up and down I can see she finds this hilarious, especially when Mark throws it back at her, shouting, 'It's alive, it's alive! Are you always like this, Bells?'

'Mark, Bells and I have to go out in a minute. I promised Emma I'd get a Christmas tree and food for tomorrow.'

'I'll help.'

'You look a mess, you can't go out looking like that.'

'So what? You always say you shouldn't care what people think.'

'Um,' I shrug my shoulders, 'yes, you're right.'

'Give me ten minutes?'

'OK. Ten minutes.'

When we get there, the supermarket is packed with shoppers and 'Jingle Bells' is playing in the background.

'Mark, what are you doing for Christmas?'

'Mum and Dad are in New Zealand this year with my brother the sheep farmer.'

'You're not going?'

'I can't. It's too expensive to fly out for a week. Anyway, I need to save a bit of money for next year,' he adds.

I nod. 'You're not going to be on your own at Christmas, are you?'

'No. I'm seeing Jess and a few friends in Edinburgh.'

'Oh, yes, of course. Edinburgh, that's a long way away.' Why is every word I say so flat and obvious?

'Excellent,' he mutters out of nowhere, looking distracted. 'Where's Bells?' We both glance around, and walk up the aisle until we see her at the delicatessen counter talking to a man behind the trays of olives and cold meats. He is wearing a hat with a silver Christmas star pasted onto the front. I can hear her asking him how old he is.

'Any more news on the book?' I sound like an interviewer. I realise it doesn't matter because Mark is not listening to me. He's watching Bells put on the man's silver-starred hat. 'Mark?' I prod him.'

'Sorry.' He turns to me. 'I've got something on my mind.'

'Anything I can help with?'

'No,' he says, as if I am the last person who can help him, followed by a calmer, 'It's school, something's come up that I need to think about.'

'What?'

He's about to tell me but then appears to have second thoughts. 'Mark, you're worrying me, why are you looking at me like that?'

'I need to work it out for myself first,' he says. Bells crashes into our trolley. 'Race you to the . . .' He looks at me for inspiration.

'We need mini-sausages and Parmesan cheese.'

'Race you to the sausages!' Mark says as he tears off with Bells.

Bells sits on my bed as she watches me get dressed. I am wearing a pale blue jumper tied at one side with a ribbon, jeans and pointed shoes with a small heel. I brush my hair in front of the mirror and see Bells in the reflection. She's rummaging through my make-up bag, picking out lip-sticks, powder and generally making a mess. 'You and Mark gonna get married?' she asks randomly.

'Me marry Mark? I don't know,' I laugh as I tie my hair back and then let it loose again. I place a large sparkling black beaded flower to the side of my head. I can't decide whether to wear my hair up or down.

'Why?'

She's now trying to put on some of my new silver nail varnish. 'Er, I don't know. He hasn't asked me,' I reply simply. 'We're not even dating.' I'm watching her carefully, to make sure she doesn't spill the polish.

'Not same as you, am I?'

She has never asked me this question directly. I don't know what to say. I can't lie and pretend she is, just to please her. Bells will see right through that anyway. I turn round and see a great circle of silver, the size of a ten-pence piece, on the white linen bedspread. 'Bells, look what you've done!' I rush over to examine the stain.

She throws the bottle across the room and it hits the wall, polish oozing out and onto the carpet.

'Bells, stop it! What's wrong? Why are you so angry?' I quickly retrieve the bottle and put the top back on tightly.

'Can't do like Katie,' she shouts, and starts punching one hand with the other, silver smudging across her palms. 'Not same,' she says firmly. 'Not normal, am I?'

I sit down next to her. 'What's brought all of this on?' I ask gently. 'Bells, you're normal to me, to Dad, Mum, to all the people who love you.'

Bells doesn't look convinced. 'Not like Katie.'

'Why do you want to be like me? I'm not half the person you are.'

'You beautiful.'

'That's not what makes a person,' I say adamantly.

'Not beautiful like Katie,' she repeats.

'Well, I'm not a good cook like you. Look at the way you ran the house when Mum was so ill. I don't think you realise how much you can do, Bells.'

She stops hitting her hands together and laughs weakly. 'Am good cook, aren't I?'

'You are. This stuff doesn't matter, it really doesn't,' I say, holding the nail polish in front of her. 'It's all superficial. You are you, don't ever change. Wave, smile, say hello to people like you always do.' I think of the time when Bells was in my shop and I was ordering her not to say hello to customers. 'That's why people love and admire you, Bells. Look at Mark, or Eddie at the deli, or Robert and Ted, Mr Vickers, or the *entire* football team for that matter. My God, I've never seen such a fan club.'

A small smile lights Bells's face.

'I feel like we are really getting to know each other now,' I stumble on, 'and I love being with you. I don't know about you, but I think that we are all looked after by an angel and I think you are looked after by an extra-special one.'

'What's her name?'

'She doesn't have a name like you and me. She's "Bells's angel". You see, she's given your name.'

Bells thinks about this. 'Mum have angel?'

'She definitely has one.'

'That's why she better. Mark have one?'

'I'm sure he does.'

'You pretty,' she says again, looking at my clothes. Bells is wearing a patchwork skirt, with a black evening top from the shop, and round her wrist is a black leather bracelet with silver studs. She's also wearing her three small stud earrings in the left ear. 'Won't ever look like you.'

'I haven't got your beautiful coloured hair.'

'Mum's hair,' she says.

'Yes, Mum's. You're very lucky. Do you still want to put some of this nail varnish on?' I ask, holding up the pot.

She gives me her hand and I carefully apply the silver over her short bitten nails. 'Look, I've made a mess too.' I smile, wiping away excess nail varnish with a tissue. 'You are you, Bells, Katie is Katie, Mark is Mark. If we were all the same, life would be pretty dull, don't you think?'

'Yes, Katie, that's right. Thank you, Katie.'

'Can I get you another drink?' I ask Eve who has brought Hector along.

'Katie, what a great party!' She's already tipsy.

'What a lovely home,' Hector adds, looking round the room.

Emma, Bells and I decorated the Christmas tree with great big silver and gold balls, silver, red and gold ribbon, and chocolate Santas wrapped in silver and gold foil. Emma put fairy lights in the kitchen and bunches of holly in the windows with fake robins nestled in the leaves. We made canapés all day: sausages, cheese puffs, mini-mince pies.

'Eve, I wanted to thank you so much for keeping the shop going these last few months. I couldn't have done it without you.'

'It is no matter. I was happy to.'

The doorbell rings again and I can hear Mark's voice. 'You must be Mark,' I hear Emma say. 'Well done about the book! I've heard so much about you.'

Oh, Emma, don't say things like that.

'I can't believe we haven't met before,' she blunders on. 'Hello,' she says to Jess.

Jess is wearing a sea-blue coloured satin top over jeans. She barely has any make-up on but her skin is flawless. Then I catch sight of Mark, and before I know it I've bolted upstairs and run into my bedroom, swinging the door shut. I don't think he saw me. My heart is beating so fast that I expect to see it jump out onto the floor. I realise I have never felt this way about anyone before. I don't know what to say or how to act in front of him any more. I don't recognise myself. Keep calm, Katie, I tell myself, only to feel my face getting redder and hotter. 'What is meant to be is meant to be,' I mutter.

I splatter on some green-coloured cream that promises to reduce the redness of my skin and spray myself with perfume that smells like lemon zest. Finally I return to the party. Bells is standing at the CD player with Mark. The Beatles start to sing. She holds a can of ginger beer towards him, her silver nails sparkling. Mark looks as if he has tumbled out of the washing machine. His hair is ruffled and he's wearing dark jeans with a loose white shirt and surprisingly trendy trainers. He puts the can down and takes Bells's hand. They start to dance. 'Can't dance very well,' she is saying.

'Doesn't matter,' Mark shouts above the music.

'Ted and I learning ballroom dance in Wales,' she adds, and laughs as Mark twists her around. 'Again!' she demands.

'You can't take your eyes off him, can you?' Emma says, sneaking up on me.

'Don't be silly, I was watching Bells dance.'

'He looks at you too, you know.'

'Really? Does he?'

'A lot, but you don't care, do you?'

'No, no.'

'Rubbish, Katie. This is me, Emma, your best friend. I know you inside out. You like him, I mean, *really like him*, don't you?'

'I can't do anything about it, though,' I sigh, still watching him. 'I've had quite a few boyfriends, but I've never had one who became a really good friend first. Like you and Jonnie. You are so lucky to be out of the rat race.'

Mark looks in my direction and smiles before turning back to Bells.

'It stinks, doesn't it? And there's nothing I can do.'

'What do you mean? Come on, you can do something.'

'He has a girlfriend.'

'OK, but why don't you tell him? Give yourself a chance, at least. What have you got to lose?'

I watch him with Bells. 'Everything,' I reply simply.

'Katie?' Mark says quietly, taking my hand and leading me out of the room. We stand alone, facing one another.

'Yes?' The music dies out.

'There's something I want to tell you.' His finger gently outlines the curve of my cheek.

'What is it?'

He takes his hand away but I long for him to touch me again.

'It's all over between Jess and me. I think it has been for a long time. I have wanted to say this since we first met but I haven't had the courage. I am hopelessly . . .' He stops. Please don't stop.

'Yes?'

'I am hopelessly . . .'

'Where are you moving to, Katie? Katie?'

'I'm sorry,' I say, shaking my head free of fantasy. Jess is standing in front of me. 'I've found a place in Ravenscourt Park,' I tell her.

'Talking of moving, isn't it wonderful news about Mark?'

'Sorry?'

'Mark? He's been offered a transfer to Edinburgh.'

'He's moving away?' Jess is watching me. 'No, I didn't know.'

She looks genuinely surprised. 'Well, he only just found out. I'm sure he was going to tell you.' There is definitely a hint of pleasure in her voice. 'I thought you saw him last night, though? I wonder why he didn't mention it.'

'When's he going?' Emma intervenes, allowing me to compose myself.

'January. This new school has great drama facilities and he'd be involved in the Edinburgh Festival. It's too good an opportunity to miss. I think it will be good for our relationship too,' she continues. 'It's hard being separated, I think Mark and I need to spend more time together.' The way she looks at me makes me feel uneasy.

'I heard my name being mentioned,' Mark says, returning. 'I don't know where Bells has gone. We need some more music.'

'Jess was telling me about your move to Edinburgh,' I tell him. 'Congratulations.'

Mark's smile rapidly disappears. 'Jess, it was my news to tell.'

'Sorry, I didn't realise it was a big secret,' she says, her eyes widening.

He shakes his head irritably. 'Katie, I've got to go.'

'What, now?' I blurt out.

'Jess, are you ready?'

She frowns. 'Right, I'll get my coat.'

I don't want him to go. I can't bear it. Mark walks ahead of me. 'I was going to tell you, Katie, I'm sorry. I've only just made the decision,' he tries to explain. I am sure he wants to say something more. 'Happy Christmas,' he finally mutters, leaning forward to kiss me on the cheek. I can hear Jess's footsteps behind me.

And then he's gone.

CHAPTER FIFTEEN

BELLS AND I are catching the train home together for Christmas. The day after the party I moved into my new flat with the help of Jonnie. It was strange leaving. I felt like I was facing my first day at boarding school as we unpacked the boxes.

My mobile starts to ring and Mark's name appears in the screen.

'Are you still in London?'

'No, Bells and I are on the train.'

'Katie, I am sorry.'

'Look, it doesn't matter.'

'No, it does. You're a good friend . . .'

There's that word I hate. Friend.

'. . . Katie, I really need to talk to you.'

'That Mark?' Bells asks. 'Hello, Mark.'

'Hi, Bells,' he says in a flustered tone. 'Katie, about the other night . . .'

Bells takes the phone from me. 'Happy birthday, Mark.'

'It's not my birthday, Bells, not quite yet, but thanks anyway. Can I have Katie back?'

'When are you leaving?' For an insane second I allow myself to imagine he is going to tell me he isn't going.

'In two weeks.' There is a pause. The line starts to crackle as the train goes through a tunnel. Mark is saying something but I can't hear.

'Mark, I'll see you in the New Year. And it's great news. I'll miss you, though.' I swallow hard.

'Hello, Mark,' Bells repeats. 'Happy birthday.'